THE HOUSE
OF
LASSENBERRY

THE HOUSE OF LASSENBERRY

DANIEL WEBB

ARCHWAY PUBLISHING

Archway Publishing books may be ordered through booksellers or by contacting:

Archway Publishing
1663 Liberty Drive
Bloomington, IN 47403
www.archwaypublishing.com
1 (888) 242-5904

ISBN: 978-1-4808-2378-5 (sc)
ISBN: 978-1-4808-2379-2 (e)

Library of Congress Control Number: 2015918007

Print information available on the last page.

Archway Publishing rev. date: 1/4/2016

CHAPTER 1. THE KIDS

In a world very similar to ours, the war on drugs had failed. The United States government had all but ignored the disastrous effect illegal drugs had on the nation. Soon after, a handful of fortune 500 executives and a few politicians from the senate and the House of Representatives decided to put a system In effect code named THE NATIONAL AGREEMENT to keep order.

Certain street gangs and drug lords were given a top secret pass to run a territory or an entire state, one such organization was the Lassenberry family who claimed the state of New Jersey as their own to distribute illegal narcotics. Out of all the gangs involved this operation, theirs was one of the few bound by blood. This is their story.

It was an early spring day when a black limousine had pulled up in front of a 3 story office facility located in Lodi, New Jersey. The chauffeur remained in the limo, while a burly black man dressed in a black suit and wearing dark shades gets out of the limo from the passenger's side. 2 white men who were not as big and wearing the same attire as the black man, exit the limo as well. One of the white guys goes into the trunk of the limo and pulls out a wheelchair. The black man carefully reaches in the limo to assist his boss into the wheelchair.

The man who needed assistance was Eddie lassenberry. About a week or so ago, Eddie had suffered from a stroke which left him paralyzed on one side of his body. Inside the office building, on the top floor, was a luxurious conference room. The room was made wall-to-wall out of cherry oak. Instead of a long conference table in the middle of the room, there were 15 leather chairs, with arm rests facing the entrance. On one side of the room where the windows were showing the view outside, was the 20 foot long conference table covered with a linen table cloth. On the table was a buffet of all sorts of food and drinks. The men who occupied the room had their choice of fresh fruit, cold cuts, baked, fried, or bar-b-que chicken, cheese and crackers, Mac-n-cheese, veal, roasted pork, bottles of wine and an assortment of liquor.

There were a total of 12 black men in the conference room. Some were standing around chatting with each other. Others were at the buffet table getting their fill of food and drink. These men were the nephews of Eddie lassenberry.

Eddie lassenberry became the drug lord of Jersey after his father had to abdicate from his position. No one could sell or buy narcotics in New Jersey without the say so of Eddie lassenberry.

Benny lassenberry, Eddie's father, started out as bootlegger in Alabama during prohibition. Benny's mother worked the fields as a sharecropper. When benny was 12 years old, his father had died of a heart attack while working out in the fields. Benny was around 18 when he and his younger sister Maggie would run corn liquor across county lines. Benny was a skilled driver when it came to out running law officials on the back roads of Alabama. Maggie was not so lucky. She died in a car crash while making a run on her own one day. In her honor, Eddie had named his first daughter after her.

It came a time when benny had to leave Alabama after the law from 5 different counties were closing in on him. He wound up a few years later in New Jersey. Not only was benny skilled at making and running booze, he was a master at the card table. Benny was making a name for himself at the gambling spots up in north jersey. It was when he had a run in with an Italian gangster named Ritchie Pavino.

Pavino happened to be a soldier in the newly formed Gatano crew of North Jersey. Pavino stood about 5 feet, 4 inches tall with a slim build. He wasn't at all threatened by 6 foot tall dark skinned black man. Pavino ran all the illegal gambling spots in North Jersey. When Pavino had gotten word that there was this young colored guy making a killing at his card games. Pavino approached benny one day. Benny was not at all intimidated by Pavino either. Pavino gave benny a slap on the chest with the back of his hand. "Listen pal! You know who I am! I have players who ain't too keen on having you people down at my card games! So, if you give me a cut of your winnings, I'll see to it that you can remain playing!" said Pavino. Benny calmly pulls out a cigar from inside his jacket. He bites off the tip and takes out a friction match. He strikes the match on pavino's wool jacket. Benny lights his cigar and plucks the match at Pavino. "Listen to me! If you don't want me at any of yo card games, just say so, but you ain't getting nothing that I won fair-n-square!" said benny. "Who the hell you think you're talking to? I'm the guy that can have a slug put in your head for that!" shouted Pavino. No one was around when Pavino said this. The 2 men were standing alone in the hallway of benny's apartment in the Ivy Hill section of Newark. Pavino just walked away after benny took a drag on his cigar and blew smoke in pavino's face. The next day Pavino sat with Luigi Gatano at a café in downtown Newark. Pavino had interrupted gatano as he was reading the newspaper. "Say boss! There's this jig on my side of town who thinks he's a tough guy!" said Pavino. Gatano puts down the newspaper. "What's this man's name?" asked gatano. "Does it matter? He's a fucking nigger!" shouted Pavino. "I asked you what's his name?" asked gatano. "I think its lassenberry or something!" said Pavino. Gatano smiled. He then reaches for his wooden can with the aid of his body guard, and struggles out of his seat. He limps over to the counter in agonizing pain and grabs a cannoli off a plate. Gatano limps back over to Pavino. "Stand up!" gatano says to Pavino. The gray haired soldier stood facing his much younger boss. "You don't touch him! Understand?" said gatano. Pavino was shocked to hear this. Gatano takes a bite of his cannoli. "Nobody touches benny lassenberry!" said gatano. The 6 guys in the café were a part of gatano's crew. All of them except for Pavino nod their heads.

Unknown to Pavino, luigi Gatano is alive because of benny. A little over a year ago, benny was making a decent living making and selling corn liquor and bath tub gin in the basement of an apartment building. Gatano at this time, was a capo to boss Alfonse Cucci of Brooklyn. During this time, Newark was open territory for illegal business. Boss Cucci had sent gatano and a crew of 10 guys over to Jersey to set up different operations. Within a few months of moving out to jersey, gatano had become one of the most feared men on the streets of Newark. It was rumored that he, gatano was the boss of North Jersey. This didn't sit well with Cucci.

It was one night when gatano, a married man with 2 children, had paid a visit to his mistress named Sandy Simpson, who lived in the iron bound section of Newark. A week earlier, boss Cucci secretly sent out 4 hired assassins called the cut throat crew to Newark to end gatano's reputation as being a boss. Not even cucci's Underboss, Tony Sangiero a.k.a tough tony new about the hit. Cucci wanted to replace gatano with his second in command, Sammy Desimone.

Sammy desimone was loyal to gatano, even though he's been in the Cucci family a couple of years before gatano. Cucci wanted all the glory of taking over Newark to himself.

Sandy Simpson was a full figured blonde who gatano met at a party out in Brooklyn over a year earlier. After a night of wild sex, gatano jumped in the shower, and then told sandy that it was time for him to go home to the wife and kids. It was around 2 in the morning when gatano was leaving Sandy's apartment. He gave her a kiss on the cheek, and then strutted down the stairs from her 3rd floor apartment. Sandy slams the door in anger. Gatano had reached the lobby. All-of-a-sudden, 4 masked men wearing black overalls jumped from behind the stairs. 2 of them grabbed gatano by the arms, while the other 2 pulled out their weapons. Instead of fire arms, these killers carried straight razors. Within seconds, they start slashing away at gatano. Gatano caught gashes on his jaw, across his chest, his scalp, on his legs and groin area while kicking to get free. At the same time, a burgundy car pulls up in front of the building. Out steps benny lassenberry. He's wearing a black fedora, a black pin striped suit, with black shoes and spats.

This address where Sandy Simpson lived, just happened to be the place where benny made his bathtub gin and corn liquor. He had made a deal with the landlord, for a huge fee, to start his operation in the basement. When on a night away from his wife and 2 sons, benny would carry a pistol underneath his jacket.

At this time, gatano was still fighting for his life. Out of fear, none of the tenants on the first floor came out of their apartments. One resident, an elderly widow watched through the peep hole.

Benny had to go through the first floor to get to the basement. When he entered the hallway, he saw 4 guys in all black standing over a man lying in a pool of blood. Benny reacts quickly. He pulls out his pistol and fires 3 shots in their direction. He purposely didn't want to kill any one. The 4 assassins ran pass benny, knocking him to the floor. They run outside, and jump into a car parked across the street. In the building, benny starts banging on doors for help. No one would answer his cry. Gatano lay on the floor drenched in blood. "We gotta get you to the hospital!" said benny. Benny picks gatano off the floor and puts him over his shoulder. Benny races out to his car. He carefully puts gatano in the back seat. He gets in takes off towards Newark City Hospital.

About a few months after the attack, gatano was still resting from his wounds in an undisclosed location down in the rural section of South Jersey. He had rented out a cabin from an elderly white couple. He gave them 5 grand in cash, not just for room and board, but to keep his whereabouts a secret. The only other people who knew of gatano's location was benny lassenberry and Frankie Depalma.

Frankie Depalma was 18 at the time. Even though he was just a kid, he had the appearance of a tough gangster. He stood about 6 feet, 5 inches and weighed around 3 hundred pounds. Coincidently Frankie was the adopted son of the elderly couple. Gatano not only spent his time recuperating, but was plotting a way to get revenge on those responsible for his near death experience.

One night at the cabin, benny and gatano were showing Frankie how to play poker. Gatano was feeling well enough to sit up. Suddenly, gatano places his cards on the table. "What the hell you doing? You gotta good hand there!" said benny. "I just want to say thank you my friend, for everything!" said gatano. Benny just smiles and nods his head. "When I get back up north, you my friend, are going to help me run Newark! I swear to you!" said gatano.

A few months had passed. Inside the den of an 8 bedroom mansion located in Buffalo, New York, a chubby gray haired Italian man sits on his leather sofa alone sobbing. Next to him, was a bottle of scotch, which he drank a lot. The man was boss Alfonse Cucci. During the 1930's, he was head of one of the most powerful crime families in the country.

His wife of 30 years stood outside the den banging on the door. Suddenly, the doorbell rings. At the front entrance of the mansion, Cucci's butler answers the bell. When the butler opens the door, there stood 3 men in the doorway. "Welcome to the Cucci residence. How may I help you?" Said the butler. The 3 men barged their way into the mansion, Pass the butler. "Where's Cucci?" asked the man walking in the rear of the group. The tall slim man who asked about cucci's whereabouts was tony Sangiero.

Tony Sangiero, or tough tony as he was called. Was cucci's right hand man. About a week ago, around mid-night while tony was walking to his limo, he was approached by a guy wearing a red bandana over his face. The man was brandishing a pistol. He had forced tony into the back of his own limo. Tony noticed that his black chauffeur was replaced by another black man in the driver's seat. Tony's chauffeur was lying next to him on the seat floor knocked out cold. "You guys don't have a clue on who you're dealing with!" said tony. "Listen Mr. Sangiero! We don't want to hurt you!" said the masked man holding the gun. The black man sitting in the driver's seat was benny lassenberry. Benny drives off. "Be a man and show yourself at least! Otherwise, pull the trigger!" said tony. The masked man slowly removes the bandana from his face. Benny looks at the rear view mirror and shakes his head. It was Frankie Depalma. Tony stared Frankie straight into his eyes for a few seconds. "What crew you're running with son? I never seen before!" said tony. Frankie had a smirk on his face. "I know who you are Mr. Sangiero, and have a high respect for you, but I also have high respect for the man who sent me too!" said Frankie.

As tony was being driven around, it took Frankie, as well as benny a couple of hours to explain the deal to tony that gatano had laid out. Near the end of the conversation, tony became more and more infuriated. "If what you say is true kid, I think me and Gatano can do business!" said tony.

Tony gave the order to his 2 soldiers to kick down the door to where Cucci was. Tony had knocked cucci's wife to the floor. She began screaming, but no one came to her aid. The 3 men enter the den where their boss was sitting in a weakened state. Tony stands over Cucci. "You had more than enough time to leave town! But, you made the choice to stay!" shouted tony. Cucci looks up at tony. "Brooklyn is my city! I built it!" shouted Cucci.

Tony didn't worry about any outsiders coming to cucci's rescue. He had 8 soldiers standing guard outside on the property.

"You were gonna let that weasel son of yours come in on my action?" shouted tony. Cucci looks up at tony with tears in his eyes. "Guess what, you fat fuck? Your son's body is chopped up into tiny pieces out in Jersey!" shouted tony. Cucci drops to his knees. "Kill me! Just kill me!" cried Cucci. "You heard him boys! Take this garbage out of here!" said tony. The 2 soldiers struggle to pick Cucci off the floor. Cucci was so terrified, that he can barely walk. They had to drag him to the cars outside. There was a caravan of 3 cars parked outside the front entrance of the mansion. Cucci was placed into the back seat of the first car. Minutes later, tony comes out of the mansion and gets into the car parked in the middle. He could see Cucci get shot in the side of the head before the cars drive off. Suddenly, black smoke appeared from the second floor windows of the mansion. There was no sign of Cucci's wife or the butler.

Tony had made a deal with gatano, that if he could prove that Cucci was double crossing him, that gatano could run North Jersey as the new boss. Gatano still had to follow the rules like any other mob boss around the country. The rules were not to deal in drugs of any kind. This is why gatano put benny lassenberry in charge of his alleged drug ring. If the law closed in on the drug operation, gatano didn't want anyone from his crew to go down. Benny was reluctant at first to take the offer, but when gatano had purchased a 7 bedroom mansion for him out in Cherry Hill, New Jersey, benny had a sudden change of heart.

Benny knew that the drug business was more dangerous than selling booze, so he comprised a crew of African American men to help him run the operation. Jimmy Jenkins a.k.a Jabbo was the first on benny's list to recruit.

Jabbo was only 17 at the time when benny offered him a job as his driver. Jabbo was a lanky kid. He was light skinned, and wore thick black frames glasses and a wild afro, which became his signature look over the years. He used to shine shoes at the barber shop benny went to on Clinton avenue in Irvington. Jabbo didn't have a driver's license due to his illiteracy. So, as a favor to benny, gatano's people supplied jabbo with false motor vehicle documents. Benny's next objective, was to find someone who wasn't afraid to pull the trigger.

Percy Williams was the guy benny had remembered from his days living in Alabama. Percy was a bouncer at the gambling spot benny used to frequent back then. Benny had sent jabbo down to Alabama with an envelope filled with cash. Percy was a bald, dark skinned man in his early 30's, standing a few inches taller than benny, weighing about 250 pounds. Percy was reputed to be one of the most feared guys in Dale County. Back then, even the Klan in neighboring counties stayed clear of him. It was rumored that Percy had at least 12 guns hidden in his surrounding areas at home and at work. One urban legend was that Percy had gotten into an altercation with a guy while talking to a woman. He pulled out a shotgun from underneath the woman's skirt and blew the guy's head off before he could react.

In a couple of days, jabbo comes back, not only with Percy in the passenger seat, but with the envelope in his jacket pocket. When jabbo pulled up in front of benny's building, where benny was coincidently standing on the porch, Percy jumps out of the car, dressed in a beige 3 piece suit, and runs on the stoop and gives benny a hug. "Man benny! I would've brought my ass up here for nothing!" said Percy.

Benny worked fast. He wasted no time rounding up his crew. There was a black man standing next to benny when Percy arrived. His name was Stanley Harrison Hart, a recent law school graduate.

Mr. Hart was in his mid 20's when receiving his degree. He stood about 5 feet, 7 inches tall, with a chubby build. Hart had a bad skin condition which appeared in dark patches on his right arm and hand. His insecurities lead him to wear long sleeve shirts, even during the hot days of summer. Later, benny had given him the nickname sleeves. Being a black man to graduate college impressed benny, and being a black man who was street wise impressed sleeves.

After jabbo parked the car, benny introduced Percy and Jabbo to hart. Benny invited the 3 men inside. Inside, was another black man sitting in the kitchen sipping on a glass of cognac. His name was Bobby Richards's a.k.a spade.

He stood at the same height as benny, but was light skinned, with a thick mustache and goatee and short wavy hair due to a process. Unlike benny, bobby wasn't married but had 2 children by 2 different women. One woman lived in Harlem, while the other lived in Newark. Bobby was only 20 years old when he met benny. Bobby was laid back, well dressed and had a pimpish swagger about him.

The kitchen table had 6 wooden chairs around it. Benny introduced spade to Percy and the others. Benny told the men to take a seat.

The meeting had lasted for a little over 4 hours. "Let me say this! If we play our cards right, we gonna be the richest niggas in Jersey!" benny said at the end of his speech. As the men were leaving the meeting, Percy leans over and whispered to benny. "Where you find the boy lawyer?" asked Percy. "When jabbo went to get you, I took a ride down to DC. I snatched him up right after graduation. Once I told him how much he could make, he packed his bags and followed me back!" benny chuckled.

Benny was the boss, jabbo was his driver and messenger, Percy was the muscle, Sleeves gave legal and personal advice and spade was in charge of all transactions.

By the 1970's, benny still had battles with lesser crews on this streets, but had no problems with the authorities. Benny was the first drug dealer in Jersey to think of paying off the cops in Newark and other surrounding cities.

By this time, benny was the father of 7 children. There was benny jr., Eddie, Jake, Maggie, mark, Lula and Danny. Eddie was the only one of benny's kids to enter the narcotics game.

Eddie grew up to be a ruthless gangster. By the time he was in his early 20's, Eddie was feared throughout the city, even more than Percy himself. In no time, Eddie was soon picked as his father's muscle when Percy's body was found in a wooded area of Weequahic Park in the south ward of Newark. It was rumored that Eddie and his crew had murdered him.

Eddie's crew consisted of 5 young black guys, but there was one in the crew who was different. This kid, who was 19 at the time, was of Italian descent. His name was Gino Massoni. Gino went to school with Eddie's younger brother Jake, but dropped out in the 10th grade.

Gino was a skinny kid fascinated with black culture. Eddie took gino under his wing and used him as his personal punching bag. One night in June, Eddie and his crew were hanging out in front of his father's safe house in East Orange. A black car pulls up. In the back seat of the car, sat Luigi Gatano himself. In the driver's seat was Frankie Depalma. "Hey boys! Shouted gatano. "Hey Mr. Gatano!" shouted the group. Gatano didn't get out of the car. Instead, someone on the front passenger side exited the car. It was gatano's son, Carlo gatano.

Just like Eddie Lassenberry, Carlo had earned his way into his father's organization. He became a made man a year earlier. Carlo looked like a younger version of his father, but was more on the chubby side.

"Hey kid! Come get in the car!" ordered Carlo. Gino looked around in a confused manner. "Who me?" asked gino. The rest of Eddie's crew kept silent. "Get over here. Now!" shouted Carlo. Gino runs off the porch towards the car. Carlo opens the back passenger door for him. Gino quickly gets into the car. After Carlo gets in, Frankie drives off. "Wait here fellas!" said Eddie. Eddie runs inside the safe house where his father was. Benny was sitting eating a cheese sandwich, while watching TV. "Pop! Mr. Gatano pulled up and took gino away!" said Eddie. Benny turns towards his son. "Just as well. That boy would be better off around his own people." Said benny. Eddie sighs, while shaking his head. "You and your crew need to go and make y'all rounds on the street." Said benny. Eddie could see a sadness in his father's eyes.

Benny was never the same after Percy was murdered, he knew it had to be someone close to Percy in order to catch him off guard. Benny didn't want to hear the rumors about his son.

From the time of prohibition, to the mid 70's, benny's family grew even more. Not only did he have 7 kids by this time, but 5 grandchildren as well. His daughter Maggie had given him 2 grandsons, Tyson and Malcolm Richards. Their father was the son of spade Richards from Newark. Benny jr. and his wife had a son named benny the 3rd. Jake's first born was a son named Larry nicknamed Big L because he weighed 10 pounds at birth. There was Mike Abbey, who was Lula's son from her first marriage to an older man named James Abbey.

Abbey was 30 years old when he ran off and eloped with Lula, who only 16 at the time. Soon after their marriage, Lula's older brother Eddie, who was 28 at the time, had Abbey murdered because he assumed that James was part of a rival crew from Jersey City looking to take over territories from the lassenberry crew. His body was never found. To Lula's and everyone else's knowledge abbey skipped town. To try and ease his daughter's broken heart, benny put up a 50,000 dollar reward for James abbey's whereabouts.

Eddie had not fathered a child at this time. He figured if he would be the heir to his father's illegal business, he didn't want any distractions in his life.

As a child, Eddie always wanted to be in the life his father was living. Benny chose Eddie to tag along with him because Eddie was the only who was too much for his mother to handle at home. One time Percy was ordered by benny to test Eddie to see if he could handle himself in the streets. Percy had hired a group of teens from the neighborhood to jump him. Eddie was being pounced by the boys. Percy hired the boys again. This time Eddie went into a rage and picked up a pipe and almost beat one of the boys to death. Luckily for the boy, Percy was hiding behind a tree witnessing the event. Percy ran out from behind the tree to stop Eddie from committing murder. The other boys took off like lightening. Percy had grabbed Eddie from behind in a bear hug. "That's enough! You passed the test! You passed the test!" said Percy. Percy released Eddie from the hold. Eddie looked at Percy with the same rage in his eyes and started trembling. "Sorry, but I had to see if you had what it takes kid! Now go to the safe house and get yo self cleaned up!" said Percy. Percy walked off, leaving the kid on the ground moaning in pain. As Eddie was walking away, he bent over and started puking his brains out. This is what led to Percy's demise.

One evening, benny arrived at café Sangiero. It was a small Italian eatery on the corner of Halstead and Edgar Street. In East Orange, New Jersey. The 20 table eatery was named by Gatano in honor of the man who gave him his start as the boss of North Jersey. Benny pulled up in his luxury vehicle alone. He was dressed in a silk 3 piece suit, wearing his signature fedora. Benny reached for a black leather briefcase in the back seat. He looks around cautiously before exiting the car. He sees 4 Italian men sitting outside of the café talking and laughing. He recognizes one of the men as old man Ritchie Pavino. Benny walks towards the café with a calm swagger. "Evening Gentlemen!" Said benny. "Hey benny!" said the guys. Pavino didn't greet benny. "Say lassenberry! Where's jabbo? He got tired of driving?" said Pavino. The other guys chuckled. Benny ignored them. "Where's yo boss?" asked benny. "He's inside, sitting in the back." Said one of the men. Benny walks inside. He removes his fedora. "Che devo essere il più fortunato uomo nero del pianeta!" said Pavino. Inside the café, benny walks to back where Gatano, Frankie Depalma and under boss Sammy desimone were sitting. "Say benny! Come, take a seat!" said gatano. Benny sits down across from the 3 men. "Always on time my friend. What? No jabbo by your side?" asked gatano. "I gave him the night off." Said benny. Benny places the briefcase on the table. He unclips the latches and opens it up. "60,000 grand as usual." Said benny. "Good! Good my friend!" said gatano. "I need a drink!" said benny. "Gino! Gino! Get out here!" shouted gatano. Gino comes running out of the kitchen wearing a gravy stained apron. "Yeah boss?" said gino. "Get Mr. Lassenberry a double shot of vodka." Said gatano. "You remembered after all this time!" said benny. "Good to see you Mr. Lassenberry!" said gino. "So, this is where they hid you?" asked benny. Benny and gino shake hands. Gino runs off to the kitchen to make the drink. "We need to have a serious talk about some work that needs to be done!" said benny. Gatano stares a benny for a few seconds. "Alright! Everybody out!" shouted gatano. Everyone in the café scatters and leaves gatano and benny sitting alone. Gino comes out with benny's drink. "Fate una pausa per circa 15 minuti bambino." Said gatano. Gino removes his apron and heads outside with the others. "So, who's the job on my friend?" asked gatano. "Spade. My son is ready to move up and spade needs to go." Said benny. "I thought you 2 were practically family. You share the same grandkids." Said gatano. "First Percy, now spade? You lassenberry men are hardcore! Or should I say your son is." Said gatano. Benny scoffs. "What's your price?" asked benny. Gatano pauses. "10 grand up front." Said gatano. "Good! You'll have it by tomorrow evening." Said benny. Gatano and benny shake hands. "So, my son will have the connection?" asked benny. "As soon as I get the money in my hands, my friend." said gatano. "Well, let me be on my way." Said benny. Benny takes the drink down in one gulp. Benny stands up. He puts on his fedora and exits the café. As benny walks outside, Frankie and Sammy walk back in the café. "What did he want?" asked Frankie. Frankie and Sammy sit down across from gatano. "Guys, I think it's time for the kid out there to earn his button." Said gatano "You mean gino?" asked Frankie. Gatano nods his head. "I want you to take the kid and find spade Richards." Ordered gatano. "Benny's top man?" asked Frankie in a high pitched voice. Gatano nods his head again. "Before noon, tomorrow." Said gatano. Frankie nods his head. "I'm on it." Said Frankie.

The day before was June 6th. Eddie lassenberry had turned 32 years old. Eddie had been dating a young woman by the name of Gloria for the past 7 months. Gloria was sort of a free spirited girl. She and Eddie were a wild pair. The 2 of them had shacked up in a luxury apartment in upper Montclair, New Jersey.

Gloria was born in Newark. She was a beautiful woman with smooth dark skin, big breasts, a small waist and long jet black hair. Men in her old neighborhood could only dream of a chance of hooking up with her. But like all human beings, Gloria was flawed. Her demon was substance abuse, which she hid from Eddie. Unknown to Eddie and everyone else, her supplier was no other than spade Richards himself.

Later that evening on Eddie's birthday, Eddie heard the door bell ringing like crazy while he and Gloria were in bed. "Who the fuck coming here unannounced?" Eddie shouted. He and Gloria were done having wild passionate sex. Eddie puts on his underwear and walks down to the lower level of his apartment to see who it was. There was a revolver Eddie kept hidden in the closet next to the main entrance. He pulls it out and checks to see if it's loaded. The doorbell rings again. "Who is it?" asked Eddie. "Open the door nigga! It's me, spade." He shouted. Eddie looks through the peep hole. "Man, I'm sleeping!" shouted Eddie. "Man, just open the door!" shouted spade. When Eddie opens the door, he sees spade standing there with a beautiful young white woman with short blonde hair. She had on a miniskirt, go-go boots and a tight tank top. She looked like she was in her late teens. Spade was holding a bottle of red wine. Spade and the young woman step inside. "Say Peggy! This joker here is my nephew Eddie!" said spade. "Hello!" Peggy said in a sweet voice. Spade slowly spins Peggy around. "Ain't she sexy?" said spade. "Not bad!" Eddie said. "I brought you over this 200 dollar bottle of wine for your birthday!" said spade. Eddie takes the bottle. He and spade hug. "Thanks." Said Eddie. "Put some clothes on! We're taking you out for a late dinner!" said spade. Before Eddie could respond to the invitation, Gloria comes to the top of the stairs wrapped in a sheet. Her nipples were showing through. "Who is it baby?" she asked Eddie. "It's my- I mean its spade and his friend!" shouted Eddie. "Oh shit! I ain't know you had company!" spade chuckled. "Yeah, you know Gloria." Said Eddie. "Hey sweetie! This here is my friend Peggy!" shouted spade. Gloria and Peggy wave to each other. "Well, since y'all ain't dressed, we can have something ordered!" said spade. "Go back upstairs baby! Man, it's too late to order anything!" said Eddie. "Oh, I forgot!" said spade. Spade reaches into his shirt pocket and pulls out a wad of cash and hands it to Eddie. "Happy birthday!" shouted spade. Spade pulls Eddie to the side. "Listen man, the white girl is a serious freak! All she need is some blow to get started and she'll do anything! I mean anything!" whispered spade. Eddie looks over at Peggy and then looks up stairs. "All y'all gotta do is watch! She'll put on a crazy ass show for ya!'' whispered spade. Eddie looks at the wad of cash in his hand. Within no time, the 2 couples were sitting in the living room. Gloria and Peggy were sitting on the sofa, with spade sitting in between them. Eddie was sitting on his beanbag chair. Gloria had put on a t-shirt and shorts before spade and Peggy came up stairs. The couples were eating leftover barbeque ribs Gloria had heated up. All 4 of them were drinking and talking all through the night. "Oh shit! We're out of wine!'' said spade. "Don't worry y'all! I got a lot of shit in the bar!'' Eddie shouted. Eddie runs downstairs to his luxurious bar he recently had installed next to the kitchen. As soon as Eddie went downstairs, spade and the girls start whispering and giggling to each other. "Ain't she sexy as hell?'' spade says to Peggy. Peggy reaches over spade and starts playing with Gloria's nipples. "You got my stuff?'' Gloria asked spade. "Yeah baby! Hold on!'' said spade. Spade reaches into his pants pocket and pulls out 3 grams of cocaine wrapped in foil. He quickly passes it to Gloria. Gloria then stuffs the cocaine in between the cushions of the sofa. Spade starts rubbing on Gloria's nipples as well. Both women start rubbing on spade's private area. All 3 start to kiss each other. They quickly stop when they hear Eddie coming back upstairs. Eddie comes back up with 2 bottles of rum and a bucket of ice. Within no time all 4 were tipsy. When Eddie was distracted in conversation with Gloria, spade reached in his back pocket and pulled out something else wrapped in foil. This powdery substance wasn't cocaine though. Eddie had placed his glass on the coffee table. Spade had poured it in Eddie's drink when he wasn't looking. Spade watched as it dissolved into the drink. "Let's chug son!'' said spade. Eddie takes spade on the dare. Eddie grabs his glass from off the coffee table and gulps his drink down faster than spade can. The girls applaud Eddie.

Earlier that day, Gloria had ran into spade down in Newark while visiting her mother. "Hey baby! Said Gloria. She and spade don't hug, and speak quickly so no one on the streets would catch on. "Today is Eddie's birthday. We're gonna be at his house tonight. Just pretend you're coming over to wish him a happy birthday and bring my stuff." Said Gloria. "Ok baby! Be cool!'' said spade. Gloria walks away. Spade looks at Gloria firm ass as she walks off.

Minutes later, Eddie gets up and starts to stagger about the room. "You ok son?'' asked spade. "Are you ok baby?'' asked Gloria. "I think- I think so!'' Eddie said before he passes out on the floor. Gloria tries to pick Eddie up off the floor. "Let him stay there! He'll be alright!'' said spade. Spade whispers in Peggy's ear. Peggy goes over to Gloria and grabs her by the hand. They start to kiss each other and caress each other's breasts. Spade starts to unbutton his shirt. He takes the cocaine from out of the sofa. He then rolls up a c-note. He unfolds the foil and takes a hit. Gloria then takes a hit, followed by Peggy. "I think we should take this to the bedroom y'all." Said spade. All 3 of them head to the bedroom. Spade noticed the bed a mess. "I see you 2 were really busy here!'' said spade. "Can you show us what you were do-ing?'' asked Peggy. All 3 get undressed. Spade lays on the bed naked. Peggy massages his erect penis, while Gloria puts it in her mouth. "Oh shit baby! Suck that dick!'' said spade. Peggy then takes his penis and puts it in her mouth next. Gloria massages spade's chest and then puts her tongue in his mouth. Peggy then sprinkles cocaine on spade's penis and sucks it off. Gloria then squats over spade's face. He begins to lick on her clitoris. Gloria starts moaning like a wild woman. Peggy then squats over his penis and inserts it into her wet vagina. Gloria and Peggy already facing each other, start to kiss. The 3 quickly switch positions with each other. Spade is taking Gloria from behind, doggy style. Peggy lays on her back as Gloria licks on her clitoris. The cocaine allows them to carry on for the next couple of hours.

The next day around noon, Eddie opens his eyes to find himself on the floor. He struggles getting off the floor. He stretches and noticed the food on the coffee table. He limps to the bedroom because his legs went numb from lying on the hard wood floor. He sees Gloria sound asleep, lying on her back in bed. He takes a closer look at her. He noticed that she has a powdery substance on her nose. This starts to infuriate Eddie. He then noticed a white crusty substance around her mouth and chin. He figured out it wasn't cocaine. In a fit of rage, Eddie smacks Gloria hard across the face. She jumps out of her slumber. "What happened?" shouted Gloria. Eddie grabs her around the throat. "You do blow now? What's that shit around yo mouth?" shouted Eddie. "I didn't do anything!" shouted Gloria. Eddie smacks her across the face again. "Bitch, don't lie to me! Get the fuck out! Get the fuck out!" shouted Eddie. "Please baby! Wait!" shouted Gloria. "I bet that's cum on your face! Ain't it? Ain't it?" Eddie shouted. Eddie then snatches Gloria off the bed by her ankles. She bangs her head on the floor. "You know what? You stay yo ass right here! I'll fix this shit!" Eddie shouted. Eddie runs to the closet and quickly puts on some clothes. "You better be here when I get back bitch!" Eddie shouted. Eddie then picks up the phone in the hallway, and dials a number. The Phone rings 4 times. Someone picks up on the other end. "Hello." Said the voice. "Yeah! It's me! Come pick me up from my spot!" said Eddie. "Got it." The voice said. "Hurry the fuck up!" Eddie shouted. Eddie then goes down stairs and pulls out his gun. Gloria slowly comes downstairs wrapped in a sheet, with tears in her eyes. "Get yo ass back in the bedroom bitch!" shouted Eddie. Gloria runs back upstairs crying.

20 minutes later, a cream colored car pulls up in front of Eddie apartment. Eddie comes outside, and runs to the front passenger seat and jumps in. "Go to my father's spot in East Orange! Quick!" said Eddie.

In the driver's seat is Eddie's right hand man Clayton Watson a.k.a Butch. Butch was born in Newark. He was 10 years younger than Eddie, but just as tough. He stood a few inches taller than Eddie, with a muscular build. The dark skinned sidekick always kept his head shaved bald. When he was in his teens, Eddie had smacked butch in the back of the head in a playful mood. This enraged butch. Butch turned and punched Eddie square in the chin, knocking Eddie out cold. Lucky for Butch, no one was around to see it happen. A few minutes later, Eddie regains consciousness. "Nice left hook man!" Eddie said while laying on the ground. Butch then helps Eddie off the ground. Ever since then, they've remained close.

Moments later, they arrived at benny's safe house. There were 2 guards standing outside the door. "Is my father inside?" asked Eddie. "Yeah." One of the guards answers. Eddie enters the house. Benny is sitting in the living room with jabbo watching TV. "Pop! We gotta talk! In private!" Eddie shouted. Benny sighs. "Ok. Let's go in the other room." Said benny. The room they entered was empty. The only items that were in there was a shot gun leaning up against the wall and 2 card board boxes filled with cash. Benny closes the door. "What's wrong?" asked benny. "Spade came by my place last night! He was all coked up!" Eddie said. "What?" benny shouted.

Benny had picked spade to be his transaction guy because he was known to be on the straight and narrow when it came to business. Benny's rule to his top guys from the beginning, was never indulge in the product.

Spade would meet his connection once a month at Port Newark-Elizabeth marine terminal. The connection was a mysterious Hispanic man accompanied by 2 body guards. Spade used to be accompanied by Percy until his death. From then on, it was Eddie. Spade would trade 2 briefcases filled with cash for a large drum filled with pure cocaine. The 2 guards would help Eddie load the drum in back of spades rental van. Spade would then drive back with Eddie to a safe house set up in Irvington, New Jersey. A small crew of benny's men would be waiting there to cut down the product for street sales.

Later that evening, benny went to gatano to put a hit on spade. Gloria had called spade as soon as Eddie left the apartment like a mad man, and warned him that Eddie might be coming for him. After the call from Gloria, spade realized his life might be in danger. Spade quickly packed a suitcase at his luxury condo out in Belleville, New Jersey. He pulls a shoe box from underneath his bed and takes out his pistol and throws it on the bed. He goes over to open the safe inside the closet. The safe is filled with stacks of cash and a velvet bag filled with diamonds. He throws all the contents of the safe into the suitcase.

Spade thought to wait until dark to make his next move. He repeatedly looked out his window to see if any strange faces were arriving at the complex. His paranoia from indulging in more cocaine made him delusional because when the sun when down, the street light from outside started casting shadows in the bedroom. It was about 2 in the morning. Suddenly, the phone rings. Spade ignores it just like he did the first 10 times before. He decided this was it. He had to leave town, and the time was now. Spade slowly opens the door and looks out into the hallway in both directions. At his right, he sees a young white couple staggering and giggling, entering their condo. Spade closes and locks his door. With suitcase in hand, spade quickly walks down the hall in the opposite direction. He approaches the back exit to avoid anyone coming or going out. He nervously looks around the dark parking lot as he approaches his car. Spade then tosses the suitcase inside the passenger side. He runs around to the driver's side and enters the car. He turns on the ignition. Suddenly, everything for spade goes silent. His vision becomes blurry. His hands fall from the steering wheel. Blood starts dripping from his mouth and nose. His body becomes weaker and weaker within seconds. He blacks out. A dark figure had approached his car. Another figure approaches the passenger side and grabs the suitcase. Spade's body is now lifeless. The 2 responsible for his death leave the scene in a nearby vehicle.

The next day after spade's death, Eddie is summoned to his father's safe house. Eddie walks pass the 2 guards benny had posted on the porch. Inside the house, there were 2 more guards sitting beside benny. The 2 black men that Eddie had never saw before, stand up. Benny then stands. "Follow me! Shouted benny. Eddie follows his father into the same empty room as before. Benny then slams the door. At first, benny doesn't notice that Eddie is carrying a suitcase. "Somebody just cost me 10 grand for a job someone didn't get a chance to do!" shouted benny. Eddie smiles at his father. "What the hell you smiling at boy?" asked benny. Eddie hands his father the suitcase. "What's this shit?" asked benny. "One hundred grand, in cash! Said Eddie. "I'm sure you took your cut off the top, huh?" said benny. Eddie chuckles. Benny gives his son a hug, but has a sad look on his face. Benny puts his hand on his son's shoulder. "It's just me and you running this now son. The only thing is, I'm really a gambler, a bootlegger, not a drug pushing gangster." Said benny. Benny leaves the room with his head down.

Before gino could make his mark on spade to become a made guy, Eddie took out spade with a slug to the temple. Actually it was butch who squeezed the trigger. Eddie grabbed the suitcase. Benny still had to pay gatano just because the deal was made. But, he came out on top when Eddie gave him the suitcase. Eddie gave butch 5 grand for the hit and kept the diamonds for himself, which was worth 60 grand on the black market.

2 days after spade's death, New Jersey crime boss Luigi Gatano, benny and Eddie lassenberry meet with the Hispanic connection out in Elizabeth. The 4 men met at a warehouse benny had just purchased. All the men were dressed in expensive formal attire. Benny like always, wore his black fedora. The 4 men didn't come alone though. The Hispanic man stood alone, but had 10 armed guards standing outside the warehouse. Gatano had Frankie Depalma wait outside by the limo, while his Underboss Sammy desimone stood by his side. At the exit, stood 2 gatano soldiers, Pete campi and mike pascolini. Benny had jabbo waiting out in the car, while Eddie, butch and a young henchman named Curtis stood by benny, armed to the teeth.

The Hispanic man shakes hands with gatano. "Buenos Dias senior gatano." Said the Hispanic man. "Buon giorno." Said gatano. Gatano never mentions the Hispanic man's name. "You already know benny lassenberry." Said gatano. "Buenos días senior lassenberry. Sorry to hear about the loss of your friend spade." He and benny shake hands. The Hispanic man gives a formal greeting to those standing around.

The Hispanic man stood about 6 feet tall, with a chubby build. He had a thick mustache that looked fake, grayish hair and a brown complexion.

"Out of all my business dealings, your organization proves to be one of the most trust worthy." Said the Hispanic connection. Eddie puts his hand on his father's shoulder. "If I wasn't for my pop, this wouldn't be possible." Eddie said as he pats benny's back. Butch, Curtis and Eddie applaud. When Eddie made the comment about his father, gatano showed a scowl on his face. Gatano's presence at the meeting was only to validate Eddie as the new connection. By this time, benny had grown tired of the business. More control of the operation leaned toward Eddie, with Jabbo and butch by his side. Benny spent most of his days watching old westerns on TV or going down to the gambling spot. But still, benny was the face of the lassenberry organization.

"You choose the location senior lassenberry, and then we can continue business as usual." The Hispanic man said. "I see no problem using this spot!" said Eddie. "Well it's official. Señior lassenberry is our new man." said the Hispanic connection. Everyone crowds around Eddie to shake his hand. The Hispanic man departs from the warehouse first, followed by Gatano and his men. "You boys wait outside." Benny said to butch and Curtis. Benny and Eddie are now alone. Benny turns towards Eddie and puts his hand on his shoulder. "Don't screw this up boy!" benny said. "You can count on me pop." Eddie said smiling. Benny gives his son a hug. They both exit the warehouse.

The next day, 2 white guys dressed in suits approach Eddie's door, passing the 2 guards Eddie had hired. One of the white guys rings the doorbell. Eddie comes down from the second level. Eddie looks through the peep hole. "Who is it?" Eddie asked. The older gentleman holds his badge up to the peephole. "It's the police!" the guy shouted. Eddie opens door slowly. At this time, both men are flashing their badges. "Yeah. What y'all want?" asked Eddie. "I'm detective Mussi, and this is my partner detective Erik from homicide division. We want to ask you a few questions." Said Mussi. "About what?" asked Eddie. "First, can you tell your friends to take a hike before I bust them for illegally carrying firearms?" asked Mussi. Eddie gives the guards the signal to walk away. "We're hear about the murder of Bobby Richards a.k.a spade." Said Mussi. "Yeah! I heard about that! That's fucked up!" said Eddie. "I know we don't have a warrant, but can we come in?" Mussi asked. "Sure! Come on in officers!" Eddie insisted. The 2 detectives enter the apartment. They head up stairs. "Have a seat officers." Eddie said with a smile. The 2 detectives take a seat on the sofa. "Can I get you gentlemen a drink?" Eddie asked. Both men shake their heads. Detective Erik pulls out a pen and pad. Mussi is staring around the apartment. He notices how lavish it is. "Wow! I'm in the wrong business!" said Mussi. "Hey man, if you looking for a new job, I got the connections!" Eddie chuckled. "I'm sure you do Mr. Lassenberry." Said Mussi. "Where were you on June 8th, around 1 or 2 in the morning Mr. lassenberry?" asked Erik. "I was at my father's place in East Orange!" said Eddie. "Ok. Were you with spade- I mean Mr. Richards at the time?" asked Erik. "No sir." Said Eddie. "Do you know a Gloria bates?" asked Erik. "Yeah! That's my ex-girlfriend!" said Eddie. "Your ex?" asked Erik. "Yeah man. We broke up on the night of my birthday." Said Eddie. "Do you mind telling us what the break up was about?" asked Erik. "Oh man! Her drug problem was getting out of control! I thought she'd stop doing blow, but she lied. I told her, it's either me or the coke! She chose the coke!" said Eddie. "So it wasn't over Mr. Richards?" asked Erik. "Hell no! What? Were they messing around or something?" asked Eddie. "We received a call coming from your house to Mr. Richards's place on the night of your birthday." Said Erik. "I don't know shit about that!" said Eddie. "I know we don't have a warrant Mr. Lassenberry, but may we search around the apartment?" asked Erik. "Only if I can follow you! I heard stories about cops planting shit in people's homes just to get an arrest!" Eddie chuckled. Mussi stands. "I think that won't be necessary Eddie. We'll be leaving now. Thank you for your cooperation and hospitality." Said Mussi. Erik stands also, but with a confused look on his face. Eddie escorts the 2 detectives to the door. "It looks like you've connected all the dots. Lots of luck." Said Mussi. "In my world, there's no such thing as luck, just skill!" Eddie chuckled. Mussi just shook his head in disbelieve. The detectives walk outside, while Eddie stands in the doorway. The detectives walk pass the 2 guards. Erik and Mussi walk to their unmarked car. Eddie tells his guards to come inside. He doesn't look happy.

Detective Stanley Mussi was on the Montclair police force for the past 30 years. Born of Italian descent, Mussi witnessed the rise of the gatano crime family. As a young man, he would frequent Ritchie Pavino's gambling spot and would see benny there from time-to-time.

After high school, Mussi attended college out in South Orange, New Jersey. He didn't come from a family with money, so he worked as a cab driver at night to pay for his tuition. Mussi developed a serious gambling habit by using his overtime money for working Sundays. He would spend at least a hundred bucks on the weekends at Pavino's spot even though he needed the money to buy books. It got to the point that Mussi would ask Pavino for credit in order to continue to play cards. One night, Mussi had come across a table where benny lassenberry was playing. Mussi joined in, and put his money in and drew his cards. It wasn't too long before benny had won the table and Mussi went bust. Mussi wanted a chance at getting his money back, but was out cash. He told benny and the guys to hold on for a moment. Mussi walks over to Pavino, who was sitting at the bar with his cronies. Mussi asked for loan. Pavino refused him. "You're a thousand in the whole kid! I'm just talking interest!" shouted Pavino. Mussi looked around feeling embarrassed. "Come on Ritchie! Just this last time!" said Mussi. Pavino grabs Mussi by the collar. Pavino had to look up to Mussi because of his small physique. "You got 2 weeks to come up with my money kid! Until then, I don't wanna see you around here or at any of my spots again! And don't leave town. If I gotta chase you, you'll wish you were never born!" shouted Pavino. Mussi puts his head down in shame. Everyone, even benny was watching. Benny gets up from the card table, and goes over to intervene. "Wait a second Ritchie! How much does the kid owe you?" asked Benny. "Mind your fucking business, you fucking coon! I don't care who your friends with! This is my joint!" shouted Pavino. Pavino changes his tune when benny pulls out a wad of cash from his pocket. "What? You're gonna pay this punk's tab?" asked Pavino. "I just asked yo ass how much the kid owes you!" said benny. Pavino cuts eyes at the patrons. He was the one embarrassed now. "2 grand, plus the vig, which comes to 3 grand!" said Pavino. Benny counts the money in front of everyone. Benny slam the cash in pavino's hand. "Let's go kid!" said benny. Benny and Mussi leave the gambling spot with the patrons in awe.

Outside, it was cold and raining. Benny pulls the collar of his overcoat up around his neck. Mussi had on a small wool jacket. "Say, I'm benny, benny lassenberry." He says to Mussi. "I know who you are! I'm Stanley, Stanley Mussi!" he says to benny. Both of them shake hands. "Why'd you do that for me back there?" asked Mussi. "Pavino is a killer. He don't care about the money. He just needs a reason to skin you alive." Said benny. "Who was your friend he was talking about?" asked Mussi. "Well, my friend runs the city." Said benny. Mussi thinks for a second. "You mean to tell me your friend is who I think he is?" asked Mussi. "Yep! That's the guys." Said benny. "What do you do for a living?" asked benny. "I go to school during the day, and drive a cab at night." Said Mussi. "What's yo major?" asked benny. "It's business." Said Mussi. Benny starts cracking up. "What happened tonight tells me you should change majors!" benny chuckled. Mussi starts laughing too. "We best call it a night kid. I'm soaked!" said benny. Benny starts to walk to his car. "How can I repay you?" shouted Mussi. Benny turns to Mussi. "Finish school! And don't gamble!" shouted benny. Benny jumps in his car and takes off. Mussi runs down the street, in the opposite direction.

As detective Mussi and detective Erik enter the car. Erik look towards Mussi. "So, we're going for a warrant?" asked Erik. "Weren't you listening kid? The man just told us we could look around! If there was something there, he'd probably gotten rid of it by the time we get a fucking warrant!" Mussi says to Erik. Erik nods his head, gazing at the dashboard. "Now scratch his name off the list, and let's move on to the next suspect." Mussi ordered Erik. Mussi pulls out a cigarette. His voice sounded raspy from years of chain smoking. Erik drives off.

Mussi and benny kept in touch over the years. When Mussi graduated from the police academy, someone had placed a brown envelope filled with cash in his mailbox. In the envelope was a letter. It said congratulations and don't gamble.

If you were in law enforcement, and were in a financial bind, you could count on benny to help you out of a jam. Benny would have card games set up in a safe house in West Orange just for cops. It cost benny almost a half million a year to fill the pockets of cops from Newark, Irvington, the oranges, Belleville, Nutley, all over Essex County.

Benny's family still lived a privileged life. His children, even when they became adults, were spoiled by their father. All benny's kids, except for Eddie, were sent to top universities around the country earning bachelors degrees and some earning their masters. Benny's oldest son, benny jr., was the spitting image of his father. He earned a bachelor's degree in history, along with a problem with alcohol abuse. Vodka was his weakness. Benny jr. worked as a high school teacher in Camden, New Jersey earning 20 grand a year. The faculty wondered how benny jr. could afford a diamond watch and have a brand new car every year on his salary. Unknown to his co-workers, benny jr. and his siblings received 5 grand a week from their father.

The 3rd son of benny was Jake. Jake played college basketball out in Kansas. He stood 6 feet, 4 inches tall, resembling his father a little, but had a lighter complexion like his mother. He earned a degree in liberal arts. His basketball career came to an end from a knee injury while playing in a championship game. Jake invested in a few barber shops and hair salons in Newark, Irvington and Camden.

Maggie was the oldest daughter of benny. She was 5 years younger than Eddie. She stood about 6 feet tall, looking like her mother, but with her father's complexion. Maggie earned a degree in math while studying in Chicago. She also earned her masters at the same place. With a 3.8 grade point average, Maggie was offered a job as head of the administration in a hospital in Chicago, but turned it down to move back to Jersey. She now serves on the board of directors of a hospital and Newark. Maggie purchased property in Atlantic City, Camden, and Vineland, New Jersey by the age of 25. By the age of 28, she was pregnant with her first child, Tyson Richards.

Mark was benny's 5th child. Mark favored his mother's side of the family. He was light skinned with curly hair and had a thin nose. When he was growing up in Cherry Hill, mark was favored over his siblings by his grandparents on his mother's side. His mother Lola came from a mulatto background. Her parents didn't care too much for benny because of his dark complexion and that he had a back woods upbringing. Mark earned a degree in dentistry, from the same school his grandfather went to. Mark set up his own practice in Wilmington, Delaware. Mark also invested in property. He has a beach house on the Jersey shore, a condo he purchased out in Wilmington and 5 bedroom house in which his grandfather purchased for him on his 18th birthday. Mark married his girlfriend Tasha of 6 years. They gave birth to 3 children. Mark jr., Corey, and terry.

Tasha Coretta Jones was born in Newark, New Jersey. She grew up in poverty, raised by a single mother. As the only child, she was lonely most of the time because her mother worked 2 jobs just to make ends meet. Tasha was often teased of her looks growing up. She had real dark skin and a wide nose. She could barely afford a hair due, so her hair was often a short kinky afro. She would be home straightening it with a hot comb. She had a lanky build and huge feet for a girl. Tasha, having GPA of 4.0, received a full scholarship in academics from the same university mark attended. Her studies became so easy to her, that she joined a sorority in her freshman year. In her junior year, she met her future husband at an on campus meeting pertaining to the civil rights movement. Tasha had no idea that her boyfriend was the son of benny lassenberry. When she found out through her sorority sisters, she ended the relationship. Mark had fell in love with Tasha. It took weeks for him to convince Tasha that he wasn't in the drug game, even though his tuition was being paid with drug money, and that he received an envelope with 5 grand in it every week from jabbo.

Jabbo would drive up to the gate entrance of the university where he would meet mark and give him the money. Jabbo had a 5 man team that did this with all of benny's children when they attended school.

In 1964, mark and Tasha were married in a big church wedding. There were at least 400 guests. Benny paid for the entire wedding, which set him back a hundred grand. Since she had no father figure, benny decided to walk Tasha down the aisle. Mark and Tasha had received a pair of his and hers gold watches from Luigi Gatano, who was also invited. 2 years after the wedding, Tasha gave birth to mark jr. on December 9th, 1966.

Lula Irene Lassenberry was born five years after mark. She had earned a degree in fine arts from one of the top schools in New York. Lula always wanted to be in the entertainment business since she was a little girl. She stood 5 feet, 5 inches tall, and had the exotic looks of her mother, but her father's complexion. Her hair was jet black and came down the middle of her back. While attending school, Lula's baby son mike, who was 3 years old at the time, was being cared for by her mother. Still distraught over James's disappearance, Lula found it hard to focus on her acting career until she met fellow actor Albert Mills Bethune.

His birth name was Alberto Vargas from San Juan, Puerto Rico. His parents came to America when Albert was 10 years old. He stood 6 feet tall, with a slim muscular build. He was brown skinned with short kinky hair. He would try his best to disguise his accent at auditions to get lead roles in the new black exploitation genre. After he and Lula both scored a small role in a zombie movie, they began dating. While Albert worked desperately to pay the rent, Lula didn't have that problem. Receiving 5 grand a week from her father, Lula was able to afford a luxury apartment on the Upper East Side. When Albert was kicked out of his Harlem apartment for being 2 months behind on the rent, Lula told him that he could stay with her and mike until he found steady work. Lula stayed at home while Albert went job hunting. One day Albert came home from another unsuccessful search for work. It was the first time in 6 months staying with Lula that he noticed an envelope filled with cash on the kitchen table. Albert picks up the envelope, takes the cash out and starts counting it. It was all in c-notes, adding up to 5 grand. Lula was in her bedroom, while little mike was in his room playing with his toys. Albert, without thinking, became angered. He storms into the bedroom. Lula was watching TV. Albert turns off the TV. "What's this?" asked Albert. "What's what sweetie?" asked Lula. Albert waves the bundle of cash in her face. "This!" he shouts. "It's for you!" said Lula. "Where or who did you get this from? Are you seeing someone else?" Albert shouted. "It's yours if you want it!" Lula said. "Yo soy el hombre en esta reación! No voy a permitir que me falta de respeto de esta manera!" Albert shouted. "English please!" said Lula. "You think I'm some kind of loser?" shouted Albert. Frightened by the shouting, mike runs into the closet with his stuffed animal. "Who gave this to you?" asked Albert. "I-I can't say! Just take the money and go to Los Angeles for a week to see if you can get an audition!" said Lula. "You know what? I don't need to play the part of the bitch!" said Albert. He throws the wad of money in Lula's face and storms out of the apartment. Lula clutches her belly.

The youngest of benny's kids was Daniel Patrick Lassenberry. But everyone just called him Danny. He was 3 years younger than Lula was. He stood at the same height as his father, with a slim physique. He had a brown complexion, sporting a mustache and goatee. Danny had went off overseas and enrolled in a university over in the U.K., where he became a Rhodes Scholar. Having saved half of his money from his father for the past 2 years, Danny came back to the states and started his own packaging company called The Lassenberry Packaging Corporation. Not only did he come back to the states with a good education, he came back with a wife and baby boy named Daniel Patrick Benjamin Lassenberry Jr. Danny met his future wife Elaine, a British secretary for the House of Lords in Parliament while on a trip to Germany. He went to visit an old high school friend who was stationed on an Army base.

Elaine was born to a white South African father and black South African mother. She was a tall slim, light skinned woman, with short curly hair. She spoke with a British accent. A year after of dating each other, Danny and Elaine were married in a small ceremony in London. Danny jr. was born a year later.

A couple of months after detective Mussi paid Eddie a visit, Eddie decided to sever ties from the Spade situation once and for all. One night in August, Eddie was driving out to Atlantic City. He was dressed in all black, wearing black leather gloves and black wool cap. He looked calm and drove within the speed limit, constantly looking through his rear view mirror. Within a couple of hours Eddie reached his destination. He pulled up to a one family house not too far from the boardwalk. This was way before the casinos came. Eddie pulls up into the driveway.

Inside the house was barely livable. There was just a couch and mattresses. 2 of the mattresses were occupied by 2 young black men. The 2 men belonged to Eddie's crew. Eddie's last orders were for them to cover all the windows with black garbage bags so no one on the outside could look in.

One of the young men was Tyrone, who was 18 at the time, and Donald, who was 22 years old. Both of them were ordered by Eddie to stay at the house, back in June to stand guard over an important matter. "Damn! Can't wait to get back home!" said Tyrone. "Yeah! This shit ain't for me!" said Donald. "Get the fuck out of here! You ain't say that shit last night, or the night before that!" said Tyrone "Shit ain't start stinking in here until now!" said Donald. Tyrone was pacing around the floor, kicking empty cans of food around. "Man, if you board, go in the room and relieve some stress like I did." Said Donald. "Man, the smell is stronger in there than out here!" Tyrone said.

Donald was a tall, muscular young man who was one of the toughest dudes in his neighborhood. He was put in charge by Eddie to run Dayton Street down in Newark. His runners pulled in 20 grand a week for the lassenberry crew.

Tyrone was another dealer working for the lassenberry crew from East Orange. He was a scrawny dark skinned kid with corn rolls in his hair. He started out as a car thief at the age of 12 until he was caught stealing Butch's car. Eddie gave the little boy a choice. Either push dope for the lassenberry crew or get pushed off the top of a building. Tyrone chose to push dope.

The 2 heard a car pull up in the driveway. Tyrone started to panic. Eddie had told them to guard what was in the other room like their lives depended on it. Eddie didn't provide them with guns, just 2 baseball bats. Donald grabs the bats that were leaning against the wall. He gives one to Tyrone. Donald tells Tyrone to stand behind the door. "Get ready to swing nigga!" whispered Donald. Donald stood in front of the entrance, waiting to beat down who-ever came through that door. Donald looked confused when he heard the sound of a key in the door knob. Suddenly, the door creeks open. The room was dark because Donald told Tyrone to turn out the lights when the car pulled up. Donald lowers his bat. Tyrone on the other hand, still has his bat at the ready. The dark figure walks in. Tyrone swings. Eddie ducked just in time. "Oh shit!" shouted Tyrone. "Nigga, is you crazy?" said Eddie. "Sorry about that ed- I mean Mr. Lassenberry! We thought we never see you again!" Tyrone chuckled. "Y'all alright in here?" asked Eddie. "Yeah! We stilling kicking!" Tyrone chuckled. "Is everything alright in the other room?" Eddie asked. "She still breathing." Said Donald. Eddie looks at Donald with disbelief. He walks pass Tyrone and Donald, straight to the back room. Eddie covers his nose and mouth because the stench is so strong. Satisfied from what he sees, Eddie shuts the door. "You boys did good!" Eddie whispered. Tyrone cracks a smile. "When we gonna get paid boss?" asked Donald. "Oh yeah, that's right! I'm glad you reminded me!" said Eddie. Eddie reaches inside of his blazer. Tyrone rubs his hand together, waiting for the payoff. Suddenly, Tyrone's happy expression turns serious. Eddie pulls out a semi-automatic pistol, with a si-lencer on the end. He takes aim and squeezes the trigger. Donald takes a bullet between the eyes. He drops to the floor. "No please! No please! Please! Please!" Tyrone screamed. Tyrone takes 2 bullets. One in the forehead and one in the chest. Tyrone drops to the floor. Eddie walks over to Donald's body. It's still twitching. Eddie puts another bullet in his forehead. His body stops twitching. Eddie puts his pistol back into the holster, inside his blazer. He kicks in the door of the room that reeked. Inside the room was the battered and bruise body of his ex-girlfriend, Gloria. Barely alive, Gloria had enough strength to smile when she saw her allege knight in shining armor. Eddie holds Gloria in his arms. "We gotta get you out of here baby!" said Eddie. "Hurry…before…they come back!" said Gloria. "Don't worry about them baby! They can't hurt you no more!" said Eddie. Eddie carefully picks Gloria off the mattress in the cradle position. He then carries her pass the dead bodies, outside to the car. He carefully places her in the back seat. Eddie then goes to the trunk and takes out a canister of gasoline. He rushes back into the house with the canister. He douses both rooms, and the bodies. Eddie then takes out a book of matches. He strike a match, then lights the whole book. He tosses it on Donald's body. Eddie runs to the front entrance and heads to the car. Within minutes, the first floor of the house goes up in flames. Eddie drives off, heading north.

The night after Eddie's birthday, Gloria was kidnapped by Tyrone and Donald. She was bound and gagged, forced into the trunk of a stolen vehicle provided by Tyrone. One the way down to South Jersey, the 2 young men stopped at a 24 hour diner down in Camden. Donald walks straight to the bathroom to wash off the blood from his hands. He had punched Gloria in the face while struggling to get her into the trunk. Tyrone sits at a booth waiting for the waitress. At another booth sat a young white couple, who became nervous when Donald walked pass to the bathroom. Sitting at the counter was a burly old white guy. He looked like a trucker. Flannel shirt, bent ball cap and chain connected from the jeans to the wallet type. He paid Tyrone no mind. The waitress was a middle-aged blonde. She was standing at the counter writing on her pad. Donald comes out the bathroom. He sits across from Tyrone. "Did you order yet?" asked Donald. "The waitress ain't come over! She just standing there!" said Tyrone. "Yo! Man the fuck up! Hey! Can we get some service over here?" Donald shouted. The waitress sighs. She comes to the booth. "Yeah. I wanna steak well done, with fries and a large root beer." Said Donald. "I'll take a tuna melt, cheese fries and a large grape soda." Said Tyrone. The waitress walks off. "Hey. You think we can start down here?" asked Tyrone. "Start what?" asked Donald. "Man, these white folks get high more than niggas! They got more money than niggas too!" Tyrone whispered. "You talking about going behind Eddie's back and hustling down here? Nigga, you done lost yo mind!" Donald whispered. "Ain't nobody really down here to stop us!" whispered Tyrone. "We'll be dead before we can sell our first dime bag! Let it go man!" whispered Donald.

Eddie lassenberry had secretly rented out an apartment on the top floor of a project housing building on Prince Street in Newark. This is where he kept Gloria after the kidnapping. Eddie had hired a registered nurse from the hospital nearby to care for Gloria.

The nurse's name was Linda Kowalski. She had a once a week coke habit, in which a guy from one of Eddie's crews supplied her. She would wear a black wig and sunglasses when she was summoned to Eddie's place. Eddie also hired 2 guards to make sure Gloria never left the building. Eddie had the place decked out with new furniture and art work. He purchased a big floor model TV for Gloria to watch in her bedroom. He bought a floor model TV for the living room as well.

Linda comes from out of the bedroom after giving Gloria a checkup. "I've have some good news. Your girlfriend seems to be pregnant." Said Linda. Eddie doesn't respond to the news. He just sits there gazing at the TV. "Did you hear me? I said she's pregnant!" said Linda. Eddie looks at Linda. "Come over here and suck my dick." Said Eddie. "What?" Linda asked. "You heard me. Come here and unzip my pants, take my dick out and start sucking until I cum in yo mouth." said Eddie. Linda scoffs. Eddie is still staring at her. The room is dead silent. Linda sees that Eddie is dead serious. She takes off her shirt. She goes over and sits next to Eddie. She slowly unzips his pants. At this time Eddie goes back to gazing at the TV. She takes his dick out, and gives Eddie a blow job.

—— CHAPTER 2. EDDIE'S PURGE ——

It was a cold dark night on January the 2nd, 1980, when Eddie called a meeting at the warehouse in Elizabeth, New Jersey. Benny had rented it out to a landscaping company. The place stored snow plows, dumpsters, log splitters and other equipment. Eddie had jabbo and butch arrange the meeting. All 40 of Lassenberry's street bosses had arrived at the warehouse. By this time, the lassenberry crew had about 153 dealers on the streets of Essex County. Butch had set up 3 folding chairs and along folding table.

When Eddie arrived, all of his street bosses were standing in a group, facing jabbo and butch, who were seated. Eddie's 2 body guards stand off in the distance behind Eddie as he takes his seat between jabbo and butch. "Quiet down people!" shouted Butch. The warehouse is silent. Eddie stood up. "I just wanna say good job over the years! It ain't no surprise we got all of Essex County in the palm of our hands! But, we gotta push forward! I'm talking Jersey City, Hoboken, Secaucus, Kearny and even here in Elizabeth! The whole county of Hudson will be ours!" Eddie shouted. Most of the guys looked shocked. "Not only are we gonna take all of Hudson county, Union county can get it too! This means more territories for you to control, which means more money!" Eddie shouted. Only a few guys applaud. "Hey don't worry! I know most of you ain't built for war! That's ok! Don't worry about it!" Eddie shouted. One young man in the crowd boldly steps forward. "What if we attack these guys, and they decide to retaliate and bum rush us? I can't sell my product and watch out for an army at the same time!" the young man ranted. Eddie walks from around the table towards the young man in the group. Eddie's guards stand vigilant. Eddie stands face-to-face with the young man. "I said don't worry about it. I say don't worry about it because it's taking place as we speak." Eddie chuckled.

The main strip on Communipaw Avenue in Jersey City was a gold mine for dealers and pimps. One such dealer was Kenneth Jenkins a.k.a juicy. No relation to jabbo. Juicy was the king of Communipaw. Juicy was also a morbidly obese black man. Weighing in at 400 pounds, standing 6 feet, 4 inches tall. Juicy owned a card dealership, 3 bars and 4 apartment buildings right on the strip. Juicy and Eddie were well aware of who each other was. That night, juicy was found dead in his apartment with his throat slit. A homeless man on the block saw 3 white guys with police badges come from juicy's apartment earlier. He noticed them jump into an unmarked car and drive off.

Peterstown is an area of Elizabeth, New Jersey that was ran by gatano crime family capo Louis Cardi. Cardi actually ran all illegal activity in Elizabeth accept for the drug trade. There were a few guys that ran dope in Elizabeth.

Ricky Dillon was a skinny 20 something year old white guy from the Westminster neighborhood who sold dope, weed and prescription pills to mostly house wives in the surrounding upper class neighborhoods. Ricky was found by his parents, dead of a puncture wound to the temple, why sitting in the driver's seat of his new sport car.

The night before, an envelope filled with cash was given to Cardi by jabbo at his estate. With the lassenberry crew running drugs in the Westminster area of Elizabeth, not even cardi could do anything while benny was under Gatano protection. The envelope was for cardi's people to do the dirty work.

Carlos Mendez was another dealer from Elizabeth who ran the downtown area of the city, which was predominantly Hispanic. He was stabbed to death by his partner in crime, Mark Vasquez the night of the meeting. 2 days earlier, butch gave mark an envelope filled with cash and an ultimatum. Get rid of Carlos, buy his product from the lassenberry crew and get to live another day.

Ezekiel Huldai was a notorious gangster from Israel. He ran a crew in the Elmora section of Elizabeth. He was into extortion, money laundering, grand theft auto and drug trafficking. The night before the purge, cardi hosted a sit down along with Huldai and Jabbo at a kosher deli in his territory. After the sit down, the deal was that Huldai would get his product from the lassenberry crew instead of being shipped from Tel Aviv. Huldai would also cut cardi in on the car theft ring.

Within no time, the lassenberry crew went from having 200 street dealers, to 320 street dealers just in a week. Eddie was also responsible for increasing the family net worth from 10 million a year, to 60 million a year. After sending his father a briefcase filled with a million in cash as tribute, benny made Eddie head of the entire drug ring in Essex County. Mark Vasquez was put in charge of Hudson, then later Union county. Mark was the key to keeping the Latino crews in check.

Although Eddie was really running the streets, the media had targeted benny as being the drug king pin. Benny couldn't walk the streets without a camera crew following him. Instead of causing a scene, benny would just smile for the cameras. To viewers watching TV, it may looked like benny walked alone, but he was totally surrounded by guards within a 50 yard radius. Benny was also being watched by 2 white men dressed in black suits and wearing dark shades. They both sat in a black van, keeping a far distance, looking through high tech binoculars.

One day, benny had ordered jabbo to have a 5 car caravan to escort him to Cherry Hill just to go home to see his wife Lola. Lola Elizabeth Lassenberry was the matriarch of the Lassenberry clan. She came from an upper middle class family. She met her future husband at the beach In Atlantic City. Benny was standing alone in his bathing suit just staring at the ocean view. Lola had pointed out benny to her girlfriends. "Good lord! He's really strange looking!" one of Lola's friends said. "He looks like a black scarecrow!" Lola's other friend chuckled

Lola was a beautiful light skinned young woman, with jet black hair that came down to her lower back. She had hazel eyes, voluptuous breasts, a small waist and curvy hips, standing 5 feet, 6 inches tall. She usually had her hair in 2 pig tails. Men were hypnotized by her beauty at first sight. She was the only child of Doctor Julius and Katherine Bash.

Julius was the first black man to have a dental practice in South Jersey at the time. His father was from Irish descent, who moved from Dublin to Jersey and married Julius's mother, who was black.

Lola was intrigued by benny at first sight. "Let's grab a hot dog from the vendor!" Said one of Lola's girlfriends. The other friend agreed. "I'm not hungry. You two go ahead. I'm going to sit here and get some Sun." said Lola. Lola unfolds her beach towel, while her friends had ran towards the boardwalk in search for a vendor. Lola had laid on her back, still watching benny from afar. Lola was getting impatient because benny didn't turn in her direction. She was always used to having all eyes on her. She then takes the initiative, and loosens her pig tails, flinging her hair to its full length. She gets up, and then slowly struts like a runway model in benny's direction. Men, young and old, married or single couldn't help notice the beauty on the beach. One white woman gave her husband a hard slap across the face for staring too hard.

Lola was 17 at the time and benny was 21. Lola was on break from college. Benny had just arrived from down south at some time earlier.

"Excuse me. Excuse me!" said Lola. She taps benny on the shoulder. Benny turns around. His eyes bulge out when he first sees the beach beauty. "You find what you're looking for?" asked Lola. "What?" asked benny. "I asked you, did you find what you're looking for?" asked Lola. Benny smiles and turns back towards the horizon for a few seconds. "Looking at you, I think I did!" benny chuckled. Lola giggles. "You must definitely be from the south." Said Lola. "Alabama." Said benny. "I've heard horror stories on how they treat colored people down there!" said Lola. "Well I seen it up close! That's why my ass up here!" said benny. "So, what's your name country?" asked Lola. "Benny Lassenberry." He responded. Just before benny could ask anything, Lola's friends return. "Who's your friend Lola?" asked one of the friends. "This is benny." Said Lola. "It's true when they say pretty girls hang in groups!" said benny. Lola and her friend giggle. Before Lola could say anything, her other friend grabbed her by the arm with one hand, while holding a hot dog in the other. "Come on girls! We have to go!" Said the other friend. Lola and her blushing friend followed the friend with the hot dog away from benny. "I have to go benny! But, look me up if you're ever in Cherry Hill under bash!" Lola shouted while being pulled away. Benny smiled, and nodded. He turns back, looking towards the horizon.

A year later after sneaking around on dates, benny and Lola eloped on January 2nd, 1934 on a Wednesday. By the time Lola's friends and family found out about the marriage, benny and Lola had already moved into an apartment. The couple were expecting their first child. Doctor bash was less than pleased with Lola's choices and did everything to make the couple's lives unbearable. The first thing doctor bash did was to cut Lola off financially. Unknown to doctor bash, benny was making a name for himself and was making good money from corn liquor and bathtub gin.

One night there was a black car parked outside of doctor bash's Cherry Hill home.

There were 3 men sitting inside. The man in the passenger seat gets out of the car, and walks to the bash's residence. He was well dressed in a gray silk suit. He rings the door-bell 3 times. At this time, doctor bash was sitting by the fireplace reading a book, while Mrs. Bash had retired for the night to bed. The doctor hears the door bell, and gets up to answer it. The doctor looks through the window, and then opens the door. "Can I help you?" asked the doctor. "Yes sir. I've been sent to tell you that your daughter and son-in-law are very happy together." Said the man. "What? Who are you?" asked doctor bash. "I'm only going to say this once sir. Leave your son-in-law alone. He's very important to people I work for that can make your life a living hell. So back off!" said the man. "Did that bum send you here?" asked doctor bash. "You've been warned sir!" Said the messen-ger. The man turns and walks back to the car. Doctor bash trembles as he sees the group of men in the car drive off. Mrs. Bash comes down the stairs in her robe. "Who was that dear?" she asked. "Somebody had the wrong address! Go back to bed!" said the doctor. "Come to bed dear! It's getting late!" said Mrs. Bash. "I'll be up in a minute!" said the doctor. Mrs. Bash turns and heads back to the bedroom. Doctor bash leans against the door, clutching his chest.

Safe houses were set up throughout the 3 counties. The lassenberry crew were moving illegal narcotics, from prescription pills such as sertraline and alprazolam of out New York, and diazepam from a pharmaceutical company in Nutley New Jersey, to Marijuana and cocaine. While other organizations were getting their supply of heroin from Southeast Asia, a.k.a the golden triangle, the lassenberry crew, were trying to figure out a way to get their hands on another source of the product.

Prescription drugs out of New York were being supplied by soldiers from the Sangiero crime family, named by the media after tony Sangiero. A crew would highjack trucks on route to retailers heading upstate. The pharmaceutical company in New Jersey was a target for a crew secretly headed by Capo Vincent Amari, a.k.a Ace. This operation was not sanctioned by gatano.

Vincent was retired from the life after serving under Cucci in New York, and then working out of New Jersey under Gatano. Pete campi was promoted to capo in Amari's place follow-ing his retirement. Amari would form his own crew as secret partners to Eddie and butch. He recruited an associate named Billy, a.k.a Wild bill, an Irish kid named Jerry O'casey and Gino Massoni.

Gino was tired of waiting tables and serving drinks at café Sangiero. Gatano would put some spending money in his pockets, but gino wanted to make his own way into the family, instead of taking handouts like a bum. Vincent had snatched these young men from obscurity.

One day, while in the basement of Vincent's home in Parsippany, Vincent schooled the boys on how to earn big and get rid of bodies. Vincent also told the young men that if they leaked any information about their unsanctioned caper, gatano would have them skinned alive. "Se mi beccano, IL boss avrebbe preso tutto da me e mi ha messo nella povera casa. Voi ragazzi, sarebbe solo scomparire." Said Vincent. "What the hell he just say?" jerry whispered to gino. "It means if you fuck up, you're dead kid!" said Vincent. Jerry gulped down the saliva in his mouth.

Eddie's crew would buy the stolen goods from Vincent and sell the product on the streets. Eddie was the connection to every jersey mob guy's dream to making big cash from drugs.

Eddie was summoned one day by his father at the safe house in East Orange. Eddie this time, was getting so big in the streets, that he would show up at meetings either late or not at all. When Eddie decided to see his father a day later after he was to meet with him, benny became infuriated. Eddie showed up in a chauffeur driven limo with bulletproof tinted windows. The chauffer was an 18 year old kid named Charlie Dalton.

Charlie was a tall skinny, dark skinned young man, with bulging eyes. He was born and raised in Newark. Charlie was a guy who was afraid of his own shadow. Charlie used to sell weed for the lassenberry crew since the age of 10 to help his mother pay the bills. Eddie took Charlie off the streets to protect him from the Prince Street crew. Whenever the other dealers wanted to party, they would take Charlie's weed and smoke it up. This would put Charlie in a financial hole with the lassenberry crew when it came time to re-up on the product. Charlie would be too scared to defend himself.

Eddie took Charlie to the DMV to get his license and made him his chauffer. Rumors of sexual relations started to spread around when Charlie was seen everywhere with Eddie, but no one had the nerve to speak out about the allegations in public.

Eddie approached the safe house where guards were standing outside. Charlie cuts off the engine and jumps out of the vehicle. "How many times I gotta tell yo dumb ass to stay in the car when I'm at a meeting?" shouted Eddie. Charlie jumps back in the car. When inside the house, Eddie walks through the empty living room. He's wearing brown 3 piece suit and brown overcoat. He approached the kitchen where his father was sitting, drinking liquor with his attorney, sleeves. At the stove, jabbo was deep frying some chicken wings. There was a back door to the kitchen, where another guard was standing. "You can leave us now." Benny ordered the guard. The guard nods his head, and then leaves. "Sit down!" said benny. Eddie takes a seat. "Evening gentlemen!" Eddie said with smile on his face. Sleeves and jabbo don't say a word. They just nod their heads. "Let's cut the shit and get to it! What's this rumor I hear that you wanna move in on South jersey?" asked benny. "Where you hear this from pop?" asked Eddie. "Just like you son, I have my sources! So, is it true?" asked benny. Why not? We ain't got anybody down there with enough muscle to stop us anyway!" said Eddie. We do business with the Philly mob! Give them a cut of the action, and we're in!" said Eddie. "That's just it son! You can't make moves like that without letting me know! I gotta go to Gatano first and make the arrangements!" said benny. Eddie jumps out of his seat. "That's what I'm talking about pop! Every time I look around, we're taking all the risks and these spaghetti eating crackers get rich off our blood and sweat! This gotta stop!" shouted Eddie. "Watch yo self boy! Jabbo want you to calm down, and take a seat!" said jabbo. Eddie looks at jabbo, and restrains his emotions. Eddie slowly sits back in his seat. "You did good so far son, but we ain't in good with them hillbilly cops down there yet!" said benny. "Well, didn't you always say to pay off the cops first?" Eddie asked his father. Benny ignored his son's last comment. "Well anyway, I set up accounts oversees in Switzerland, and in Singapore, just in case the feds move in on us. This family ain't going to the poor house under my watch!" benny said. Benny turns towards sleeves. "Go ahead. Show him." Benny said to sleeves.

Sleeves pulls out a few forms from his briefcase. He hands them over to Eddie. "What hell is this?" Eddie asked. "These forms state that you, your mother, and another lassenberry male of your choosing, have access to the accounts." said sleeves. "The fine print says the male heir must be of lassenberry blood." Said benny. "I ain't getting no bitch pregnant pop! You know that!" said Eddie. "You gotta whole shit load of nephews with the name lassenberry to choose from!" said benny. Sleeves hands Eddie a pen. Eddie sighs, and then signs the paperwork. He hands the paperwork back to sleeves. Sleeves puts the forms back into his briefcase. "I'll have copies for you by the end of week." Said sleeves. Jabbo sets 3 plates on the table. He grabs some paper towels and lines a bowl with it. He then places the chicken wings on top of the paper towels to soak up some of the grease. "Jabbo made a lots chicken wings boy! You want jabbo to fix you a plate?" Jabbo says to Eddie. "Nah, old man. I ate already." Eddie said. "Good! More for jabbo." Jabbo chuckled. Eddie shakes his. "Say pop. How much we holding in these accounts?" Eddie asked. Benny smiled. "Just say, my grandkids college is already paid for." Said benny. "But none of yo grandkids are in college yet!" Eddie says to his father. Benny just stares at his son, smiling. "Wow!" Eddie said. "If you ain't got any news for me son, you can be on yo way." Said benny. "Well, there is one important matter. I hear New York and other crews across the country are being supplied from the Golden triangle. I wanna tap into a new source." Said Eddie. "The only other well-known source son, is Afghanistan, and the Russians trying to take that for themselves." Said benny. "Why can't we find a way to creep on over there and get our hands on some of that opium?" asked Eddie. "Hold on son! You're getting in way over your head now! We can take over a few cities, but getting in between 2 countries is way out of our league." Said benny. Eddie shakes his head. He stands from his chair. "You old timers take care. I'm out." Eddie said to the trio. Eddie pats his father on the shoulder, then leaves the safe house.

About half a block away, a black van is parked on the street. Its windows are tinted on all sides. 2 white men in black suits are sitting up front watching Eddie as he leaves the safe house and get into the limo. In the back of the van, sits a black man wearing the same suit and wearing headphones hooked up to sophisticated audio equipment. "The feds would love to get their hands on this information." The man in the driver's seat said.

A week later, about 2 in the morning inside the Elizabeth warehouse, 5 men stand around a man bound to a chair. The man bound to the chair was Ezekiel Huldai. His face was swollen, covered in blood. Standing in front of him smiling was Eddie lassenberry. The other men were Clayton Watson, a.k.a butch, his younger cousin William Watson, a.k.a Dubbs, and Dubbs's childhood friend Robbie Davis, a.k.a bullet proof. Watching in the back ground stood a scrawny kid named Hakim.

CHAPTER 3. HAKIM

Hakim was the son of Eddie's ex-girlfriend Gloria. Hakim now at the age of 14 was adopted by Eddie when Gloria passed away 10 years earlier from a drug overdose. Rumor has it, that it was no accident. Hakim lived in the project housing building Eddie rented right before hakim was born. By pulling strings with the Newark housing authority, Eddie had purchased the 15 story building as his personal lair for one million dollars. Eddie had offered all the tenants a grand a piece to move out. Knowing who Eddie lassenberry was, the tenants realized the wise thing to do was to take the money and run. After all the tenants had moved out, Eddie hired a construction crew to seal off the first 10 floors. The construction team was provided by Union official Paul Valdese, who happened to be a soldier in the Gatano crew.

The floors were sealed off by center blocks. The elevators were dismantled except for the freight elevator. It was the only easy access to the building, except for the fire escape. Eddie always had 2 guards posted at the freight elevator 24/7. A few months after the construction job, Eddie decided to post 4 guards on the roof 24/7. Eddie gave the entire 11th floor to hakim.

Every year, one of hakim's rooms, which was an entire apartment, was filled to the ceiling with toys and new clothes. There was always a crowd of people from the neighborhood around the building receiving gifts from Eddie and hakim during the holiday season.

Hakim was a handsome kid, who looked just like his mother, but with a lighter complexion with soft curly hair. Eddie built a firing range in the basement of the building. He would bring hakim down there and have him sharpen his skills with all types of fire arms. By the time hakim was 12, hakim's marksmanship was near perfect.

At the warehouse, Ezekiel was begging for his life. "Oh god! Eddie I swear to you, I'll leave town! Fuck it! I'll leave the country! Please! Please!" cried Ezekiel. "I'm not doing this for me buddy! Cardi said that you were cheating him out of his share of some jacked cars! He said you owe him 100 grand! On top of that, you were pushing dope from philly to Baltimore! You could've started a war between us and philly for that!" Eddie shouted. "Please! Get cardi over here! I swear I can get him the money by tomorrow!" cried Ezekiel. "Too late for that Hebrew!" Eddie said. Ezekiel tries desperately to get out of the ropes. "Hakim! Get over here!" shouted Eddie. Hakim comes from out of the back ground. He stands next to Eddie. Eddie pulls out a hand gun, giving it to hakim. "No! No kid!" Ezekiel shouted. Before Ezekiel could utter another word, a loud pop goes off. Ezekiel's head falls back staring into the light fixture. As blood was trickling from his the hole in his forehead, hakim hands the gun back to Eddie. "How you feeling son?" Eddie asked hakim. Hakim didn't say anything. He just shrugged his shoulders. Eddie smiled even though he could see hakim's eyes start to tear up. Eddie looks at bullet proof. "I want you to chop this peace of shit up and get rid of it before the sun comes up!" Eddie said to him. Bullet proof just nods his head and unties the body. Butch walks over to hakim at pats him on the shoulder. "Welcome to the club kid!" said butch. Eddie puts his arm around hakim. "Let's get the fuck out of here son! You got school in the morning!" Eddie chuckled. Everyone but bullet proof leaves the warehouse.

Hakim attended the high school a few blocks away from his home. He was chauffeured to school by Curtis every day. Hakim was treated like a celebrity at school. He wore gold chains and gold rings to school before it became popular in the hood. When lunch time came on Fridays, he would buy every kid in the cafeteria cookies, ice cream and donuts. He was the only kid that could pull out at least a grand from his pockets. His clothes were always the latest fashion. He always had a fresh haircut every 2 weeks. Hakim was more interested in dealing with college girls than with the girls in high school. During the summer, Eddie would let him throw parties at the building. The only thing that Eddie didn't tolerate was the kids using drugs where he rested his head.

One time hakim threw a party, when one kid pulled out his own little supply of cocaine and started doing lines. One of Eddie's guards saw this and grabbed the kid by the arm to escort him out of the building. A group of young men, who were friends of the kid had interfered. Suddenly, a gun was drawn. "He's got a gun!" one girl screamed. The crowd ran for the exit. People were being trampled on. At this time, hakim was in another apartment on his floor having sex with 2 college girls. One was white, the other black. Both of them were giving hakim oral sex, when one of the guards burst in. "What the fuck nigga?" hakim shouted. "Sorry hakim, but these kids going crazy out here!" said the guard. Hakim jumps up from the sofa and pulls up his pants. "Shit! You bitches better be here when I get back!" said hakim. The 2 girls started giggling. "Come on nigga!" hakim said to the guard. The guard follows hakim down the hall. As they make their way down the hall, another guard walks towards them. "Stay here man! We got it under control! We got the kid that started this shit!" said the guard. "Bring him down the hall in apartment 11a!" hakim said. "Got it!" said the guard. "Make sure you strip that nigga down to his underwear and tie him up!" said hakim. "No problem!" said the guard. "Go with him!" hakim says to the other guard. Hakim walks back to the apartment where the 2 girls are. Outside the building, the crowd lingers on into the streets. The police show up. 6 squad cars with lights flashing and sirens wailing to be exact. One cop gets out of his car and pulls out a bullhorn. "I want everyone to clear the area! Now!" the officer shouted. A young white girl, looking in her early 20's, runs up to the officer with the bullhorn. "Officer! My friend is up in that building! I think he's being held hostage!" the girl shouted. "What's your name miss?" asked the officer. "It's Amy Koehler! I was the one who made the 911 call from the pay phone across the street!" said Amy. The officer reaches into his squad car and pulls out a clipboard with report forms attached. "Now tell me exactly what happened again?" asked the officer.

Back in the building on the 11th floor, "Y'all can go now!" hakim said to the girls. The 2 girls leave the apartment, heading towards the freight elevator. Hakim leaves out, heading in the other direction towards apartment 11a. In the apartment, 2 of Eddie's guards have the white kid tied up and stripped down to his underwear. Hakim enters the apartment. "Is this the punk bitch that fucked up my party?" hakim shouted. "Come on dude! Please let me go! I'm sorry!" the kid cried hysterically. Before hakim could respond, another guard enters the apartment. "Damn nigga! Y'all don't believe in knocking?" hakim shouted. "Yo man, cops outside!" the guard shouted. "Alright! Untie him and give him his clothes back!" ordered hakim. With tears in his eyes, the white kid quickly puts his clothes back on. "I don't wanna see yo ass around here again!" said hakim. The kid rapidly nods his head out of fear. "If the cops start asking you questions, do don't know shit! Understand?" said one of the guards. "Ok! Ok! You got it!" the kid stuttered. The kid trots out of the room, tucking his shirt into his pants. Hakim and the guards start laughing hysterically.

Minutes later, the kid comes running out of the building. "There he is!" shouted Amy. "Amy! What's up?" said the kid. The kid had a nervous smirk on his face. "Are you ok son?" asked the officer. "Yeah! Why wouldn't I be?" the kid asked. The officer could see the kid trembling. "Your girlfriend here says you were in some trouble up there!" said the officer. "I just got lost! Everything is cool" said the kid. "Are you sure you don't want to make a statement of any kind?" asked the officer. "I just want to go home!" said the kid. "Your girlfriend said someone pulled a gun on you." Said the officer. "No one pulled a gun on me! Why'd you tell him someone pulled a gun on me Amy?" said the kid. The kid was giving Amy the signal with his eyes, not to say anything. "What's your name son?" asked the officer. "It's josh! Josh Peterson!" said the kid. "The people that live here are a bad bunch josh! All you have to do is make a complaint, and we'll take it from here!" said the officer. "For the last time! I'm ok officer! Let's go Amy!" josh shouted. Josh grabs Amy by the hand, pulling her away from the officer. The officer could see josh and Amy bickering all the way to their car. The officer looks up at building, and shook his head.

A few days later, at the lassenberry estate, family members sit at the long marble, kitchen table eating breakfast. It was Lola sitting at the head of the table. Her grandsons mark jr., who was 12, benny the 3rd, who was 15, Larry a.k.a big L. was 13, mike abbey, who was 13, Tyson Richards 13, his younger brother Malcolm 12.

The maid had approached the table, giving Big L. a fresh hot stack of pancakes. He then drowns the pancakes in syrup. "Are my handsome babies enjoying their breakfast?" Lola asked. "Rosa can cook her ass off grandma!" said benny the 3rd. Lola smacks her grandson upside the head. "Don't use that kind of language young man! Understand?" said Lola. "Yes ma'am." Said benny the 3rd. Big L. chuckles with a mouth full of food. "You guys wanna get a game of 3 on 3 after we eat?" asked Tyson. "Hell yeah!" said benny the 3rd. Lola gives him an evil look. "I mean heck yeah." Said benny the 3rd.

Benny had a regulation size basketball court built on the property. It was surrounded by a 30 foot chain linked fence. The basketball court wasn't the only thing benny provided for his grandkids. Another guest house was built on the property after benny the 3rd was born. The second guest house had 4 bedrooms, living room, oak wood walls, marble floors, studio lights and a state of the art entertainment system. Next to the second guest house was an Olympic size swimming pool surrounded by a 3 foot fence. Benny spared no expense on his grandkids. A half acre jungle gym was built on the property as well. Around this time, the estate was appraised by a friend of the family for 10 million dollars.

"I have to tell you boys something before you all go out and play ball." Said Lola. "What's that grandma?" asked Malcolm. "I don't thinks it's good for you boys to be around hakim the next time your uncle brings him over." Said Lola. "I thought pop-pop said family should stick together." Said mike abbey. "Hakims' not really family sweetie. He was adopted." Said Lola. "So, we're not his cousin?" asked Big L. "No, but you can call him your cousin to make him feel good about himself." Said Lola. "You gonna come watch us play ball grandma?" mark jr. asked. "Oh no sweetie! My favorite show is coming on in a half hour!" said Lola. "I saw pop-pop on the news the other day. They said he was a gangster." Said mike abbey. Lola slams her hand on the table. "Your pop-pop is a successful business man and works hard to give his family a nice living!" said Lola. Rosa the maid enters the kitchen. "Rosa! Could you make sure the kitchen is clean after the boys leave?" asked Lola. "De inmediato señora." Said Rosa. Lola gets up from the table, and then kisses her grandson benny the 3rd on the forehead. "I'll see you babies later! Love you!" Lola said as she waves to her grandsons. "By grandma!" The boys all shout. "You boys put your dishes in the sink when finished." Said Rosa. "Ok! Damn!" said benny the 3rd. Big L. starts chuckling. "Don't be fresh!" said Rosa. "Don't be fresh! Don't be fresh! Don't be fresh! Don't be fresh!" some of the boys chant. "Estos niños son un dolor en el culo!" Rosa said as she storms out the kitchen. The boys start laughing hysterically.

The boys talk freely now that the adults have left the kitchen. "I heard hakim got a lot of pull at school!" said mike abbey. "I even heard he killed somebody!" said mark Jr... "All I know, if he try something here, homie gonna get knocked the fuck out!" said benny the 3rd. "Yeah, you beat his ass, then he comes up to your school with his boys to jump yo ass!" said Tyson. Benny the 3rd punches the palm of his hand. "Then it's on! But, I don't think Uncle Eddie gonna let it go down like that!" said benny.

Later that evening, Eddie and hakim are sitting on the roof of their home. Eddie sent his roof top guards down to the 13th floor. Eddie had remodeled the entire 13th floor into a cafeteria and lounge. All the walls were torn down to each apartment to create one giant facility. There were 30 long cafeteria tables, 10 vending machines filled with sandwiches, junk food, juices and sodas. There were dozens of 32 inch TV's mounted on the walls of the facility from one end, to the other. Eddie was the first person to have cable TV installed in Newark. One Sunday out of the month, Eddie would host at the cafeteria a free meals program for the kids in the neighborhood. None of the guards were permitted when the kids came to the 13th floor.

"So son, what you do today?" asked Eddie. "Took a walk around the neighborhood, then made Curtis take me to the mall to pick up a few things." Said hakim. Eddie was holding a bottle of expensive brandy in his hand. He takes a swig straight from the bottle. "I bought a whole new wardrobe for school! I can't wait to go back man!" said hakim. "So you really like school, huh?" asked Eddie. "Hell yeah! I'm like a god in school!" said hakim. Eddie chuckles, then takes another swig of brandy. "I get good grades, all the bitches on my dick, and the guys either scared of me or wanna hang with me!" said hakim. Eddie takes another swig. "Get that education son. Don't be like these fools that work for us! If this whole operation crumbles, they ain't got nothing to fall back on!" said Eddie. "I already know that shit pop!" said hakim. "You ain't gotta worry about college. It's already paid for." Said Eddie. "Did you finish school?" asked hakim. Eddie takes a swig. "No. I'm where I'm supposed to be son. Not too many men can do what I do." Said Eddie. "I can!" hakim chuckled. Eddie lightly punches hakim in the arm. "Yeah, right!" Eddie chuckled. Eddie takes his last swig, and then gets out of his seat. He yawns and stretches. "I'm tired. I'm about to go in." Eddie yawned. Eddie leaves the bottle of brandy next to hakim. "Tell them knuckleheads to get back up here when you go down." Eddie ordered hakim. Hakim nods his head. Eddie exits the roof through the staircase. Hakim looks up at the night sky. He takes the bottle of brandy, and then takes a swig. He scowls from the taste. He walks to the ledge of the roof and pours the brandy over the side. He looks up to the sky again. He then tosses the empty bottle over the ledge into the foliage below.

The next morning, Eddie was up and dressed in a 2 piece suit, ready to take a ride out to Cherry Hill. 2 days earlier, Eddie had made a call to his mother, informing her that he was stopping by the estate.

"Go down stairs and tell Charlie to start the car." Eddie said to his body guard. The guard leaves the apartment. When Eddie steps out into the hall of his apartment, there are 2 more guards waiting to escort him to the elevator. All 3 men walk towards the freight elevator. Eddie pushes the button to go down to the 11th floor. Once the elevator hits the 11th floor, Eddie tells the guards to wait inside the elevator. Eddie then walks down to 11b. Apartment. He knocks on the door. "Hakim! You up?" shouted Eddie. "Hakim!" Eddie shouts again. Suddenly, the door opens. Hakim comes out wearing pajama bottoms. "Yeah?" hakim yawned. "I'm on my way to Cherry Hill. If you need anything, Curtis is in the kitchen making you breakfast. See you later." Eddie explained. Hakim just nods his head, and heads back inside the apartment. Eddie walks back to the freight elevator.

Outside the building, Eddie approaches Charlie. "All the car's tanks filled?" asked Eddie. "Yup!" said Charlie. "They better be!" said Eddie. All the guards enter their assigned cars. The caravan drives off.

Almost 2 hours later, Eddie and his security team reach their destination. Only Eddie's car drives pass the main gate, while the other cars stay parked outside the gate entrance. Charlie drops Eddie off in front of the door to the mansion. Charlie and the guard drive down the pathway to the guest house to relax. Eddie straightens his neck-tie, and then rings the doorbell. 30 seconds pass. Eddie sighs. He rings the bell again. Suddenly, the door opens. Standing there, was an elderly dark skinned man wearing a black cardigan sweater, bow-tie and gray dress pants. "Mr. Eddie lassenberry I presume." He says. Eddie looks the old man, up and down, from head to toe. Eddie noticed that his black shoes were polished to perfection. "You gotta be kidding me!" Eddie said. "Pardon me sir?" said the old man. "Never mind! Where my momma at?" Eddie asked. "She's in the den sir." He says. Eddie opens the door even wider, storms through the door, and down the corridor. The old man scoffs. Eddie makes his way to the den where his mother is. He opens the double doors. Hey momma!" shouted Eddie.

"Quiet!" Lola whispered. Eddie quietly closes the doors. Lola just happened to be cradling her grandbaby in her arms.

Theresa Madison Lassenberry, nicknamed terry was born the same night of the purge on Hudson County. She's the youngest child of Mark Lassenberry sr. and Tasha. She and her brothers, Mark jr. and Corey stayed over at the mansion while their parents went on a trip to Rome for a couple of weeks. "Hey princess!" Eddie said to his niece. Lola is gazing at the TV as usual. "What you watching momma?" asked Eddie. "I don't know why I watch the news! It's just terrible stuff going on!" said Lola. Lola picks up the remote, and turns off the TV. "What's with Jeeves?" Eddie asked. "Who's that?" asked Lola. Eddie sighs. "I meant the butler momma!" said Eddie. "Oh cooper! Your father thought there was just too much work for Rosa, so he called an agency a few weeks ago." Said Lola. Eddie sits down next to his mother. He gives her a kiss on the cheek. Eddie just stares at his baby niece. "She looks just like that knucklehead brother of mine!" said Eddie. "I can't wait until he comes back from Rome! These kids are driving crazy! I'm too old for this now!" said Lola. "Did he go first class?" asked Eddie. "I think so. I don't know!" said Lola. "I know if I was going to some place like Rome, I would take a private jet!" said Eddie. "Your father said you were spending like a wild man!" said Lola. The double doors open. "May I offer Mr. Lassenberry some refreshments?" asked cooper. "No thanks Jeeves!" Eddie said. Lola elbows her son's ribs. "Just playing with you cooper! No thanks." said Eddie. "Can I offer you anything ma'am?" asked cooper. "No thank you cooper. Just go to the kid's guest house and tell those grandkids of mine to come here." Said Lola. "While you're there! Tell my driver not to get too comfortable!" said Eddie. "Yes sir." Said cooper. Cooper closes the double doors as he leaves. "You've only been here a few minutes! Here! Hold your niece!" said Lola. Eddie gently takes his niece from his mother's arms. "So, how's that boy you're taking care of?" asked Lola. "His name is hakim momma! He's doing fine." said Eddie. "Last time he came here, he just had evil in his eyes! I told your nephews to be careful around that boy!" said Lola. "Oh momma! Ain't nothing wrong with that boy! I don't know where you get your information from!" said Eddie. "Ok! I'll just keep my mouth shut then!" said Lola. Eddie hands the baby back to her grandmother. "I'll be back in a minute." Eddie said to his mother. Eddie exits the den, closing the doors behind him. Lola shakes her head, and then turns back on the TV.

Eddie walks down the corridor of the mansion, heading towards the staircase. Eddie walks up the long flight of stairs viewing the pictures on the wall. He stops at one portrait. It was a black and white portrait of Eddie and his siblings when they were young. Eddie's eyes tear up. He takes a few steps more, and sees another black and white photo of his sisters dressed up when they were little. When he gets to the top of the stairs, Eddie walks down the hall, pass his parent's room. 2 doors down, he reaches his old bedroom. He opens the door slowly. He sees that the room is empty. Eddie walks over towards the window. He looks out the window, and sees Charlie and the guard walking towards the mansion. He also sees some of his nephews playing on the jungle gym. Eddie then walks over to the closet. He opens it, and sees nothing inside but wire hangers on a rod. He leave the room, closing the door behind him. Eddie heads back down stairs. On his way back to the den, the doorbell rings. Eddie stops. He sees cooper going to the door and opening it. Standing in the doorway was Eddie's older brother benny jr.

"Your mother is in the den Mr. Lassenberry." Said cooper. Benny Jr. pats cooper on the shoulder. He walks pass cooper staggering. Benny Jr. walks right into his brother standing in the hall. "Hey, little brother! How the hell are ya?" benny jr. shouted. Eddie could smell the liquor on his brother's breath. "Why can't you come see momma without drinking?" shouted Eddie.

"You only come around once in a blue moon! You have no right to come here and talk to me like that!" benny jr. shouted. Cooper just stands there, watching the 2 brothers go at it. "What the fuck you looking at Jeeves? Get the fuck outta here!" Eddie shouted. Cooper leaves the scene as fast as a man of his age could. "Yeah cooper. Run before he kills you." Benny jr. shouted. At that moment, Eddie balls up his fist and punches his brother straight in the chin. Benny Jr. falls back like a wooden board, on to the floor. Eddie just stands there. In a split second, he shakes his head, realizing what he had done. Eddie steps over his unconscious brother, and storms out of the mansion. A few minutes later, Lola comes out of the den, with her grandbaby in her arms. She could see from down the hall, her son laid out on the floor. "Cooper! Cooper! Eddie!" shouted Lola. The yelling wakes the baby.

Benny jr. was an occasional drinker until he lost his wife Karen to breast cancer 5 years earlier. The family helped out with looking after his children benny the 3rd, Joseph and daughters Sandra and Sarah.

Eddie walks over to Charlie and his guard. Eddie's nephews see him, and run over in his direction. It was Jake's son Krayton, who was 7 years old at the time, and Joseph, who was 8, racing to see who could get to Uncle Eddie first. Joseph wins the race. "Hey Uncle Eddie! Where you going?" asked Joseph. Eddie puts his arms around Joseph and Krayton. "I gotta go now boys! Uncle Eddie got some important business to get to!" Eddie explained. Eddie kneels down in front of his nephew Joseph. "Before I go, I wanna tell you that I love you and your father. He's a good man. When I leave, go tell him that his brother loves him. Can you do that for me?" Eddie says to the boy. Little Joseph nods his head with a smile on his face. Eddie stands, and reaches into his front pocket. He pulls out a wad of cash. Eddie gives his nephews each a c-note. "Make sure y'all go tell grandma that I gave it to you!" Eddie ordered. The 2 boys race towards the mansion. "Get the car!" Eddie says to Charlie. Charlie makes a dash to the car. Within moments, the car pulls up. The guard opens the back door for his boss. The guard goes around, and gets in the front passenger side. Charlie drives off towards the gate. Eddie looks back at the mansion and sees his mother standing in the doorway. She looked sad. She steps back inside, slamming the door.

Later on, Eddie's caravan arrives back at the building. When Eddie enters his apartment, he loosens his tie. He flops back into his leather recliner.

Moments later, there's a knock on the door. "Come in! Eddie shouted. The door opens. In comes hakim and Curtis. Hakim is dressed in a money green sweat suit, and wearing a big gold chain around his neck. "Where you 2 been?" Eddie asked. Hakim slaps Eddie on the lap, and then takes a seat across from him on the sofa. Curtis remained standing, with his arms folded. "So, what's going on in Cherry Hill pop?" asked hakim. "You answer my questions first, then I'll answer yours!" said Eddie. Hakim seemed nervous. "We just took a ride around town!" said hakim. Eddie looks at hakim. He stares hakim up and down. He noticed a blotch of what looked like dried blood on one of hakim's white sneakers. He then looks over at Curtis.

"I'm hungry. Go outside and tell Charlie to order me some Chinese food. He'll know what I want." Eddie says to Curtis. Curtis looks at hakim. "Go nigga!" Eddie yelled. Curtis storms out the door, slamming it shut. There's a dead silence in the room after Curtis leaves. "I want you to listen to me very carefully! Go to your apartment, and get out of those clothes! Take a long hot shower! Put your clothes, underwear and sneakers in a garbage bag, and then bring it to me!" said Eddie.

An hour after Eddie had left for Cherry Hill, hakim was dressed, standing out in front of the building. Moments later, Curtis pulls up in a luxurious ride. Hakim hops in the passenger seat. "I don't know why you told me to bring over a suit to wear!" said Curtis. "You're my chauffeur, right? So you gotta play the part!" said hakim. "So that means you gotta sit yo ass in the back!" said Curtis. Hakim looks at Curtis and smiles. Hakim then gets out of the car, and jump in the back. "Man, you was supposed to open the door for me!" said hakim. Curtis scoffs at hakim, and then drives off. "Where the fuck I'm taking yo ass anyway?" asked Curtis. Hakim pulls out a piece of paper from his sock. "Go to 24 Essex Avenue, in Glen Ridge." Hakim said. "What's at 24 Essex Avenue?" asked Curtis. "Man, I met this bad ass white chick when we went to the mall the other day! She's married, but I don't give a fuck!" said hakim. "What if her husband at the house?" asked Curtis. "Man, she said he goes to work at 8 in the morning, and don't come home until 8 at night!" said hakim. "You sure about that?" asked Curtis. Hakim sucks his teeth. "My father paying you to guard my ass, not to ask questions!" said hakim. Curtis just shakes his head, and continued driving. "Hurry up nigga!" hakim chuckled.

In no time, Curtis and hakim reach their destination. Curtis slows down checking the numbers on the houses. He then stops in front of 24 Essex Avenue. "I'm not leaving until I see her ass at the door, and you go inside." Said Curtis. "Just chill until I'm done!" said hakim. "I can't be sitting in this car, in these white folks neighborhood! They'll end up calling the cops!" shouted Curtis. "What, you strapped?" asked hakim. "You know goddamn well I'm strapped! Just get out!" said Curtis. Hakim gets out of the car. He turns to Curtis. "Just be out here in an hour!" hakim whispered. Hakim walks up to the front door and knocks. He peeks through the little window on the side. He sees the door bell, and then pressed it. Hakim looks back at Curtis smiling. Curtis gives hakim the finger. Hakim looks through the side window again. He sees a figure approaching. The door opens.

Standing in the doorway was a beautiful woman in a pink bathrobe. She had natural long red hair, which appeared as if she just stepped out of the shower. When she sees hakim, she smiles from ear to ear. "What are you doing here, young man?" she asked. "I told you I was coming over! When I saw you in those tight ass jeans the other day, I couldn't wait!" hakim said. "You are insane!" she giggled. Hakim steps in closer to the woman. He gently pushes her inside the house, while kissing her on the lips. Curtis figured it was his cue to drive off. The tires screech as he hits the gas.

Inside the house, hakim pushes the door to close it, but it remained ajar. The woman tries to resist at first. "Come on Janie! You got my dick all hard!" hakim whispered in her ear. "You are so bad!" said Janie. Hakim starts squeezing on her breasts. Janie starts breathing harder and harder, but stops hakim before he puts his hand down her private area. They both back up towards the couch. Janie falls back on the couch, with hakim landing on her. Janie finally gives in to her desires. She takes off hakim's sweat jacket, and then pulls off his t-shirt. Hakim forces his tongue into Janie's mouth. Janie then puts her hand in hakim's sweat pants, and starts massaging his erect penis. Hakim gets up and takes off his sweat pants and underwear. He grabs Janie's hair, and forces his penis into her mouth. Janie starts gagging. "Ready for a real woman?" asked Janie. She turns over on her hands and knees. "Come on baby! Put in me!" shouted Janie. Hakim smacks Janie on the ass. He tries to put his penis in her vagina. "No! Put it in my ass!" said Janie. "What the fuck?" asked hakim. "Put it in my ass, quick!" shouted Janie. Hakim tries his best to squeeze his penis in her. "Oh shit! I'm gonna cum!" hakim shouted. "Hurry! Put it in!" shouted Janie. It was too late. Hakim relieved himself on her butt cheeks. "Sorry, but damn that shit felt good!" said hakim. "How good, asshole?" said a male voice. Hakim jumps up. He turns, and sees a man standing at the entrance. Janie jumps off the couch. "Oh baby! I'm sorry! I'm sorry! Oh Herman! I'm so sorry!" said Janie.

Janie's husband Herman was a chubby toupee wearing business man, standing 5 feet, 5 inches tall. He looked in his late 50's, while Janie looked in her mid-20.

Herman slams the door shut. "I don't believe this shit!" shouted Herman. Janie runs over to her distraught husband. She tries to embrace him, but he smacks her across the face and pushes her back. "He tried to rape me!" shouted Janie. "That's bullshit!" shouted hakim. "That's right! Bullshit! I saw you with his filthy black cock in your mouth!" shouted Herman. Hakim is standing there, butt naked, wearing nothing but socks and sneakers. There was a small dresser next to the door way. Herman opens dresser drawer, scrambles through piles of junk and pulls out a hand gun. Herman could see the terror in hakim's eyes. "Wait a minute man, shit!" shouted hakim. Herman points the gun at Janie, and starts sobbing. "I spent all that money on tits, ass and vagina, so you could fuck this animal?" cried Herman. Hakim's jaw drops. "What the fuck you mean, you spent money on vagina?" asked hakim. "Tell him bitch! Tell him!" shouted Herman. "I-I-I used to be a man!" said Janie said, as tears trickled down her cheeks. Hakim begins to gag. He grabs his knees, and pukes on the floor. "Always check the Adam's apple kid!" shouted Herman. Hakim pukes some more.

Down the street, about a block away, Curtis was on his way back to pick up hakim. "That nigga don't need an hour!" Curtis says to himself.

Back at Glen Ridge, Herman starts to cry hysterically. "I gave you everything!" Herman cried. "But, baby! I brought him over for you!" cried Janie. "What the fuck? Y'all some crazy white people!" shouted hakim. "You want to see crazy, you filthy piece of shit?" shouted Herman. Herman points the gun at hakim, but Janie jumps in the way. "No Herman!" Janie shouts. The gun goes off. Janie clutches her throat. She falls to the floor. Janie goes into convulsions. She starts to choke on her blood. Herman screams. "My wife! My beautiful wife!" Herman shouted. Hakim thinks he's the next victim, so he puts his hands up in front of his face fearing for his life. Hakim then noticed that Herman had put the gun to his head. "I'm sorry Janie! I love you!" shouted Herman. He pulls the trigger. Blood and pieces of brain tissue splatter on the wall. Herman falls to the floor. At this moment, Curtis kicks in the door with pistol drawn. Curtis looks at Herman's body on the floor. "I heard a gun go off! What the fuck happened? Curtis shouted. Hakim is speechless. He slowly walks over to Janie's trembling body. "What the fuck you doing?" Curtis shouted. Janie spits up blood on to hakim's sneakers. Her body became still. "Get your clothes on nigga! Quick!" shouted Curtis. Hakim snaps out of his daze. He turns and grabs his sweat suit off the couch, and gets dressed. They both run out to Curtis's car. As Curtis starts the car, he noticed the brand new car parked in the driveway. "Hey, is that his car?" Curtis asked. "I guess! Come on man, and lets the fuck out of here!" shouted hakim. "Yo! We can get paid big time from that shit!" said Curtis. "Man, I just wanna go!" said hakim. "This what we gonna do! You get behind the wheel, and I'll go inside and get the car keys!" said Curtis. "This is fucked up!" shouted hakim. "Just get be-hind wheel!" said Curtis. Curtis gets out the car, and makes a quick dash back into the house. Hakim slides over behind the wheel. Inside the house, Curtis runs through Herman's pockets. He finds the car keys in his front left pocket. The house keys were attached as well. Curtis had took the whole set of keys. He goes outside and pulls the door closed. He then runs toward the driveway. Curtis checks the key ring. Disables the alarm, and jumps in the car. He pulls up beside hakim. "Just stay close behind me! If you gotta run the light to keep up, then do it!" said Curtis. Curtis takes off, with hakim following close behind. They head down Broad Street in Bloomfield, and get to Bloomfield Avenue. They make a left, heading south. About 25 minutes later, Curtis and hakim arrive at a garage out in Elizabeth. Curtis parks at the front entrance. Hakim parks behind him. Curtis gets out and heads to the front entrance because the garage is closed. The door is locked. He bangs on it. A few seconds later, out comes a burly white guy. "Hey, Vincent my man!" shouted Curtis. "What the fuck you want?" asked Vincent. "Come on brother! I gotta fine specimen of a vehicle out here for ya!" Curtis chuckled. Vincent looks over Curtis's shoulder. He sees the car. He grabs Curtis by the collar. "You know better than to bring stolen shit down here without notifying me first!" Vincent shouted. "Listen, but that shit just came out this year! It's practically new!" said Curtis. "I don't give a fuck if it's a space ship! You don't bring hot shit around here without a heads up!" Vincent shouted. He let's go of Curtis's collar. "Come on Vince, man! I'm just asking for 6 grand! You gonna get that on the doors alone!" said Curtis

Vincent was an associate of the gatano crime family. He ran the chop shop for capo Louis Cardi.

"Alright then! If you take the car, I'll cut you in on some lassenberry business!" Curtis said. "What? You want me to sell powder from my garage?" asked Vincent. "Yeah why not? "Look! How much money can you really make from car parts, compared to what I can do for you?" asked Curtis. "Listen kid! Do you think I'm stupid? I know you ain't got connections to benny lassenberry like that!" said Vincent. "Bullshit! I got his grandson sitting in the other car! He'll vouch for me!" said Curtis. "Bring him over here then!" said Vincent. Curtis turns around, and then signals hakim to get out of the car. Hakim gets out of the car, and walks over towards Curtis. "What's up?" asked hakim. Vincent looks at hakim. "I know you kid! You're a lassenberry, huh?" asked Vincent. Hakim nods his head. "Give me the word man, so we can do business!" said Curtis. Hakim looks at Curtis, and then looks at Vincent. "Hey, whatever the man says." Said hakim. "That's it?" asked Vincent. "You heard the kid!" said Curtis. Vincent looks at Curtis. "Come on inside and get your money!" said Vincent. Curtis smiles, while rubbing his hands together. Hakim follows them inside the garage.

As they walk towards the back of the garage, hakim looks around, and for the first time sees the inner workings of a chop shop. They enter Vincent's office. Vincent goes into his safe and takes out a bundle of cash. He holds the cash in his hand before giving it to Curtis. "So, 50/50, right?" asked Vincent. "What?" asked Curtis? "We split the profits from the deal!" said Vincent. "Oh, uh the deal! Yeah, right! 50/50!" said Curtis. "6 grand my man." said Vincent. He hands if over to Curtis. Curtis takes the cash and then tosses Vincent the keys to the stolen vehicle. "When am I gonna see the goods?" asked Vincent. "Oh, by the end of the week! See ya!" said Curtis. Curtis grabs hakim by the arm and rushes out of the garage. When they get outside, Curtis starts cracking up. "What was that shit about?" hakim asked. "This fool think I'm going into dope business with him!" Curtis chuckled. "That's what you needed me for?" asked hakim. "Hell yeah! Once he saw a Lassenberry, he thought he won the jack pot!" Curtis chuckled. They both get in Curtis's car and drive off.

Hakim arrives back Eddie's apartment with the garbage bag filled with his clothes and sneakers. Hakim is now wearing blue jeans, and a light blue sweat jacket. He still has on his jewelry. By this time, Charlie had arrived with Eddie's food. Eddie undressed down to his underwear. "Go hang my clothes in the closet." Eddie says to Charlie. Charlie puts the food on the coffee table and grabs Eddie's clothes. He goes into Eddie's bedroom and neatly hangs up his suit. Charlie comes back out of the bedroom, at the same time Curtis enters the apartment. Eddie picks up the garbage bag and gives it to Charlie. "Take this down in the basement and burn what's inside." Eddie said. Charlie takes the garbage bag and leaves. Eddie orders Curtis and hakim to sit. They both sit on the sofa. "Now tell me what happened while I was gone! If I find out you're lying, I will murder both of you!" Eddie said. Curtis looked terrified. "You wanna tell him?" Curtis asked hakim. "It's like this pop! I met this white chick at the mall the other day, and I went over to her house today to get me some! The husband busts in, and pulls out a gun! He shoots her, and he shoots himself! Curtis takes the husband's car and we take it down to Elizabeth and chop it up!" said hakim. Curtis drops his head, shaking it in disbelief. Eddie looks at Curtis. "So, you got greedy and took the car?" asked Eddie. "I only got 6 grand for it!" said Curtis. Eddie walks over to Curtis. "Don't I pay you enough so you don't have to do shit like that?" Eddie asked. Curtis looks up at Eddie, scared to death. Curtis was about to speak, but Eddie puts his finger over Curtis's lips. "This is what I want you to do. I want you to go back to the house tonight and get rid of the bodies, ok." Eddie said as he gently strokes Curtis's head. "You want me to go with him?" asked hakim. "Nah, you stay yo ass here! You done did enough for the day!" Eddie said in a calm voice. Eddie looks at Curtis. "What you sitting around for? You got a lot of work to do tonight! I guess you should go get prepared!" Eddie said to Curtis. Curtis doesn't say a word. He gets up and leaves the apartment.

Down in the basement, Charlie had dumped all the contents in the garbage bag into a steel drum. He takes a book of matches from out of his pocket. He strikes the match, and lights up the whole book. He stands over the drum and watched as the clothes and sneakers go up in flames. The fumes from the sneakers overwhelm Charlie. He goes over to the janitor's sink and fills a bucket up with water. He then douses out the flames. He puts the drum over in the corner, and fills the bucket again. He douses the drum just to be on the safe side. He puts the singed contents back in the garbage bag, and leaves the basement with garbage bag.

Later that evening, Curtis leaves his apartment in Newark, dressed in all black. He even has on black sneakers. Curtis was a slim dark skinned guy with corn rolls in his hair, which he covered with a black ball cap. He walks 3 blocks from his house, where he finds a dark blue muscle car. Curtis was particularly fond of these type of vehicles. He walks pass it. He looks around, then turns back towards the car. He then pulls out a slim Jim from his pant leg. He looks around again, and then slides the tool between the side door and the window. Once the lock pops up, he then puts on a pair of black leather gloves. He jumps into the car. He takes out a flathead screwdriver and pops the ignition. Within seconds, Curtis has the car in drive and takes off. It was about 12:30 am when Curtis arrives on the block of the deceased couple. The street was dead silent. Curtis looks around, and then circles the block. He arrives back at the house, cutting off his head lights. He then backs the car into the driveway. Curtis is startled when the security light at the side door comes on. Lucky for Curtis, he remembered to separate the house keys from the car keys. He reaches into his front pocket and pulls out the keys. He enters the house through the side door after jumping out of the car. He finds the switch that turns off the security light. He bumps into furniture, until he finds the light switch to the living room.

Down on Broad Street in Bloomfield, a man stands at a pay phone making a call. The black man wearing a dark blue jacket and jeans, dials 911. "911 what's your emergency?" asked the operator. "There's a black man looking through someone's window on Essex Avenue in Glen Ridge I think!" said the caller. "Do you have a specific address?" asked the operator. "I think its 25 or something!" said the caller. "Can I have your name sir?" asked the operator. "Hurry! He has a gun!" the caller shouted. The caller then hangs up the phone, and jumps into a pick-up truck and drives off.

Moments later, a glen Ridge police car arrives on Essex Avenue. The 2 cops get out of their vehicles and walk up the porch of 22 Essex Avenue. One of the cops, a balding white guy, rings the doorbell. The much younger cop stays at the bottom of the steps, with his hand on his holster. Suddenly, and elderly man comes to the door in his bathrobe. The porch light comes on. "Good evening officer. Can I help you?" the elderly man said. "Yes we have report of a breaking and entering." Said the officer. "There's no one breaking in here!" the old man chuckled. The cop at the bottom of the steps sees a shadowy figure walking around the house next door. "We got something! Next door!" the officer shouted. The older officer runs over to 24 Essex Avenue, while the younger officer gets in his squad car and blocks the driveway. The older officer rings the doorbell. He looks through the window and sees a figure duck behind a sofa. He calls in for back up. The officer blocking the driveway gets out of the squad car. He sees someone trying to exit the side door. "Freeze! Don't Move!" the officer shouted. Curtis sees the cop and runs back into the house. "Oh shit!" said Curtis. Curtis pulls out his pistol. Minutes later, 4 more Glen Ridge police cars show up, along with 3 Bloomfield Squad cars. The street was bright with flashing lights. All the streets nearby were blocked off. An unmarked car pulls up on the scene. The detective flashes his badge to the officers. "What we got?" the detective asked. "The call we've received earlier says it was a black man breaking and entering! He ran back into the house at the side door as soon as he spotted us!" the officer said. "Is he armed?" asked the detective. "We don't know!" said the officer. "Are the streets secure?" asked the detective. "Yes!" said the officer. The detective goes back to his car. He then pulls out a bullhorn. "This is detective Allen of the Glen Ridge police! "We have the entire area surrounded! Come out with your hands in the air!" shouted detective Allen. "Oh shit! This is it!" Curtis whispers to himself. "This is your last chance! Come out with your hands in the air!" shouted detective Allen. "Fuck this shit!" Curtis says to himself. "I'm coming out! Don't shoot!" said Curtis. "Come out with your hands in the air, and lay face down on the grown!" the detective shouted. "Just don't shoot!" shouted Curtis. Curtis lays his gun on the floor next to the dead bodies. Curtis slowly opens the front door. All the officers have their guns aimed at the front entrance. Even detective Allen has his gun drawn. Curtis puts his arms out in front of him. "Don't shoot me!" Curtis shouted. The front porch was dark. "Gun!" shouted detective Allen. Guns go off. It sounded like the 4th of July. "Cease fire!" shouted detective Allen. Suddenly, the shots cease.

Curtis feared the police for most of his life ever since he was 8 years old. He stood witness to his father's death at the hands of the police. Curtis's father, Ralph Hanes was a drug runner for the lassenberry crew. One day, Ralph took his son on a run with him to drop off 5 pounds of marijuana and half a brick of cocaine to Upper Montclair. Ralph was secretly getting high during his run. He pulls over the car, with his son in the passenger seat. He dips into the product and started snorting in front of his son. "Daddy! Let's go!" little Curtis shouted. In a fit of rage, Ralph smacks his son in the mouth. "Don't ever tell me what to do!" shouted Ralph. An elderly white woman walks by and witnessed the man strike the boy. "You shouldn't hit that boy!" she shouted. "Mind yo goddamn business! This is my son!" shouted Ralph. Ralph wipes the coke from his nose. "You should be ashamed of yourself, doing that stuff in front of your son!" said the woman. Ralph jumps out of the car, with a gun in his hand. He points the gun at the old woman. "Say one more word! Say another fucking word!" shouted Ralph. Other pedestrians on the street take cover. A police officer pulls up on the scene. Ralph stands in the middle of the street, waving his gun around. "That's right! Y'all run! I run these streets!" shouted Ralph. "Police! Freeze!" shouted the officer. "Fuck you!" shouted Ralph. Ralph takes a bullet in the chest. Ralph's body was numb from doing huge amounts of cocaine. He goes charging at the officer. The officer squeezes off 3 more shots. Ralph drops to his knees, and falls to the ground. Curtis screams. He jumps out of the car and covers his dying father. "Please don't kill my daddy!" the little boy cried. It was too late. Ralph Hanes had died. Curtis sees his hands stained with his father's blood. He goes into shock, and passes out on his father.

Curtis's mother has died a year earlier from heart disease. He was taken in by his Uncle Roy and Auntie Rita after the incident.

Curtis's body tumbles down the front porch. The officers still approach Curtis with caution. All of their guns are drawn on him. Detective Allen stays in the background. One officer flips his body on his back. "He's gone!" said the officer.

The next morning, Eddie and hakim are sitting in the living room eating breakfast. I called Curtis this morning. He didn't answer." Said hakim. "He's probably drunk somewhere. Getting rid of a body is harder than taking somebody out." Said Eddie. "I wanna get a gold tooth." Said hakim. "Boy, I tell ya! You kids today!" Eddie chuckled. Suddenly, one of Eddie's guards enter the room. "You can't knock?" asked Eddie. "You need to turn on the TV boss!"

said the guard. "Turn on the TV then nigga!" said Eddie. "We were watching in the cafeteria!" said the guard. The guard grabs the remote from off the coffee table, and turns on the TV. "Allege drug dealer Curtis Hanes was killed early this morning from multiple gunshot wounds, battling the glen Ridge police." Said the news reporter. Eddie orders the guard to turn off the TV. Hakim's plate falls from his hands. He pukes on the carpet. "Take it easy son!" said Eddie. "I can't believe this shit!" hakim shouted. He covers his face, and starts sobbing like a baby. "Get the fuck out!" Eddie says to the guard. The guard leaves. Eddie gets up from his seat and rubs his son's back. Eddie puts his hand on hakim's shoulder. "Look at me son. Curtis was a good man, a good soldier. He chose this life. He knew the consequences. Now all you can do, is let go and keep moving forward." Eddie says to hakim. Hakim looks up at his father, and wipes his tears away.

It was August 14th 1980, when funeral services for Curtis Hanes were held at Porter's funeral home in Newark, New Jersey. It was an open casket. Curtis's hair was styled with fresh corn rolls. His neck was covered by an ascot to hide the gunshot wound. The room was filled to the ceiling with flowers. The casket had a gold plated appearance.

Benny Lassenberry stopped by only for a few minutes to his pay respect. He went over to Curtis's aunt and uncle, embracing them with hugs. Benny left the funeral home escorted by a least 15 armed body guards. The police had the street blocked off by order of the mayor of Newark.

Different crews from the lassenberry organization showed up to pay their respect. This was the place where Essex, Hudson and union county crews were meeting for the first time. One kid, whose nick name was pork chop, was in awe when seeing benny lassenberry for the first time. "Oh shit! Benny lassenberry just walked by me!" pork chop says to another kid.

Standing off in another area of the funeral home were 4 men dressed in black suits, whispering to each other. Eddie Lassenberry, Butch, Mark Vasquez and attorney Stanley Hart, a.k.a sleeves were discussing the future of the organization.

There were federal agents outside the police barricade snapping pictures of allege dealers and street bosses. But, half a block away were 2 men in black suits standing on the roof of a building looking at the crowd outside the funeral home through high tech binoculars.

Outside sitting in his limo, benny patiently waits for sleeves to come out. "What's taking this guy?" benny sighed. "You want ol' jabbo to send somebody in there to get him?" asked jabbo. "No. just give him a few minutes more. I don't wanna embarrass him in front of the troops." Said benny. Finally, sleeves arrives at the limo. Sleeves gets in. "Sorry to keep you waiting benny!" said sleeves. "Let me guess. You were talking business with my son." Said benny. "Can't get anything pass you!" sleeves chuckled. Sleeved leans in towards benny. "He's talking about taking Sussex and the other surrounding counties." Sleeves whispered. "Oh really!" said benny. "There's a lot of Wall Street types doing tons of blow, and rich house wives with too much money and time on their hands popping pills like candy." Sleeves whispered. "So, what's our opposition out there?" benny whispered. That's just it! There's really no one to take us on!" sleeves whispered. "Who's gonna run things for me out there?" asked benny. "The guys want your blessing to give it to Butch." Whispered sleeves. Benny shakes his head. "I don't know about this sleeves! Butch will end up scaring the shit out of them white folks up there." Said benny. ""Butch is scary alright." Sleeves chuckled. "Jabbo! Honk the horn." Said benny. Honking the horn gives the guards standing outside the limo, the signal to get it. The other guards walk to their designated limos. The guards enter, and jabbo drives off. The police remove the barricades so benny's caravan can drive thru.

Back inside the funeral home, Eddie greets and shakes hands with different factions of the lassenberry organization. He's being closely watched by his body guards. They surround him in a semi-circle as if he was president of the United States.

Standing on the opposite side of the funeral parlor was the boss of Hudson and Union county, Mark Vasquez. He's also backed by a group of body guards. Standing next to him was his 11 year old son, Mark jr., a.k.a Mookie. "¿quién es ese hombre negro por allá padre?" Mookie asked his father. "Esa hombre de ahí es responsable para nosotros tener una buena vida." Mark sr. explained. Mark sr. turns to one of his men. "Tony. Después caminamos hasta el ataúd para ver el cuerpo, nos vamos." Mark sr. ordered. Mark sr. and his son walk up to the casket, and both give the sign of the cross, then leave.

Butch and his cousin Dubbs decide to leave as well. Butch straightens his black neck tie, and then approaches Eddie. "I got this chick across town waiting for me. You know how it is man." butch explained. He and Eddie shake hands. Butch pulls Eddie in towards him. "I hope your pop approves this deal man." butch whispered. "Don't worry. You got it." Eddie whispered. Butch and Dubbs make their way through the crowd to leave.

Later that evening at Eddie's building, Eddie stands outside the door to hakim's apartment. He knocks on the door. "Hakim! It's me!" Eddie shouted. The door opens. Eddie steps into the apartment. Hakim walks back to his sofa. There are no lights on. Eddie clicks on the light. He looks around the apartment. "You been sitting in the dark all this time?" Eddie asked his son. Hakim didn't answer. "I see you put up new posters." Eddie said. "Man, they been up there for months!" said hakim. "You sure?" asked Eddie. "If you came down here more often, you would know!" said hakim. "Watch yo mouth boy!" Eddie shouted. Eddie takes a seat a few inches away from hakim. He takes a deep breath. "It was a good service. We put a picture of him on his head stone." Eddie said. Eddie scratches his head. "We gotta see about getting you a new driver." Said Eddie. Hakim jumps out of his seat. "I don't wanna fucking new driver!" hakim shouted. Eddie remains seated. "Listen son. You know it ain't safe out there. You're the future of all this. I can't let anything happen to you." Eddie said. "I can get around by myself!" hakim shouted. "No, you can't! You're a 14 year old kid that's worth millions! You have to have protection where ever you go! "That's just the way it is!" Eddie shouted. "I said I don't need a driver!" hakim shouted. Hakim storms out the room and heads to his bedroom, shutting the door behind him. "You can't run from who you are son!" Eddie shouted. Eddie leaves the apartment.

Time passed on. Eddie granted hakim his wish. He didn't hire him another driver, but hired a couple of body guards to follow hakim where ever he went.

It was the mid 80's, when benny had control of the most affluent counties in New Jersey. Warren, Sussex, Passaic, Morris and Bergen county were his now. Benny had a different approach to take over these counties than his son. For example, the town of Oxford, New Jersey, located in warren county, anonymously received a half million dollars in contributions from benny to restore a historic manner.

This manor was a Georgian style home built in colonial times. It was in much needed repair. Before legislators could lift a finger, benny used his mob connections to take over the construction project. Once again, with Gatano's permission, benny used union official Paul Valdese for the operation. The county freeholders were more than delighted to see envelopes filled with money on their desks just to turn a blind eye. It was no sweat off of benny's back to make payouts. Benny thought about the long term. Within months after the completion of the manor, tourism increased by 3 percent. Restoration of historic sites were repeated throughout the 5 counties over a period of 2 years. This put benny in a13 million dollar financial hole. Weekly allowances to lassenberry family members were put on hold for a few months. In time, benny started to invest in bed and breakfast lodging next to these historic sites. Obviously benny didn't want his name or face attached to a business endeavor where 95 percent of the customers were upper class white people.

Benny went into business with a couple of lawyers named Allen J. Sunn and Kent Mooney, who ran a small firm out in Alpha, New Jersey. They were introduced to benny by sleeves. All 3 men were members of the American bar Association.

Allen and Kent were a couple of yuppie white guys who borrowed money from sleeves years ago to start up their firm. Kent had a reputation for being a degenerate gambler, going back to his law school days. Allen had an addiction to cocaine which almost cost him to lose his license to practice law. Still in debt to sleeves, The 2 young men didn't hesitate to meet with benny. They were put in charge of the day-to-day operations of all 30 bed and breakfast establishments. As promised, butch was put in charge of running narcotics throughout these counties.

Butch would supply his front men, Allen and Kent with illegal prescription drugs, cocaine and marijuana. Allen and Kent would recruit a small army of blue collar workers that worked on college campuses in the surrounding areas.

Kent and Allen came to butch just a year after butch took over, with another business venture. They told butch to invest in dive bars. The meeting took place in the basement of one of the bed and breakfast establishments out in Dover, New Jersey. It was March 8th, 1984. "These college kids need a place to go off campus to do their dirt." Said Kent. "We just need the funding, and we're in!" said Allen. "Calm down white boy!" said butch. "He's just excited. That's all." Said Kent. "How much this shit gonna cost me?" asked butch. Kent reaches into his briefcase and pulls out a folder. In the folder was an 8 month business plan that he and Allen had drew up. Butch snatches the paper work from Kent. He skims through the 3 page plan with a confused look on his face. "Is there a problem?" Kent asked. Butch quickly folds the paper work and stuffs it inside his jacket pocket. "What hell are you doing?" asked Kent. "Hope you made copies!" said butch. Butch zips up his jacket. "I'm taking this to the big man. I'll get back to you." Said butch. Butch leaves the 2 men standing there in awe.

It was hakims last year of high school at this time. He just turned 18, and was ready to take his final exams for graduation, which was a few months away.

One day while hakim was coming home from school, he decides to stop at his father's apartment. 3 of Eddie's body guards greet hakim in the hallway by giving him dap. Hakim knocks on the door. "Come in!" Eddie shouted. Hakim enters the apartment. Eddie is sitting watching TV in his oak wood rocking chair hakim bought him as a joke for his birthday a while back. "What's up old man?" said hakim. "I got your old man right here!" Eddie said as he grabbed his crotch. Hakim slumps on the sofa. Something on the coffee table catches hakim's eye. It was a small black vial. Hakim grabs the vial. "What's this pop?" hakim asked. Eddie stops rocking. He gets up and snatches it from hakim. "This shit here, is the future! It's called rock cocaine! We decided to call it crack!" Eddie explained. "Where that shit come from?" asked hakim. "From what butch told me, some whacked out college professor created it in a lab! All I know is that this shit is 10 times more effective than regular blow! We cut it so we can sell it 10 times cheaper too!" Eddie said. Hakim looked confused. "Alright! Let me show you!" Eddie as he put the vial down. Eddie goes to the door, and opens it. "T-bone! Get in here!" Eddie shouted. T-bone comes running down the hall. "What's up boss?" he asked. "Get in here." Eddie ordered. Eddie closes the door. "Take a seat!" he says to T-bone. Eddie goes into the kitchen. "What's going on?" T-bone asked hakim. Hakim just shrugged his shoulders. Eddie comes out of the kitchen with a glass tube and a lighter. He takes the vial and puts a piece of the drug in one end of the tube. "I want you to put your mouth on the other end of the tube!" Eddie said. "Come on boss! You know I don't fuck with the product!" said T-bone. "Don't let me have to tell you again, nigga!" Eddie shouted. T-bone sighs. He reluctantly puts the tube in his mouth. "Now light up!" Eddie shouted. Hakim sits up. T-bone takes the lighter and lights up the rock. He inhales. "Pull it! Pull it! Now hold it!" Eddie said. T-bone's eyes begin to bulge. T-bones spews out white smoke. Moments later, he starts trembling, his lips tighten up. Eddie is giggling. T-bone looks around the apartment in a paranoid state. Eddie takes the tube from him. Eddie then goes to the door. He opens it. "Rick! Get in here and take T-bone outside to get some air!" Eddie ordered. T-bone starts fidgeting around, pulling away from rick. "My head spinning y'all!" T-bone shouted. Rick grabs him by the arm and leads him out of the apartment. Minutes later, T-bone was taken outside. At this point he became more erratic. T-bone punches rick in the face and began running down the street across an empty lot. He then runs out into the street into oncoming traffic. Cars are honking their horns, swerving around him. It was too late to swerve for one car. T-bone ends up being thrown 15 feet into the air, landing on his back. The vehicle that struck him kept on driving, actually speeding down the street. Moments later a crowd gathers around his body, when all of a sudden, T-bone gets up and rips off his shirt. He starts running down the street like a mad man.

2 days later around 3 am, after his meeting with Kent and Allen earlier, butch gets a sit down with his boss at the safe house in East Orange. Also at the meeting was family attorney sleeves. "So what's the deal with these white boys?" asked benny. "These jokers wanna know if you can invest in dive bars in my territory." Said butch. Butch pulls out the business plan Kent and Allen drew up. He hands it to benny. Benny takes out his reading glasses from his suit jacket. He takes a moment to read over the details. "So, how is it running your own thing?" benny asked butch as he continues to read. Butch chuckles. "I tell ya, these white folks spend 10 times more on blow then niggas! As for pills, those uppity white chicks devour

those things like breath mints!" Said butch. Sleeves starts laughing. Benny stops reading and looks up at butch. "You put money in the right people's pockets I hope." Said benny. "What people?" asked Butch. "The police son!" said benny. "Oh shit! You're right! I'm on it!" said butch. Benny shakes his head, giving butch the look of disappointment. He folds the paper up and gives it back to butch. "So boss, we in?" asked butch. "Well, I have to call our friends in on this one again. I think we can do this." Said benny. Butch nods his head. "This means I'm gonna have to be reimbursed. That means according to this business plan, you and them 2 white boys gonna pay me 100 grand each, every month for the next 2 years. You still wanna go ahead with this?" said benny. "Those white boys ain't got it like that boss! But listen! I'll come up with your offer out of my pocket!" said butch. "Either way, I just want my money back! Can you handle that? Don't tell me yeah boss, and don't have my money at the end of the month!" said benny. Butch rubs his hands together. "I got you! I got you!" said butch. Benny extends his hand. Benny and butch shake on it. "Soon as the project is finished, the payments start." Said benny.

Outside the safe house, Butch's cousin Dubbs is waiting by the car. Butch comes out. He approaches his cousin. "Listen up! The boss man said it's a go! But, I need startup money!" said butch. "How much we talking?" asked Dubbs. "I need one million in my hand before the week is out! I don't care how you get it! White boys, niggas! I want you to turn everybody upside down and shake'em if you have to! I want that money!" said butch. Dubbs sighs. "Ok. You got it." Said Dubbs. "Now, let's get the fuck out of here!" said butch. Dubbs opens the car door for his cousin. Butch gets passenger side. Dubbs gets in the driver's seat, and they drive off.

About a half block away, 3 men in black suits, 2 white guys, the other one Asian, are sitting in a black van. They see Dubbs pull off in the middle of the night using night vision binoculars. The white man in the back of the van was hooked up to a sophisticated listening device. "These people are expanding." Said the man with ear phones on. "They're probably going for the entire state." Said the other white guy. "Let's not assume agent, and get this information back to the boss." Said the Asian guy. The van drives off.

It was a Monday when hakim was on his way to school to take his exams. 2 of Eddie's guards are sitting in a car, and watch as hakim enter the school. At this time, 2 young black men had entered the school. Their names were Shane Collins, a.k.a shank and his twin brother Sheldon, a.k.a raw dog. These 2 sophomores had made a reputation for themselves over the past semester as being bad asses.

They were both tall, slim identical twins, once asked by their phys. Ed teacher to join the basketball team. They both refused. Instead, they spent their time in school trying to emulate hakim.

While hakim had bodyguards and pockets always filled with cash, these 2 were taking lunch money from the kids in school. They also would take items such as new pairs of sneakers and jackets right off their victim's backs.

When it was time for lunch, Shane walked into the cafeteria with a couple of his boys, where the seniors were eating. He walked down the aisles with a gold chain in his hand he had just snatched from some kid. "Anybody wanna buy a gold chain?" he shouted. At this time, hakim was sitting eating lunch with a couple of females. "I said anybody wanna buy a gold chain?" Shane shouted. Shane struts over to hakim's table. He taps hakim on the shoulder. "Yo, hakim! 200 bucks, and it's yours!" said Shane. Hakim looks up. "I don't need it man." said hakim. "Come on nigga! We know you can afford it!" said Shane. Hakim gets out of his seat. Hakim stood about 6 feet, but Shane stood a few inches taller. One of the girls sitting with hakim, tries to pull him away from the trouble. Hakim yanks his arm away from her. "I'm gonna say it again man! I don't need it!" said hakim. "You gonna dis me like that?" said Shane. The whole cafeteria goes silent. One of Shane's boys balls up his fists. "Walk away kid! You ain't ready for me!" said hakim. Shane looks straight into hakim's eyes with a scowl on his face. "What nigga? It's a new day around here!" said Shane. Hakim removes his gold chains and rings and gives it to his female friend to hold. "Yo! Hold this!" Shane says to one of his boys. As soon as Shane hands over the chain, hakim throws a left jab at Shane, striking him in the chin. Shane falls to the floor. Shane is dazed. Before Shane can get back up, hakim throws a couple of more punches. Shane falls again. One of Shane's boys grabs hakim by the shirt. The school security guard runs over and pull the boys off of hakim. Students are hollering, and standing on tables to get a good view. Before the guard could separate the 2 boys, Shane's boy swings, missing hakim's face. Hakim sneaks in a punch while the guard is between them. The guard puts hakim in a bear hug. "Hakim, chill man!" the guard whispered to hakim. Shane's boy, who was holding the gold chain, tries to make a dash for the exit, but is stopped by 2 more security guards. Shane's other boy takes a swing around the security guard and punches hakim in the jaw. A guard grabs the kid from behind. The assistant principle runs in and tries to restore order in the cafeteria.

Minutes later at the principal's office, hakim is sitting in a chair watching the school secretary type, while Shane and his boys are behind the glass door being scolded by principle Bruno. Hakim rubs his jaw. He looks up and sees his friend Kenya standing in the door way. "You ok?" she asked. "Oh yeah! I'm cool!" said hakim. Kenya takes a seat next to hakim. She reaches into her book bag and pulls out hakim's jewelry. "I know you want these back." Said Kenya. Hakim gently pushes her hand away. "What's the matter? You don't want your stuff back?" Kenya asked. "You keep it baby. I got a lot more at home." Hakim boasted. "You sure? You realize how much gold you have here?" Kenya asked. "About 5 or 6 grand." Said hakim. Kenya's jaw dropped. "Yeah, I'm thinking about moving up a notch to diamonds!" hakim said. "Yeah right!" Kenya said. "For real!" said hakim. They both smile at each other. Kenya shakes her head. "You are something else!" she chuckled. Suddenly, the principle's door opens. Shane and his boys exit the office. All 3 of them stare down hakim as they leave. "Hakim! In my office please!" shouted principle Bruno. "I'll get with you later." Hakim says to Kenya. Kenya gives hakim a peck kiss on the lips, then leaves. Hakim stands, and then heads to the office. Bruno closes the door behind hakim. "Take a seat young man." said Bruno. Bruno goes around his desk and sits down. "From now on, you're going to stay as far away from those jerks as possible! I'm not stupid! I know what would happen if your father gets wind of this! So, let's keep things quiet!" said Bruno. "To be honest Mr. Bruno, there ain't enough room at this school for me and Shane!" said hakim. "But you're graduating in a few months! You shouldn't even think twice about them!" said Bruno. Hakim reaches into his pocket, pulls out a wad of cash. He starts counting the bills. Principle

Bruno starts salivating. Hakim slams a stack of hundred dollar bills on Mr. Bruno's desk. "I know 2 grand can make things happen Mr. Bruno!" said hakim. Mr. Bruno reaches for the cash. Hakim slams his hand on the cash before Bruno grabs it. "So, we understand each other?" asked hakim. Mr. Bruno smiles. We sure do son! We sure do!" said Bruno. Mr. Bruno takes the cash off the desk. He folds it and stuffs it into his pocket. "You can go back to class now." Said Bruno. Hakim and Bruno shake hands. Hakim leaves the office.

Bruno was the school's principle for the past 8 years. He stood 5 feet, 9 inches tall, with a chubby build. He was 45 years old at the time, but looked in his 60's from stress. He kept a bottle of anti-depressants in the top right drawer of his desk, while keeping a bottle of pain killers called ultracet in his bottom left drawer. Unknown to hakim, Mr. Bruno was being supplied these painkillers by the Lassenberry's Elizabeth crew, ran by Mark Vasquez. Mr. Bruno pops a couple of pills without chasing them down with water. Suddenly, there's a knock on Bruno's door. "Come in!" he shouted. Enters school guidance counselor Ms. Starr. "Excuse me Jimmy. Do you have any more posters left sent by the superintendent?" she asked. "Oh yes!" said Bruno. Bruno gets up from his chair grabs a couple of 12" x 18" posters that were behind his file cabinet and gives them to Ms. Starr. "Thank you. I want to pin these up in the office, not just for the students, but for the faculty as well." Said Ms. Starr. Both Ms. Starr and principle Bruno chuckle. "You never know!" said Bruno. "Well, you have a good day jimmy." She said. "You do the same!" said Bruno. Ms. Starr leaves his office. Mr. Bruno closes the door. He walks over by the file cabinet and sees one poster left. He holds it up. He has a look of sorrow on his face. The words on the poster read, JUST SAY NO.

Later that evening at Eddie's apartment, Eddie hakim and Charlie were sitting around watching TV and eating ice-cream. Eddie was eating vanilla, while Charlie and hakim were eating chocolate. There was an old black-n-white sitcom on the tube that was so funny, it made Charlie laugh with a mouth full of ice-cream. "Cover yo damn mouth man!" said hakim. Charlie covers his mouth. "Sorry about that!" Charlie muffled. "It looked like somebody took a shit in yo mouth!" said hakim. Eddie burst out laughing.

"How was school today?" Eddie asked. "Shit was crazy today!" said hakim. Hakim looks over at Charlie, who was wearing only a t-shirt and underwear. "Go put some clothes on man! I wanna talk to my father for a minute!" said hakim. Charlie looks over at Eddie to get confirmation to leave. "Yeah! Go check on the cars after you get dressed." Eddie said. Charlie puts his ice-cream on the coffee table and runs in the room to put some clothes on. Hakim and Eddie are silent, just sitting there eating ice-cream and watching TV. Minutes later, Charlie comes out the room fully dressed. He grabs his ice-cream, with the spoon still in it and heads to the door. "Tell Mikey and pee-wee I wanna see them first thing in the morning!" said Eddie. Charlie leaves. "So what happened?" Eddie asked. "I got into a fight with these clowns from school!" said hakim. "Did you win?" asked Eddie. "I dropped this one nigga pop, but his boy caught me with a jab to the face!" said hakim. "Did you get in trouble?" Eddie asked. Hakim didn't say a word. He just rubbed his fingertips together. "What I tell you? You pay the right people, anything's possible!" Eddie said. "Word up!" said hakim. "You want me to send somebody to the school and take care of that boy who socked you?" asked Eddie. "Nah! I won't have to worry about his punk ass anymore!" said hakim.

About a week later, Shane and his boys were expelled from school for possession of cocaine in their school lockers. They were held by the security guards and later hauled off by the police. Shane claimed his innocents and had no idea how the drugs got into his locker. For some reason, principle Bruno did a random locker search that day.

Months later, somewhere in the remote area of Death Valley, 2 elderly men sit at a card table in a cramped, but air conditioned motorhome facing each other. Outside the motor home, were 5 men sitting under a giant shaded tent. The men under the tent were Carlo gatano, Frankie Depalma, jabbo, butch and union official Paul Valdese.

"How you fellas enjoying this weather?" Carlo chuckled. "You lost yo fucking mind?" said butch. Frankie stands from his seat. "Watch your mouth!" said Frankie. "Man, sit down! I gotta fucking gun on me too!" said butch. Frankie slowly takes his seat. Everyone who was packing were exposed. The men had to dress down because of the intense heat. It was 95 degrees in the shade. Both the Gatano crew and the Lassenberry crew arrived in separate private jets. The pilots flew back to LAX, leaving the 2 crews to settle their business. They were ordered to return within an hour.

Inside the motorhome, "This is the worst place to hold a meeting!" said benny. I received word that the feds are up our asses! Big business has to be discussed out in the middle of nowhere now!" said gatano. "Funny, you can offer me protection from everything else but the feds!" benny chuckled. "No one is untouchable my friend!" said gatano. "Never mind that! I'm here to talk about why your goons are shaking down my people in Warren and Bergen county!" said benny.

After the grand opening of the second dive bar, located in Cliffside Park, New Jersey, front men Allen and Kent were bombarded by the local patrons that night. Due to the success of the first dive bar, Allen and Kent became local celebrities. Money was coming in so fast that the 2 decided to quit practicing law and shut down the firm. Allen and Kent were making 200 hundred grand a piece in one month from the legal side of bed and breakfast business and the fledgling dive bar business, while butch was bringing in a half million every 2 weeks from drug trafficking.

Kent treated himself after the Cliffside grand opening by buying himself a brand new 1985 candy apple red sports car, which didn't come out on the show room floor yet. It was fully loaded with a phone and state-of-the-art sound system. Kent had real alligator interior installed, with monogram seats. He purchased a condominium out in Parsippany, bought a new wardrobe of tailor made suits, and purchased a beach house for his parents on the Jersey shore.

Allen unfortunately fell off the wagon. After the grand opening, he purchased 2 kilos of cocaine from one of Butch's top runners named Tim Russert. There was a big party thrown by Allen at a country club out in West Orange, New Jersey, where the ratio of women to men was 10 to 1 that night. In attendance were Hollywood big shots, corporate executives and those in the porn industry. Allen went over the top by having a plush throne made for himself. There were condoms spread out all over the floor. At this time, the AIDS epidemic was told to the public that it was confined to the gay community. So, the condoms on the floor were ignored. Allen went as far to have a line of beautiful women take turns snorting blow off of his erect penis.

Months later, one late afternoon at the first dive bar in Ramsey, New Jersey, 3 men walked into the bar. They notice Allen standing around giving out orders to the workers. He looked scrawny and pale. People say it was from too much indulgence of the product. One of the men approached Allen, while the other 2 went to take a seat at one of the booths. The man taps Allen on the shoulder. "Pardon me buddy." The man said in a polite voice. Allen turns around. "My friends and I would like to have a word with ya!" the man said. "I'm kind of busy right now sir!" said Allen. Allen gives the man a business card. "If you have any complaints, call our main office and leave your name and number and I'm sure someone will get back to you!" said Allen. The man turns to his acquaintances smiling. He turns back to Allen. He grabs Allen by the collar and pulls him over to the booth where the other 2 men are. He shoves Allen into the booth and sits next to him, blocking Allen in so he couldn't leave. "Now that we have your attention! We wanted to tell you that you have to be taxed in order to do business around here!" the man said.

The man that grabbed Allen was a burly Italian guy who was a soldier in the gatano crew named Joe Muccio. The other 2 men were Alfred Amato, a.k.a A-man from the same crew, and the older looking gentleman with the receding hairline was Salvatore Fiore, capo from the Sangiero crew out in New York. "Listen gentlemen! The people that run this place are dangerous! I don't want any trouble from either side!" Allen said. The men started laughing. Salvatore puts his finger in Allen's face. "Listen! We know all about you Mr. Sunn! We know this place is ran by Lassenberry's people! I'm speaking for me now! I want 50 percent partnership in this place starting tomorrow! If you have to go back to benny, tell him Salvatore from Brooklyn said it's a whole new ball game in this neck of the woods! Salvatore shouted. Salvatore gets up from the booth and leaves the bar. His driver was waiting outside. Joe puts his arms around Allen. "Now what we're looking for my friend, is 5 grand a piece every week, starting today!" said Joe. Allen was trembling. Alfred Amato unzips his jacket to unveil a pistol. "Just hold on one second guys!" Allen stuttered. Allen runs over behind the register and takes out a wad of cash from underneath the bar. The cash was meant for butch. Allen runs back over and starts counting the cash. He divides exactly 5 grand a piece. "Good man!" said Joe. Joe gives Allen a hard pat on the back. The 2 gangsters leave the bar. Allen breaks out into a sweat. He then turns his spike haired, flamboyant, looking bartender. "Tommy! Bring me a double scotch, no ice! Quick!" shouted Allen. Seconds later, tommy the bartender brings his boss the drink. Allen takes the drink down in one gulp. "Another one tommy!" said Allen. Tommy takes the empty glass to fetch Allen another drink. Moments later, tommy comes again with another drink. "Are you ok Mr. Sunn?" tommy asked. "Bring the phone over here and plug it in for me!" Allen said. He gulps down his second glass. Allen feels a sharp pain in his chest. Tommy brings over the phone. Tommy gets down on hands and knees to plug the phone into the jack underneath the booth. "Good boy tommy! Now go get me another drink and take a 10 minute break." Said Allen. Tommy runs to fetch his boss his third drink. Allen picks up the phone, but drops the receiver out of jitters. He picks up the phone again and dials out. The phone rings 4 times. "Come on you bastard! Pick up!" Allen said. Finally, someone answers. "Hello!" said the voice. "Butch! It's me, Allen! You gotta get out here quick!" Allen said. "Where the fuck you at?" asked butch. "Ramsey!" Allen shouted.

"Shit! Call Kent!" butch shouted. Tommy arrives with Allen's third drink. Allen gulps it down like it was his first drink. "Kent can't help me on this one!" Allen said. "You can't tell me over the phone?" asked butch. "Just get out here, please!" Allen cried. "Ok! Ok fool! This better be worth the trip!" butch said.

Back at the meeting in Death Valley, "It's been a week since your people dipped their hands into my business." Said benny. "Listen my friend. I said a long time ago that as long as I'm alive, no harm would come to you and your family." Gatano said. "I remember that! But, I'm talking about my business right now! Tell them to back off, or they'll end up with their throats slit!" benny said. "Are you serious?" asked gatano. "I'll give you 20 grand for each body, but one things for sure, they won't rob me again!" benny said. "I don't know who I'm talking to right now! Is it you or your son?" gatano asked. "You best believe it's me!" said benny. Gatano and benny stare each other down, until benny cracks a smile. They both share a quick chuckle. "I'll tell my crew to back down, and you give them the 20 grand a piece you were going to give me." Said gatano. "What about New York?" benny asked. Gatano shrugs his shoulders. "I'll just tell them I bought you out." Said gatano. The 2 bosses shake hands. "Now, is there anything else my friend?" gatano asked. "Nah! I'm still pissed this dive bar franchise is costing me over 15 million to build!" benny said. "You said 15 million?" asked gatano. "Yeah why?" benny asked. "Never mind!" gatano shouted. "Ok. I guess this meeting is over." Said benny. Both men stand and give each other a firm hug. "Hai bisogno di andare su una dieta il mio amico! Che stai ricevendo grande come una casa!" gatano chuckled. "I might be fat, but you're still older than me, you crippled fuck!" benny chuckled. Both men burst out laughing, and hug each other again. Gatano grabs his cane. Benny and gatano leave the motorhome. The men outside rise from their seats when the 2 bosses come out. "Well gentlemen! Ready to get out of this heat?" gatano asked. Gatano walked over to Paul. He just stares at him. "Abbiamo molto di cui parlare quando arriviamo a casa, è IL Serpente!" gatano said. "What's wrong Mr. Gatano? Did I do something wrong?" Paul asked. Gatano doesn't answer. His just walks off in the other direction. Out of fear, Paul makes a dash to save himself from a possible death sentence. Frankie reaches for his pistol. "Frankie! Lasciarlo andare!" gatano shouted. Frankie puts his pistol away. "Questo calore Del deserto lo finirà." Gatano said. Jabbo and butch have confused looks on their faces. Benny on the other hand, knew why Paul was running nowhere fast. Suddenly, benny's private jet appeared in the sky. Following a few miles behind, was Gatano's private jet.

It was on a Friday, when hakim's life would change forever. It was the day of the prom at his high school. The students of the class of 1984 were getting closer to the real world. Earlier that day, hakim was standing in front of the mirror admiring the tuxedo he was wearing. Standing behind him in the doorway, with his arms folded, was Eddie. "You look sharp kid!" Eddie said. "Thanks pop!" hakim said. "What's with this young lady you're taking?" Eddie asked. "Oh, Kenya? She's cool." Hakim said.

The tuxedo hakim wore was a black tailcoat, with a white ruffled shirt, burgundy bow-tie, burgundy cummerbund and black patent leather shoes. At the last minute, he went to get a fresh haircut at his Uncle Jake's barber shop.

"I can't believe yo ass got accepted to an Ivy League college!" said Eddie. "I told you I liked school!" said hakim. Eddie walks over to hakim, and turns hakim to face him. He puts his hands on hakim's shoulders. "I'm very proud of you son. I mean it." Eddie said. "Come on pop! Don't be getting all soft on me! You're Eddie lassenberry! The biggest bad ass on the planet!" hakim said. "Don't ever forget that shit either!" chuckled. The 2 share a hug.

Elsewhere, Sheldon Collins, a.k.a raw dog was in his bedroom of his mother's apartment in Newark, New Jersey. He paces around the room holding a semi-automatic pistol in his hand. His rage is magnified by the combination of crack cocaine and gangster rap music. After the incarceration of his brother Shane, Sheldon was out for blood. The young man stares at the mirror, dancing around the room reciting the words of the loud music blasting. Sheldon squeezes the trigger of the weapon, but there's no bullets in the gun nor chamber. Sheldon falls back on his bed, coming close to hitting his head on the head board. All Sheldon could think about was putting an end to his rival hakim.

Back at hakim's apartment, hakim takes off his tuxedo. Eddie had already left to go back upstairs to his own apartment. Hakim puts on a pair of jeans and t-shirt. He sits on his new leather couch. He reaches for the phone. He makes a call to his soon to be prom date Kenya. The phone rings 4 times before someone picks up. "Hello." The voice said. "Hey Ms. Green! How's everything? Hakim asked. "Hello hakim! If you're calling for Kenya, she's out at the salon getting her hair done for tonight." Said Mr. Green. "I just called to ask her if she wanted to be picked up in a limo or a horse-n-carriage." Hakim asked. "I thought you 2 already talked about this!" said Ms. Green. "We did, kind of! But, I also wanted to ask her what color she wanted to ride in!" hakim said. "I'm sure she would love a cream colored one." Said Ms. Green. "I'll get right on you, I mean it!" said hakim. Ms. Green just giggled. "I'll see you tonight at the house." said hakim. "'Can't wait to see you in your tux cutie." Said Ms. Green. "See you!" hakim said. Hakim hangs up.

Ever since their first encounter, hakim would get tongue tied when talking to Ms. Green. A month earlier, hakim took Kenya and her mother out to a fancy Japanese restaurant in Livingston, New Jersey. Ms. Green was not only impressed with hakim's good looks, she was also fond of his style of dress. That night, hakim was dressed in a gray silk 2 piece suit, a pair of dark gray alligator shoes. He wore his gold chain, his gold watch and gold cuff links. Ms. Green had lust in her eyes for the young man.

Just like her daughter, Ms. Green had an hour glass figure, and bedroom eyes. Hakim also couldn't help but notice her long sexy legs, and long jet black hair. Hakim found Ms. Green's perfume alluring, but had to stay focused on the daughter.

After dinner and small talk, hakim ended the night off by tipping the geisha hostess a c-note. Ms. Green couldn't help but give hakim the eye. Before exiting the restaurant, hakim opens the glass door for mother and daughter. Ms. Green walked passed hakim following her daughter, then quickly squeezed his private parts. She noticed that hakim was already erect. As the 3 of them entered a chauffeur driven limo, the groping continued. This time, it was hakim doing the groping to mother and daughter... Kenya and her mother were both wearing tight mini dresses. They both could've passed for twins. Hakim purposely positioned himself between mother and daughter. It was obvious that Ms. Green was a free spirited woman. She found nothing wrong with hakim sticking his tongue down her daughter's throat. While the young couple were making out, Ms. Green was discretely rubbing on her own voluptuous breasts. Hakim had one arm around Kenya, while Ms. Green took his other hand and slid it up her dress without Kenya noticing. The chauffeur could only enjoy the moment by looking through the rear view mirror. Unknown to Kenya and Ms. Green, they were being followed by 2 of Eddie's body guards in a blue economy size car.

Finally, the party to end the school year was drawing closer. Earlier, Charlie was ordered to pick up the corsage. The cream colored limo was parked outside the building. Out of fear of the neighborhood, the chauffeur waited inside the limo, with windows rolled up.

Eddie had asked Butch, Mark Vasquez sr. and Dubbs to stop by hakim's apartment. Eddie wanted to show the other top guys how proud he was of his son.

"Man, you better tare that ass up tonight boy!" said butch. All the guys start laughing. "Hombre busca afilado como una tachuela!" mark sr. said to hakim. Hakim turns and looks at mark senior. "What the hell you say?" hakim shouted. "Easy son. I think he was just giving you a compliment." Said Eddie. "Se refresque mi amigo!" mark sr. said as he gives hakim a pat on the back. "Whatever man!" said hakim. "Hey Charlie! Where's the fucking corsage man?" Eddie shouted. "I put it in the ice box!" said Charlie. "Can you believe this nigga still calls a refrigerator an ice box?" Eddie chuckled. Everyone in the room start laughing. Charlie runs to the kitchen and retrieves the corsage. Eddie pulls hakim to the side to talk to him in private. "You sure you don't want any body guards to go with you?" Eddie asked. "Come on pop! I told you a thousand times, I wanna be a normal kid like everybody else at the prom!" hakim said. "Ok son!" Eddie whispered. Eddie gives his son a hug. They go back into the other room with the others. "Well y'all, this is it!" hakim said. "Man, you talking like you going to jail!" butch shouted. Hakim just laughed it off. Hakim leads the way outside the building, while a professional photographer, hired by Eddie snaps pictures. People from the neighborhood gather around to see how hakim looked. Some people even applaud. Hakim enters the limo, followed by the photographer. Eddie and the crew cheer hakim on. Hakim sees his father giving him a thumbs up. The limo drives off.

Moments later, the limo arrives on the corner of Tremont Avenue and South Orange Avenue in Newark. The chauffeur parks the limo. There's already a crowd standing outside of Kenya's building. People start to applaud as hakim steps out of the limo. The photographer takes pictures of the crowd as well. Hakim was being coy, and trotted pass the crowd without saying a word. He was just all smiles. "When you gonna take me to the prom?" an elderly woman in the crowd shouted. Crowd starts laughing. Hakim enters the building. He walks to apartment A6, on the first floor. He knocks on the door. The door opens. It was Ms. Green standing there.

Ms. Green stood at the door wearing sweat pants, a tight t-shirt and flip flops. Her hair was pinned up in a bun.

When she sees hakim, she screams with excitement. "You look so sexy!" Ms. Green shouted. She gives hakim a big long hug. "You gonna get me in trouble!" hakim whispered in her ear. "Whenever you're ready!" Ms. Green whispered in his ear. Ms. Green Let's go of hakim when she sees the photographer. "Come on in guys!" Ms. Green said. "You have to excuse the way I look." Said Ms. Green. "Everything's fine from where I'm standing!" hakim commented. Ms. Green just smiled.

There was a small crowd in the apartment. All the ladies in the room were giving hakim compliments. Everyone becomes silent as the young lady of the hour comes out of the bedroom. The photographer immediately starts taking pictures.

Kenya stepped out in a long burgundy, strapless gown. Her hair was pinned up, with long curls flowing down the side of her face, just above her huge breasts. The color of her 3 inch heel shoes matched her gown.

Hakim stood in awe. Kenya showed off her beautiful smile. Hakim walks up to Kenya and gives her a big kiss on the cheek. The photographer snaps the picture. "Damn girl, you're beautiful!" hakim said. "Yo ass better not get pregnant girl!" a voice behind the crowd shouted. Hakim looks over and sees a dark skinned, over weight elderly man sitting in the recliner. "Hakim. This is my uncle Sluggo." Kenya said.

Sluggo couldn't get up to greet hakim because his left leg was amputated due to diabetes. Sluggo used to be a dealer for benny lassenberry back in the early days when Eddie was a little boy. After 10 years of incarceration, and bad health, Sluggo left the life behind. Benny let Sluggo off the hook by giving him some sort of severance package of 6 grand in cash. Sluggo eventually ran through the money on booze and women and ended up on welfare.

"Hey son, get over here!" Sluggo said. "Oh uncle Sluggo, they have to go soon!" said Ms. Green. "Its ok!" said hakim. Hakim walks over to where the old man was sitting. He reaches his hand out to Sluggo. Sluggo doesn't return the gesture. Hakim could smell the liquor as he got closer to Sluggo. "You know I used to be the man on these streets back in the day! Yeah, boy!" Sluggo chuckled. "I don't know nothing sir." Said hakim. "I know who you are! Tell benny and them guys to pay me a visit sometime!" said Sluggo. Sluggo finally decides to extend his hand to hakim. They shake hands. Hakim could feel that Sluggo was deliberately trying to tighten his grip. "Yeah boy! We used to run this city together!" Sluggo chuckled. "Like I said sir, I don't know nothing." hakim said. Sluggo releases his grip on hakim. "Just stop it uncle Sluggo!" Kenya said. "Can everyone get together for a group picture?" asked the photographer. The ladies in the room try to fix themselves for the picture. "Let the prom couple in the middle!" shouted one of the ladies. 8 people, including hakim and Kenya, stood still for the picture. Uncle Sluggo decided to remain out of the picture. The photographer snaps the picture. More pictures were taken of hakim and Kenya together, Kenya by herself, hakim putting the corsage on Kenya's wrist, and then hakim by himself. The last picture taken before the couple left was of hakim, Kenya and her mother, Ms. Green. The couple heads outside to the car. Kenya waves to the crowd. The chauffeur opens the door for the couple. Kenya gets in, then hakim. The photographer sits across from them and starts snapping pictures. There were a small group of guys staring from across the street. They were small time dealers from Eddie's crew. "Oh shit! Wasn't that hakim?" one of the guys said. "Fuck that nigga!" another guy said. "Man, don't say that shit too loud! You don't know who's listening!" the first guy said.

Back in Kenya's apartment, uncle Sluggo sits in his chair with a scowl on his face. "Shit! He knew who the fuck I was! I had this city in the palm of my goddamn hands!" Sluggo says to himself.

It took less than 10 minutes for hakim's limo to arrive at the school. The chauffeur parks in the front of the school. He gets out and opens the door for hakim to get out first. Hakim then takes Kenya's hand so she could exit the limo. There were dozens of limos out front. There were other luxury cars, a few sports car and one horse and carriage. "Ah man, I think we should've got the horse and carriage instead! That is so beautiful!" said Kenya. "I rather ride in a car!" hakim said. Kenya sees her girlfriends walking in her direction. She and the girls huddle and start screaming for joy. Kenya give hugs to her 4 girlfriends. "You look so pretty!" one girl says to Kenya. "You know you look fly too!" said Kenya. The girls look over at hakim. "Hi hakim!" they all said simultaneously. The girl's dates were huddled in their own group. They weren't too fond of their dates praising hakim. Moments later, hakim is gently shoved from behind. He turns around quickly. Hakim starts grinning when he sees that it was Leonard.

Leonard was not part of the in-crowd. He became cool with hakim a year after Curtis passed away. Leonard was short and a little chubby. A number of times Leonard had fell victim to bullies because his mother was hooked on drugs. She passed away from an overdose a while back. Hakim witnessed the bullying one day and put a stop to it. This meant a lot to Leonard, but hakim didn't want a close friendship. Hakim did do Leonard a favor, by setting him up with a date for the prom. He asked one of his college chicks that he used to mess with to take Leonard.

The 6 couples enter the gymnasium where the prom was being held. The gymnasium was decorated with big cardboard stars covered with shiny colors of foil. They were dangling from wires connected to the ceiling. There were strobe lights mounted to the walls. There were giant photos all around the walls of students from the senior class. The buffet served all kinds of food and soft drinks.

Kenya received so many hugs, that she had to fix her dress. Most of the guys at the prom couldn't help but gaze at Kenya's huge breasts. She was just that sexy. Hakim noticed the guys staring "What you looking at?" hakim says to Leonard. Leonard had fear in his eyes. Hakim smiles and starts throwing fake jabs at Leonard's rib cage. Leonard tries to block the jabs, but hakim proves to be too fast. Hakim then stops and pats Leonard on the back. "You're alright with me brother!" hakim said to Leonard. Suddenly, the music changes to fast paced club music. "Hey y'all! That's my song!" one of Kenya's girlfriends shouted. The young lady grabs her date by the hand, and they hit the dance floor. Soon the other couples in Kenya's group follow them on the dance floor. Hakim just stood there. "You don't wanna dance?" asked Kenya. "Man, this song is corny!" hakim said. "Stop being so grumpy! Kenya grabs hakim by the hand, then pulls him on to the dance floor. After a few minutes, hakim started to loosen up. The kids start forming into a new brand of line dancing as the DJ mixes the music. Hakim wasn't familiar with this dance. He felt out of place. Kenya grabs him by the hand, and guides him so he stays in step. Hakim was getting the hang of the dance until the strobe lights came on. It totally throws off his equilibrium. He becomes clumsy, stumbling on Kenya's shoes. Kenya started laughing hysterically. "These lights keep fucking with my eyes!" hakim shouted. "Let's go outside then!" Kenya shouted. Hakim grabs Kenya's hand. They both make their way through the crowd. They come upon the exit. One of the chaperones happened to be Ms. Starr at the exit. "Where do you 2 think you're going?" Ms. Starr asked. "I need to get away from these strobe lights Ms. Starr!" hakim shouted. Ms. Starr looks at her watch. "As soon as they stop with the light show, I'll be coming out looking for you!" said

Ms. Starr. "Oh, come on Ms. Starr! We're grown now!" said hakim. "You'll always be kids to me! Stay where I can find you!" Ms. Starr shouted. Ms. Starr shakes her head as the young couple exits the gymnasium.

Outside, Kenya pulls hakim in closer to her. She then plants a big kiss on his lips. Hakim starts giving Kenya tongue action. His hands go down the small of her back. He starts rubbing on her firm ass. Kenya gently pulls away smiling. They holds hands. "So, this means you're my girl from now on!" said hakim. Kenya just nods her head, smiling. Hakim takes a quick glance over Kenya's shoulder and sees someone standing yards away from them. Hakim was in shock to see this person. Hakim quickly went from shock to anger. The person hakim saw, or least he thought he saw caused him to have a traumatic flashback. The person standing there was Sheldon Collins, a.k.a raw dog. Without hesitation, hakim pulls Kenya to the side, and makes a dash towards Sheldon. Before Kenya realized what was going on, hakim had Sheldon on the ground, with his hands around his neck. Hakim continuously slams the back of Sheldon's head into the concrete. The puddle of blood on the ground where Sheldon's head was, had spread, getting bigger. Kenya starts screaming for hakim to stop. Ms. Starr could hear her screams over the loud music. It was like hakim was in a trance. Kenya runs over and grabs hakim by the shoulders. If a fit of rage, hakim smacks Kenya with the back of his hand, causing her to fall backwards on the ground. Ms. Starr and a small crowd of teens witness Kenya's fall. Kenya lands on the grass. It took at least 3 students and a security guard to get hakim off of Sheldon. One of the students noticed that Kenya wasn't moving. He and Ms. Starr ran over to check on her. Ms. Starr noticed the grass was soaked with blood underneath her. Ms. Starr took a closer look and saw that a nozzle in the sprinkling system had pierced the back of Kenya's skull. Ms. Starr started trembling and shut her eyes tight, not wanting to believe the inevitable. Hakim was breathing erratically as Sheldon's body laid lifeless. Hakim was finally coming to his senses, but it was too late.

Back at Eddie's apartment, Eddie was up watching TV eating a snack. He hears someone banging on the door, as if they were going to knock it off the hinges. "Stop banging on my goddamn door like that, and come in already!" Eddie shouted. The door opens. "What the fuck you want?" Eddie asked. Standing in the doorway was Bilal Rahman, a.k.a cutty rock. Cutty just stood there in a daze. The guard at the door stood close, making sure cutty didn't try to do harm to Eddie. "Speak nigga!" Eddie shouted. "Something bad happened at hakim's school!" said cutty. Eddie started breathing heavy through his nose. "Is hakim, dead?" Eddie asked. Cutty shakes his head. "Then what is it?" Eddie shouted. "Hakim's been arrested for murder!" said cutty. Eddie starts rubbing his chest. He collapses on the sofa. "What precinct they got him in?" Eddie asked. "More than likely, they have him at the one on 16th avenue!" cutty said. "What time is it?" Eddie asked. Cutty looked at his watch. "Its 8:35!" cutty said. "Alright. Go and do your job." Eddie ordered. Cutty leaves. The guard stays with Eddie inside the apartment. Eddie goes to the phone, and dials a number. The phone rings 3 times. Someone picks up. "Hello!" said the voice. "Hey sleeves! I need you to meet me at the park in my area, by the jungle gym within an hour!" said Eddie. "Are you ok?" sleeves asked. "It's not me! It's hakim! Just be there!" Eddie ordered. Eddie hangs up the phone. "Have a car ready for me within 15 minutes!" Eddie says to the guard. The guard nods his head, and then leaves. Eddie heads to his bedroom to get dressed.

The next day around 10 a.m. outside the police precinct, Eddie sits in his limo alongside the family attorney sleeves. "So what we're looking at old man?" Eddie asked. "It doesn't look good for the kid. Murder in the first degree, involuntary man slaughter, and numerous witnesses that saw it happened. The kid could be looking at life without parole!" Said sleeves. "So, we have a talk with these witnesses then!" said Eddie. "Not a good move! The feds might get involved, and that's the last thing we want! Plus, there are too many witnesses!" said sleeves. Eddie starts rubbing his chest and breathing heavy. "Take it easy son! Control your breathing!" said sleeves. "This is not good sleeves! Not good at all!" Eddie said.

Hakim was transferred to a maximum security F.C.I in Fairton, New Jersey. He was being held without bail until his trial on November of 84.

Back at Eddie's apartment, Eddie was sitting in his living room alone with a glass of Vodka. There was a knock on the door. "Come in!" Eddie shouted. The guard opens the door and enters, followed by butch, mark Vasquez, and Dubbs. Butch goes over to Eddie and pats Eddie on his shoulder. "Hey man!" said butch. Mark sr. shakes benny's hand. "Take a seat guys. I got some serious shit talk about." Eddie says to his crew. All 3 men take a seat on the sofa. "Get back to your post!" Eddie says to his guard. The guard leaves the apartment.

"What's the deal? Why'd you call us?" asked butch. Eddie rubs his chin, and then takes a deep breath. "There might be a civil war." Eddie said. "With who? Asked butch. "I talked to my father earlier. He's afraid hakim might talk to keep from doing hard time. He's talking about taking him out." Eddie said as tears trickled down his cheek. "Dios mío! I know where you're going with this, and I have to say, going against your father, not good mi amigo!" said mark Vasquez. "You're just talking crazy now!" said butch. "Is it crazy to let him just kill my boy?" Eddie asked. The best thing to do, is to let go, unless you can come up with a better plan than war!" butch said. "Lo siento, pero no puedo participar en esta lucha! Estoy fuera!" said mark Vasquez. Mark storms out of the apartment. "Mark! Vuelve aquí! Eddie shouted. Mark ignores him. Butch taps Dubbs on the shoulder. Both cousins stand from their seats. "Sorry brother, but we can't be a part of a battle that's already lost! Everybody and they momma know that benny keeping this thing we got going because of the cops and the mob!" said butch. "So, y'all letting me deal with this alone?" Eddie asked. "Let's go Dubbs!" said butch. Butch and Dubbs leave the apartment. In a fit of rage, Eddie throws his glass of vodka across the room, shattering it on the wall. His guard comes running into the apartment, with gun in hand. "Nigga! Get back to your post!" Eddie shouted. The guard leaves.

Eddie picks up the phone and dials a number. The phone rings 3 times. Someone picks up. "Jabbo!" the voice said. "Yeah jabbo. It's me. Let me speak to my father." Eddie said. "You speak to ol' jabbo from now on!" jabbo said. "Listen old man! Stop fucking with me!" Eddie shouted. "If this call about the boy, you meet ol' jabbo in person!" Jabbo said. Meet me at the park around my way over by the jungle gym tomorrow night at 11 sharp!" Eddie ordered. Both men hang up. Eddie goes into his bedroom. He removes a large oil painting of a black couple from off the wall. Behind the oil painting was a huge safe. Eddie dials the combination, and opens the safe. He pulls of a briefcase. He lays the briefcase on the bed. He opens the briefcase to unveil a disassembled high powered rifle with scope. He then goes to the phone. He dials a number. The Phone rings 5 times, until someone picks up. "Salaam." The voice said. "It's me!" said Eddie. "Eddie?" asked the voice. "Nigga! How many times I gotta tell y'all not to say my name over the phone? Just be here tomorrow by noon!" Eddie said. "Got it!" said the voice. Eddie hangs up the phone.

The person on the other end of the phone was Bilal Rahman, a.k.a cutty. He was sort of a spy. It was cutty's job to secretly record conversations he would have with runners and street bosses in Eddie's crew. Every week Eddie would want to hear the recordings of those in his crew who might be a threat.

It was 12 years ago when cutty became involved with the lassenberry crew. Before that, there was an upstart Islamic group in the neighborhood. Cutty had joined this group after getting out of the army. He was recruited into the Islamic brotherhood by a childhood friend nick named munk. The Islamic brotherhood had sent munk and cutty around the neighborhoods of Newark to persuade young drug dealers to get out of the life and turn their lives around for the better. Munk's teachings of the Koran effected a lot of the black youth to the point where it got the attention of the man who was in charge of running Newark's drug trafficking. Eddie lassenberry went to his father for permission to shut down the Islamic Brotherhood. Benny told his son that he couldn't just get rid of the Islamic Brotherhood by force. Benny told Eddie, the best way to shut down a belief system is to find dirt on them. So, Eddie put a private investigator on his payroll. Eddie found out what his father said was true. Within months, the private investigator found out that the imam of the Islamic Brotherhood had a craving for prostitutes, and he had the pictures to prove it. Eddie's next plan was to divide and conquer. Cutty and munk were the only 2 from the Brotherhood who saw the pictures. Without explanation, cutty and munk left the Islamic Brotherhood. Cutty and munk tried to raise money to fund their own mosque. Eddie approached the 2 men and offered to give them the money to build their own mosque, in return that they expose the imam of the Islamic Brotherhood. A week later, pictures surfaced at the imam's home, via the mail of him engaging in sex acts with prostitutes. A note came with the pictures basically telling him to shut down his mosque and leave New Jersey.

A year had passed, and Akbar Muhammad, a.k.a munk had become imam of an elaborate mosque on Springfield Avenue in Newark. Construction had went over budget on the mosque. Monk told Eddie that he would pay him the remainder of the cost over a period of time, if he would just finish construction. The cost came to 200 grand. Eddie had munk sign a contract that sleeves had drew up, saying that they would pay the 200 grand in a period of 2 years. Munk agreed, then signed.

It was on the night of April 1st, 1972 when the mosque mysteriously caught fire. Munk was awaken from bed by a phone call. He got dressed and rushed to the scene. Munk stood back in the safe zone with other onlookers. All he could do was drop to his knees. Suddenly, he felt a hand on his shoulder. The hand grabbed munk by the ear, tugging on it real hard. Munk looked up to see that it was Eddie lassenberry. Eddie had a sinister grin. The mosque couldn't be saved. The fire was too intense. "2oo grand, remember? Follow me brother." Eddie said to munk. Munk gets up off his knees and follows Eddie to a car. Eddie tells munk to get in the back seat. 5 of Eddie's guards had surrounded munk. Munk entered the back seat. He sees cutty sitting in the back too. Cutty just looks forward trembling. "What's going on brother?" munk whispered. Cutty turns towards munk. "I have a feeling we've just sold our souls, brother!" cutty whispered. Suddenly, Eddie enters the car, sitting in the front passenger seat. Eddie turns to face the 2 men. "This is how it's going down gentlemen! You either finish paying me off for the mosque, or you can come work for me and forget about this whole mess!" Eddie explained. Cutty looks at munk, then looks outside the car, at the guards. Cutty gives in. "I…I guess so!" cutty said. "What about you big man?" Eddie asked Monk. "Nothing you do can make me stray away from Allah and his prophet Mohammad!" munk shouted. Eddie chuckles. "So that's how you wanna play it!" Eddie said. Eddie reaches into the glove compartment of the car, pulling out 2 items. One was a pistol and the other a camera. Eddie realized at that point that cutty's faith wasn't as deep as Munk's faith. Eddie points the gun at munk. Eddie then holds the camera up. "Now cutty! I want you to lean into your friend over there and plant a big kiss on his lips!" Eddie said. "The teachings of the Koran forbids such behavior!" munk said. "If you don't kiss him, I'll kill both of you!" Eddie said to Cutty. Munk looks at cutty. "In the name of Allah and his prophet Mohammed, don't fall victim to his treachery my brother!" said munk. Eddie just chuckles, pulling back the hammer on his pistol. "Forgive me brother!" cutty cried. Cutty grabs munk by the shoulders and plants a long kiss on his lips. "Hold it! Hold it!" Eddie said as he snaps a few pictures. "Perfect!" said Eddie. "In the name of Allah and his prophet Mohammed, think about what you're doing!" said munk. Eddie scratches his head with the barrel of the pistol. "I thought real carefully!" Eddie says to Monk. Eddie then points the pistol at munk. He squeezes the trigger. The guards standing outside, heard a loud popping noise from within the car. Inside the car, cutty was covering his ears from the deafening noise of the weapon. He could see Eddie laughing, but he couldn't hear anything, but the ringing in his ear. Eddie takes the camera and the pistol, and gets out of the car. "When he gets his hearing back, tell him he belongs to me now!" Eddie says to one of the guards. The guard just gives Eddie a nod. Eddie then walked down the street, with camera in hand towards a limo. He gets in, and the limo pulls off.

The day after Eddie had made the call to meet with jabbo. Cutty arrives at the apartment as scheduled. Cutty is in the living room, while Eddie is in the bedroom. Eddie comes out carrying the briefcase containing the high powered rifle. "Follow me!" Eddie says to Cutty. Both men leave the apartment. Moments later Eddie and Cutty are in the basement of Eddie's building. The 2 men are alone in an area where Eddie and the guards would do some target practice.

The basement of the building was so huge, that it was separated into 4 compartments. Eddie takes the weapon out of the briefcase. "You know how to use one of these?" Eddie asked Cutty. "No…I don't!" cutty said. "Well you're about to get a crash course. Eddie explains the different parts of the weapon, shows cutty how to assemble the weapon, and adjusts the scope. At the other end of the basement, about 30 yards away, were a couple of silhouette targets. Eddie grabs a couple of acoustic earmuffs, and hands a pair to cutty. "Now, we only got until tonight to get this shit right! My life depends on it! Your life depends on it!" Eddie said. "Understood!" cutty said.

Later that evening, Eddie and Cutty arrive at the park, just down the street from his building. The 2 men are sitting in a car just yards away from Eddie and jabbo's rendezvous point. "Now, I want you to go over into those bushes over there! If you spot anybody from jabbo's crew with a weapon, pull the trigger and take down the old fucker! Just remember, those pictures from back in the day will surface if you try any funny shit! Understand?" Eddie said. "Understood!" cutty said.

Cutty still embraced Islam, even though he'd sold his soul to Eddie lassenberry to avoid persecution. Cutty was an informer, not a killer. This was the first time he'd had ever held a weapon. Cutty takes the rifle and runs over and hides in the bushes. Eddie takes out a snub nose revolver from his pants belt, checking it again.

15 minutes later, a luxury car pulls up on the opposite side of the jungle gym. Cutty gets nervous, breaking into a sweat. Eddie sees the driver's side door open. Out comes a light skinned black man, looking in his late teens or early 20's wearing a 3 piece suit. The young man opens the back passenger door, and out comes jabbo. He was dressed in a brown silk suit. His wild afro had turned gray. Eddie steps out the car. He waves to jabbo. The only way they saw each other in the night, was from the light pole nearby. Jabbo stands in front of his car, with his driver standing next to him. Out of respect, Eddie makes his way over to jabbo. Eddie embraced jabbo with a hug. "So jabbo, how can I save my boy's life?" Eddie asked. Over in the bushes, cutty tries to stay still as possible, but suffers an allergic reaction from the bush he was hiding in, which causes him to scratch all over.

Back at the rendezvous point, jabbo scratches his gray goatee pondering on how to settle the problem between Eddie and his father. "Since yo daddy left it up to ol' jabbo, I say come up with enough money so the boy can live a good life in the joint." jabbo said. "How the hell I'm gonna get that kind of money to him while he's locked up?" Eddie asked. "Jabbo know this judge that owes me a favor. Maybe he can get ol' jabbo in contact with the warden at the prison where yo boy staying at." Said jabbo. "How soon can you make this happen old man?" Eddie asked "Jabbo promise before the boy's trial." Said jabbo. Pleased at what Jabbo had proposed, Eddie and Jabbo shake hands. "Listen now! A hand shake is good, but payment is better to ol' jabbo!" jabbo chuckled. Jabbo holds out his hand. Eddie scoffs, reaches into his pocket and pulls out a wad of cash. Eddie starts counting out the bills as he placed them in jabbo's hand. "Don't be shy! Keep it coming son!" jabbo chuckled. Eddie shakes his head. "There you go old man! 4 grand, and not a dollar more!" said Eddie. Jabbo folds the wad and stuffs it in his pants pocket. Eddie and jabbo embrace with another hug. "Now get!" jabbo shouted. Eddie walks back to his car, while jabbo's driver opens the door for him. As soon as jabbo's car drives off, cutty comes running from the bushes. He tosses the rifle in the back seat, and jumps in the passenger side. "You did well." Said Eddie. "Thanks! I don't know why you called on me of all people! I don't do this kind of stuff!" said cutty. Eddie grins at cutty. "I brought yo ass out here to tell you yo services are no longer needed." He tells cutty. Cutty can't believe his ears. "You…you mean I'm free to go?" asked cutty. Suddenly, Eddie takes out the snub nose revolver. He points it at cutty's head, and squeezes the trigger. "Now, you're free." Eddie chuckled. Eddie drives off.

It was October and Eddie decides to pay a visit to his son for the 2nd time. Eddie first signs in at the front gate of the F.C.I. facility. He walks through the metal detectors, then he goes through a physical search by an armed guard. Eddie then follows 2 guards down a corridor. They make a right down another corridor. They approach an electronic door, which can only be accessed by pressing in a 4 digit code. Once the guard hears a buzzing sound, he opens the door, where Eddie sees another guard sitting a desk watching 6 small monitors. "Right thru here Mr. Lassenberry. The guard said. "Things changed a lot since last time." Eddie says to himself. The guard punches in a code to another door, leading to a room.

Inside the room, Eddie sits patiently at a long folding table. He sees another chair, a light fixture above and a video camera hanging high on the wall, with a red light indicator. Eddie noticed the door on the opposite side of the room. Moments later, hakim enters the room from that door, wearing an orange jump suit. Eddie noticed hakim hair grew into a curly afro. Hakim comes in shackled by his hands and ankles. He takes a seat across from Eddie. "You look good boy! Put on a couple of pounds I see!" Eddie said. "Whatever! Listen! I only been in here a few months pop, and I'm getting death threats like crazy in here!" hakim said. "Listen! We gonna fix all that!" Eddie said. "What? They're gonna transfer me?" hakim asked. "No. I fixed it so you can live like a king in here." Eddie told hakim. Hakim slams his fist on the table. "I don't wanna live like a king in here! I wanna go the fuck home!" hakim screamed. "Listen to me! The reason why they put us in this room, is so I can tell you how to run this fucking place!" Eddie shouted. Hakim's eyes start to tear up. "I know for a fact, that you won't do no more than 15 years!" he says to hakim. Hakim puts his head on the table, crying like a baby. "I cut a deal with some very important people! You'll get your own cell, 10 times bigger than a regular one. You can have food from the outside. Refrigerator, stove, TV, king size bed, your own weight room. You can have bitches up in here! You'll be far away from general popula-tion!" Eddie chuckled. Hakim wiped the tears from his eyes. He felt a little better after Eddie had ran down the list of perks. But, it doesn't it last for long. "Oh shit! Kenya!" hakim said as his head drops on the table. Eddie scoffs. Eddie puts his hand on hakim's shoulder. "We all know it was an accident son! It's gonna come a time when you have to realize it!" Eddie said

A couple of days earlier, Eddie, Jabbo and jabbo's driver, were at the Elizabeth warehouse. It was 2 in the morning. Minutes later, they hear a car horn outside. "Go open the door." jabbo tells his driver. The driver runs over to the control panel on the wall, pressing the green but-ton. This causes the warehouse's overhead door to automatically lift. Eddie and jabbo stand 20 yards away from the door, when a black sedan comes riding in, with headlights beaming. Jabbo's driver closes the entrance. The headlights on the sedan turn off, but the engine was still running. Out steps a white guy wearing shades and a beige trench coat. He approaches Eddie and Jabbo. "Good evening, or should I say good morning." the man said as he and jabbo shook hands. Jabbo turns to Eddie. "Now Eddie. You need to go with this man." said jabbo "Who the fuck is this?" Eddie asked. "That's not important Mr. Lassenberry. Just strip down naked and get in the trunk of the car." the man ordered. "Fuck you!" Eddie shouted. The man looks at jabbo. "I can't take chances of a wire jabbo. These are the terms. Take it or leave it." The man says to jabbo. Jabbo pats Eddie on the back. "Just do it son! Trust ol' jabbo on this one!" jabbo said. "Alright then, damn!" Eddie shouted. Eddie gets undressed. "The socks, shoes and jewelry too." Said the man. "Hold this!" Eddie says to jabbo's driver. Eddie had handed the driver his diamond watch, diamond bracelet and diamond pinky ring. Totally naked, Eddie follows the man to the sedan. The man pops open the trunk. Eddie reluctantly hops in the trunk, laying on his side. The man closes the trunk. He gets in the car. Jabbo's driver opens the overhead door so the man can back out. After the car leaves, jabbo's driver closes the overhead door again. Jabbo places Eddie's belongings on the tool bench. Jabbo and his driver sit and wait for Eddie to return safely. Jabbo pulls out a deck of cards from inside his jacket. "Let's see if you can whip ol' jabbo in some 21!" jabbo said.

Meanwhile, Eddie is in the trunk of the car feeling the impact of every bump and pothole on the road. The man suddenly speeds up, causing Eddie to bounce around even more. The man then sees flashing lights in his rear view mirror. He smiles as the patrol car gets closer. He then pulls over on the side of the road. The patrol car pulls up and parks behind the sedan. The police officer gets out, and walks toward the car with one hand on his holster and carrying a flashlight with the other. The man rolls down his window. The officer approaches. "Going pretty fast there sir! Can I see your license and registration?" asked the officer. The man pulls out his wallet and flips it open to the officer. The officer shines his light on it. "Oh, sorry about that sir! When I ran the plates, dispatch said you couldn't be identified!" the officer said. "That's quite alright buddy. Keep up the good work." The man said to the officer. The man rolls up his window, puts his shades back on and drives off. The police officer scratches his head, then walks back to his car.

About a half hour later, the sedan pulls off the road, and drives into a wooded area. The car comes up to a clearing in the woods. The man keeps the headlights on, but turns off the engine. He gets out and opens the trunk. "Follow me Mr. Lassenberry." The man ordered Eddie. "Where the fuck are we?" Eddie shouted. The man doesn't answer. Eddie follows the man, holding his genitals. Eddie is tip toeing because his feet are sensitive to the rocks, leaves and twigs on the ground. About 50 yards away from the sedan, the man stops. Suddenly, a pair of bright headlights come on. Eddie blocks the light with his hand. The man's eyes are protected from the light by his shades. 2 figures step out of the car with high beams wearing clown masks. "We know your situation! We want 1 million dollars apiece in separate briefcases dropped off to our associate standing next to you by noon today." Said masked man. "Wait a minute! I have a few demands!" shouted Eddie. "Well, talk!" the masked man said. "I want my boy to live like a king while he's incarcerated!" Eddie said. "Jabbo already explained that part to us!" said the masked man. "I mean I want him to have a TV, a king size bed, food served from the outside, refrigerator, stove, his own weights, his on private place in the prison,10 times bigger than any cell! He's allowed to have conjugal visits! I'm talking the works!" Eddie shouted. "Are you finished?" asked the masked man. "So, you're telling me for just 2 million the boy can live like a king?" asked Eddie. "No Mr. Lassenberry! The 2 million is for us! For 1 million dollars more, then the boy can live like a king!" said the masked man. "You greedy bastards!" Eddie shouted. "You have until noon today Mr. Lassenberry!" said the masked man. "Let's go!" the masked man says to the other man wearing a mask. "Get me the fuck out of here!" Eddie shouted to man with the shades.

The time of the trial had arrived. There were dozens of news reporters outside the Newark courthouse. Dozens of local and state police had the entire courthouse secured. The streets were barricaded by officers wearing riot gear.

It was 8:35 am on November 5th 1984 when a black unmarked car is allowed to break the barricade and drive next to the side door of the courthouse. 3 plain clothed detectives step out of the car, followed by hakim. Hakim is wearing a blue suit, and handcuffed from the front. He is being escorted by the officers through the side door. The reporters couldn't get close enough for questions.

Back at Eddie's apartment, Eddie is sitting down watching the media circus on TV. Charlie is sitting across from him. "You made sure to tell all our people not to show up at the courthouse, right?" Eddie asked Charlie. "Yep! Sure did." Charlie answered.

Elsewhere at café Sangiero, mob boss Luigi Gatano watches the news with his son Carlo and 5 of his capos. "These fucking niggers! Who do they think they are, us?" Carlo chuckled. Boss gatano doesn't laugh. "Say pop! You think that scumbag Eddie lassenberry would clip his own kid to keep him quiet?" asked Carlo. "Mai può dire con quel tipo!" gatano replied.

At the lassenberry safe house in East Orange, about 20 young black men, who were runners in Eddie's crew stand around a big floor model TV watching the news. "That kid is toast!" one kid shouted. Someone in the crowd smacked the kid in the back of the head. Before the kid could respond, there stood jabbo in the doorway. "Why y'all ain't out on them streets?" jabbo shouted. Everyone scattered like roaches.

At the lassenberry estate in Cherry Hill, benny is in his custom made king size bed, sleeping like a baby.

As meticulously planned, Hakim received 15 years for 2nd degree murder and with the possibility of parole in a maximum security correctional facility. Sleeves was not needed for the trial because Eddie had paid off the right people.

A month later, hakim was due in court on a civil suit for the accidental death of his girlfriend Kenya Green. Since hakim was already serving his sentence, there was no need for him to show up in court. The Green family was awarded 10 million dollars for Kenya's death. Eddie had purchased in hakim's name, 50 acres of land in South Jersey. Hakim had 100 hundred grand in gold coins in a safety deposit box. Eddie also invested in hakim's name, 25 thousand shares of pharmaceutical stock. All of it had to be surrendered to the courts for the green family.

A couple of weeks after the civil suit, Kenya's family started receiving death threats. Graffiti was spray painted on Ms. Green's car and apartment door and windows. Uncle Sluggo would sit out in front of the building in his wheelchair, when cars driving by would fire shots to scare him. It got so bad, that Ms. Green had to go to the F.B.I because local police had turned a blind eye. Benny had got wind of Eddie's threats towards the family. Eddie was told to cease with the threats.

CHAPTER 4. GINO

It was a bright sunny day on July 30th 1987, but a sad day for Luigi Gatano. Everyone from both the gatano crew and the Sangiero crew had come together to pay their respects to long time capo Vincent Amari, a.k.a Ace. The 91 year old died peacefully in his sleep 2 days earlier. The funeral was held as a cathedral out in Brooklyn. There was a 50 car caravan leaving Newark for Brooklyn where Vincent was born and raised.

Vincent was one of the original 10 sent by boss Cucci to New Jersey. His job was to aid the young capo Luigi Gatano in taking over the underworld in Newark. It was Vincent who led the hunt for the cut throat crew after the death of boss Cucci. Gatano demanded different body parts of his victims. Gatano would take these dismembered parts to an undisclosed place and perform some sort of ritual. This ritual was done on 2 occasions by gatano. First, at the age of 17 back in Sicily. He was brought into the last remaining assassins guild located in the province of Caltanissetta. The practitioners of this order believed that you become more powerful in social status 3 years after the ritual is performed.

Benny lassenberry and jabbo were the only 2 blacks to arrive at the cathedral to pay their respects. All eyes were on him as he and jabbo made their way through the crowd. Benny came in wearing a black pin striped suit and black shoes. He wore his signature black fedora, which he removed at the entrance. "Hey benny! Nice suit!" shouted boss Francesco Sangiero. Benny sees the new mob boss and walks over towards his entourage. Benny and boss Sangiero shake hands. At that moment, benny could hear chatter from Sangiero's men standing behind him and jabbo. "Non posso credere che New Jersey fatto queste scimmie a parte del loro equipaggio! The gangster chuckled.

Benny spent a great deal learning the Italian language once he and gatano became friends. Benny kept his composure and ignored the insult. "It's been a while." Said boss Francesco. "Right! Since your uncle's funeral.

While Sangiero and benny were talking, a stocky figure walks out from behind Sangiero. It was Sangiero capo, Salvatore fiore. He was the one who tried to muscle in on benny's dive bar. "It's the famous benny lassenberry!" said Salvatore. Salvatore extends his hand. "You must be Salvatore. The guy who tried to rob me!" benny said. Salvatore keeps his arm extended.

"It was just business! No hard feelings, right?" said Salvatore. Benny just stared at him for a few seconds with anger in his eyes. He then extends his hand, and the 2 men shook hands.

Benny becomes sickened by the sight of the Sangiero crew. "Excuse me gentlemen. I see my boss over there. Come on jabbo." Benny ordered. As benny and jabbo were walking away, benny could hear more insults in Italian. This time coming from Don Francesco himself. "Questo portico nero scimmie dovrebbe lavorare per noi" said Don Francesco. "I've been saying the same thing for the longest!" said Salvatore.

Benny makes his way over to Gatano and his entourage. Instead of using his walking cane, gatano decided to show up in wheelchair. He was being strolled around by Frankie Depalma. Benny shook Gatano's hand. Jabbo does the same. "How you feeling old man?" asked benny. "Hey, show some respect, will ya?" gatano chuckled. "Frankie. I can't see how you put up with this guy?" benny asked. "Years of practice." Frankie said. "I'm demoting the both of you!" gatano chuckled. Everyone laughs.

Gatano yanks on benny's suit jacket. Benny leans down to gatano. "We need to have a walk talk." Gatano whispered. "Stay here jabbo and keep Frankie Company." Ordered benny. Benny takes control of the wheelchair. He slowly pushes gatano through the crowd, towards the exit. There were a lot of wise guys whispering as the 2 men went buy. When they finally reached outside, benny struggles to kneel down next to gatano. "You're the only one I can talk to about this for now! I found out Gino was dealing pills for Vincent to your people! I wanted to have him clipped, but it turns out he put a lot of money in Vincent's hand! So, that means he can put a lot of money in my hand!" gatano whispered. "So what's that gotta do with me and my people? I make sure you always get your cut!" benny whispered. "Listen, my friend. I want control of those pills. I decided to officially bring him into the fold, to get his button. I want you 2 to be partners." Whispered gatano. "What about the Irish guy and that wild bill, what's his name?" benny asked. "That's where you come in! Those 2 punks have to go!" Gatano whispered. Benny didn't say a word. He just nods his head.

Later that evening, benny had called for a meeting with Eddie and Jabbo. All 3 men were sitting at the kitchen table eating a late supper jabbo had prepared. Benny wipes his mouth with a napkin. "Here's the deal son. Gino's 2 pill pushing partners have to go! You'll be his new partner from now on! The thing is, he's gonna be a made guy! That means you can't fuck him like you used to! That means you'll be working for him from now on, when it comes to the pills! You get a crew together, and help him jack the Pharmaceutical Company from now on! He'll make sure gatano gets his cut, and you'll give us ours!" said benny. "All I gotta do, is clip 2 people?" Eddie asked. Benny and jabbo look at each other. Benny turns to Eddie. "Haven't you been listening to me?" benny shouted.

Outside, about a block away. 3 men in black suits and dark shades are sitting in a black van listening to every word the lassenberry crew is saying, through advance audio equipment.

It was a week later after capo Vincent Amari was laid to rest. Gino was sitting in one of his hangouts in Montclair, New Jersey. It was around 10 pm when he and his partners, Billy Cozzielle, a.k.a Wild Bill and Jimmy O'casey were counting the money they'd made that night from the pills score. Earlier, they dropped off a whole truck load of prescription drugs to Mark Vasquez sr., and walked away with 100 grand. Even though they did well that night, Gino looked depressed. "I can't believe I'm 48 years old and still running around like some punk kid! I should've gotten made a long time ago!" said gino. "You? What about me?" shouted Wild bill. "But I've been close to Gatano since I was a kid! You're just an outsider!" shouted Gino. "Hey! Non dimenticare, sono italiano anche tu stronzo egoista!" shouted wild bill. Gino scoffs. "Whatever!" said gino.

Wild bill was the ringleader of the trio. He wasn't obsessed with being a made guy like gino was. He thought as long as he was under Vincent's wing, he was safe. Now that Vincent had passed away, he didn't feel safe anymore.

Jerry O'Casey attended grade school with gino. Years later, gino introduced jerry to Vincent.

The money was split 3 ways. "33 thousand a piece! The good thing is that we don't have to give that old fuck his cut anymore!" said O'Casey. "I don't like this! Sooner or later, we'll have to fall under somebody's flag!" said gino. "Bullshit! It's just us 3, and that's it!" shouted wild bill.

Jerry looks up. "What's wrong?" asked gino. "You hear that?" whispered jerry. "Hear what?" asked gino. "I thought a heard someone moving around outside!" jerry said. "It's an apartment building! You're gonna always hear something outside! Mio dio! Non posso credere che ho appendere intorno a questi ragazzi! Said bill. Gino had a pistol next to him on the end table. Suddenly, someone dressed in all black, wearing a ski mask bursts into the apartment wielding a sub machine gun. "Get the fuck on the floor!" shouted the intruder. At that moment, 2 more people with ski masks enter the apartment, also holding machine guns. Gino goes for the gun, but the intruder grabs it first. "I said get on the floor!" shouted the intruder. Jerry quickly dives on the floor, while wild bill takes his time kneeling down. He tries to get a good look at masked men. The second masked man goes over and kicks Billy in the stomach. Billy falls to the floor in the cradle position, holding his stomach. The third intruder is wearing a fanny pack. He pulls out 3 sets of handcuffs. Gino and his crew are cuffed from behind. "Grab the money!" said the leader. The third intruder takes the cash and puts it into a garbage bag that he brought with him. The third intruder also had a small roll of duct tape in his fanny pack. They taped over the mouths and eyes of gino's crew. They quickly force them outside into a white moving truck.

About a half hour later, the moving truck pulls up to a house on a dead end street in Linden, New Jersey. The driver of the moving truck, who was also wearing a ski mask, honks the horn 3 times. 2 white guys come out and grab Gino from the truck. Gino is trembling. "What about the other 2?" the masked man asked. "The old man said wack'em!" said one of the white guys. Wild bill and jerry start jumping and squirming around trying to get free. The masked man lowers the overhead door to the truck. The 2 white guys take gino into the house, through the side entrance.

Inside the truck, one of the masked men has a pistol with a silencer attached. Wild bill gets a shot through the eye. Jerry takes a bullet in the forehead. The truck drives off.

Inside the house, gino is forced down into the basement. He had the duct tape stripped from his eyes. To his surprise, gino was standing in the middle of the basement, surrounded by at least a couple of dozen members of the Gatano crew.

Standing out from the crowd were capos Mike Mancuso, who ran the waste management and carting business in Essex and Union county. Joe Liacono ran all the illegal gambling in North Jersey after Ritchie Pavino passed away. Louis Cardi ran a crew out of Elizabeth who stole everything from cars to frozen foods. Carlo Gatano, who was the boss's son, ran a prostitution ring, which involved human trafficking. Sammy Desimone was the Underboss.

One of the soldiers took a pair of bolt cutters and freed gino from the handcuffs. Some of the guys were chuckling, noticing gino had wet himself. Gino turned red from embarrassment. "Don't worry kid! After tonight, that'll be your biggest problem!" Sammy said.

From out of the crowd came the boss of the crew. Luigi Gatano had limped over towards gino. "What you're about to go through tonight, is what every man down here had to go through. Are you ready to be reborn kid?" said Gatano. "Yes!" said gino. "Once you are reborn, you will belong to this organization until death. Are you ready to reborn?" asked gatano. "Yes!" said gino. You are to obey and carry out the orders of the boss of the organization, even if it means your demise! Are you ready to be reborn?" asked gatano. "Yes!" said gino. Gatano gives Sammy his cane to hold. Sammy gives gatano a switchblade. "Hold out your hand." Gatano says to gino. Gino extends his right hand. Gatano makes a gash in the palm of gino's hand. Gino flinches a little. Gatano gives the switchblade back to Sammy. Sammy gives gatano a card of a saint. Gatano takes a lighter and burns it. He places it in gino's bloody hand. Gino is told to hold the card until it burns itself out. "From this day on, your soul is no longer yours! Do you understand?" asked gatano. "Yes!" said gino. "Welcome to the family!" said gatano. The boss gives gino a kiss on both cheeks. Gino's eyes start to tear up. "Get over hear, ya big baby!" shouted mike Mancuso. Mancuso gives gino a kiss on the cheeks. Everyone approached gino and embraced him with a hug. Carlo grabs gino by the arm and pulls him to the side. "Congratulations! But, let's get something straight! You work under me now! I gotta a little strip club in Newark I want you to run for me! The thing is I expect 10 grand a week! The rest is yours! So don't be late with the payments! Capire?" said Carlo. Gino nods his head. "Capito." Said gino. Carlo hugs gino again. Sammy Desimone cuts his eye over at Gino and Carlo. "Hey fellas! I left the bar-n-grill open over in Bloomfield! Everything's on the house!" said soldier Nick Rago. Well, since you put it that way, let's go!" Cardi chuckled. Everyone follows Rago out of the basement. Sammy grabs gino. They are the last 2 in the basement. "Whatever you do. Watch your back with that guy! He may be the boss's son, but he's a fucking evil low life!" said Sammy. Gino nods. They both leave the basement.

CHAPTER 5. F.C.I

Back in January 1985, hakim was serving his first year of a 15 year sentence. He was sitting in his cell. But his cell wasn't like anyone else's cell. As promised by Eddie lassenberry, hakim's living conditions were impeccable.

The cell itself was 10 times the size of the standard cell. It was custom built by contractors hired by the Warden, Paul A. Benedict. The funding for the construction project came not from F.C.I, but from hakim's account. The total cost of the project 50 grand, which was deducted from the 1 million dollars originally given to him by Eddie lassenberry. The lair as it was called, was located on the top floor of F.C.I in a distant area from general population. There were 2 huge windows that didn't have bars on them, instead they were casement windows with a crank to open with. The first thing hakim did when he entered his lair, was open the windows and take a deep breath.

The floor was made of parquet on one half of the lair for the king size bed, dresser drawers, coffee table, sofa and a floor model TV. The cemented floor side supported the electric stove, refrigerator, and the weight set.

The bathroom was located near the weights. It was equipped with a full bathtub and separate shower made of beige tile all around. It had a medicine cabinet filled with shaving equipment, clippers, band aids and cotton swabs. There was a separate urinal installed from the toilet, a linen closet with fresh sheet, towels and wash clothes. There was even an automatic hand dryer in the bathroom.

Just like his home was in Newark, hakim had the whole floor to himself. There was a thick metal door that separated hakim from the rest of the world. Outside that door stood a corrections officer posted around the clock. The officer's salaries were paid for by F.C.I, instead of Eddie lassenberry. There were 6 giant ceiling fans for when it became hot, and baseboard heaters all around the lair for the cold weather.

As for food, hakim's meals weren't made in the chow hall like the other inmates. His food came from restaurants. His refrigerator was stocked with beer, juices and sodas and condiments. He even had his own spice rack by his sink. His first meal there was light. Hakim had to get used to the fact that he wasn't coming home anytime soon. After a week he regained his appetite. He ordered a double cheeseburger, fries and a chocolate shake.

Hakim kept himself well groomed. He hired a personal barber, inmate Reggie Mills, a.k.a Mush. Mush was a tall, skinny light skinned brother from Camden, with 5 years left on his sentence. Mush was serving 10 years for a bank robbery. He was 12 years older than hakim. The first time mush cut hakim's hair, there was a silence in the lair. The 2 were trying to feel each other out. Hakim already saw in mush that he wasn't a brawler. He was just someone who talked slick all the time. When mush was done with hakim's hair, he grabbed the broom and started sweeping up the hair. Hakim gave him 10 bucks for the job. "Hey! This place you got here is a palace!" said mush. Hakim looked around with a smile on his face.

The second time mush came up, hakim offered him a cold beer. There was some small talk going on between the 2 guys during the cut. Before hakim could tell mush about himself, mush interrupted him. "Listen brother! Mostly everybody from C, D, and E block either know you or heard about you! Every big shot in here wanna meet you!" said mush. "Yeah! The C.O. told me already." Said hakim. "I just wanna know, how it is being a lassenberry?" asked mush. Hakim chuckled. "You looking at it" said hakim. "This place is tight brother! I'll keep the place clean and won't charge you for the cut! I just wanna hang out here!" said mush. "Let me sleep on it!" said hakim. "Oh, no problem brother!" said mush.

The next day, both hakim and mush take a stroll around the yard. Part of Eddie's deal with the warden was hakim could have the entire yard to himself for a couple of hours. Hakim had to ask for special permission to let mush roll with him. Mush and hakim looked around as they strolled the yard. There were armed guards in each of the 4 towers with high powered rifles. "Damn! So this how quiet it is when nobodies out here!" said mush.

Later that evening, hakim, mush and the C.O. that was on the graveyard shift were playing dominoes. The guard, whose name was Officer Wade O'Boyle, was a 20 something year old white guy who worked that shift, while going to community college during the day. "Where you from wade?" asked hakim. "Nearby Greenwich." Said wade. Hakim and mush had took down a few beers earlier. "You wanna beer man?" mush asked wade. "No can do. I'm on the clock!" wade chuckled. "Come on! Ain't nobody gonna talk!" shouted mush. "Well, ok!" wade chuckled. "Yo! Go and get a beer for wade!" mush orders hakim. "What's that?" hakim asked. Mush was buzzing. "Go get the man a beer!" said mush. Wade could see the anger in hakim's eyes. With much restraint, hakim reluctantly went to get wade a beer. "Yo! Lift y'all bottles up! I wanna make a toast to the coolest fucking C.O. at F.C.I!" shouted mush. Hakim scoffs at mush, but he and wade lift and clank bottles. More drinking continued. Mush had commented on how wade looked, and that he should be in movies. Hakim's eyes bulge as he sips on his beer. Mush gently puts his hand on wade's shoulder. Wade doesn't flinch one bit. Hakim quickly puts his beer down. "Alright fellas! It's getting late! Y'all got to get the hell up out of here!" shouted hakim. "The night is still young!" said mush. "I said get the fuck up out of here! Yo wade! Get this nigga out of here, before I do!" said hakim. Wade grabs mush by the arm and escorts mush from the lair.

A couple of months had passed. Mush hasn't been to the lair since. Mush asked a few of the officers have they seen hakim lately. One of the officers just laughed at mush. He was a burly bald black guy. "Get yo bitch ass back out in the yard before I fuck you up!" the officer says to mush. Mush didn't say a word, and just walked away.

Later that evening, while mush was sleeping in his cramped cell, he gets woken up by the burly, bald officer. "Hey mills! Mills! Wake up!" the officer said as he shines the flashlight in mush's face. "What?" asked mush as he puts his hand over his eyes. "Get yo shit on! They want you at the main desk!" shouted the officer. "What for?" asked mush. "Bitch! I don't know!" the officer shouted. Mush gets dressed in his orange jumpsuit. A few inmates are awakened from the all the shouting. "Open 12 E!" the officer said on his 2-way radio. Mush's cell electronically opens. Mush exits the cell and is escorted by the officer. "Yo mush! Where they taking you?" asked the inmate. Mush just shrugged his shoulders. Mush and the officer reach the main desk of E block. There was another officer at the desk. "I got it from here Jones!" said the officer. At that moment, mush became nervous. "Turn around mills! I have to cuff you!" said the other officer. "Why y'all got me up in the middle of the night? I ain't do nothing!" shouted mush.

The second officer was elderly white guy named Carl Baker. He was a year shy of retirement. "Let's go mills! You've been sent for!" said officer baker. "Don't hurt'em too much baker!" officer Jones chuckled. Moments later, mush starts to calm down as he and officer baker approach familiar territory. "What hell he want with me at this hour?" asked mush. Officer Baker didn't answer. Minutes later, they approach the entrance to hakim's lair. "What happened to office O'Boyle?" asked mush. "He was transferred for drinking on the job. Now they have me doing this shit until I leave this hell hole!" said officer baker. Baker punches in a code to electronically open the door. Baker takes off mush's cuffs. Baker leaves him, and closes the heavy steel door behind him. Hakim comes out of his lair. Mush is nervous again. "Whatever I did man, I apologize!" said mush. Hakim doesn't say a word. "Come on, and tell me what I did wrong!" much cried. "Just shut the fuck up and get in here!" said hakim. Mush enters the lair. "Have a seat!" hakim ordered. Mush takes a seat at the table. "First thing nigga, if you wanna be a part of my world, you better recognize that I give the orders!" said hakim. "You got it! I'm sorry!" mush cried. "Second thing! Ain't none of that fag shit going on in here!" said hakim. "With-all-due-respect hakim, I ain't no fag! I just wanted have some dirt on that white boy! That's all!" said mush. "If you'd came to me first, I would've told you that I already had things under control!" said hakim. "So what now?" mush asked. "All I want is your loyalty!" said hakim. "You got it! You most definitely got it!" Said mush. "You can move your stuff up here this week. I'll get the warden to get you a bed up here." Said hakim. "Thank you! Thank you!" shouted mush. "Just remember who's the man, and it'll all work out." Said hakim.

CHAPTER 6. DUBBS

near the end of 1987, it was decided by the Lassenberry hierarchy to make William Watson, a.k.a Dubbs boss of the newest territories in Jersey. Hunterdon, Somerset, Middleton, Mercer and Monmouth County now belonged to him.

The Watson faction of the lassenberry organization worked for benny for a long time. There was another Watson that worked for benny a few years back. Anita Watson was Dubbs's older sister who used to work on the streets as a look out for her cousin Butch. He then gave her a job at one of the dive bars as Allen's assistant manager. She lost her battle with diabetes back in 84, at the age of 30.

It was hours before Christmas day when benny, Eddie, sleeves, mark Vasquez sr., butch, jabbo and Dubbs were in the executive suite of a 5 star hotel in Upper Manhattan. They were all dressed up in their Sunday best.

A couple of year's earlier, benny had monogrammed diamond pinky rings made for the top guys in his crew. The rings were white gold with white diamonds shaped into the letters B and L.

Down in the lobby of the hotel, were a dozen guards from the crew dressed in fine suits as well. There were 2 guards that were ordered to stand outside the revolving door, where it was freezing cold.

Back at the executive suite, benny was making an announcement. "Today is a good day for us gentlemen! We get to expand the family business! There ain't nobody to come close to what we have achieved over the years! Raise your glasses!" said benny. They all raise they're glasses. "13 down, 8 more to go!" shouted benny. "13 down, 8 more to go!" everyone shouted. "Que todos podamos prosperar en los años venideros!" Mark Vasquez sr. shouted. "Whatever he said!" butch shouted. Everyone laughs. Everyone gulps down their champagne. Dubbs leans over to butch. "What he meant by 13 down and 8 more to go?" Dubbs whispered. Butch shakes his head. "He's talking about the counties. There are 21 counties in New Jersey! Do I have to do all the thinking little cousin?" asked butch. Benny reaches into his coat pocket and pulls out a little velvet box. Dubbs sees the box and rubs his hands together. "Calm down son! You don't get the ring until you can prove yourself!" benny chuckled. Benny walks over to

Dubbs and puts his hand on his shoulder. "You sure you ready for the big league son?" benny asked. "Damn right I am!" said Dubbs.

A week after the lassenberry family had brought in the new year of 1988, the matriarch of the family, Lola lassenberry was hospitalized due to a serious illness. Benny was able to give his wife everything, but a cure for cervical cancer. After she was first diagnosed, she kept it a secret for about a month. It took the housekeeper Rosa to realize how serious the illness had stricken Lola, when she found heavy blood stains on Lola's panties when during the laundry. That same day, Rosa was changing the sheets in the master bedroom and found the sheets soaked in blood as well. Rosa went down to the den and found Lola unconscious. Rosa dialed 911 first. After she hangs up she makes a call to benny.

By the time benny arrives at the estate, the guards at the gate told him that his daughter Maggie had showed and jumped in the ambulance, taking Lola to the nearby hospital in Camden. Benny gave the order to his driver to turn the car around and head to Camden.

At the hospital, there were a few family members sitting in the waiting area, while Maggie and benny jr. were in the room with their mother. Lola was still unconscious. She was hooked up to an intravenous tube and an EKG machine. She was quickly moved into a room by herself in the cancer treatment ward. Maggie sat down beside her stroking her long gray hair. Benny jr. sat on the other side holding his mother's hand.

In the waiting area was benny the 3rd, who had picked up his father after work and Mike abbey who was on break from college. At the front desk, the receptionist was approached by benny's driver. "Excuse me. What room is Lola lassenberry in?" the driver asked. The receptionist checks the file. "She's on the 5th floor, room 512." Said the lady. "Thank you!" said the driver. At that moment, benny was standing behind his driver. Benny walked passed the security without a pass. "Wait sir! You can't go through the halls without a pass!" the security guard said. The security guard had to be 6 feet, 5 inched, but it didn't matter to benny's driver. He steps face-to-face with guard. "You heard of benny lassenberry man?" asked the driver. "Yeah, so?" said the security guard. "Well, that's him over there!" said the driver. The security guard looks over at benny. His jaw drops. "Sorry about that! I didn't mean any disrespect Mr. Lassenberry!" shouted the security guard. Benny doesn't pay him no mind. He just heads to the elevator. "Please tell him I meant no disrespect!" the security guard pleads with the driver.

Moments later, benny gets off the 5th floor. He asked nurses where is room 512. The nurse points in the direction. Benny walks as fast as his ageing body could. Benny walks pass the waiting area. "Pop-pop!" shouts benny the 3rd. benny looks back. Benny the 3rd walks towards his grandfather and gives him a hug. "Damn! You a grown man now!" benny shouted. "Just turned 23!" said benny the 3rd. "How is she?" benny asked. Just then, benny's other grandson comes out of the waiting room. "Hey pop-pop!" shouted mike abbey. "Damn! I got too many grandkids! Whose kid are you?" benny asked. "Lula's my mother pop-pop!" said mike abbey. Benny gives his grandson a hug. He then heads to room 512.

Down stairs in the lobby, a horde of lassenberry children and grandchildren approach the front desk. There was Maggie's sons Tyson Richards and Malcolm Richards, Jake sr., mark sr. and his wife Tasha, followed by mark jr., Corey, his cousins Joe-Joe, and Big L. and benny's youngest daughter Lula, who just walked in the front entrance. Benny's driver recognized some of the family members. He goes over to the security guard. "Look! You see that group of people over at the desk?" said the driver. "Let me guess, they're Lassenberry's people." Said the security guard. The driver nods. "Well, send them up!" said the security. Everyone heads toward the elevator. The elevator ride was silent. The elevator door opens on the 5th floor. Everyone exits. They all rush down to 512. "Hey Ma, over here!" mike abbey shouted. The family members enter the waiting area. In the waiting area were benny the 3rd, Maggie benny jr. and mike abbey. "How's grandma doing?" asked Malcolm. "We don't know yet. The doctors took some tests and she's still unconscious." Maggie said as she fights back the tears. "Where's pop-pop?" Big L. asked. "He's in there with mamma." Said Maggie. "If she dies, then you gonna be the queen of the family Aunt Maggie!" Big L. said. Tyson turns towards his younger cousin, and smacks him upside the head. "Shut the hell up! You're always saying something stupid!" Tyson shouted. Big L. looked heated, but didn't do or say a thing. Lula and her nephew Joe-Joe start chuckling. Everybody be quiet!" Maggie shouts. The room becomes silent. "Nobody is dying! Mamma just a little sick that's all!" Maggie said.

Larry, a.k.a Big L., grew from a pudgy kid, to a 6 foot, 4 inch, 300 pound offensive tackle for a southern university, which was his father's alma mater. The scars on his bald head came from head butting team mates during practice games. His team warned him about head butting without a helmet, but he didn't listen. His GPA was low. The only 2 reasons Big L. was allowed to continue playing was that he became a powerhouse on the field, and that the athletic department received a 5 million dollar donation under the name of lassenberry. Big L. displayed a jovial, childlike mentality. At one point, his uncle Eddie wanted to make him his body guard. Benny and jabbo had to put an end to that idea quick.

Finally, after hours of MRI and CT scanning, the doctor tending to Lola enters the room. It was only benny sitting there, holding his wife's hand. Benny stands to greet the doctor "Mr. Lassenberry. I'm Doctor Berger. The doctor and benny shake hands. Benny seems to lose control of his breathing, anticipating bad news. "Cut to the chase doc! You know who I am! I can take it!" said benny. Doctor Berger looked puzzled. "I thought you knew!" said the doctor.

Doctor Berger was one of the most respected physicians in cancer research on the East Coast. His team worked longs hours and days looking for treatment to fight many forms of cancer. Uterine, Cervical and Ovarian were his priority. Due to the outbreak of the AIDS epidemic, government and corporate funding for his research had dwindled.

Back in the waiting area, everyone is sitting around silent, until Lula breaks the silence. "So, how's school baby boy?" Lula says to her son, mike abbey. "It's a cake walk ma!" he answered.

Mike abbey attended an Ivy League university in Jersey on a full scholarship. Mike was pampered by his grandmother growing up, while his mother was off pursuing her acting career. He was considered a mamma's boy by his older cousins. He had that lassenberry look of bulging eyes and thick lips. He was light skinned like his father, standing 5 feet, 5 inches tall, with a beer gut. He was the total opposite of his younger brother Bert Bethune, a.k.a BB.

Standing a 6 feet, 3 inches tall, BB took after his mother and father, going into the entertainment business. Not as an actor, but as a stuntman for a particular movie studio. Only 20 years old, BB had already performed stunts for 4 films so far. BB wasn't desperate for work like other black stuntmen. He managed to save a half million dollars provided by his grandfather over the course of 2 years.

It was a little after 8 pm. The family occupying the waiting area grew even more. Benny's youngest son Danny had arrived with his wife Elaine. They managed to catch a flight back to the states on a private jet.

Minutes later, benny and Doctor Berger had left the Lola's room and walked towards the waiting area. Everyone stood to their feet, when the head of the family walked in. the room was silent. "Ok everybody! Doctor Berger here, is gonna explain to you what's going on with yo mamma!" said benny. "You look tired daddy. Come over here and sit down." Said Maggie. Benny listens to his daughter.

"Mrs. Lassenberry for some time now has been diagnosed with Cervical Cancer. At this stage, the cancer has spread throughout some of her vital organs. Due to her age, a trachelectomy wouldn't matter at this point. I can provide medication to slow down the process, but it all really remains on her will to fight." Said the doctor. Benny sits there just twiddling his thumbs. He then gets up. "Listen everybody! If you have nothing else to do, head back to the estate! I'll call up and have food and drinks for you when you get there! I have some business to attend to, then I'll be back here in the morning!" said benny. Benny walks over to his son benny jr. before he leaves. "I want you to stay here until I get back. She needs to see a familiar face if or when she wakes up." Said benny. Benny jr. nods his head, and then gives his father a hug. Maggie helps her father put on his overcoat. He hugs all of his kids and grandkids, and then heads for the elevator by himself. Before benny can push the elevator button, Lula comes running down the hall. "Daddy! You sure it's a good idea to leave junior here alone with mamma?" asked Lula. "As long as he's here, he can't run to the liquor store and act a fool." Said benny. He kisses his baby girl on the forehead and steps into the elevator.

It was about 10:30 pm, when benny shows up at the Irvington safe house to check on things. Benny's driver opens the door for his boss. When benny walks up the porch steps, he is greeted by 4 black men. These men were not armed with any weapons. They were there just to warn the real danger inside.

Each of the 4 guys had a specific code to alert the armed guys inside. One at a time, the men would knock on the door with a specific knock to let someone on the inside know that Eddie, Jabbo or benny lassenberry had arrived. If there was no knocking code, and the door opened, the person or persons standing outside would end up like Swiss cheese. Benny had the knocking code changed every week. Benny's back up plan was having a sharpshooter posted at the second floor window.

Rodger Eagle Eye Red feather joined the lassenberry crew back in 1975 after coming home from Vietnam. His father, Tuvi Red feather, was on the tribal council until his death a few years earlier. Rodger going against is family's wishes, joined the army due to his conservative views. During boot camp, Red feather was faced with ongoing prejudice. But, his marksmanship skills on the firing range made him an asset during the war. When he arrived back home to the states, it wasn't to a hero's welcome. He wasn't even allowed back into the tribe for his participation in Vietnam. Red feather left Arizona, heading east. He ending up in a bar out in

Montclair, New Jersey, drinking his sorrows away. Eddie lassenberry, who was 39 years old at the time, was at the same bar that night looking for an escape from everything. He noticed the strange looking man sitting 3 seats down from him wearing army utility jacket. Eddie had asked him what each patch meant. The conversation led from one thing to another.

When benny entered the safe house, he was surprised to see Eddie standing there overseeing the count team. "What the hell? Everybody out!" shouted benny. The 5 cash counters drop the money and rush out of the room. The door closes. "Where's jabbo?" benny asked. "I gave him the night off." Eddie said. "You gave him the night off?" benny shouted.

Eddie was all decked out that night, wearing a tailor made silk suit and plenty of jewelry. He was to rendezvous with some fashion model out in New York until he received word about his mother's condition. "We all just came from the hospital visiting your mother, and yo ass here worried about some goddamn money!" benny shouted. Eddie slowly picks up a wad of cash rapped in a strip of paper with $5,000 stamped on it. "I'm just doing the job you trained me to do pop." Eddie said calmly. "Don't get cute with me boy!" benny shouted. "Pop. I got over 40 envelopes to give out to the cops. I gotta fill up those envelopes over there, for the family. And we can't forget your old pal gatano and his briefcase over there in the corner. I know it sounds disrespectful, but jabbo ain't as sharp as he used to be." Eddie said. "Bullshit! Jabbo is as sharp as a razor! I know you son! You used this as an excuse not to show up at the hospital! You didn't want the family to see you break down!" said benny. Eddie turns away from his father. Benny puts his hand on Eddie's back "I'll tell yo brothers and sisters that you got caught up in business, and that your flight was delayed. In the future, leave the count room to jabbo. Oh, by the way. You need to spend more time with that gino character. My old pal gatano didn't put him with us for nothing." Benny chuckled. He leaves Eddie in the room alone. Outside the count room. "Y'all get back in there and finish counting my money!" benny said.

About a block away in a dark alley on 18th avenue, a black van with tinted windows is parked with the engine and lights turned off. There is a Latino man and a black man sitting up front, and another black men sitting in back at a computer monitor and console. All 3 men are wearing black suits and dark shades. They only acknowledged each other by numbers, not names. "Agent 3, any sign of the feds?" asked agent 1. "Negative, but there is an Irvington patrol car about .09 miles heading in our direction." Said agent 3. "Set frequency scrambler and activate voice simulator." Said agent 1 as he reaches for his infrared binoculars. Within seconds the patrol car receives a call from dispatch to pursue a drunk driver on the other side of town.

Back at the lassenberry estate, the family is gathered in the main mansion. Everyone decides to hunker down for a couple of days.

Danny sr. and his wife head up stairs to his old bedroom. They enter the room. Elaine gives her husband a hug. "Everything will be fine sweetie." Said Elaine.

Danny's room hasn't been touched since he left for college. Danny sr. was always interest in science fiction and space as a kid. There were posters of galaxies, planets. Aliens from another world. "As you can see, I was a nerd growing up." Said Danny. "You're still a nerd. But, you're my nerd." Elaine says to Danny. She gives him a peck kiss on the lips.

At the same, mark sr. and his wife Tasha enter mark's room down the hall. Tasha noticed old black and white photos of family members, past and present spread out on the bed. After Tasha hangs up her coat, she takes one of the pictures off the bed. "Who's this?" Tasha asked. "That's a picture of my great-grandmother on my mother's side." Said mark. "She looks white." Said Tasha. Mark takes the picture. "That's because she is." He said.

It was around mid-night when benny's grandchildren were still up in the guest house built for them by their grandfather. Benny the 3rd, Tyson and Malcolm Richards, Mark jr., Mike Abbey, Big L. stayed in this guest house, while the others stayed in the other guest house.

Big L. had grabbed the remote and turned the TV on. He kicked off his size 13 sneakers and placed his feet on the coffee table. Seconds later, his cousin's start complaining about the stench coming from his feet. "Damn! Put your shoes back on or go take a shower!" said Tyson. Mike abbey chuckles. "I'm serious man!" said Tyson. For a joke, Big L. puts his foot on Tyson's leg. Everyone is laughing. Tyson jumps up from the couch and punches Big L in the jaw. Mark jr. knows what was about to go down, so he gets up, and stands between Tyson and Big L. "Take it easy cuz!" said mark jr. said to his gargantuan cousin. Big L stands, towering over his cousins. Big L takes one hand and shoves mark Jr. Out of the way, knocking him over the couch. Tyson puts his fists up to defend himself. Big L. swings at Tyson with a right, but Tyson ducks. Tyson instead, is caught with a left. Tyson drops to the floor like a rag doll. Big L. straddles Tyson. And begins pummeling Tyson. It takes mike abbey and Malcolm to pull Big L. off Tyson. Tyson's face was covered in blood as he lay on the floor unconscious. "Come on and do that to me, you punk bitch!" Malcolm shouted. Mike abbey jumped between Big L. and Malcolm, knowing that Malcolm would receive the same beat down as his brother. "Mark Jr. gets off the floor. "Take him outside mike, and let him cool off!" said mark jr. "Come on lets go outside!" said mike. Mike takes Big L. for a walk a walk outside. Seconds' later benny the 3rd comes out of the kitchen with a sandwich in his hand. "What the fuck y'all doing out here?" asked benny the 3rd. "It's ok! We got it under control now!" mark jr. said. "Oh shit!" benny the 3rd said when he spotted his cousin Tyson on the floor out cold. "Mike! Bring him back in here!" said benny the 3rd. "Benny wants us back inside big. Let's just see what he wants." Said mike. Mike gets Big L. to turn around. Mark jr. and Malcolm try to revive Tyson. "Y'all done lost y'all minds!" benny the 3rd shouted. Tyson regains consciousness. They sit him on the couch. Benny goes into the bathroom and comes out with a head towel. He gives it to Malcolm to wipe the blood off his brother's face. "Whatever happened in here, better be squashed by morning! I don't want the guards outside see us acting like this towards each other! We're lassenberry men! We're better than this!" said benny the 3rd.

The next morning at the F.C.I, hakim was in his lair bench pressing. By this time, he had 5 guys in his crew. Mush had introduced hakim to them. Hakim took him on his word that they were ok. There was this Spanish kid named Oscar Deltoro, a.k.a. OZ, and 2 black guys named jimmy Reed, a.k.a Fixxx, and Kyle Zane, a.k.a Zane the insane. Just recently, hakim brought in another inmate on his own to end the lineup. Morris Bissen, a.k.a tiny stood 6 feet, 5 inches tall, weighing about 350 pounds. Mush had warned him about tiny being unstable, but hakim saw that tiny was heavily into weights like he was. Mush didn't really want to be around tiny because mush was caught cheating at cards one day, and tiny caught wind of it. Tiny was about to kill mush until the officers intervened. Tiny was sent to the hole for a week because of it. Hakim told tiny he could be a part of his crew and live a cushy life if he'd promised not to lay a hand on mush. Tiny agreed. Hakim had ordered another twin bed be put in his lair for tiny.

Oz was a puny looking kid that used to run cocaine for mark Vasquez faction of the lassenberry crew, until he was busted selling to an undercover cop. Fixxx was from Irvington. He was busted for breaking and entering. He would only take VCR's and cable boxes and try to sell them back on the streets. Zane was a tall scrawny brother, who received 6 years for statutory rape. Hakim saved him from the other inmates when mush convinced him that he was a doormat type, but was good at telling funny outrageous stories. Hakim was the one who gave him the nickname insane as a joke.

"Come on, and give me one more! Shouted tiny. Tiny was spotting hakim as he struggled to bench press 250 pounds. Hakim rests the bar on his chest. "Push it! Push it!" tiny shouted. Hakim pushes the weights up, and locks his arms. "Come on and give me one more!" tiny shouted. Hakim was trembling, trying his best to press the weights one more time. Hakim is at the half way mark. Tiny let him off the hook and aided him to set the bar on the rack.

The next day around 8 in the morning, caterers had come into the lair, escorted by officers, and dropped off breakfast for the 6 inmates. There was pancakes, eggs, cheese, sausages, steaks, has browns, cereal, fresh fruits, milk and juice. The crew ate like kings. Lunch and dinner was no different. It was all funded by hakim's million dollar account. It cost hakim up to 500 dollars a week to feed his crew. By the time hakim arrived at F.C.I back in 84, he had spent at least a hundred grand.

Hakim's main way of keeping his crew in check was to have conjugal visits from beautiful call girls. These women were searched thoroughly by female corrections officers before entering hakim's lair. Hakim spent at least 5 grand a month for 5 sexy ladies to come and please him and his crew. It didn't take long for hakim to realize that tiny had other interests.

Tiny used to be an instructor at a gym out in Asbury Park, New Jersey. One night after closing up the gym, tiny was paid a visit by one of its members. The member was a young flamboyant white guy who took a liking to tiny. The feeling was mutual with tiny even though tiny had a girlfriend and baby daughter at home. After he and the guy finished romping around, tiny went to hit the shower. He had asked the guy to join him, but the guy decided to leave. Tiny insisted that he stay. He wrestled with the guy, until they both tumbled over and landed on the edge of some gym equipment. The guy landed and punctured his neck, hitting a vital organ. Blood was spewing everywhere. The next morning, the owner opened up, and saw tiny sitting in a daze next to the dead body.

As the weeks followed, hakim was depressed that his father hadn't come visit him once sine the lair was constructed. Hakim made phone calls, wrote letters, and even asked officers to relay messages. But there was no type of feedback.

One day out in the yard, hakim gathered his crew together. Since mush would be the first to be released, hakim wanted him to set up their own drug ring for when he gets out.

It was the middle of March 1988, when the lassenberry family had to lay to rest one of their own. It was at the lassenberry estate, the head of the family was sitting in the den alone, holding his head, sobbing like a baby. Benny held his head up, staring at a giant portrait of all his children when they were young. There came a knock on the door. "Hey pop! It's me Danny!" the voice yelled. The door slowly opens. In comes benny's youngest child. "Pop, you Ok?" asked Danny. Benny nods to his son. "I'm coming out son!" Benny said in a soft voice. Benny comes out the den, followed by his son Danny and sees Malcolm Richards, mark sr., Danny jr., Jake and benny the 3rd standing out in the hall. They were all dressed in black suits, with sad looks on their faces. "Everybody ready?" benny asked his family. "Yeah pop!" said Jake. Jake hands his father his black fedora. Benny puts his hand on jakes shoulder. "Well, let's go." Benny says to everyone. Cooper the butler opens the front doors for his boss. Benny's sons and grandson follow him outside in front of the mansion.

Parked out front were 6 black limousines. In the first 3 limos sat more members of the lassenberry family, outside the gate of the estate, 30 cars were parked, filled with friends, distant relatives and associates of the family. Sitting in one of the cars was Albert Mills Bethune, his girlfriend Fiona and their 12 year old twin sons.

Albert came all the way from Pasadena when he received word about the Lassenberry's loss from Lula. Lula and Albert kept in touch over the years for the sake of their son BB. Albert 's acting career only led to B rated movies and a few cigarette commercials down in South America where he met Fiona. Except for a few gray hairs, Albert looked the same. He would call his son BB from time to time asking for a handout to pay bills. After BB turned 18 and received his first envelope from his grandfather, he didn't mind helping out his father, until BB stopped returning his calls. "Todavía no entiendo por qué estamos aquí! Su hijo ni siquiera quiere hablar con usted!" said Fiona. "He's my son regardless of how our relationship is!" Albert shouted. "Acaba de ser honesto y decir que estas aquí por dinero!" Fiona shouted.

Benny is escorted to the first limo. A body guard opens the limo door for him. Benny the 3rd, his sisters Sandra, Sarah, his brother Joe-Joe and their aunt Maggie get in afterwards. Benny looks over to his right. "You sure you can handle this sweetie?" asked benny. "For the last time, stop asking me that! That's my first born being buried today! There's nothing going to stop me from sending him off to his eternal resting place!" Lola said.

Lola's health had improved a little due to her medication and change of diet. The family got a second opinion from a Holistic doctor, who was into natural herbs and meditation.

Benny jr. had finally lost his battle with alcoholism. Just weeks after visiting his mother in the hospital, benny jr. collapsed at his home while sipping on a double shot of vodka. He actually passed on a Friday, but his body wasn't discovered until Monday. His next door neighbor saw his body through the patio door laid out on the floor. Benny the 3rd arrived at the house with his wife Bridget that day. They saw flashing lights from police cars and ambulance. Benny the 3rd saw the coroner there too. He knew it was too late. Benny the 3rd told his pregnant wife to stay in the car before he went towards the scene. His aunt Maggie and uncle's Jake sr. and mark sr. were already on there.

The funeral procession had arrived at the church benny jr. had spent most of his life attending. Jabbo had a twenty 20 man security team posted all around the church. All the body guards wore trench coats. The police had the main street blocked off. All motorist had to make detours. Boss gatano was being assisted out of his limo buy Frankie Depalma and a soldier in his crew. Lola and benny were already seated in the front pews when gatano approached them in his wheelchair. He gives Lola a kiss on the cheek. Benny stood, leaning over to give gatano a hug. As he strolled by, gatano shook hands with benny's remaining sons. When he got to mark sr., he grabbed mark sr. by the arm, and tears came running down his cheeks. "Tirami fuori di qui Frankie!" gatano ordered. Frankie quickly strolled his boss towards the exit. Eddie was sitting next to benny the 3rd. when he noticed Gatano leaving in a hurry. He gets up and makes his way to the exit. Eddie gets to the door way and sees Gatano's people helping him get back into his limo. He also sees gino in another car parked across the street. Eddie was going to make his way over there to him, but changed his mind. Eddie and gino weren't allowed to be seen together due to their prescription pill connection. Eddie goes back into the church.

After the sermon and the eulogies, Maggie screamed out her brother's name when the gold plated casket was sealed. After the huge volume of flowers were removed, the pall bearers got into formation. Butch and 5 guys from his crew carried the casket out to the hearse. After the casket was loaded into the hearse, people started to vacate the church. Everyone had loaded up into their vehicles. The caravan didn't move until Benny and Lola finished their conversation with the pastor. About 15 minutes later, benny and his wife are escorted to the limo.

About a half hour later, the caravan arrives at the cemetery located on the outskirts of Cherry Hill. The caravan parks in front of an enormous mausoleum, which took up half an acre of land. The mausoleum had a 100 foot obelisk stand on both sides. The obelisks had the name Lassenberry carved vertically in big letters. Above the double doors to the tomb was also carved Lassenberry. Underneath the family name were the words Familia in Saeculum, which meant family is forever in Latin. Benny's grandson Krayton was in awe of this structure. "Damn! When pop-pop has this built?" Krayton asked. In another limo, "I always thought I would be the first one in the family to be put in here." Benny said to his wife. Once the cars stop, all the chauffeurs open the doors for everyone in the limos. It took 4 groundskeepers to open the heavy double doors to the mausoleum. After the pall bearers enter with the casket, everyone else was instructed to form a line of 3 abreast. Benny, Lola and Maggie lead the way. The crowd walked all the way near the rear of the tomb.

The walls and floor were made of marble with designated spots on the floor for family members were to be placed. Benny jr. was placed on the right side of his father's space. On the left side of benny's space was a space designated for Lola. After the pastor said the final prayer, flowers given out to everyone to be placed on the casket. The line was then instructed to make a U-turn out of the mausoleum. There were people standing outside, waiting to get in to lay down their flowers as benny, Lola and Maggie exited.

After the funeral services, everyone arrived at a lodge hall for a feast. There was a huge selection of food and drinks laid out in a buffet. There was fried, baked and bar-b-que chicken, a tray of sliced roast beef, 3 pans had salmon steaks over a bed of wild rice. There were 4 different pasta dishes, 3 pans of macaroni and cheese, sautéed meatballs and all different types of soft drinks. In his son's honor, benny didn't allow any alcoholic beverages on the menu.

Charlie Dalton had walked over to the corner of the hall with 2 plates of food in his hands. One plate was for his boss Eddie, who stood away from the crowd. Eddie was admiring the portraits and symbolism on the lodge's walls. He liked the way the men looked in their lodge uniforms. "This is how we should be set up!" Eddie said. What's that's boss?" asked Charlie. "Nothing! Just eat yo damn food!" Eddie said.

Sitting at one of the tables were 3 of Eddie's nephews. It was Krayton, Danny jr. admiring Corey's gold watch he'd just purchased. "Damn, that shit fly as hell! I can't wait until next to my first envelope!" Krayton said. "What envelope?" Danny jr. asked. "What? Your father ain't tell you?" said Krayton. "Man, when you turn 18, you get an envelope with 5 grand every week for the rest of your life!" Krayton said. "Get the hell out of here!" Danny jr. said. "How you think I paid for this watch?" said Corey. "Shit! I ain't going to no damn college or getting a job!" Krayton said. "I don't know cuz! If pop-pop and uncle Eddie get busted, we're all gonna be some broke ass niggas!" Corey said. "All they gotta do is let me run shit, and I'll keep the cash flowing!" Krayton said. "Nigga please! You don't know nothing about how the drug game works!" Corey chuckled. "Damn! 5 grand a week! That's 260 grand a year! Doctors don't even make that kind of money!" said Danny jr. "And it's all tax free cuz!" said Krayton.

As Eddie stands in the corner eating his food, out of nowhere a little girl in a black dress runs up to Eddie, giving him a big hug around his waist. She nearly knocks the food out of his hand. "Hey Uncle Eddie!" the little girl shouted. "Hey young lady! Be careful!" Eddie chuckled. "Do me a favor sweetie, and go get your father. Tell him I wanna talk to him." Eddie says to his niece. "Ok Uncle Eddie!" said the little girl. She releases Eddie from her hug. And skips away. Eddie shook his head smiling.

Moments later the little girl's father, Danny sr., approaches his big brother. "Hey there little brother!" said Eddie. "You making Samara a messenger now?" Danny sr. chuckled. The 2 brothers hug each other. "You knew about the mausoleum?" Eddie asked. "I didn't have a clue!" Danny sr. said. "I wonder what else he's keeping from us." Eddie said. "It seems like pop is taking it harder than mom!" said Danny sr. "He just lost his first born son! What you'd expect?" Eddie said. "I mean it's just strange. He never expressed how he felt before!" Said Danny sr. "You been oversees too long! You sounding all mushy and preppy!" Eddie said. Danny sr. felt insulted. "I have to go find my wife now!" Danny sr. said. "Yeah. You go do that." Eddie said sarcastically. Danny sr. gives Eddie a weird look and walks away. Eddie is done eating. He folds his paper plate in half and gives it to Charlie. "Throw that away and go start the car. I'm leaving. "Eddie ordered. Charlie runs off and tosses the plate in the trash. Eddie walks over to the table where his mother and father are seated. Also at the table was jabbo, sleeves, boss gatano, Frankie Depalma, sleeve's wife, butch, and an elderly white guy who happened to be Cheery Hill police chief Todd Dannon. "Listen everybody! I got some stuff I gotta handle! Eddie shouted. Eddie goes over and gives his mother a kiss on the forehead and waves goodbye to everyone else.

In another part of the hall, mark Vasquez sr. is sitting at a table with fellow king pin Dubbs. Watson. "How does it feel running things out there with the Gente Blanca?" mark asked. "What you say?" Dubbs asked. "I meant white folks man!" mark chuckled. "Well, then say that!" Dubbs shouted "I just like fucking with you amigo!" mark chuckled.

Before Dubbs gained control of his territory, he received word of a 10 man crew from Belmar, New Jersey who were running cocaine from out of Peru. Dubbs and his older cousin butch assembled a team of hired guns to take out the Belmar crew. The hit team consisted of guys butch knew who desperately needed the job. There was former police sergeant Dennis McNally, who was in debt after his wife of 20 years left him. McNally was an overweight grumpy Irish guy who was kicked off the force for accepting bribes from the neighborhood brothel. McNally hung out at one of the lassenberry dive bars in Palisades Park. It was Kent Mooney who pointed out McNally to butch about his financial problems. Butch approached McNally with an offer to make 30 grand to take out some rouge dealers. McNally jumped at the chance.

The second guy for the job was Jackie Toomer, a.k.a the joker. Toomer was a childhood friend of hakim's that wanted to be involved with the top brass of the lassenberry crew because he thought he and hakim were real close. Eddie gave him a job as his father's driver, but it didn't last long because of toomer's immature antics. Eddie wanted to put a bullet in the kid's head, but butch convinced him not to. Butch told Eddie he could use him for other things. Toomer didn't hesitate to go to work for butch.

The last man on the list was Jarvis Thompson, who happened to be the harbor master down in Belmar. His position was most important. Jarvis had to convince Dirk Duncan, who was head of the Belmar crew and who owned a 3 hundred yacht, that he needed to come aboard for a safety inspection. It was a week before the funeral of benny jr. when Jarvis gave Dirk a call to warm him that there was a foul odor coming from where his yacht was docked. Dirk and Jarvis had a trusting relationship for the past few years.

Both Jarvis and Dirk went on board the yacht to investigate the problem. Toomer, Dubbs and McNally were already on board hiding down in the engine room. McNally brought along his trusty double barrel shot gun. Dubbs and toomer both were armed with sub machine guns. Butch hid on the pier armed with a rifle with scope just in case the victim would try to escape. Once Jarvis had lured Dirk down into the engine room, the 3 men, who were wearing ski masks grabbed Dirk from behind. Dirk was tough. He didn't go down without a fight. He punched one of the masked men in the jaw. Another masked man grabbed Dirk while Jarvis made a run for it topside. Dubbs and team had to make Dirk's demise look like an accident. Finally, one of the masked men covered dirks mouth and nose with a cloth soaked in chloroform. Dirk fought to the end until he passed out. Toomer took off his ski mask, and started rubbing his jaw. "That old dude hit hard as hell!" said toomer. "Put your mask back on dip shit!" McNally shouted. "Who the fuck you think you're talking to?" said toomer. "What if someone comes down here before we can torch the place?" said McNally. "Oh, I see!" said toomer. "Where you find this kid?" asked McNally. Dirk's body was laid down next to 6 kilos of raw cocaine Dubbs had brought along in a duffle bag. Within minutes the 3 men make a break for it top side. McNally was slowing everyone up because he was leading the way and was out of shape. They finally made a break for the pier. Jarvis stayed behind as an alibi. Minutes later, butch, Dubbs, toomer and McNally reached the getaway car, which was a black jeep. McNally calmly drives away. "Well that's that!" said McNally. Moments later, a loud explosion goes off. Butch and McNally could the night sky light up in the rear view mirror.

The crew drive all the way out to Butch's territory out in Hampton Township of Sussex County. There, they arrive at a lassenberry dive bar ran by Kent Mooney. Butch and the crew get out of the jeep and head for the back of the bar, which was closed for the night. They all go down into the basement. They all hand over their ski masks, undress out of their overalls and give them to Dubbs. Dubbs puts everything in a garbage bag. There's just one more thing you gotta do before we leave cousin!" butch said. Dubbs nods his head. Dubbs reaches behind the staircase and pulls out a revolver. Toomer takes a bullet between the eyes. He falls to the floor, which was covered with plastic. McNally realized he was next. Dubbs points the revolver at McNally. "You fucking niggers." McNally said in a calm voice. McNally takes a bullet in the forehead. He falls to the floor. "Let's clean this shit up!" said butch.

A few days later, the rest of Dirk's crew came under the thumb of Dubbs. Dirk was the only connection to the Peruvian cartel. The Peruvian cartel didn't make a move against Dubbs when they found out he was under the protection of the Jersey mob and the Columbians.

It was December 1988 when benny was introduced to his great-grandson Benjamin Daniel Lassenberry the 4th. Eddie was at the estate when his nephew paid a visit to show off his son. Seeing the 4th generation of lassenberry being born made Eddie proud. While everyone was gathered around Bridget and the baby in the family room, Eddie pulled his nephew benny the 3rd to the side. "Now that there's another generation of us, we need to start something bigger, something more powerful! Your son is the future of an empire!" Eddie shouted. Benny the 3rd was dumbfound. "With all due respect uncle, I'm not allowing my son near the life you lead! So get that out of your mind!" benny the 3rd shouted. He leaves his uncle standing alone in the hall.

January of 1989 was the year that a member of hakim's crew was on his way to being a free man, and go back out into the world. It was around noon that mush was dress in civilian clothes that hakim had purchased for him. As an extra gift, hakim had ordered a thick gold chain for mush to wear out in style. Hakim had arranged a grand feast for the crew.

Food had come into hakim's lair on silver platters rolled in on fancy designer carts by 3 men in waiter's outfits. They had to be checked for weapons and contraband before entering. For this special occasion, the crew dined with gold plated utensils. Hakim also ordered for a long oak wood table to be sent in for the event. Hakim sat at the head of the table, with mush on his left, tiny on his right. Hakim tells the waiters to leave. "Before we begin to eat, I would like to say it truly breaks my heart to see someone I consider a brother to leave us!" hakim says to mush. Tiny stands to say a few words. "I just wanna say keep that ass tight!" tiny chuckled. There was a dead silence for a few seconds. Fixxx stands. "Whatever you do man, don't come back!" said Fixxx. Zane stands up. "Represent man! Get these streets ready for us!" said Zane. The last to make a speech was OZ. "I just wanna say no te olvides de nosotros!" said OZ. everyone applauds. "Now, let's eat!" said hakim.

Mush's favorite meal was prepared for him. He had a thick juicy T-bone steak with seasoned potatoes and collard greens seasoned with bacon. Minutes passed as the guys were eating. Suddenly, mush noticed his left hand starts to shake. Soon, he drops his fork. The other guys don't take notice and continue to chow down. Mush clutches his chest. He stumbles out of his chair, leaning over the table. The other guys still keep eating. He grabs his nose and then starts screaming. Blood started trickling out of his nose. "Something's wrong with me! Somebody help me!" mush screamed. Hakim stands from his seat, while the others continue to eat. Mush slumps back into his chair as blood trickles from his ears and eyes as well. Hakim wipes his mouth with his napkin. "This punk bitch thought he was gonna just walk out of here, and get back on the streets so he could disrespect me!" hakim shouted to the crew. Mush goes into convulsions. "You thought you were smarter than me? I'm the smart one! Now you about to die cause you didn't recognize!" hakim shouted. Mush's body falls to the floor. OZ looks down at the body. "He's gone poppy!" said OZ. Hakim walk over to the body. He snatches the chain from mush's neck. Hakim then spits a huge wad of mucus on the body. Hakim returns to his seat. "Somebody get this bitch ass nigga outta my house!" hakim shouted. Tiny gets up from his seat and tosses the body over his shoulder. He leaves the lair and takes the body to the main entrance. Tiny bangs on the door real hard. The officer opens up once he sees its tiny carrying the body. The 3 servers come in, and place the body on the dining cart. They cover the body with a couple of sheets that were folded underneath the cart. The body is then rolled down the corridor, never to be seen again.

Time and time again, Hakim stood by patiently as Mush showed disrespect to him in front of others. Even inmates in general population were starting to doubt hakim's rule over his crew because of mush's undermining behavior. A year earlier, hakim arranged the hit on mush with the assistance of the warden and a few corrections officers. Hakim had informed the crew that this was mush's last supper, and that he had to go. It cost hakim 100 grand to get away with a hit of this caliber, and to walk away clean.

Months after the death of mush, hakim's crew dwindled down to 2 guys. Oz stayed around because of protection. Tiny stayed around because he enjoyed the lavish life of the lair. Fixxx and Zane wanted out. They were terrified of hakim and the power he possessed on the inside. It cost hakim another 50 grand to make sure that Fixxx and Zane didn't become a liability. Fixxx was found in his cell hanging from a top bunk by his t-shirt. Zane spent the rest of his days in the hole, dying of starvation.

Paul Benedict, warden of F.C.I, had summoned hakim to his office. Hakim was told to arrive in his orange jumpsuit to keep up appearances. Hakim was under orders that he had to arrive at the warden's office in shackles. 4 officers arrived at hakim's lair at noon. Hakim was taken to the D.O.C bus to make the trip over to the warden's office.

Paul A. benedict, like other wardens, loved to have big shot gangsters in their prison. It was lucrative for the warden to have big shots wanting special privileges such as women, contraband, and the occasional hit to be put out on someone. It was back in 1984, when Warden Benedict landed a big shot named hakim.

The bus arrived at the warden's facility. Hakim noticed the flag pole with the United States flag waving in the breeze, with the state of New Jersey flag waving underneath.

Hakim was escorted to the main office where Warden Benedict was waiting. The corrections officers stated his name and badge number in order to gain access inside the facility. The officer and hakim were buzzed in.

Warden Benedict ran F.C.I close to 30 years. The last inmate who occupied the prison that was considered a big shot was a man named Mike Bixby. He was a gun for hire by the gatano crew until being caught with 2 dead bodies in his house one Christmas morning. The gatano people sent him cigarettes, women and booze until his death in 1979.

"Come in and have a seat Mr. Lassenberry!" said the warden. Still shackled, hakim slowly sits in the chair across from the warden's desk. "It's Mr. bates!" hakim said. "Ah yes! That was your mother's last name!" said the warden. "Fuck lassenberry, and fuck you!" hakim shouted. The warden smiled. "You can leave us." The warden says to the officer. The officer leaves the room, shutting the door behind him. The warden leans forward in his chair. "The only reason you've survived in hear is because you're considered a lassenberry." The warden explained. "Listen you sick old fuck! The thing with mush and the others is over! Now, tell me what the fuck you want!" hakim said. "You're right son. Let's cut the bullshit. I just received word that the lassenberry crew expanded their territory, and their heading in this direction." The warden said. "So what the fuck that gotta do with me?" hakim asked. "I say we do business together!" said the warden. "What kind of business?" hakim asked. The warden puts on his reading glasses. He skims through hakim's file. "I have a lot of connections in the court system and parole board. Mr. Lassenberry. Oh excuse me, Mr. bates. With the stroke of the pen and a phone call, I can take 5 years off your sentence. You can walk the streets again in 1994, instead of 1999." Said the warden. "What this deal gonna cost me, if I decide to play with whatever you wanna do?" hakim asked. "Just the rest of the money in your account." The warden said. Hakim scoffs. "You gonna take all what I have left in my account, and keep me locked up in here for the next 5 years?" Listen son, very carefully. I can take all of your money, and kick your ass out of that palace of yours and keep your black ass in the whole for the rest of your sentence! But, I'm a business man, and I made a deal with Eddie lassenberry." Said the warden. Hakim looked defeated. "So what you want me to do?" hakim asked. "Ok! Now we're talking!" the warden chuckled. Once you're out of here, I can set you up in Vineland and Millville. Get some retired cops to back you, and we split the profits 60/40. I get the 60 of course." The warden chuckled. Hakim starts laughing. "Listen you clown! I was brought up in the business by the best! The shit you talking, don't even make sense! First you take my money, then I can't afford the good life in here, and can't take care of my crew! I end up in general population, and get a shiv stuck in me! Even if I do survive the 5 years, going against the lassenberry crew, is suicide! Man, take me back to my palace!" hakim said. The warden frowns. "Ok son, have it your way! But, that big gorilla looking nigger won't be receiving anymore conjugal visits from the pretty boys anymore! Let's see how long you and your pal Deltoro last when he's craving for man ass! And just so you know, if he's harmed in any way, you and Deltoro will spend the rest of your days in the hole, together, without food and water! You'll be ripping at each other like cannibals! Trust me! It's been done before!" the warden said with a serious look. Hakim looks around the office. "You're still a clown!" hakim chuckled. The warden's face turns red. He hits the buzzer underneath his desk. The guard enters the room. "Take Mr. Lassenberry back to his palace!" said the warden. Hakim insults the warden before leaving by spitting on his desk. After the guard and hakim leave, the warden swivels his chair towards the corner of the room. There laying on the floor, was a clown mask.

A month after Dubbs took control of his new territory, he and his cousin butch relaxed one night at Dubbs's home in Bradley Beach. The house sat about a hundred yards from the seashore. There were no dunes to protect the houses from the rough seas at the time. Dubbs and butch were sitting outside on beach chairs guzzling down a few beers, while their wives and children were inside. Dubbs married his longtime girlfriend right after benny lassenberry gave him the green light to be a boss.

"It's about time you shaved off that jerry curl nigga!" Butch chuckled. "Alright already!" Dubbs said.

Dubbs looked like a younger version of his cousin butch after shaving his hair. Butch had decided to shave his head many years ago.

Butch looked through the patio doors to see if any of the kids were coming out. Once the close was clear, he turns to Dubbs. "Listen little cuz, this area down here is yours now! I can't be coming down here all the time putting these crackers in line for you!" butch said. "I got it! I got it!" Dubbs said. "Don't forget to pay off the cops, judges, politicians or whoever you gotta pay to keep shit running smoothly!" butch said. "Damn man, how am I supposed to eat then?" Dubbs asked. Butch moves in closer to Dubbs. "Listen nigga, this ain't coming from me! It's coming from up top, and that's the way it is! How you think benny lasted this long?" butch explained. Dubbs nods his head. "Now, let's have a toast!" butch shouted. They both raise their bottles. "To the Watson clan!" butch shouted. "To the Watson Clan!" Dubbs shouted. They tap bottles.

At the same time butch and Dubbs were sitting on the deck, 10 miles straight ahead, sat 3 white men in a black motor boat watching the 2 cousins through night vision binoculars. "The Watson men must be secure in their position on the food chain" said agent 2. "Why you say that?" asked agent 1. "They have only 1 body guard patrolling the perimeter." Said agent 2.

The motor boat was equipped with state of the art surveillance equipment. Even from a far distance out to sea, Dubbs and butch voices came in crystal clear.

Back at F.C.I, within 2 weeks, the warden's prediction came to fruition. Hakim was laying in his bed one night. He could hear the moans and groans of his cell mate OZ. "Stop squirming bitch, before it comes out!" shouted tiny. "Hakim, come help me!" OZ screamed. The more OZ screamed for help, the harder tiny dug into him! Hakim couldn't see it, because the lair was pitch black. The fact was he kept the lights off because he didn't want to see it. Hakim covered his ears with his pillow while staring at the ceiling.

When tiny was done with his business, he turns on the lights. "Let's hit the shower now!" tiny said to OZ. Hakim closes his eyes, pretending to be asleep. OZ is being pulled towards the bathroom. Tiny looks over at hakim and starts licking his lips. When tiny and OZ enter the bathroom, tiny slams the door shut. Hakim opens his eyes and exhales.

The next morning, hakim jumps out of bed from having a nightmare. He sees that OZ and tiny are not in their beds. He sees the light is on in the bathroom. He gets out of bed and slowly walks towards the bathroom. He pushes the door open slowly. His jaw dropped. Laying on the shower floor naked, was OZ and tiny. Cuddled up together. Tiny was snoring loud. OZ looked pale. He wasn't moving at all. Hakim looked in closer and saw that OZ had a towel tightly wrapped around his neck. He also saw a trail of blood coming from OZ's anus. Hakim thought he saw it all, but he covered his eyes because he didn't want to see this scene anymore. Hakim snaps into madness. He goes to the weight bench and grabs a 50 pound weight. He comes back to the bathroom. He stands over tiny. Hakim lifts the weight above his head and slams it on tiny's head, crushing it. He then slams the weight on his head once more, until tiny's eye pops out of his head on to OZ's body. Hakim drops the weight, which the loud noise alerted the guard outside. Hakim sobs like a baby.

Within a half hour, hakim is stripped of his clothes and hauled off to the hole. Hakim bangs on the steel door until his knuckles bleed. "Let me out! Let me out!" he screamed.

About a month later, hakim is awaken when a guard opens the door to the hole. Another guard splashes hakim with his own piss bucket. The guards put on latex gloves. A guard tosses hakim his jumpsuit. "Hurry up and get dressed pal! The warden wants to see ya!" the guard shouted. "Fuck all y'all!" hakim shouted. The 2 guards start kicking hakim in the ribs. Hakim was too weak from hunger to fight back. Next to hakim was pieces of crusted white bread and a cup of water. Hakim, even in his weakened state, manages to get dressed. He is cuffed from behind and is taken back to his lair. When he arrives at his lair, he sees the warden Benedict sitting on his couch with his legs crossed. The warden had a deviant smile on his face. "Cuff him to the weight bench and leave us." ordered the warden. Hakim was so weak, see couldn't stand. He just squatted on the floor. The guards leave. The warden walks over to hakim and kneels down to face him. "I like you hakim. I really do. You just have to know your place in the world and stay there. What I'm going to do to keep you from the parole review board and having your sentence extended for murder. I'm going to take 200 hundred grand from your account, leaving you approximately 250 thousand dollars. If you can stretch that amount of money until 1999, god bless you." The warden chuckled. The warden gets up and leaves the lair. He orders the guards outside to take the cuffs off hakim.

A year later, sitting in a car a parked in an alley off of Frelinghuysen Avenue, was drug lord Eddie lassenberry and Gatano soldier gino Massoni. The 2 men sat alone, with no body guards around. "I appreciate you meeting me out here like this!" Eddie says to Gino. Eddie takes a swig from a bottle of expensive Cognac. He offers gino a taste. "Get the fuck outta here!" said gino. "This reminds me of the good old days!" Eddie said. "What good old days? You used to make my life a living hell!" said gino.

A week before they hung out of Frelinghuysen avenue, Eddie paid a visit to gino's X-rated theatre. Down in the basement of the theatre was a place where men could go and pay for sex. Gino had about a dozen girls working for him. Eddie came in a disguise wearing a beard and mustache with dark shades. One of the girls in a black dominatrix outfit asked Eddie if he wanted to party. Eddie declined. "Well take yo broke ass upstairs and watch the fucking movie!" said the girl. Eddie just smiled and threw a crumbled up c-note at the girl. The girl didn't get upset, and just picked the money off the sticky floor. As Eddie goes upstairs, he nearly runs into gino. Gino was standing over by the cigarette machine talking to his crew boss, Carlo gatano. Eddie doesn't look directly in their direction, but noticed Carlo smacking Gino upside the head. "Listen dummy! Every time I come down here, you got some fucking excuse!" Carlo shouted. Carlo pauses for a moment. He looks at the johns walking back-n-forth, to see who is being nosey. "Quando vengo qui! Voglio tre sexy ragazzi bianche solo per me! Capire?" Carlo shouted. "Sto cercando Carlo, ma è difficile trovare buoni che cercano donne bianche di venire qui!" gino explained. Within that moment, the 2 men walk away. Eddie caught bits and pieces of the Italian dialect. Eddie then rushes out of theatre before being spotted.

At Frelinghuysen Avenue, Eddie lights a cigar. "Let me get one of those." Gino said. Eddie smiles, then hands over another to gino. Eddie lights gino's cigar first, then his own. "So what you wanted to see me about?" gino asked. "I need 5 cases of them GBL pills. These college kids go crazy over that shit!" Eddie said. "That's it? You could've told me this at the next refill spot!" gino said. "Really, I wanted to apologize for all the dumb shit I put you through when we were kids. You're a made guy now. You deserve respect." Eddie confessed. Gino looks at Eddie and starts chuckling. "You are a real bullshitter, you know that?" gino chuckled. Eddie starts to chuckle. "No, seriously brother! We out here making a shit load of money together! That's just beautiful! And the best part is, we've known each other since forever! If I gotta beef with someone, I'm coming to you first for help! And I hope you feel the same about me, brother!" Eddie says to Gino as he stuffs another cigar into gino's pocket. Gino looks at Eddie, with tears in his eyes. "Shit! I never realized you've felt that way!" gino said. "I mean that shit from the bottom of my fucking heart, brother!" Eddie said as he hands over the bottle of cognac to gino. Reluctantly, gino takes a swig. Eddie looks at his watch. "Oh shit! I gotta go!" Eddie shouted. Eddie holds gino's hand. Remember brother, if you need me, just call me!" Eddie said sincerely. Gino gives a nod. Eddie jumps out of the car. "Don't forget your booze!" gino said. "Ah man, you keep it!" Eddie said as he gets out. Eddie starts trotting down the street as the rain starts coming down.

A couple of days later, gino stops by one of benny's dive bars. This one was located out in Succasunna, New Jersey. When gino pulled up in the parking lot, he spotted Allen J. Sunn, who was talking to a very sexy young lady. Gino didn't stop to converse. He just walked into the bar.

It was a Saturday night, and the place was packed, considering it was the only social hangout in 20 miles. The place made tons of legit money on Friday and Saturday night. But, the back door led to another world. The back door led to upstairs, where a dealer from the lassenberry crew resided.

His name was Brendan Colt. He was an obese white guy in his late 30's at the time, who sold weed and cocaine to some of the locals. He was a friend of Kent Sunn but a runner for butch. Pulling in about 15 grand a week in drug money, Brendan handed over half his profits to Sunn, who in turn handed it over to butch. With Gino and Eddie's recent partnership in pills, Brendan made an extra 10 grand a week.

It was only 10pm, and Gino already was on his fifth drink. With the combination of being a made guy and a lot of booze, he acted like he was entitled to push his weight around. He swivels his stool towards a young white couple sitting at the bar counter. "Hey pal! Is your lady for sale?" gino asked. The guy gets up out of his seat. He stands a foot taller than gino. "Listen buddy! You had too much to drink! I think you should go home!" the guy shouted. The girl gets in between gino and her boyfriend. Gino looked at the girl from head to toe. She was a blonde beauty. "Hey sweetheart! You wanna make some real money?" gino asked. "That's enough buddy! Leave now or get hurt! Said the boyfriend. Gino gently pushes the girl to the side. "Do you know who the fuck I am kid?" gino shouted. The boyfriend grabs gino by the collar and balls up his fist. Suddenly, Allen walks in and sees what was about to go down. He rushes through the crowd and over to the bar getting in between gino and the boyfriend.

"Pete! You have no idea who this guy is connected to!" whispered Allen "What the hell are talking about?" Pete asked. Gino swings on Pete and punches him in the jaw when Pete wasn't looking. Pete's boys coming rushing through the crowd. Gino was about to pull out a snub nose revolver when Allen snatches it away from him. Allen pulls gino away from the crowd, towards the back of the bar. Allen bangs on the door screaming for Brendan to come down stairs. Finally, Brendan unknowingly comes to the rescue. He's breathing heavily from coming down the flight of stairs. Somehow Allen moves Brendan out of the way, rushing through the door, dragging gino with him. "What the fuck Allen?" shouted Brendan. "Just shut the damn door, please!" shouted Allen. Brendan shuts the door, and hears multiple hands banging on it to get in to get at gino. All 3 guys head upstairs. "Get the fuck off me!" shouted gino. Brendan helps Allen by grabbing Gino. "Keep him here! I have to go and cool down the crowd before they tare this place apart!" said Allen. Soon after Allen leaves, Gino starts talking gibberish, calling Brendan Carlo. Gino swings on Brendan. Brendan slams gino on to the bed, causing him to hit his on the head board. Gino is knocked out cold. Brendan feels his neck for a pulse. He's relieved that gino is still breathing. Down stairs, Allen maneuvers through the crowd as Pete's people are yelling at him. He gets to the bar and tells his 3 bartenders to give everyone drinks on the house.

The next day, around noon, Allen Sunn is sitting at the bar counting the take from last night's crowd. His eyes are blood shot red from not getting any sleep. Moments later, gino comes down stairs, holding his head, followed by Brendan. "Fuck! My fucking head is killing me!" said gino. "Brendan. There's an ice pack under the bar counter. Do me a favor and fill it with and give it to gino." Said Allen.

Minutes later, butch walks in all decked out in a blue silk suit. "Hey gino! What brings you out here?" butch asked. Butch walks over towards the bar. He and gino shake hands. "You look like shit!" butch says to gino. Brendan runs back upstairs out of fear of being harassed by butch. "That's right! Take yo fat ass back upstairs!" butch chuckled. Butch then walks over to Allen. "You got that for me?" asked butch. Allen hands butch an envelope filled with cash. Butch doesn't bother counting it. "17 more pick-ups, and I'm done for the day." Said butch. "I wish I could say the same thing!" Allen complained. Butch gently smacks Allen upside the head with the envelope. "Give teddy a call! Tell him I'm on my way to collect!" butch says to Allen. "Alright already!" Allen said. Butch leaves the bar, followed by his body guard. Gino is in a trance by all the cash Allen is counting. Gino goes over and takes a stack of money. "Oh, come on!" Allen said. "Shut up! This is just a little going away present to myself!" gino said. "How am I going to pay my employees?" Allen asked. "Not my problem. Like I said, you don't have to worry about me coming around here anymore." Gino said. "Yeah, right!" said Allen. Gino walks out of the bar smiling with cash in one hand, and an ice pack in the other.

CHAPTER 7. SWITZERLAND

It was near the end of 1991, when the Soviet Union had fallen, and the lassenberry crew dominated 60 percent of the drug trafficking in New Jersey. The most southern part of the state was still open territory to other crews. Benny couldn't get the ok from gatano to go after the 8 remaining counties. The mob family out in Philadelphia was in cahoots with certain crews down there.

Eddie, mark Vasquez sr., Dubbs and Butch had their areas secure, but Eddie wanted the rest of New Jersey. Eddie was telling his father that mark Vasquez's son Mark jr. would be perfect for the job.

Mark Vasquez jr., a.k.a Mookie had followed his father into the life. Mark sr. had his son started as a look out on the streets of Elizabeth. Now at the age of 22, Mookie was given the job to drop off the take in Irvington, so the Vasquez faction could get their refill.

Mookie was the spitting image of his father, but a little taller. At the age of 16, Mookie was hauled off to juvenile detention for assaulting a kid with a sharpened pencil at the prep school he attended. The kid survived, but was left with a permanent gash in his neck.

When Mookie returned home, he was greeted to a to a huge welcome home block party in the streets of Elizabeth. His father spared no expense. The event was bigger than New York's Puerto Rican day parade.

Antonio Diaz, a.k.a Tony Diablo was second in command of the Vasquez faction. He ordered a group of runners from his crew to greet and show Mookie respect. Mookie never met any of these guys, who were low level runners on the corner. Mookie spent his childhood only around street bosses. Angel Salazar, a.k.a Tigre negro, Hector Rosa, a.k.a The Shark, Gregory Thomas, a.k.a Tip, a black guy who ran drugs in the Hoboken, Bayonne and Secaucus area, and another black guy named Brian Cooper, a.k.a Wiz, who became the new king of Communipaw avenue, were just a few of the top guys allowed to come to the Vasquez house.

The party went on all through the night. The chief of police received a wad of cash so the cops wouldn't try to shut down the festivities.

It was around 1996 when one of Butch's people spotted Mark Vasquez sr. down in Miami in the company of a known Peruvian cartel leader.

Most of the crews around the country, like the lassenberry crew, did business with the Columbian cartel. There were few that did business with Peru and Mexican cartels.

When word got back to butch, he notified benny and jabbo about what was going on. Coincidently the Colombian connection got wind of Mark Vasquez's secret meetings as well. The Columbian kingpins didn't like the fact they might lose business to the Peruvians, so they summoned boss gatano and benny to a sit down to straighten matters out.

The Columbian drug lord and his entourage arrived in Switzerland on October 20th, 2:35 am CET time in a private jet. He told boss gatano the meeting would be held on October 22nd.

At the safe house in East Orange, benny had Eddie, Jabbo and butch gather around for a discussion. "I just got word that we're having a sit down with the Columbians about Vasquez! In a half hour a limo is gonna come for me! It's gonna take me to Teterboro airport! I was told to bring butch and his witness to the meeting! Jabbo, you're coming too!" said benny. "You sure you don't need me in on this pop?" Eddie asked. "No, if shit hits the fan, they'll still wanna do business with someone from Jersey! I rather it be you!" said benny.

The limo was to arrive in 10 minutes. The room was silent. Butch was pacing back-n-forth. "I knew we couldn't trust that beans and rice eating mother fucker!" butch shouted. "Relax boy, and sit yo ass down!" jabbo said. "How can I jabbo? We might get snuffed out because of this guy!" said butch. "Just do what ol' jabbo said, and sit down!" said jabbo. Butch stops pacing, and takes a seat on the couch next to Eddie. "Is that witness of yours still on the porch?" benny asked butch. "Yeah, he's out there." Butch said.

Minutes later, Charlie comes running in. "The limo outside! The limo outside!" Charlie shouted. "Calm yo dumb ass down, yelling like that!" Eddie shouted. "Ok people! Its show time!" said benny. Benny puts his hand on Eddie's shoulder. "Remember. If we don't make it back, put aside the personal shit and still do business with these people." Benny says to Eddie. Everyone heads outside. All of the guys are dressed in fine tailor made suits. "Where's my hat"? Benny asked. Benny forgot he left his fedora on the TV, and grabs it.

Benny, jabbo and butch are all dressed in fine tailor made suits, except for the witness. He's dressed in jeans, a t-shirt, a black leather blazer and wearing a fat gold chain around his neck. Butch walks over to him. "You look like you're going to a fucking rap concert! Get in the damn limo!" butch ordered. Butch gets in the limo, followed by jabbo. "Don't forget what I told you son!" benny shouted. Benny then gets in the limo. The chauffeur closes the door, and goes around the driver's side. Within moments, the limo drives off.

A couple of hours later, 5 miles above the Atlantic ocean, benny and his crew share a private jet with members of the gatano crew. Carlo gatano, Frankie Depalma, Carlo's new bodyguard Anthony Pasolini, a.k.a T.K.O accompanied boss gatano to the meeting.

Butch and his witness sat across from Frankie and Anthony as the sexy looking Hispanic flight attendant was serving drinks. Butch and Anthony just stared at each other. Anthony started smiling. "What the fuck you smiling at?" asked the witness. "Be quiet Mikey!" "Say butch, let me introduce T.K.O from Paterson." Frankie said. "I know who he is! Middle weight with 30 wins, 3 loses!" said butch. "I heard about you too old man! I heard you knocked out 40 guys, each with one punch!" said Anthony. "You wanna be number 41?" butch asked. Anthony and Frankie start chuckling. "Good thing for me, I'm not some punk drug dealer!" Anthony said.

At the other end of the jet sat boss gatano and Carlo. Across from them sat benny and jabbo. "I swear to Christ old man, if you fucked up our business relationship with the Columbians, don't bother going back home!" Carlo says to benny. Jabbo leans forward, face to face with Carlo. Jabbo looks Carlo straight into his eyes. "Show some respect boy, or you gonna deal with jabbo later! You don't wanna deal with jabbo!" said jabbo. Carlo saw that jabbo was for real. "Fuck you old man!" Carlo said before he got up to go to the bathroom. "Hai scelto l'uomo giusto per guardare le spalle il mio amico." Boss gatano said. "E'il migliore." Said benny. "You better not be talking shit either!" jabbo says to gatano. Benny and gatano start laughing. 6 hours had passed, benny and gatano were the only 2 passengers awake. Benny was reading a travel magazine, while gatano was admiring to view over Europe.

About an hour later, the jet lands at Bern airport. A limo pulls up on the tarmac to pick up the 2 crews. The limo takes them to the Federal Palace. The men were in awe of the beautiful scenery of this country. "I could live here for the rest of my life!" Mikey said. "Not me! You'll stick out like a piece of coal in the snow!" said butch. Mikey chuckled.

Moments later, they arrive at the palace. They are escorted through a back entrance that leads to the east wing. "Ti prego mi segua signori." Said the escort. They all enter a room with a long wooden table. On the table were bottles of vintage wines, fresh fruit, pastries and bars for the famous Swiss chocolate. "Il vostro ospite sarà con voi signori." Said the escort, who was a short old white man dressed in a black suit. The escort leaves the room, closing the thick wooden double doors to give the men from Jersey some privacy. Butch takes an orange from the glass fruit bowl. He then takes a piece of the Swiss chocolate. "This shit don't taste sweet!" butch said. "I didn't know they speak Italian here!" Anthony said. "Not only that, they speak German, French and Romansh here too." Gatano said. Jabbo pops the cork off of a bottle of wine. He sniffs the cork. He first pours a glass for benny, and then for himself. Carlo takes the bottle from jabbo and pours his father a glass of wine as well. "Salute!" benny and gatano say as they raise their glasses.

A few minutes later, the double doors open. In steps the assistant of the man who set up the meeting, followed by the man himself. His name was Oscar Deltoro Santos. He came into the room with 5 armed bodyguards carrying semi-automatic machine guns. Mikey is startled. "Take it easy boys. We just came to talk." Benny says to his people. Non fare un figlio si muove all' improvviso! Siamo venuti a parlare!" boss gatano says to Carlo.

Mr. Santos is dressed in a black tuxedo. "Ci lascia." Mr. Santos says to the assistant. The assistant leaves the room. Mr. Santos took control of the infamous Caballeros de Fortune cartel back in 1990 from the mystery man before him. Mr. Santos was tall and slim with a pale complexion. He looked like he was in his late 30's.

"Have a seat gentlemen." Said Mr. Santos. Everyone grabs a seat. Mr. Santos remains standing. "So what's the problem gentlemen? Haven't I made you all wealthy beyond your wildest dreams?" Mr. Santos asked. Benny stands from his seat. "With all due respect Mr. Santos, we're just as shocked and upset as you! The reason why it took so long to address the issue, was that the man being accused worked for me for over a decade! I just wanted to make sure that the rumors were true!" said benny. "Now that you know these rumors to be true, what are you prepared to do about it?" asked Mr. Santos. Benny taps but butch on the shoulder. "Yeah, right!" said butch.

Butch stands from his seat. "My man next to me said mark's contact is part owner of one of the hotels on Miami Beach. I say if we get the contact to talk, we can shut down mark's Peruvian connection." Butch explained. Very well then. You gentlemen must excuse me. I have an important dinner date to attend to. You gentlemen can stay here for the night at my home in Zurich." Said Mr. Santos. Before benny could utter a word of gratitude, boss gatano speaks. "We would be delighted Don Santos!" said boss gatano. "Good. I'll have my assistant Giuseppe escort you back to the limo." Said Mr. Santos. 2 of the armed guards open the door for Mr. Santos to leave. The other guards stand at attention. Minutes later, the assistant Giuseppe enters the room. "Vi prego di seguire nuovo verso la limousine." Said Giuseppe. "Kid. If we pull this off, I'll give you your own town to run." Butch whispers to Mikey.

The next day, benny wakes up in a king size bed. He rubs his eyes to clear his vision. There's a knock on the door. "Yeah! Who is it?" benny asked. "Giuseppe Mr. lassenberry!" he shouted. "Come in!" shouted benny. Giuseppe comes in the room. Benny can hear his bones crack as he stands from the bed and stretches. "Mr. Santos expects you and your people to join him for breakfast within an hour at the south patio sir." Said Giuseppe. Benny looked confused. "Where the hell is the south patio?" benny shouted. "As soon as you're dressed, one of my staff members will come and show you where to go sir." Said Giuseppe. Benny nods. Giuseppe leaves the room.

Later on, benny meets with the rest of his crew, Gatano's crew and Mr. Santos at the south patio. They all sat at a long table covered with a white linen table cloth. Santos sits at the head of the table, with gatano at his right side, and benny on his left. There were 4 butlers waiting on the side to be called upon.

"Tell me something Mr. Lassenberry. Have you decided who to replace Mr. Vasquez with?" asked Mr. Santos. "I have someone in mind, but it ain't written in stone." Said benny.

After breakfast, Mr. Santos had to depart from his guests. "Now if you gentlemen would excuse me, I have to fly out to Madrid. My son has a championship game this evening. I hope you gentlemen have a safe journey back to the states." Said Mr. Santos. Everyone stands as Mr. Santos leaves the patio.

Before the lassenberry crew and the gatano crew leave for Bern airport, benny and butch take a walk down the corridor of the Santos mansion. They notice all the vintage art work a life size statues lining the halls. "You know, Eddie love shit like this." Said benny.

A day later, everyone arrives back at Teterboro airport. There on the tarmac, are 2 limos waiting to take each crew to their point of interests. When benny arrives back at the East Orange safe house, he just stands at the bottoms of the porch just staring at his surroundings. Eddie comes out of the house. "Pop! Pop! You ok?" said Eddie. "I can't believe I just came from Switzerland!" said benny.

It was late February of 1997, when Mark Vasquez jr., a.k.a Mookie was sitting at a booth in a bar he owned called la fábrica de rumores in Union City, New Jersey. It was around 8: 35 pm. sitting with him was a beautiful Latino woman. She was dressed in real provocative clothing, showing off her curves and voluptuous breasts.

The bar was purposely empty that night. Mookie wanted to show off the power he had to the fine young lady. Mookie allowed his bartender to stay of course to serve drinks.

The bartender's nick name was Beanz. He was Mookie's cousin on his mother's side of the family. Beanz was a short and chubby guy who dropped out of high school in the 9th grade because of making descent money working for his cousin.

"Yo Beanz, obtener mi Amiga aquí una cerveza y me consigue UN Ron con Coca-Cola!" Mookie shouted. Beanz looked behind the bar, but couldn't find one beer. Mookie was agitated. He gets up and goes over to the bar. "I thought you put in an order for 20 cases last week!" Mookie shouted.

Seconds later, 4 men burst in wearing ski masks. Armed with pistols with silencers, they take out Beanz with 2 shots to the body causing him to fall to the floor. One of the masked men turns to the young lady and puts 4 bullets into her. She slumps over in the booth. Mookie tries to makes a run for the back entrance, but is tackled by 2 of the gun men. They pick Mookie up off the floor. "Please don't kill me!" Mookie shouted. "Shut the fuck up!" said one of the masked men. Mookie is then handcuffed from behind. A black sack is placed over Mookie's head. "Get rid of the bodies and clean up any blood stains!" said one of the masked men. 2 of the masked men take Mookie out front to where a white van is parked. Mookie is shoved into the side door of the van. The driver, who is wearing a ceramic mask, drives off.

Back in the bar, the other 2 hit men locked the doors and moved the bodies into the bathroom. They found rags and detergents in the cleaning locker.

Back in the van, one of the mask men takes off his disguise. It is revealed that the masked man is Butch's guy Mikey. He took off the mask because of feeling smothered. "I better get my own territory after doing this shit!" Mikey said.

45 minutes later, the van pulls up in front of an office facility in Lodi, New Jersey. Mikey gets out of the van, and slides the side door open. The other hit man, still wearing his ski mask, grabs Mookie and drags him out of the van. Mikey and the masked man take Mookie inside the facility. The van drives off. The driver was ordered to go back to the bar and pick up the other 2 hit men, and the bodies. Mikey and the masked man take Mookie to the elevator. Mikey could hear Mookie breathing heavily under the sack. Once inside the elevator, Mikey pushes the button to go down to the basement.

The basement of the facility was more of a storage place for damaged and outdated office furniture. Mookie was taken passed the storage area to a back room. Standing at the door of this back room was a black guy I a suit. There were 2 office chairs in the room facing each other. Mookie is forced to sit in the chair where his back is facing the entrance.

Moments later, benny lassenberry, Jabbo, butch, Dubbs, Eddie lassenberry and 2 body guards enter the room. Benny takes off his suit jacket and hands it to one of the bodyguards. Jabbo holds the chair as benny sits down. Benny gives Mikey the signal to remove the sack from Mookie's head. Mookie sits there trembling like a leaf. "Take it easy son. Ain't nobody gonna hurt you." Said benny. Everyone is standing around the room. "Take off the cuffs." Said benny. Mikey takes out the key, and takes off the cuffs. Mookie grabs his wrist, rubbing it to ease the pain. "You shot my fucking cousin!" Mookie screamed. "What I'm about to tell you, is gonna be more of a shock." Said benny. The room is silent. Benny takes a deep breath, then exhales. "Sorry to tell you this son, but yo father been going behind our back, making deals with the enemy. The people up top says he gotta go." Said benny. Mookie drops his head in shame. "Nothing to say? Asked benny. Mookie starts crying. "So you knew about this?" benny asked. Mookie sniffles. "I knew it was wrong, but he's my dad!" said Mookie. "Everybody but jabbo, leave the room now!" said benny. The guard opens the door, letting everyone out. "I'm sorry Mr. Lassenberry, but, I would follow my father off a cliff if I had to!" said Mookie. Benny scratches his chin. Funny you should say that son, my own Eddie said the same thing about me." Benny chuckled. Mookie's leg starts trembling. "I can't believe this shit is happening!" said Mookie. "I hate to say this, but in order to keep your family's status, you'll have to remove your father from his seat." Said benny. Mookie frantically shakes his head, putting his hands over his ears, trying to block out benny's voice. "Listen. Ain't no way around it son. This is the life we live. You know this." Said benny. Benny leans back in his chair. Mookie removes his hands from his ears. "Even if I wanted to do it, my uncle Diablo will kill me!" said Mookie. "Well then yo uncle might have to go too! It's either that, or your family will lose all its territories, and have to leave the state! It's up to you! By the way, don't even think of running to the Peruvians. They're being taken care of as we speak." Said benny. Benny rolls his chair in closer to Mookie's. "Usted es el Único que conozco que puede hacer felices a loss dioses de nuevo." Said benny. Mookie was in awe. Benny smiled. "To be a boss son, you have to know a thing or 2, about a thing or 2." Said benny. Mookie bends over, and vomits on the floor, barely missing benny's shoes. "Vamos! Usted tiene que tomar una decision aquí, ahora mismo!" said benny.

Over a thousand miles away, about a hundred armed guerillas hired by Colombian drug lord Oscar Deltoro Santos, just stormed the mansion of the Peruvian drug czar who lived in the Amazonas region of the country. The charge was led by boss Gatano's son Carlo, who begged his father for the mission. Carlo was so involved in the job, that he wore camouflage army fatigues to the purge.

Carlo had the Peruvian drug lord tortured in the most grotesque way imaginable. Not only did he torture the unsuspecting drug lord, but his family consisting of his wife, young son, 2 teenage daughters and mother. Grenades were duct taped to his children's faces. Carlo personally pulled the pin on his son before leaving the room he was tied up in. Carlo slowly peeled the skin off his wife's body, as the Peruvian drug lord watched. His plea for mercy fell on deaf ears as Carlo stripped her legs of its flesh. Even some of the guerillas were disgusted with Carlo's tactics. "Creo que este tipo es el mismo Diablo!" one guerilla said to another.

At the end of the battle, only 10 of Santos's soldiers were killed compared to the hundreds of soldiers that died on the Peruvian side. The mansion was burned to the ground. The remaining members of the Peruvian's drug lord family heads were decapitated and put on spikes. Carlo walked away from the burning mansion soaked in blood, carrying a blood stained machete.

Back in Lodi, benny stands from his chair and puts his hand on Mookie's shoulder. "You gotta week to make it happen." Said benny. The guard hands benny his coat. Benny and jabbo leave the room.

2 days later, back at Eddie's home. Eddie had invited gino over to have a couple of drinks. It was around mid- night, when gino came over. There was a bottle of scotch on the coffee table almost empty. Eddie's glass was on the table still full, while gino was holding his empty glass

on his lap. "I heard rumors that prick went down to South America and whacked somebody." Said gino. "Who you're talking about?" Eddie asked. Gino is drunk by now and getting agitated. "Fucking Carlo! Weren't you listening?" gino shouted. Eddie remains silent. "What's that noise?" gino shouted. "What noise man?" Eddie asked. Before gino said anything, a figure comes out of Eddie's guest room. The person coming out of the room was wearing brown dress pants, and a white button up shirt. The shirt had blood stains on it. The person was holding an ice pack on his head. "Who the fuck is that?" gino shouted. "Oh, that's my nephew Danny Jr. over there!" said Eddie.

The day before, Danny jr. had paid a visit to his parent's estate in Livingston, New Jersey. Danny jr. had just graduated from his father's Alma Mata with a degree in business.

During his stay in south East England after graduation, Danny jr. lived in a loft with his roommate Nigel Quarter, his cousin on his mother's European side of the family.

Nigel entered the British Naval College. His specialty was in underwater demolition. Nigel also took training in PE4 plastic explosives

While in England, Danny jr. became irritated by the fact he didn't receive any envelopes for the past 5 months from his grandfather or Uncle Eddie. "I don't believe this shit! I called my father about my envelopes and he tells me he has no control over that!" Danny jr. shouted. Nigel was laying on the couch reading a magazine. "Why don't you take a trip across the pond and get your bloody money mate!" Nigel chuckled. Danny jr. goes over to where his pants are hanging on a hook. He pulls out wad of cash and counts it. "Shit! I only have 2700£ on me!" Danny jr. said. Danny jr. hands over half to Nigel. "This should help out with the rent until I get back." Danny jr. said. "How long will you be gone?" Nigel asked. "Hopefully, just a week." Said Danny jr. Nigel stuffs the money in his front pocket. Danny jr. goes to the closet and pulls out his suitcase. He stars emptying his dresser drawer of a few items.

The next morning, Nigel gives Danny jr. a ride to Heathrow airport. The weather was cold and dreary. Nigel walks Danny jr. to the departure area. "Well mate. Have a safe trip." Nigel said. Danny jr. and Nigel shake hands. "Thanks! I'll be back in a week." Said Danny jr. Nigel yanks a strand of hair from his small afro. "What hell man?" shouted Danny jr. "They had on the Telly that scientists are cloning sheep! I thought if I had a strand of your hair, I could clone you if the plane crashes!" Nigel chuckled. "You're a sick puppy!" said Danny jr. said.

It was around 10pm when Danny jr. landed at Newark airport. He leaves the terminal, and hails a cab. "495 Morgan drive, Livingston." Danny jr. said.

Within a half an hour, the cab pulls up to the front entrance of the estate. "Nice place!" the taxi driver said. Danny jr. grabs his suitcase, and pays the fee. Danny Jr. walks pass the gate, on to the property. He walks up to the front entrance, and rings the doorbell. Danny jr. turns the knob. The door is unlocked. Danny jr. peeks inside. "I saw you coming up the driveway!" said the housekeeper.

The woman's name was Emma. Emma worked for Danny sr. and his family since he came back to the states. Danny jr. drops his suit case. He goes over and gives Emma a hug. "Good to see you my sweet little boy!" said Emma. "Where's my parents?" Danny jr. asked. "Oh, they're down in Belmar fishing with friends. They should be back tomorrow sweaty. Your brothers' in the kitchen. Emma said.

Donald was in the kitchen eating a late night snack. Danny jr. enters the kitchen. "What's the word?" Danny jr. said. "What's up big brother?" said Donald. The 2 brothers shake hands. "Where's Samara?" Danny jr. asked. "Man, she's out in California, hanging out with that actress chick." Said Donald. Emma walks in the kitchen. "Y'all ain't gotta stop talking cause I'm in here! Y'all been running off at the mouth since y'all was babies! Emma chuckled. Emma takes a basket of laundry to the laundry room. "What you doing in the states?" asked Donald. "I just came home to get paid!" said Danny jr. "I just bought myself a fly ass jeep!" said Donald. "When you get your envelope?" Danny jr. asked. "2 days ago, old man Jabbo brought it over!" said Donald. "You bought a new jeep with 5 grand?" asked Danny jr. "Hell no!" we all gotta raise! It's 9 grand now!" Donald said. "God damn!" Danny jr. said as he slams his hand on the kitchen counter.

Benny recently put Eddie in charge of the family finances. Eddie took it upon himself to give his siblings and their children a boost in payment without properly checking the numbers. This resulted in Danny Jr. not getting not getting an envelope for the past 5 months. "What cars in the garage right now?" Danny jr. asked. "I think its mom's sports car." Donald said. "Where's the keys?" Danny jr. asked "I think they're on her dresser." Donald said. Danny jr. runs upstairs to his parent's room. The keys are where Donald said they'd be. He runs out to the garage and hops in the car.

About 20 minutes after, Danny jr. arrives on the streets of Newark. Danny jr. new the name of the street his uncle lived on, but didn't know which turn to make to get there. He sees a pay phone on the corner of West Bigelow Street. He also noticed the young people hanging out this late at night. He parks the car and gets out to make a call. Across the street, 4 young black men, 3 whom happen to be low level members of the lassenberry crew, were checking out the sports car. "Yo! Y'all know that nigga?" asked one of the dealers. The other guys shake their heads. "He out here driving that new shit!" said the dealer. There was one kid that wasn't a part of the lassenberry crew. He couldn't been no more than 15 years old. This kid was a car thief. He pulls out a pistol. "That fucking ride is mine!" said the car thief. The car thief was walking towards Danny jr., while he was on the phone talking to his brother Donald. Danny jr. is approached by the young man. "Hey, nice ride man!" the kid said. Danny jr. turns towards the kid. The kid takes out the pistol. He whacks Danny jr. across the head. Danny jr. falls to his knees. The kid whacks Danny Jr. upside the head again. Danny jr. falls to the ground. The kid goes through Danny Jr's pockets and takes his wallet and the car keys, while people on the street are watching. On the other end of the phone, Donald calls out for his brother. A lady witnessed the kid take the keys from Danny and grabs the phone. He unknowingly hangs up on Donald. The crowd grows bigger. The car thief jumps in the car and takes off. He tosses the wallet out of the car. A little boy picks up the wallet. One of the dealers grabs the little boy. "What's in that wallet?" asked one of the dealers. "Get off me!" the little boy shouted. The dealer grabs the wallet. He looks through the wallet and reads the name on the drivers' license His jaw drops when he realizes who the unconscious man was. "Oh shit! Oh shit!" he shouts. He drops the wallet. And then runs back over to the other dealers. He shows them the driver's license. "Oh shit! He's a lassenberry?" shouted one of the dealers. They all scatter from the corner.

About a half hour later, Eddie lassenberry is nodding out on his recliner with a drink in his hand, while Charlie Dalton is sleeping on the couch, when he hears a knock on the door. "What the fuck? Come in!" Eddie shouted. The door opens. In comes Eddie new guard Pete Bey, a.k.a peanut. "We gotta talk boss!" said peanut. Eddie staggers from his seat. "This shit better be important!" Eddie said. "They got your nephew Danny Jr. over at the hospital! He was robbed on the corner of West Bigelow!" said peanut. "How you know it's my nephew?" Eddie asked. Peanut pulls out a wallet from his pocket. Eddie takes the wallet, and opens the contents. Eddie kicks the couch and wakes up Charlie. Charlie jumps up in a frightened state. "I want you and Peanut to go down to the hospital, get my nephew out of there and bring him back here! Matter of fact! Bring rick with y'all! If the lady at the desk give you shit? Just tell her benny lassenberry wants him!" Eddie said. "Got it boss. Hurry up and get dressed man!" Pete says to Charlie. After Pete and Charlie leave, Eddie makes a phone call. The phone was ringing on the other end. "Hello?" said the voice. "Yeah Chewie! It's me! I want you and Mackie to round up everybody from the West Bigelow crew before the week is out, and bring'em down to the Kearny warehouse!" said Eddie.

Danny jr. walks over to gino to shake hands. "How's it going?" Danny jr. asked. "I should be asking you that? What happened to your head?" gino asked. Danny jr. looks over at his uncle. "Wrong place, wrong time." Danny jr. said. "He just slipped on a banana peel! Eddie chuckled.

Gino gets uncomfortable with the presence of Danny jr. in the room. "Well it's time for me to take my ass home!" gino said. Gino struggles out of his seat. He starts staggering to the door. "You want one of my guys to walk you to your car?" Eddie asked. "I got it." Said gino. Out in the hallway stood peanut. "Peanut! Tell a couple of the guys to walk him to his car!" ordered Eddie. Once Gino and peanut leave out, Eddie looks over at his nephew. "What?" asked Danny jr. "You're a Lassenberry? Don't ever let anybody think you got your ass whipped!" said Eddie

The day after Gino left Eddie's place, Eddie gets a knock on the door. "Come in!" Eddie shouted. At this time, Danny jr. was ordered to stay at his uncle's place to recuperate. Eddie's guard Leon, a.k.a 2 Gunz enters the apartment. "What is it?" asked Eddie. "The West Bigelow boys! We got'em!" said 2 Gunz. "Where's the sports car?" Eddie asked. "It's back in Livingston, at your brother's house." said 2 guns. Eddie puts on his leather blazer. "Let's go nephew. It's time for some pay back." Eddie says to Danny Jr... Danny jr. quickly grabs his jacket and follows his uncle out the door. Peanut closes the behind them. Eddie and Danny Jr. follow 2 guns down the hall towards the freight elevator. Standing there, are the elevator guards. Jerome Peters, a.k.a pinky and David Thompson, a.k.a Tiki were both packing shotguns. Tiki opens the door for his boss. Mike, a.k.a black mike. Tony, a.k.a boom. Jason, a.k.a J. Big and Troy a.k.a smooth are the main guards always posted outside the building. They stand at the elevator doors, each carrying concealed hand guns. Black mike being the guy in charge of the outside crew, gets on the walkie-talkie. "He's coming out of the elevator now." Mike says to Toby on the roof.

Toby was a black guy in his late 40's at the time, who was in charge of roof security. Also on the roof was Kent Foxx, Corey Diamond, a.k.a cee-cee and Rodney, a.k.a R2.

About 40 minutes later, Eddie's limo arrives at the Kearny warehouse. Boom gets out the limo. He opens the door for everyone in the back. Black mike, Eddie, Danny jr. and 2 Gunz. All enter the warehouse. Inside the warehouse were boxes filled with stuffed animals. The toys were used years ago when benny's old connection had millions of dollars of pure cocaine smuggled into the country. Today, Eddie uses this place for torture.

Inside the warehouse sits 4 teenage boys bound to chairs. Danny jr. stands nervously in the background. Hit men Chewie and Mackie stand behind the young men wielding shotguns. "Hey fellas!" Eddie said to the young men. When the boys see Eddie, they start to panic. 2 of them start crying. Eddie pulls out a pair of latex gloves. Out of fear, the boys rat out the car thief. The car thief starts crying like a baby. "I'm sorry Mr. Lassenberry! I didn't know who's car that was!" the car thief cried. Chewie hands Eddie a pistol. Eddie walks over to one of the dealers. "Why didn't y'all stop him?" Eddie asked. "I ain't got nothing to do with that?" the dealer shouted. Eddie puts the gun to the dealer's right eye and squeezes the trigger. There's was a loud pop. The dealer's head hangs back. Blood starts pouring from the back of the young man's head, while other 3 young men start jumping around in their seats crying like babies and begging for their lives. "Hakim! Damn, I mean Danny! Get over here!" Eddie shouted Danny Jr. walks over towards his uncle. Eddie gives the gun to Danny jr. as the young men are jumping around in fear. "Don't embarrass me!" Eddie whispered to his nephew. Danny jr. is shaking a little. Danny Jr. takes aim at the car thief. Everyone can see his hand shaking. "Shoot!" Eddie shouted. Danny jr. shoots. The kid takes a bullet in the forehead. Danny jr. runs over in a corner and pukes his brains out. Chewie and Mackie start laughing. "Alright. Let's get the fuck out of here!" Eddie shouted.

Everyone leaves the warehouse except for Mackie and Chewie. While Eddie, his nephew and his guards leave the warehouse, they could hear 2 shotguns blasts go off.

After Charlie drops off Eddie and the crew, he is told to take Danny jr. to his parent's estate. Once they arrive, Danny gets out of the limo. "You ain't gotta worry about the mess in the back!" said Charlie. Danny jr. became sick again. He walks up the driveway as Charlie drives off. Danny jr. walks up to his parent's driveway. He looks around to see if anyone was watching. He's stands at the front entrance. He falls to the ground, balled in the fetal position, sobbing like a child. The front door opens. It's Danny sr., who sees his son lying there. Danny sr. kneels down to his son. He doesn't ask any questions. He just cradles his son.

At the end of the week, Danny jr. is standing on the curb outside his parent's estate talking to a neighbor from down the road. "It's good to see you Daniel!" said the neighbor. "It's good to see you too doc!" said Danny jr. "Your father tells me that you're thinking of coming back to the states to stay." Said the doctor. Yeah, I was thinking about it." Said Danny jr. "So, thinking of joining the family business?" asked the doctor. "Family business?" Danny jr. asked. "Yes. Your father's packaging business." Said the doctor. "Oh! That family business!" said Danny jr. "What did you think I was talking about?" asked the doctor. "Uh, nothing!" Danny jr. says to the doctor. Suddenly, a black SUV pulls up. Danny jr. and the doctor can't see inside of the vehicle because it had tinted windows. Both Danny jr. and the doctor step back a few steps in fear. The passenger window rolls down. Danny jr. recognizes that it's black mike, who stares at Danny jr. with a deviant smile. "Yo uncle wanna talk to you!" black mike said. Black mike steps out of the vehicle, wearing a burgundy suit. "Come on man, and get inside! I got this bitch I'm meeting up with!" said black mike. "Is everything alright Daniel?" asked the doctor. "Mind yo business old man! Come on Danny! Get in!" said black mike. "Want me to call the police?" asked the doctor. "No, no doc!" said Danny. "Are you sure son?" asked the doctor. "Shut up old man, before I snuff yo ass!" said black mike. Danny jr. walks towards the car, and gets in the back seat. "Enjoy the rest of your day old man." said black mike. Black mike gets in, and the vehicle drives off, leaving the doctor standing there.

Later, Danny jr. is taken to his Uncle Eddie's place in Newark. Charlie parks the car right in front of the building. Black mike and Charlie escort Danny jr. to his uncle's apartment. Some of the guys from the crew shake hands with black mike, but none care to address Charlie. Black mike, Charlie and Danny jr. approach Eddie's apartment. Standing there was body guard 2 Gunz. Black mike and 2 Gunz shake hands. 2 Gunz then knocks on the door. "Come in!" Eddie shouted from inside. 2 Gunz opens the door, letting all 3 guys inside. "Hey nephew!" Eddie said, standing there in a t-shirt and sweat pants. Eddie gives his nephew a hug. "Y'all can wait out in the hall." Eddie said. 2 Gunz and Charlie leave the apartment. "Follow me." Said Eddie. Danny jr. follows his uncle to the bedroom. Eddie pulls out a briefcase from underneath his bed. Eddie places the briefcase on the bed. He opens it. Danny jr. was gasping from what he saw. There were stacks of cash inside the briefcase. Eddie grabs a stack of cash and tosses it to his nephew. "I tell ya nephew! Getting rid of bodies cost a lot of money! So I'm deducting from your allowance what it cost me to pay my people to avenge you! That's 10 grand in yo hand! The next time you go to yo daddy about me, I'm gonna forget we're family and you will disappear! Understand?" said Eddie. Danny jr. was so scared, the only thing he could do was to nod his head repeatedly.

Suddenly, there's a loud banging on the door. "What the fuck?" Eddie shouted. Eddie grabs his revolver. From the closet. Eddie goes out in the room. 2 Gunz bursts in the apartment. "What happened?" Eddie shouted. "They found Mark Vasquez dead!" shouted 2 Gunz. Eddie is standing there, showing no emotion. Back in the bedroom, Danny jr. was still shaken up by his uncle's threat, but his greed took control of his fear. Danny Jr. grabs 4 stacks of cash and starts stuffing it in inside pant legs.

Eddie calls Danny jr. from out of the bedroom. Danny jr. was about to stuff another stack of cash in his pants, until he dropped it on the floor. He quickly puts the stack of cash back into the briefcase. He comes running out of the room. "Tell black mike to take my nephew back home!" Eddie says to 2 Gunz. Eddie hugs his nephew. "Remember what I told yo ass!" Eddie said. Danny jr. nods. Eddie is now in the apartment by himself. He makes himself a drink, a slumps back in his recliner.

A day before, Danny sr. and his older brother Eddie met at a diner in West Orange. Danny sr. arrived first. His older brother had arrived with an entourage of 10 body guards.

Eddie had the manager and the 2 waitresses shut down the diner, and go into the kitchen. The patrons inside, seeing all of these black men, decided to leave voluntarily. Eddie's men were all wearing black trench coats. Outside the diner were 2 more guards standing at the entrance. Inside the diner, the guards had spread out, sitting in random booths. The 2 brothers hug each other. "Always cautious, huh brother?" said Danny sr... "Can never be too careful."

Eddie said to his brother. They both take a seat at the booth Danny sr. had already ordered a sandwich and fries. "Now tell me what's on your mind little brother." Eddie said. "My son was sitting in front of my door step crying the other day. He had called earlier complaining about not getting his envelopes sent to for past 5 months! That's why he flew out here from overseas! Listen! I don't want to know what kind of evil shit you showed him, but just pay him already!" Danny sr. said. Eddie leans forward and takes a French fry from his brother's plate and eats it. "Listen! If you ever talk to me like that again, I'll have to show you my dark side little brother!" Eddie whispered. "Fair enough!" said Danny sr. "It was just a misunderstanding in dispersing the cash, that's all. "You should be grateful at least I gave the family a raise!" said Eddie. "So, my son is going to get what's owed to him, and we can move on, right?" asked Danny sr... "Alright!" Eddie chuckled. The brothers shake on it. "So how's the packaging business?" Eddie asked. "Business is doing well!" Danny sr. said. "That's good!" Eddie said.

About a block and a half away, a black van was parked, occupied by 3 men in black suits and dark shades. The first agent is looking at the diner through high tech binoculars, while another agent is hooked up to advanced audio and video device. The agent spots 2 F.B.I agents on top of a building across from the diner. "You think Daniel lassenberry is being recruited by his brother?" asked agent 2. "If the Feds take him in, then we'll find out. Said agent 3.

In the beginning of March, the weather was warm enough to melt the snow on the ground. It was also a dark day for the Vasquez faction. At an Episcopal church in Elizabeth, close to a thousand people turned up to pay respect to the untimely passing of Mark Vasquez sr., king pin of Union and Hudson County. All you can hear are the cries and screams of women, mostly Hispanic, in the streets.

Elsewhere, Dubbs was sitting in his living room at his Bradley Beach home eating a ham and cheese sandwich. He was reading his favorite comic book. His trusted second in command, Robbie Davis, a.k.a. bulletproof came in through the sliding doors from outside. "Yo, your cousin coming." Said Robbie. Dubbs washes down his food with a glass of juice. "Tell him to come in!" said Dubbs. "I'm already here nigga!" butch chuckled as he stood in the doorway. Dubbs gets up and wipes the crumbs off his hands and goes over to hug his cousin. "Come sit down cuz!" said Dubbs. They both sit down on the sofa. "Proof, go and get butch a beer!" said Dubbs. Butch turns to Robbie. Forget that. Take a break outside and let me talk to my cousin for a minute!" butch ordered. Robbie nods his head and goes outside to Butch's guards. "Why ain't you dressed and got yo ass over in Elizabeth?' butch asked. "Man cuz, I'm trying to stay off the tube and out of the papers!" said Dubbs. "Wrong move! We show our faces so the Vasquez people don't think we had anything to do with his death." Butch said. "Fuck'em! We got 2 territories under our belt! We make our own rules now!" shouted Dubbs. Butch leans back in his seat. "You talking about a war we can't win cuz! The lassenberry people will back them, and the Italians will back the lassenberry people!" said butch. "This is bullshit!" shouted Dubbs. "What's really wrong cuz?" asked Butch. Dubbs looks outside and shakes his head. "Man, besides my people, I'm paying off 8 judges, 15 politicians, and a whole army of cops and sheriffs! After all that! I'm only putting 5 million a year in my pocket, while that Spanish nigga was pocketing at least 12 million!" Dubbs shouted. "15 million a year, but who's counting?" butch chuckled. "What the fuck?" said Dubbs. Butch puts his hand on his cousin's lap. "You gotta understand something. These good ol' boys out here don't wanna see you get rich. Just be lucky you're a millionaire." Said butch. "So how much you making a year?" asked Dubbs. "None of yo goddamn business!" butch chuckled. Dubbs punches his cousin in the arm. "Speaking of good ol' boys! This white boy moved out here from California over a month ago, bringing out some new dope called crystal method or some shit! I told him he could set up his lab out here for 30 grand a month!" Dubbs said. "You should've waited to see if you could get more from him. Lassenberry gotta get his cut from it." Said butch. "Nah, not this one! This my deal! Mine alone!" said Dubbs. Butch looks at his cousin, then bursts out laughing. I'm just fucking with you cuz! You keep that chump change." Butch chuckled. "You always gotta be an asshole!" said Dubbs. "But seriously, I need you to get dressed and come out to Elizabeth with me." Butch ordered. "Got you. Just give me a few minutes to get dressed." Dubbs said.

Back in Elizabeth, the crowd coming to view the body was getting bigger. Local and state officials showed up to pay their respects. Inside the church, 4 out of 9 freeholders of Union County greeted the grieving widow of Vasquez. The mayors of Secaucus and Jersey City, who were up for reelection, showed their faces, as well as mayors from Kearny, Roselle, Rahway and Elizabeth.

The media was out and about as well. A sexy Latino journalist stopped Mayor Frank P. Albert of Kearny. "This is Sonya Vega of channel 15 news here with Mayor Albert from Kearny. Mr. Mayor, what brings out here today sir?" asked Vega. "Well, Mr. Vasquez was a major contributor to our educational system. He was financially generous to start a full scholarship program throughout Hudson County. "What do you say about Mr. Vasquez's alleged ties to organized crime?" Asked Vega. "I say if Mr. Vasquez was involved in such endeavors, I wouldn't be here talking to you. Now if you would excuse me." Said Mayor Albert. "Thank you for your time Mr. Mayor." said Vega. The mayor nods and walks away with his aide. "You've heard it here first. This is Sonya Vega coming to you live from Elizabeth. Back to you Linda and David." Said Sonya Vega.

Inside the church, Eddie lassenberry surrounded by a 10 body guard detail, hugs Mookie, who is backed up by an armed detail as well. Mookie is then hugged by Charlie Dalton." Meet the boss is the bishop's office in 10 minutes." Whispered Charlie. Mookie nods his head.

Minutes later, Mookie makes his way through the crowd, followed by his body guard Victor Nunez. Mookie opens the door to the bishop's office. "Quedarse en la puerta y asegurarse de que nadie entra." Mookie whispered to Nunez. Mookie walks in to find Eddie lassenberry already in there, sitting behind the bishop's desk. Charlie was leaning up against the bookcase trying to look cool. "You can leave now. Go start the car." Eddie says to Charlie. Charlie leaves the office with his head down from embarrassment. Mookie had anger in his eyes as he paces the floor. "How does it feel to run your own territory now?" Eddie asked. Mookie stops pacing. "It's gonna take some getting used to!" Mookie said. "I see you got yo father's ring on." Said Eddie. "It fits like a glove." Mookie said softly. "Let's get down to business kid! I just wanna know can everything get back to normal after today?" asked Eddie. Mookie just nods. "Ok then. You'll pick up your refill of 50 kilos of cocaine, 100 pounds of weed, and 10 cases of assorted prescription pills, already labeled for you at Port Elizabeth the first of every month. That means my father expects a briefcase at the port with no less than 2 million for the connection. Mookie's eyes tear up. He doesn't say a word. He just nods his head. I guess the meeting is over!" Eddie chuckled. Eddie leaves the office. Mookie stays behind to wipes the tears from his eyes. Mookie then leaves the office. He sees Eddie leaving the church. Suddenly. He's approached by Tony Diablo and his boys.

"Después de loss servicios, tenemos que volver a grupo y mantener una reunión con las-senberry." Said Diablo. Mookie sighs. He then shows Diablo the back of his right hand. "I'm wearing my father's ring now. That means I call the shots." Mookie said. Mookie then walks through Tony Diablo and his crew, towards the casket.

It was near the end of February when Mookie invited his father over for a one-on-one dinner. No wives, no body guards, nobody, just father and son. "¿Está todo bien, hijo?" mark senior said. "Everything couldn't be better pop." Said Mookie. "Qué pasa? Que no le gusta hablar español más?" asked mark sr. Mookie sighs. It's a new day pop. Things change." Said Mookie. Mark gives his son a look of disappointment. There is a dead silence in the dining room. "We're out of beer pop. I'm going to get some more. You want anything?" asked Mookie. "Yo me quedo con el vino." Mark sr. tells his son. Mark sr. just sits there at the table chewing on his food. Before he could react, Mookie had pierced the back of his neck with a syringe. At the end of the syringe was an 18 inch rubber hose. Mookie quickly blows into the hose, then yanks the syringe from his neck. Mark sr. jumps from his chair, knocking the dinner ware and food off the table. He runs frantically around the room until he runs into the wall. Mark sr. just lays there on the floor still. Mookie just stands there with the syringe and hose in his hand. He calls out his father's name, but there's no answer. Mookie walks over to his father's body. He kneels down over his father and screams at the top of his lungs. The night before the murder of his father, Mookie was visited by Eddie lassen-berry. Eddie showed him what tools to use to get the job done.

At the F.C.I, hakim now at the age of 31, was alone in his lair marking off another day on his calendar. Wearing nothing but a t-shirt, sweat pants and flip flops, he decides to leave his lair. He walks to the exit. He bangs on the heavy metal door to get the attention of the officer. "Jones! Open the door!" hakim shouted. Jones opens up. "You know the routine bates." Said Officer Jones. Every time hakim wanted to leave the lair, he had to be thoroughly frisked. Hakim hadn't left his lair since the tiny incident. 10 minutes later, another officer arrives on the scene after being called over the walkie-talkie. The officer's name was Washington. "All this time up here by yourself, now you wanna meet-n-greet!" said Washington.

Washington was a black officer that had been on the job for 15 years. He didn't care too much for hakim and his privileged life on the inside. "Don't fuck with me! I'm not some reg-ular punk ass inmate!" hakim shouted. Washington was raised in Newark and new of the lassenberry crew. "Man, you know I was just fucking with you!" Washington said. "Man, just take me down to Gen pop!" hakim said.

Officer Washington remained at the E block entrance. "I'll wait here until you're ready to go back." Said Washington. Hakim just strolled down the corridor without a care in the world. The rumors about him murdering everyone in his crew, made him a force to be reckoned with.

There were a group of black inmates playing Texas hold'em for cigarettes at the table. "Yo!

Hakim man, come jump in this!" said one inmate. "You fellas go ahead with that! I'm looking for a chess game right about now!" said hakim. As he kept walking, hakim noticed one inmate sitting at a table by himself, with a checker board all set up looking for someone to get a game with. Hakim walks over to the guy. "Yo man! Gotta switch it to chess if you wanna a game!" hakim chuckled.

The inmate sitting at the table was bald, well built and light skinned. Hakim extends his hand to greet the inmate. "I'm hakim man." he said in a daunting voice. "I heard about you. I'm Biron Eric Xavier, but they call me Bex." Said Bex. They both shake hands. Hakim takes a seat across from Bex. "You gotta thick ass country accent! You from down south?" asked hakim. "Nah man, Bridgeton." Bex said. "You got chess pieces in the bag over there?" asked hakim. "Yeah, but I ain't never played no chess before!" said Bex. "Get rid of this checkers shit!" said hakim. Bex pushes the checker pieces to the side. Hakim shows him how to set up the chess pieces. "Now listen! Chess is like life itself! You gotta learn to survive in this game!" hakim said. "Got it!" said Bex. "First things first. This is a pawn." Said hakim.

It was around 2 in the morning, Eddie had just finished entertaining a sexy young woman. He went into his briefcase to give her a few bucks to send her on her way, when he noticed stacks of cash missing. He remembered when the last time he went into the briefcase. It was when he was in the company of his nephew. Eddie had realized it was Danny jr. and yelled for 2 Gunz. Eddie runs to the door. 2 Gunz was sitting in a chair outside in the hallway, fast asleep. "Wake yo ass up nigga!" Eddie shouted. 2 Gunz jumps out of his seat. "Make a call to Mackie and Chewie, and tell them to be here in an hour! By the way! Escort this bitch off my property" Eddie ordered. "Got it boss!" said 2 Gunz. 2 Gunz grabs the lady by the arm, taking her down the hall to the freight elevator. Eddie slams the door and rushes over to his liquor cabinet and pours himself a drink.

Exactly at 3 in the morning, there's a knock on the door, but Eddie couldn't hear it from being wasted. After a minute of banging on the door, Eddie wakes up from his drunken slumber. "Who that?" Eddie shouted. "It's me boss! I got Mackie and Chewie with me!" said 2 Gunz. "Come in!" Eddie shouted.

Rufus Forte, a.k.a Chewie and McClain Foxx, a.k.a Mackie were Eddie's 2 personal hit men. They both stood about 6 feet tall. Chewie was the muscle bound one, while Mackie was real slim. Chewie served 19 years in a maximum security prison out in Pennsylvania. He got himself involved with the lassenberry crew by meeting butch through a mutual friend once he was released. Mackie was Chewie's cellmate, who was let out of prison a few years earlier. Mackie was broke and homeless until he ran into Chewie, who introduced him to butch. Chewie vouched for Mackie, and the rest is history.

"What's the word old man?" asked Mackie. "Go back to your post." Eddie says to 2 Gunz. Mackie frowns from the smell of alcohol on Eddie's breath. "I want you 2 to suit up and go my brother's house in Livingston and bring my nephew Danny jr. to the Kearny warehouse! Now!" Eddie shouted.

Every time Eddie told Mackie and Chewie to suit up, he meant ski masks, bullet proof vests and pistols with silencers. 15 years working for Eddie, the 2 guys never missed their mark.

It was around 4:35 in the morning, when the 2 hit men arrived in a brown van at the upscale neighborhood in Livingston. The van was parked adjacent to the gate at the lassenberry estate. All you could hear were the crickets and the power from the street light. Mackie saw the street light as a nuisance. He screwed on the silencer to his pistol, while Chewie was on the lookout. Mackie took aim and shot out the street light and the block went pitch black. "You got 5 minutes to bring his out here and throw him in the van!" Chewie whispered. Mackie nods. Mackie dons his ski mask. He jumps out of the van. Chewie slowly drives off on a side street. Mackie climbs over the electronic gate and runs towards the front entrance. He kicks the door open on the second attempt. With pistol in hand, he runs up the stairs. Mid way up the stairs, he runs into Emma the housekeeper, who was in her robe. Mackie grabs her by the arm. He puts his hand over her mouth. "If you scream bitch, I'll kill you!" he whispered. The excitement was too much for Emma. She clutched her chest and passed out. Mackie released her, causing her to fall down the stairs. He continues upstairs. He heads the first room on the right. He kicks the door in. the room is empty. He creeps to the next door on the right. He kicks in the door too. He sees the room is empty as well, but it looked as if someone was sleeping in the bed. Suddenly, Mackie looks out the corner of his eye. He takes a whack in the head with a baseball bat. "Get the fuck outta my house!" Donald shouted. Dazed, Mackie tries to crawl to the staircase to escape. Donald whacks him across the back. "Pop! Wake up!" Donald shouted. Mackie crawls down the stairs with great speed. At this moment, Danny sr. comes running out of his room holding a revolver. He told his wife to stay in the bedroom. Mackie tumbles down the stairs and makes his way outside. He staggers to the gate, and then climbs over it. Coincidently, Chewie drives up. Mackie staggers to the van. He gets in "so you got'em?" Chewie asked "No! The fucking old lady, just go!" Mackie shouted Chewie drives off.

The next morning, benny lassenberry was sitting at the edge of his bed at the lassenberry estate. He was in his pajamas, clutching his wife's hand as she lay there lifeless. Lola lassenberry had finally lost her battle with cancer. Earlier, he told cooper and Rosa to notify his children and grandchildren. The last time benny sobbed so much was the death of his first born. He grabs his walking cane and heads for the elevator.

Eddie had installed an elevator in his father's mansion a year ago so benny and his wife could get around the mansion easier. The door to the elevator was made of glass. The elevator could travel from the second level basement, all the way to the attic.

Benny had reached the main level of the mansion. He could see some family members standing around before he stepped out of the elevator. He smiled when seeing his grandson Mark Jr.

Now at the age of 31, mark jr. had grown into this 6 feet 2 inch tall, man about town. Mark jr. was a playboy, who spent most of his time jet setting between New Jersey's posh locations, Aspen, Beverly Hills and South America. He was an articulated, and well groomed extrovert. He and his siblings were sheltered from their uncle Eddie, so all mark jr. knew how to do was enjoy the finer things in life.

Tyson Richards, Mike Abbey and benny the 3rd were standing alongside mark jr. to greet their grandfather. Benny couldn't hold back the tears in front of his grandsons this time.

Eddie finally shows up at the mansion with a hangover. He hugs his sister baby sister Lula.

"Did anybody go over Danny's? Elaine just called saying someone broke into the house and gave housekeeper a heart attack!" asked Maggie. "I'll send some of my men over there to check on him. Jake sr. turns to Eddie. "We don't need body guards to solve all our problems. Mark and I will see about our brother." Jake sr. said. Eddie has rage in his eyes. "Listen here! I'm the oldest! What I say goes, mother fucker!" Eddie shouted. Jake sr. scoffs at Eddie. "Let's go mark!" Jake sr. shouted. Eddie steps to his brother. "I take care of this family! Even that pretty wife of yours!" Eddie says to Jake sr... "Fucking bastard!" Jake sr. shouted. Jake sr. lunged at his brother, but was stopped by his brother mark sr. "Y'all stop now! Jake, mark, y'all go see about your brother!" benny shouted. Mark sr. gets Jake sr. to calm down. Suddenly, the doorbell rings. Cooper answers the door, and there stands Danny sr. Elaine and Donald. As soon as Danny sr. sees Eddie, he jumps at him as well. "You tried to kill my family?" Danny sr. shouted. Danny sr. runs through the crowd and slugs his brother in the face. "You son-of-a-bitch!" Danny sr. shouted as he gets 2 more hits off Eddie before mark jr. and Tyson get between them. At this moment, Big L. comes running out of the kitchen with a sandwich in his hand. "Everybody ok?" big L. asked. Mark sr. paused for a moment, looking at his behemoth of a nephew, then goes back to the matter at hand. "What the hell are you screaming about?" asked mark sr. "Your Brother here sent some goons to my house and put my housekeeper in the hospital!" said Danny sr. "That's bullshit!" Eddie shouted as he cups his hand over his swollen eye. "You did or said something to Danny jr., because he packed his bags and left for the UK like a goddamn lightning bolt!" Danny sr. said. Eddie lips start to swell up. "I don't believe this shit! After all the shit I do for y'all, this is how y'all treat me!" Eddie said as the tears roll down his cheek. I would never hurt anybody in my family! I love all y'all, and that's why I gave everybody a bonus!" Eddie cried as he goes over and sit at the bottom of the staircase. Eddie buries his head in his lap, sobbing like a baby. Danny sr. scoffs at his brother's moment of weakness. "Y'all mother's body is upstairs! I want y'all go up there now before the coroner comes! Now go!" benny shouted. Everyone heads upstairs, some taking the glass elevator, and some walking right pass Eddie, taking the stairs. It infuriates Eddie that the attention was taken away from him. Benny walks over to his son. He hits Eddie upside the head. "Get over yo self boy, and get yo ass up them stairs!" benny ordered Eddie. At this point, Eddie's face was swelling up even more, but he obeys his father and takes the stairs up.

Moments later, the coroner arrives, escorted by 2 Cherry Hill police cars. The guards at the gate let them pass through. Everyone heads downstairs to let the coroners do their job. Big L. finds a pair of sunglasses from out of one of the bedrooms and gives it to his uncle Eddie. Eddie takes the glasses and puts them on.

3 days later, the funeral procession was taking place for Lola Elizabeth, queen of the lassenberry clan. Her body was placed in the family tomb, positioned one space over from her son. Boss Gatano, Frankie Depalma and 2 associates were the only ones from the gatano crew came to pay their respects.

Lola's granddaughter Samara came out from California with her super model girlfriend. Now at the age of 19, Samara lassenberry had grown into the image of a sexy black goddess. She looked like the younger version of her grandmother, but with an almond complexion. She couldn't have weighed no more than 120 pounds at the time, standing at 5 feet 7inches tall without heels. She had long jet black hair, which came down to the middle of her back. Her rear end lacked the curves of the average black woman which her mother told her she inherited from her side of the family. What she lacked on the bottom, she definitely made up on the top. Arriving on a private jet from Teterboro airport just a day before the funeral, Samara and girlfriend named Ariel cassata stopped by the lassenberry mansion, both dressed in scantily clad outfits. The mansion was swarming with relatives and friends of the family. Samara trotted around in her stiletto shoes giving hugs and kisses to family and friends. Her size D breasts were bouncing around, barley restrained by her tight burgundy Minnie dress. Her friend Ariel wore the same identical outfit, but it was turquoise. Samara grabs Ariel by the hand and drags her over to meet Aunt Lula. Samara hasn't seen her aunt since the funeral of her uncle benny Jr... "Hey auntie Lula!" samara screamed as she hugged her aunt. "Hey sweetie!" Lula screamed. "I've missed you so much!" samara yells. "What are you doing these days young lady? I see you're a grown woman now!" Lula said as she poked Samara's breast. Embarrassed, samara folds her arms to cover up her huge breasts. "Oh auntie, this is my best friend Ariel from Los Angeles!" said Samara. "Hello!" Ariel says to Lula as they wave to each other. "Ariel models, but wants to get into acting as well!" Samara said. "So how long you've been modeling?" Lula asked. "5 years now!" Ariel said. "I told her that you were nominated for best supporting actress back in 77!" Samara boasted. "Wow! That's the year I was born!" Ariel said. Lula looked like she was insulted, but said nothing. She just rolled her eyes. "Well anyway girls, I have to go see how my father is holding up! There's more than enough food! So get yourselves something to eat! You look so thin!" Lula says to Ariel. "Nice meeting you!" said Ariel.

The 20 year old model Ariel was the same height and was thin as samara. She had a light complexion. Her hair was jet black, soft and curly, cut at shoulder length. Her breasts weren't as huge as samara's but she had the ass of a stripper. Every time she walked, it looked like she was purposely making her ass jiggle. People would always ask her about her ethnicity. She had a thin nose and lips of a white girl.

Samara looked around the crowded room as she and Ariel walked towards the buffet table. Suddenly, she spots someone across the room that she was dying to meet all day. "Oh my god!" Samara screamed. "What?" asked Ariel? "Oh you have got to meet my uncle Eddie!" Samara said. "Eddie. Eddie lassenberry is your uncle?" asked Ariel. "Yeah girl! Come on! He is the coolest dude on the planet!" said Samara. Most of the men in the room couldn't help keep their eyes off of Ariel. Friends and family members had glanced at Samara as well. There was no doubt that they were the eye candy at the mansion. Samara spoke to family members as she and Ariel made their way through the crowd towards Eddie. "Hey Cousin Bert! Hey Cousin Larry!" Samara shouted. Just like a dozen other guys in the room, Big L. was hypnotized by Ariel's beauty as she walks by. Krayton comes from behind Big L. and Bert. "Damn, that bitch gotta nice ass!" Krayton said.

Eddie had arrived at the mansion wearing a more fashionable pair of shades to cover his black eye. He and Charlie were dressed in expensive silk suits. "Damn boss! Who that with your niece?" Charlie asked. The closer and closer Samara and Ariel came, the more Charlie's eyes bulged. "Hey Uncle Eddie!" Samara shouted as she gave him a big hug. "Hey baby girl!

How's my favorite niece doing?" Eddie said. "I'm good! Why are you wearing those shades in doors?" Samara asked. "Something got in my eye yesterday, and I rubbed it until it got infected!" Eddie said. "Oh thanks! I got my envelope last week!" Samara said. "You know I always take care of family!" Eddie says as he rubs his hands together. Samara grabs Ariel's hand and pulls her in closer. "Uncle Eddie, Ariel Cassata! Ariel, Uncle Eddie!" Samara chuckled. Eddie gently grabs Ariel's hand and kisses it. "Cassata? You part Italian?" Eddie asked. "My mother is from the Dominican Republic and my dad is from Verona Italy." Ariel said. "Ok! Hai avuto modo di essere la donna più sexy del pianeta! Mi piacerebbe dare al mondo un giorno!" Eddie said with a sinister grin. Both girls started giggling. "I'm sorry, but I know very little Italian! My father passed away when I was 8, so he didn't get a chance to teach me much of it." Ariel said with a sad but sexy look. Eddie also became hypnotized. "Oh well, in that case! Mi piacerebbe roccia quel corpo sexy tutta la notte!" Eddie said. Ariel gently hits Eddie on the arm. "I know some of what you were saying! You are bad!" Ariel giggled. "Hey Samara!" Charlie said in a timid voice. "Hey Charlie. Last time I saw you, was at uncle benny's funeral. We've gotta stop meeting like this!" Samara giggled. It took Charlie a few seconds to catch on to the joke. "Oh yeah!" Charlie chuckled. The girls looked embarrassed for him. Eddie lightly smacks Charlie upside the head. "Go fix me a plate!" Eddie ordered. Charlie walks away like a dog with his tail between his legs. Samara shakes her head as she watches Charlie walk away. She turns back to her uncle. "So how's pop-pop taking it?" asked Samara. "He'll be fine in no time! That old man seen it and done it all!" said Eddie. Across the room, Eddie could see his little brother Danny sr. coming in his direction. Eddie takes a deep breath. Danny sr. is known to be unpredictable. Danny sr. had rage in his eyes as he makes his way through the crowd. Danny sr. grabs his daughter by the arm. "Come with me young lady! I need to talk to you!" Danny sr. whispered. "Ok Daddy! Damn! I'll be back Ariel!" Samara said. Danny sr. takes his daughter out to the terrace where there are fewer guests. "Listen young lady! I don't want you near that man ever again! Danny sr. ordered. Why, what's wrong?" Samara asked. "He's the reason why your brother skipped town that's why!" Danny sr. shouted. Samara shook her head. "No daddy! I talked to Donald and mommy about it already! We don't know if that's true!" samara said. "I know my brother and what he's capable of, regardless what the rest of the family thinks!" Danny jr. said. "Daddy! You have to relax!" samara said. "One other thing! Don't take anymore envelopes from him either!" Danny sr. said. "What?" Samara said in shock. "When jabbo's people come and give you an envelope, don't take it! If you need any money, I'll give it to you from now on!" Danny sr. said. "But daddy!" yelled Samara. "Don't but daddy me! Just do what I tell you!" Danny sr. shouted. Samara pouts. She folds her arms and looks out at the scenery in the yard. She then turns to her father. She nods her head. "Good! Now go find Donald! We have to go to Emma's wake, or have you forgotten?" said Danny sr. Maggie comes out to the terrace with a plate of food in her hand. Whatever you 2 are talking about, you need to keep it down! My mother just passed away, and this is her house!" said Maggie. Danny sr. doesn't say a word. He and samara walk back inside. As Danny sr. makes his way through the crowd, Eddie comes up from behind, grabbing his arm. Danny sr. turns around. "What do you want?" Danny sr. asked. Eddie clears his throat. Charlie Dalton comes over and gives Eddie his plate of food.

"Go start the car!" Eddie orders Charlie. Danny sr. shook his head. "Does he roll over and play dead too?" Danny sr. asked. Eddie stuffs a deviled egg in his mouth. "I'm gonna say this once little brother! Anything you say about me from this day on, just drop it!" Eddie said. Danny sr. unfolds his arms. "Drop what?" Danny sr. asked. Eddie didn't say a word. He just walked pass his brother towards the exit.

Days after the passing of the queen of the lassenberry clan, her children, including Eddie, went on hiatus from their professions to reminisce on their memories of her.

Maggie spent her time on hiatus at the lassenberry estate in Cherry Hill tending to her father's needs, even though benny had a live in butler, a live in housekeeper and private chef. She convinced her father to stay at home and not go back to running the streets. Maggie stayed in the same old bedroom since her childhood

2 weeks later, Maggie and her father sat down in the dining room at the long oak wood table to eat. The chef, was a middle-aged Haitian man named Jean Paul Beauvais. He was handpicked by jabbo years ago. Jean Paul was required to wear the traditional chef's uniform at all times when preparing food. Like all employees that worked inside the mansion, Jean Paul had to go through a thorough background check. And was searched when entering the mansion. Jean Paul used to have a Sous-chef working for him until it was found out that she was an F.B.I informant wearing a wire. Due to the professionalism of the mansion security, the Sous-chef and the wire that was taped to her body disappeared without a trace.

After Lola's death, benny became comfortable at the dinner table by not wearing any pants. He only liked wearing his pajama top. "So when you looking to retire little girl?" benny asked. Maggie sighed. "I'm 56 years old dad! I'm far from a little girl!" Maggie said. "Nonsense! As long as I'm alive, you'll always be my little girl." Said benny. Maggie used her linen napkin to wipe the tears from her eyes.

Jake lassenberry, along with his second wife Janis. Rented a RV to travel across the country. He left his son Jake sr. in charge of all his businesses until his return.

Janis Hernandez Lassenberry, who was 30 years younger that Jake sr., were married for only 5 years. She looked like she came straight out of a fashion magazine. Jake purposely dressed her in the finest scantily clad outfits. Unknown to Jake sr., Janis used to mess around with his older brother Eddie back in the day when was in her teens. Out of all of benny's sons, Jake and Eddie were the closest. This was why Janis and Eddie kept their fling secret.

"This is the life baby! Just us 2 cruising down the road without a worry in the world!" said Janis. Janis grabs Jake sr. by the hand and kisses it. She noticed that he had a sad look on his face. "I know you miss your mother sweetie, but you have to realize that she was in poor health for a while!" Janis said. Jake took a deep breath. "It's not that. It's something my brother said to me the day my mother passed." Jake said. "What's that sweetie?" Janis asked. Jake sr. pulls the RV over on the side of route 60 in West Virginia. He turns off the Ignition. "My brother and I got into it that day, and he brought you into the argument!" Jake said. Janis turns her head the other way for a couple of seconds, then she turns back towards her husband. "What did he say?" Janis asked. "Nothing directly about you, but it was like he… forget it!" Jake sr. said. Jake sr. starts the engine. Janis turns off the ignition, and takes the keys, and then reaches over and unzips Jake's pants. "Oh woman! You done started something now!" Jake sr. chuckled. Janis gets out of her seat, and then crawls on her husband's lap.

Mark sr. spent his time after closing his dental practice with his wife Tasha at their cabin out in aspen, Colorado. Mark sr. and his wife would only visit their home in the mountains to celebrate their wedding anniversary.

The cabin was nestled in a remote area, miles away from tourism. Mark had the luxurious cabin built from the ground up. The cabin was surrounded by an 8 foot iron gate. Out of his 15 acres of land, 70 percent of the property was covered by forest.

Danny sr. spent his time over in the UK getting to the bottom of his son's problem. Danny sr. met his son Danny jr. at a pub one night in Camden town. They hug each other tightly before being seated. Danny sr. orders a dark logger he used to drink back in his college days. He persuaded his son to order the same drink. Once their drinks are served, Danny sr. raises his glass. Danny jr. raises his glass. "Here's to being a lassenberry!" Danny sr. shouted. Father and son tap glasses. "So, how you feeling?" Danny sr. asked. "To be honest pop, I'm scared to death!" Danny jr. said. "Did you steal from your uncle?" Danny sr. asked. Danny jr. is silent for a moment. He takes a sip of his beer. "A hundred grand! Danny jr. whispered. Danny sr. scratches his head. "How did you know it had anything to do with money?" Danny jr. asked. Danny sr. chuckled. "I heard rumors about my brother growing up, and the only 2 things I know that motivates him, is money and pussy!" Danny sr. said. Danny jr. sips his beer. "I know I should've been there for grandma's funeral!" said Danny jr. "Let me go back to the states and try to make things right." Said Danny sr. Danny Jr. looks around at the other patrons. "There's something else pop!" Danny jr. whispered. "What?" asked Danny sr. "He made me kill someone!" Danny jr. whispered. Danny sr. puts his head down. He then looks at his son. His eyes start to tear up. "Well, if that's the case, you should keep your ass here! I'll tell your mother and brother that we'll have to visit you from now on!" Danny sr. said. Danny jr. sips his beer. "How you and Nigel getting along?" Danny sr. asked. "Oh, Nigel is good! He's a cool guy!" Danny jr. said. "I was hoping you'd be home so I could teach you the packaging business. Now, I have to show Donald the ropes." Said Danny sr. "Donald? Pop, come on!" Danny jr. shouted

CHAPTER 8. THE N.A.

A week had passed. 2 white gentlemen in black suits and wearing dark shades walk down the corridor of an undisclosed facility. They approach 2 huge double doors guarded by 2 guards wearing black suits as well. They walked another 40 yards pass 6 more guards standing at attention on either side of them armed with the sub-machine guns. They come to a solid iron gate with foreign writing on it. Next to the gate, was an electronic panel. One of the men places the palm of his hand on the panel. A red laser light scans his hand. The gate slides open. They then come to a set of double doors that automatically opens. They enter a lavish room with wall-to-wall red carpet.

In the middle of the room was an elderly white guy with a full head of gray hair. He was wearing a blue jogging suit. He had a putter in his hand hitting golf balls into a drinking glass. "You sent for us sir?" asked one of the agents. "Yes. Phase 2 of operation National Agreement will commence June 6th of this year. Your orders are on the desk over there. One of the agents walks over and takes the folder marked Top Secret. The 2 agents exit the room.

The elderly man happened to be Dr. Alfred Zachmont, chief of research and development for the National Agreement. To the public, he was on the board of directors of a major pharmaceutical company based in Maryland.

It was in May of 97 when hakim felt comfortable enough to allow Bex to room with him in his lair. The 2 guys found out over time that they were born a few weeks apart in 1966, with hakim being the eldest.

Bex was serving 5 years for armed robbery of a convenience store located in South Jersey. "Man, I still can't believe after a few months, I'm hanging out in this spot!" Bex said "Go grab a beer for us man!" hakim said.

Hakim spared no expense partying with his new friend and cell mate. Hakim had the warden bring in 4 hot call girls, a live DJ, food and liquor which cost hakim 15 grand.

"Can't believe my ass gonna be free in a few months!" Bex said. "You can't believe a lot of shit!" hakim chuckled. Bex starts laughing. "Listen! If you ever need a place to stay when you get out, just come thru and crash for as long as you want! It's just me and my mom! She's cool people!" said Bex. Hakim rubs his eyes. Thanks, but when I get out, I'm gonna be running the streets!" hakim boasted.

It was near the end of May when 2 old friends were sitting in an old burgundy van out in the Eagle Rock Reservation in West Orange, New Jersey. It was a breezy spring evening. Eddie lassenberry and Gino Massoni were drinking from their own bottle of liquor. Eddie as usual, would listen to gino rant about how he was being mistreated by Carlo gatano. Unknown to Gino, Eddie would fill his bottle mostly with water just enough to leave an alcohol scent. Eddie had to stay sober to get enough information from gino about the gatano crew. Benny realized once boss gatano croaked, his family would fall under the thumb of his son Carlo.

"That fucking Carlo literally took 10 grand off my desk last week while I was counting the take! On top of that, he takes his cut afterwards!" said gino. "You should know better than to count the take in front of the boss!" Eddie chuckled. "He said he's taking extra from everybody so he can pay for his fucking daughter's wedding. I overheard Larry Russo and Tony Asaro complaining about this shit too!" gino said. "Who the fuck is Larry and tony?" Eddie asked. "These kids who just got their button! They're good guys, but they ain't never gonna make any real doe working under Carlo!" said gino. Gino takes a swig from his bottle. Eddie sat there for a moment rubbing his chin. "What if you were running the crew?" Eddie asked. Gino spews alcohol from his mouth, all over the dashboard. "Are you fucking insane?" gino chuckled. "According to you, these guys might as well get 9 to 5 jobs because of Carlo!" Eddie said. "I didn't say that! I'm just saying they could live better!" gino explained. "I'm just saying, if you were in charge, hypothetically speaking, they would live better, right?" said Eddie. "Yeah, I would!" said gino. "See! You should be running the crew then!" Eddie suggested. Gino slams the bottle on the dashboard. "Listen! Get that idea out of your head now! We both could get whacked just for thinking about it!" gino shouted. "Damn! Carlo got you spooked! Huh?" Eddie chuckled. Gino just gave Eddie an evil look. "Alright! Forget I brought it up! Shit!" Eddie shouted. Gino wanted to end the conversation, but the alcohol in him wouldn't let him. "You know how many people I gotta whack to get to that prick?" gino asked. "Get to who?" Eddie asked. "Fucking Carlo!" gino shouted.

About 35 minutes later around 10 pm, Eddie arrives at his home after dropping gino off. Eddie stops the van at the end of the block, and is greeted by one of his guards, Tony Taylor, a.k.a Boom and Moses Nolan, a.k.a Big country. Both guys are packing sawed off shot guns. Eddie gets out of the van while the engine is still running. "Everything alright boss?" asked Big country. "Get somebody to take the van to an empty lot and burn it!" Eddie ordered. "We didn't even know you left!" Big country said. Eddie steps to big country. "Didn't I just say get rid of the fucking van?" Eddie shouted. Big country just nods. As Eddie walks towards his building, he is greeted by 2 more guards who escorts him back.

Just recently, Eddie invested in a state-of-the-art surveillance system throughout the building. There were 6 cameras on the roof top facing the ground level, placed in different directions. There were 4 cameras on each of the remaining floors that weren't sealed off. All the cameras were wired to a couple of 17 inch monitors. One monitor was in the hallway on 2 Gunz's desk. The other monitor was in Eddie's bedroom.

Just a half mile away, 2 men in black suits were standing on the roof of an elementary school. The agents had in their possession a couple of night vision binoculars. Both agents watch as Eddie enters his building.

A couple of days had passed, when Eddie lassenberry was home watching TV with Charlie Dalton. It was around 11:00 pm, when an inebriated Eddie hears a knock on the door, while Charlie was sitting across from him just about to sniff his third line of cocaine. Eddie gets off the sofa, wearing nothing but boxers and sweat sox. He staggers to the door. "What you want?" Eddie shouted. "I got 2 chicks on the monitor talking about they need to see you!" 2 Gunz shouted from out in the hall. Eddie opens the door and goes over to the monitor. On the monitor Eddie and 2 Gunz could see body guard Troy Cotton, a.k.a Smooth rubbing on Ariel's arm. "Send them up!" Eddie says to 2 Gunz. Eddie goes back in the apartment and tells Charlie to go into the other room and lay a pile of cocaine and weed on the coffee table.

Eddie always kept half a brick of cocaine and a couple of pounds of weed in the house for Charlie's habit. One time Eddie got a heads up about a raid about to take place by the feds. He made Charlie and 2 Gunz flush all the weed and cocaine down the toilet.

Minutes passed, and the girls were escorted before 2 Gunz by Tiki. "God damn! God damn girl!" Tiki shouted. Ariel blushes. "Yo! Take yo ass back down stairs!" said 2 Gunz. Gunz opens the door for the young ladies. "Hi Uncle Eddie!" Samara shouted. "Hey, baby girl!" Eddie shouted. Eddie gives his niece a hug. "You remember my girlfriend Ariel!" said Samara. "Hell yeah! Come on and give Uncle Eddie a hug! You just like family too!" Eddie said.

As usual, the girls were dressed sexy as ever. Samara had on a tank top barely supporting her huge breasts. She was wearing cut-off jeans which hugged her hips and stiletto shoes. Ariel was wearing a sheer body suit. You could see her black bra and black tight mini shorts underneath. Of course, she wore stiletto shoes as well.

"Come on and take a seat! Eddie said to the girls. Samara and Ariel sit on the sofa, while Eddie sat in his favorite chair. He orders Charlie to sit on the floor next to him. Ariel can't help but notice the mountain of cocaine and weed on the coffee table. Eddie notices her staring. "Go ahead girl, and help yo self!" Eddie said. "That's ok! I'm good for now." Ariel said. "Well, can I get y'all something to drink?" Eddie asked. The girls look at each other and start to giggle. "I'll have vodka." Said Ariel. "I'll have the same." Said Samara. "Go to the bar and make them a drink nigga!" Eddie orders Charlie. Charlie jumps up and runs over the bar. "Y'all want ice?" Charlie asked. Both girls give a nod. Charlie then runs to the kitchen, straight to the refrigorator. Charlie then comes out with a pale of ice. Ariel is impressed that Eddie has a flat screen TV. "Wow! I never saw a TV like that!" Ariel said. "Yeah baby girl! That's one of those plasma TV's!" Eddie boasted. Ariel gets up and looks behind the TV. "It looks just like a picture frame!" said Ariel. "You should see the one I got in the bedroom! It's 55 inches!" said boasted. Ariel turns to Eddie and smiles. "I bet it is!" said Ariel. Eddie grabs the remote and flips to a porn station. It showed a man eating a woman's pussy. Samara had the look of embarrassment. "Oh my goodness!" Ariel said as she gazed into the TV. Eddie changes the channel. "That's enough of that shit!" said Eddie. Ariel starts giggling. "So what y'all doing in my neck of the woods?" Eddie asked. "You don't have a neck of the woods!" Ariel said in sassy tone. "I see I'm gonna have to teach you lesson in manners young lady!" Eddie chuckled. "Anyway Uncle Eddie. Ariel needs to borrow some money until she gets her next audition." Said samara. Eddie leans back in his chair. "Why didn't you go to your father?"

Eddie asked. "Daddy don't have the kind of money she's asking for!" said Samara. "How much you talking?" Eddie asked. "A hundred thousand." Ariel said. Eddie sat up straight in his seat. "Damn girl!" Eddie shouted. Charlie shook his head. "I just bought a new sports car, and rented a beach house out in Malibu." Said Ariel. Eddie puts his glass down. "You mean to tell me you can't get anything from them Hollywood cats?" Eddie asked. "I don't wanna get into owing someone in the business! That could ruin my career down the line! The less they know about my private life, the better!" said Ariel. Eddie scratches his head. "You gotta point there." Eddie said. "You think you can do it uncle?" Samara asked. Eddie gets out of his seat. He goes over to Ariel and lightly strokes the side of her face. "Damn! You fine as hell!" Eddie said. Ariel just smiles. Samara turns her head in the other direction. Eddie slides his hand down Ariel's left breast. Ariel doesn't make a move. "Go and take a hit!" Eddie said. Ariel turns towards Samara. "You gonna take a hit with me?" Ariel asked. "Charlie! Set the girls up with a few lines!" Eddie said. Charlie goes over to the coffee table and takes the razor to cut the cocaine up into 6 lines. "I'll be back." Eddie said to the girls. Eddie goes in the bedroom and takes out his briefcase. "Y'all gonna like this shit! This here quality shit!" Charlie said. Eddie comes out of the bedroom with a big brown paper bag. "Here girl. That's 200 grand in there. You ain't gotta pay it back." Eddie said. Ariel jumps up and gives Eddie a hug. "Thank you! Thank you! I'll pay you back as soon as I can!" said Ariel. "I said you don't have to pay me back!" Eddie whispered. Ariel nods. "Charlie. Fix the girls another drink." Eddie said. While still having his arms around Ariel's waste, Eddie sticks his tongue in Ariel's mouth. Ariel starts sucking on his tongue. Eddie released her. "Go on and take a hit with my niece." Eddie said. Ariel and samara both roll up 20 dollar bills and start doing lines of cocaine. Eddie goes over to his entertainment system and turns on some jazz music. Ariel, Samara and Charlie are busy doing lines, while Eddie stands there rubbing his erect penis.

Meanwhile, down stairs near the freight elevator, Troy Cotton, a.k.a Smooth is standing with fellow guard Travis Ellis. "You know the one in the shorts his niece! Right?" said smooth. "Damn! She fine as hell!" Travis said. "I bet yo ass a grand right now, he's fucking both of them!" smooth said. "Eddie crazy, but I don't think he'll do some shit like that!" said Travis. "Yo! Eddie crazy like that!" said smooth. "Maybe, but I ain't betting! I need my money now! My kids wanna go to the amusement park next week!" Travis explained. "You full of shit!" said smooth. "Whatever nigga!" said Travis.

The next day, around 11 am, Eddie steps out of the apartment, into the hall wearing nothing but a silk bathrobe and leather flip flops on his feet. He kicked the chair where 2 Gunz was sleeping with his feet kicked up on the desk. Eddie was pissed off to see 2 Gunz had his shot gun out in plain sight. "Wake up knucklehead!" Eddie shouted. 2 Gunz falls out of his chair, on to the floor. "How the fuck you guarding me if yo ass asleep?" Eddie shouted. "I'm up! I'm up! Everything good boss!" 2 Gunz said. "When my niece and her friend comes out, I want you to get somebody to escort them to their car!" said Eddie. "Got it boss!" said 2 Gunz. Eddie goes back into the apartment. Ariel comes out of the bedroom fully dressed, fixing her hair. Charlie was on the sofa naked, snoring in a deep sleep. Feeling a little groggy, Ariel walks over to Eddie and puts her arms around his waist. "Damn baby! That was intense last night!" Ariel chuckled. She gives Eddie a peck kiss on the lips. Moments later, Samara comes out staggering out of the bedroom with shoes in hand and her zipper down on her shirt. "Morning everybody! It's still morning, right?" said Samara. All 3 start laughing. Samara staggers over to Ariel and Eddie. "That was crazy as hell uncle!" said Samara. "You're crazy as hell girl!" said Ariel. Samara sticks her tongue down Ariel's throat. Samara and Ariel start feeling each other up. Charlie wakes up to what he thinks is a dream. "Ok! Break it up girls!" Eddie said. The girls stop kissing. "I gotta a business to run!" Eddie chuckled. Both girls put their arms around Eddie. "We need to do this again!" said Ariel. "I see no problem with that!" said Eddie. "Oh! I forgot my shoes!" said Ariel. She runs back into the bedroom. "You know what happened last night better not get out!" said Eddie. "I know uncle!" said Samara. "Just make sure yo friend know!" Eddie said. Samara nods. Eddie hugs her and gives her a kiss on the cheek. "Oh listen! Tell yo brother that I'm not mad at him, and that he can come back from overseas. Tell him he's family and family is forever." Eddie said. "Ok uncle." Said Samara. Ariel comes out of the bedroom. Eddie hands her the bag of money. Samara noticed that Charlie looked depressed. "What's wrong Charlie?" Samara asked. "Don't pay that fool no mind! He just mad he ain't get no pussy last night!" Eddie said.

After his niece and her friend left, Eddie decided to take to pay a visit to a group of his soldiers whose job was to patrol the roof top. There were a total of 7 men assigned to the roof top

Toby Willard was put in charge of both of the roof top. He was in his mid-40 at the time. He worked for Eddie for about 25 years, first being a look out, then moving up to dealer. After doing 5 years for being busted for possession of cocaine, Toby was promoted to body guard for not snitching on Eddie and the crew. After seeing that his guys on the roof top had everything under control, Eddie heads back down to the apartment. Once Eddie enters his apartment, he sees Charlie sitting on the sofa doing a couple more lines of cocaine off the coffee table. "You got a call." Charlie said. "What they say?" Eddie asked. "This guy said to meet him at the usual spot at 10 pm sharp." Said Charlie. Eddie looked pissed. "I told that Guido to hang up if I didn't answer!" Eddie says to himself. "What's that?" asked Charlie. "Nothing! I'm about to take a nap! I need you wake me up at 8. I want this place cleaned up too! Get that shit off the coffee table!" Eddie said. "Got it!" Charlie said. Eddie heads to the bedroom.

Later that evening, Eddie is awaken by 2 Gunz. Eddie slowly gets out of bed. "Is 8 o'clock boss." 2 Gunz said. "Where the fuck is Charlie?" Eddie asked. "He left out an hour ago." 2 Gunz said. Eddie looks at the clock on the wall. Eddie goes to the bathroom, and turns on the shower.

The time is now 8:45, and Eddie stands in front of the mirror straightening his neck –tie. Eddie leaves the apartment and is escorted to the freight elevator by 2 Gunz. Standing at the elevator was Darnell Washington, a.k.a Clip and Pete Bey, a.k.a Peanut. "If I don't make it back tonight, tell Charlie to call my father, butch and jabbo." Eddie whispered to 2 Gunz. When Eddie reaches the ground level, he is then escorted to his car by Tony Taylor, a.k.a boom and Jason Curtis, a.k.a J. Big. Boom opens the driver's side door for his boss. Eddie starts the engines and takes off. At the end of the block, Travis Ellis and David toomer remove the barricades blocking the street. Eddie drives off to rendezvous with gino, or so he thinks.

While driving down Avon Avenue, Eddie stops at a red light. He notices a black van pull up beside him. Eddie slowly grabs his revolver from under his seat. Eddie always notified 2

Gunz to plant a weapon under his seat when he went off alone. Before the light turns green, another black van pulls up on the opposite side of Eddie, arousing panic on Eddie's part. Eddie grabs his mobile phone to call for help. The phone is dead. No signal at all. Eddie is blocked off on all sides by vans. Eddie's emotions go from fear to rage. With gun in hand, Eddie jumps out of his car. "Y'all know who the fuck I am? I'm Eddie lassenberry! Let's do this!" Eddie shouted. Eddie takes another shot. "Come on! Eddie shouted. Suddenly, Eddie is struck from behind, not by a bullet, but in the back of the neck from a syringe. Eddie's body falls to the ground. There's not another vehicle driving on the streets, as if all streets in every direction were blocked off. Eddie's body was placed in one of the vans. His hands were bound behind him with zip tie. His face was covered with a cloth sack. In the same van, the agent takes out a mobile phone. "This is agent 2 in vehicle 4, with package in route. I repeat. Package is in route." Said the agent.

A few hours later, the 4 vans pull up to the gate of an industrial facility in a remote area of Upstate New York. On the outside, the facility looked like it was abandoned for a long period of time. The outside was rusted. You could hear the shrieking noises of dangling pipes and gutters outside. There were old abandoned cars and piles of used tires all over the property. Outside the gate was a huge rusted sign telling outsiders, private property keep out.

The vans pull up to the main gate. "This is agent 1 in vehicle 1." Said the agent on the intercom. Suddenly the gate automatically slides open. The convoy enters passes through the gate. The convoy then approaches a huge hangar door, with 5 surveillance cameras hanging above. The agent in the first van leaves his vehicle and goes over to open a metal flap on the side of the hangar entrance. He places his hand over digital screen. A laser light reads his palm print. He then punches in a 6 digit code on the key pad below. The hangar door slowly rises. The agent quickly runs back in his van. When the hangar door is fully opened, the convoy is greeted by 6 heavily armed agents. The first van and the van carrying Eddie make a left, driving into the facility, while the other 2 vans make a right and park.

The facility was so spacious on the inside that the 2 vans had to drive for a few minutes to get to the opposite side of the hangar. There were about a dozen agents, heavily armed, spread out on the cat walks above watching the 2 van's every move. The 2 vans drive over a metal platform that was wide enough for the vans to park side-by-side. After another laser light from up above scans the contents of both vehicles, the vans are slowly lowered down as if they were on a huge freight elevator. The 2 vans are lowered into darkness. Moments later, bright lights come on. The 2 vans are facing a giant vault door about 60 x 60 feet in height. The agent in van 1 punches in 4 digit code on the dashboard of the van. The heavy steel door slowly opens. The 2 vans proceed down a narrow slope about a mile long. There was a trail of blue light guiding the 2 vans deeper into the earth. The 2 vans approaches a barricade where there are 4 agents in black jump suits, armed with sub machine guns. One of the agents approach the vehicle that was carrying Eddie inside. The agent pulls out a small sensor. The sensor has a laser light coming from it. He scans the eye of the agent in the van. Once cleared. The van carrying Eddie proceeds as the other van stays put. The van then descends further down another slope. After a 10 minute drive, the van comes to a halt. The 3 agents exit the van. One of the agents takes off his shades and stares into a digital panel. The laser light scans his eye, causing a metal door to automatically open. The other 2 agents take Eddie out of the van. They all go through a door leading of an office corridor. They enter a room that was fully furnished like an office. There was a couch in the corner of the room, like the one someone would see in a physiatrist's office. They lay Eddie on the couch. Eddie is then unbound and has the cloth sack taken off. The 3 agents then leave the room.

Time passes. Eddie slowly rises from his slumber. His vision is a little blurry. He sits up rubbing is eyes. He slowly stands to his feet. Eddie looks around the room he sees shelves with stacks of books and encyclopedias. There's a long mahogany office desk across from him with a globe sitting on it. Eddie staggers towards the door. He can't get the door to open. "What the fuck? He shouts. Eddie starts banging on the door. "Whoever the fuck is out there, better open up!" shouted Eddie. "Good morning Mr. Lassenberry." The voice said, coming from the ceiling speakers.

The voice didn't sound intimidating. It sounded like a youthful chipper young man. "Whoever the fuck you are! You better be ready for war! You just fucked with the wrong nigga!" Eddie shouted at the ceiling. "I hate to say it since I admire you Mr. Lassenberry, but you're in no position to make any threats." Said the voice. Eddie hears movement outside the door. Eddie takes off his jacket to prepare for a fight. "You're going to have visitors come into the room Mr. Lassenberry. Just follow them please." Said the voice. The door opens. Enters 3 agents. Dressed in black coveralls and jack boots. They were armed with high tech light machine guns. "Follow us Mr. Lassenberry." Said the agent. Eddie sees there's a no win situation. He puts his jacket back on. Eddie follows the agents down the corridor to an elevator. One of the agents punches in a 4 digit code on the key pad next to the elevator. The elevator doors open. They all enter. Inside the elevator, the walls are covered with mirrors. The digital readout on the panel indicated they were on the B4 level. Seconds later, they reach B6 level. They get out of the elevator. They head down the corridor. "What? We in a fucking maze?" Eddie shouted. There was no response from the agents. About 2 doors down, they reach their destination. "In here Mr. Lassenberry." Said one of the agents. Eddie noticed that the room he entered was identical to the one he'd just left. The only difference was that there was no physiatrist's couch. There was a young white man sitting at a mahogany desk, facing the entrance. He looked like the stereotypical preppy, Ivy League school type. He wore reading glasses, dressed in a brown cardigan sweater and brown dress pants. His hair was well groomed with a part on the side.

Also in the room were 2 other people sitting in chairs with their backs to the entrance. There was an empty chair next to the men. Eddie moves in closer and realizes it's his father and jabbo sitting there with drinks in their hands. "Welcome Mr. Lassenberry! Have a seat please!" the young man said. "Who the fuck are you?" Eddie shouted. "Just have a seat Mr., lassenberry." The young man said. "Son. Just sit down!" benny said. "Fuck this shit!" Eddie shouted. Jabbo stands up. "Just do what you daddy said, and sit yo ass down boy!" jabbo shouted. Eddie looks at jabbo. He calms down, and takes his seat. "Forgive me for the rude invitation Mr. lassenberry. Like I told your father, we can't reveal our location." The young man chuckled. "Like I said! Who the fuck are you?" Eddie shouted. The young man gets up from his seat comes from around the desk. He goes over and extends his hand to Eddie. "Yes!

My name is Terrance Haggerty! Assistant Director of the National Agreement, New Jersey Division!" Terrance chuckled. "National what?" Eddie asked. "We've informed your father and Mr. Jenkins a little bit on whom we are." Said Terrance. Eddie refuses to shake Terrance's hand. Terrance shrugs his shoulders and heads back to his seat. "They snatched me out of bed and grabbed jabbo from the guest house." benny said. "So that's why y'all sitting there in pajamas?" Eddie asked. "The reason why we've made the false call to you Mr. Lassenberry was because we just couldn't get pass that roof top crew of yours without being detected!" Terrance chuckled. "Forgive me Mr. Lassenberry. Can I get you a drink?" Terrance asked. "No! But I would like one of those cigars on your desk!" Eddie said. "Nothing like a fine cigar, huh?" said Terrance. An agent walks over to Terrance's desk and takes the cigar from Terrance. He then hands it to Eddie. Eddie bites the tip off. The agent lights it for Eddie. "Now that we're all here, let's get down to business." Terrance said. Terrance looks at the agents standing guard by the entrance. "Leave us, but stay close outside!" Terrance ordered. The agents leave. Terrance opens the drawer to his desk and pulls out a nickel plated automatic pistol, he places it on the desk, with the barrel facing the 3 men. "Just a precaution gentlemen." Terrance chuckled. "Just get to it!" Eddie said. "Our organization has been watching the lassenberry crew for a long time. A very long time! According to our data, you've taken control of 65 percent of the drug trafficking in the state of New Jersey. That's impressive!" Terrance chuckled. "You ain't seen nothing yet!" Eddie said "Quiet son!" said benny. "The war on drugs in this country is a joke. I know it. You know it. Certain government officials know it. With that said, the National Agreement Program is the only solution to such a scourge." Said Terrance. "So by kidnapping us, you think you can stop it?" Eddie asked. "On the contrary Mr. Lassenberry. We want to control it!" Terrance chuckled. "So you want to kick us out so you can control the drug trafficking in New Jersey?" benny asked. "Of course not Mr. Lassenberry! You'll just be under our thumb, and our protection!" Terrance chuckled. "We already have protection!" said Eddie. "The mafia! Yeah right!" Terrance chuckled. "Did I say something funny?" Eddie asked.

"Mr. Lassenberry, soon this country will head into financial turmoil. Due to the fact no one is investing in America anymore. Everyone is buying foreign because it's cheaper. From wrist watches to automobiles. Not only are that, the Arabs with their billions of barrels of oil, draining the pocket of Americans with their high gas prices. "So what's that gotta do with us?" benny asked. "Let me finish!" Terrance said. "So get on with it nigga!" Eddie said. "In the 80's, the Russians tried to invade Afghanistan due to the fact that Afghanistan is the largest supplier of opium in the world because of the poppy fields. With the help of the C.I.A, the Afghans were supplied with enough military support to send the Russians running back home with their tails between their legs. The problem now is that this militant group the C.I.A created, now calling themselves the Arab freedom League have taken control of the country where the poppy fields are. Lucky for us the C.I.A and certain big businesses have allied themselves with a group Afghans Called the northern Islamic group. Their goal is to stop the A.F.L from destroying the poppy fields. Our job is to make the A.F.L look like the bad guys, and the Northern Islamic Group look like the good guys. On that note, we have to convince the free world that the A.F.L are terrorists and are going to destroy our freedoms." Terrance said. "Still! What's that have to do with us?" Eddie shouted. "Well Mr. Lassenberry, your people have 2 jobs. First, you will purchase goods in large quantities from a list of American corporations I have on a list of. Your purchases will help improve their stock value, which in turn will improve the economy. Second, your people will start trafficking heroin for us. Once we get our grips on the poppy fields, which will be real soon. "If we refuse?" asked benny. "Oh that's quite simple Mr. Lassenberry. If you don't comply with our demands, your whole operation will be shut down, your overseas accounts will be frozen and you and the other top guys in your organization will be sent off to jail for a long, long time. We have our hands deep in government and in the private sector. The mafia won't be able to help you. They'll be too busy trying to find a crew to replace you. Luckily for you, the mafia has a rule not to touch dope directly, or you and your people would've been wiped out a long time ago." Terrance chuckled. "If we agree. What's in it for us?" benny asked. "Glad you asked. You become untouchable." Terrance said. "What about our wise guy friends?" asked Eddie. "Well, that's your problem. Something you have to deal with. We'll just make sure the lassenberry crew stays out of jail." Terrance said. "That's it?" benny asked. "Just one more thing. We have to let the American public think that the war on drugs is not a lost cause. One of you have to sacrifice yourselves to the law." Terrance chuckled. There was a dead silence amongst the 3 men. "Can I speak with my father for a moment in private?" Eddie asked. "Why certainly. You can go out in the hall and talk it over, and long as you come back in with an answer." Terrance chuckled. Eddie and benny stand from their seats. Jabbo was about to stand. "No jabbo! You stay here!" Eddie said. Jabbo looks at benny. "It's ok jabbo. We'll be back." Benny said. Jabbo sits back down.

Out in the hall, benny places his hand on his son's shoulder. I know what you're about to say son! I already know!" said benny. "Pop! I can take the family to the next level with this guy on our side! That means we don't have to pay off the cops!" Eddie whispered. "What about the gatano people?" asked Benny. "I'll think of something! Trust me!" Eddie said. "This just don't sit right with me!" benny said. "Pop! These people have the power to freeze our assets! Didn't you say the family won't go broke not as long as you live?" Eddie said. "So what do you suggest?" asked benny. "Let's go back inside, and just follow my lead!" Eddie says to benny. Benny hands Eddie his walking cane. Benny takes off his ring. He gives it to Eddie. "I'll go against my better judgment, and let run the family business now! Just find someone you can trust to take over your territory!" benny said. "Pop!" Eddie said. "Go on and take it!" benny shouted. The agents standing in the hall stare at the 2 men. Eddie's eyes tear up. He hugs his father.

After Eddie puts his father's ring on, Eddie takes his off, putting it in his pocket. Benny and Eddie head back into the office. Benny and Eddie take their seats. "Well gentlemen. What's the verdict?" Terrance asked. "You can talk to me from now on! I run the organization now!" said Eddie. Jabbo turns to benny. "It's true old friend. Listen to Eddie now." Benny said. "I have a few demands for our benefit!" Eddie said. "And that is?" Terrance asked. 'First thing! I want my father to live comfortably in exile on an island after you stage his arrest to the public! Second, I want our family! The lassenberry bloodline to have aristocratic status! A coat of arms, like the royal families in Europe!" Eddie said. "A what?" Terrance asked. "You heard me! And I want a ceremony done to make it official! I want someone of royal blood to do it. I want the lassenberry family to have this, divine right!" Eddie said. "You are a sick man! I think

I like you!" Terrance chuckled. "Can you do it or not kid?" Eddie asked. "It looks possible. You sure that's all now?" Terrance asked. "You got a pad and pen?" asked Eddie. Terrance reaches into his drawer and pulls out a pad and pen. He hands it to Eddie. "After I write this, that'll be it." Eddie says to Terrance. After Eddie jots down his demands. He hands the pad and pen to Terrance. "That's a tall and dangerous order Mr. lassenberry!" said Terrance. "Listen kid! From what I can tell, you and whoever yo ass is connected to, can start world war 3! So, don't bullshit me!" Eddie shouted. Terrance chuckles and nods. "Good! I want the delivery done quietly at that spot I just wrote down!" Eddie said. Terrance sighs. "Just one more thing!" Eddie said. "Are you sure Mr. Lassenberry?" Terrance asked. "I have whisper this one in your ear!" Eddie said. Terrance looks at jabbo and benny. "Very well!" Terrance sighed. Eddie gets up and walks over towards Terrance's desk. Terrance grabs his pistol as a precaution. Eddie leans over the desk. Terrance leans forward as well. Eddie whispers in his ear. He then extends his hand in a friendly gesture. The 2 men shake on it to seal the deal. Terrance doesn't release Eddie's hand just yet. "You must understand Mr. Lassenberry, that this handshake binds our 2 sides together! Forever!" Terrance chuckles hysterically. He then releases Eddie's hand. Eddie looks at his hand, and sees a bruise developing on it. Terrance continues to laugh. Eddie massages his hand to ease the pain. "Now remember! You'll receive a list from us soon, of all the businesses you'll be involved with!" said Terrance. Before Eddie, benny or Jabbo can utter a word, Terrance calls in his agents over the intercom. The agents enter the room. Terrance gives them the signal. Eddie, benny and jabbo are injected from behind with syringes to the back of their necks. All 3 men pass out.

Eddie wakes up, finding himself in the back seat of his car, parked at the corner of Avon and 16th street in Newark. It is a bright and sunny day. There's a little kid staring at Eddie through the window. The kid takes off running when Eddie sees him. Still groggy, Eddie grabs his mobile phone next to him. His vision starts to clear up. He looks at his wrist watch. It's 1:35 pm. "Red feather! Gotta call red feather!" Eddie says to himself. Eddie dials a number. The phone rings 5 times. Finally, red feather picks up. "Yeah!" said red feather. "It's me! Meet me at the warehouse in Kenilworth within an hour!" Eddie said. "I'm out of town at the moment." Said red feather. "I don't give a fuck if you're on the moon! Get yo ass to the warehouse within an hour!" Eddie shouted. Eddie clicks off the phone. Eddie then makes another call. The phone rings 2 times. Someone picks up. "Yo! Who this?" said the voice. "It's me! I want you and Chewie on the first plane back here!" Eddie ordered. "You want us to suit up?" Mackie asked. "No! Just get y'all asses out here! Quick!" Eddie ordered. Eddie clicks off the phone and tosses it in the passenger seat. He sees the keys are already in the ignition.

Within 40 minutes, Eddie arrives at the Kenilworth warehouse. He gets out of the car and walks around to the side of the warehouse to where the dumpster is located. Underneath the dumpster was a key, which he opens the double doors to the warehouse. Eddie gave instructions to Terrance to where the key was hidden and the numbers to the combination lock as well.

Minutes later, red feather shows up dressed in his old Vietnam foul weather jacket and ding jeans. He parked his 1990 station wagon down around the corner to make sure he wasn't being followed. Red feather bangs on the door of the warehouse. Eddie lets him in. Eddie looks around outside to see if red feather was being followed. Eddie shuts the door. Eddie leads red feather to the back of the warehouse. They both are standing in front of 2 metal drums. "Grab that crowbar over there!" Eddie said. Red feather runs over and grabs the crowbar off the tool bench. "Open it man!" Eddie ordered. What's in here?" red feather asked. "I don't pay you to ask questions! Just open it!" Eddie shouted. Red feather pried open one of the drums with little effort. Red feather views the contents. "Is this what I think it is?" red feather asked. Eddie looks into the drum. "Yes it is! Yes it is!" Eddie chuckled. Red feather removes some of the contents. "This is C4! Plastic explosives!" red feather said. "It looks like you have enough here to blow up a city block!" red feather said. "Open the other one!" Eddie ordered. Red feather pries open the other drum. The second drum has explosives inside too, with an arm full of detonators on top. "I want you to go that burger spot on Elizabeth avenue tonight! There, you'll see a black van parked in the lot! The keys will be above the sun visor! Get yo ass back here by midnight! Don't tell a soul about this! Your life depends on it!" Eddie said. Red feather nods. He leaves the warehouse. As soon as red feather leaves, Eddie gets on his mobile phone. He dials a number. It rings 4 times. "Hello." Said the voice. "Hey baby girl! It's your uncle!" Eddie said. "Hey Uncle Eddie!" Samara said. "Did you straighten things out between me and your brother yet?" Eddie asked. "Oh yeah! When I told him, he sounded relieved for some reason!" Samara said. "Good! That's real good! I want you to call him again and tell him that I'm going wire him and that white boy he staying with some money to catch the first plane back to the states!" Eddie said. "Oh, you mean Cousin Nigel?" Samara asked. "Yeah, that's him! Tell Danny Jr. I wanna see both of them at my at my place tomorrow night! No later!" Eddie said. "I'll give him a call as soon as I hang up with you." Said Samara. "Remember! They gotta be at my place by tomorrow night!" Eddie said. "Ok! I got it!" Samara sighed. "You can't tell anybody what I've just told you!" Eddie said. "Ok uncle." Samara said. "Thanks baby girl!" said Eddie. "Oh! I was wondering if I could have some money so Ariel and I can travel to Tunisia." Samara asked in her sexy voice. Eddie shook his head. "How much we talking?" Eddie asked. "$40!" Samara said. "40 thousand?" Eddie shouted. "Yeah! We want to stay for a week to go shopping and sight see!" Samara said. "Ok! I'll have jabbo send it to you before the week is out!" Eddie sighed. "Can we use the private jet too?" Samara asked. "Let's not get crazy girl! That's yo granddaddy's jet! Y'all will be just fine flying first class!" Eddie said. "It was worth a shot!" samara chuckled. Eddie doesn't respond. He clicks off the phone.

Elsewhere, jabbo pulls up to the lassenberry estate in a taxi. He gets out of the taxi, still wearing his pajamas. The guards are shocked to see him outside the gates in his pajamas. "What y'all looking at? Somebody get out here and pay jabbo's cab fare!" jabbo shouted. 2 of the guards come running out the gate. "How did you get pass the gate without us knowing?" one of the guards asked. "Don't worry about that! Just get me inside!" jabbo shouted. "I'll get a car to drive you up to the house!" the other guard said. "I swear y'all some useless ass niggas!" jabbo shouted.

The next day around 10 pm, Eddie is sitting in his apartment with Charlie Dalton, both doing lines of cocaine and listening to the blues, with the volume turned up loud. Eddie's mobile phone rings. Eddie answers his phone. "Yeah!" Eddie shouted. "Yo nephew and some white guy that talks funny, down here to see you boss!" the voice said. "Good! Take'em to Charlie's car, and tell them to wait until I come down!" Eddie said. "Got it boss!" the voice said. Eddie clicks his phone off. "Give me yo car keys!" Eddie says to Charlie. Charlie reaches into his pocket and takes out his car keys. He hands them over to Eddie. "Watch the place until I get back. Eddie runs to the bathroom. He stands in front of the mirror to see if he had any residue of cocaine on his nose. Eddie then comes out the bathroom. "You ain't taking your gun?" Charlie asked. Eddie grabs Charlie by the collar. "Don't worry about what I take and don't take!" Eddie shouted. Charlie is trembling from fear. Eddie then leaves the apartment.

When Eddie reaches the ground level, he walks towards Charlie's car, escorted by his 3 of his guards. "I want all y'all to stay here until I get back! If I don't make it back, look out for Charlie and report to Butch to run things! Understand?" Eddie said. All 3 guards nod. Eddie approaches his nephew. "Hey nephew! Eddie shouted. Danny jr. has fear in his eyes. Eddie gives him a hug. "Hey uncle!" Danny jr. said. Danny jr. starts to relax more after hug. "I finally get to meet you Nigel!" Eddie shouted. Eddie gives Nigel a hug as well. "Pleasure to meet you Mr. Lassenberry!" said Nigel. "Man! Get outta here with that formal shit! We family nigga! It's Uncle Eddie to you!" Eddie said. Nigel is flabbergasted. "Ok! It's Uncle Eddie then." Nigel chuckled. The guards walk away. "Come on and get y'all ass in the car! We're gonna paint the town red, after I take care of some business first!" Eddie said. "Alright then!" Danny jr. chuckled. Danny Jr. gets in the passenger side of the car, while Nigel gets in the back. Eddie gets behind the driver's seat. He drives off.

Eddie jumps on interstate 280 west. "Listen guys! All bullshit aside! I need y'all help real quick! There's 50 grand a piece in it for y'all!" Eddie said. Nigel's jaw dropped. "What is it uncle?" Danny jr. asked. Eddie doesn't say a word. He keeps driving

About 15 minutes later, Eddie parks the car in an empty lot of a shopping center in West Orange. "Y'all see that manor we just passed?" Eddie asked. Danny jr. and Nigel nod their heads. "Good! Eddie said. Eddie reaches in the glove compartment. Danny jr. looks nervous. Eddie pulls out an instant camera and a revolver.

Earlier, Eddie took Charlie's keys while he was sleep on the couch. Eddie placed the camera and revolver in the glove compartment. Eddie then goes back to the apartment and lays the keys on the coffee table without Charlie knowing a thing.

Eddie points the revolver at Nigel. "Listen bitch! I want yo ass to lean over the front seat and ram yo tongue down my nephew's throat!" Eddie shouted. "What, what's going on Uncle Eddie?" Danny jr. stuttered. Eddie cocks back the hammer on the revolver. "I ain't gonna tell you again white boy!" Eddie shouted. Nigel was shaking, he looks Danny jr. in his eyes. Out of total fear, Nigel grabs Danny jr. by the back of his neck, and presses his lips to Danny junior's lips. Eddie lightly whacks Nigel in the back of the head with the butt of the revolver. "Y'all better open y'all goddamn mouths and give each other a real kiss!" Eddie shouted. Nigel's eyes start to tear up. Both he and Danny Jr. open up their mouths. "I wanna see tongue!" Eddie shouted. Danny jr. and Nigel's tongues trade saliva. Eddie grabs the camera with his other hand and starts snapping photos. 5 photos fall on the front seat. "That's enough!" Eddie shouted. Danny jr. quickly pulls away from Nigel. Nigel wipes hid lips and spits out the window. "Now I want you 2 bitches to get the fuck out and walk back down to the manor! I want you to hide in the bushes until I get back!" Eddie said. "Come on uncle! Why you're doing this to us?" Danny jr. asked. "Don't ask why! Just get the fuck out and do what I told you, or these pictures get out to everybody!" Eddie shouted.

Later that evening, red feather is sitting in a lawn chair fast asleep in the Kenilworth warehouse. He is exhausted from moving the heavy load of explosives to the van by himself. Suddenly, he's awakened by a car horn. He jumps out of his seat. He runs to the door and sees it's his boss. Red feather then opens the overhead door to the warehouse, allowing Eddie's car to pull inside. Eddie gets out of the car. "Is everything loaded up?" Eddie asked. Red feather gives a nod. "Good! Let's go!" Eddie ordered. Eddie jumps into the driver's seat, while red feather jumps into the passenger side. The van exits the warehouse. Red feather gets out and closes the overhead door.

Back at the manor in West Orange, Danny jr. and Nigel are hiding in between the bushes just off the edge of the manor property. "What the hell mate? What's going to happen to us?" asked Nigel. "I don't have a clue!" Danny jr. whispered. "I think we should make a break for it!" Nigel whispered. "Are you sick? You've forgot about the pictures already?" Danny jr. asked.

Danny jr. and Nigel could only hear the sounds of crickets under the clear night sky. A car passed on the road about every 10 minutes. There was only 1 car parked on the manor property. "Who the hell is in there at this hour?" Danny jr. whispered. "More than likely, the grounds keeper mate!" Nigel whispered.

About a half hour later, Eddie and red feather pull up across the road from the manor. Danny Jr. And Nigel get nervous. They squat deeper into the bushes, hoping not to be detected. Red feather gets out of the van and runs across the road. Danny jr. and Nigel watch as red feather jumps over the 12 foot gate of the manor. At this time, Eddie had cut off the head lights of the van.

Red feather creeps around towards the windows of the manor to see if anyone is inside. He sees that the coast is clear and heads to the guest house. Red feather sees that the lights are on. He peeks in one of the windows. He sees a middle aged white male in a custodian's uniform sitting in a lounge chair reading a newspaper.

Back at the van, Eddie can see the bushes moving from across the road. He gets out of the van and gives off a loud whistle. Danny jr. Nigel sees Eddie signal them to come over to him. Danny jr. and Nigel make a break for it and run across the road in Eddie's direction.

Red feather grabs a few pebbles from off the ground. He tosses them one at a time at the window. The grounds keeper looks up from his newspaper. He sees nothing and continues to read. Red feather reaches into one of the pockets of his foul weather jacket. He pulls out a handkerchief from his pocket. He then reaches into another pocket and pulls out a small dark bottle. He takes the cap off the bottle and soaks the handkerchief with the liquid contents. The bottle happened to be filled with Chloral Betaine. It was given to red feather by Eddie earlier. Red feather tosses a few more pebbles at the window. "God damn raccoons!" the grounds keeper shouted. The grounds keeper grabs a wooden bat out of the closet. He also grabs a flashlight from his toolbox. He steps outside and clicks on the flashlight. He walks further away from the entrance. Suddenly, red feather sneaks up behind the groundskeeper and covers his nose and mouth with the handkerchief. Within moments, the blacks out and falls to the ground. Red feather picks up the groundskeeper and tosses him over his shoulder he takes the groundskeeper back inside and props him in his chair. Red feather makes his way back towards the gate.

Back at the van, Nigel and Danny jr. are sitting in the back of the van, next to the explosives. Nigel stares at the C4 in awe. "I heard you was good at handling that shit!" Eddie said. "Well, I've been trained by the best in her majesties military!" Nigel said reluctantly.

Red feather had grabbed the keys from the groundskeeper and opens the gate. He runs across the road, back towards the van. Red feather jumps in the van. He turns around and sees Danny jr. and Nigel. "Who's this?" red feather asked. "Don't worry about them! Is everything good?" Eddie asked. "Yeah!" said red feather. Eddie starts the van and drives across the road on to the manor property. Red feather gets out and shuts the gates. Eddie drives up to the main entrance and shuts off the engine. "Everybody out!" Eddie shouted. Danny jr. and Nigel get out of the van. "Empty all your pockets boys! I don't want anything left behind after we're done!" Eddie said. Danny jr. and Nigel empty their pockets. "The watches too!" Eddie ordered. They place all their items into the van. Red feather comes running back. "Now, we're gonna unload all this stuff into the main hall!" Eddie said. Red feather opens the door to the main hall. It takes Danny jr. and Nigel 12 trips to unload the explosives and detonators inside the main hall. Red feather stands guard at the van, while Eddie oversees the boys hauling the explosives.

Inside the manor, Eddie instructs Nigel on what his job is to be done. "I want you to wire this place from top to bottom!" Eddie ordered. Nigel stood in front of Eddie surprised. "This is insane! You can reduce this place to ashes with this amount of explosives!" Nigel said. Eddie puts his hand on the back of Nigel's neck. "Listen! If you don't do it, you and your whole family will regret it! Besides, you get to walk away with a shit load of cash!" Eddie said with a sinister grin. Nigel puts his head down. He looks up at Eddie. "I understand!" said Nigel. "Good! Now get yo ass to work!" Eddie said. Nigel runs back to the van and takes the tools needed for the job.

Red feather is told by Eddie to run back to the guest house and check on the groundskeeper. He sees that he is still unconscious.

Back at the manor. Eddie was standing guard with his pistol in hand. "Come on, and hurry this shit up!" Eddie shouted. Danny hustles back and forth assisting Nigel in wiring up the place. Danny jr. notices a 6 foot metal rod in the van, about 2 inches in width. At the end of the rod was a round target with letter x on it about 4 inches in diameter.

Finally, it was about 5 in the morning. "Alright! Let's clean up and get these tools back in the van!" Eddie shouted. Eddie walks out into the hall where Nigel is finishing up wiring the last detonator inside a vent at the base of the wall. "This should it do it mate! All I have to do is reinstall the vent cover!" Nigel explained. Danny Jr. walks pass his uncle carrying a power drill in one hand and the toolbox in the other. "When you go back to the van, bring a broom and dust pan! Yeah I forget! Bring that metal rod with you too!" Eddie says to his nephew.

Back at the guest house, red feather is standing over the groundskeeper, watching him as he snores. He has the handkerchief soaked and ready to place over the groundskeeper's mouth if need be. Red feather looks out the window, watching as the sun comes up.

Minutes later, Danny jr. comes running towards the guest house. He opens the door. "What now?" asked red feather. "My uncle said he wants you to put the cherry on top. Whatever that means!" Danny jr. said. "It's about time! Here! Takes this handkerchief and bottle! It this guy starts to wake up, cover his mouth and nose up at the same time! Got it?" red feather explained. Danny nods. He takes the handkerchief and bottle. Red feather leaves the guest house.

Minutes later, red feather arrives at the main hall. "Ready to set the rod, I heard?" asked red feather. Nigel shows up. "You have enough wire left for the roof top?" red feather asked Nigel. Nigel nods. "Ok then! Come with me to the roof!" red feather ordered. Red feather takes the metal rod from Eddie. He and Nigel make a dash for the staircase. On the roof, red feather mounts the rod to one of the chimneys, with the bull's-eye pointing due north. Nigel has with him a 4 gauge wire that leads down the sides of the chimney. Nigel then lines the wire to the rod. He splices one end behind the bull's-eye. He drops the remaining wire into the chimney. Nigel then runs back down stairs to the main floor.

Moments later at the guest house, Danny jr. can hear the birds chirping as the sun comes up. He sees the van pull up out front. Danny jr. comes running to the front entrance. He sees his uncle giving him the signal to come on. Danny Jr. grabs the bottle off the table, but ends up dropping the handkerchief on his way out. Danny Jr. jumps in the back passenger seat nest to Nigel. "The bottle and handkerchief! You have it?" red feather asked. Danny jr. frisks himself for the handkerchief. "Oh shit!" Danny jr. shouted. "What?" Eddie shouted. "Let me guess! You left the handkerchief in the guest house!" said red feather. Red feather brought the van to a halt. He makes a U-turn. Danny Jr. runs back to the guest house and spots the handkerchief on the floor and grabs it. He noticed the groundskeeper was still unconscious. Danny jr. runs out of the guest house, closing the door behind him. Eddie breathes a sigh of relief. Red feather drives pass the gate. Eddie gets out and makes sure the gate is secure. Eddie jumps back in the van, and red feather takes off.

Red feather calmly drives down interstate 280 east. Eddie turns around. "You boys did a hell of a job back there! You can pat yourselves on the back!" Eddie said. Danny jr. and Nigel high 5 each other. "Hey red. I want you to keep focused on the road." Eddie ordered. Eddie reaches down by his side. He then turns back towards the guys in the back seat. Red feather cuts his over for a split second to see what Eddie was about to do. Before red feather could blink, a loud popping noise goes off be red feather's ear. Nigel ends up with a bullet hole between his eyes. Danny jr. goes into shock. His jaw dropped. He starts to tremble. Eddie then points the pistol at his nephew. "Uncle Eddie! Uncle!" Danny jr. screamed. "Sorry nephew." Eddie said in a calm voice. Red feather flinches as he hears another popping noise. Eddie faces front in his seat. "Drop me off at the corner of Avon and Bergen Street. After that, I want you to pick up Mackie and Chewie at the Kenilworth warehouse. They'll know what to do with these 2." Eddie said as he wiped a tear from his cheek. There was a dead silence in the van for a moment. Red feather continues to drive. "What about me? Are we good?" red feather asked. Eddie starts chuckling. He looks at red feather. "Shit man! Yeah, we good! You're my trigger man!" Eddie chuckled. Eddie pats red feather on the shoulder while laughing. Red feather has a dead serious look on his face. "What if the kid didn't rig the explosives right?"

red feather asked. Eddie looks ahead down the street. "That means I won't get the chance to curse his ass out!" Eddie chuckled.

Later on, Eddie arrives back his building. He's standing in the hall just outside his apartment. As soon as he enters the apartment, a pungent odor rushes in his direction. Sitting on the sofa was Charlie Dalton in his underwear. He was snorting line after lines of cocaine off the coffee table. "Nigga, jump yo ass in the shower! In here, smelling like an animal! Eddie shouted. Charlie jumps up, wiping his nostrils. He makes a dash to the bathroom. Eddie shook his head in disgust. He goes over and sits in his favorite chair. Eddie grabs the remote and turns on the TV, just flipping channels. His favorite show is on. Suddenly, the program is interrupted. The local news comes on. "This is breaking news! Alleged drug czar of New Jersey, Benny Lassenberry has just been taken into custody by F.B.I agents this morning! Mr. Lassenberry was caught on a surveillance camera along with 2 unknown accomplices discussing movement of vast quantities of cocaine throughout New Jersey! The surveillance camera also catches Mr. Lassenberry standing next to 3 crates filled with the illegal substance!" the news reported said. Eddie's eyes almost pop out. He couldn't believe his ears. He starts flipping channels. Just about every channel is showing the same news coverage. Another news anchor had the same story, but with video. The video shows benny being hauled off in handcuffs. Escorted by 2 federal agents. There are 2 federal agents walking ahead of benny, as well as 2 more following carrying sub machine guns. Benny wasn't handcuffed like the average criminal. He was cuffed with his hands in front of him. There were dozens of reporters trying to shove their microphones in benny's face.

Eddie's landline phone rings. Eddie has to force himself away from the TV. He picks up the phone. "Hello?" Eddie said. "It's your sister! I'm watching the television! What the hell is going on?" Maggie Shouted. Eddie turns down the volume of the TV with the remote. "Now ain't the time to talk to you sis! Just sit tight until tomorrow! It ain't safe to talk on the phone right now!" Eddie says to his sister. He quickly hangs up the phone. Eddie turns the volume back up.

Elsewhere, Antonio Diaz, a.k.a Tony Diablo is sitting behind the counter of a Bodega that he owns, watching his small screen TV. "El mundo apenas terminado!" said Diaz. The grabs his mobile phone off the counter. He quickly dial a number. After 4 rings, someone picks up. "¿ tú TV de observación ahora?" Diaz asked. On the other end of the phone was his boss Mookie. "¡Por supuesto! ¡esta en cada estaión!" said Mookie. "Ahora que el Viejo tipo es historia! Podemos conseguir nuestro propio ir de la cosa! Apenas como tu padre querido siempre!" said Diaz. Mookie paused for a second. "Apenas descubramo qué Eddie que va a hacer primero antes de que decidamos ir abajo de esa carreteras! Recuerda, él todavía consiguió la conexión!" Mookie explained. In a fit of rage, Diaz slams his mobile phone on the floor, shattering it into pieces.

Elsewhere in a pizzeria in Belleville, New Jersey, gatano soldiers Larry Russo, Tony Asaro and Joey Muccio are sitting in a back room watching the breaking news on TV. "Holy shit! You think he'll rat out the boss?" Joey asked. "As soon as Carlo gives us the word, he's gone!" said Larry.

Not just in the states, the news was heard throughout the globe. "La tête de l'une des plus grandes operations de traffic de drogue aux États-Unis, Benny Lassenberry, an été tout simplement été placé en detention par des agents fédéraux." A French journalist from Paris said.

"Nach jahren der lauf einer der größten droenhandel operationen in den vereinigten staaten, wurde drogenkönigszapfen Benny lassenberry von FBI-Agenten festgenommen." Said the young lady reporting from Berlin. Reports came from parts of South America as well.

"Traficante Americano, Benny lassenberry foi apenas levado em custódia por agentes federais depois de estar em posse de grandes volumes de cocaína." The Brazilian reporter said.

It was June 30th, when the big event for the Gatano family had arrived. Carlo's only daughter Danielle was getting married to her high school sweetheart.

The young groom was of Italian descent, but had no affiliation with organized crime. Carlo was pleased with the fact that his baby girl would lead a normal life. His future son-in-law and his daughter decided to get engaged after graduating from college. The groom received a degree in medicine.

It was around 2 in the afternoon, when the people started to arrive at the manor. There were close to 4 hundred guests invited to the big event. Top aide to Don Luigi Gatano, Frankie Depalma was being hospitalized after suffering a major heart attack the day before. Mob bosses as far as Palermo, Sicily had arrived to the event. A few politicians and city officials reluctantly accepted their invitations. A couple of professional athletes and celebrities were invited to the grand wedding as well.

According to Gino Massoni, no one under capo status was invited to the wedding. This didn't sit well with most of the soldiers and close associates of the Gatano crew. Eddie absorbed all of this information from Gino through their many conversations. As far as Eddie lassenberry was concerned, anyone inside the manor would not live to see July 1st 1997.

About a mile away, Vietnam veteran Rodger Red feather was positioning himself on top of a high office building. Red feather had arrived at the roof top a day earlier to study the target mounted to the manor's chimney. He came prepared wearing the proper attire. During the night, red feather was wearing a black coveralls.

Red feather came equipped with a huge duffle bag that consisted a small disassembled tent, a thermos filled with hot soup, container filled with cold drinking water, a roll of toilet, plastic baggies, a bag of beef jerky, a Barrett M82 high powered rifle with folding bipod, 4x rifle scope and 2 BMG cartridges. Red feather had purchased the weapon and ammo from an illegal gun dealer from Mississippi. "If I find out this weapon is being used on anyone I know, I will skin your red ass alive! Understand?" said the scruffy looking dealer. Red feather nods his head and hands over a wad of cash the gun dealer. It was about 10 grand to be exact. The purchase of the weapon was funded by Eddie lassenberry. Red feather and Eddie were to rendezvous at a motel 10 miles away after the job was completed.

The couple of days before the wedding, Eddie found out the gun dealer's whereabouts. Wearing thin leather gloves, Eddie crept over and placed the gun he used on his nephew Danny jr. and Nigel and securely placed it underneath the chassis of the gun dealer's pick-up as he was getting piss drunk in a bar. Miles from the motel. After doing so, Eddie took off running through the woods. He made his way back to the motel within a few hours. The desk clerk at the motel didn't give it a second thought that Eddie had arrived back at the motel covered in twigs and leaves. When day break came, Eddie checked out of his room. He returned his room key to the front desk and left a hundred dollar tip for the clerk.

Back at the roof top of the office building, red feather was shading his face from the heat of the sun by sitting under a small camouflage canopy as he assembled the high powered rifle. He looked through his scope and sees his mark mounted on the chimney of the manor. He also sees guests arriving.

It was going on 4pm. The last of the guests started trickling into the manor. Red feather spotted the bride and groom arriving in their limo. Red feather took a swig of water. He looks at his wrist watch. He takes a deep breath. The bride and groom enter the manor, escort by small entourage. "Here we go!" red feather whispers to himself. He recalibrates his scope. He has the target clear in his sights. He holds his breath. He fires. Five seconds later, red feather could see a flash of bright light. He pulls back. Red feather quickly disassembles the rifle, putting all the parts in the duffle bag. Breathing heavily, he looks around to see if he dropped before leaving the scene. Red feather makes a dash to escape with the heavy duffle bag on his bag.

Moments later, the West Orange fire department arrive. One firefighter jumps from his truck. He is in shock to see the devastation from the blast until his chief tells him to snap out of it and get to work.

The blast turned the entire manor into a pile of rubble. Limousines were flipped on their sides due to the explosion. Fire fighters make their way through the debris. As the fire fighters were hosing down small pocket of flames, rescue teams were searching for signs of survivors. The fire chief looked across the road and saw body parts stuck in the smoldering trees.

Within an hour, fire fighters, police and EMT workers from the surrounding cities arrive on the scene. It was like a war zone in a third world country. Debris from the blast were found over a mile away from ground zero. Camera crews from the media were barred at least 2 miles from the disaster area.

Later that evening, Eddie was sitting alone in his apartment with a glass of vodka in his hand, watching the breaking news. Video footage showed a gray cloud of smoke rising from the disaster area. Eddie chuckles. He grabs the bottle of vodka from the coffee table. He pours some of it on the carpet. "Here's to you Don Gatano! Rest in pieces!" Eddie chuckled.

The next day around 2 in the afternoon, Eddie arrives at the lassenberry estate with a terrible hangover. Earlier, he made a call to his sister Maggie to gather some of the family members to the mansion.

Around 4:30 Maggie's oldest son, Tyson Richards drives up to the main gate. After being fired by jabbo, there were only a garrison 4 men left on duty. There were only 2 officers at the main gate and 2 at the second entrance. "Is my mother still inside?" Tyson asked. "Yes sir. She's been there since noon." Said one of the officers. "I love the new set of wheels you got here!" said the other officer. "Yeah. It cost me a nice chunk of change." Said Tyson. "I bet the car payments must be through the roof!" said the officer. Tyson scoffs. "I don't make car payments." Said Tyson. The overweight officer starts laughing. Suddenly, another luxury car pulls up behind Tyson. It was his cousin Joe-Joe. "Move that shit!" Joe-Joe shouted. Tyson gives his cousin the finger. Joe-Joe starts laughing. "You lassenberry people are crazy!" the officer chuckled. Tyson turns toward the officer with a serious look on his face. "I'm a Richards! Now let us through!" Tyson ordered. The officer quickly opens the gate, letting both cars through. Joe-Joe gives the officers the peace sign.

Cooper the butler opens the door for Tyson and Joe-Joe. "Your uncle is waiting in the family room." Said cooper. "How's everything coop?" Joe-Joe asked. "My bones aren't what they used to be Mr. Lassenberry!" said cooper. Tyson and Joe-Joe make their way down the hall to the family room. Tyson opens the door. He sees other members of the family sitting around facing Eddie, who is standing behind a podium. "Take a seat boys!" Eddie said.

Already seated were Jake sr., Jake jr., Corey, Lula, mike abbey, benny the 3rd, Maggie, mark sr., mark jr., Danny sr., BB and Krayton. Cooper enter the room with a tall glass of ice water Eddie had asked for. Eddie was gulped down most of the water due to dehydration. Standing behind Eddie was Charlie holding a long cardboard tube. Both he and Eddie are dressed in expensive suits. Eddie takes another swig of water. He hands the glass to cooper. "You can leave now old man!" Eddie says to cooper. Cooper leaves the room and shuts the door behind him. "Now! I know you all have questions about this, that and the third! First I wanna talk about pop!" Eddie said. "You're damn right we want to talk about daddy!" Lula shouted. "Take it easy little sis! Pop is alright! I can't tell you where they've taken him, but I can assure you he's in the best of care!" Eddie said. "Is he sick?" asked Joe-Joe. "Nah! Not at all! That old man is strong as an ox!" Eddie said. "Is he in jail?" benny the 3rd asked. "He's not in jail nephew! But, I still can't tell you where they have him at!" Eddie said. "You mean we can't see him anymore?" Lula asked. Lula's eyes start to tear up. Her son BB puts his arms around her. "I know it hurts little sis! We're all hurt! Pop did what he had to do to keep for us to keep our status in the world!" Eddie says to the family. Krayton raises his hand. "Yeah nephew?" Eddie asked. "I wanna know uncle. Do those Italians getting blown up have anything to do with pop-pop going away?" Krayton asked. The room becomes silent. "We know he was doing business with them for a long time." Krayton said. "I can assure you all, that pop had nothing to do with that shit! As a matter of fact, the lassenberry family has cut all ties with the Gatano people! Old man Gatano was ok in my book, but that's a tragedy those people have to deal with! Not us!" Eddie said. Krayton nods. "You can write your pop-pop letters, just give them to me and I'll make sure he gets them!" Eddie said. "Boss! You ready to tell them?" Charlie whispered in Eddie's ear. "Oh yeah! Now listen! 2 weeks after the fourth, a ceremony will be held at the luxurious Hardenbergh hotel!" Eddie said. "Wow! That's the hotel of all hotels!" said Tyson. "You damn right, nephew! Charlie show'em!" Eddie ordered. Charlie pulls out a poster size paper from the tube. He unrolls it and holds it up in front of his face. The poster shows a drawing of a shield with all kinds of designs around it. "What the hell is that?" Jake sr. asked. Eddie smiles. "This what pop sacrificed his freedom for! It's our family coat-of-arms! This right here above the fedora is the New Jersey state bird, the Eastern Goldfinch! The 2 men on either side of the shield represents our new army!" Eddie said. "What do the words mean at the bottom uncle?" asked Krayton. "Oh, that's our family motto in Latin! FAMILIA IN SAECULUM! It means family is forever! That's how we're gonna run this family from now on! This is beginning of the Lassenberry Empire! New Jersey is mi- I mean ours! Eddie shouted. Danny stood up and stormed out of the room. Everyone looked confused. "Don't worry about him! He'll be alright!" Eddie chuckled. Maggie leaves the room to go after her little brother. "If there are no questions, I'd like to speak with all my nephews in private!" Eddie said. "Anything you have to say to my boys, you can say to me!" mark sr. said. "Can I say something to you in private?" Eddie asked. Mark sr. walks up to the podium. "Listen man! I know you all educated and shit, but pop ain't gonna be around no more, and benny jr. is dead! That means I run the family! In all matters! Including the finances!" Eddie whispered in his brother's ear. Eddie could see mark sr. turn red. "Jake! Lula! Let's go!" mark sr. shouted. Mark sr. storms out of the room just as Danny sr. did. Jake sr. stands before Eddie. "Whatever you're doing brother, I just hope you know what you're doing!" Jake sr. said as he shakes his brother's hand. Lula walks up to her big brother and gives him on the cheek. "Take us to the promise land big brother. Take us there!" Lula shouted as she gave Eddie a big hug. Both Jake sr. and Lula leave the room, followed by Charlie.

Eddie looks around the room at his nephews. "After the ceremony, you will address me by standing at attention when I enter the room!" Eddie says to everyone. Krayton and Joe-Joe nod their heads. Eddie shows his nephews his ring. "This ring I have on, will be passed on to one of you some day! When the time is right, the chosen one will continue to lead this family into the future! In the meantime, go back to your everyday lives and enjoy your wealth! I got things under control! Now, the meeting is over!" Eddie ordered. Eddie's nephews form a single line a shake their uncle's hand as they leave the room. "Benny! Tell Charlie to come here!" Eddie says to his nephew.

Outside the main entrance of the mansion, Maggie tries to calm Danny sr. down. "Stop being silly Danny!" Maggie said. "Silly? He's not pop! He's either going to get us all killed or put us in the poor house!" Danny sr. said. "He's been by daddy's side for a long time!" Maggie said. "That may be true, but pop was a business man! That man in there, is a cold blooded killer!" Danny sr. shouted. Maggie scoffs. "My son Danny told me he had him kill some kid!" Danny sr. explained. "You can't be serious." Maggie chuckled. Both Maggie and Danny sr. become silent as Eddie and Charlie exit the mansion. "I'll catch you later sis." Eddie says to Maggie as he gives her a hug. "You be careful out there!" Maggie says to Eddie. Eddie turns to his little brother. Danny sr. turns his head as Eddie extends his hand in a friendly gesture. Danny sr. walks away, heading to his car. "What's his problem?" Eddie asked. Maggie folds her arms and sighs. She goes back into the mansion.

A week later, Frankie Depalma is lying in bed at his estate, recovering from his illness. He prayed while bed ridden with his wife by his side for the loss of his former boss and his family.

Laying low after the attack on the West Orange manor, 10 soldiers from the Gatano crew had gathered at a cabin out in the Adirondack Mountains. The cabin belonged to Nicky Rago, a.k.a noodles. He and his brothers arranged the meeting with 7 other soldiers. Nicky, carmine and Bernard Rago sent for Bruno Aiosa, Jimmy Caruccio, Mike Pascolini, Santino Riviello, Tony Asaro, Sal cotucci and Gino Massoni. Gino being the last one to show up, felt an uneasiness in the room. He was greeted with hugs and kisses on the cheek from each member. The men sat around a table filled with fine Italian cuisine. Nicky sat at the head of the table. "Grazie signori per presentarsi presso la nostra ora più buia." Nicky said. "Say Nicky! Everybody ain't from the old country!" said Bernard said. "Fair enough! I'll speak English for all you Yankees!" said Nicky. A couple of the guys starting laughing. "We're here because a terrible tragedy has fallen upon us! We've had more than enough time to grieve! Now it's time to get back to business!" said Nicky. Nicky's brother Bernard stands. "Let's just cut to the chase and make my here the new boss! We go to the commission and get back to business!" Bernard shouted. "Not so fast! I don't think it's that simple! We don't know who's responsible for carrying out a hit of that magnitude!" said mike. Bernard Rago slowly reaches for his pistol from inside his jacket. Mike's number 2 guy Bruno Aiosa beats Bernard to the draw. "Non pensi nemmeno Rago!" shouted Bruno. Bernard releases his weapon. "Take it easy! If we kill each other in here, the mancuso crew is sure to take over!" said mike.

With Mike Mancuso dead from the explosion, his crew had become a bunch of rouge gangsters. The thing about business now, there was no one in the hierarchy to kick up trib-ute to.

"Listen! If we don't get organized right here, right now, the mancuso crew more than likely gonna run through our businesses!" Gino said. "If that happens, the New York families gonna see us as weak! And if they come over here, we're fucked! Remember! They out number us 20 to 1 now!" said mike. "How in the hell you know the Mancuso crew or New York gonna try something like that?" Nicky asked. Mike walks up to Nicky, standing a few inches from his face. "Wouldn't you?" mike asked.

It was July 18th, about 5pm, when members of the lassenberry family, gathered at the front entrance of the Cherry Hill estate. They were all dressed in formal evening attire. Maggie and her Lula were dressed in long sexy evening gowns. They both were wearing diamond earrings and necklaces, while the men were all dressed in black tuxedos. "I love your earrings sister girl!" Lula says to Maggie. "Hell! I'm taking them back to the diamond dealer as soon as this thing is over with!" Maggie said. "Well, I'm keeping mine!" Lula giggled.

Suddenly, 2 limos pull up in front of the estate. They get clearance to go pass the gates. Everyone spreads out and occupies both vehicles. The limos were sent by Eddie to pick up the family and take them to the Hardenbergh hotel in New York. Maggie, Lula, Tyson, Mike abbey, mark sr. and Jake sr. get in the first limo, while Joe-Joe, Krayton, Corey, BB, mark jr. and benny the 3rd hopped into the second limo.

The limos turn on to the Garden State parkway. "Why Uncle Eddie ain't coming with us?" Krayton asked. "Think about it kid. This supposed to be a legit gathering, and Uncle Eddie is the only one in the family that's not legit." Mark jr. explained.

In the other limo... "I just found out this morning ma, Cindy pregnant!" Tyson said. Maggie quickly turns toward her son. "I'm gonna be a grandmother again?" she screamed. Maggie jumps on her son and gives him a big hug. She releases Tyson and punches him in the arm. "Why in the hell are you with us boy? You should be home with your wife!" Maggie shouted. "Damn ma! That hurt!" Tyson shouted. Tyson massages his arm. "We have las-senberry babies coming out of the wood work! First Big L. having twins, Bert just had a girl a month ago, and now you!" Maggie chuckled. Tyson gives his mother a serious look. "Just like my first kid, ma. This child is a Richards. Not a lassenberry." Tyson said.

With an hour, the 2 limos pull up to the front entrance of the Hardenbergh. The uni-formed doormen walk to the limos and open the doors for the guests. Everyone exits their limo.

Suddenly, a tall elderly white man, dressed in a tuxedo approaches the family. "Let me guess! You're are the Lassenberry party, are you not?" he said in a British accent. "Yes we are." Jake sr. said. "Welcome to the Hardenbergh. Follow me please." The man said. "And, who are you?" Jake sr. asked. The man turns toward Jake sr., and steps closer to him. "With all due respect sir. That's not of importance. My job is to escort you and your family to your appropriate seating arrangements. So, please follow me." The man said. Jake sr. just shrugged his shoulders and followed the man. The others followed as well. People started gawking at the lassenberry party as they through the lobby. The escort led them to a banquet hall. Inside the hall, there were 20 huge round tables.

The table ware and décor looked as if it was prepared for royalty. The women of the family were properly seated first. The men sat afterwards. Corey picked up his steak knife. "Is this real gold?" he asked. "Corey!" Maggie shouted from embarrassment. "They're gold plated sir." Said the escort. Krayton looks around the hall and noticed other people at their tables scattered about. All of the attendees hadn't arrived yet due to many empty seats. "You'll have to excuse me ladies and gentlemen. I have to attend to other matters. Our waiters will be out just a moment. Please feel free to visit our bar over there." Said the escort. He smiles, then walks away.

Moments later, a middle-aged white couple approach the table. "Good evening everyone!" the man said. "You look familiar. My goodness! You're the CEO of Galaxy Appliances!" Maggie shouted. "Guilty as charged!" the man chuckled. Jake sr. stands from his seat to greet the couple. "Oh! No need to stand! Mr.?" the man paused. "Jake Lassenberry." He answered. The 2 men shook hands. "I'm Edgar James Phine, and this is my wife Edith!" Edgar chuckled. Jake sr. shakes the wife's hand as well. "This is the rest of the lassenberry clan!" Jake sr. chuckled. Instead of going around the table to greet everyone, the couple just wave. Each member of the family introduces him and herself. "We'd just like to say congratulations on this heraldic event!" said Edgar. "Why, thank you!" Jake sr. said. "Would you gentlemen like to accompany me to the bar and leave the ladies to chat for a while?" Edgar asked. "Hey! I'm way ahead of you!" Jake jr. chuckled. All the men at the table leave their seats. Jake sr. offers Edith his seat. "Why thank you!" she said in a raspy voice. The men head to the bar. "Bring me a ginger ale with ice!" Lula says to mike abbey. Mike rolls his eyes and scoffs. Edgar pats Jake sr. on the back. "You look like a scotch man!" Edgar chuckled. "I go no higher than red wine!" Jake sr. chuckled. There 2 bartenders on duty. Mike abbey jumps in front of everyone. "Let me have a ginger ale with ice, and a rum and coke!" he said.

The new comer to arrive at the bar, was a tall slim white guy with a receding hair line. Just like all the men at the bar, he also wore a black tuxedo to this special occasion. "Peter!" edger shouted. The 2 men rushed towards each other and shook hands. The lassenberry men turn to see who Edgar was so excited to see. "You son-of-a-gun! How long has it been?" Edgar asked "The last gathering!" peter chuckled. Edgar winks at peter. "Oh! How rude of me! Peter! This is the lassenberry family!" said Edgar. "Dr. Mark lassenberry." Mark sr. said as the 2 men shake hands. "I'm Peter Boeman! Founder of Boeman motor company! Peter goes around and shake the hands of other members of the family. "How's business?" Jake sr. asked. Peter sips his cognac first. "Well Jake! We've only been in business for 5 years! But, this year shows a lot of promise! We expect a major increase in sales after tonight!" peter chuckled.

Edgar changes the subject. "Say Pete! Isn't that Daphne Pallenti and her husband Scott?" Edgar asked. "Yeah, that's them!" Peter said. Edgar turns towards Jake sr. and his nephew Tyson. "Could you gentlemen excuse us for just one moment? Peter and I must confront our colleague at the other end of the bar." Edgar said. "Why sure, go ahead!" Jake sr. said. Edgar and peter leave the lassenberry group. Mark Jr. leans over to his father. "There's something creepy about that Boeman guy pop!" mark jr. whispered.

Back at the lassenberry table, Lula noticed Daphne Pallenti from across the room. "Hey Maggie! You know who that tall lady is over there" Lula asked. Maggie shakes her head. "My god! That's Daphne Pallenti of Blush Cosmetics! My make-up guy uses her product all the time!" said Lula. "Take it easy! It's our night, not hers!" Maggie said. Edith leans into Maggie. "I hear her husband Scott just paid for his mistress's implants!" Edith whispered. Maggie covers her mouth in awe. "You think she knows?" Maggie asked. Edith scoffs at Maggie. "Please! It's part of their arrangement!" Edith whispered. "I wonder if I should go over and introduce myself!" Lula said. "I don't think that'll be necessary! She's coming over here!" Edith whispered.

Daphne Pallenti is CEO and creator of Blush Cosmetics. Daphne has been in business for the past 10 years. Her cosmetics and skin care products are sold throughout the Tri state area.

At the entrance standing by the double doors, the elderly gentleman that escorted the lassenberry family to their seats stands with another white male, who is dressed in a tuxedo as well. The elderly man pulls out a gold hunter-case pocket watch. "How long until their arrival sir?" the other man asked. "Within a half hour. Get everyone to their assigned tables at once." The elderly man ordered. "Very well sir." The other man said.

The gentleman receiving the orders was much younger and didn't have an English accent. With the snap of his fingers, he summoned 10 young Caucasian men wearing white tie and tails with white gloves. These men weren't servers, but more like ushers. The servers wore black tie and tails, with white gloves.

The 10 men walk over to the young man in a single row, standing at attention. Mark jr. took notice of what was happening. "Get all of the guests, especially the lassenberry party to their seats as swiftly as possible." The young man ordered. The hall has approximately 200 invited guests, not including the lassenberry party. The 10 men scatter throughout the banquet hall escorting the guests who are not seated. One blonde kid, looking like he's in is his early 20's, rushed over to the bar where the lassenberry men and a handful of other gentleman had gathered. One of the elderly men in the group, who was smoking a cigar happened to be a magistrate from England. He recently told brothers' Jake sr. and Mark sr. he was interested in investing in medical imaging machines.

"Excuse me gentleman!" one on the ushers bellowed. All the men at the bar quiet down. "The ceremony will begin shortly. Would everyone be so kind in taking their seats, while the lassenberry party please, follow me." The usher said. "Come on guys! Let's get this over with!" mark sr. shouted to his family. At the lassenberry table, Edith and Daphne congratulate Maggie and Lula one more time, and then part ways to their assigned tables.

Seated at the Scott and Daphne Pallenti table were Justin Steigalhoff, who was the biggest independent brewer in New Jersey. Seated next to him on his right was his wife Ida. There was

Chuck Randal and his wife Christine sitting to his left. Chuck was owner of Petrol-world gas stations of North Jersey. There was the Honorable Senator Kelsey brown of New Jersey with his wife Shelly. Essex county Executive Anthony Rago-Molino and his wife Brenda.

Anthony Rago-Molino just happened to be a distant relative of the infamous Rago boys. County executive Molino had no criminal ties to the Rago crew.

At the lassenberry table, Maggie leans over to her nephew mark jr. talk about the people in attendance. "I have a feeling before tonight, uncle Eddie didn't know any of these people existed!" mark jr. whispered to his aunt. Maggie looks around the hall. She looks in the direction of Edith and Edgar. They see Maggie. Edith waves at Maggie. Showing all her teeth. Maggie nervously waves back. "Let's just get this ceremony over with and get the hell out of here!" Maggie whispered to her nephew.

While the waiters were serving appetizers, Maggie and Lula notice a bald white man with a thick beard, wearing white tie and tails, walking on the stage. The stage had a throne placed dead center of the stage. Which was pushed out by 3 ushers a few minutes earlier. Mark sr. turns toward the entrance and noticed the elderly man that escorted them in earlier gave the man on stage the signal to proceed on with the event. The man on stage approached the podium, and adjusts the microphone. "May I have your attention ladies and gentlemen? At this time, I would like everyone to stand to their feet!" said the man on stage. The elderly man at the entrance swings open the huge double doors allowing 20 men, dressed in beefeater garb, to march in rows of 2 inside the banquet hall. When the last 2 men enter the hall, another man dressed in a black robe enters the hall, carrying a 3x3 foot plaque with the lassenberry family coat of arms imprinted on it. He marches between the 2 rows of men, stopping in the middle. "Custodes Ordinis! Intrinsecus!" the man on stage shouts. The Beefeaters turn in unison facing each other. The man holding the lassenberry plaque marches towards the stage.

At this time, there were 3 trumpeters on stage. "Ladies and gentlemen! It is my privilege to announce his majesty, Prince Erik of Denmark!" the man shouted. The trumpeters began to play. 3 officers dressed in formal Danish military garb enter the hall, followed by the prince of Denmark. As everyone is still standing, the 3 officers march towards the stage, following the man carrying the plaque. The prince follows the officers on stage and takes his seat.

The prince is dressed I white tie and tails, donning the sash of his homeland. He was decorated with 2 rows of medals on the left side of his chest.

The trumpeters stop playing once the prince is seated. The man with the plaque stands to the far right of the prince, while the beefeaters line the stage. The man at the podium gives the trumpeters the signal to play once more. Suddenly, the man of the hour enters the hall dressed in white tie and tails. The man is no other than Eddie Lassenberry. The trumpeters continue to play as Eddie walks towards the stage.

When Eddie reaches the stage, he stands before the Prince of Denmark. The trumpeter's introduction halts. The man at the podium places a red velvet pillow before the prince. The prince stands facing Eddie. "Kneel Mr. Lassenberry!" ordered the prince. Eddie slowly kneels down with one knee on the pillow. The man who placed the pillow down, hands the prince a ceremonial sword. "I dub thee, knight of the Order of the Elephant! Må jeres familie tjene tusind år!" the prince shouted. He taps Eddie on each shoulder with the blade of the sword.

"Rise Mr. Lassenberry!" said the prince. Eddie stands to his feet. The man at the podium takes the sword from the prince. The prince receives a case from the man holding the plaque. The prince opens the case, unveiling a medal representing The Order Of the Elephant. The prince then pins the medal on the left side of Eddie's chest. The gentleman holding the plaque, hands it over to Eddie. Everyone in the hall goes wild with applause. Everyone but the table where Eddie's family is seated. Jake sr. slowly starts to clap as he looks around the banquet hall. The rest of the family reluctantly follows Jake's lead. The prince is immediately escorted out of the hall by the beefeaters. Eddie then leaves the stage as the crowd continues to cheer. Eddie makes his way through then crowd as men shake his hand and the women embrace him with hugs and kisses on the cheek. Eddie passes a table where an elderly white male, who looked in peak physical health, grabs his hand and pulls him in. "I'm General Theodore J. Magus! We'll be doing business soon!" the general whispered in Eddie's ear.

Eddie finally comes to the table where his family is. Maggie hugs Eddie. "This is really creepy!" Maggie whispered in Eddie's ear. Eddie goes around the table and is hugged by the other family members. "After this uncle, I'll follow you through hell!" Krayton shouted.

"If everyone would please take your seats! The waiters will be around to serve the main course." Said the announcer. "Y'all gonna have to excuse me! I gotta take my seat over there!" Eddie said. "Oh! You're too good to dine with us now?" Lula chuckled. "It's just business sis!" Eddie said. Eddie pats the back of his nephew mark jr. as he walks away.

Eddie heads over to his assigned seat a couple pf tables over. At this table was C.W. Winters, head of Winter Movie Studios. Sitting next to Winters was a beautiful young woman, who happened to be his fourth wife. Also at the table were Asian porn superstars, Luv Shyne and Paris tea. They were both wearing skimpy outfits, turning the heads of most of the men in the hall. There was bank president Ira Bergstone, of Bergstone savings and loan and his wife. There was "A" list movie star Jett Connors. Hardenbergh C.E.O Mitch Tomicino and his wife were seated at the table as well. Last but not least was Chief of Research and development of the National Agreement, Doctor Alfred Zachmont and his wife.

Everyone stands and applauds as Eddie comes to the table. "The goose with the golden egg!" shouted Dr. Zachmont. "Please! Please! Sit everybody!" Eddie modestly shouted. "Hey! That's my line!" Dr. Zachmont chuckled. Everyone takes their seat. Eddie sits next to porn star Luv Shyne. Sitting on the other side of Eddie was Jett Connors. "Man, I must've watched your last movie 10 times!" Eddie says to Connors as they shake hands.

Jett was tall and slim, sporting a Mohawk for his next movie role, which would be filming in his native land of Australia. Jett came dressed in a white dinner jacket and black bow tie.

"Say man! We gotta hang out in my neck of the woods soon!" Eddie says to Jett. Jett looks over to Mr. Winters as if he was looking for approval. Mr. Winters nods his head. "Of course mate!" Jett says to Eddie.

Luv Shyne tugs on Eddie's arm to get his attention. "Oh! I like yo movies too baby!" Eddie chuckled. All the guys at the table start laughing

2 of the waiters come over to the table and start serving the main course. On the plates were sirloin steaks, baked potatoes with sautéed onions. 2 more waiters come over pouring red wines in everyone's crystal glasses. "Let's dig in people!" said Dr. Zachmont.

At the lassenberry table, "I don't know why, but this whole thing don't sit right with me!" mark jr. said. "I think this whole thing is cool as hell!" said Krayton. "Man! You wish you was Uncle Eddie anyway!" said BB. "I'd rather be called Eddie then Krayton! Why the hell you named me Krayton anyway?" Krayton asked his father. "Listen! Your mother gave you that name! You damn well better appreciate it!" Jake sr. shouted. Krayton rolls his eyes. Feeling embarrassment from her family's bickering, Maggie changes the subject. "This steak is delicious!" said Maggie. "Forget the steak! I still can't believe I'm in the same room with C.W. Winters!" Lula whispered. "What? Is he some big shot actor?" Corey asked. "Better than that! He can make or break an actor's career!" Lula said.

After desert was served, Dr. Zachmont stands from his seat. He taps his glass with a fork. "Attention everyone! Attention!" Dr. Zachmont shouted. The hall becomes silent. "Would everyone stand please!" said the Doctor. Everyone stands. "I would like to make a toast to our new friend! May I officially introduce to you all, Sir Edward lassenberry!" said the doctor. Everyone in the hall applaud, except for mark jr., who just stood there. Eddie stands and waves to everyone. "Speech! Speech!" Dr. Zachmont shouted. The applause starts to simmer down. "I would just like to thank you all for welcoming me into the fold! I promise a profitable future for years to come!" Eddie shouted. The people who would profit cheer. Porn star Luv Shyne grabs Eddie and gives him a long kiss on the lips. Everyone oohed and aahed! Eddie pulls away from her. "So, this what a thousand dicks taste like?" Eddie chuckled. Everyone laughs. Luv Shyne shows no sign of humiliation. She just laughs along with everyone else.

About a half hour later, the crowd trickles out of the hall, just like they trickled in earlier. The family is standing around Eddie chatting, until Dr. Zachmont comes over. He puts his hand on Krayton's shoulder. "You all should be proud. Eddies' going to help change the structure of this country." Said Dr. Zachmont. The doctor could see mixed feelings on the faces of the family members. "Well, get home safe everyone. And thank you for an eventful evening." Said the doctor.

Eddie had one too many drinks. Before Dr. Zachmont could leave with his entourage, Eddie walks over and hugs the doctor. "Thank you! Thank you!" Eddie cried. The doctor pushes Eddie away. He was disgusted when Eddie put his arms around him. Dr. Zachmont's facial expression quickly switched to a smile when he realized he was surrounded by people who were his minions, to say the least. The doctor walks off, towards the exit.

Eddie walks toward his family, yelling for the lassenberry plaque. "Where the fuck is my plaque?" Eddie shouted. "Its right here sir!" one of the servants said as he cradles it in his arms. Eddie snatches the plaque from the servant. Eddie walks over to his brother mark sr. and puts his hand on the back of his neck. "See! Now I'm considered a god to these fuckers!" Eddie whispers. He then kisses mark sr. on the cheek. Mark sr. pushes away from his brother. "Let's get the hell out of here!" mark sr. said. "You can't deny it little brother! I'm the man!" Eddie chuckled as he staggered to stand in one spot. Maggie grabs her brother. "Go home and get some sleep!" said Maggie. Eddie scoffs at his sister and gives the plaque to his sister Lula. "Make sure the plaque gets hung up in the family room!" said Eddie. "You sure you're going to be ok?" Lula asked. Eddie looks over towards the exit and sees the 2 porn stars standing around mingling. "Oh, I'm gonna be fine little sis!" Eddie chuckled. He staggers towards the exit.

Outside the hotel, across the street was parked a black car, with 2 federal agents sitting inside. The federal agent sitting behind the driver's seat was a black man snapping pictures with a long lens. The federal agent in the passenger seat who was Hispanic was staring at the crowd through binoculars. They witness Eddie lassenberry staggering to the limo with both porn stars underneath his arms. They all enter the limo. The limo drives off. The feds make a U-turn and stay 2 car lengths behind.

In the limo, Eddie and the girls pop open a bottle of expensive champagne, spilling it all over the upholstery. The chauffeur on the hand, was no hired stranger. It just happened to be Charlie Dalton.

Charlie was one of the few guys in Eddie's crew that didn't have a criminal record. Charlie's paper work as a chauffeur was legit. There was a phone in the limo. Charlie had to call Eddie on the limo because the Eddie had put up the patrician. After 8 rings, Eddie picks up the phone. At this moment, Paris tea was giving Eddie a blow job, while Luv Shyne is doing lines of cocaine. Eddie is so wasted, he drops the phone and passes out.

The next morning, Eddie is out cold in his bed with the 2 porn stars. It was 9:35. "Boss. Boss! Wake up! Boss!" 2 Gunz shouted. Gunz pulls out his pistol. He taps Paris tea on the head with the barrel of his weapon. Paris tea jumps up. She's startled to see the black man standing over her with a gun in his hand. "Wake your girlfriend up. Get your clothes on and get the fuck out before I kill you and her." Gunz said in a calm voice.

About a half hour later, Eddie slowly rolls out of bed. He sits at the edge of the bed holding his head. "Charlie! Charlie!" Eddie shouted as his voice cracked. There is no Charlie. Eddie gets up from the bed, butt naked. He stumbles to the bathroom. Holding his head. He stands over the toilet to take a leak. He goes to the sink and splashes water on his face and the back of his neck. Eddie goes to the kitchen, opens the refrigorator and drinks straight from the pitcher of ice water. There's a knock on the door. "Come in!" Eddie shouted. 2 Gunz walks in. Eddie walks in to the living room still naked. He falls back on the couch. "You alright boss?" 2 Gunz asked. "What happened to them 2 bitches?" Eddie asked. "I put them out." Gunz said. "Good!" Eddie said. "You need anything?" Gunz asked. "Where the fuck is Charlie?" Eddie asked. "He went to get breakfast for the roof top crew." Gunz said. "Fuck it! You can do it then. I want you to get the word out to all the crews everywhere I'm to be called Sir Edward from now on. Understand?" Eddie said. "Gunz gives a nod. Seconds later, Gunz thought for a moment. "Wait a minute! You want me to what?" Gunz asked.

CHAPTER 9. SIR EDWARD

"You heard me! It's Sir Edward from now on!" Eddie said. Gunz nods his head again. "Make sure Butch, Mookie and Dubbs get the message too!" Eddie ordered. Eddie then heads back to the bedroom. 2 Gunz leaves the apartment. As he is leaving, Charlie enters the apartment with of bag of takeout breakfast. Charlie goes into Eddie's bedroom. "I got a couple of bacon, egg and cheese sandwiches." Said Charlie. He lays the bag of food on the night stand. Eddie takes out a sandwich. He takes it out of the wrapper. Eddie takes a bite. "God damn it! This shit is cold!" Eddie shouted. Charlie is terrified. Eddie throws the sandwich at Charlie, hitting him in the chest. "You know I got food in the refrigorator! I bet the boys on the roof food is hot! Now go fix me a hot breakfast!" Eddie shouted. Charlie makes a dash for the kitchen.

Minutes later, Eddie's mobile phone rings. Eddie picks up the phone. "Hello?" said Eddie. "Mr. Lassenberry. August 13th, Teterboro airport 2 Am." the voice on the phone said. "Hello! Hello!" Eddie shouted. There was no answer. The person on the other end had hung up.

Thousands of miles away, 3 men stand beneath the art work of the Sistine Chapel admiring its beauty. All 3 elderly men are of Italian descent, were walking around dressed like tourists, wearing Bermuda shorts and t-shirts with either Vatican city or Rome written on them. One of them had a camera dangling around his neck. "Ogni volta che vengo qui, questa non cessa mia di stupirmi!" said the man with the camera. He happened to be a big shot from Palermo, called boss Fernando Domenico. The man standing across from him looked agitated. "Ho pensato che siamo venuti qui per dare il via libera per vendicare Don Gatano!" the man says to boss Domenico. The man whom lacked patience was a distant cousin of the late Luigi Gatano. The same man was also related to the late Don Alfonse Cucci.

The 3 men belonged to a secret order within the Sicilian mafia that sent soldiers to America that shared the same bloodline. Don Cucci was the 3rd mob boss assigned to America. Cucci's Underboss, Anthony Sangiero was his nephew, while Gatano was a distant cousin. As close as they were, not even Frankie Depalma nor Benny Lassenberry new of Gatano's true agenda.

"Mio fratello poalo è sempre ansioso!" said the impatient man, who happened to be Bramante Cucci. The other man to make up the trio was a big shot from the Camorra crime syndicate, Luigi Carafa. "Siamo qui solo per far capire che luomo che si proclama capo, è il bersaglio." Said Carafa. The 3 men agree, and then go their separate ways.

Back in the U.S., Gino Massoni is relaxing at his adult theatre located in Newark. He shut down the place for the night for a little private time with 2 of his whores that give lap dances in the basement. He gets off by masturbating while the 2 naked women are feeling on each other for his enjoyment. Suddenly, he hears a noise upstairs even though the music was loud and he was pissy drunk. He pulls out a handgun from his vertical shoulder holster. The women are so high and so in to each other, that they don't notice gino leaving the basement. Gino creeps up the carpeted stairs. "I know I locked that fucking door!" gino whispered to himself. He makes his way to the top of the stairs. With gun in hand, he quickly pushes open the door. Standing in the shadows are 4 figures. "Who's there?" Gino shouted. One figure steps out away from the group. He has his hands in the air. "Take it easy Gino! It's me, Mario!" the man said. "Mario the cat? How the hell you get in here?" Mario asked. "I'm known for being a cat burglar pal! Now put the gun away! You're making me nervous!" said Mario. Gino slowly puts his weapon back in the holster. "Wait a minute! How come you fellas ain't show up at the meeting?" gino asked. Mario puts his hands down. "What for? So we can get ambushed by the Rago boys?" Mario said. "I gotta admit that I was on edge when I got there, but we walked away in one piece!" said gino. Gino staggers over to the light switch. He clicks it on. The guys start laughing. Gino looked down and noticed his dick was hanging out. "Fuck you!" Gino shouted. He then fixes his pants. He sees standing behind Mario, 3 other soldiers from the Mancuso crew. Federico Gali, Paul Rita and Enrico Scholia. "What you guys want with me?" Gino asked. Mario pulls out a cigar from inside his jacket. He bites the tip off and then lights it. "We need real structure back in the family. We need a boss, an Underboss. Last time we checked, Frankie Depalma ain't in good health." Mario said. "I don't the Rago boys!" gino said. "Neither do we!" said Federico. "Out of respect. We're gonna get the go ahead from Depalma to take out the Rago crew. You with us?" Mario asked. Gino looks up at the ceiling for a moment. "All I know, is that Gatano was like a father to me! When I find out who was behind all this, believe me, they're dead!" gino said.

The next day at Frankie Depalma's residence, Gino pulls up to the driveway. There, stood 2 body guards dressed in suits at the main entrance. Wearing a suit jacket, silk button-up shirt, sharp pressed dress pants and wing tipped shoes, gino steps put of his car, approaching the guards with his hands in the air. "I ain't got time for this fellas! Make it quick! I called Mr. Depalma earlier, and I got fucking hangover!" gino said. "Just keep your hands up pal!" said one of the guards. Gino sighs. The guard pats him down. "Following me." The guard says to gino. Gino follows the guard down the long driveway. "Why couldn't I just drive up to the front door, for Christ's sake?" gino asked. "Since the attack on the manor, the boss don't want cars parked too close to the house!" said the guard. Within moments gino and the guard stand at the front entrance. The guard knocks on the door in a coded pattern. The door opens. Standing in the doorway, another guard dressed in a suit. "He's here to see the boss." Said the escort. Gino follows the indoor guard through the extravagant home of Frankie Depalma. The 2 men head the staircase. At the top of the stairs, the guard leads gino 3 doors down to the left. The guard knocks on the door. "Boss! It's me, Sal!" he shouted. "Is gino with you?" frank shouted. Sal turns towards gino. "You're gino right?" Sal whispered. Gino scoffs at Sal. "Yeah! Yeah! Come on!" said gino. Sal opens the door, allowing gino to enter. He sees Frankie in bed, covered from his chest down with a comforter. There was a teenage girl sitting by his side. "If you need anything boss, I'll be outside." Said Sal. "Go down stairs and make me a drink pumpkin." Frankie says to the girl. "Now, you know you're not supposed to be drinking grandpa!" said the girl. Frankie smiled. "Ok pumpkin. Make it a glass of milk." Frankie chuckled. His granddaughter gives him a kiss on the forehead. "You want anything to drink Gino?" Frankie asked. "No Mr. Depalma." Said Gino. Frankie's granddaughter leaves the room. "Come sit down! Frankie ordered Gino. Gino goes over and sits next to Frankie. Feeling uncomfortable, gino moves his chair a couple of inches away from Frankie. "What, I smell or something? Move the chair back this way!" Frankie shouted. Gino moves the chair back. Frankie was watching his favorite cartoon. For a moment, there's silence between the 2 men. "I remember like it was just yesterday. Me, the boss and benny lassenberry sat at a table in a small room talking about how we're going to start our own family." Frankie said. "Mr. Gatano told me the stories." Gino said. Frankie starts to cough repeatedly. He grabs the glass of water off the night stand. After he takes a couple of sips, his cough stops. "With all due respect Mr. Depalma, I didn't come to reminisce about the past. I came to talk about the future of this family." Gino said. "I'll tell about the future of this family! It'll never be the same again! Last I checked, we've got crews invading each other's territory!" Frankie shouted. He starts coughing again. He sips his water. His granddaughter enters the room with a glass of milk. "Just leave it on the night stand, and leave us please." Frankie said to his granddaughter. She leaves the bedroom, closing the door behind her. "I just had a meeting with the Mancuso crew yesterday. It seems they're the only obstacle keeping the crews getting back together. Once we get them out of the way, with your permission of course, we can get back to business as usual." Gino explained. Frankie is silent for a moment. "I remember when the boss took you off the street, and gave you purpose. Now that the boss is gone, I'm giving you the opportunity to walk away." Frankie said. "I can't leave! This is my life!" gino cried. "That's all I need to hear!" Frankie said. Frankie starts coughing again, and again he sips his glass of water. "Something's gotta be done! My envelopes are getting smaller! I tell ya what kid! You get boys together and deal with the Rago crew, and I'll see to it that you move up. Way up!" said Frankie. "You can count on me, boss! Sono qui per servire voi fino allá morte!" gino said. "Good! You can leave now!" Frankie ordered. Gino nods his leaves the bedroom. He chuckles as he walks down the hall.

It was August 13th, a little after midnight. Eddie was in his apartment standing in front of the mirror. He was all decked out in a brown 2 piece silk suit. He had on brown gator shoes. His hand was clustered with diamond rings, including the signature ring is father gave him. He was fastening his diamond studded cuff links, when came a knock on the door. "Come in Gunz!" Eddie shouted. Gunz enters the apartment. "Mr. Jabbo down stairs waiting in the limo for ya boss!" said Gunz. "Charlie! Get out here!" Eddie shouted. Charlie Dalton comes running out of his bedroom. "I need you to stay here until I get back!" said Eddie. "When you coming back?" Charlie asked. "None of yo monkey ass business!" Eddie shouted. Gunz was trying his best to hold back the laughter. "Just be here when get back! Now go in my bedroom and get the bottle of smell good off the dresser." Eddie said. Charlie runs in Eddie's bedroom. He grabs one of the 3 bottles of cologne. He runs back into the living room. Eddie snatches the bottle from him. Eddie sprays into the air, so the mist lands on him. Eddie runs to the bar, and pours himself a drink. He frowns from the taste. Eddie pours another drink. "Now I can go!" Eddie said.

Down stairs in front of the building, Eddie is escorted to the limo by 2 of his guards, Jason Curtis, a.k.a J. Big and Troy Cotton, a.k.a Smooth. Eddie approached the limo. As soon as the guard opens the door, everyone could hear jabbo shooting off his mouth. "You got ol' jabbo waiting down here like a damn fool! Y'all must lost yo minds!" jabbo shouted. Embarrassed, Eddie turns to his body guards. "This is what happens when you get old!" Eddie chuckled. The guards chuckle as well. Eddie gets into the limo. The chauffeur shuts the door. "Listen old man! Cut it out!" Eddie shouted. Jabbo becomes silent. He stares out the window. "I'm jabbo! I been in this shit too long! Remember that! Jabbo says to Eddie. "OK! Jesus Christ!" Eddie shouted. The chauffeur drives off.

It was around 1:23 am, when the limo arrived at Teterboro Airport. Before the limo stops, Eddie noticed a helicopter and 6 national agreement agents standing guard around it. He also noticed another limo parked near the helicopter as well. "This must be some serious shit!" jabbo bellowed. Eddie takes a deep breath. "Let's go old man!" Eddie said. The chauffeur gets out of the limo. He helps jabbo out of the limo. Eddie hands jabbo his walking cane. Eddie exits the limo.

In the other limo, one of the agents opens the rear door, allowing the passenger to exit. Out of the limo comes general Theodore J. Magus. He was dressed in camouflage military fatigues. The general looked in his late 50's, with broad shoulders and tall in stature. He and Eddie meet at middle ground and shake hands. "Mr. Lassenberry! Ready to take a trip to the other side of the world?" the general shouted over the noise of the helicopter. "It's Sir Edward now!" Eddie shouted. "Whatever floats your boat!" shouted the general. Getting out of the general's limo was a petite beautiful exotic woman, wearing a tight suit jacket and tight skirt stopping just above her knees. Her brown hair was, but she had it pinned up in a bun. The glasses she wore, made her look even sexier. She wore high heeled shoes that showed off her painted toe nails. Eddie was hypnotized by this sexy woman as she walked towards the helicopter. The general smirked. "That's my personal secretary! She'll be coming along for the duration!" the general shouted. "Whatever!" Eddie shouted. Jabbo comes over and shakes the general's hand. "Mr. Jenkins! I finally get a chance to meet you!" the general shouted. Eddie was in awe. "You already know jabbo?" Eddie asked. "Oh! Your father and Mr. Jenkins are legends in the business!" said the general.

The helicopter they were about to board was a twin- engine, tandem rotor heavy-lift helicopter. As all the passengers boarded, the rear rotor speeds up to catch up with front rotor.

6 NA agents board the helicopter. The signalman on the tarmac gives the pilot the go ahead to lift off. The helicopter takes off into the night sky.

Within a couple of hours, the helicopter reaches Wright-Patterson Air force base in Dayton, Ohio. Before the sun comes up over the horizon, the crew and passengers transfer to a cargo plane. The NA agents stripped off their black suits to expose military jump suits and false badges. Again, Eddie was in awe. "You sure our paper work is in order?" Eddie asked the general. The general chuckled. Take it easy Mr. Lassenberry! All you have to do is meet the contact face-to-face!" said the general. "It's Sir Edward!" said Eddie. "Next stop, Karachi Air Base!" the general shouted. One of the agents walks to the cargo plane. He shows the military official in charge a roster sheet and the manifest of what was to be transported in the plane.

The manifest showed that a couple of tons of medical supplies would be sent to Karachi, Pakistan to help Afghan refugees from a terrorist menace. The senior officer in charge just glanced over the paper work, and then saluted the agent. As soon as the engines start, the passengers from the helicopters board the cargo plane. The agent with the copy of the manifest signals another agent to come over. Both agents head board the cargo plane, and head towards the cockpit. Minutes later, Sir Edward, jabbo the general, the secretary and the remaining agents strap themselves in. it was about 4 in the morning, when general magus and team were thousands of miles over the Atlantic. "When we arrive Sir Edward, show respect for the custom, so this operation can run smoothly." Said the general. "What you trying to say there general? I don't know how to act around folks?" Eddie asked. The general changes his tone. "Oh, no! I didn't mean anything by it!" the general shouted. Sir Edward turns and looks out the window.

Once the passengers are notified by the cockpit, they unbuckle their straps. The general's secretary walks pass the general and Sir Edward, heading towards the restroom. The gets a palm full of ass as she walks by. She doesn't flinch one bit. She just smiles at the general and keeps walking. "She's going to beat a great treat for the master!" the general whispered to Sir Edward. Sir Edward had a baffled look on his face. "What master?" Sir Edward asked. The general just smiled.

Hours later, the cargo plane arrives over the District of Karachi. The pilot sees the lights of a private air strip just ahead. He is given orders over the plane's communication's system that he has the green light to land.

The cargo plane then comes to a halt. When the engines cease, an oil truck appears over the horizon. It is followed by and another truck filled with hard hats and coveralls. Eddie jumps out of seat, with the look of paranoia. "Calm down Sir Edward. They're just the refueling detail." The general chuckled. Sir Edward turns towards the general. "I knew that!" he shouted. Jabbo noticed 2 sport utility vehicles pull up alongside the cargo plane. General Magus greets a Pakistani representative dressed in regulation Pakistani army fatigues. "Good evening general." The man said. "It's a good thing your English is exceptional or I'd be lost out here!" the general chuckled. The 2 men shake hands. The general then introduces Sir Edward and jabbo to the Pakistani representative, but doesn't mention the reps name to Sir Edward.

General Magus, Sir Edward, jabbo, the Pakistani rep, and the general's sexy female companion pile up in one SUV, while the NA agents get into the other.

Sir Edward noticed that the Pakistani rep was doing a hundred miles per hour down the dirt road. He and the others brace themselves as the speed increases. "Forgive me for the uncomfortable ride! We must make haste to the Afghani border before day break!" said the rep. "This remind ol' jabbo when I was young, being chased by the cops down Frelinghuysen ave!" jabbo chuckled. Sir Edward didn't a word. He was feeling a little car sick.

An hour later, both vehicles arrive at the Pakistan, Afghanistan border. At the check point, they are stopped by a garrison of Afghani men. These men weren't in military fatigues, but in traditional afghan garb. "Who the hell are these jokers?" Sir Edward asked. "These jokers as you call them Sir Edward, are future allies of the U.S." said the general. "How's that?" asked Sir Edward. The general smiled. "It's classified. All I can say that they're from the north." The general explained.

The men were armed with AK-47 machine guns. The Pakistan rep and the head of the garrison went back and forth verbally in their native language. Minutes later, they were given the signal to pass beyond the check point. "That was easy!" said Sir Edward. "Everything is easy when you have the same interests!" said the Pakistan rep.

A few hours later, Sir Edward watched as the sun was coming up. The general and jabbo were fast asleep. Sir Edward was sitting behind the general's secretary. He starts playing with her ear lobe. She closes her eyes, and starts moaning. He leans forward to whisper in her ear. "I'm gonna show you a good time when we get back to the states! You're gonna get the best fucking in the world, bitch!" Sir Edward whispered as he rubs on her huge breasts. The secretary moans as she's rubbing between her legs.

"We're here gentlemen!" the Pakistani rep shouted. General Magus jumps from his slumber. Jabbo does the same. Sir Edward just leans back in his seat with a smile. The secretary quickly fixes her blouse. The general looks out the window and sees huge snow Cap Mountains.

2 men wearing Khet partug, approach the convoy. They are armed with AK-47 machine guns. They exchange words in their native language with the Pakistani representative. The 2 men seemed upset. "What's wrong with these guys?" the general asked. "Your lady friend's attire is very disrespectful." Said the Pakistani rep. "So, I'll tell m her to wait here! But, we're doing business!" said the general.

General Magus, the Pakistani rep, Sir Edward and jabbo exit the vehicle. They all follow the 2 men to a huge tent.

The temperature was about 90° Fahrenheit. Sir Edward removes his jacket, unbuttoning his shirt to try and cool off. Sir Edward noticed off in the distance 3 huge transport vehicles. The 2 Afghani men lead the group to the tent. Inside the tent sat the man in charge of the operation. He looked like he had lived a hard life. He was surrounded by 8 other men, who were also armed with machine guns. "Salaam!" said the Pakistani rep says to the man in charge. "Salaam!" said the man in charge. General Magus steps forward. "Salaam Mr. Qadir." Said the general. "Mr. Qadir just nods at the general. Qadir speaks to the Pakistani rep in Arabic. After a few seconds, the Pakistani rep tells Sir Edward to come forth. Sir Edward walks towards Qadir. His men have their weapons at the ready. "Take it easy guys!" Sir Edward shouted. Qadir raises his hand. His men stand down. Qadir speaks to the Pakistani rep. "I'm told to translate to you as commanded by Rasul Qadir." The rep explained. "No problem!" said the general. Sir Edward just shrugs his shoulders. Qadir speaks to the rep. "He asks if you are the one to carry the merchandise back to America?" the rep says to Sir Edward. Sir Edward just gives a nod. Qadir speaks to the rep. "Qadir will like you to leave us alone for a moment." The rep says to the general. The general looks infuriated. "Hold on a minute god damnit! I'm in charge of the operation on the American side!" said the general. Qadir's men point their weapons at the general. Sir Edward raises his hands in the air. "Wait a minute! Tell them I'm a business man, and I need the general to get me back to the states!" Sir Edward shouted. The rep speak with Qadir. The rep turns to Sir Edward. "Qadir implores that you leave the tent immediately!" said the rep. "I got this! I got this!" Sir Edward says to the general. The general storms out of the tent with rage in his eyes. Qadir speaks to the rep. "Qadir says he sees deceit in the general's face." the rep said. "What does he see in my face?" Sir Edward asked. "He said he sees a man who wants to do business, and go home." Said the rep. "What now?" Sir Edward asked. The rep speaks with Qadir. "Qadir says we should get you loaded up and back to America." The rep says. Before they exit the tent, Sir Edward stops the rep. "Tell Qadir that my name is Sir Edward of New Jersey, and if one day we can't do business with each other, that I have his word that another member of my bloodline continue our agreement." Said Sir Edward. The Pakistani rep gives Sir Edward a confused look. "Go ahead and tell him!" Said Sir Edward. The rep translates to Qadir and his men. Qadir smiles. He approaches Sir Edward. Qadir grabs Sir Edward by the arms and gives him a kiss on both cheeks. Qadir then translates to the rep. "He says he can't help but admire a man that values family as much as he does." Said the rep.

Moments later, everyone exits the tent. Qadir points to the 3 transport vehicles. Qadir's men waste no time and trot over to the vehicles. Sir Edward grows impatient. "Why the hell they have the trucks parked way over there?" asked Sir Edward. "They feared being bombed alongside 3 trucks before you arrived." Said the rep. "Whatever." Sir Edward says to himself.

Sir Edward and General Magus watched as the 3 vehicles come towards them. "You got that paper work?" jabbo asked the general. General Magus signal one of NA agents to get the paper work from the secretary, who was waiting in the SUV. Moments later, the agents' trots back to the general dripping of sweat. He passes the paper work to the general. The general then gives it to jabbo.

Before they made their trip to southern Asia, General Magus contacted Qadir's people to find out where and when he wanted his pay to be wired. Afterwards, Sir Edward would have sleeves make contact with an Afghanistan bank of Qadir's choosing through one of its directors. The bank director would create a business account in the name of a false company. When sleeves gets the word from Sir Edward, 20 million U.S. dollars would be electronically wired to that account.

Through the dark of night, the 3 trucks follow the general's convoy across the afghan border back into Pakistan. The trucks would then be loaded onto the cargo plane. Once the cargo plane reaches the states, the trucks would already be empty. In mid-air, the heroin is transferred into huge crates marked textile products.

2 days later, about 4 in the morning, Sir Edward enters his apartment. He was so exhausted, he drops his jacket on the floor. He drags himself to the bedroom, where he belly flops on to his king size bed. Suddenly, the phone rings. "Shit! What now?" he shouted. Sir Edward answers the phone. "Yeah!" he shouted. "It's me! Where the fuck you been? I need a refill out here!" the voice shouted. The voice on the other end was Butch. "Calm down!" shouted Sir Edward. "These fiends eaten this shit up like candy!" Butch said. "Man, you think that's

something? I got some quality shit coming in real soon!" said Sir Edward. "Make it Quick!" Butch shouted. Sir Edward hangs up. He closes his eyes. Minutes later, the phone rings again. "Fuck!" Sir Edwards shouted. "Charlie! Charlie!" Sir Edward shouts. Charlie didn't answer. After 5 rings, Sir Edward picks up the phone. "Qué pasa? ¿Necesitas una recarga aquí!" the voice shouted. Still groggy, Sir Edward barely understood the language. "What the hell?" Sir Edward shouted. "I said I need a refill out here!" the voice shouted. The voice on the other end was Mookie Vasquez. "I'll call you back in a few hours!" sir Edward shouted. He hangs up the phone. Sir Edward shut his eyes. Seconds later, the phone rings again. Sir Edward picks up the phone. "I'm fucking tired! Call back later!" he shouted. He then hangs up.

On the other end of the phone was Charlie Dalton. He was arrested for lewd behavior the night before, coming out of a night club in Patterson, New Jersey.

It was around 3 in the afternoon when Sir Edward wakes up. The phone rings. "Yeah!" Sir Edward shouted. "What the hell? The boss wants you to pick up your product! Your people must be starving by now!" the voice shouted. Sir Edward rubs his eyes. "Ok! Ok!" said sir Edward. We hate holding on to this stuff beyond the transaction period! Get it together!" the voice shouted. "Goddamn man! I'm coming!" sir Edward shouted. "Don't let it happen again!" the voice shouted. Sir Edward hangs up.

Sir Edward was supposed to meet with his cocaine connection a few days ago, but got caught up in the new afghan connection, which he thought was more important. With a new shipment of pure heroin coming to the states, Sir Edward needed a place to store it for processing. That's where Tasty Burger C.E.O Jacob Tanner was instructed by the National Agreement to let Sir Edward use his abandoned meat processing plant. The plant was shut down due to a drastic reduction in business after an Escherichia Coli epidemic a couple of years earlier. Mr. Tanner was sought out by the National Agreement and given financial refuge for his absolute obedience. Accusations came to Mr. Tanner by his team of lawyers that the E. coli outbreak was due to sabotage.

The plant was an area of 15,000 sq. ft., located just outside the Pine Barrens in South Jersey. It was already well guarded by 2 dozen NA agents for months.

Sir Edward hits the shower. He just stands under the shower head, letting the water just run down his body. Seconds later, he grabs the soap. After his shower, he hears the phone ring. "Shit! Everybody just leave me the fuck alone!" he shouts to himself. Sir Edward drops the towel, and picks up the phone. "Yeah!" Sir Edward shouted. "Your presence is requested by your new business partners Mr. Lassenberry." The voice said. When and where?" Sir Edward sighed. "There will be a car waiting for you at the corner of Frelinghuysen and Dey Street." The voice said. Sir Edward hangs up. Sir Edward walks to the closet and picks out a gray silk suit to wear.

Sir Edward paces back-n-forth, thinking of what business to take care of first. There's a knock on the door. "Come in!" sir Edward shouted. Entering the apartment was 2 Gunz's right hand man and younger cousin, David Thompson, a.k.a Tiki. He was filling in for his cousin guarding outside the apartment. "I just got word from rick boss man, that Charlie got locked up out in Patterson last night." Said Tiki. "What?" Sir Edward shouted. "That's what rick told me! He's standing guard at the elevator!" said Tiki. "Close my door and get back to your post!" Sir Edward said. Tiki shuts the door. "Charlie! Charlie! Charlie!" Sir Edward whispers to himself. He picks up the phone. He calls the only other man that can go down to the Patterson precinct and spring Charlie out within minutes. The phone rings 3 times. "Jabbo!" the voice said. "Hey old man! I need you to go out to the Patterson precinct and get that fool Charlie out. Jabbo chuckles. "How much this gonna cost ol' jabbo." Jabbo asked. Sir Edward sighs. "Come on old man! I got too much on my plate as it is! Just go get him out!" Sir Edward says before he hangs up. Sir Edward puts on his suit jacket. He steps out into the hall. "Listen. When Charlie gets back, tell him I said to keep his black ass here until I get back." Said Sir Edward. "Got it boss man." said Tiki. "Now call the boys outside and tell them I'm coming down." Sir Edward ordered. Tiki gets on the walkie-talkie and gets in contact with Sir Edward's guards outside. Sir Edward heads to the freight elevator. Standing at the elevator were guards Pete Bey, a.k.a peanut and rick.

It was around 5 pm when Sir Edward and his guards showed up at the refill spot In Port Elizabeth. The 4 four guards that escorted him were carrying 2 suitcases a piece. Sir Edward had collected the funds from his 3 generals, Butch, Dubbs and Mookie.

Sir Edward and his men stand face-to-face with 5 heavily armed Latino men guarding the merchandise on the truck. The Latino man in charge steps forward. "Buenas tardes Eddie. ¿Dónde Está jabbo? The Latino man asked. "Oh jabbo? I sent ol' jabbo on an errand." Sir Edward explained. Jabbo was usually the one to taste a sample of the product before the transaction. This time, it was Sir Edward who dipped his fingers in the product. He approved of its quality. The transaction was over within minutes. Sir Edward received his refill to take back to the processing spot to cut the product for street sale, and the Latino connection received their 8 suitcases filled with cash. "La próxima vez, no tienen nos espera. Obtenemos sospechoso." The Latino man said. "I'll keep that in mind." Sir Edward said as the 2 men shook hands.

Back at Sir Edward's apartment, Sir Edward sits in his favorite chair drinking a glass full of vodka straight. It's about 6:45 pm. "Don't come out that room until I tell yo black ass!" Sir Edward shouted in a slurred voice. Moments later, there's a knock on the door. "Come in!" sir Edward shouted. Tiki steps in. "Butch is down stairs boss." He said. "Send him up nigga!" Sir Edward said. Tiki leaves.

In the freight elevator, Darnell Washington, a.k.a Clip and Jerome Peters, a.k.a Pinky escort butch to Sir Edward's floor. "You boys keeping Mr. Lassenberry safe, right?" butch said with a smirk. "No doubt!" said Clip. "Good! I don't wanna come back here and start knocking niggas out!" butch said as he holds up his fist. The 2 guards laughed off the threat. "I'm serious!" butch said as he stands face-to-face with Clip. The elevator comes to a stop. Butch exits the elevator. Tiki stands from his seat as he sees butch coming down the hall. "What's up kid?" butch says to Tiki. "Hey butch!" said Tiki. Tiki knocks on the door for butch. "Come in!" sir Edward shouts. Butch enter the apartment. Butch sees Sir Edward sitting in his chair. "Say man! Ain't you supposed to be showing me something?" butch asked. Sir Edward nods out for a moment. Butch taps Sir Edward on the shoulder. "Wake up man!" butch shouted. Sir Edward wakes up. Suddenly, Charlie comes out from his bedroom. His face was so battered, he looked unrecognizable. "Please help me!" Charlie mumbled. "What you talking about fool?" butch asked Charlie. Sir Edward looks at Charlie with hate in his eyes.

He jumps from his chair and chases Charlie back into the bedroom. Charlie slams the door to separate himself from his tormentor. "Better run bitch!" sir Edward shouted. "Come on man, before you kill that boy!" butch chuckled. Butch grabs Sir Edward's jacket. Sir Edward gets himself together, by tucking his shirt back into his pants. "We'll take my ride." Said butch as he and Sir Edward leave the apartment. "Everything alright boss?" Tiki asked. "Stay at your post and make sure Charlie don't leave!" sir Edward ordered. Tiki notified the crew downstairs that the boss was on his way down. Sir Edward and butch are escorted to Butch's car by Mike Dunji, a.k.a black Mike and Troy Cotton, a.k.a Smooth. Butch jumps in the back seat with Sir Edward. Butch's driver takes off.

It was 5 minutes to 8pm. Butch and sir Edward arrive in Burlington County. This county was untouched by the lassenberry crew, along with Ocean, Camden, Gloucester, Salem, Atlantic, Cumberland and Cape May counties. Sir Edward wanted all of New Jersey under his thumb. Nothing stood his way, except for the fact that the Philadelphia mob had control of all the small time dealers in that region.

Only 5 minutes from their destination, Sir Edward tells Butch's driver to pull over on the side of a desolate road just off interstate 295. "Why the fuck we're out here?" butch asked. "We're gonna walk the rest of the way." Sir Edward said. "You ready to walk?" butch asked his driver. "Fuck that! You stay yo ass in the car until we get back!" Sir Edward says to the driver. The driver looks over at his boss. "Stay in the car." butch sighed. Both Sir Edward and butch exit the vehicle and start their trek. "That wasn't cool what to you did back there!" butch said. "What the fuck is your problem?" sir Edward asked. "I know since the old man was sent up the river, you're the big man now! You can't be talking to my people like that in front of me!" butch shouted. Sir Edwards turns towards butch. "Your people? Remember this! All of you are my people! All of you!" sir Edward shouted. Sir Edward continues to walk. Butch follows closely behind.

15 minutes later, butch and Sir Edward come in sight of a huge industrial facility. They only hear the sound of crickets in the weeds off the side of the road. There were no street lights, but lights coming from the facility. "Damn man! I'm getting old! All this fucking walking is killing my back!" sir Edward said. "Nigga! We barely did any walking!" butch shouted. Sir Edward bends over grabbing his knees. Butch just shook his head. "You using the product man? I know you drink like a fish, but I wanna know, are you using?" butch asked. Eddie stands tall. "Fuck you! I got this! Let's go!" sir Edward shouted.

As they walk closer, the facility looks more enormous. They notice a tall metal fence with coiled barbed wire on top surrounding the facility. 2 NA agents, dressed in black suits, become vigilant when they see the 2 black men approach the fence. "Can I help you gentlemen?" asked one of the agents. Sir Edward straightens his neck-tie. "Yes. I'm Sir Edward from the house of Lassenberry." He said proudly. The agent pressed on side of his wrist watch. He speaks onto it. "Agent 1 at entrance 5. Mr. Lassenberry just arrived." The agent said. "Sir Edward?" butch chuckled.

There were surveillance cameras posted all around the fence. One automatically shifts at the gate's entrance, zooming in on Sir Edward and butch. "Smile for the camera man!" sir Edward said to butch as he winks at the camera. The gate automatically slides open at a slow pace. "You may enter Sir Edward." Said the agent. Sir Edward walks pass the gates. Butch on the other hand, was stopped. "It's ok! He's with me!" said Sir Edward. "Sorry sir. Our orders are to only to let you enter." Said the agent. Butch looked pissed. "Hold up! I didn't come all the way out here in the middle of nowhere just to get turned back!" butch shouted. The other agent reached inside his suit jacket for his pistol. "It's ok!" sir Edward pleaded to the agents. "Calm down." Sir Edward says to butch. "Ours orders are to get you to the meeting on time sir." Said the agent. "Can you at least get him a table and chair?" sir Edward asked. "I'm hungry too!" butch mentioned. The 2 agents look at each other. "Can you get him some food too?" sir Edward asked. "Very well sir." Said the agent. Sir Edward pats butch on the arm. "This won't take long." He said. "I hope not!" butch sighed. One of the agents escorts Sir Edward to the main entrance. The other agent gets on his com link to order butch what he desired to eat.

After the huge double doors slide open, Sir Edward and the agent walk through the dimly lit factory area where Sir Edward sees nothing but pallets stacked on top of each other and mostly rusty pipes lining the walls and ceiling. The agent leads Sir Edward to another door where the only way to open it was with a key card. He swipes the card on a control panel located on the side. The agent then punches in a 4 digit code. The door makes a clicking sound. The agent opens up. On the other side of the door leads to the actual facility. Sir Edward smiled when he saw the 3 transport vehicles that were in Afghanistan. "I see the Arabs got their money." Sir Edward says to himself. He approaches the trucks. He walks around the back of the vehicles. "Where's the stuff man?" he asked the agent. He then walks up to the agent and grabs him by the collar. The agent doesn't budge or reaches for his weapon. "Listen you punk! If I don't get my shipment, I'm gonna rip yo damn eyes out of yo head!" he shouted. "There won't be any need for violence sir Edward!" a voice from out of nowhere shouted. Sir Edward looks around. "Who the fuck said that?" he shouted as he released the agent. "I did!" said the voice. Sir Edward sees a tall slim white man in a suit standing at the doorway on the opposite end of the facility. The man walks toward Sir Edward. He extends his hand out to greet Sir Edward. Sir Edward walks pass the agent. "Who the fuck are you?" he shouted. The man still had his hand out to greet Sir Edward, but realized that Eddie wasn't in a friendly mood. At this time, 2 more agents enter the room dressed in black suits as well. "Y'all gonna stiff me out of my product now?" sir Edward asked. Not at all!" the man said in a calm voice. "Better not, or you might as well kill my black ass!" sir Edward said. "Take it easy. No one is going to do you any harm." He says to Sir Edward. The man stood a few inches taller than Sir Edward, placed his hand on his shoulder. "Relax and just listen to what I have to say." The man says to him. Sir Edward finally calms down. "I'm Peter bellum. I'm National Agreement's products and services transportation C.E.O, North- Eastern division."

Peter Bellum is a conservative lobbyist from New Jersey. He was recruited by the National Agreement back in the early 90's when he started on doctor Zachmont's research team. Impressed with his work, doctor Zachmont recommended him to the council for promotion.

"Where's my dope? Sir Edward asked peter. We have your product here in the facility." Peter said. "We had a deal! I paid them Arabs 20 million U.S. dollars! Now I want my shit so I can mix it and put it out on the streets!" Sir Edward shouted. Peter had a smirk on his face. "You forget about the NA part of the bargain? Peter asked. "What bargain?" sir Edward asked. "It's true that you fulfilled your end to the Afghans, but our people are in this business to make a lot of money as well. The only way to make it happen overnight is through you. Nothing's for free. Peter pulls out a folded piece of paper from inside his jacket pocket. Sir Edward looked confused. "The day you received your knighthood and family coat-of-arms, you took a life oath to those in attendance. Nothings for free. You must understand." Peter says to Sir Edward. Peter unfolds the paper. He then takes out his reading glasses. "Can't read a darn thing without them." He chuckled. "Come on, and get on with it!" Sir Edward shouted. Peter clears his throat. "Let's see. Ok. I'm going down the list. Your are to purchase one thousand units from Galaxy Appliances which includes 2 hundred refrigerators, 2 hundred washing machines, 2 hundred dish washers, 2 hundred range ovens and 2 hundred water heaters at retail prices. Items are subject to change. This will be done on a quarterly basis." Said peter. "What the fuck you mean by quarterly?" sir Edward shouted. "That means every 3 months. Let me continue, please." Said peter. "You are to purchase one hundred contemporary modeled automobiles from Boeman Automotive Corp. at retail prices on a quarterly basis. You are to purchase 20 thousand U.S. dollars of cosmetics from Blush Cosmetics Inc. on a month to month basis at retail prices. You are to purchase 5 thousand dollars U.S. dollars of office supplies from Upgrade Office Supply Company. Peter pauses for a moment when he sees Sir Edward sweating and rubbing his chest. "Are you ok?" peter asked. "Go man! Just go on!" Sir Edward panted. "You are to purchase 50 thousand U.S. dollars' worth of small arms from Stock & Barrel Defense Company on a month to month basis at retail prices." Said peter. "Why the hell would I buy legal guns? I'm a criminal!" sir Edward said. "We know you're a criminal. You know you're a criminal. Hell, even the most of the country knows you're a criminal! But you have no arrest sheet, and no convictions. So according to the judicial system, you're a regular citizen. Bravo, Sir Edward." Said peter. A sense of pride falls upon Sir Edward's face. "Continue!" he says to peter. "You are to purchase a hundred cases of Steigalhoff beer from Steigalhoff Brewery on a month to month basis. Here! You take the list and finish reading over it. I have copies." Said peter. Sir Edward reads the rest of the list. "Goddamn! You got like 30 businesses on here!" he shouted. "Once you've made your first purchase of these items, which will be this coming Monday, then and only then will you receive your shipment. Any questions?" Said peter. Sir Edward folds his arms in a bold manner. "How do I know you people won't take my shipment and sell it yourselves?" Sir Edward asked. "Why would we? We're not drug dealers. We'll leave that to you. Just do what's expected of you and I assure you and your family will prosper way beyond your imagination." Said peter. Peter extends hand again in a friendly gesture. Reluctantly, Sir Edwards shakes his hand.

Outside the gates, butch is sitting at a folding table, drinking a soda and eating a ham sandwich. He looks at his watch. It was about 9pm, when Sir Edward exits the facility. Butch stand to his feet. He sees Sir Edward has the look of disappointment on his face. "Everything good, man?" butch asked. "Let's go. I need a drink. Don't I own a dive bar around here somewhere?" sir Edward asked. "Yeah! About 10 miles! Let's go get that drink!" butch chuckled.

It was 3 days later on a Monday, when lassenberry family attorney, Stanley Hart, a.k.a Sleeves is being driven by a young man to the Elizabeth warehouse. He was summoned by Sir Edward earlier that day. The elderly man sat in the passenger seat, rotating the ring on his finger that benny had given him. "What you think he called you for grandpa?" the young man asked. Sleeves sighs. "Who knows with this guy? He's not his father!" said sleeves.

The young man driving was sleeve's eldest grandson Brandon Stanley Hart. He was tall and slim with a light complexion. He inherited his mother's good looks, but was cursed with his grandfather's skin condition on his feet. Brandon was unemployed living off of his trust fund provided by his grandfather.

They finally arrive at the warehouse. Brandon noticed a fleet of cars parked outside the warehouse. "What the hell is this?" sleeves said to himself. Brandon gets out and walks over to the passenger side and assists his grandfather out of the car. Brandon and his grandfather slowly make their way through the maze of brand new cars. They all had the bill of sale documents in the side windows, and were all made by Boeman Automotive. Brandon noticed federal agents, or what seemed to be federal agents taking pictures off in the distance. "Don't pay them any attention! Let's just get inside!" said sleeves. There was just one of Sir Edward's guards posted at the entrance. It was a young black man in his early 20's named Terrance Washington, a.k.a Bitty. He wasn't armed. His job was just to watch the fleet of cars so none of them were stolen. "What you want old man?" bitty asked. "Do you have any idea whom you're talking to son?" sleeves asked bitty. Bitty sticks out his chest. "I don't give a fuck who you is!" bitty shouted. "Listen! I'm going to forget what you've just said! Just go in there and tell your boss sleeves is here!" he said. Bitty's jaw dropped. "Oh shit! I'm sorry Mr. Sleeves!" bitty stuttered. Bitty quickly opens the door for sleeves and Brandon. They enter the warehouse. Brandon looks back at bitty with a smirk on his face. Inside, sleeves sees nothing but wall to wall merchandise. "What the hell is all this?" sleeves asked Sir Edward. There were a couple of guys walking around auditing the items. Sir Edward comes over to sleeves. "Uncle sleeves!" he shouted. Sir Edward gives sleeves a hug. "What, you into high jacking now?" sleeves asked. "Trust me! All the shit is legitimate!" said Sir Edward. Brandon walks over to a long table displaying all sorts of small arms weaponry. He picks up a high powered rifle. He aims it at the wall, peering through the scope. "You're trying to sell all of this stuff?" Brandon asked. "You gotta gun license?" sir Edward asked. "Ah, no!" said Brandon. Sir Edward snatches the weapon away from him. "Who the fuck is this kid?" sir Edward asked. "You remember Brandon! My grandson!" said sleeves. Sir Edward squints at Brandon. Then his eyes widen. "Get the fuck outta here! Little Brandon? Last time I saw yo ass, you was riding a tricycle!" Sir Edward shouted. "I guess it's been a long time then." Said Brandon. "Man, get over here and give me a hug! Shit! We family!" shouted Sir Edward. Brandon looks over at his grandfather. Sleeves just shrugged his shoulders. Brandon and Sir Edward give each other a hug. Sir Edward puts the rifle back on the table. "Refrigerators stoves word processors, boxes of skin care products. It must be on the level if you won't sell my grandson a rifle." Said sleeves. "That's what I called you for old man!" said Sir Edward. "What are talking about?" sleeves asked. "You 2! Get out! Don't come back in until I call for you!" said Sir Edward. The 2 guys doing the auditing, drop their clipboards and next to a case of hand lotion and rush out of the warehouse. "I'm running out of room here! Since you're the only friend of my father that ain't got the feds tailing him, I thought you should be the one to help me set up shop and sell all this shit!" said sir Edward. "No! No son! That's too much work for me! I just want to spend the rest of my days on the beach with a Daiquiri!" sleeves said. "Come on, sleeves man!" he shouted. "The answer is still no son! Get one of your brothers or sisters to help you!" said sleeves. "I already bought all this shit using their names so the tax man don't come after me!" said Sir Edward. "The first thing you can do is to put an ad in the newspaper and sell the refrigerators and stoves." Said Brandon. Sir Edwards looks impressed. "What you do for work kid?" sir Edward asked. "Being his grandson!" Brandon said with a bewildered expression as he pointed to sleeves. "Well, now you work for me!" sir Edward said. "What about the cars outside?" Brandon asked. "What about them?" Sir Edward asked. "Come on! Boeman? Get real!" Brandon said.

Boeman Automotive had the reputation of not being the best of American made cars. Peter and Helen Boeman attached their company to the National Agreement out of desperation. Sir Edward would be their meal ticket to an IPO on the market.

"I got an idea! If you can put up the money for an empty lot, I can get a couple of friends of mine in the used car business to sell them for you." Brandon said. "Didn't you just say that these cars couldn't sell?" sir Edward asked. "Maybe if you cut the cost a little. In fact, cut the cost on all this stuff! I guarantee you'll attract a younger crowd looking for their first car!" Brandon explained. Sir Edward thought about it for a moment. "How soon can we get started?" sir Edward asked. "You find the empty lot, and I'll place the ads. I'd say, within a week?" Brandon said. "You kinda smart kid!" Sir Edward said. He comes from good stock." Said sleeves. "Deal?" Brandon said as he waits for Edward's hand shake. "Deal!" he said as he shakes Brandon's hand.

Besides Kent Mooney and Allen J. Sunn, Brandon Hart was the next to work as a front man for the Lassenberry organization. In no time, Brandon sold most of the first shipment of Boeman cars faster than expected. Sir Edward cut the cost of the vehicles by a small percentage. A $32,000.00 Boeman Sedan would be sold for $23,000.00 off the lot. This resulted in Sir Edward opening 5 more dealerships throughout the Tri-state area, going by the name of Hart Boeman dealers. The public had no idea that Sir Edward was the man behind it all.

It was December of the same year, when Maggie had decided to put the family estate up for sale. The lassenberry estate was appraised as t 18 million dollars.

The whereabouts of Danny jr. were still unknown. Sir Edward promised his father that he'd use all of his power on the streets to find him. Danny senior's faith in his brother was growing thinner by the day.

Popularity in what was left of the Gatano crime family was waning more towards Gino Massoni at this time. The Rago boy's aggressive and underhanded ways towards other crew members was the last straw. It was settled. The whole Rago crew had to go. To show that he wasn't out to be the big boss, Gino decided on a 3 man ruling panel. Gino, Mario Felini and the ailing Frankie Depalma would bring stability back to the family.

It was February of 98 when the Rago crew were hanging out at a sports bar ran by brother Carmine. The actual owner of the sports bar was former drug dealer Brendan Colt, who fell victim to Carmine after failing to pay the vig on a loan. There were only members of the Rago crew, and about a dozen strippers hired to entertain them. For some reason, the catered food arrived a couple of hours after the party began. Carmine was pissed. He had his brothers and

14 soldier and associates to impress. Once the food arrived, everyone was buzzed and starving. Carmine grabbed Brendan and pulled him in the back room. "I'm drunk and hungry right now! But, tomorrow we're gonna have a talk about who's the boss around here! Understand?" Carmine shouted. Brendan just frowned from the smell of alcohol on Carmine's breath. "Do you understand?" Carmine shouted. "I got it Carmine! I understand!" Brendan said as he trembled. "Now get the fuck out of here before I rip your head off!" Carmine shouted. Brendan decided to use the back door to leave in order not to get harassed by the others in the bar. Carmine staggers back to the party. He already sees a few of the guys and strippers passed out. "Cock suckers can't hold their liquor!" Carmine said to one of his soldiers. Carmine helped himself to the food as well. "You have to try this garlic bread sweetie!" one of the stripper said to carmine. Carmine was so drunk, that he grabbed a handful of garlic bread and sopped it in a small container of gravy. While eating, carmine didn't notice his brother Bernard slumped over the bar counter, or one of the strippers standing behind him drop to the floor. As carmine kept eating, bodies kept dropping. He began to feel dizzy and nauseous. He looked at the bartenders, and pulled out his pistol. "You fuckers trying to kill me?" carmine shouted. The bartenders put their hands up and looked terrified. Carmine grabbed a glass that someone was drinking out of. "Alright! Drink it! Drink it or I'll blow your fucking heads off! He shouted. The bartenders were scared to drink after looking around the bar, but were more scared of getting shot. Carmine was getting so weak, that he had to lean on the bar counter. "That's it! Keep drinking out of every fucking glass! If I go, you go!" carmine slurred. One of the bartenders noticed him foaming at the mouth. The bartenders look at each other. "Are you getting sick?" one bartender asked the others. "No. just buzzed a little." One of them uttered. "I'm fine too." Said the other bartender. Simultaneously, all 3 bartenders look over at the display of food. One of the bartenders quickly grabs the phone and dials 911.

The next day, news reporters on the scene were standing outside the sports bar. They were told by local authorities that the deaths were caused by the combination of Cyanide and Arsenic poisoning.

The bartenders, in their police report stated that the only person that was there that night besides the dead was the owner Brendan Colt. Brendan was hiding out a few miles away in the basement of Gino's adult cinema down in Newark, he was told that the doors would be unlocked, and to make his way to the basement after the job was done. Moments later, gino shows up. He goes down into the basement. "Now, we gotta get you outta the country!" gino said. "When you said I could make a million bucks from this, how could I fucking resist?" Brendan chuckled. "I got your passport! I made it myself!" Gino said. "You did what?" Brendan shouted. "Take it easy! I've been making fake documents for the family since I could remember!" gino said. Brendan was nervous. Gino could see it in his eyes. "Hurry man!" Brendan shouted. "Ok! It's right here in the bag of money!" gino said as he walks toward the duffle bag. Instead of pulling out a passport, he pulls out a pistol with a silencer attached. He then points it at Brendan. Brendan starts breathing uncontrollably. "Hey man! I did what you told me to do!" Brendan cried. "And I appreciate it! But, I can't risk anything coming back full circle pal. Gino said calmly. Brendan drops to his knees, and starts begging for his life. "Sorry." Gino said after he pulled the trigger.

There was a small room in gino's basement. He enters the room and comes out with a bundle of plastic. He neatly lays it flat on the floor. He goes back into the room and comes back out with a butcher's knife. Gino gets undressed down to his underwear. Being out of shape, it became a chore for him just to get on his knees. He struggles to roll the body on to the plastic. Gino starts dry heaving after he raises the knife above his head, hesitating for a moment. He then brings the knife down with hard force. The blow severs the head causing blood the spew from the neck. Gino struggles to his feet. He runs as fast as he can back into the small room. He comes out with an arm full of dirty rags and trash bags. He then drops some of the rags on the floor next to the pool of blood. With his feet, he tries to soak up the blood so it doesn't spread across the floor. He pulls a muscle in his lower back trying to pick up the blood soaked rags. He stuffs the rags into a trash bag. He shoves the rest of the rags in the opening of the neck. While wrapping the body up, he hears the phone ring off in the distance. "Son of a bitch!" gino shouted. His recent weight gain tires him out before he could get to the top of the stairs. He finally gets to the phone. "Hello!" he shouts. "The sick man wants to see us, now!" said the man on the other end. Gino slams the phone down. "Shit!" gino shouted.

An hour had passed. Gino finally arrives at Frankie Depalma's estate. Parked across the street, he surveys the area. Gino sees a half dozen men he doesn't recognize dressed in suits standing outside the gates. He's relieved to see 3 of Mario's boys standing over in the distance smoking cigarettes. Gino turns off the engine. He checks himself in the rear view mirror. He exits the car. "Mr. Massoni! Can you bring the car through the gate?" one of the soldiers shouted from across the street. Gino was shocked. He didn't expect that kind of welcome. He gets back into his car and drives up to the gate. The gates open and gino drives through. One of the soldiers opens the car door for gino. "Follow me Mr. Massoni!" said one of the soldiers. Gino fixes his neck-tie with a smile on his face and follows the man to the main entrance. He leads gino down into the basement, down a dark corridor. "Where the hell we're going? To china?" gino chuckled. They approach a door. "Here we are." The soldier said. The man opens the door where he and gino see Frankie Depalma and Mario Felini sitting across from him at a table. "You're late!" Mario said. The man that came in with Gino leaves the room, closing the door. "Take a seat." Frankie said. Next to Frankie was as box of tissues, a glass of water and a bottle of prescription pills. He grabs a couple of tissues to cover his mouth when he coughs. Gino takes a seat. Frankie clears his throat. "So, it's done?" Frankie asked gino. He doesn't answer. Frankie turns to the video monitor. I see you came alone. That's not good." Frankie said. "I'm a boss now!" Gino said. "That's even more of a reason to have men guarding you!" Frankie said while coughing. "Come on! You see my people outside!" Mario said. Frankie takes a sip of water. "Listen! What's done is done, as far as I'm concern! Let's just split everything 3 ways and be done with it!" Gino said. "Well for starters! I'm taking the Montclair strip!" said Mario. "I don't give a shit. Take it. Gino said nonchalantly. "I'm bumping Paul Rita up to capo." Mario said. "I think you should hold off on that for now." Frankie said. "What for?" Mario asked. "I think we gotta enough chiefs for now." Said Frankie. "How many men we got on the roster anyway?" Gino asked. "Including the guys outside, about 40." Mario said. "Jesus!" Frankie said. "Funny, hearing the media yesterday still calling us the Gatano crime family, when every gatano was blown to smithereens!" said Mario. "Good! It keeps our names out of the papers." Frankie said. "Well, since we cleared that up, let's talk about the Lassenberry matter." Mario said while rubbing his hands together. "What about it?" Frankie asked. "Correct me if I'm wrong, but rumor has it those mooks were kicking up mill a year to the old man! 5 million a year! I say we go knock on some doors and tell them to pay up!" Mario said. Gino looked nervous. He knew if the crew went after the lassenberry people, he'd be found out being a part of the conspiracy. "It's true about the amount. But, I think we should let that deal die with the Don. If it weren't Benny Lassenberry, there wouldn't be a Gatano crime family." Frankie said. "I second it!" Gino said with haste. "So drop it!" Frankie said. "Fuck!" Mario shouted as he slammed his hand on the table causing Frankie's bottle of pills to topple over. A sigh of relief falls upon Gino. "So what else is there?" Frankie asked. Well, since it's just us running things now. Don't you think it's time to arrange a sit down with the commission?" gino said. "Yeah. We gotta let them know we're still alive and kicking." Frankie said while coughing. Frankie taps gino on the arm to get his attention. Frankie points toward a bottle of Sambuca and 3 shot glasses over in the corner of the room sitting on a wooden stand. Gino goes over to retrieve the items. He comes back and fills each shot glass. All 3 men stand and raise their glasses. "Viva la famiglia Gatano!" Frankie shouted. "Viva la famiglia Gatano!" Mario and gino shouted. Salute! All 3 men shout. They tap glasses and gulp down their drinks.

CHAPTER 10. DIAZ

lsewhere in the back of a bodega in Elizabeth, New Jersey, Mark Vasquez jr., a.k.a Mookie sits with his second-in-command, Antonio Diaz, a.k.a Tony Diablo. Diaz had just arrived with 2 grocery bags filled with cash. "Esta lassenberry venta mierda se debe hacer de la magia! Imagínese si nos encontramos todo!" said Diaz. "I know what you saying, but we gotta good life. I don't wanna screw it up cause of greed." Said Mookie. He gets up from his seat and grabs a candy bar from out of one of the boxes. "Data prisa sobrino! Vamos a contar este dinero para que podamos alimentar a las tropas!" said Diaz. "Chill! I didn't eat all day!" Mookie shouted. Mookie not only takes the candy bar, but opened another box filled with bags of potato chips. He takes out 2 bags. He walked towards the front of the store to grab a bottle of soda from the refrigorator. He walks back to where Diaz was sitting. Diaz just emptied the bags of money on the table. Mookie licks the chocolate off of his fingers and helps Diaz count the money. "My son got an A in his science class!" said Mookie. "Yo sabía que ese chico era inteligente." Said Diaz. "My little is girl smart too, but she's stubborn as hell like her mother!" Mookie said. "Ningún hombre! Ella se parece a su padre!" Diaz chuckled. "Fuck you!" Mookie chuckled. As Mookie is counting the money, he noticed something odd about some of the bills. "Some of these 20's and 10's look like play money!" he said to Diaz. Suddenly, they hear the bell chime at the front entrance. "I thought you locked up out front?" said Mookie. Diaz didn't utter a word. Mookie reaches into one of the pockets of his jacket that was hanging on the back of his chair. He pulls out a snub nose revolver. He stands to his feet. "Why ain't you pulling out your piece?" Mookie whispered. Diaz sighs. He pulls out his pistol that was stuffed in the back of his belt. "Quédate aquí! Voy a ir echar un vistazo!" Diaz whispered. Diaz slowly walks out between the isles of food with his gun raised at the ready. He walks out of Mookie's line of sight. "Diablo! Diablo!" Mookie whispered. Before Mookie could get a response, he is ambushed by 2 gun men.

They both wore black leather gloves and ski masks with goggles having darkened lenses. They both were dressed down in black army fatigues and wearing Kevlar vests. Their weapon of choice were 2 AK-47 machine guns.

When Mookie saw these 2 gun men coming towards him, he screamed out for Diaz. He could hear his own heat beat out of fear. Mookie took aim and got off 2 shots. The gun men were still charging at him. They stopped and the shots started. Mookie was sprayed with a barrage of bullets. The force of the gunfire threw Mookie back into the air. He ends up landing on boxes of toilet paper. The gunfire ceased. One of the gun men makes the sign of the cross. The other gun man walks over to the body and kneels down. "Vamos hombre! Vamos Ahora!" the gun man in the back ground shouted. The gun man kneeling over Mookie's body snatches his diamond studded chain from around his neck and then takes off the diamond pinky ring given to his father by benny lassenberry. The 2 gun men then make a dash for the exit, where a car with tinted windows was waiting out front. They both jump in the car, which starts spinning its tires for a few seconds because of the snow covered ground. From out of nowhere, Diaz comes running out side and tosses his gun down the storm drain in the gutter. He screams for help. "Ayuda! Ayuda! Alguien por favor ayuda!" he shouted.

A couple of hours later, Sir Edward is sitting in his favorite chair watching TV. He has the remote in one hand, and a glass of vodka in the other. It was about noon.

Breaking New! Streams across the bottom of the TV screen. "This is Carmen Santiago of channel 12 news! Just when you thought the drug war has ceased on the streets of New Jersey, a brutal shooting here in Elizabeth leaves one alleged drug dealer in critical condition!" she said. The camera man showed the bodega owned by Mookie blocked off with tape. 2 uniformed police officers stand guard by the entrance.

Sir Edward clicks the mute button on the TV. He fills his glass to the rim with vodka. He starts pacing back-n-forth. There's a knock on the door. "Come in!" he shouted. 2 Gunz bursts in. "Oh shit! I just got word Mookie got hit!" Gunz shouted. "Calm down nigga! I just watched it on TV!" said Sir Edward. 2 Gunz pounds his fists together. "We gonna war boss?" he asked. Sir Edward takes a sip of his drink. "Let the Latinos handle that. Just get the word out to our people to stay on high alert, and get ready for anything. Now go." He said. 2 Guns nods his head, and then leaves. Sir Edward sits and thinks for a moment. He picks up the phone he presses one button. He hears 3 rings. "Jenkins residence." The voice said. "It's me! Put the old man on the phone!" said Sir Edward. A few seconds pass. "Jabbo speaking!" he said. "Get the others together and meet me at the number 3 spot at 8pm, sharp!" Sir Edward ordered. He hangs up the phone.

After the last encounter with National Agreement, sir Edward told his guys Jabbo, Mookie, Butch and Dubbs to meet at one of the 5 secret meeting places in case of an emergency situation. The Kenilworth warehouse, the old Elizabeth warehouse, the new spots were inside a gas station in Newton. New Jersey a garage in Ocean View and the generator room at Cherry Hill Mall.

Sir Edward goes to the door and opens it. "I'm gonna take a nap. Wake me up at 6 and have the car ready for me." He ordered. "Got it boss!" said Gunz. Sir Edward slams the door shut. He enters Charlie's bedroom. Charlie is lying in bed with a black eye and swollen lip watching TV. "Be dressed before 6! We gotta meeting!" he says to Charlie. Sir Edward heads to his room. Falls back on his king size bed. He stares at the ceiling. He hears a thump outside his room. Suddenly, the door is kicked open by Charlie. He comes running in the bedroom wearing nothing but his boxers. "You bitch! I do everything for you! Charlie screams. Charlie then tackles Sir Edward before he can get out of bed. Charlie balls up his fists and starts pounding on his boss. Sir Edward grabs on to Charlie's wrists. He flips Charlie on the bed. Sir Edward had a smile on his face, while Charlie has tears in his eyes. Outside in the hallway, Gunz can hear the bumping around in the apartment. He does nothing. He just sits there reading a magazine. He turns the page and sees an ad for Galaxy refrigerators at discount prices. Inside the apartment, Charlie gets one hand free and grabs Sir Edward by the testicles. He screams. He released Charlie. Charlie starts pounding away at his boss's face. "I hate you! "I hate you!" Charlie shouted. He gives Charlie a karate chop to the neck. Charlie starts gasping for air. Sir Edward falls to the floor, cradling his sore private parts.

It was around 7:30 pm. Butch arrived at the number 3 spot first. It was the gas station in Newton. At the spot, was an over the hill, scruffy looking biker named Tex who managed the gas station. Since this was part of Butch's territory, Tex has been buying dope from him since Butch took over. Tex had a good set up. He would make a transaction with customers when they'd come to fill up their gas tank. Tex fooled everyone that drove by the station. 95% of his customers were locals. His customers lived in an upper middle class to moderately wealthy community. A top executive working on Wall Street, who was one of his most lucrative customers, spent at least 5 grand a week on cocaine. From Doctors to soccer moms. Tex had them all hooked. The dive bar nearby, which was managed by Allen J. Sunn, was packed every Friday and Saturday by these patrons.

"What up my man?" Butch said to Tex. Both men shake hands. Butch noticed Tex wearing dingy oiled stained jeans, worn down hiking boots with a torn long sleeve flannel shirt. "For a guy making a shit load of money, you sure love the homeless look." Butch said. "Gotta keep up appearances!" Tex chuckled. Tex walked over and retrieved a soda from out of the vending machine. "Want one?" he asked butch. "No, I'm cool." Butch said. "You're kinda early. I don't need a refill yet." Tex said. "No man. I need this place for an hour at least." Butch said. Tex sips his soda. "Saw on TV about that Spanish kid getting shot up. He should be dead! AK-47 was it?" Tex asked. "I guess some people just lucky. Damn, it's cold out here!" said Butch.

My people gonna be here any minute. That means you gonna have to check out for a while." Butch said. "Ok! Ok! Just let me lock up the office! You can use the garage!" said Tex. Butch went checking out his surroundings and sees nothing but wooded area and road. The sun was setting. "Ok now! Just lock up when you're done! I'm about to go get a drink. Sent the wife and mother-in-law to Hawaii for 2 weeks! Now I'm in paradise!" Tex chuckled. Butch just shook his head smiling. Tex hops in his pick-up truck. As soon as Tex drives off, 2 vehicle approach in the opposite direction. The first car is driven by jabbo's driver, with jabbo sitting in the back seat. The second car, which was a jeep, was being driven by Butch's cousin Dubbs. Jabbo's driver pulls up to the garage. Dubbs drives up by one of the gas pumps. Dubbs gets out of ride and approaches his big cousin. They hug each other. "Shit! My man still alive!" Dubbs said. "Yeah! But for how long?" Butch responded. Jabbo's driver gets out of the car, then opens the door for jabbo. He grabs jabbo's cane and assists him out of the back seat. Jabbo gets out laughing. "This fool tell you he done got lost on the way here?" jabbo chuckled. "You got lost man?" Butch asked Dubbs. "No man! It was no fucking sign on the exit!" Dubbs said. "He tried to make a U-turn off the fucking ramp! He almost made ol' jabbo piss his pants!" jabbo chuckled. "You probably pissed yo self anyway, and just don't know it! Goddamn fossil!" said Dubbs. Jabbo looked at butch. "What he called ol' jabbo?" jabbo asked. "Come on y'all! Let's get inside out of the cold!" butch said as he gets between his cousin and jabbo. "No! I wanna know what the hell he called ol' jabbo!" jabbo shouted. "He ain't mean nothing by it!" butch chuckled. All 4 men, including jabbo's driver enter the garage.

Minutes later, Sir Edward pulls up in a brand new 98 Boeman Sedan. His is sitting in the back seat, while Charlie drives. Charlie parks right next to Dubbs's jeep. Sir Edward is wearing dark shades to cover another black eye. Charlie looks in the rear view mirror. "I'm sorry!" Charlie said to Sir Edward. He says nothing. Sir Edward just puts his hand on Charlie's shoulder. Charlie grabs his hand, and then kisses the back of it. "Keep the heat on so you don't freeze to death." Sir Edward said as he exits the vehicle. Sir Edward buttons up his trench coat while walking to the garage door entrance. He sees everyone has shown up. "You! Go wait in the car!" Sir Edward says to jabbo's driver. The driver looks over at jabbo. Jabbo gives him the signal to leave. The driver leaves. "Nobody comes to these meetings without wearing my father's rings! You know better old man!" sir Edward shouted. Jabbo stays silent. He just gives a nod. "We all know why we're here. "I'm telling y'all now, I ain't had shit to do with what happened to that kid!" sir Edward shouted. He looks at Butch. "Come on now! Hell no!" Butch shouted. Sir Edward points to Dubbs. "Wasn't me!" said Dubbs. He then points to jabbo. "Boy! You better get yo finger outta jabbo's face!" said jabbo. "Well it's settled then! We're all innocent!" said Sir Edward. "The only one I could think that would do some shit like that is Diablo! Word on the street, was Diablo would always try to punk Mookie in front of everybody!" said Dubbs. "Jabbo thinks he's right!" said jabbo. Sir Edward folds his arms. Suddenly, a station wagon pulls up to the pump. The guys hear the horn blowing. "Go tell whoever it is, we're closed!" Sir Edward ordered Dubbs. Dubbs runs outside. Know says a word. They wait for Dubbs to come back. Seconds later, Dubbs returns. "It was some old white couple." Dubbs said. "So, if it's true about Diablo, we gotta handle it!" Butch said. "Well, somebody from that crew gotta approach me with a shit load of cash in order to get a refill." sir Edward said as he strokes his goatee. "I guarantee Mookie was on his way to get a refill too!" said Dubbs. "Whoever comes with the money better be wearing my father's ring!" sir Edward said. "What's that gonna prove?" Butch asked. "Simple brother. If they don't come with a ring, I can refuse the refill and give them a day or 2 to come back with a ring. We question how they got their hands on the ring, and take it from there." Sir Edward said. "Ok then! Everybody agree?" butch shouted. Dubbs and jabbo both give a nod. "Ok then. This meeting is over." Said Sir Edward. All the guys leave the garage. Butch locks up the garage. They all get in their vehicles. Jabbo's car leads the way down the road, heading south. "I want you to go to the hospital where Mookie is staying tonight, and find out if he's wearing my father's ring." Sir Edward ordered Charlie. Charlie nods.

It's was 10pm when Sir Edward and Charlie arrive at the trauma center in Elizabeth. Charlie pulls into the underground garage. "Now go find Mookie and see if he's got the ring." Sir Edward said. Charlie takes the underground elevator to the main level. He heads to the receptionist's desk. "Ah, could you tell me what room Mark Vasquez is in?" Charlie asked.

The receptionist checks the computer. "Sorry sir. Mr. Vasquez is under tight security. Only immediate family can visit." The receptionist explained. Charlie walks away. He sits in the visitors section of the lobby. He knows going back to the car without the information is unacceptable. He sees a custodian walking by. He follows the custodian down the hall. Charlie sees the old black man head to the cleaning locker. The custodian grabs a handful of trash bags. Before he slams the door to the locker shut, Charlie runs behind him and grabs the door knob before it slams shut. The custodian didn't notice a thing. Charlie ducks inside the cleaning locker. He sees a pair of coveralls hanging on a hook. He puts them on. He found it difficult to wear because he tall and slim. The coveralls were made for someone short. Charlie comes out of the closet pushing a bucket and mop. Instead of asking someone for Mookie's whereabouts, he takes the elevator to every floor until he gets to the 4th floor. He finds that Mookie's room is being guarded by 2 uniformed police officers. Charlie quickly sneaks pass the nurses sitting at the desk. He walks up to the police officers. "Excuse me! Gotta empty the waste can?" Charlie stuttered. "I think somebody already came in and did it." Said one of the officers. "Looks like you need a new pair of coveralls!" the other officer chuckled. Charlie starts laughing too. "I gotta check to make sure! I'm the new guy around here! My supervisor crazy as hell!" Charlie chuckled. The officer cracks open the door. He looks inside the room. "Make it quick." Said the officer. Charlie runs in real quick. He sees Mookie lying in bed unconscious with a tube coming out of his neck. He sees that Mookie is dependent on the machine to keep him alive. Charlie then focuses on the mission. He checks both of Mookie's hands and sees there is no ring. He checks the stands and sees nothing. He rushes out of the room, right pass the officers. One of the officers just shook his head. "That guy is weird!" said one of the officers. Charlie takes the elevator down to the main lobby. He finds the cleaning locker was locked. He had to get his pants out of there. He also had to wait until the custodian showed up to open it. After 15 minutes of ducking the hospital staff, a custodian opened the locker to retrieve something. Charlie saw the chance to make his move. Just like before, he runs behind the custodian, into the cleaning locker and grabs his close. He makes a dash for the elevator. Inside the elevator he takes off the coveralls and puts on his pants. He hits the G button on the elevator panel. When he gets down to the garage, he runs around like a chicken with his head cut off looking for the car. He even runs outside the garage. He hears a screeching sound of tires coming from around the corner. The car pulls up in front of him. "Get in fool!" sir Edward shouted. Charlie jumps in the passenger side. Sir Edward pulls off. As they were driving down the street, Sir Edward turns to Charlie. "So, what you see?" he asked Charlie. "Nothing!" said Charlie. Enraged, Sir Edward punches the middle of the steering wheel. "Ok! Now we know!" he said.

The next day around 10 in the morning, Eddie and jabbo take a ride out to Lincroft, New Jersey. This was where Mookie's girlfriend and kids resided.

Mookie purchased a 2 million dollar home for his kids' right after his father's demise. Buying the house for his kids took his mind off the horrible act he had committed.

Sir Edward called in advance before visiting Mookie's family. He and jabbo arrive at the house he tells Charlie, who was the driver to stay in the car. "Where are all the bodyguards?" Sir Edward asked jabbo. Charlie gets out and assists jabbo out of the car. Jabbo and Sir Edward walk up to the main entrance. Jabbo presses the doorbell. Seconds later, a little girl opens the door. "Sir Edward and jabbo smile at the girl. "Hola princesa! ¿Dónde Está tu mama?" sir Edward the little girl. She runs back inside. A few seconds later, Sir Edward and jabbo eyes pop out of their heads when they see this sexy, beautiful, almond skinned young woman come to the door. "Can I help you?" she asked. Sir Edward noticed that her eyes were all puffy from crying. "I'm jabbo and this is my boss." Jabbo said. "I know who you are! What do you want?" she asked. "Usted debe ser Rita." Sir Edward said. "Oh! Usted habla el idioma!" Rita said. "Can we come in for a moment? He asked.

Rita was of Afro-Cuban descent. She and Mookie hooked up right after he came home from incarceration. She like all the other young Latino girls in the old neighborhood were rushing in line to be with Mookie.

"Podemos hablar aquí!" Rita said. Voy a ir directo ai punto. ¿Tomaste un anillo del dedo Mookie Después de lo que pasó? He asked. "Su madre y me preguntaban unos a otros donde estabas el anillo!" she said. "Could y'all speak English while ol' jabbo standing here?" jabbo asked. "¿Podemos hacer este Viejo tonto un favor por favor?" Sir Edward asked Rita. Rita smiled. "See! I knew there was a smile in there somewhere!" Sir Edward chuckled. "Mookie did tell me that it was a gift from your father to his." Rita said. "It was. Whoever took the ring, must have something to do with Mookie being shot. Did you see any one in his crew wearing it?" Sir Edward asked.

At that moment, Mookie's son, Mark the 3rd comes running to the door. "¿Quiénes son estas personas mommy?" the little boy asked. "Retrocede en la casa con su hermana!" Rita tells her son. Little mark runs back in the house.

Everyone suddenly hears salsa music blasting down the street. The music gets louder and louder. Sir Edward turns to see 2 pimped out low riders coming up the driveway. One was rust colored, the other was dark green. Both vehicles looked custom built. In the first car were only 2 guys. The one in the passenger seat was Diablo himself. The other car had 4 of Diaz's soldiers in it

"You packing old man?" Sir Edward whispered to jabbo. "Fuck yeah!" jabbo whispered. Sir Edward slowly undue the top 2 buttons on his trench coat, to gain access to his pistol. Charlie is sitting in the car. He sees the 2 cars. Terrified, he finally gains enough courage to reach into the glove compartment and grab a small revolver. He quickly checks to see if it's loaded. Diaz gets out of the car wearing a long leather shearling coat. ¿Qué pasa señor lassenberry!" Diablo shouted out really loud. Diablo had a big smile on his face. "That's Sir Edward to you!" he says to Diablo. "Hola Rita! ¿Podría entrar en la casa por un minuto? Quiero hablar con el Sr. lassenberry!" Diablo says to Rita. Sir Edward turns to Rita. "Just give us a few minutes. Ok?" he asked Rita. Rita slowly goes back into the house, closing the door. "How many times I gotta tell you son, it's Sir Edward!" he shouted. At this time, Diablo's boys step of out of their car. One of the guys walks to the back of the car and pops open the trunk. Sir Edward pulls out his pistol and points it at the guy. "If you pull out a weapon, you die son!" Sir Edward shouted. "Yo Johnny, frio! Diablo said to his boy. "Así es Johnny, frio!" sir Edward shouted. Diablo opens his coat to show that he's not packing. "See, everything's cool!" Diablo shouted. Antonio Diaz, a.k.a Diablo, slowly walks toward Sir Edward and jabbo. Jabbo pulls out his pistol. "You stay yo ass right there! Ol' jabbo can hear you real good!" jabbo shouted.

Diablo stops in his tracks. "I just came to check on rita and the kids!" he shouted. "She's good! They're all good!" sir Edward shouted. "Since you're here, I just wanna say I'll be running things until Mookie pulls through!" Diablo shouted. "Cover me!" sir Edward whispered to jabbo. Sir Edward walks toward Diablo. He doesn't see a ring on either hand. They come face-to-face. "Until I see my father's ring on your finger, no refill!" sir Edward said. "What the fuck you talking about, no refill! I got a million in cash to give you old man!" Diablo said. "I wipe my ass with a million dollars." Sir Edward said. Diablo starts to look desperate. "Listen! I'll throw in a hundred grand out of my own pocket! I need that refill!" Diablo pleaded. Sir Edward puts his mouth to Diablo's ear. "No ring! No dope! And don't even think about looking for another connection!" he whispered in Diablo's ear. "Jabbo! Let's go!" said Sir Edward. Jabbo puts away his pistol. He and Sir Edward walk back to the car. Charlie breathes a sigh of relief. Diablo looked fired up. "Vamos a conseguir el infierno fuera de aquí antes de que mate a Alguien!" Diablo shouts to his crew.

It was March 15th, and the snow started melting all around. Mark lassenberry sr. decided to gather his wife and 3 kids to go out for a ride to visit some friends in Alpine, New Jersey.

At this time, mark jr. was 34, Corey was 28 and his only daughter terry, was18 years old. Mark sr. had rented a stretch limousine so he could enjoy the scenery of this lavish part of the Garden State. Mark sr. was sitting next to his wife Tasha, while mark Jr. Corey and terry sat across from them.

Mark sr. told the chauffeur to pull over on the side of the road. His kids looked confused. Daddy! Why are we pulling over? I thought your friends lived a couple of miles away from here!" Terry asked. "I just feel like going for a walk with my family through this beautiful town! I can lose a couple of pounds as well!" mark sr. chuckled. They all get out of the limo.

Mark jr. was wearing a Taylor made suit, with a mock turtle neck sweater. He was wearing a watch worth about 30 grand, a matching pinky ring worth about 15 grand. He kneeled down to wipe off his gator shoes he said he paid a grand for. Corey was wearing jeans and a leather jacket he paid 2 grand for. He had a pair 600 dollar pair of sneakers on. The thing that made Corey stand out, was the 18 inch diamond necklace he was wearing. He was the first on the urban club scene to wear diamonds of the magnitude. A certain hip hop artist saw Corey at a night club and mimicked his style in a rap video. The artist's rented a diamond necklace for his video. This caused a chain reaction for other rap artists to step up their jewelry game. Corey was also the first to have a custom medallion with his likeness on it. The medallion made totally out of diamonds. Corey told his brother mark that he saved all of his envelopes for a year to purchase the necklace and medallion, which came to the total of $250 thousand dollars. He also had a matching diamond ring and watch which totaled 50 grand. Corey and his siblings never worked a day in their lives and enjoyed splurging on the money they've received from their grandfather, now their uncle.

Terry stepped out of the limo sporting a chinchilla jacket, her parents bought her for a birthday present worth about 18 grand. She was wearing regular jeans she had tucked into her knee high, spiked heeled boots worth about 2 grand. Terry grew up to be a very attractive young lady. Friends and family members told her that she looked like her grandmother on her father's side. When she went off to school in Europe, she decided to cut her long wavy hair.

When she walked, it was like looking at a runway model. She stood about 5 feet, 7 inches tall with an hour glass figure. Her father would always tell her that she was her grandmother with a tan.

The family walked down the quiet road reminiscing how it was before terry left for school. Mark sr. stopped in front of the gate of an estate. The driveway had to be as long as 2 football fields, leading to an enormous mansion. "Why are we stopping daddy?" terry asked. Her mother Tasha just smiled. Corey and mark jr. had a confused look on their faces. "Oh, I almost forgot!" said mark senior. He reached in the inside pocket of his Gabardine trench coat and pulled out a thick white envelope. "Jabbo dropped this off a few days ago, and to tell you happy belated birthday!" mark sr. chuckled. Terry takes the envelope. "Daddy! Is this what I think it is?" she asked. "It sure is baby! Your first envelope!" her father chuckled. She opens the flap of the envelope and sees it was stuffed with cash. "Welcome to the club little sis!" Corey said. "Thank you daddy!" she screamed as she hugged her father. "Don't thank me! Thank your uncle Eddie!" her father said. " I got my first envelope! I got my first envelope! " terry chanted as she danced around her family. Mark jr. just sighed. "That's not all young lady!" said her father. Mark sr. unlatched the hook on the gate of the estate. He starts to walk up the driveway. His wife Tasha follows. "Hey pop! Where're you going?" mark jr. asked. "You kids ask too many questions! Just follow me!" mark sr. shouted.

The driveway was made of cobble stone. There were shrubs lined up on either side that needed trimming. There were many tall trees on the property that shaded most of the area. "Man, this looks like the set of a haunted house movie!" Corey said. "You sound like a bitch!" Mark jr. whispered to his brother. Corey punches his brother in the arm. "You hit like one too!" mark jr. chuckled. Feeling fatigue, mark sr. finally comes within sight of the mansion.

The mansion resembled the white house in one form or another, having 4 giant columns. The 2 level home displayed a loggia on the upper level, supported by columns. The front steps were grandiose, with only 7 steps that stretched from one end of the mansion to the other. The entrance to the mansion had double doors measuring close to 20 feet in height. The mansion's had a sold sticker covering the for sale sign.

"Who lives here daddy?" terry asked. Mark sr. pulled out a set of keys from his pocket and handed them over to terry. She started jumping up and down, screaming at the top of her lungs like crazy. She hugs both of her parents and makes a dash to the front entrance. Terry almost fall trying to run in her spiked heels. "Be careful sweet heart!" her mother shouted. The first thing terry noticed when entering the house, was the spiral staircase. Her family calmly walks enters the mansion. "When did you do this pop?" mark sr. asked. "I tried to have it ready before her birthday, but I couldn't seal the deal in time." Mark sr. explained.

A few weeks had passed, and Diablo was approached by all 10 of Mookie's street bosses. They had collectively given Diablo a quarter of a million dollars for the refill after the scene at Rita's house. Diablo felt a sense of hostility in the air. They all met at a Latino night club in Union City owned by Diablo called Salsa 100. "Diablo hombre, ¿qué Está tomando tanto tiempo? Tengo personas que padecen hambre a la calle!" Ricardo Salazar said. "Yo man, y'all niggas gotta talk English!" said Brian Cooper, a.k.a Wiz. "Yeah, you Spanish boys gotta change it up when we come around!" said Greg Thomas, a.k.a Tip.

Wiz and Tip were the only 2 black guys in Mookie's crew. Wiz ran Communipaw Avenue in Jersey City at first. He was then told to split Hillside, New Jersey with tip, who had control of Hoboken, Bayonne and Secaucus.

Diablo was pissed at what wiz said. "You black boys only here because Mookie let you stay around! Guess what? Mookie ain't here!" Diablo said. Wiz and Tip finally realized they were surrounded by Latinos. Wiz didn't care, even though he was scrawny, weighing no more than 150 pounds. He was about to rush Diablo until Tip, who was burly and 6 feet, 5 inches tall jumped in between them. Diablo reached for his pistol. "Chill! I'm here to get my refill, not die!" Tip said to Diablo. Diablo slowly puts his gun away. "I'm running low on product!" Wiz said. "I need my shit too!" Tip said. Hector Chavez grabs Diablo's attention. "Mi hermano y yo decidimos darle 10 días o que van a las personas lassenberry nosotros mismos!" said Hector.

The Chavez brothers, Hector and Pablo ran the streets of Union City for Mookie. The brothers were of Cuban descent. Their youngest brother Joe, a.k.a Pescado was killed last summer at a house party out in the Bronx. It was said that Latino gang members were behind it. Hector wanted to take a couple of his runners to the Bronx and settle the score, but Diablo told hector to stand down because it might affect business. Diablo eased the pain of the Chavez family a little by funding an elaborate funeral service and having a family plot constructed for him.

"Recordamos lo que hizo por nuestro familia, pero loss negocios son los negocios." Hector said before both brothers leave the club. Diablo becomes fired up. He starts lashing out. "Todo el mundo obtener el infierno fuera de aquí! Voy a tener tu maldito rellenar!" Diablo shouted. The rest of the crew leave as well. "Usted tiene 10 días hombre! 10 días! Ricardo Salazar said before he spits on the floor. He's the last to walk out.

Diablo paces back-n- forth. He felt the weight of the world on his shoulders. Mookie was in a coma, the crew wanted their refill in 10 days, and Sir Edward wanted to see a ring before the Vasquez crew gets the refill.

The next morning, Sir Edward orders Charlie to get the car ready. He wanted to go out for a ride. He told Charlie he wanted to drive out to his parent's estate. About 45 minutes later, they arrive at the estate. Sir Edward tells Charlie to drive up to the gate. Even though the estate was for sale, Sir Edward kept an armed guard on the payroll the patrol the grounds to keep out thieves and vandals.

Sir Edward didn't visit the estate much, but when he did, he loved to see his nieces and nephews runs around playing. He told Charlie to stay in the car as he entered the mansion. He walks around. He reminisces on the early days when the house was full of life. He reminisced on seeing his mother sitting in the den watching her favorite TV show. He remembered the time his father sat at the head of the table during the holiday season when they were kids. He missed seeing the 10 foot tall Christmas tree standing in the middle of the living room. After walking through the mansion from top to bottom, Sir Edward becomes infuriated when he sees the family coat-of-arms in the corner of the basement covered with tarp. Sir Edward carries the precious art work out of the basement. He wipes off the thin layer of dust and props it on the mantle of the fireplace. Still outraged, he storms out of the mansion. He walks over to the car, Charlie is sitting and reading a magazine. "Where's my phones?" he asked Charlie.

"You left it in the back seat!" said Charlie. Sir Edward reaches through the window and grabs his mobile phone. He punches in digits. After 4 rings, someone picks up. "Royalty Realty. Carol Haims speaking." The lady answered. "Yeah! This is Sir Edward Lassenberry!" he said. "Excuse me!" Carol said. "I said this is Sir Edward lassenberry, calling about the lassenberry estate in Cherry Hill! He shouted. "Could you please hold for a second?" she asked. Sir Edward sighs after the elevator music comes on. "Hello! Mr. Lassenberry?" the voice asked. "It's Sir Edward! He shouted. "Yes, of course! This is the Customer service manager Robert Williamson. How can I help you sir?" he asked. "Yeah. I wanna take the lassenberry estate off the market." Said Sir Edward. "But sir! We have 2 possible buyers!" said Williamson. "I don't give a good goddamn! I'm not selling!" he said. "I promise you sir, Royalty Realty will have the estate sold by the end of the week!" said Williamson. "You don't listen, do you?" he said to Williamson. "There is a clause in your contract of a termination fee sir." Williamson said. "Whatever! I'll wire you the fee in a couple of hours!" sir Edward shouted. He hangs up. He gets in the car and tells Charlie to drive up to the security guard. Sir Edward sticks his head out of the window. "Make sure no one comes pass this gate!" he says to the guard. Sir Edward thinks for a moment. He picks up the phone, and dials. The phone rings 3 times. "Jabbo!" the voice said. "I want you to get all my brothers together at the estate Saturday at noon." Sir Edward ordered. "You know you and Danny ain't on good terms." Jabbo said. "Just do what I tell ya!" Sir Edward shouted. Jabbo hangs up. "Let's drive over to that guy who makes our suits for us. What's his name again?" sir Edward asked Charlie. "It's Stephan." Charlie said. "Yeah, that's him. It's time for us to get a wardrobe change Charlie!" sir Edward chuckled.

While Charlie was driving back up north, Sir Edward turns around, looking out the back window. At exit 138 on the Garden State Parkway, he sees something suspicious. "Charlie! Pull over!" he shouted. Charlie quickly dips off to the shoulder of the road. "Keep the engine running!" sir Edward ordered. As cars are zooming by, Sir Edward exits the car. Walking about 20 yards back, a he flags down a black van. The van pulls over. Sir Edward walks toward the passenger side of the van. The tinted window rolls down. Sir Edward see 2 National Agreement agents sitting up front, while the 3rd agent is sitting in a swivel chair facing a control console. "Sir Edward chuckles. "You guys gotta change your routine!" he said. The agent s didn't utter a word. "Look here! Tell your boss that I need to see him tonight around midnight! It's urgent." Sir Edward ordered. He walks away. The agent rolls up the window. The driver pulls off pass the exit. Sir Edward gets back in the car. "To the tailor Charlie." Said sir Edward chuckled.

It's about 3pm, when Charlie and Sir Edward arrive at Stephen's House of Style. It was an upscale men's apparel shop located in the garment district in Manhattan. Stephan's took walk in customers, but his cheapest suit to design cost around 3 grand. Stephan's has fitted suits for mob bosses, A-list celebrities, politicians, Europe and Middle-East royalty. Charlie opens the door to the shop for his boss. They could hear soft jazz music coming from the speakers in the ceiling. The floor was made of thick glass, with different color lights flashing through it. Sir Edward starts snapping his fingers to the music. This place wasn't like a regular men's shop. There were no suits hanging off any coat hangers. They did see mannequins made out of porcelain. The mannequins came in different sizes to represent real men.

Charlie hits the bell on the desk. Seconds later, coming out of the pattern room was no other than Stephan himself. He was way ahead of his time in the fashion world as far as critics were concerned. He was dressed in tight blue jeans, with the cuffs folded up. A plaid long sleeve shirt, with the sleeves rolled up pass his elbows. He wore a suit vest over it and a bow-tie. His shoes were leather winged tips.

"Charlie!" Stephan shouted. "What's up kid?" Charlie shouted. They both give each other a hug. "How's tricks dude?" Stephan asked. "Living life baby!" Charlie chuckled. Sir Edward clears his throat to get attention. "Oh Stephan man, this is my boss sir Edward!" Charlie said. "Well alright!" Stephan said as he lightly shakes Sir Edward's hand. "We can talk about old times later, but Sir Edward got business to discuss with you!" Charlie said. "So sir, what kind of business we're talking?" Stephan asked. "I wanna know how far your fashion sense is in military uniforms?" sir Edward asked. "Ok then!" Stephan said with a confused look on his face. "I want the new uniforms made exclusively for me and my people. No questions asked." Sir Edward "As long as you're paying sweetie, you got it!" Stephan said. "I want me and Charlie to big the first to be outfitted with them." Sir Edward said. "Ok then! First I have to get your measurements." Stephan said as he takes the tape measure from around his neck. He starts with Charlie first. "Would you prefer double breast or single breast jacket?" Stephan asked. "Let's go all out! Double breast." Said Sir Edward. "So what kind of sash would you like?" Stephan asked. "What kind of what?" asked Sir Edward. "It's like a wrap that goes around your waist or over your shoulder." Stephan said. "Oh! You talking about that thing they wear in beauty pageants!" said Sir Edward. "Exactly sweetie!" Stephan sighed. "Well, we'll do both." said Sir Edward. "Now for the colors. What you prefer?" Stephan asked Sir Edward. "Simple black uniform, green and red sash. Oh yeah! I want us to be outfitted with those boots the Germans wore back in World War 2!" sir Edward mentioned. "Oh! You're talking about jack boots?" Stephan asked. "That's what I was thinking about!" said Sir Edward.

An hour later, outside the men's shop, 2 men make themselves known to Sir Edward as he and Charlie leave the shop. They flash their badges. They were federal agents. "Mr. Lassenberry! We're curious. What type of people you're involved with? I ran the plates on that black van and nothing came up on our records." The fed agent said. "I don't know what you're talking about! I thought you feds had yo shit together!" sir Edward said. He and Charlie just walk away.

It was around eight in the evening, Sir Edward was at his place in his underwear and a drink in his hand. He just sent Charlie out for Chinese food. He hears a thumping noise out in the hallway He grabs the remote and turns down the volume. Suddenly, there's a dead silence. Until the door is kicked opened. Sir Edward falls back to the floor. Enters a figure dressed in all black from head to toe. Sir Edward couldn't see the person's face, who was wielding a high powered rifle with a silencer on it. Sir Edward screamed when he saw 2 Gunz slumped over his desk. The dark figure lowers the weapon. Just when Sir Edward thought his demise was at hand, another figure walks through the door. "Terrance?" sir Edward shouted. "Good evening Sir Edward!" Terrance Haggerty chuckled. "What? How did you get up here?" Sir Edward asked. "Didn't you want to have a meeting with me? Well I'm here!" Terrance chuckled. Terrance was dressed like an NA agent. "You killed my men?" sir Edward asked.

"Tranquilizers sir Edward. Tranquilizers. You need to tighten up your security. Now, how can I help you?" he asked Sir Edward. Sir Edward picks himself off the floor, laughing like a mad man. Terrance snaps his fingers and the mysterious figure steps out into the hallway. "You're a deviant after my own heart! Can I get you a drink?" sir Edward chuckled. "Sir Edward. Your people will be awake in about an hour. What do you want?" Terrance said in a more forceful voice. "I need to hire at least 8 of your agents!" sir Edward said. Terrance looked puzzled. "What the hell do you mean hire?" he asked. "I really mean rent them. For Saturday!" Sir Edward said. Terrance sighs. "Very well!" Terrance said. "I need them in their regular black suits, Saturday at my parent's estate!" sir Edward explained. "Your parent's estate? I thought you and your family were selling the place!" said Terrance. Terrance starts laughing. "I'm kidding you! I received word today that you called the realtor!" Terrance chuckled. Terrance looks at his wrist watch. "Well, if there's nothing else, I'll be on my way." He said. "What about my door you kicked in?" sir Edward asked. "Buy a new one! You can afford it!" Terrance chuckled. Terrance turns to leave the apartment. He then stops and turns back facing Sir Edward. "If you ever approach another black van again, I'm gonna make you suffer just a little bit. Those damn feds are hard to shake, ya know." Terrance said in a calm voice. He and his hit man leave and walk down the hallway. They head to the freight elevator. Sir Edward looks at 2 Gunz slumped over the unconscious, and shakes his head. He pours himself another drink.

Up on the roof, Solomon Ellis, a.k.a Church, is just waking up from being shot with a tranquilizer dart. Church has been working for the lassenberry people for 10 years, while serving 2 jail sentences. He worked out on the roof by doing 100 push-ups and a 100 sit-ups. He looked through the scope of his high powered rifle and sees the ground crew waking up off the ground. They were all shot by the tranquilizer gun.

Back at the apartment, Charlie returns with a bag of Chinese take-out. "What happened? A lot of the guys are waking up now off the ground and the floor! What happened to the door?" Charlie asked. Sir Edward sits in his chair and sips on his drink. "If anybody ask. You did it!" sir Edward said.

The day sir Edwards had been waiting for finally arrived. It was Saturday around 1pm. On the Garden State Parkway, a limo filled with passengers heads north to Cherry Hill. The ride to Cherry Hill originated from Delaware. Mark sr., Jake sr., and Danny sr., who was reluctant to come was persuaded by jabbo, who was sitting across from him.

The limo finally arrives at the lassenberry estate. "Who the hell are those guys?" Jake sr. asked jabbo.

The guys Jake sr. were referring to, were 4 NA agents standing at the gate entrance. The limo pulls up to the gate. Jabbo rolls down his window. "Sir Edward is waiting for you inside." Said one agent. The limo pulls up to the main entrance. "Sir Edward?" Danny sr. asked. "You got me little brother!" Jake sr. said as a NA agent opens the limo door for him. "Follow me gentlemen." The NA agent said. "Wait a minute! Who the hell are you people to lead us into our own parent's house?" said Danny sr. to one of the agents. "Danny stop it! I think they're just doing their job!" said mark sr. "Don't let yo mouth get into trouble son!" jabbo whispered in Danny senior's ear.

Inside the mansion, the Lassenberry brothers are told to stand at one side of the bottom of the staircase, while jabbo and his driver Tony stand on the opposite side. There was one agent standing at the top of the steps. He pulls out a folded piece of paper from inside his suit jacket. "Good afternoon gentlemen!" said the agent. The agent unfolds the paper. "For the past 6 decades, the lassenberry name has always been synonymous with great state of New Jersey! It is with honor that I introduce a man with the vision, integrity and drive to take the Lassenberry name and the Great state of New Jersey to new heights! I give you Sir Edward, patriarch of the House of Lassenberry!" the agent shouted. He and the other agents applaud. Jabbo and his driver Tony follow suit. The lassenberry brothers just stand there in awe. Slowly, the man of the hour appears at the top of the staircase. Sir Edward descends from the stairs like some demi-god.

His uniform was all black, in a Gestapo styled fashion. He sported a red shoulder sash, with a green sash around his waist. On his left breast was a medal representing the Order of the Elephant given to him by the same man that knighted him, HM prince Erick of Denmark. His pant legs wear neatly inserted into his polished jack boots. Followed behind him was Charlie wearing the same identical uniform, minus the sashes and the medal. 2 agents followed Charlie down the stairs, both carrying the polished Lassenberry coat-of-arms. Sir Edward stops at the bottom of the stairs. Charlie stands by his side, while the 2 agents stand mid-way on the staircase holding up the coat-of-arms. Sir Edward looks up at the coat-of-arms, and then looks at his brothers. "I found this beautiful work of art in a dark corner of the basement! From this day on, any form of desecration to this work of art, is considered disrespect for what my father spent his life working for!" he shouted. Sir Edward walks over to his brother Danny, with his hands folded behind his back, and stands before him face-to-face. "Anyone showing disrespect to this fine work of art, is showing disrespect to me, continuing my father's work!" he shouts. Sir Edward walks away and stands next to Charlie.

The Jake and mark sr. started to take their brother serious when they see the 6 agents stand at attention as Sir Edward walks by. "I'll only ask each of you once and once! Do I have your undying loyalty and obedience as head of the family?" he said to the lassenberry brothers. He looks toward his brother mark for a response. "Of course brother!" mark sr. said the haste. He then looks at his brother Jake. Jake sighs. "You are the way brother!" he chuckled. He looked over at his brother Danny. Danny doesn't give him the answer he's looking for. "What about my son? What about Nigel? Where the hell are they?" Danny sr. shouted. "Just make things easy son, and show yo loyalty to yo brother! You can trust ol' jabbo!" "I promise to do everything within my power to find them!" said Sir Edward. Sir Edward walks over towards his little brother and gives him a firm hug. He kisses Danny sr. on the cheek. "Help me, please! Danny sr. cried. "Just let go and believe in me little brother!" Sir Edward cried. Danny sr. starts sobbing. At this moment, Charlie goes in the dining room. He soon comes out carrying a silver platter, with 6 shot glasses filled with scotch placed on top. Both Jake sr. and mark sr. grab a glass. Jabbo and his driver Tony grabs a glass. Sir Edward grabs his glass. Danny sr. refuses to take one. Charlie takes a glass and hands the platter with the last glass on it to one of the agents. Charlie raised his glass. "Long live the house, of lassenberry! Long live Sir Edward!" said Charlie. Everyone, except for Danny sr. raise their glasses. "Long live the house of Lassenberry! Long live Sir Edward!" jabbo, Tony, Jake sr., and mark sr. all shout simultaneously. They all gulp down their drinks. Sir Edward puts his hand on his brother's shoulder. "Just say it little brother, and everything will be alright from here." He says to Danny. "Long live the house…of lassenberry. Long live…Sir Edward." Danny sr. mumbled. Sir Edward accepted that, and hugs his brother. Sir Edward pulls jabbo to the side away from the group. "What's the deal with Diablo?" sir Edward whispered. "Last anybody seen him, he was heading to the airport. That was a few days ago." jabbo whispered. "Did he leave the country or what?" sir Edward asked. "Man, Jabbo don't know!" said jabbo. "This is what you do. Get someone to go to the airport and find out if he left the country. And if he did, I wanna know when and where." Said Sir Edward. "Got it." Said jabbo.

Sitting in a room recovering from a dizzy spell at the Hotel Plaza Grande, Antonio Diaz, a.k.a Diablo had just crossed out the name of a place he'd just visited. The time is 8am, ECT. On his bed he had a duffle bag of Ecuadorian Sucre. Coming from the province Guayas, Diablo had made big payouts for information to the whereabouts of 2 low leveled gang members León Arteaga and Jorge Ortiz. His search was narrowed down to the city of Ibarra in Northern Ecuador.

Diablo walks to the bathroom and splashes his face with cold water. He hears a knock on the door, "Quién es?" Diablo said "Servicios a la habitación!" the voice said. "No me acueurdo de llamar para cualquier cosa!" Diablo said as he walks to the door. As soon as diablo cracks the door open, a man bursts in. Diablo is sacked to the floor. There was another man that ran in the room and locked the door behind him. Before Diablo could react, there was an automatic pistol shoved in his face. "Oímos que estabas buscando para nostros! Nuestro negocios se hizo de nuevo en los Estados Unidos!" Jorge shouted. "Era! Era! Sólo Estoy aquí por una cosa!" Diablo said. "Qué es Eso?" Jorge asked. "Estoy aquí por ese anillo en su dedo Eso es todo!" Diablo said. "No me mientas perra!" Jorge said. "¡Escucha! Tengo una bolsa llena de dinero en la cama! Es tuyo, para el anillo! Diablo said. "León! Ir a ver la bolsa!" Jorge shouted. León runs over to the bed. He checks the bag. He sees the money inside. "Es aquí!" León said. Jorge puts the gun to Diablo's eye. "¿Qué pasa si tomo el dinero y quedarse con el anillo!" Jorge said smiling. "Vamos hombre! Usted puede comprar Diez anillos y un coche con ese dinero!" Diablo said. "No vale la Pena que el hombre! Sólo dale ese anillo estúpido! Tomamos el dinero y nos vamos!" león said. Jorge looks at Diablo. He throws it in Diablo's face. "Si me dicen de ti volver a Ecuador, estás muerto!" Jorge said. León grabs the bag of money. Before Jorge and león leave the room, Jorge shoots Diablo in the knee cap. Diablo screams at the top of his lungs. Jorge and león go running down the hall of the hotel. Diablo ignores the pain just enough to place the ring on his finger. He drags himself over to the bed. He pulls himself off the floor by using the bed. An elderly couple walks by, and sees Diablo in agonizing pain and his pant leg soaked with blood. "Que consigue a un medico! ¡Por favor! Diablo cried.

A half hour later, Diablo is being cared for at the Hospital Eugenio Espejo. Nurses have stopped the bleeding. He's been given morphine to kill the pain. At this time, Diablo is feeling euphoric. Moments later, a doctor enter the room "Buen señor días. Eres un hombre con suerte. Hay una buena probabilidad de que Podemos salvar la pierna." The doctor said. "Gracias doctor!" Diablo said in a slurred voice. "Vamos a tener que aplicar primero que la anesthesia general en la mania." The doctor said. Diablo just nods his head. "Una vez que tenaganos esa babosa de su tapa de la rodilla, se le multa." Said the doctor. The doctor sees that Diablo is out of it. He just smiles and leaves the room.

The next morning, Diablo awakens from a good night's sleep. The first thing he checks, if the ring is still on his finger. He then looks around until he finds the next important thing he wants. The bed pan. Moments later, the nurse's aide strolls in with breakfast. "Bueno Mr. mañana Diaz! Su hora del desayuno!" the nurse's aide said. "Me siento como que puedo comer un cabala!" Diablo said "Usted no lo oyeron de mí, pero he oído que el anestesiólogo no puede hacerlo hoy!" the nurse aid said. Diablo shakes his head. "Tengo que salir de aquí! Tengo que conseguir mi culo de nuevo a loss Estados Unidos!" Diablo shouted. His yelling could be heard down the hall. The nurse comes running in. "Enfermera! Tengo que volver a Estados Unidos! No puedo quedarme aquí!" Diablo shouted. Diablo started acting belligerent. The nurse tries to calm him down, "Sr. Diaz que no puede salir hasta que Tomamos la posta de la rodilla!" said the nurse. The nurse calls the orderlies in to hold Diablo down to give him sedative. The 53 year old was throwing a tantrum like a child. The medication finally calmed him. "Don't touch my ring." Diablo mumbled.

Having his hair tied into a pony tail, Diablo stood out like a sore thumb in a population of much shorter and darker Latinos. The tattoos that were covering most of his body made it obvious as well.

Back in the United States, sitting at his breakfast table eating a bowl of fruit, jabbo was gazing at the wooded area just outside is home. He had purchased a 5 bedroom colonial home in the first Mountain area of West Orange, New Jersey. Jabbo lived alone most of the time. Very few people new about the small island he had purchased off the Florida Keys for his wife and 2 daughters. Being an important figure in the lassenberry crew, jabbo thought it would be safer for his family to keep sort of a distance from him. He does take a private jet to the island and stays about 4 months out of the year unless called upon by the lassenberry hierarchy. The only ones that knew about jabbo's family was benny and Sir Edward.

It was quiet and peaceful at 6 in the morning, until jabbo's driver Tony Kerouac walked into the kitchen. "We've found him." Tony said. Jabbo almost chocked on his food from hearing the news.

Tony Kerouac had been jabbo's driver, body guard and chef since the purge back in 1980, after being a nickel-n-dime pot dealing kid from Jersey City. Tony was born in Baton Rouge, Louisiana. He and his mother moved to New Jersey when he was 2 years old. His mother lost her inheritance to a plantation for being pregnant by Tony's African American father. The 200 acre property was passed on to a cousin of hers.

"Where this fool at?" Jabbo asked. "South of the border. Way south of the border." He said. "How's yo Spanish?" Jabbo asked while chewing on a grape. "I'm Creole boss. It's French." Said tony. "Well, go book us a round trip flight to wherever we gotta be." Jabbo said. "Ecuador boss." Said tony. "Well, Jabbo going to Ecuador then!" said Jabbo. "Anything else boss?" tony asked. "Yeah, hire one of them translators when we get out there." Said Jabbo.

Later on that day, Sir Edward takes a ride out to Cedar Grove to see Brandon hart. The sun was setting. The street lights in the neighborhood were getting brighter. Charlie pulls up to Brandon's driveway in a brand new 98' Boeman LXE. Sir Edward was proud to see about a dozen Boeman cars in the parking lot. He tells Charlie to stay in the car, while takes the elevator. Sir Edward gets the second level. As soon as he gets out of the elevator, he hears the muffled sound of club music coming from down the hall. The music was coming from Brandon's condo. Sir Edward can hear women laughing over the music before he even knocks. The door opens. It's Brandon who answers it. "Hey! Uncle Eddie!" Brandon shouted. "Now, you know damn well what they call me!" sir Edward chuckled. "Sir Edward! I'm sorry! Please come in!" said Brandon. Sir Edward walks in to see a sofa with 3 beautiful black women sitting on it. There were empty wine bottles all over the floor. Sir Edward also noticed the place was lavishly fixed up. "Hey everybody! This is my uncle Sir Edward!" said Brandon. Everyone either waved or shouted hello. Sir Edward waves back. "You gotta a beer?" sir Edward asked. "Oh, sure!" Brandon said. Brandon runs in the kitchen to the where 2 couples are standing. Brandon maneuvers his way around his guests a grabs 2 beers. Brandon makes his way back to Sir Edward. "Let's go out on the balcony." Said Brandon. On the balcony, Sir Edward opens his beer and takes a big gulp. "How's business?" he asked Brandon. "The units are selling like crazy! Most of the people inside own a Boeman!" said Brandon. Sir Edward puts his hand on Brandon's back. "I don't want most of the people to own a Boeman. I want all the people in there to own a Boeman!" said Sir Edward. Brandon looks into Sir Edward's eyes and can tell that he wasn't kidding around. Brandon takes a deep breath. "Let me sleep on a way to increase sales." Brandon said. "You got 24 hours young man." he says to Brandon. Sir Edward takes another swig of his beer, and hands Brandon the bottle. He heads back inside. "Enjoy the rest of the evening people!" Sir Edward said. "Goodnight!" said most of the crowd. Sir Edward leaves the condo. Brandon heads to the kitchen and pours out the rest of Sir Edward's beer into the sink. One of Brandon's female friends approach him. "You never mentioned before that Eddie lassenberry was your uncle!" she said. "He's pushing me to sell more Boeman cars even faster!" Brandon said. "He looks too gangster to be into Boeman cars!" she said. Brandon thought for a moment. "Holy shit! That's it!" Brandon shouted. "What's it?" she asked. Brandon starts laughing like a wild man. He gives his friend a long kiss on the lips. He then makes a dash to the bedroom. Before he shuts the door, he turns to the crowd. "Hey everybody! I just came up with a fresh idea! Just continue on with the party and see yourselves out! Good night!" shouted Brandon. The crowd looked bewildered at first, but continued to party the night away.

It was a half hour after Diablo's surgery, and he was still unconscious. Outside the hospital, a cab pulls up to the main entrance. The passengers of the cab notice that the streets are busy with locals going about their business. Stepping out of the cab first was a young Ecuadorian man, wearing torn jeans, and a short sleeve shirt and sandals. Tony Kerouac is the next to step out of the cab. He's was wearing a white strew fedora and white linen shirts and pants with sandals. Both men enter the lobby to the hospital. The cab driver doesn't take off. He turns the engine off, gets out of the cab and walks over to a fruit stand across the road. The Ecuadorian man was paid to be Tony's tour guide. The young man walks over to the receptionist's desk, while tony stands behind him a few feet back. "Discúlpeme. ¿podría decirme en qué habitación demi primo Antonio Díaz es en?" the young man asked the receptionist. The receptionist checks the computer. The computer was running slow. Suddenly, information on

Diaz surfaces. "Está en la habitación 114 en el pasillo. Pero, no se le permite a loss visitants Después de la cirugía." The receptionist said. 114 was the only thing tony needed to hear. He walks pass the desk, while the receptionist is being distracted by the young tour guide. Tony makes is way down the hall. He sees room number 112 on his right, room 113 on his left. He comes to the room. Tony looks around to see if anyone is looking his way. Except for an orderly passing him in the hall with trays of food, it seemed clear. He cracks the door open to room 114 and peaks in to see Diablo in bed fast asleep. Tony enters the room and closes the door. He walks over to the bed and is standing over Diablo. Tony sees the ring on his left hand. Tony removes his fedora. Inside the rim of the fedora, tony removes a straight razor.

Moments later, tony leaves room 114 as he puts back on his fedora. He walks straight down the hall to the exit. As tony is leaving, jabbo comes limping in with walking cane in hand, heading straight to the lobby. He takes a seat next to a portly Ecuadorian woman tending to her 2 little children. Outside, Tony hops in the cab. The cab driver sees him and comes walking back across the road. He gets in the cab. Tony's tour guide walks up to the cab. "Llevarlo de regreso al hotel! ¡Rápido!" the tour guide says to the cab driver. The cabby drives off.

It's around 7:30 pm, exactly 24 hours after Sir Edward and Brandon had their little meeting on the balcony. Brandon is sitting at his desk in his bedroom. There are empty beer bottles everywhere in the room. There is a waste basket filled with crumbled up paper. He hears his door bell. All Brandon is wearing are boxers and sweat sox. He runs to the door, then stops. He runs back to the bedroom and puts on a pair of pants. He runs back to the door and presses the intercom. "Who's there?" he asked. "Sir Edward wants to talk to you!" the voice shouted. Brandon hits the buzzer. He opens the door waiting for Sir Edward to come up. Soon Brandon sees Charlie coming through the door, followed by Sir Edward. "Sir Edward!" Brandon said nervously. He tries hard to ignore Charlie's and Sir Edward's uniforms. Sir Edward goes up to Brandon and gives him a hug. Sir Edward then takes 2 steps back. Charlie on the other hand, helps himself to the refrigorator. "You need help, man?" Brandon asked Charlie. "Never mind him! What idea you came up for me to sell more cars?" Sir Edward asked. "Yeah, right! Hold on!" Brandon said. Brandon runs back into the bedroom. He comes back out with a wrinkled up piece of paper. "I've written down a lot of stuff, but this shit here is golden!" he boasted. Sir Edward sighs. "Ok! Ok! We have billboards put up in every urban area on the East coast! I'll show a late model Boeman, with you standing in front of it, dressed in a pin striped suit, wearing a pinky ring! The logo would say, BOEMAN! IT'S GANGSTA!" Brand said with a big smile. Sir Edward scratches his gray goatee. He thinks about it for a minute, then smiles. "I like it! But, what I rather have is somebody else's face on the billboard!" sir Edward suggested. Brandon folds his arms, and starts pacing and pondering a solution. He looks at Sir Edward and starts smiling. "Your father!" Brandon shouted. Sir Edward looked pissed. He grabs Brandon by the throat. "What the fuck you just say?" he shouted. "I mean he should represent what a gangster is!" Brandon said while gasping for air. Sir Edward releases Brandon and calms himself. Charlie starts laughing while eating a sandwich he'd just made. "Shut the fuck up!" sir Edward shouts to Charlie. Brandon catches his breath. "Think about it! Benny lassenberry is truly the original gangster, as far as the homeboys in the hood are concerned!" Brandon explained. This time sir Edward folds his arms. He gives a little smirk. Sir Edward reaches in the pocket of his uniform pants. He pulls out his wallet. He pulls a card out of the wallet and hands it to Brandon. "Call this number. This is the number directly to the C.E.O of Boeman Automotive. Tell him you work for me, and then tell him your idea. I guarantee he won't refuse you." Said Sir Edward. "Come on knucklehead! Let's go!" he says to Charlie. Eddie slaps Brandon on the shoulder. "Good job man." said Sir Edward. Charlie opens the door for Sir Edward. They leave the condo. Brandon quickly closes the door behind them. He leans up against the door, and breathes a sigh of relief.

Elsewhere, an orderly is on his way to give Diablo his breakfast. Jabbo is still sitting in the lobby of the hospital. This time, an old man is sitting next to him with gash above his head waiting to be seen by a doctor.

The orderly is a pudgy, dainty type of fella. "♪ Mr. Diaz, es hora para el desayuno! ♪" the orderly sang. The orderly pushes the door to Diablo's room open. The receptionist hears a high pitch scream. The kids in the lobby quiet down, hearing someone louder than themselves. More orderlies come running down the hall, followed by an elderly security guard. They burst through the door of room 114 seeing the pudgy one standing in the corner covering his mouth. He points towards the bed. They all look to see Antonio Diaz, a.k.a Diablo dead. They get a closer look and see he has his throat slit, with his own finger lodged in it. Blood had spilled on to the floor before it dried. As soon as jabbo hears that Diablo is dead, he walks outside where the young tour guide is sitting on a crate. Jabbo gives him the signal. The tour guide hails a cab for him. Jabbo gets in the cab. It just so happens, that the cabby is the same guy that took tony back to the hotel. "Llevarlo de regreso al hotel!" the tour guide said.

It was July 15th, when Mookie was released from the hospital Mookie was given sort of a hero's welcome. All his top crew members stood outside in 2 parallel lines with new second in command Ricardo Salazar on one side, and Hector Chavez standing on the other side. Mookie was being wheeled out by Gregory Thomas, a.k.a tip.

The channel 12 news van was on the scene. "This is Brian Garner of channel 12 news standing outside Elizabeth medical center, where allege drug kingpin Mark Vasquez jr. has been released from the hospital after being shot multiple times by masked gunmen back in early February. As you can see, numerous uniformed police officers are patrolling the scene to make sure Mr. Vasquez's departure from the hospital is a peaceful one. This is Brian Garner, in Elizabeth. Channel 12 news." He said.

Camera crews and other reporters tried to get up close to the allege drug lord to ask questions, but were deterred by Salazar's boys by covering the lenses. Rita was standing right by Mookie's side when the limo pulls up in front of the hospital. Mookie's people carefully ease him into the limo. Once in the limo, Ricardo, Rita, hector, tip, Jorge Morales and Angel Salazar, a.k.a tiger Negro jump in as well. The chauffeur was the one who fold the wheelchair and placed it in the trunk. "Respaldamos en bebé de negocios!" Ricardo shouted. "Come on, man! English!" Mookie said as he points to Tip. "Thanks boss!" Said Tip. Mookie stares at his ring. "Hey Ricardo. Set up a meeting with Eddie lassenberry for this weekend." Mookie ordered. "You got it!" said Ricardo.

That evening, inside his mansion located in Chappaqua, Westchester County. Don Francesco stands in a candle lit chamber naked. The elderly mob boss holds up the head of one of his victims, which was given to him by one of his men. "Al dio Romano delle tenebre si combinano quegli spiriti al mio!" Don Francesco chants 3 times while smelling the stench of the dead flesh. After he was done performing the ritual, don Francesco leaves the room, locking the door to the chamber. He goes down the hall, still naked, to one of his 5 bathrooms. He stands over the sink and turns on the faucet. He then splashes cold water on his face to snap out of his trance. He hears his mobile Phone ring in the next room. He goes to answer it. "Si, sono io!" the don said. "Qualsiasi modifica nel New Jersey?" the voice asked. "Ci sono 3 di loro. Quello avido sarà l'ultimo uomo in piedi." don Francesco explained. "Buona. Noi Abbiamo la persona giusta pronti a pulire casa." Said the voice. Don Francesco hangs up the phone. He goes to his closet and puts on a bathrobe. He makes his way to the front lawn where one of his guards is standing, smoking a cigarette. "Jimmy! Get over here!" the don shouted. The guard runs over to the don. "I want you to hang around Jersey for a couple of weeks. Keep an eye on those 3 bosses. That Frankie Depalma ain't doing so well. Send him a gift basket on my behalf." Said the don. "You want me to bring along a crew?" jimmy asked. "No. we don't need to make them nervous." Said the don. Jimmy nods his head and walks off. "If I find any cigarette butts on my lawn, all hells gonna break lose!" the don yelled. Jimmy nervously looks for butts before he leaves.

It was the last day of July, on a 90° afternoon. Clayton Watson, a.k.a Butch was on his way to the Watson family reunion out in Monmouth, New Jersey. His wife, sons and daughter were in the car with him, while 3 of his body guards were following in a luxury vehicle. Butch and Dubbs were the main attraction at the family gatherings. Everyone wanted to see who would show up in the freshest ride. In the back of his truck, butch had 4 garbage bags filled with one dollar bills. He would MC contests for the kids. Last year he hosted a potato sack race for the kids and one of his nephews was awarded 500 dollars. Butch was driving down the road, then suddenly he hits the brakes. He skids off the side of the road. His wife and daughter were screaming like crazy. Butch jumps out of his vehicle. His body guards pulled over behind him. His wife kept asking him what was wrong. Butch didn't answer. It was like he was staring off into space. His guards run up to him. "Boss! What's up?" one of the guards asked. "Oh shit!" butch said. He points at the bill board on the side of the road. It read, BUY BOEMAN! IT'S GANGSTA! It had an old black & white picture of benny lassenberry posing in front of the car. "That nigga crazy!" butch said to himself.

At the end of 1998, 1 out of every 3 people in urban areas were driving a Boeman vehicle. A lot of street hustlers would spent their last dime on getting a Boeman. Some would customize their rides with tinted window, sound systems, chrome rims and hydraulic systems.

It was August of 98 when Sir Edward decided to make another major change. He was at his place sitting in his favorite chair, with Charlie sitting across from him. They both were getting high. "You know what? This place ain't fit for someone of my status! I belong in a castle! Like the ones they have over in Europe!" Sir Edward said. "You're moving to Europe?" Charlie asked. "Fuck no! I'm gonna build me one right here!" Sir Edward said. "Where at?" Charlie asked. "You'll see!" Sir Edward chuckled.

The next morning sir Edward and Charlie were standing outside of the Lassenberry estate. Sir Edwards dials his mobile phone. After 3 rings, someone picks up. "Valdese Construction!"

the voice said. "Yeah! Let me speak to Frank Valdese." Sir Edward said. "Speaking!" said Valdese. "Yeah frank, its sir Edward." He said. "Who?" Valdese asked. Frustrated, Sir Edward walks away from Charlie so he can't be over heard. "It's Eddie lassenberry!" he shouted. "Oh, ok! What can I do for you?" Valdese asked. "Yeah, I'm calling because my father did business with your father in the past. I was wondering would you be interested in a major construction project?" sir Edward asked. "What type of project?" Valdese asked. "Demolition to an old house, and building a new home from the ground, up!" said Sir Edward. "What type of home we're talking about?" Valdese asked. "I'm talking about a castle! I mean a European style castle!" Sir Edward said. "A castle? Are you fucking nuts?" Valdese shouted. Valdese hangs up the phone. "Bitch ass nigga!" shouted Sir Edward. He redials the number. Valdese picks up. "Hey! Why you hang up?" Sir Edward asked. "I run a serious business here! I don't have time for bullshit!" Valdese said. "This ain't no bullshit!" said Sir Edward. There was a silence on the phone. "Listen. I have your number. Let me call you back in, 10 minutes." Valdese said. "Don't be leaving me hanging!" said Sir Edward. "Alright! Alright!" Valdese hangs up the phone. Sitting at his desk, he makes a phone call. The phone rings a couple of times. "Fell." The voice said. "Hey fell! That Eddie lassenberry character just called me saying he wants me to do a major demo job, and listen to this! He wants me to build him a European style castle!" Valdese chuckled. "Are fucking with me Frankie?" fell shouted. "No fell! I shit you not!" Valdese said. "Here's what you do! You tell him to meet you at your office tomorrow morning, 8 sharp! Understand?" fell ordered. "Sure thing." Valdese said. Valdese hangs up the phone with fell and calls Sir Edward back. After a few rings, Sir Edward picks up. "Yeah?" he answered. "Could you come down to my office tomorrow morning at 8?" Valdese asked. "You still at that old spot?" sir Edward asked. "We're out in Wayne now! Across from the mall!" Valdese said. "Ok. Got it." Sir Edward said. "See you then!" said Valdese. Sir Edward hangs up the phone. He starts laughing hysterically. He kisses Charlie on the cheek. "So you really gonna build a castle?" Charlie asked. "Hell yeah! What the fuck you think I been telling yo ass!" sir Edward shouted. "I believe you!" Charlie said. "It's time to celebrate!" sir Edward chuckled. He dials a number. The phone rings 5 times. "Hello?" the soft voice answered. "Hey girl! It's yo uncle!" sir Edward said. "Hey, what's up?" the voice said. "What you and yo girlfriend Ariel doing tonight?" he asked. "We're in Vancouver right now! I came here to do a photo shoot!" said the voice. "Fuck all that! I'm gonna send a private jet to pick y'all up!" he said. "Hold on one second!" the voice said.

Samara told her uncle to hold look for her friend Ariel. She and Ariel were actually at a party in Vancouver, thrown by a big shot film producer. The party was wall-to-wall super-models, "A" list celebrities and filmmakers. The party took place in an art deco mansion where the floors where made of marble and glass. It had a giant water fountain in the middle of the room.

Samara was wearing nothing but a silk sheet to cover her body. She went searching for Ariel with her mobile phone in hand. A couple of old white guys squeezed on her ass as she walked by. She responded with a smile. She finally sees Ariel getting double teamed by 2 guys. One guy was a well-known porn star, and the other was "A" list movie star Jett Connors. "Wow!" samara said. She sees Ariel taking both penises in her mouth. "Ariel! Ariel!" she shouted. Ariel put her finger in the air, signaling samara to wait. Within minutes, both men simultaneously shoot loads of cum on her face and tits. The 2 guys were worn out and moaning. Samara starts giggling. Ariel grabs a handkerchief from Connors and wipes herself off. "Come answer the phone bitch!" samara chuckled. "Who is it?" Ariel asked. "It's my uncle!" said samara. Ariel goes running over to Samara wearing nothing but stilettos. She grabs the phone. Samara walks away. "Hi baby!" Ariel shouted. "Hey girl! I told my niece that I'll send a private jet out there to come get y'all!" he said. Ariel looks around the mansion. "Awe baby! You want me? Ariel said in a sensual voice. "You know the deal! I got everything you need and want here!" sir Edward chuckled. "I'm sure you do baby!" Ariel said. "So, I'm gonna make a phone call and the jet should be out there in a few hours!" said Sir Edward. Ariel sighed. "Can I take a rein check on that? We're really busy and everything!" said Ariel. Sir Edward dropped his smile. "Listen bitch! I want yo ass out here tonight Eastern standard time!" he shouted. "What the fuck you just say?" Ariel shouted. Suddenly, a pretty blonde woman, wearing nothing but bra and panties goes over to her and starts sucking on her tits. "Come on girl! You know I'm just fucking with you! But seriously, I want you out here, tonight!" he said. "I promise I'll be out there this weekend baby." Said Ariel. She starts moaning a little from the touch of the woman. Sir Edward gets furious. He hangs up the phone. "These young ass bitches!" he shouted. Ariel gently shoves the woman's head away. She walks over to where samara is. With a martini in her hand, samara was flirting with Jett Connors. "What my uncle say?" samara asked. "I told him I'll be out there this weekend. Then hung up." Ariel said. "Excuse us!" Samara said as she hands Connors her martini glass. She grabs Ariel by the wrist. She takes Ariel into another room so they could talk in private. "What's wrong with you girl?" Ariel asked. "Listen! My uncle is kinda crazy! He'll send the private jet out here, filled with a bunch of niggas that will kill everybody in this place! Fore real!" samara whispered. "Why are you making me do this? You see where we're at?" Ariel whispered. "You need to see where we're at, because it might be the last time we see these people alive!" Samara whispered. Reluctantly, Ariel calls Sir Edward back. He answers the phone. "Hey baby. I'm sorry. You can send the jet." Ariel said in a sweet voice. "Good! It'll be in Vancouver in a few hours!" he said. "Happy now?" Ariel said to Samara after she hangs up.

Sir Edward makes a phone call. The phone rings a couple of times. "Hello, Platinum Jets." The voice said. "Yeah. Put teddy on the phone." Sir Edward ordered. "Hold please." The voice responded. 30 seconds later. "Hello?" said teddy. "Yeah, teddy. It's me, lassenberry." He said. "Yes, Mr. Lassenberry! How can I help you?" teddy asked. "I need you to fuel up, and pick up a couple of my people from Vancouver ASAP." Said Sir Edward. "Just give me the details and I'll get right on it!" said teddy.

Platinum jets had served the lassenberry crew for years. Teddy is the only executive at that company who does spare of the moment flights for the crew. After a last minute job like this, Sir Edward would throw a 5 to 10 grand tip teddy's way.

By 10pm, there was a limo waiting for Samara and Ariel at Teterboro airport. Wearing nothing but terrycloth bathrobes and stilettos, they both hop in the limo. When the limo reaches Newark, it's aloud to pass the barricades on Sir Edward's block.

The next morning around 8:05 Sir Edward's phone rings. He was lying in bed between

Ariel and his niece Samara butt naked. Charlie was fast the asleep on the floor next to the bed. The phone awakens Ariel. She pushes Sir Edward to wake up. "Get up baby." Said Ariel. Sir Edward wakes up and looks at his watch. "Oh shit!" he shouted. The noise scare Samara out her sleep. Sir Edward answers the phone. "What the fuck? I'm sitting here waiting for you!" Valdese shouted. "I'm coming! I'm coming!" said Sir Edward. He hangs up and makes another call. Butch answers after 3 rings. "Yeah what?" butch said. "Get strapped! Meet me outside Valdese Construction Company, less than an hour! Across from the mall in Wayne!" he said. "Alright!" butch shouted as he sits on the edge of his bed.

After everyone gets dressed, Sir Edward gives the girls a few bucks and tells the limo driver, who was waiting down in hakim's apartment, to drop the girls off wherever they want.

It was 9:45am when Sir Edward arrived in front of Valdese Construction. He sees Butch pulling up across the street in the mall lot. Butch is sitting in his truck and pulls out a .38 revolver from under his seat. He gets out of the car, and stuffs the gun inside his belt. Butch then walks over to where Sir Edward is. Frank Valdese peeks through his the blinds and sees butch over at Sir Edward's car. "What's this shit?" Valdese says to himself. Valdese opens a drawer to his desk and pulls out a semi-automatic pistol. He checks the clip, and then takes the safety off. In the bathroom, Valdese can hear the toilet flush. Outside, Sir Edward gets out of the car and greets butch with a hand shake. Inside, the person who flushed the toilet comes out of the bathroom. Sir Edward and butch enter the office. "Hey frank!" sir Edward shouted. "You finally got your ass down here!" Valdese said as he and Sir Edward shake hands. Sir Edward introduces Valdese and to butch. "This is Mr. Felini. My business partner." Valdese said. "I know Felini!" said Sir Edward. Both Felini and Sir Edward shake hands. "It's good to see you after all these years. Sorry about what happened to your father. Real standup guy. They don't make'em like that anymore." Felini said.

Mario Felini was one of the 3 bosses of the Gatano crime family. He was a tall skinny guy in his early 50's looking more wasp that Italian. He always wore a 1930's paper boy cap. Felini took control of all the construction businesses in north jersey after the gatano massacre. Felini went from steeling import goods from Port Elizabeth, to running a 50 million dollar a year operation. Regardless of making all of that money, he was still resentful of the lassenberry crew for not paying tribute from the drug business.

Felini sits next to Valdese. "Can I get you guys' coffee?" Valdese asked butch and Sir Edward. They said no. "So you want a castle built to cover all the grounds of the estate?" Valdese asked. "Just about." Said Sir Edward. "I'll have to get an appraiser, zoning permission from the city, call the gas and electric company, the water department and that's just the tip of the ice berg!" Valdese explained. "I want it made out of those big stone blocks like the castles in Europe." Said Sir Edward. "Stone masonry ain't big in the states. We might have to import the stone blocks from overseas." Said Valdese. "No problem!" said Sir Edward. Valdese takes out a pen and pad from the desk drawer. "Shall we go take a look at the property and see what we're dealing with?" Valdese said. "Ok. Let's go." Said Sir Edward.

Butch gives his car keys to Charlie, while he jumps in the car with Sir Edward. Valdese and Felini follow behind Charlie. "I see lassenberry got himself a Boeman." Said Felini. "Me personally, I think they're crappy. But I see a lot of them on the road these days." Said Valdese.

"I really think you lost go damn mind!" butch shouted. "What the hell you talking about?" asked Sir Edward. "I'll talk about the castle thing in a minute! But I wanna talk about the bill boards! What the hell you doing putting your father's image on these shitty ass cars?" butch asked. "The less you know, the safer you are!" said Sir Edward. "If it involves my family's safety, boss or not! Supplier or not! I'll pull this car over and we'll have it out in the streets until I get an answer!" butch shouted. "Alright! I'll tell you, but not now! You just gotta trust me for now, and follow my lead! After I do business with these guys, I'll fill you in!" said Sir Edward. Butch stares out the window. "Ok! I'll give you time to get your story together!" butch said.

After a few hours looking over the property, Frank Valdese conjures up some figures. "After looking at everything, I'm estimating at least 50 million." Said Valdese. Sir Edward takes a deep breath. "I can have my lawyer draw up a contract within a week. With a down payment of 25 million, I can get a demolition team here in no time!" Valdese explained. Sir Edward looks at the home he was raised in, and starts reminiscing about his childhood playing with his siblings. "You sure you wanna do this?" butch asked. Yeah! I'm sure!" said Sir Edward.

Valdese and Felini head back to Wayne. "This deal is golden!" Felini shouted. "When I'm done with this cock sucker, we'll own the shirt on his back!" said Valdese.

Sir Edward takes out his mobile phone. "You ready to go?" butch asked. "I'm calling sleeves." Said Sir Edward. The rings. "Hello." Sleeves said. "Hey old man. I know you're retired, but I need to you. Meet me at the Lodi office within an hour." Said Sir Edward. He hangs up. "Ready to go, now." Butch asked. "Now I gotta call jabbo!" said Sir Edward. Jabbo picks up. "Yeah. Be at the Lodi office within an hour!" said Sir Edward. He hangs up. "Now are we ready to go?" butch said. "Damn nigga! I love ya, but you sounding like a fucking little kid right about now!" sir Edward shouted. "Whatever man!" butch said. "I gotta get something out of the house! Come help me take down the coat-of-arms." Sir Edward ordered Charlie. "What coat-of-arms?" butch asked Sir Edward. Charlie and butch follow Sir Edward into the mansion. Sir Edward looks up at the coat-of-arms above the mantle. "So that's what yo ass talking about!" butch said. "Yeah, that's it! Charlie! Find something to cover it with!" sir Edward shouted. "No problem." Said Charlie. "Help me take it down!" sir Edward said to butch. Charlie comes back with comforter he found in one of the bedrooms. They take the coat-of-arms and cover it with the comforter. Butch and Charlie carry it out of the mansion, while Sir Edward locks up the mansion. "We'll meet in Lodi!" sir Edward said to butch.

It was about an hour later, when jabbo and Tony Kerouac arrived at the Lodi office. Butch was sitting in his truck waiting when they arrived. "Damn old man, you slow!" butch chuckled. "You don't want jabbo foot in yo ass!" jabbo said. Suddenly, sleeves pulls up next to butch. "What's this all about?" sleeves asked. "I have no idea." Said butch as he exits his vehicle. Jabbo leads the group to the basement of the facility to one of the conference rooms. In the room was a 20 foot long wooden table. "What do you know about this coat-of-arms?" butch asked jabbo. "What coat-of-arms?" sleeves asked them. Before jabbo could answer, in comes Charlie wearing his uniform. "Everyone stand and recognize Sir Edward of lassen-berry!" Charlie shouted while standing at attention. "What the fuck?" butch shouted as jabbo and the others stood up. "On yo feet son!" jabbo said to butch. "But jabbo!" butch said. "I said stand up!" jabbo shouted. Butch eventually stands. The 8 NA agents sir Edward rents recently rented, enter the room wearing their usual black suit and dark shades. They line up against the wall. "What the hell is going on?" butch asked. "Quiet!" shouted jabbo. Slowly the man or the hour enters the room. "No! You stay this time!" jabbo orders tony. Sir Edward didn't say a word about tony this time. Tony pulls out Sir Edward's seat. "Everybody sit!" sir Edward shouted. Everyone sits. Sir Edward remains standing. "Today, August 20th 1998, is the dawn of a new day! We are on a level far more than we've been in the past 60 years! No respect to my father, but we in this room will lay down the foundation of this organization for the next thousand years! As head of this organization, I make into law that we support and aid all future male lassenberry leaders for generations to come! The Jenkins bloodline, the Watson bloodline and the hart bloodline will prosper and have secure position under the rule of all lassenberry male heirs! It's a known fact that I don't have any sons to pass on my leadership! That means one of my nephews will have to take my place one day! That also means the male heir of the lassenberry bloodline possessing my ring will rule this organization! The same rules apply to your families regarding your rings as well! Question?" sir Edward shouted. "I have a question." Said butch. "Go ahead." Said Sir Edward. What about Mookie and his crew?" butch asked. "I already had a sit down with him and his people as soon as he came home from the hospital. He looked me in the eye, and told me that I had his undying loyalty." Sir Edward said. "I guess it ain't no need to mention Dubbs! He'll follow my ass off a cliff!" butch chuckled. They all laugh. Jabbo raises his hand. Sir Edward acknowledges jabbo. "Old jabbo getting old! I need somebody to replace me soon so I can rest my bones!" jabbo said. "That's between you and Tony." Said Sir Edward. Tony showed a sigh of relief. Sir Edward looks over at sleeves. "Your grandson Brandon is a valuable asset to me. So, I'll be looking forward to seeing him playing a major role in the organization's legitimate side of the business for years to come, under your discretion of course. "Fine by me!" sleeves said. "We still have 8 counties left in the state to grab! Believe me when I tell you, we will grab them! If there are no more questions, comments or concerns, I order we close this meeting!" said Sir Edward. No one said a word. Jabbo stands from his seat. "Long live the house of Lassenberry! Long live Sir Edward!" he shouted. Sleeves, tony and butch stand. "Long live the house of Lassenberry! Long live Sir Edward!" they all shout. Everyone remains standing. Charlie opens the door. 4 NA agents step out first, then Sir Edward and Charlie. The remaining 4 agents follow behind Charlie. Jabbo and the crew then leave. Outside, Sir Edward pulls sleeves to the side, far away from the group. "Listen old man. I need your services. There's this guy who owns the Valdese construction company I don't trust. I want you and your team of pencil pushers to spy on him by any means necessary as of today." Said Sir Edward. Sleeves nods, then walks away.

It was around 10 in the morning when frank Valdese received the lassenberry contract through express mail. He takes it out the large envelope. The paper work had to be about an inch thick, not counting the carbon papers in between. Frank calls his lawyer on his landline. The phone rings 3 times. "Berger & Berger!" the voice said. "Hey sol! It's Frank! It just came in!" he shouted. "Frankie baby! I'm quite sure it's to your liking!" Sol chuckled. "This fucking lassenberry guy! He's a piece of work!" said frank. "Remember, its pages 3 and 5! Soon as he sings, we've got him!" sol shouted. "Great! I'll call you later!" said Frank.

In between the piles of paper work are hidden forms perfectly sealed between sheets of carbon paper. According to sol, once lassenberry signs the forms, he'll being paying 3 times more than the job is worth.

Frank makes a call to Sir Edward. The phone rings 6 times. The answering machine is activated. "Yeah Eddie! It's Frank Valdese! I have your contract! It just came in this morning! See ya soon!" frank said.

About an hour later, frank car hear the door buzzer. He looks through the blinds. He sees 2 preppy looking white guys in suits. Frank goes to the door. "Can I help you fellas?" he asked. "Yes, Mr. Valdese?" one guy asked. "Yeah, I'm him! What is it?" he asked. "We represent Sir Edward Lassenberry." The guy said. "Where is he? Why ain't he here?" Frank asked. "We were told that you have the contract in your possession." The guy said. "Listen pal! I don't know what's going on here, but Eddie should be here to sign this contract!" frank shouted. "We are part of Mr. Lassenberry's legal team. We're here to thoroughly go over the details of the contract. May we come inside?" the man asked. Frank looks frustrated. "Come in!" Frank said reluctantly. The 2 men come inside and introduce themselves. They both take a seat at frank's desk. Frank goes into his file cabinet and pulls out the contract. He hands it over to them. One of the men starts reading the paper work word for word. Frank gets nervous. The other man sees the sweat trickling down frank's face. "Do you have a copy Mr. Valdese?" the man reading asked him. Unknown to frank, a telephone operator was wrapping up his equipment at the top of the telephone pole across the street. "No, no I don't, but give me another day, and I can get my lawyer to wire another contract!" Frank pleaded. "Sorry to disappoint you Mr. Valdese, but our client wants the contract to be signed today." One of the men said. The other legal rep started reading page 2 of the contract. Frank starts to get nervous. He realized that if they found out that page 3 has been illegally tampered with, it could end the deal. Frank starts to distract the men with humor. "I love coming in this office every morning! Even more than my wife's pussy!" frank chuckled. He doesn't get any response from the 2 men. They show strict professionalism. The legal rep is just about to flip over to page 3. Frank starts to sweat. He quickly snatches the contract from the legal rep. "That's it! I don't need this shit! Tell, lassenberry the deals off if he can't wait until tomorrow!" Frank shouted at the men. They both stand simultaneously. "Well Mr. Valdese. We thought we'd could do business. I guess not. You have a good day sir." Said one of the men. As the 2 men head to the door, frank stops them. "Hold on a minute! What can I do to change your minds?" frank asked. "Nothing, Mr. Valdese." They leave the office. Frank looks out the window. As they jump into a 98 Boeman hatchback. So frustrated, frank flips his desk over. He screams at the top of his lungs.

It was Saturday, and demolition has started on the lassenberry estate anyway. The whole perimeter of the estate was taped off. There are 4 roll-off dumpsters lined up next to each other on the basketball court. A construction trailer is sitting off to the far side of the second guest house for management. On the trailer reads New World Construction.

The C.E.O was Charles Scott. He was a short white haired old man, who happened to be on the council of the National Agreement. None of Mr. Scott's 1,200 employees new of this involvement of this secret society. What frank Valdese had wanted, Mr. Scott had achieved. Mr. Scott and Sir Edward were standing outside of the construction zone, wearing construction hard hats. "I wish I was there to see the look on Valdese's face! Mr. Scott chuckled. "He and Felini wanted to rape me of everything! Thanks to my people inside the phone company, I had the heads up on that asshole!" said Sir Edward. Mr. Scott put his hand on Sir Edward's back. "You don't have to worry about working for those people anymore. You are a part of our family now." Said Mr. Scott.

Charles Scott came all the way from California on behalf of peter Boeman of Boeman auto industries. Mr. Scott won the construction project through bid rigging.

Boeman auto industries stock had skyrocketed on behalf of Sir Edward's people and other drug organizations around the country. Through advertisement, the Boeman auto company flourished because of the gangster image. Even oversees, the Boeman auto craze was a huge success. In urban areas all over Europe, Asia and certain parts of the middle east. Boeman surpassed all the other major auto business in sales.

Sir Edward's mobile phone rings. He answers ti. On the other end was his sister Maggie. Maggie was in Europe on business at the time. She had accompanied a team of medical researchers to Paris on new Developments on cancer research. She had received word from her son Tyson Richards about her brother's shenanigans. "Eddie! What's this I hear about you building a castle?" she shouted. "Hey sis! Ain't hear from you in a while!" he said. "I thought we'd decided to sell the estate and divide the profits amongst the family!" Maggie shouted. "First of all, it's Sir Edward now. Second of all, pop left me in charge of the family fortune before he went away." He said. "You could've at least informed me!" Maggie shouted. "Sis! Sis! Did you get your envelope before you left?" sir Edward asked. Maggie paused for a moment. "That's beside the point!" Maggie shouted. "Relax sis! When you come home from whatever you're doing, you'll see I made a lot of changes." Sir Edward told her. He hangs up before Maggie could utter another word. "Family! I tell ya!" sir Edward chuckled. "Yeah. I know the feeling. Oh! Speaking of envelopes! My old mind is fading! I forgot to give this to you!" said Mr. Scott. Mr. Scott reaches inside his jacket pocket. He pulls out a shiny gold envelope with engraved writing on it. He gives it to Sir Edward. "What this?" Sir Edward asked. "The gods thought it was time for you to be shown a good time!" said Mr. Scott. Sir Edward looked at Mr. Scott and saw a sinister smile on his face. "All the information is inside." Said Mr. Scott. "I wanna bring my right hand man jabbo with me." Said Sir Edward. "Well, ok. But, one thing you must do after you open and read it. You must burn it! That letter, that envelope should only exist in your mind after you read it! If you make the mistake of leaving it lying around, well! I won't be able to save you! No one will!" Mr. Scott said with a devilish look in his eyes. Suddenly, Mr. Scott bursts out laughing. He starts coughing as well. Sir Edward shook his head as he and Mr. Scott continue to stroll the premises. "How does a moat sound?" Mr. Scott asked. "A moat?" Sir Edward asked. "Yes, a moat!" it's not costing you a dime" Mr. Scott chuckled.

That evening at the Valdese construction, frank was sitting at his desk on the phone. "Ok Ms. Kelly, you said you wanted new siding?" frank asked. While frank was on the phone, in comes Felini and his sidekick Paul Rita. "Ms. Kelly! Let me call you back! Yea ma'am! As soon as I'm done here! Bye!" frank said before he hung up. Felini walks up to the desk rubbing his hands together. "So what you got for me pal?" Felini asked. Frank leans back in his chair. "It makes me sick to my stomach! He didn't bite!" said frank. Felini stops rubbing his hands. "What you mean he didn't bite? You said, now this is coming from you! You said this was full proof!" Felini shouted. "I swear to god fell, every other time we did this, it worked like a charm!" frank cried. "But all of a sudden, the biggest job you come across, you can't seal the deal!" Felini shouted. "For some fucking reason, it's like they read my mind!" frank cried. "Who are they?" asked Felini. "His fucking legal team!" frank cried. Felini removed his cap and started scratching his head for a moment and puts it back on. "Ok! What you got on ya?" Felini asked. "Ah, what you mean?" frank asked. Felini walks up to frank and grabs him by the collar. "I'm not walking out of here empty handed!" Felini shouted. Frank was scared as shit. He went through his pockets to give Felini something. He checks all 4 pockets, giving Felini a total of 2 grand. "You sure this is all you have?" Felini asked. "Yeah, yeah!" frank cried. Felini shook his head. "Well, I'm gonna come back every week and expect twice as much out of your pockets!" Felini shouted. Come on fell! You already hitting me for 10 grand a week as it is! "Frank cried. "That spook lassenberry just made a jerk out of ya! Now you gotta pay for your fuck up!" Felini shouted. Paul Rita steps forward. "Hey! Where's my cut?" Paul asked. "What?" Frank asked." I didn't come down here for nothing either pal!" Paul shouted. "But, but I don't have anything on me!" frank cried. "I'll tell you what then this can be my new hangout! You can pay the gas and electric bill!" Paul said. "Sounds fair to me!" Felini said as he counts the money. "Now get the fuck out of my office!" Paul shouted. "What in the world you gonna with my office?" frank asked. Paul grabs a binder from off the desk and throws it at frank. Frank ducks. "I said get the fuck out!" Paul shouted. Frank quickly grabs his keys, jacket, hightailing it out there. He jumps in his truck and takes off.

It was October 13th around 8 in the evening, when Sir Edward was at his apartment standing in front of the mirror. He was dressed in a black tuxedo, white silk shirt with diamond cufflinks. He takes his small comb and starts combing his goatee. There's a knock on the door. "Come in Gunz!" he shouted. 2 Gunz walks in. "Your brother Danny down by the barricade." Sir Edward rolls his eyes, sighing. "Send the word that I left town for a couple of days." Sir Edward ordered. 2 Gunz nods.

Every time Danny sr. wanted to talk to his brother about finding his son Danny jr., Sir Edward would assure him that he'd always had team searching for him. On another occasion, Danny sr. threatened to go to the feds. Sir Edward had to always remind him never go to the feds due to the fact that he's a drug lord.

Moments later, Charlie arrives. He's assigned to be the chauffeur tonight. "I just called jabbo, and he's ready for us to come pick him up." Charlie said. "Ok then." Said Sir Edward. They both head out the door. "Gunz! Radio down to the street that we're handing to the car." sir Edward ordered. 2 Gunz nods. Sir Edward and Charlie head to the freight elevator. "Have everybody on the street stand tall! He's coming down!" 2 Gunz said over the walkie-talkie. "Jason Curtis, a.k.a J. big met Sir Edward and Charlie at the bottom floor. J Big escorts them to the car.

Sir Edward had recently purchased a vehicle that was not even on the market yet. A 1999 XLR stretch Boeman limo. The difference about this was the doors were flexible to slide up and down like a garage door and would notify the driver by computer voice what exactly needed repair.

There was a dead silence when Sir Edward and Charlie walked to the limo. Charlie lifts the door for his boss. Sir Edward enters the car. Charlie shuts the door and hops in the driver's seat. He drives off, heading to West Orange to pick up jabbo.

Over an hour and a half later, the limo arrives at Teterboro airport. There at the airport, was a private jet waiting for sir Edward and jabbo on the tarmac. A couple of NA agents approach the limo. Charlie gets out and opens the door for his boss and jabbo. "I'll give you a call when we get back." Sir Edward said to Charlie. Sir Edward and jabbo climb aboard the jet. Sir Edward takes a seat and takes a magazine from the book rack. The pilot comes out of the cockpit. "Sir Edward, jabbo, I'm Captain Bennett. This young lady is your flight attendant tiffany. She's here to serve you in any way possible. I mean any way! We should arrive at our destination with a couple of hours." Said the captain. Bennett returned to the cockpit. The seatbelt sign comes on. Jabbo buckles up. "Excuse me tiffany! Could you help me with my seatbelt?" sir Edward asked her. The petite blonde goes over to Sir Edward and fastens his seatbelt. Sir Edward could see her cleavage and noticed that she had a good boob job done. "Nice work!" sir Edward said. "Thank you!" tiffany giggled. "Damn girl! You can make a man explode in his pants!" said Sir Edward. Tiffany rubs on Sir Edward's private area. Sir Edward goes even further by feeling on her breasts. "You are bad!" tiffany giggled. Sir Edward smiled. "I have to go strap myself in, but I'll be back!" she giggled. Sir Edward rubs on her ass as she walks away. Within seconds, they are air bound. "Where you taking ol' jabbo anyway?" jabbo asked. "Now you ask, old man?" Sir Edward shouted. "Well, where we going?" jabbo asked. Man, I don't know! The invitation said to get my black ass on the jet!" said Sir Edward. "It really said yo black ass?" chuckled. "No, but it would be fucked up if it did!" sir Edward chuckled.

Just like captain Bennett said, the jet did arrive at its destination on schedule. It landed beyond the forest on a secluded well lit runway located in the state of Maine. The jet came to a halt. The door opened and there was a NA agent waiting on the ground. "Please, follow me Sir Edward." said the agent. The agent leads them to a limo. The agent gets in the driver's seat, taking jabbo and his boss to their destination. The drive took about an hour until they arrived at a huge clearance beyond the forest. What sir Edward saw made his jaw drop. His eyes laid upon an enormous palace. There were night lights beaming on certain parts of the palace. The agent drives up to a 20 foot iron gate that surrounded the entire perimeter. The agent enters a 5 digit code a small control panel located at the entrance. The gate automatically slides open. The agent drives through. The limo drives up a winding road made of cobble stone. About a 100 yards from the main entrance of the palace, stood a huge bronze statue of a woman on her knees bound and gagged. "Jabbo think that somewhere shit!" jabbo said as he gazed upon the statue. As the limo pulls up to the main entrance, there stood another agent. He opens the limo door for Sir Edward and jabbo, escorting them to the huge oak double doors. "Just one moment sir." The agent said before punching a 5 digit code located on a control panel above one of the metal door knobs. After they enter the hall, the agent steps up to a podium with a microphone posted on it. "Please welcome Sir Edward of New jersey!" he announced. Out of nowhere appeared Terrance Haggerty.

He was dressed in purple tuxedo and wearing purple high heel shoes. The sound of his shoes echoed as he approached Sir Edward and jabbo. "This fool is done definitely lost his mind!" jabbo whispered to Sir Edward. "Sir Edward! Welcome to the palace!" Terrance chuckled. He snaps his finger, and summons one of the servants over. The servant approached them offering Sir Edward and jabbo drinks. They each take a drinks. "Astonishing place, isn't it?" Terrance chuckled. "Jabbo thinks it looks like a home for vampires!" jabbo said. "Oh, jabbo! Pleasure to see you again!" said Terrance.

Sir Edward noticed the odd décor. There were of life size statues all around the hall of people in tortured positions. The huge oil paintings on the walls were just as grotesque.

An elderly light skinned black man, with long gray hair pulled back in a ponytail approached Sir Edward and jabbo. "So, I finally get to meet sir Edward of New jersey!" he said. "This is Bruce Le harve of New Orleans!" Terrance chuckled. Le harve and Sir Edward shake hands. "I always been a big fan of your father." Le harve said. "Me too!" Sir Edward chuckled.

Coming down the long double helix staircase with a drink in his hand, was a familiar face to Sir Edward. "Hey O'Neil!" sir Edward shouted. O'Neil goes over and shakes hands with Sir Edward and jabbo. "How the hell you get pass the gate?" Sir Edward chuckled.

Maury O'Neil was an Irish gangster, with a thick accent operating out of Hell's Kitchen. He ran dope in all the 5 boroughs. His supplier used to be supplied by the Peruvians until Gatano put an end to that. The National Agreement introduced him to the Afghan connection.

"How you doing you there lassenberry? Want to thank you for the gift." O'Neil said. "What gift?" jabbo asked. "Hey there jabbo! Eddie here bought me a brand new Boeman!" "It's Sir Edward. Sir Edward!" he shouted. "Please! You're always going to be little Eddie to me!" O'Neil chuckled. Sir Edward balls his fist and grits his teeth, but plays it off with a smile. "You didn't get a chance to meet Lawrence Hall from Chicago, did ya?" Terrance asked Sir Edward. Terrance signals Lawrence to come over to the group.

Lawrence hall was once a black nationalist. He broke away from his beliefs and started importing dope to street gangs back in the 60's. Mr. Hall supplied the north and south side of Chicago. Only to those in the underworld, his territory was known as Kingdom Hall. He was a tall burly, dark skinned man, who suffered from respiratory illness. His companion, was an oxygen tank that he wheeled around with him.

Sir Edward and Hall shake hands. "It's been long time jabbo!" hall said as he embraced jabbo with a hug. "Jabbo got nothing but love for ya!" jabbo chuckled. "Damn man! Who don't you know?" sir Edward asked. "Me and jabbo here had a run in back in the day! But we're good now!" hall chuckled.

Lawrence Hall was part of a crew in Newark that benny and his people ran out of town. A then young hall escaped gun fire from an even younger jabbo. Lawrence and his crew had spread out in difference parts of the country. Lawrence ended up in Chicago.

Sir Edward looked around at all the well-dressed men mingling. He recognized Bert Holmes over at the other end of the room, who had a group of men around him listening to him ramble. Mr. Holms was a white guy who was dope king of Detroit. As far as law officials in Michigan were concern, Holmes didn't exist. All the media new that the streets were ran by the black gangs. One of the men surrounding holms was Fernando Domenico.

Domenico belonged to a sect that actually ran the Sicilian mafia. His bloodline secretly ran the 26 mafia families in the United States. Domenico was sent to gathering to find out who was behind the death of Luigi Gatano and his entire family.

Suddenly, the doors from the corridor opened. 2 NA agents held the doors open for a harem of sexy women dressed in bikinis. They come out and start mingling with the gentlemen in the room. One of the butlers came out carrying a platter with a colorful display of condoms. Some of the men wasted no time grabbing asses and tits. Some of the girls grabbed condoms off the platter and went to work. Sir Edward looked at the top of the stairs and saw a shadowy figure in a hooded cloak staring down at everyone. His curiosity was distracted by a sexy redhead with huge breasts, as she stroked the side of his face. "What's your name baby?" she asked. Sir Edward didn't answer. He grabs the young lady by her long hair, shoving her head south.

Again, the doors open to the corridor were opened. This time, a group of chiseled men came out wearing Speedos. Some of the guys like Holmes, eyes lit up with excitement. Dance music was coming from the sound system hooked up into the walls and high ceiling. These flamboyant men started dancing, and feeling up some of the guests. At least the ones that wanted to be felt up. Jabbo slowly stepped back away from the on looking crowd. Sir Edward embraced what was taking place while the red head was kneeled before him. One of the male dancers approached Sir Edward and gave him a long kiss on the lips. Those among the gathering that fancied that type of behavior applauded. A man wearing a ceramic mask came out of nowhere with a video camera started recording all the sexual acts. Jabbo couldn't believe what he saw next coming out of the corridor.

The next morning, Sir Edward had awaken to a painful hangover. He crawled out of bed realizing it wasn't his bed. He was in a huge Victorian styled bedroom where the windows were covered with velvet maroon drapes. The furniture looked like it was fit for royalty and a very expensive looking crystal chandelier hanging from the ceiling. He sat at the edge of the bed naked. Feeling nauseous, he runs to the bathroom and kneels before a gold plated toilet. He comes out of the bathroom failing to puke up what was ailing him. He noticed the red head girl lying naked in the bed. Sir Edward tried his best to wake her, but realized she was lifeless. Lying next to her, was one of the male strippers. He too was naked and lifeless. Sir Edward smiled, then started laughing when he realized it we he who ended their lives. The girl had hand prints around her throat. The man was castrated and beaten to a pulp. Sir Edward's tuxedo was on the floor stained with blood. Grabs a towel from the bathroom and wraps it around his waist. He then goes out into the hallway. He sees trails of blood covering the floor. Sir Edward looks to his left and sees bodies being carried down the stairs, wrapped in bloody sheets. He was tapped on the shoulder, which startled him, it was one of the butlers. "May we enter your now and dispose of the contents Sir Edward?" the butler asked. "Yeah sure!" said Sir Edward. The butler claps his hands twice. 2 figures dressed in hazmat suits come walking down the hall. They enter Sir Edward's room. "We have a men's apparel shop at the other end of the palace sir Edward." Said the butler.

Walking down the hall still wrapped in a towel, Sir Edward spots other guests lingering around the palace. He walks pass one room and sees another man in a hazmat suit performing CPR on Chicago drug lord Lawrence Hall. Sir Edward peeked into the room, but was shut off when one of the NA agents slammed the door on him. As he continued his trek to the other side of the palace, he comes across Terrance Haggerty dressed in 19th century European attire. He had in his hand a fencing sword. "Ah, sir Edward of Lassenberry! I see you're up all bright eyed and bushy tailed! At least bright eyed! A good breakfast will do the trick! The cafeteria is located that way! Make a left down the short flight of stairs!" Terrance chuckled. "Where's jabbo?" he asked Terrance. "He was last seen out back in the white garden." Said Terrance. Sir Edward noticed the Terrance's sword had blood on the blade. He continues his journey through the palace. Sir Edward finds his way outside to the white garden.

This white garden had acres of beautiful patterns of white Camellia, Shasta, Daisies, White Lilac, Madonna Lilies and a patch of White roses within the center of all of it. Sir Edward was amazed at the display of flowers. He looked to his left and saw jabbo sitting on a stone bench with his walking cane in his hand. It was a sunny breezy morning. Jabbo was watching as the white flowers were swaying back-n-forth. "Jabbo! Jabbo!" sir Edward shouted. Jabbo didn't respond. He just sat there quietly, staring at the flowers. Sir Edward walked over to him, and shouted once more until he got his attention. "When I call for you old man, I suggest you answer!" sir Edward shouted. "Jabbo ain't never seen this kind of evil! I been out here all night! This place is sick!" said jabbo.

The next day, Sir Edward and jabbo landed back at Teterboro airport. Like a faithful dog, Charlie was sitting waiting in the limo. Whether he stayed at the airport or went back home, no one knew. No one cared. Charlie is startled when Sir Edward taps on the window. "Open the door knucklehead!" he shouted. "I'm up! I'm up!" Charlie shouted as he rubbed his eyes. He noticed that his boss was wearing a different set of clothes. "Open the damn door!" sir Edward shouted again. Charlie quickly scrambles to get out of the vehicle. He opens the passenger door for his boss and jabbo. "Dubbs called. He said he needed a refill on weed." Charlie said as he put on his seatbelt.

It was the 16th of October around 8 in the morning. 2 of Sir Edward's nephews are playing basketball in an indoor court not too far from Alpine, New Jersey. Cousins Corey and Krayton were doing more talking then playing the game. "Hey cuz! That's a bad ass crib your sister got!" Krayton said. "It's alright!" Corey said. "Man, I could turn that place into night club!" Krayton said. "Shit! My sister ain't playing that! These white folks out here ain't playing that shit!" Corey said. "Man, we're lassenberry! We do whatever the fuck we want!" said Krayton as he out maneuvers his cousin and makes the basket.

Krayton was Jake's youngest son. Even though he grew up in a lavish lifestyle since birth, Krayton thought of himself as a tough guy from the hood. He stood 6 feet, 2 inches tall, with a slim build. The first time he received an envelope from his grandfather, he blew it all on dice out in Atlantic City. Krayton was never fond of the name his parents gave him. He'd rather be called K Big. Only his father called him Krayton. His mother fell victim to cancer a couple of years earlier. Her body was entombed in the lassenberry mausoleum.

After the game, which Krayton won 21 to 15, they left the indoor court and jumped into Corey's 98 Boeman. "You heard Uncle Eddie building a castle?" Krayton asked. "Yeah! I road pass there last week. That's fucked up what he's doing!" Corey said. "I don't think so. When the castle gets finished, that means he'll be moving from Newark to Cherry Hill. I'm thinking about turning the building into a night club." Krayton said. "What's with you and night clubs? I'm calling you crazy Krayton for now on!" Corey chuckled. "Man, fuck you!" Krayton said. They drive over to terry's estate. She wasn't home, but Corey had the key to get in anyway. The only furniture inside was terry's bed, a TV and a sofa. They spent the rest of the morning watching TV.

The next day at Sir Edward's apartment, Sir Edward had just come back from distributing the refill to Butch, Dubbs and Mookie. He was about rest in his favorite chair, until suddenly he felt a pain running from his chest to his neck. He became nervous. The pain became more excruciating. He struggled towards the door, falling to his knees. 2 Gunz heard a big thumping noise coming from inside the apartment. He bursts into the apartment seeing his boss on the floor in the Fetal position. "Boss!" Gunz shouted. "Call...doctor!" Sir Edward cried. 2 Gunz ran out into the hallway. "Pinky! Call an ambulance quick!" he shouted

It took the EMT a half hour to arrive at the apartment. Luckily Charlie was asleep in his bedroom and was there to perform CPR until help arrived. This also gave Charlie a chance to step up as leader. Sir Edward was rolled out of the apartment on a gurney. Outside the building, Charlie jumps in the back of the ambulance. "Call jabbo! Quick!" Charlie ordered 2 Gunz.

About a half hour later, jabbo and Tony arrive at Newark General Hospital. The receptionist at the desk was on the phone. Jabbo limps over to the desk, snatching the phone from her and hangs it up. "Excuse me!" the young black woman shouted. "Jabbo wanna know what room sir Edward in!" he said. "What? What's a jabbo and who is Sir Edward?" she asked. The security guard came running over. "What's going on here sir?" asked the guard. Tony pulls the guard to the side. "You know this is jabbo Jenkins you're talking to, right?" tony said. The guard looked over Tony's shoulder. "Oh shit! My fault! My fault! I didn't know, man!" the guard whispered. The guard kept repeating that he was sorry. "Calm down! It's ok!" tony said. Tony walks over to the desk and stands in front of jabbo. "Could you tell us what room Eddie lassenberry is in?" tony asked the receptionist. He reaches into his front pocket and pulls out 500 dollars. He laid it on the desk. The receptionist looks around and snatches the money. She checked the computer. "He's in intensive care right now. Just have a seat and I'll let you know when you can see him." She said. "Thank you!" tony said to her. Tony gently grabs jabbo by the arm and pulls him away from the desk. The receptionist gave tony a seductive look, but he didn't give it a second look. Tony was used to women coming on to him all the time. They both went over to waiting area. Minutes later, Charlie comes from the lobby with a coffee in his hand. "Jabbo!" Charlie shouted. "What happened now?" he asked Charlie. Tony helps jabbo out of his seat. "They said he had a heart attack! I mean like major!" Charlie said. "God damn!" shouted tony. "Jabbo hate to say this, but if he dies, jabbo gotta get his ring and put it on a Lassenberry's finger!" said jabbo. "Don't worry about that for now boss!" tony said. "He'll make it! I know he will!" Charlie said as tears trickled down his cheek.

After a few hours, the receptionist calls tony over. "Good news. Your friend is out of intensive care. They're moving him to a room where he can rest. I'll call you when he's ready for visitors." She said. "Thank you sweetie!" said tony. "So, when can I get your phone number?" the receptionist asked tony. Tony started blushing. "You have a pen?" tony asked. "Of course silly! I'm a receptionist!" she giggled. Tony smacked himself on the forehead. "True! True!" tony chuckled. He takes the pen from her and writes his name and number on a piece of copy paper.

A couple of hours later, the receptionist calls tony over again. This time, Charlie and jabbo walked over as well. "You can go see him now. He's in room 324. I can only give out 2 passes." She said. "You stay here!" jabbo said to tony. Charlie takes the passes. He and jabbo head toward the elevator. Tony turns toward the receptionist. "You guys must be big shots! You had that guard shaking in his boots!" she said. "Nah, that man lying in room 324 is the big shot." Tony said. "What about the old man with the cane?" she asked. "Oh! That's jabbo sweetie! Nuff said!" he told her.

When Charlie and jabbo reached the 3rd floor, Sir Edward was sitting on the edge of the bed in a gown. They come into the room. "What the doctors say?" jabbo asked. "Get my clothes out of the closet." Sir Edward said Charlie. Charlie goes over to the closet and retrieve his clothes. Within minutes, the doctor enters the room. "Mr. Lassenberry. What are you doing?" the doctor asked. "It's Sir Edward! Didn't you say I'll be fine?" he asked the doctor. "Yes, but you need to rest!" said the doctor. "I know you Indian people are smart, but I know my own body doc!" said Sir Edward. "Remember Mr. Lassenberry, because of that young man standing next to you, is the only reason you're still here!" the doctor said about Charlie. Sir Edward looked at Charlie, then dropped his head in shame. He lifts his head back up. "Just send me the bill doc." He said.

Almost an hour later, Sir Edward is wheeled out of the main entrance by an orderly. "Where tony at?" Charlie asked. "Go find him!" said jabbo. Charlie leaves his boss and jabbo and takes a walk to find tony. Suddenly, he sees tony coming out of the employee lounge zipping up his pants. "You didn't do what I think you did, did you?" Charlie asked. "Don't worry. She was off the clock." Tony chuckled.

Back at the apartment, jabbo, tony and Charlie sit with sir Edwards. "I wanna thank you men for your support. Now I wanna speak to jabbo alone." Sir Edward said to Charlie and tony. They both leave the apartment. Sir Edward leans forward in his chair. First thing to-morrow I want you to contact all my nephews with the last name lassenberry. I need them to meet me hear this Saturday. I need you to understand something. My body ain't what it used to be. I burned myself out!" said Sir Edward." He said to jabbo. "Jabbo wants you to rest." He said to Sir Edward.

The next day at Danny senior's estate, Donald is playing his video game on his 60 inch floor model TV. Elaine was in the den getting a massage from her masseur Antwan. Danny sr. was in the guest room reading the owner's manual on a new Boeman SUV he just pur-chased. The doorbell rings. It rings multiple times. "Someone answer the bloody door!" Elaine shouted. Frustrated, Donald puts down the controller to the video game to go answer the door. Donald first checks the video monitor that was hooked up to a motion camera. He sees its jabbo. "What the Fuck?" Donald said to himself. Donald goes to the door and presses the buzzer to open the gate. Jabbo's car enters the property. Donald opens the back door of the vehicle for jabbo. "It's kind of early for the next envelope Mr. jabbo!" Donald said. "Jabbo ain't here to give nobody no god damn envelope!" he said to Donald. Suddenly, Danny sr. comes to the door. "What is it Mr. Jabbo?" Danny sr. asked. "I'm here for yo son, not you! Yo uncle gonna have a limo come here Saturday morning. Be ready to go!" jabbo said to Donald. Jabbo walks back to the vehicle. The car makes a quick U-turn and leaves the property. "What was that all about?" Donald asked. "All I know is you better not leave in that limo Saturday!" said Danny senior. "Dad! I'm a grown man! I can take care of myself!" Donald shouted. "I'll pay for you and your girlfriend to go to Hawaii for a couple of weeks!" said Danny sr. "I have enough money to stay in Hawaii for the whole year!" Donald said. "Oh, look at Mr. big timer over here!" Danny sr. chuckled. "Hey! What can I say? I'm a lassenberry." Said Donald. Danny sr. grabs his son by the shoulders. "Seriously son! Don't get in that limo this Saturday! Please!" he says to his son. Donald sighs. "Ok dad. I won't go. I'll take the money for Hawaii though." Donald chuckled. Danny sr. gives his son a hug.

Finally, Saturday came around. A Boeman limo was on its way to Sir Edward's apartment. In the limo was Larry, a.k.a Big L., Joe-Joe, benny the 3rd, Krayton, Jake jr., mark jr. and Corey. These were the young men who carried the lassenberry name sir Edward wanted to see. The other nephews were excluded from the invite, either they were too young or their fathers weren't a lassenberry. There were strict instructions given to the limo driver to stop at the barricade and let the nephews walk the rest of the way to the apartment. "This is where you get out and walk!" the driver said, who happened to be tony. "This guy done lost his mind!" benny the 3rd said to himself. "You're gonna have to drive us to the front door, my man!" said Krayton. Tony didn't said a word. He reached under his seat and pulls out a pistol. He lowers the divider between passenger and driver. "Now I have orders to execute every last one of you, if you don't exit this vehicle right now!" tony shouted. "This dude ain't fucking around! Let's go y'all!" Joe-Joe said. "1, 2, 3!" tony said. "Fuck this shit!" Joe-Joe shouted as he jumps out of the limo. He's followed by his older brother and cousins. Mark jr. was the last to leave the limo. He just stared at tony, showing no fear. Tony had the pistol pointed directly at his face. "You got a lot of balls man." tony said. Mark jr. slowly exits the limo.

As the lassenberry men walked toward the apartment, a small army of Sir Edward's guards stood by quietly, armed to the teeth as they walked by. "Hey y'all! We're just here to see our uncle!" Corey stuttered. There was no response from the guards. "Let's just get to the apartment quick!" Joe-Joe whispered to Corey. Once the lassenberry men entered the freight elevator, the guards broke character and burst out laughing. "You see them, man?" steel chuckled. "I can't see myself working for those punk ass niggas!" black mike chuckled.

In the freight elevator, the lassenberry men are accompanied by Clip and J. Big, who are armed with shot guns. The elevator reaches Sir Edward's floor. When the elevator door slides open, there stands 2 Gunz. "Y'all follow me!" he said to them. Reluctantly, the lassenberry men follow Gunz down the hall. When they reach the apartment, Charlie is standing in the doorway. "Y'all come in and take a seat." Charlie ordered. Everyone took a seat, either on the sofa or in a folding chair. Charlie told them not to sit in his boss's favorite chair.

Minutes later, Sir Edward comes out of the bedroom. He was wearing a blue silk bathroom and flip flops. "I'm glad y'all came! It warms my heart to see I still got family!" sir Edward said. "We always got your back uncle!" Krayton shouted. "This shit is crazy." Mark Jr. whispers to himself.

Charlie goes into the kitchen. He comes out with 2 platters. One with catered sandwiches, and the other with a mount of cocaine and marijuana on it. He puts both platters on the coffee table. "There's a bar over in the corner guys. Help yourselves." Charlie said. Big L. wasted no time grabbing a turkey sandwich from the platter. Joe-Joe goes over to the bar and makes himself a drink. Charlie puts in a movie.

The movies Charlie had in his hand were pre-selected by Sir Edward. 2 of the movies were considered the most popular in the gangster genre. One of the about 4 hours long. As soon as the opening credits appeared, Krayton became excited. "Oh shit! This my favorite flick y'all!" Krayton shouted. Corey grabbed a joint from off the coffee table and lit it. Charlie pulled out cut straws from his pocket. He places them on the table next to the small pile of cocaine. "Y'all can use the straws, but I prefer rolling up a hundred dollar bill!" Charlie chuckled. Big L. pours himself stiff drink, filling it to the rim. Suddenly, benny the 3rd makes himself a drink. Joe-Joe wets his pinky finger and dips into the pile of cocaine. "I always wanted to do that! I saw a pimp do it at a party I went to!" Joe-Joe said. "Go ahead nephew! Help yo self!" Sir Edward said. Jake jr. grabs his first sandwich, while Big L. is chomping on his third. Thinking that no one was watching, Corey starts putting joints in his pockets. Joe- Joe went from dipping his finger in cocaine, to grabbing a straw. Krayton helps himself to a sandwich while gazing at the TV.

About 5 minutes left into the movie, Krayton is sitting on the floor eating another sandwich. Benny the 3rd is out cold, snoring in his chair. Joe-Joe and Corey are in deep conversation about current events. It sounded more like gibberish due to the effects of cocaine. Sir Edward noticed that one of his nephews didn't indulge in anything but a cold glass of water. Mark Jr. Kept looking at his watch. Krayton gets up and inserts another movie. After his third trip to the bathroom, Big L. didn't come out this time. Sir Edward was still observing everyone. Charlie joined in the conversation with Joe-Joe and Corey. Joe-Joe and Charlie did a couple of more line together. Corey sat this one out due to the looks he was get from his older brother. He instead makes himself a drink.

Hours later, the second movie comes to an end. Krayton applauds. "I don't care how many times I watch that shit, it just make a nigga wanna smoke somebody!" Krayton clamored. "It's just a movie cuz!" mark jr. sighed. Krayton gave his cousin the finger. Mark Jr. heads to the bathroom to check on Big L. he opens the door to find his cousin laid out on the bathroom floor next to the toilet. The toilet bowl had no vomit in it, but the floor was covered in it. "Come help me pick his ass up!" mark jr. says to Corey. It took all the strength they had to pick up the dead weight off the floor. It made things even harder when Corey started slipping on the vomit. Benny the 3rd wakes up from the noise caused by Corey falling on the bathroom floor. Joe-Joe walked out of the apartment. Benny the 3rd continuously stomps his feet after losing feeling in his leg. Sir Edward looks at his watch as he yawns. "It's been fun my nephews but I'm about to call it a day! I got shit to do!" sir Edward shouted. Mark jr. becomes agitated by the combination of what his uncle just said and the weight of his enormous cousin. Krayton repeatedly thanks his uncle for his hospitality. Mark jr. a d Corey struggle to take Big L. out of the apartment. "Yeah! Get his fat ass home into a cold shower!" sir Edward said.

Once they reach outside, the lassenberry clan are being heckled by a group of guards, all orchestrated by Sir Edward himself. After too much consumption of cocaine, Joe-Joe. Was basically walking around in circles talking to the guards at a fast rate. "Fake ass niggas!" someone from the crowd yelled. Krayton goes on the attack, but is stopped by his cousin Corey. "Man, I'm too fucked up to be out here fighting! Let's just get to the limo and get the fuck out of here!" Corey said. The nephews of Sir Edward enter the limo. "Take us to my place." mark jr. said. "Man, take my ass home!" said Krayton. "We're going to Delaware!" mark jr. demanded.

It was around 8pm, when the limo dropped off the lassenberry group at mark junior's 2 bedroom condo in Delaware. Mark's place was lavish. His walls were covered with oil painting by famous African American artists.

Big L. was still out cold from too much drinking. They lay him on the sofa. He belts out a monstrous snore. The effects of cocaine use makes Joe-Joe paranoid. He peeks through the wooden blinds, thinking he's being followed. Jake Jr. pulls out a pack of cigarettes. "No smoking in here cuz! You know better!" said mark jr. "Somebody get me an aspirin with a glass of water, please!" benny the 3rd said as he sits holding his head. "Somebody get him an aspirin! Never mind! I'll get it! Joe-Joe! Get away from the blinds! There's nobody out there!" mark jr. said. "We should've fuck those dudes up back at Uncle Eddie's place!" Krayton said to Corey. Mark jr. comes out of the bathroom with 2 aspirins and a cup of water. He gives it to benny the 3rd. "Unless you guys are retarded, there's no way couldn't tell Uncle Eddie was testing us!" mark jr. explained. The room was quiet. "You heard what his guards were saying about us! If they wanted to, they could've kicked all our asses!" mark jr. said. "If you would've followed my lead, we could've scrapped with them and won!" Krayton said. "They had guns, you idiot!" mark jr. said.

Back at Sir Edward's place, Charlie was busy cleaning up the mess. Sir Edward heads to the bathroom. "Charlie! Come here!' he shouted. Charlie comes running. "Look at this shit!" said Sir Edward. Charlie looks at the bathroom floor and sees chunks of dried vomit all around the toilet. "Clean that shit! I'll be back in a few minutes!" he ordered. Sir Edward leaves the apartment, and heads down the hall to what he called his spare pad. He punches in the code on a digital console. The door unlocks. The apartment is empty. He runs to the bathroom to his business.

The next day around 4 in the evening, Mario Felini pays an unexpected visit to Gino at his hangout in Newark. The place is quiet. "Hey gino!" he shouts. Gino doesn't answer. Felini walks through the lobby, towards the movie theatre. Its pitch black. He heads to the door leading to the basement. The door is locked. "Gino!" he shouts. There's still no answer. Felini decides to leave. Before he leaves, he hears a toilet flush. Gino comes out whistling with a newspaper folded underneath his arm pit. He's startled to see Felini. "What the fuck? You almost gave me a heart attack!" gino shouts. "You left the fucking door open!" said Felini. Gino catches his breath. "What you want?" gino asked. "I'm here for a sit down." Felini said. "Where's Depalma?" gino asked. "I think this is something we can do without the old man." Felini said. "You're talking crazy! There's 3 bosses, not 2!" gino said. "There's 2 bosses and one sick old man with 2 feet in the grave!" Felini shouts. "You realize what the other families would do if they found out we're planning to take out Depalma?" gino said. "I'm not talking about clipping Depalma! I came here to talk about that low life nigger, Eddie Lassenberry!"

Felini said. "We all decided to leave the dope alone!" gino said. Felini calms himself. "Listen! All we gotta do, is find out where his next shipment is coming in, then bam! We clip him and his crew, make a deal with the supplier, then it's ours!" Felini said. "Ok genius! Who are we gonna send in to do recon?" gino asked. "Just to make sure everything goes smoothly, I'll do the spy work!" Felini said. "It sounds too risky!" gino said. Felini gets frustrated. "I can't believe this! All your life you've been a stooge for Eddie lassenberry! Now you got the opportunity to take him out! Sembri una vecchia paura!" Felini shouts. Gino scratches his head. "Ok! You do the recon. I'll get a crew together, and once I get the word from you, we'll take'em out." Gino said. Felini pats gino on his head let a pet. "See! I knew you were smarter than you look!" Felini chuckled. Felini extends his hand. Gino reluctantly shakes his hand. "Next time we meet, I'll have all the information for ya." Felini said. Felini leaves with a smile on his face, while Gino stands there with a scowl on his.

It was the first week of November, when every member of the lassenberry family over the age of 18 was expecting an envelope of cash. Jabbo and his dispersing team would find the family members no matter how difficult.

Danny sr. and his son Donald were home waiting for jabbo to send someone over to deliver their envelopes. Usually, jabbo's team would be around at this time like clockwork.

It was going on 10pm, and no sign of jabbo or his team's members. Danny sr. checked his watch. Donald came downstairs. "Hey dad! Nothing?" Donald asked as he looked out the window. Danny sr. shook his head.

As promised, Sir Edward told his brother that he would deliver Danny junior's envelopes to him until they found out his whereabouts. It's been a year and 4 months since Danny junior's disappearance. Danny jr. accumulated an over a half million dollars. His father kept his envelopes in a safe, hidden somewhere in the basement. The following day, Danny sr. realized he and his son were financially cut off. A couple of day's later, Danny sr. gave his daughter a call about her envelope. Samara told her father that she had received hers the day before. Danny sr. wanted to contact his brother about the situation, but was told a long time ago by his father benny, never notify anyone about the envelopes.

Besides having a 5 million dollar estate in Livingston, New Jersey, Danny sr. owned a cottage just outside Paris, France. He owned a hundred foot yacht and belonged to a yacht club down the Jersey shore, which he paid $25,000 a year in dues. His 4 cars and motorcycle were paid off, but Danny sr. wanted that envelope money to finance purchasing property in North Africa. His annual salary from his packaging company came to a half million dollars. He would now have to depend on that salary to pay his property tax, his club dues and maintaining his yacht.

It was in mid-December when Sir Edward drove up to the construction site of the castle. The outer walls were completed, being made of huge stone blocks. After grabbing a hard hat from the trailer, he was given was given a tour by the site manager. Sir Edward witnessed the electricians running wire through small holes in the interior of the castle. Another team was digging to create a moat to surround the perimeter. The site boss told Sir Edward that the upper levels will be installed with clerestory type windows.

Coincidently, Danny sr. pulls up in his truck. He drives up the 200 yard driveway to the construction site. Danny sr. sees his brother off in the distance. After maneuvering through construction workers and heavy equipment, he finally catches up with his brother. "Can I speak to you alone for a moment?" Danny sr. asked his brother. Sir Edward sighs. ""You can get back to work." Sir Edward told the site manager. "Listen. I know you're not going to give me an envelope anymore, but what about Donald?" Danny sr. asked. "What about him?" Sir Edward asked. "He's a good kid! It's also embarrassing that my son being treated like an outcast!" Danny sr. shouts. "It was embarrassing and disrespectful to me, your son didn't show up to a meeting I arranged! I run this family! That includes you, and your son!" sir Edward shouts. "I have a question little brother. Did you tell your son not to come to the meeting?" he asked. Danny sr. gives a nod. "I was just looking out for my son's safety! God only knows where my other son is!" Danny sr. shouts. "I'll say it again. I run this family. I make the rules for this family, and that's it." Sir Edward explained. He walks off, leaving Danny sr. standing there, alone.

It was January 3rd, 1999 when Sir Edward had sent jabbo to get mark jr. from Delaware. Mark jr. was entertaining a young lady friend at the time. Jabbo and tony came knocking on his door. "Who the hell is that?" mark jr. whispered. "Maybe it's your other woman!" said the young lady. "I told you a hundred times, I don't have another woman!" he chuckled. He walks to the door in his bathrobe. Mark Jr. looks through the peep hole. He opens the door. "Your uncle wants to see you, now!" said jabbo. "Uncle Eddie?" mark jr. asked. "You call him Sir Edward, boy!" jabbo demanded. Mark Jr. turns toward his lady friend. "Jabbo giving you 10 minutes to get dressed!" jabbo ordered. Mark Jr. Leaves the door open, too afraid to close the door on jabbo. "Listen baby! My uncle sent for me! I have to go!" mark jr. sighed. "I thought we had the whole day together?" she cried. "I know, but this is my uncle we're talking about! He can get crazy we he doesn't get his way! I mean dangerously crazy! I promise to take you to Greece like I said I would! Fuck it! We'll do the whole Mediterranean!" mark jr. promised her. Those words put a smile on her pretty face. "Now, let's get dressed and get out of here!" mark jr. said after he kisses her on the lips.

Minutes later, mark jr. comes outside with his lady friend. "The dude has good taste!" tony said to jabbo. "Jabbo seen better." Mark Jr. Get in the back seat, next to jabbo. "So, what's the reason my uncle wants to see me about?" mark jr. asked. "He just told ol' jabbo to go get yo ass!" jabbo said.

Within a few hours, they arrive at Teterboro airport. Mark Jr. saw a private jet on the tarmac, with the engines revved up for takeoff. "Why are we at the airport?" mark jr. asked. "Come on boy! Let's go!" jabbo shouts. Mark jr. gets out of the car and sees a couple of white guys in black suits, wearing dark shades standing next to the boarding steps of the jet. Tony assists his boss out of the car and hands him his walking cane. Mark jr. has the look of terror in his eyes. "Follow me!" jabbo said to Sir Edward's nervous nephew. The 2 agents follow them on board the jet. Mark Jr. starts sweating something awful. Sitting all the way in the back of the jet, was Sir Edward and General Theodore J. Magus. Mark Jr. walks his way towards them. "How's it going nephew!" said Sir Edward. "Hey uncle! Is everything good?" mark jr. stuttered. "This here is General T. Magus!" said Sir Edward. The general stands. "So, you're the future?" the general asked mark jr. as he shook his hand. "Have a seat nephew and strap in!" said Sir Edward. Mark Jr. takes a seat across from his uncle and the general. The 2 NA agents sit at the other end of the jet. Jabbo and tony sit on the other side of the isle from Sir Edward. The sexy blonde stewardess closes the hatch. "Kinda overdressed there nephew." Sir Edward said. "Overdressed for what?" mark jr. asked his uncle. He noticed that everyone on board, except for the agents were dressed like it was the middle of June. "Its 40 degrees outside uncle!" mark jr. said. "Not in Afghanistan!" said Sir Edward.

CHAPTER 11. SIR MARCUS

Mark jr. was making a pilgrimage that would change his life forever. He was introduced to people of real power through his uncle. He was reborn into a new world unknown to most people.

It was the first week of February, when Sir Edward had to make to get his refill from Port Elizabeth. This time he brought along his nephew mark jr. and jabbo. Off in the distance, spying with binoculars was mob boss Mario Felini. Felini could see 2 Latino men exiting a white van. "Got you now you fucks!" Felini says to himself. All of a sudden, Felini felt something in the back of his neck. "You move, and you're dead!" said the voice from behind him. It was jabbo's right and man, Tony Kerouac. Tony jumps in the back seat of Felini's car. He takes a walkie-talkie from inside of his leather jacket. "I got the fish." Said tony. "Hey pal! Do you have any idea who I am?" Felini said. "Shut the fuck up and drive down the pier!" Said tony. Felini puts the car in drive. He heads towards the pier. By this time, the Latino connection had made the transaction with Sir Edward and left the scene. Tony forced Felini to drive over to where his boss, mark jr. and Sir Edward were.

It was cold and blistery that day. Sir Edward, mark jr. and jabbo were standing at the edge of the pier stomping their feet and pacing back-n-forth to keep warm. Felini's car pulls up. "Get the fuck out!" tony said. Felini turns off the engine and exits the car. Felini and Sir Edward look dead in each other's eyes. "Come on kid! There ain't no need for this! Just let me go, and I'll forget I ever saw you guys!" Felini pleaded. "Get the fuck out!" tony said to Felini. They both exit the car as tony has the gun pointed at the back of Felini's head. "I see you got to me first." Felini says to Sir Edward. Sir Edward looks up at the sky. "The whole thing is gray! Damn!" Sir Edward said. "So. You were gonna take me down? Well, here I am, you piece of shit!" Sir Edward shouts.

It was a Sunday. That meant no worker on the dock. No witnesses. "I just have one question! Did that fucking fat piece of shit gino rat me out to you?" Felini asked Sir Edward. Sir Edward just smiled. "If you shoot me, you're a dead man!" said Felini. Sir Edward started chuckling. "I'm ain't gonna shoot a made guy! But, I have no problem watching yo ass freeze to death!" said Sir Edward. "Tony! You know what jabbo want you to do!" said jabbo. "Got it boss." Said tony. Tony walks Felini to the edge of the pier, then pushes him over the side. They all watch Felini struggle for air as he flaps around in the freezing water. He could barely scream for help. Mark jr. was shaking like a leaf, not from the cold weather, but from watching a man die before his eyes. Mark Jr. runs over to the other side of the pier and pukes his brains out. Sir Edward and others start laughing hysterically.

The following week on a Monday, Sir Edward's health took a turn for the worse. He was sitting in his apartment watching TV with a glass of vodka in his hand. Suddenly, the left side of his body went numb and gave out on him. The drink fell from his hand. He screamed for help. Gunz came running in the apartment and finds him on the floor. He was carried down to the freight elevator. J. Smooth and Gunz put him the car and rushed him to the hospital. Gunz contacted Charlie, Charlie called jabbo, and then jabbo called mark jr. a half hour later. A couple of hours later, mark jr. arrives at the hospital. A few minutes later, Dubbs and Butch show up as well. Charlie told them what room Sir Edward was in. "What we gonna do now?" Dubbs asked jabbo. Suddenly, Jorge Morales arrived wheeling in Mookie. Jabbo pulled tony away from the crowd. "Jabbo don't care how you do it, but you gotta go get the ring off the boss's hand!" ordered jabbo. "Got it!" tony said. "What room is he in?" Mookie asked butch.

Tony made his way to room 503 in the intensive care unit. He looked inside the room and saw Sir Edward unconscious and hooked up to a heart monitor, with tubes coming out of his nose. Sir Edward had an I.V. hooked up to his hand as well. Tony makes a quick dash to Sir Edward's bedside. He carefully pulls the ring off of his finger. "Rest easy." tony said to Sir Edward. He heads back to the waiting area. He sees everyone standing around. Tony taps jabbo on the back of his shoulder. He gives jabbo the ring. Jabbo tells everyone to follow him to an empty corridor for privacy. Jabbo holds the ring up. "On this day, leadership of the lassenberry organization goes to Sir Edward's nephew! What you want us to call you son?" jabbo asked. "Mark I guess!" mark jr. said as he shrugged his shoulders. "I got it! So they don't confuse our names with each other, you should call yourself Marcus!" Mookie said. "Ok!" mark jr. said as jabbo hands him his uncle's ring. "Put it on son!" jabbo ordered. Mark jr. slowly puts the ring on his left pinky finger. "Perfect fit!" Dubbs said. "So it's settled! Long live the house of lassenberry! Long live…Sir Marcus!" jabbo shouts. "Long live the house of lassenberry! Long live Sir Marcus!" they all shout simultaneously. Sir Marcus's eyes tear up. "Make a call to my family and tell them to get out here!" ordered Sir Marcus. Jabbo grabs his mobile phone from his pocket and starts making calls.

A couple of days later, Sir Edward was still laid up in the hospital unconscious. Jabbo was sent to the apartment with 2 NA agents. It was his job to inform Sir Edward's crew at the apartment that their services were no longer needed. 2 Gunz, Tiki, Kent Fox and especially Rick didn't take the news easily. Out of respect, Mackie and Chewie were confronted by jabbo, but with 2 briefcases filled with a million dollars each as a severance package. They were all replaced by a small garrison of NA agents on orders of Sir Marcus. This was revenge for humiliating his brother and cousins when they last visited the apartment. Jabbo gave 2 Gunz his final orders before he departed from the apartment. "Jabbo want you and the boys to lay low! Jabbo think these new people ain't human!" jabbo said before he embraced 2 Gunz with a hug.

Later on that evening at the East Orange safe house, Sir Marcus had a meeting with jabbo,

Charlie and tony. "First thing tomorrow, I want a moving company at my uncle's place to move all his belongings into storage." He ordered jabbo. "Jabbo think you should wait until Sir Edward come out of his coma." Said jabbo." "Ok then! Charlie will watch over things at the apartment until my uncle recovers." Sir Marcus ordered. Sir Marcus pulls jabbo over for a one on one conversation. "If my uncle has any important items, such as weapons, cash and documents I want you to bring them to my place! Understand?" Sir Marcus whispered. "No problem." Said jabbo.

It was the first week of April. The exterior of the castle was near completion. The castle had a north, south, east and west wing. The west wing was near completion for occupancy. The only thing needed was the décor. It was an around 8 in the morning when Sir Marcus visited the construction site. An interior designer hired by Sir Marcus, had an office desk made of teakwood placed in what was to be Sir Edward's office. Sir Marcus sat himself down in a chair made of teakwood as well. The arm rests and seat were padded with the feathers of a rare bird according to Sir Edward's written specifications. Jabbo showed up at the castle a few hours later with a binder in his hands.

The binder was 4 inches thick filled with all the information of what and who was involved with the lassenberry day to day operations. For 5 decades jabbo was the keeper of the binder. He recorded every event pertaining to the business. He presented the B.O.I as he called it, to Sir Marcus. The B.O.I had the names of every Street boss and runner in the lassenberry organization. Jabbo's last entry read that there were 653 dealers and 50 street bosses spread throughout the 13 counties that the lassenberry crew controlled. The binder showed how much everyone was paid. It also had the names of every politician, judge, police officer and media contact that was on the lassenberry payroll. Jabbo didn't have too much information on the National Agreement. Even jabbo's resources couldn't get that close to them.

As Sir Marcus was flipping through the pages of the B.O.I, jabbo was explaining to him the ins and outs of the drug game. Sir Marcus came upon an entry that was written in 1997 with hakim's name in it. His name had a question mark next to it. "What's this about?" he asked jabbo. "Oh! That was a dream yo uncle had at one time. He wanted hakim to run things at one point, but that idea went out the window." Said jabbo. "It's been a long time since I've seen that joker!" Sir Marcus said. "Jabbo forgot to tell ya. Hakim coming home soon." Jabbo said. "When?" Sir Marcus asked. "Soon! Real soon!" he said.

The next day jabbo and tony went to the hospital to see Sir Edward. After coming out of his coma a few days earlier, Sir Edward was ready to come home. The stroke left the most powerful drug lord in New Jersey paralyzed on the left side of his body. His left eye was closed shut, and his face drooped as he laid in bed. Jabbo grabbed some tissue from his bedside and wiped away the drool from Sir Edward's mouth. "Listen here. Jabbo gonna take care of you now son." He said as a tear trickled down his cheek. Tony had to turn away. He couldn't bare to see the man that was once so powerful, look so helpless. Suddenly, Sir Edward's lip struggle to move. His speech was slurred. Jabbo had to put his ear to Sir Edward's lips after he wiped away more drool from his mouth. "I understand boss. Jabbo want you to rest now." He said to his boss. He then kisses Sir Edward on the forehead. "Let's go!" jabbo said to tony. Outside the room, jabbo explains Sir Edward's orders to tony.

It was at the Lodi office building where 12 of Sir Edward's nephews were to gather, dressed in formal attire. Tyson Richards, Malcolm Richards, Mike Abbey, Big L., Joe-Joe, BB, Benny the 3rd, Krayton, Jake jr., Corey, Donald and Mark jr., who was not known to anyone as Sir Marcus yet. They were all there by orders of jabbo for a big announcement. Big L. headed straight for the buffet table. "What's this shit about?" Tyson asked benny the 3rd. "I have no idea!" said benny. Sir Marcus was sitting in one of the lounge chairs sipping on a glass of wine. Donald comes over and sits next to him with a bottle of beer in his hand he grabbed from the refrigorator. When he opens it, beer spewed out on his suit. "Shit!" Donald shouted as he wiped the beer off of himself. "You ok little cuz?" Sir Marcus asked. "I don't know, maybe! I guess you heard Uncle Eddie cut me and pop off." Donald said. "Cut what off?" Sir Marcus asked. "He stopped sending us envelopes because of some beef he got with my father!" Donald said. "What's the beef about?" he asked Donald. "Something about my brother! My father thinks he got D.J. on the run about some money, I think!" Donald whispered. Sir Marcus didn't say a word. He just sipped on his wine.

At another part of the room, Joe-Joe, Krayton and Corey are standing together, each with a plate of food in their hands. "That jabbo dude one crazy nigga!" Krayton chuckled. "Maybe he called us here to bump us off!" Joe-Joe whispered. "Shit! I'll punch that old man in his neck!" said Krayton. "After you do it, then where you gonna live?" Corey chuckled. "Oh, you funny as hell!" Krayton said. "Check this out! You still wanna buy Uncle Eddie's apartment? I don't think he'll be staying there for long!" Corey whispered. "Oh, now you wanna go into business with me now!" Krayton said. "I thought about it! Like you said before! Everybody and their mother would wanna party at the place the legendary Eddie lassenberry once lived!" Corey whispered. "Why y'all ain't tell me about this?" Joe-Joe asked. "You wanna come in on this?" Krayton asked. Joe-Joe thought about it for a second. "Not really! It's just fucked up you didn't ask me!" Joe-Joe said. "Awe! His feelings hurt!" Krayton said as he squeezed Joe-Joe's cheeks. Joe-Joe smacked his hand away. "That's alright! When y'all get in a beef with them Newark niggas out there, don't call me!" Joe-Joe said. Krayton starts laughing hysterically. "We're lassenberry! We run Newark!" Krayton said. "Correction! Uncle Eddie runs Newark!" Joe-Joe said.

Mike abbey and his brother BB were standing, staring at a replica of the lassenberry coat-of-arms hanging on the wall. "So, we're royalty or something now?" Bert asked. "I guess so!" mike said.

Suddenly, there's a hard knock on the door. "Somebody else was invited?" Big L. asked as he was chewing his food. Corey looked nervous. He slowly steps back behind Joe-Joe. The room is silent. The door slowly opens. The first to step through the door was a tall burly NA agent. Coming in next was another NA agent. Jabbo comes strutting in afterwards with his walking cane. "Jabbo want all y'all to stop what you doing, and stand as greatness enters the room!" he shouted. "You heard the man!" said Sir Marcus. His brother and cousins stand facing the entrance, waiting to see who was coming in next. It was the man himself being strolled in a wheelchair by another agent. Sir Edward was wearing his uniform with his Order Of the Elephant medal pinned to him. His head was tilted to the side. The agent wheeling him in took out a handkerchief and wiped the drool from his mouth.

Jabbo takes out a sheet of paper from inside his jacket pocket. He unfolds it. "Y'all listen up gentlemen! This is coming from Sir Edward himself!" said jabbo.

"I Sir Edward, on this day, April 20th 1999, will cease as the head of the lassenberry organization! I will cease as overseer of the 13 counties in New Jersey! I will cease as financial provider of the lassenberry bloodline! I pass on all duties and territories under lassenberry control to my nephew mark lassenberry! Step forward son!" jabbo ordered. Sir Marcus stood before jabbo. Corey and his cousins stood in awe. "What the fuck?" Krayton whispered to himself. "Now turn and face your family!" jabbo ordered. He turned around facing everyone. "From this day on! You will not call him mark lassenberry jr. anymore! You will address him as Sir Marcus!" jabbo shouted. "I want you all to repeat after jabbo! Long live the house of lassenberry! Long live Sir Marcus!" jabbo shouted. "Long live the house of lassenberry." They said. "Louder!" jabbo shouted. "Long live the house of lassenberry! Long live the Sir Marcus!" all shouted at the top of their lungs. One by one, Sir Marcus's brother and cousins approach him. "Oh shit! We got this now brother!" Corey chuckled. "Take is easy." Sir Marcus said as he hugged his brother. Benny the 3rd was next. "I'd rather it be you cousin!" he said. "Thanks." Sir Marcus said as they hugged. Next was Joe-Joe. "I wanna raise!" Joe-Joe said jokingly. "We'll talk." Sir Marcus chuckled as they hugged. Next in line was BB. "Good luck cuz." He said as they hugged. Krayton then faces his cousin. He had a scowl on his face. "Don't fuck it up cuz!" Krayton then chuckled. Sir Marcus lightly taps Krayton on the cheek. They both hug. Donald makes his way to Sir Marcus next. "Look out for me big cuz!" Donald whispered in his ear as they hugged. "Don't worry." Sir Marcus said. Donald gets teary eyed then walks away. Mike abbey was next in line. "Congratulations cousin!" he said as they hug. Next was Big L. "Hold on a second!" Big L. said as he wiped mayonnaise off of his hands with a napkin. The hug he gave Sir Marcus was so tight, everyone could see the pain in Sir Marcus's eyes. "Let him go man!" shouted Corey. Big L. releases Sir Marcus. "Oops! Sorry!" Big L. said. "Don't worry about it!" Sir Marcus said as he tried to catch his breath. He pats Big L. on the shoulder. "Next!" Sir Marcus shouted. Malcolm hugs Sir Marcus. "Good luck man." he said. "My turn!" Tyson said as he approached his cousin. He grabs Sir Marcus by the shoulders. "Listen. If there's anything the Richards boys can do for you, just ask. You hear me! Huh?" Tyson said. "Alright! Alright!" Sir Marcus chuckled. Tyson steps to the side. Jake jr. was the last to approach his cousin. He hugs Sir Marcus. "We're here for you cousin!" he said.

"Alright! Now it's time for Sir Marcus to go and take care of some business!" said jabbo. "Yeah! You guys stay and help yourselves to more food and drink, and I'll catch you all later!" said Sir Marcus. Tyson breaks through the crowd. "You already knew you was the chosen one, didn't you?" he whispered in Sir Marcus's ear. He could see the hate in Tyson's eyes. "I said I'll catch you later, cuz" Sir Marcus said. "Sir Marcus. Let's go, please." Jabbo said. "Make way." The agent said as he wheels Sir Edward out of the room. Sir Marcus, jabbo and the other 2 agents follow them out.

Moments later, Krayton, Tyson and Malcolm huddle together at the buffet table. "I just figured out why Uncle Eddie invited us to a meeting at his apartment a while back!" Krayton said. "What meeting?" Tyson asked. "Holy shit!" Krayton said. "Holy shit, what?" Tyson asked. "It was because we had the name lassenberry!" Krayton said to himself. Tyson looks at his brother

Malcolm with fury in his eyes. Tyson deliberately knocks a tray of food on to the floor. Everyone turns when they hear the loud noise. "Come on! Let's get the fuck out of here!" Tyson says to Malcolm. Both brothers storm out of the room. Corey walks over to Krayton. "What's with them?" he asked Krayton. "Jealously is a mother fucker, I guess!" Krayton sighed.

It was June 23rd when hakim was being released from prison after serving 15 years for murder. Hakim looked like a new man from head to toe. He was strictly muscles from a vigorous exercise regimen during his last 5 years. He let his hair grow back and got tatted over parts of his body.

He had a coiled snake tatted on the left side of his chest, a pair of demon wings covering his back, the words God Of Fire on his right forearm, a skull with flames shooting out of its eyes on his right calf, a picture of Africa on his left forearm with the word Home written underneath and the words HOOD KING written across his torso.

The process for release was different for hakim than any other inmate. He was called to the warden's office after all of his forms were filled out. As he was leaving his cell block, he had the privilege of saying goodbye to certain inmates. "Y'all keep ya heads up!" he shouted down the tier. A lot of the inmates cheer and holler as he leave the cell block.

Hakim was escorted to the warden's office by 2 corrections officers that grew fond of him. One of them was lieutenant wade O'Boyle. "So, the infamous hakim bates is finally on his way to freedom!" O'Boyle said. "It's been a long fucking time, man!" said hakim. "Think you're ready for the world out there?" O'Boyle asked. "The question is the world ready for me?" hakim boasted. "Don't go do something stupid and end up back here." Said O'Boyle. "You know you want me to stay!" hakim chuckled. "Bullshit!" said O'Boyle. Hakim turns to O'Boyle. "What made an educated white boy like yourself decide to stay?" hakim asked. "This might sound insane, but the world makes more sense in here, then out there." He answered. "I believe this place done drove you insane, man! Hakim said.

The prison bus carrying hakim and the guards arrive outside the warden's facility. O'Boyle follows hakim inside the facility. Inside stood a corrections officer waiting for their arrival. "Hey Hardy! Go take a 5 minute smoke break! I got it from here!" O'Boyle ordered. Hardy gives O'Boyle the peace sign and takes a pack of cigarettes from his shirt pocket. Hakim and O'Boyle approach the warden's office. O'Boyle knocks on the glass part of the door. "Almost home free, man!" hakim said. The warden buzzes them in. O'Boyle opens the door. "Sir." He said. "Bring him in O'Boyle." The warden said as he was playing a game of solitaire. Lying on the warden's desk was a revolver and a check written out to hakim bates. "You can step outside Officer O'Boyle." Said the warden. O'Boyle leaves the office. He steps outside where hardy was. He takes the pack of smokes from out of hardy's pocket and takes out a cigarette. Hardy lights it for him. "What's the deal with that bates guy?" hardy asked. "I hope I'm wrong. But, this ain't the last we're gonna see of hakim bates." O'Boyle said.

Back in the office, the warden tells hakim to take a seat. Hakim sits. "Let's cut to the chase old man! Where the fuck is the rest of my money?" hakim asked. "Take it easy young man." The warden said in a calm voice. "I just wanna get the fuck out of here!" hakim said. "Guess what? We both have something in common!" the warden said. "And what's that?" hakim asked. "We're both leaving this god awful place!" he said. "What, you retiring?" hakim asked the warden as he opens the drawer to his desk and takes out a bottle of scotch and 2 glasses. "After 50 years of babysitting, I deserve it!" the warden said. "50 years? Oh, you definitely need a drink!" hakim said. "This is top shelf shit here! Thanks to you!" the warden said as he's pouring hakim and himself a drink. "Cheers nigga!" hakim said as he gulps down his drink. The warden gives off a smirk and gulps his drink down as well. "I haven't heard from your father in the past 2 years." The warden said. "If you're talking about Eddie lassenberry, well I haven't heard from him in 14 years!" hakim shouted as he pours himself another drink. The warden had a deviant smirk on his face, as he realized he dug underneath hakim's tough exterior. "I have to say, you let this job get the best of you. You like you came out of an Egyptian tomb." Hakim said. "Ooh! Nice comeback kid!" he chuckled. Hakim smiled. "So what's your plans for the future?" the warden asked. "I plan to take over the world, or at least New Jersey." Hakim said with a serious look on his face. "Are you trying instill fear into me, Mr. bates?" the warden asked. "Nah, man! I just want that check right there, and be on my way!" hakim responded. The warden puts his finger on the check and slides the check to hakim. "That's the remainder of your dowry. Spend it wisely." Said the warden. Hakim looked at the check. It was made out to him for one hundred thousand dollars. "Hold on man! Where's the rest of my money?" hakim asked. "Let's see. Fancy dining, living conditions, women, and oh yes! Murder for hire!" said the warden. Hakim slowly puts the check inside his pants pocket. "I tell you Mr. bates, covering up a crime scene for someone doesn't come cheap.

Outside the prison gates, hakim stands until a taxi pulls to the curb. Hakim was dressed in a burgundy jogging suit, white sneakers and wearing the same jewelry had when he first stepped into prison. Besides his check, hakim was given a sum of 3 thousand dollars in cash courtesy of the F.C.I

"Where you headed son?" the cabby asked. "Newark. Eddie lassenberry territory." Said hakim. "Whatever you say." Said the cabby. Hakim looks over at the prison and saw O'Boyle still standing behind the gate. He gives O'Boyle the thumbs up before the cabby drives off.

About a half hour into the drive up north, hakim noticed a billboard on the side of the road advertising the new Boeman Sedan. The words above the vehicle read, STILL GANGSTA! A couple of hours later, the cabby makes a turn on his hakim's street. Hakim noticed there were no guards, no barricades. As they come closer to the building, hakim noticed that the building and the whole block was barren. "You sure this is where you wanted to be dropped off son?" asked the cabby. Hakim's ostentatious attitude was quite the opposite from the time he started his journey home. "Damn! Take me back down to South Jersey. Bridgeton to be exact!" hakim ordered the cabby. "Ok! It's gonna cost another hundred and twenty bucks!" the old man said. "Don't worry! I got the money!" said hakim. "Don't you think you should call your people up before taking that long ride back?" the cabby asked. "I wish I could." Said hakim.

A couple of hours later, hakim is just waking up from the long drive. They drive up to a one family shanty in a rundown rural neighborhood. "This is it young blood! That'll be 220." The cabby said. "No sweat." Hakim said as he pulled out a wad of cash. He also pulled out the check warden benedict had given him. He was so confident after seeing the check, he gave the cabby a tip of 20 bucks. "Damn son! Thanks!" the cabby said. "Be good old man." hakim said as he exits the cab. Hakim grabs his duffle bag. Hakim just stands there and watched as the cabby drives off.

CHAPTER 12. ANNIE

It was 4 in the afternoon on a breezy summers day, as a group of African American children were playing tag in the field across the road from the house hakim had his eyes on. He looked to his left and saw an old light skinned black woman next door, sitting in a rocking chair on the porch. He walks up the steps of the house he came to visit after passing a rusted 4 foot tall fence. The concrete steps were crumbling from neglect. The front lawn was over powered by weeds. On the porch was a night stand that had an ashtray on it filled to the rim with cigarette butts. There were empty beer bottles on the porch next to the night stand. The wooden porch itself was rotted from neglect as well. Hakim couldn't ring the doorbell because the button was dangling by the wires. There was a door knocker though, so he used it instead. The door opens. It was a short white woman who came out. Hakim could smell the strong stench of cigarettes as the door opened wider. Hakim could tell from that instant that she found him attractive. He received the look from women since he was a teenager. "Can I help you handsome?" she asked. "Yeah! Is Bex here?" hakim asked. "Oh Biron? He just left not too long ago, on his way to the liquor store! He'll be back in a few! May I ask who wants to see him?" she asked. "I'm a friend of his from F.C.I." hakim said. "Oh, is that right?" she said. "He said if I was ever in town, to pay him a visit." Hakim said with a big smile on his face.

The woman looked straight up hill Billy. She wore cutoff jeans and a wife beater t-shirt with no bra. Hakim could see her tits sagging and that her nipples were hard. When she spoke, hakim noticed that she had dentures. She looked in her early 50's, having short blonde hair with streaks of gray around the edges. Any person who lived the street life could tell she was sexy as hell in her younger years.

"You ain't dressed like someone who was on the inside! You look more like a big shot to me!" she said. "I had sort of a good life before everything went to shit." hakim said. "Anyway. I'm his mother Peggy, and your name is." She said as she extended her hand to greet hakim. "Oh, my fault! I'm hakim." he said as they shook hands. "Well come on inside!" she said.

Hakim follows her into the house. Peggy slams the door shut. They walk pass the living room. It looked like someone used it as a bedroom. There were sheets and a comforter on the sofa. The coffee table had more empty beer bottles on it, with one filled with cigarette butts. There were black-n white photos of Peggy when she was younger on the dusty shelves in the corner. She posed in most of them like she was a super model. The rest of the pictures were mounted on the wall were of Bex when he was a baby and toddler. They entered a small cramped kitchen. The kitchen has just enough room to fit a frig, a table with 4 chairs and a 32 gallon waste can.

"Go on and have a seat!" Peggy insisted. Hakim sits and places his duffle bag on the floor next to him. "You wanna soda or glass of water?" she asked. "A beer sounds much better!" said hakim. "Sorry, I'm all out! Biron should be back with a case though!" she said. "Can't wait!" said hakim. "You wanna listen to some music?" Peggy asked. "Cool!" hakim said. Peggy goes into the living room and retrieves a boom box. She places it on the counter next to the sink and plugs it in to the outlet. As soon as she presses the button on the boom box, rap music started blasting through the speakers. Peggy started dancing and snapping her fingers. Hakim noticed she had the dance moves of a black woman. Hakim nervously taps his fingers on the kitchen table, then sees the front door being pushed open. He stands to his feet. In comes Bex with a case of beer under his arm. Right behind him, was a short light skinned, pudgy black woman carrying a grocery bag. "Hey baby boy! You have a guest!" Peggy shouts. Bex squints his eyes at hakim. "Oh snap!" Bex shouted. He rushes into the kitchen and puts the case of beer on the floor. He gives hakim a hug. "My nigga! My nigga!" Bex chuckled. Hakim hugs him back. "Didn't you tell me to come see you when I was in town?" hakim chuckled. They hug each other again. "Boy, move so I can put this heavy ass bag down!" the pudgy woman shouted. Bex releases hakim and takes the bag from the woman. "All you had to do was to the shit on the table!" Bex shouted. "Don't yell at her!" Peggy said. "Yeah! Don't yell at me!" the woman shouts. "Y'all got my cigarettes?" Peggy asked. "Damn ma! Here!" Bex shouted as he takes the carton of cigarettes out of the bag. "I hope you bought cups! I ain't washing them damn dishes you left in the sink!" Peggy shouts. "Yeah! We got cups!" the woman shouts.

The woman name was Annie Stevens. She lived next door with her grandmother, who hakim saw before he came into the house. Annie was in her early 30's with Down's syndrome.

When she was a little girl, the kids in the neighborhood used to tease her until Peggy made Bex play with her. Since then, she and Bex were like brother and sister. When she was 11 years old, a couple of boys down the street tried to rape her until Bex found out and beat both of the boys to a pulp.

Peggy and Annie start dancing together to the rap music. "Give me a beer man! I'm thirsty as hell!" said hakim. Bex passes him a beer. "Hakim, this is Annie. Annie, hakim." said Bex. Hakim waves at Annie. Annie waves back with a smile. Hakim noticed Annie was missing her some teeth. "Where you from?" she asked hakim. "Oh, I'm from Newark." Hakim said. "Where the hell is Newark?" Annie asked. "It's in this state, but up north." Hakim said. "Turn up the music!" Annie shouts as she and Peggy start doing the bump. Annie bumps her hip into hakim's shoulder. Hakim starts laughing. Hakim noticed that Bex had on a dingy t-shirt, and a pair of saggy jeans with paint stains on them. Bex noticed him staring at his clothes. "This dude down the road gave me a grand to do his house!" Bex said. "You driving all the way back to Newark tonight?" Peggy asked hakim. "I was hoping I could stay the night so I can get some rest." Hakim said. "Sure you can stay! I'll get a sheet and a pillow for ya, after we party the night away!" Peggy shouted. Peggy turns up the volume on the boom box. Bex takes out a bottle of vodka from the grocery bag and fills there cups. "I wanna make a toast!" Bex shouts. "Yeah! A fucking toast!" Annie shouted. "To my friend hakim! Welcome home!" Bex shouts. Peggy, Annie and hakim raise their cups. Everyone gulps down their drinks. Hakim's eyes start to tear up. "What? The drink too strong for ya?" Annie asked. "Hell no!" hakim chuckled. Bex refills everyone's cups. Hakim pulls a few bucks from his pocket. "Put yo money back in your pocket! It's on me, man!" Bex said.

Suddenly, they hear someone banging on the front door. Bex goes to the door and opens it. An elderly black couple enters the house. "Hey y'all! Come on in the kitchen!" Bex shouts. They follow Bex into the kitchen. "Hey y'all! I want y'all to meet my friend hakim!" Bex shouts. "What's up man? I'm Toby. This my wife jenny." He said as he and hakim shake hands. Hakim shakes jenny's hand as well. Jenny gives Annie and Peggy a hug. "We gotta head back to the liquor store!" said Bex. "I'll go with you!" hakim said. "Come on Toby! It's on me! You women stay here!" said Bex. "Bring back some chips!" Peggy shouted. "Yeah! Bring back some chips!" Annie shouted. Bex, Toby and hakim leave the house and jump in Bex's rusty old jeep. Hakim jumps in the back seat. "They gave you yo license back that quick?" Toby asked. "Don't worry old man! I got this!" Bex chuckled. Bex drives off.

Inside the house, jenny grabs a beer. "Do me a favor Annie, and put the rest of the beers in the refrigorator!" Peggy said. "That's one good looking man!" jenny said. "I don't why that boy looks so familiar!" Peggy said.

Jenny was short, brown skin and skinny. She had a short afro. Usually when jenny came over, which was every weekend, she would give Bex 10 dollars to go get her a bag of weed. She kept it a secret from Toby. He would get angry when drunk, sometimes abusive if he caught her with drugs. Bex would have to calm Toby down and take him home to sleep it off.

At the liquor store, Toby and Bex are walking down the aisle, each with a case of beer. Hakim was at the counter telling the elderly white guy at the register wanted the most expensive cognac. The guy told his young assistant to watch register so he could go in the back. Bex and Toby approach the counter. The man comes back with a bottle in his hand. "Listen kid. This is a 12 year old cognac, I only buy it one case at a time." The man said. "Cool! I'll take 2 bottles!" hakim said. "Damn man!" Bex shouted. "That'll be 500 bucks." The man said. "You're sure you can handle that?" Toby asked. "I got it!" hakim said as he pulls out a wad of cash. He pays for the bottles. The old man lifts one of the hundred dollar bills to the light. "Don't worry old man, it's real." Hakim said. "Everything checks out." The man said. "Are you serious?" hakim sighed. The young assistant runs to the back storage area, and quickly runs back out with a second bottle. The bottles came in small black velvet sacks with a gold draw string sealing it closed. The old man hands hakim the 2 bottles. "Make sure you don't drop that shit!" said Toby.

Outside the liquor store, they all head towards the jeep. They all load up in the jeep. Bex was having a hard time starting the vehicle. "Damn! It's the fucking starter again!" Bex said. "What? We gotta walk now?" hakim asked. "You know I got bad knees!" said Toby. "If our ass gotta walk back, yo ass gotta walk back!" Bex said to Toby. Hakim sees a young black woman coming out of the liquor store with a bottle of wine in her hand.

The woman was light skinned with dreadlocks coming down her back. She was wearing a traditional African dress that came down to her ankles. Hakim struts over to her as she is unlocking the door to her car. "Excuse me. Excuse me." Said hakim. The young lady turns around. "Can I help you?" she asked. "Yes you can. I know this might sound strange, but my friends and I are stranded here because our car just broke down. We would be ever so grateful if you give us a ride." Said hakim. "Have you lost your mind? I don't know you, or your friends!" she said. "No disrespect, but I can give you a hundred dollars if you do us this one favor. I'll throw in this bottle of expensive cognac!" Hakim said. "What's your name?" she asked. "I'm hakim, and you are?" he asked her. The young lady doesn't say her name. "Well hakim, here's a lesson from me to you. Everybody can't be bought!" she said before she gets in her car. "This is a nice ride! What is it, one of them new Boeman cars?" hakim asked. "Have a nice day hakim." the young woman said before she drives out of the parking lot. Hakim walks back over to Toby and Bex with his tail between his legs. Toby laughs so hard, he starts coughing. "You thought you had that pretty girl in yo back pocket!" Toby chuckled. "That car she was driving is real popular now!" Bex said. "Fuck her, and her car!" hakim shouts. "Come on y'all! Let's get back to the house!" Toby said.

The 3 men start their trek heading west down a dark road. "When I get a chance, I'm buying one of those cars, man!" Bex said. "Never mind that! The first thing you do tomorrow is get a new starter. I'll put it in myself." Toby said.

All the guys could hear while walking down the road were crickets. There were light posts every 1000 feet, making it dark and gloomy. They come upon a huge lavish house. "Man, that's a nice crib!" hakim said. "That's buddy's house." Bex said.

Buddy was a skinny dark skinned kid in his early 20's, who was the neighborhood drug lord. Buddy had the most immaculate house in the area. He had a 3 door garage with automatic door sensors. His front lawn was the size of Peggy's entire property. The house looked like it belonged in Beverly Hills instead of South Jersey. "You guys stay here." Bex said. Bex puts the case of beer on the ground next to Toby. Bex walks up to the front door and presses the buzzer. Within seconds, the door opens. "What up nigga?" buddy shouted. "What up B?" Bex said as they shook hands. "Want the usual?" buddy asked Bex. Buddy looks over Bex's shoulder and sees Hakim and Toby standing in the distance. "Yo! Who that nigga over there with old man Toby?" he asked. "Oh! He ain't nobody!" Bex said. "Listen nigga! Next time, don't bring no strange faces around here! You lucky I'm up in some pussy right now, or I would smoke his ass and yo ass just for bringing him around here!" buddy said. Bex doesn't say a word. He puts his head down in shame. Bubby steps back into the house. Minutes later, buddy comes out with an ounce of weed wrapped in a plastic baggie. Bex takes the baggie and stuffs it in front pocket. "When you gonna come work for me nigga?" buddy asked. Bex starts chuckling. "Man, I'm good right now!' Bex said. Buddy puts his hand on the back of Bex's neck. "If you decide to get in the game nigga, you better come see me first, ya feel me?" buddy said. Bex feels the pressure from buddy's boney fingers getting tighter. "I got you man! I got it!" Bex said. Buddy releases his grip. They shake hands. Bex walks toward the gate, buddy went back into his house, slamming the door shut. Bex walks picks up the case of beer from off the ground. "Man, you let that skinny little punk bitch handle you like that?" hakim said. "Man, it's all good!" Bex said in a trembling voice. "Let's go boys. Toby said.

Finally, a half hour later they arrive at the house. "It's about time!" Bex said. Toby was crossing the road. Bex and hakim were already on the porch. "You know why it took us so long, right?" hakim whispered. "Why?" Bex asked. "Because that old man walking with us!" hakim chuckled. Bex just shook his head and went into the house. "Where the hell y'all been?" Peggy shouted. Bex takes the bag of weed out of his pocket and discretely passes it to jenny. Toby walks in the door out of breath. Hakim then walks in the kitchen with the cognac. Jenny and Annie make them themselves a drink. Hakim makes himself a drink and heads out on the front porch. Bex grabs one of his mother's cigarettes and make a drink and heads out to the front porch. Hakim is looking up at the night sky. Bex sits on the cracked steps. He takes a drag off of his cigarette. Hakim sits down next to him. He takes a sip of cognac. "Hey! You realize that nigga sell shit from his house?" hakim asked. "Who?" Bex asked. "That little nigga that grabbed you by the neck!" hakim said. Bex looks around to see if anyone was in hearing distance. "Quiet man!" Bex whispered. "I'm just saying that nigga doing something dumb as hell!" hakim said. "I guess you would know!" Bex said. "If you gonna live that life, you don't to the product! I would just check to see if the shit was good enough to put on the streets. Sit back, and collect the cash!" hakim said. "Whatever!" Bex said. Bex heads back into the house.

In the kitchen, Peggy is sitting on a folding chair she got from the back yard. Everyone is sitting around listening to R&B music. Annie gets up and starts dancing. She doesn't notice that her drink is spilling over as she dances around. No one tells her either.

The next day around 3 in the afternoon, it was raining hard. Hakim was waking up from a terrible hangover. He leans over rubbing his head. He noticed that he was sleeping on the sofa in his underwear. His clothes were hanging over the arm of the sofa. Even though his head was throbbing, he quickly checks his pockets. He was relieved the check and his money was still in pockets. His nostrils started flaring from the smell of food. He looked across the living room and saw Bex sleeping on the floor under a blanket. Hakim puts on his pants. He gets up and stumbles towards the kitchen. He sees Peggy in there whipping up some eggs and pancakes. There were sausages already on a serving dish. "Afternoon handsome! How about a late breakfast?" Peggy asked. Ok, thanks." Hakim said in faint voice as he heads to the bathroom. He closes the door tight. The bathroom downstairs was so small and cramped, there was only room for a sink and toilet. After taking a leak, he flushed the toilet and washed his hands. "Sit down and get some food in you!" Peggy said as he comes out of the bathroom. Peggy grabs a plate from the cabinet and places it in front of hakim. Peggy fills his plate with scrambled eggs and sausages. "Can't nobody whip up eggs like me sweetie!" Peggy said. Peggy sits across from hakim and lights up a cigarette. Hakim starts to chow down. "God damn! Slow down handsome! I can makes some more!" Peggy chuckled. Hakim ignores her and continues eating. She looks at hakim with curiosity. "When is your birthday sweetie?" she asked after she takes a drag of her cigarette. "March 5th, 1966." Hakim said while chewing his food. "What's your mother's name?" she asked. Hakim looked at Peggy and stopped chewing. "My mothers' dead!" he said. Peggy takes another drag of her cigarette. "She still gotta name, don't she?" she asked. "Gloria. Gloria bates." He said. Peggy's jaw dropped. She placed her cigarette in the ashtray. She slowly rises out her seat. "What's your daddy's name?" Peggy asked him. Hakim drops his fork in the plate and wipes his mouth, leaning back in his chair. "My biological father I don't know. My adoptive father is Eddie lassenberry." He said. Peggy stumbles backward, losing her balance. "Biron! Biron! Biron!" Peggy screamed as she caught herself. Bex hears his mother's screams and comes running in the kitchen in his underwear. "Ma! What the fuck?" Bex shouted. Peggy looks at hakim as if she'd seen a ghost. "I knew you looked familiar! You look just like her!" Peggy shouts. "Like who ma?" Bex asked. "Gloria bates! Biron! Say hello to your brother!" Peggy said. Hakim stands he backs up, until he hits the wall. "Oh shit!" Bex shouts. "I can't believe this! After all these years!" Peggy said. "Sit down boys and finish eating! We gotta talk later! We really gotta talk!" Peggy chuckled.

After they finished eating, Bex sat in the kitchen across from hakim. "Why didn't you tell me you was the son of Eddie lassenberry?" Bex asked. "First of all, I ain't his son! Not anymore!? Hakim said. "Now I get why nobody fucked with you while we was in lock up!" Bex said. Peggy comes into the kitchen. "If y'all finished, come follow me." She said. Bex and hakim follow her into the living room. "Why I gotta feeling this conversation gonna get very uncomfortable?" Bex asked. Peggy turns off the TV. She turns to Bex. "You already know your father is spade. Right?" Peggy says to Bex. "So, you trying to say my father is spade too?" hakim asked. Peggy sits down. "This is what happened! It was me and Gloria was messing around with spade at the same time! Since Eddie lassenberry had a vasectomy, the only other man had to be spade!" Peggy said. "That still don't mean we brothers because you and my mother was fucking spade!" hakim said. "I swear to god, on my parent's grave, you're spade's son! If you don't believe me, y'all go take a DNA test!" Peggy said. "I don't know about this." Hakim said. "I got a phone call a week after spade's body was found, to leave town! I tried to get in contact with Gloria, but it was like she disappeared off the face of the earth!" Peggy said. "So you came down here?" hakim asked. "Not right away! I stayed until Biron was born! After my parents died, I was alone with Biron, living in Nutley! Nobody wanted to help me because I was a single mother with a half black baby! I moved down here when Biron started talking! I worked odd jobs until I could put money down to get this house!" Peggy said. "This is crazy!" hakim said. "So, you think we should get this DNA test?" Bex asked. "Fuck it! Let's do this and see what happens!" hakim said.

The following Monday, Bex and hakim made an appointment to see a doctor. They were referred to a specialist who conducted the test.

Back at Peggy's house, both Bex and hakim sit on the porch watching the kids playing in the middle of the road. "I can't believe we gotta wait 2 weeks for those damn test results!" Bex said. Bex spots Annie coming towards the house. "Where Peggy at?" Annie asked. "She took the jeep and went to the store." Bex said. "I hope she bring back some chips! Grandma love her some chips!" Annie said. Annie sits down next to Bex. "I heard y'all brothers." Annie said. "We'll find out soon enough." Bex said. "That means you gotta get a house down here!" Annie chuckled. Hakim just shook his head. "Y'all got beer?" Annie asked. "Yeah. Bring me one too." Bex said. Annie goes running in the house. "I gotta get back up north soon." Hakim said. "What's up there?" Bex asked. "I gotta find out way my building was boarded up!"

hakim said. Annie comes back out with 2 beers. She gives one to Bex. They hear the phone ring from inside the house. Bex gets up to answer it. Annie sits on the porch and moves closer to hakim. "How many beers can you drink in an hour?" Annie asked hakim. "A lot!" hakim said. "I don't know how much a lot is, but I bet I can drink more!" Annie said. Hakim starts laughing. Bex comes running out of the house. "Ma got stuck again! That damn jeep!" Bex said. "It's about time you got another car." hakim said. "Who can afford a car? I already called Toby! He's on his way!" Bex said after he gulps his beer. Minutes later, Toby pulls up in his truck. "Annie, let's go!" Bex said. "Oh yeah! Let's get on the good foot!" Annie sang. Hakim starts laughing hysterically. They all jump in the truck. Toby drives off.

About 40 minutes later, they arrive at the mall where Peggy is. "The gangs all here!" Annie chuckled. Peggy was waiting in the jeep when they pulled up. "Everybody come grab a bag!" she shouts. "You got chips?" Annie asked. "No baby girl. We can get some on the way home!" Peggy said Peggy jumps in the passenger seat. Hakim, Bex and Annie sit cramped up in the back.

Driving along the highway, the group pass a couple of car dealerships. "So you calling a tow truck?" Peggy asked Bex. "Fuck that jeep!" Bex said. "Watch your mouth!" Peggy said. "Hey Toby! Pull into that car dealership up there!" hakim said. "Ok." Toby said. Toby pulls into the parking lot of the dealership. Everybody but Toby gets out. "Alright everybody! Let's go car shopping!" hakim shouts. "Oh yeah! Let's go car shopping!" Annie said. "You buying a car?" Bex asked. "No. I'm buying you a car." hakim said. "Oh yeah!" Annie said. "Let's all split up and go searching. Hakim said as Peggy puts her arm around his waist. Bex goes one way, hakim goes off in another direction and Annie follows Peggy.

After a half hour of car hunting, Peggy comes upon the car of her dreams. It was the newest Boeman model. Peggy Annie jumped inside the mahogany colored luxury vehicle after asking the dealer for the keys. The dealer explained to them specifications of the vehicle. Annie loved the automatic seats. Minute's later hakim and Bex walk over to where Peggy and Annie were. They see that Toby sound his way over to ladies. "I see y'all found something y'all like!" hakim said. "Isn't pretty? It even gotta sun roof!" Peggy said. Toby goes over to stand next to Bex. "This is a bass ride boy!" Toby said. "Well if my mother wants it, then we'll take it!" Bex said. "How much we talking man?" hakim asked the dealer. "For you good people, I'll let it go for 33 thousand." The dealer said. "That's all?" hakim said. "30 grand, and we'll take it off your hands today!" Bex said. "You sure you can handle that sweetie?" Peggy asked. "Don't worry! It got it!" hakim said. "How would you be paying for it sir?" the dealer asked. "I have a bank check right here man." hakim said. The dealer takes the check. "Do you have I.D. sir?" the dealer asked. "Here you go!" hakim said as he hands the dealer his I.D. card. "Follow me then." The dealer said to the group. They all follow the dealer to inside the office.

Inside of the office, the dealer takes the check in the back to where his manager was. "It looks like we're gonna drive out of here in style ma!" Bex said. "Oh, I can't wait!" Peggy chuckled. "Oh, I can't wait!" said Annie. Moments later, the dealer comes from the back office. He hands hakim the check. "What's the problem?" hakim asked. "Sorry sir, but the check is invalid." The dealer said. "What? Check again!" hakim said. "We've checked it 3 times sir. It seems there are no funds in the account to back up this check." The dealer said.

"Well, how much is in there then?" hakim asked. "To be honest sir, nothing." The dealer said as he shrugged his shoulder. "This is bullshit!" hakim shouted. "Calm down sweetie! It's ok!" Peggy said. "I'm sorry sir. If you can all chip in and make a down payment of 15 thousand, then we can discuss a deal!" the dealer said. "Man, ain't nobody here got that kinda money!" Bex shouted. "Well, here's my card. If you change your minds, give me a call." The dealer explained. Hakim storms out of the show room. The rest of the group follow hakim outside. "We ain't buying a car?" Annie asked. "Not today baby girl!" Peggy said as she rubs Annie's back. Every one jumps into Toby's truck. He drives off.

Later that evening on Peggy's porch, Bex and hakim are having a few beers. "That's fucked up how that warden robbed you!" Bex said. "What's really fucked up, is that I can't do anything about it!" hakim said. Hakim sips on his beer. "Not only did the warden jack me, my so called father ain't never paid me a visit! Not one damn letter!" hakim said. "Know what? No matter what the DNA tests say, we family now!" Bex said. Hakim's eyes tear up as they tap beer bottles.

A week later, hakim is still a guest at the Xavier house. After helping out with food, bills and having the jeep towed again, hakim has no more than 500 bucks left. Feeling depressed, he consumes more and more alcohol over time. It was about 10 in the morning one day, when Bex went off to do a landscaping job. Peggy is in the house fast asleep. The mailman comes driving down the street. Hakim was sitting on the porch with a beer in his hand. The mailman hands him the pile of mail. "Thanks." Hakim said. "Have a good one." Said the mailman. Hakim goes through the mail, when he comes across a large manila envelope. The envelope is addressed to him. It was the DNA test results. He reads half way through the letter and shows a sigh of relief. He goes into the house and heads to the refrigorator. He pours himself a glass of water. Peggy wakes up from the noise in the kitchen. She sits up from the sofa. She grabs a cigarette from off the coffee table. Hakim is heading back on the porch with the glass of water. "What time is it?" Peggy asked. Hakim looks at his watch. "It's noon time." Hakim said. "We get any mail?" Peggy asked. "Yeah. I got some good news." Hakim said. "What's that?" Peggy asked. "I can officially call you Aunt Peggy." Hakim said. Peggy stands up, running over to hakim and giving him a hug and a big kiss on the cheek. "I told you!" Peggy said.

Later that evening, Bex comes home sweaty, grimy and tired. He enters the house and sees his mother, Annie and hakim at the kitchen table drinking. "How was your day baby boy?" Peggy asked. Bex leans against the refrigorator. "I'm still breathing." Bex chuckled. Hakim holds up the letter with the DNA results. Bex takes the letter and reads it. Peggy has a big smile on her face. Annie is busy guzzling her beer. "Oh shit! This cool!" Bex shouts. Hakim gets up from his chair. He hugs Bex. Peggy starts crying tears of joy. "I wish had a camera!" Peggy said. "Even though we were born on the same month and year, I'm the oldest!" hakim said. "You're only 5 days older!" Bex said. "That's right!" hakim chuckled. Bex thought for a moment. "Damn! I got a big brother!" Bex said. "Oh shut up and grab a beer, fool!" Annie said. Everyone starts laughing.

The next morning, Bex is up and ready to go to work. He puts on a pot of coffee. Peggy comes from down stairs in her robe. She goes into the kitchen. She grabs a cigarette. She lights it and takes a long drag. "You want bacon and eggs or pancakes, baby boy?" she asked

Bex. "Ma. You wanna stop calling me baby boy? I'm 33 years old!" Bex said. "As long as I'm alive, you'll always be my baby boy!" she said as she pinched his cheeks. Hakim comes into the kitchen wearing a t-shirt and sweat pants. "Bacon and eggs or pancakes?" Peggy asked hakim. "Ah, bacon and eggs." He said as he heads to the bathroom. Suddenly, there's banging noise at the front door. "Who the hell?" Peggy shouts. The banging continues. Bex gets up from the table and opens the door. Annie is standing in the doorway in her pajamas crying like a baby. "Grandma won't wake up!" she screams. 'Call 911!" Peggy tells Bex. The toilet flushes. Hakim comes out of the bathroom "What happened?" he asked. Bex looks at hakim while holding Annie's hand. "Stay here with Biron!" Peggy tells Annie. Peggy runs next door over to Annie's house. She covers her nose and mouth from the smell of urine and death. She walks over a pile of clothes on the floor and sees Annie's grandma in the living room slumped over in her wheelchair. Peggy didn't cry, but was sad. Back at the house, hakim stands on the porch with Annie and Bex, waiting for the EMS van.

The next morning, Bex, hakim and Annie sit at the kitchen table in silence. Peggy is next door at Annie's cleaning up as much as she can.

"Who wants pancakes?" Bex asked. Annie raised her hand. Hakim raised his hand. "I don't know if I can make it like ma, but I'll try!" Bex said. "Get me a beer fool!" Annie says to Bex.

Later that evening, Bex comes home from another odd job. Peggy and Annie are sitting in the living room watching Annie's favorite TV show. As soon as Bex enters the house, Peggy asks him a question. "I just realized baby boy. You paint everybody else's house. Why not paint this one?" she asked. "What?" Bex asked. "You heard me!" Peggy said. "When you pay me, I'll paint!" Bex chuckled. Peggy pulls out a cigarette, lights it and takes a drag. "Oh! I gotta pay you to paint your own god damn house?" Peggy shouted. "Yeah ma! About time I get started doing it, I could've painted 2 houses, did 3 lawns and paved 4 driveways!" Bex shouts. "Bullshit!" Peggy shouts. Bex just laughs and heads to the refrigerator and grabs a beer. He comes back in the living room. "Tell hakim to do it!" Bex said. "I should." Peggy said. "Where is he?" Bex asked. "He got bored and went for a walk." Peggy said. Moments later, in comes hakim. "Speak of the devil!" Peggy said. "What happened?" hakim asked. "I need you to paint the house." Peggy said to hakim as soon as he walked through the door. "Uh ok. But I ain't good at it!" hakim said. "It's 3 cans of white paint in the shed. "You got brushes, rollers and a pan?" hakim asked. "We can go to the hardware store and get that shit tomorrow." Bex said. "Hello!" Toby shouted as he and jenny come through the door. What's up old? Wanna beer?" Bex asked. "Oh of course!" Toby said. "The funeral is tomorrow." Peggy said. "Damn! I gotta get me a suit!" Toby said. Annie jumps up crying and runs upstairs. Peggy and jenny go running after her. "I ain't me no harm!" Toby shouted. "Shut up old man!" Bex said as he gives Toby a beer. Hakim goes over and sits on the floor with his back leaning against the sofa. He grabs the remote and changes the channel. Bex brings in 2 chairs for Toby and jenny. They take a seat. "I done seen something that ain't feel right on my way over here!" Toby said. "What's that?" hakim asked. "I swear before god, I seen a black van down the street with 2 white guys in black suit, wearing shades sitting up front!" Toby said. "So what?" Bex said. The crazy thing was, there was no license plates neither on the front or the back of the van!"

Toby said. "You sure old man?" Bex asked. "Damnit! I circled the block to make sure!" Toby shouted. Bex starts laughing. "All the years I lived around here, I ain't never seen no shit like that!" he chuckled. "That shit was just strange! That's all!" Toby said. "Toby done saw a U.F.O!" Bex said. "Don't you mean U.D.O?" hakim said. "Whatever man!" Bex said. Jenny comes walking down the stairs. "Well, Peggy got her to calm down." Jenny said. "You seen a black van too?" Bex asked. "What black van?" jenny asked. "She ain't seen shit!" Toby said. Hakim gets up and peeks through the blinds. He sees nothing.

Friday came, and the gang jump into the trap and head off to the cemetery in Bridgeton. Bex, Hakim, Annie, Peggy, Toby and jenny all had a drink before leaving.

Grandma made sure the house was paid off, so that Annie wouldn't lose it to foreclosure. Peggy spent a month at Annie's cleaning out grandma's belongings. Annie had no other relatives to look out for her. Even though Peggy cleaned out the house to make it more livable, Annie felt safer staying at the Xavier house.

It was September of 1999, and Peggy was watching TV. Hakim just finished painting the house. Peggy went into the kitchen to make lunch for hakim and Annie. Annie came down stairs wearing jeans and a sweat shirt Bex had bought her. As usual, she had a cigarette in her mouth. Annie came into the kitchen. "Can I ask you something Ms. Peggy?" Annie asked. Peggy takes the cigarette out of her mouth. "What you want sweetie?" Peggy asked. "I was wondering, could I call you momma?" Annie asked. Peggy stopped cooking. She tried to fight back the tears but couldn't. "Yes you can baby girl!" Peggy said. Annie and Peggy hug each other. Hakim walks in the kitchen. "What's going on?" he asked. "Finally, I have a daughter!" Peggy cried. "Hey! That's cool." Hakim chuckled. Peggy starts coughing. "Well, I'm done painting." Hakim said. "I gotta see this!" Annie said. Hakim and Annie go outside to see the finished work. "Give me a minute!" Peggy shouted. Peggy takes a paper towel to cover her mouth as she continues coughing. Peggy looks down at the paper towel. It had specs of blood on it. Peggy gets nervous, but tosses the paper towel in the trash can. She comes running outside. Peggy stands out on the curb. She nods her head and smile. "Not bad! Peggy said. "Not bad! Annie said. Peggy puts her arm around Annie's waist.

Later that evening, Bex comes home exhausted. He just finished mowing 5 lawns. He went into the bathroom downstairs. He looked into the toilet and saw blood and tissue in it. He became infuriated. He runs upstairs into his mother's bedroom. He sees Annie in there watching TV. He grabs Annie by the arm, yanking her out of the room. "Ouch! Stop it!" Annie shouts. "Come on! I'm sick of this shit!" Bex shouted. Bex drags Annie down the stairs and through the kitchen as she falls to her knees. He still drags her to the toilet. He pushes her head towards the toilet. "You gotta learn how to flush the goddamn toilet after yo ass is finished! This shit is nasty girl!" Bex shouted. Annie is crying and screaming. Peggy was on the porch smoking a cigarette. She hears the commotion and comes running in the house. Peggy jumps on Bex's back, pulling him off of Annie. "What the fuck you're doing to her?" Peggy shouted. Bex turns toward his mother with hate in his eyes. "This gotta stop ma! If she's on her period, she's gotta flush the toilet!" Bex shouted. "You bastard! That's not her! It's me!" Peggy shouts. Bex releases Annie. Annie falls to the floor, crying like a baby. "It's me! I've been coughing up blood and forgot to flush the toilet!" Peggy shouts Bex just stands there in shock. "You sick ma?" he asked. "I might be! I made an appointment to see the doctor tomorrow!" Peggy said. Bex's eyes tear up as he runs out of the bathroom, out the front door. "Biron!" Peggy shouted. She gets down on the floor and cradles Annie in her arms. "Hush! Hush! Baby girl. It's ok. He didn't mean it." Peggy whispered. She flushes the toilet.

Outside the house, Bex goes for a walk to calm down. He sees his brother coming from the opposite direction. Bex has fury in his eyes. Hakim walks up to him. "How you like the paint job?" hakim asked. Bex enraged, gets up in hakim's face. "Why don't you go look for a fucking job?" Bex shouted. Bex pushes hakim out of the way and storms down the street. Hakim has a confused look on his face at first, then he gets angered.

About an hour later, Bex comes walking through the door and sees hakim watching TV. Hakim looks up at him. "After we find out what's wrong with Aunt Peggy, I'll go look for a job." Hakim said in a calm voice. Bex doesn't say a word. He just heads upstairs. He opens the door to his mother's room. He sees Peggy and Annie fast asleep. He then leaves, shutting the door behind him. Bex heads back downstairs and heads to the kitchen. He gets a beer out of the frig. He goes into the living room and sits on the floor with hakim and watch TV.

That dreadful Monday came around, when Bex had to drive his mother to the doctor's office. Peggy was wearing a wool jacket over a turtle neck sweater, jeans and tennis shoes. The drive wasn't an easy one. The roads were wet and the fog was dense. "It's my own fault!" Peggy cried. "Ma stop! We don't even know what's wrong with you yet!" Bex said. "I know. I always knew." Peggy said as she starts coughing. Bex pulls up into the parking lot of the doctor's office. Peggy gets out of the jeep. "I'll call you to come pick me up." Peggy said. "No ma! I'll find a parking spot and meet you inside!" Bex said. Peggy smiles then shut the door to the jeep. She heads to the front entrance of the facility. She heads to the front desk and signs in. Peggy was on time for her appointment. Within minutes, she was called in to see the doctor. Bex walks in the waiting room moments later. He approached the receptionist's desk. "Excuse me. Did Peggy Xavier go in to see the doctor yet?" he asked. "She just went in." the lady said. Bex takes a seat. He grabs a magazine out of the rack. He just skims through it, tapping his feet uncontrollably. Bex occasionally stared at the clock on the wall.

It was about an hour and a half later from the time Peggy first stepped into the facility. Finally Peggy comes from out of the examination room. Bex noticed she had fear in her eyes. "Everything ok ma?" he asked. Peggy went to the receptionist's desk to reschedule for another appointment. "Come on! Let's go!" she said to Bex. He grabs his mother by the arm. "Ma! Is everything ok?" Bex said. "I'm fine baby boy! Just take me to the liquor store!" she shouted. "The liquor store ain't open yet!" Bex said. "When then, just take me home!" Peggy shouted

There's a dead silence on the ride back home. When they get to the house, Peggy gets out of the jeep. Bex stays inside, keeping the engine running. "Where you going?" Peggy asked. "This guy owes me a couple of hundred for a paint job I did last week. I'll be back in a little bit." Bex said. "Well stop at the liquor store and get some beer and a carton of cigarettes!" Peggy shouts. "Ma! Why you still wanna get cigarettes?" Bex shouted. "Boy, don't argue with me! Just go and get my shit like I told you!" Peggy shouted. Peggy goes into the house.

Inside the house, hakim is teaching Annie how to play chess. Peggy walks in. "Why you ain't tell me you had a chess set in the shed?" hakim asked. "I done forgot all about that. I tried to teach Biron when he was little, but he wasn't interested." Peggy said. "This is the game of all games here!" hakim said. "Y'all daddy taught me when we was dating." Peggy said. "Eddie taught me when I was little." Hakim said. Peggy went to the refrigorator and took out something for dinner that night. "Spade told me he and Eddie used to go at it all the time! He said he taught Eddie how to play!" Peggy shouted from the kitchen. She goes over to the sink and washes her hands. She starts coughing. Peggy can see the blood go down the drain like a whirlpool. She says nothing. "Your move." Hakim says to Annie.

Not too far away in Cherry Hill, Sir Marcus, tony and jabbo are at meeting in the west wing of the Lassenberry castle. Sir Edward, still bound to his wheelchair, was in the east wing of the castle with his physical therapist. The east wing was just completed a week ago to accommodate the ailing boss. Sir Marcus also purchased furniture under his new fiancée's discretion.

Her name was Kimberly Jenkins, youngest daughter of jabbo Jenkins. She was 30 years old at the time. She was light skinned, with dreadlocks flowing down her back. She was the spitting image of her father. Kimberly was deeply fascinated with African culture. She was always wearing traditional African clothing, in fact, her favorite clothing to wear was kanga. Kimberly studied abroad a t Kampala international University in Uganda. While over there, she learned to speak fluently in the Luanda Language.

Jabbo introduced her to Sir Marcus a few months earlier. The 2 hit it off quickly. Part of it was due to jabbo influencing Sir Marcus to keep their family ties strong. Sir Marcus's parents and siblings embraced her immediately into the family. Mark sr. was especially thrilled because she came from wealth and that she was the daughter of his father's closest ally. Sir Marcus was so sure that she was the woman for him, that he emptied his own personal account and purchased the engagement ring for 2.5 million dollars.

The meeting in the west wing was about Sir Marcus receiving 2 medals. The first was the Order of Friendship from the Russian government. Years after the cold war ended, the former Soviet Union's finances started to decline. Sir Marcus was advised by the National Agreement to purchase a stock pile of small arms from their Russian counterpart's worth in the millions. There was to be no ceremony due to the fact it would get out to the main media that American businessmen were dealing in gun trafficking. Payment for the weapons were electronically transferred in the name of a fake charity.

The second medal sent to Sir Marcus was the Colombian Order of San Carlos Knight (Caballero). The lassenberry organization were the 3rd largest importers of cocaine in the eastern part of the United States next to Florida and New York City. The Caballeros de Fortuna Cartel, still under the leadership of Oscar Deltoro Santos, persuaded the corrupted Colombian government to present the award to Sir Marcus for continuing to do business between their 2 organizations. This award too was under the guise of lassenberry charitable work in Colombia. Sir Marcus would have 2 more medals than his uncle. Sir Marcus was also eligible to wear the Order of the Elephant medal because he and Sir Edward shared the same bloodline.

At the meeting, jabbo warned Sir Marcus not to except any invitations from the National Agreement. Sir Marcus didn't pay too much attention to what jabbo had to say concerning that. He was just interested in the family finances.

"Anything else on the agenda?" he asked jabbo and tony. Tony was about to speak, but before he could utter a word, jabbo slumps over in his chair. His eyes were wide open. A stream of saliva ran out the corner of his mouth. "Jabbo?" Sir Marcus said as he stood from his seat. Tony was looking down at his notes. Sir Marcus was in a daze at first. Tony looks up, and is stunned. "Boss! Boss!" tony shouts. Tony drops his writing pad. He runs over to jabbo. Sir Marcus does the same. Tony shakes jabbo a little to get a response from him. Jabbo's glasses fall off of his face, on to the floor. Sir Marcus's eyes start to tear up. "Let's lay him on the floor!" tony shouted. "Call 911!" Sir Marcus shouted. Oh god! Please no!" Sir Marcus shouted as tony ran to the phone on the desk. Sir Marcus performed CPR on jabbo, but nothing was working. "Tell the agents to let the EMS workers in when they arrive!" sir Marcus ordered tony. Tony presses a button on the phone, which connected to the main gate. At the gate, 2 NA agents guard the gate. The agent answers the phone in the security booth. "Jabbo is down! Jabbo is down! I want you to let the EMS truck in when they arrive!" tony shouted. "Understood sir." The agent said. "Is he breathing?" tony asked after he hangs up the phone. Sir Marcus shakes his head as tears trickled down his cheeks. Tony runs over to jabbo's side and drops to his knees. They both realize that the inevitable has happened. "Don't leave me! Please don't leave me!" Sir Marcus cried as tony stood to his feet. Tony wipes the tears from his eyes and looks down at Sir Marcus. "Long live the house of Lassenberry! Long live Sir Marcus!" tony shouted.

Moments later, the paramedics arrive at the castle. They are given permission to enter the property. The construction detail working on the north wing are confused when they spot the Ambulance pass the gates. The paramedics follow the agents to the west wing on customized golf carts. They drive down the corridor of the castle. The paramedics are in awe of their surroundings. The agent in the lead cart gets on the walkie-talkie "Agent 12 is in route with medical assistance. I repeat. Agent 12 is in route with medical assistance." The agent said.

It was September 11th 1999, at 1:35pm. James Jenkins, a.k.a jabbo, the back bone of the lassenberry organization for over 6 decades, breathed his last breath.

Later that day, Sir Marcus was preparing for his fiancée to arrive at the castle. She was called upon 20 minutes after the ordeal. Sir Marcus ordered tony to arrange for jabbo's wife Elma, daughter Jenna to come up north. All the lassenberry family were notified through phone calls.

Once jabbo's wife Elma received the horrible news, she retrieved jabbo's will from the safety deposit box in a bank in southern Florida. In his will, jabbo was worth close to 80 million dollars in cash, which was to be split between his daughters Kimberly and Jenna. He owned a private island in the Florida Keys which he left to his wife. Jabbo also owned property in West Orange, an apartment out in Los Angeles, which he rarely visited, a ranch out in Texas only because he had side deals going on before the National Agreement came into the picture.

Jabbo was buying cocaine from the Peruvians way before Mark Vasquez sr. was. Jabbo would have a crew of 3 guys living out in Texas to mix and sell the product. After mark Vasquez sr. was found out, jabbo abandoned the operation. The guys in his crew just disappeared off the face of the earth.

A couple of hours after his death, jabbo's body was removed from the castle by the coroners.

Sir Marcus, escorted by 2 NA agents, waited at the main entrance of the west wing for his fiancée. She pulled up in a Boeman limousine. The Chauffeur passes the gates. One of the agents opens the door to let her out. She kept a calm facade. Sir Marcus walks up to her and gives her a big firm hug. Kimberly was really consoling Sir Marcus by patting and rubbing his back. "He didn't suffer!" Sir Marcus said. Kimberly wipes the tears from his eyes. "He lived an adventurous life from what I hear!" Kimberly said. "Let's go inside." Said Sir Marcus. An agent had golf cart waiting for them.

These golf carts were 6 electric driven carts were designed. So that all 4 seats faced forward. The top speed for these indoor vehicles was 25 miles per hour. In each wing had a recharging station which kept the carts operational.

Sir Marcus told the agent to drive to the east wing of the castle. Within a few minutes, they arrive at the east wing. "Baby, let me go in alone. My uncle is kind of weird around strangers." Said Sir Marcus. Sir Marcus kisses her hand. He gets out of the cart. There was an agent already posted at the huge wooden double doors. "Open up agent!" Sir Marcus ordered. Sir Marcus passes through the double doors and walks down the corridor. He comes to another his uncle's dwelling. He taps the door knocker. "Uncle! I'm coming in!" Sir Marcus shouts. When he enters, Sir Marcus can't believe his eyes. Sir Edward's physical therapist, who was an attractive young black woman, was giving Sir Edward a hand job. He claps his hands together to get her attention. "Alright young lady! You can take a break!" said Sir Marcus. Embarrassed, the young lady trots out of the room. "Sorry Mr. Lassenberry!" she said before leaving. Sir Marcus stands before his uncle, who was in his wheelchair. Sir Edward had a droopy smile on his face. Sir Marcus pulls out a handkerchief and wipes the drool from his uncle's mouth. "This… better…be good…boy!" said Sir Edward said in a slurred speech. Sir Marcus kneels down in front of his uncle. "I have some bad news uncle! Jabbo, jabbo dies earlier today." He said to Sir Edward. There was a silence for a few seconds. The screaming from Sir Edward's mouth was so loud, that Kimberly and the agents could hear it from the main corridor. Sir Edward's eyes filled with tears. "I have to go finish making the arrangements uncle." Sir Marcus whispered. Sir Marcus runs into Sir Edward's elaborate bathroom and fetched a towel. He runs back and wipes Sir Edward's face of all the tears and slobber. He then kisses his uncle on top of the head and leaves the room. He sees the young lady standing outside. "You can go back and finish up what you were doing." Sir Marcus chuckled.

A couple of days later, Sir Marcus was playing host to a gang of his future in-laws. Not only did he fly in Elma and Jenna Jenkins, he was persuaded by Kimberly to bring in Elma's 4 brothers, their wives and kids from out west. Jenna's husband Sheldon and their 3 kids came from the island. Kimberly's best friend Carmen, from south Miami came in.

Sir Marcus was dressed in a jogging suit and tennis shoes. He gave the family a tour of the finished areas of the castle. Everyone was in awe of the beautiful architecture. Standing off in the distance, were a couple of NA agents. Sir Marcus took them to his office in the west wing. "What's the giant plaque on the wall behind Sir Marcus's desk?" one of Kimberly's nephews asked. "That's the Lassenberry coat-of-arms. Our family crest." Said Sir Marcus. "That's what those kings and queens got over in Europe?" the nephew asked. "That's exactly right!" said Sir Marcus.

About an hour later, the tour had ended. Kimberly took all 25 members of her family, including Carmen to a nearby hotel to settle in before the funeral. Sir Marcus goes back to his office. He gets on the phone. Someone answers. "Lassenberry residence." The voice said. "Yeah Thomas. It's me. Let me speak to my father." ordered Sir Marcus. "Right away sir." Thomas said as he straightens his neck-tie. A few seconds later, mark sr. gets on the phone. "Hey pop! I've received your message earlier. "Yeah son. Your uncles and I want to have a meeting with you tomorrow" mark sr. said. "About what time? I'm entertaining Kimberly's family until the funeral." Sir Marcus said. "Does 9 in the morning sound good?" said his father. "That's sounds great pop!" said Sir Marcus. "I'll see you here then." Said mark sr.

After Sir Marcus hangs up the phone, he goes over to his leather sofa across from his desk. He takes off his sneakers and kicks his feet up, then closes his eyes. Within a few minutes, there's a knock on the door, which awakens Sir Marcus. "Damn! It's like I've been asleep for days!" Sir Marcus says to himself. "Enter!" Sir Marcus shouted. "Hello! Boss!" tony says as he walks in the office wearing an expensive looking suit. "Everything is set. I've got the ok from the mayors of Newark, Irvington, and East Orange through financial influence of course. Starting on Broad Street in Newark, going through East Orange and ending up just outside Irvington Park, where jabbo's body will be placed in the hearse, on its way to Teterboro airport. A team of white horses will parade the casket through the main streets of these cities." Tony said. "What about a police escort?" Sir Marcus asked. "It's been taken care of too." Said tony. "Oh! There's one thing a want to do!" Said Sir Marcus. "What's that?" tony asked. "I want to bring Charlie Dalton back into the fold." Said Sir Marcus. "If you say so!" tony sighed. "We know Charlie. This young therapist has an agenda, I think." Said Sir Marcus.

After Sir Edward's stroke, Sir Marcus decided to move into the castle with his future wife. Charlie Dalton was left out of the equation because Sir Marcus had immediately hired a live in physical therapist.

The next morning, Sir Marcus was getting dressed to go meet with his father and uncles. Kimberly rolls over in bed, facing Sir Marcus. "You sure you'll be back in time to entertain my family?" Kimberly asked. "As soon as I get back from my father's house, I'm yours for the rest of the day!" he said and then jumps in the bed, giving Kimberly a peck kiss on the lips. "Get out of the bed, with your shoes on!" Kimberly chuckled. Sir Marcus tosses a pillow in her face. "I'm gonna kill you!" Kimberly chuckled. He quickly hops out of bed and runs out of the room. Sir Marcus gets into the golf cart, and is driven to the main entrance. He goes outside where 2 agents were waiting by the limo for him. One of the agents opens the door of the limo for him. The iron gates are open and the limo leave the premises.

Within an hour, the limo arrives in Atlantic City. The limo drives up to the gate of the estate. The agent pushes the button to the intercom. "Lassenberry residence." Thomas said. "Sir Marcus is here to see his father." said the agent. The electronic gate slowly slides open. The limo proceeds up the driveway. Sir Marcus could see 2 other cars in the lot. The limo stops. The agent gets out of the car and opens the door for Sir Marcus. He exits the limo and walks up to the main entrance. There stood the Thomas the butler. "Your family is waiting in the lounge Sir Marcus." Said Thomas. Thomas takes his overcoat. He follows Thomas to the lounge. Once at the entrance, Thomas opens the door to the lounge. Mark sr. comes from out of the bathroom. "Good to see you son! You can leave us now." mark sr. says to Thomas. Thomas leaves the room. "So you like what I've done to the lounge? I turned it into my own private man cave to get away from your mother!" mark sr. chuckled.

This was the man cave of all man caves. It has 2 professional billiard tables, a solid oak bar with 12 rotating stools lined up along the bar counter, huge oil paintings of scantily clad women, autograph pictures of celebrities he'd come across in his travels. There were 4 pinball machines, a cigar bar in the next room, dart boards on each wall, 2 foosball tables and a stage holding a drum set, key board, and a couple of guitars.

Since when you joined a band?" Sir Marcus asked. "Hey! Sometimes I hire a band! It's relaxing to have live music! Come on in the cigar bar!" mark sr. said.

Inside the cigar bar sat Jake sr. and Danny sr. sitting like kings smoking cigars. "The air seems fresh in here!" said Sir Marcus. "Yeah. I had a ventilation system installed in the ceiling. Can I offer you a stogy son?" mark sr. asked. "I'll pass." He said. "You sure? I've ordered a box of 8 from Spain, 5 hundred bucks a piece!" said mark sr. "A stogy is considered cheap, pop." Sir Marcus said. "You know what I meant! Don't get cute!" said mark sr. said with a scowl. Sir Marcus walks over to greet his uncles. "Uncle Dan, Uncle Jake!" he said as he shook their hands. He takes a seat across from them. Mark sr. sits next to Jake sr. in other recliner. "Wow! I feel like I'm on trial here!" Sir Marcus chuckled. His elders have serious looks on their faces. "The reason why we called you here son, is to resolve this silly feud between your uncles Danny and Eddie." mark sr. said. "Listen pop! I hope you didn't ask me over here to change Sir Edward's mind! That's between them!" Sir Marcus said. "That's all well and good you respect my brother's words, but I'm your father, and these are your uncles too." He said. "Let's cut the bullshit! I think my son is dead, and that piece of shit brother of mine knows something! On top of that, he disrespects my household by stopping the envelopes from coming every week!" Danny sr. said. "With all due respect uncle, is this about Danny or the envelopes?" Sir Marcus asked. "So, you're going to leave your uncle here destitute?" mark sr. asked. "The man owns a million dollar company!" Sir Marcus shouted. "I won't for long, thanks to your uncle!" Danny said. "What the hell are you talking about?" Sir Marcus asked. "That brother of mine sent his Italian friends to shake me down! They're killing my business!" Danny said. "I don't know about that!" Sir Marcus said. "Since you know about it now, what are you going to do about it?" Danny asked with rage in his voice. Sir Marcus sighs. "Ok. I'll get some people I know to get them to lay off then! As far as me getting directly involved, I can't!" Sir Marcus said. "What about my son?" Danny asked. "We're still working on it!" said Sir Marcus. "We've also noticed that you have sleeve's grandson in the appliance and auto business." Said his uncle Jake. "Yeah. That's something Sir Edward started." Sir Marcus said. "I've been thinking. Could he be sort of demoted so Jake jr. can run that part of the family business?" Jake sr. asked. "Like I said, that's sir Edward's doing. Not mine. Jabbo told me before he passed, that it was Brandon's idea and that he's doing an exceptional job." Said Sir Marcus. "You're telling me you won't let your own cousin run the business?" Jake sr. shouted. "I can call Brandon, and tell him to give Jake a management position or something." Sir Marcus said shrugging his shoulders. "Just see to it that he doesn't get his hands dirty!" Jake sr. ordered. Sir Marcus gets irritated. He gets up out of his seat. "I gotta go! I promised Kimberly I'd entertain her family!

So I expect to see all of you at the funeral, right?" Sir Marcus said. "Yeah, of course." Jake sr. said. "Good! Pop. Could you walk me to the door?" Sir Marcus asked. "Give us a minute." Mark sr. says to his brothers. Sir Marcus and his father leave the man cave. They walk to the main entrance. "Before you say anything son, I just want to say how proud I am of you!" he said to Sir Marcus. He puts his hand on his father's shoulder. "I love you pop, but don't ever ambush me like that again!" Sir Marcus says before storming out the door.

It was 10am on a Friday when one of the most respected and feared men in New Jersey was being laid to rest. Services were being held at the Eternal Life funeral Home in downtown Newark. The entire block was barricaded off. There were about 20 uniformed police officers on detail. There was a huge crowd of people that stretched about a block to get a view of the departed. Inside, friends and family were standing around reminiscing about jabbo and his influence he had on people. There were a couple of news vans outside hoping to get an interview those on the inside. There also FBI agents outside doing surveillance to see was the who's who coming out of the funeral home.

Clayton Watson, a.k.a Butch had arrived with 10 men from his crew. Mark Vasquez jr., a.k.a Mookie was being strolled in his wheelchair by his second in command Ricardo Salazar, while 5 of his top guys followed close behind. William Watson, a.k.a Dubbs entered the funeral home with his boys as well. Gino Massoni and a few of his soldiers showed up to pay their respects. Rufus Forte and McClain Foxx, a.k.a Chewie and Mackie were allowed access into the funeral home. 2 Gunz and the crew from the old building were not allowed access. They were treated like the average spectator.

This was the opposite for the mayors of Newark, East Orange, Irvington, Elizabeth, Cherry Hill, Jersey City and other public officials, who were reminded by Tony Kerouac about jabbo's involvement in their political success. Longtime family lawyer, Stanley Hart, a.k.a Sleeves arrived with his family and associates Allen J. Sunn and Kent Mooney. Bruce Le harve from New Orleans flew in the night before with an entourage to pay respect. Dope runner Maury O'Neil from New York showed up as well. Mob bosses including Don Francesco from New York made a brief appearance to view the body.

About an hour into the viewing, 2 Boeman limousines made their way through the barricades. Both limos drove around the back entrance of the funeral home away from the crowd. Charlie Dalton steps out of the driver's seat of the first limo in his uniform that was designed by Stephan. He holds open the door for his new boss, Sir Marcus and his fiancée Kimberly. In the second limo were 6 NA agents armed with automatic weapons at the ready. Their instructions were to stay in the limo unless there was an immediate danger.

A hundred miles away, Bex is sitting in the kitchen at his mother's house eating a bowl of cereal. He suddenly hears loud laughter coming from the living room. He gets up from the table and rushes in to the living room to see hakim laughing at the TV. "What's so funny man?" Bex asked. "Man! I'm laughing at this shit on the news!" hakim shouted. Bex walks over and stands next to his brother. "You're sitting laughing at somebody's funeral service?" Bex asked. "You heard of jabbo, right?" hakim said. "I heard a little something about him on the streets." Bex said. "This bitch ass reporter is talking about him like he was god or something! They saying he was as important business man and philanthropist!" hakim chuckled.

"So what?" Bex said. "That nigga was evil as hell! He killed a whole army of people! Eddie told me when I was a kid, all the shit he did behind the scenes!" hakim said.

Upon his request, Sir Edward wanted to stay at the castle. Charlie Dalton now back in the picture, was his new care taker. When Tony found Charlie, he was staying at a homeless shelter down in Newark. Sir Edward never paid Charlie a salary or put any money away from him.

Later that evening, stragglers came in wanting to view the body, were leaving. There was one homeless man outside the barricades earlier standing on a plastic crate condemning the event. "Why y'all standing out here for this nigga? He wasn't nothing but the devil!" the man shouts. Some of the people in the line were laughing. He kept on ranting about how bad of a person jabbo was until police officers yanked him off the crate and put him in Squad car.

The next day, pall bearers carry the body of jabbo to the horse and carriage. Once on the carriage, all in attendance jumped into their vehicles. The carriage was being pulled by a team of 4 white gelding Clydesdales. Newark police escorted the convoy all the way to the border-line of East Orange. From there, East Orange police became the escorts. Finally, the convoy came to the Irvington borderline. There, funeral employees quickly move the casket from the carriage to a Boeman hearse. The hearse was on its way to Teterboro airport. The Jenkins clan were to arrive at the airport the next day to leave with the departed back to the Jenkins Island.

It was around 7pm when the lassenberry and Jenkins family met back at the hotel where Sir Marcus put the in-laws up for their stay. Tony already had food and drinks prepared in the banquet hall of the hotel. This was the first time Elma had a chance to meet Mark sr. and Tasha.

Elma was a curvy, elderly light skinned woman with soft curly gray hair. She had tiny moles around her hazel eyes. At the gathering. Elma only socialized with her daughters, which was partially due to being isolated on the island with Kimberly, Jenna and the help.

Benny the 3rd, Tyson Richards, Samara and Ariel were on the other side of the dining hall mingling with Kimberly's friend Carmen. Their behavior was that of a group of young people hanging out at a night club.

The food and drinks were placed on 2 long folding tables. the menu consisted of bar-b-que chicken, sautéed meatballs, baked Mac- and-cheese, pasta salad, sliced Virginia ham, seafood salad smoked salmon, wild rice and dinner rolls. The drinks were red wine, scotch, vodka, rum, all sorts of fruit juices and soda. Tony spared no expense.

Sir Marcus was standing over in an area of the hall with a plate of food in his hand. He was in a conversation with only member left of his grandfather's original crew. Sleeves also had a plate full of food. "These meatballs are good!" sleeves said. "Tell me something about that Allen Sunn guy. He seems jittery." Sir Marcus said. "What do you wanna know, about his coke habit?" sleeves asked. "You're just telling me about this, now?" Sir Marcus whispered. "Don't worry! I've been going over the books since your grandfather hired him!" sleeves whispered. "I don't like this one bit! You gotta get rid of him!" Sir Marcus whispered. "Listen son. If it ain't broke, don't fix it. Check your books tonight before you rest your head. 15 million went into an offshore account last year." sleeves said. "15 million? Damn! I gotta check the books!" Sir Marcus whispered. "Check your books kid, but don't worry. You're very wealthy." Sleeves said.

It was around 2 in the morning, when Sir Marcus was sitting in his office wearing nothing but his pajama bottoms. His eyes were blood shot red after reading financial documents from his uncle's safe. Sir Marcus realized that the family was losing money dealing with such corporations such as Boeman and Galaxy appliances. It dawned on him that these corporate entities were protecting the family from incarceration in exchange for selling their products for them. "It seems you got us sucked into a powerful vacuum uncle!" sir Marcus says to himself. He realized that the family was actually surviving off drug money, and breaking even with the bed and breakfast chain. Sir Marcus neatly stacked the paper work, placing it back into its binder. So exhausted, Sir Marcus fell asleep at his desk.

It was mid-December, when the north wing of lassenberry castle was completed. There wasn't any furnishing of décor as of yet. Sir Marcus and Kimberly haven't decided on the décor. Sir Marcus immediately decided to recreate another family coat-of-arms above the marble fireplace which measured 8 ft. x 20 ft. in width. This replica of the coat-of-arms would be twice as big as the one in his office. While standing in front of the fireplace, he pondered some more, and decided to place huge oil paintings of his grandfather benny and his uncle Sir Edward right underneath the coat-of-arms. Luckily for him his uncle Eddie had a picture of himself wearing his uniform with his Order of the Elephant medal on him.

The north wing had 2 levels. The first level had a 20ft high ceiling with hand carved floral décor, supported by 8 Ionic order columns, with the appropriate ratio to prevent buckling. Kimberly enters the room, and after a short conversation with her fiancée, decides that it should be the ballroom. She would hire world renowned Jamaican artist, Huie Abrahams to do the oil paintings of Sir Edward and benny lassenberry.

Like the north wing, each wing had 4 bathrooms. Sir Marcus gave strict orders to remodel 1 bathroom in each wing to have handicap accessible ramps and toilets installed for his uncle. This order was not in the original blue print of budget, so he tapped into the family account once more, which cost him a hundred grand.

It was the day before Christmas, and the roads of Bridgeton, New Jersey were covered with a foot of snow. Bex and hakim were outside shoveling in front of the house for the past half hour. Hakim just cursed out the driver of a snowplow passing by. The plow had pushed the snow back on to the jeep he and Bex shoveled out. Hakim threw the shovel into a pile of snow like a spear and hops through the snow on to the porch. "Come on Bro! We gotta finish this before sun down, before it starts to freeze!" Bex shouted. "Fuck this shit! I'm taking a break!" hakim shouted. Frustrated and breathing heavy, Bex looks around and drops his shovel. They both head into the house. Bex stomps his feet to get the excess snow off of his boots. Hakim walked pass the living room where Peggy and Annie were sitting watching TV. He went into the kitchen and turned on the stove. He takes off his leather gloves to heat his hands above the burners. Bex takes off his wool gloves and does the same thing. "If we get done soon, we can make a few extra bucks doing a couple of houses!" Bex said as hakim cups his hands together to blow his hot breath into them. "Man, I ain't used to this shit!" hakim said. "What snow?" Bex asked. "No! Hard work!" hakim shouted. Bex hears the sound of a nasty cough coming from the living room. He rushes in there to see his mother lying on the couch covered in blankets. Annie had passed a couple of tissues to cover her mouth. Peggy looked at the tissue in her hands and saw clumps of blood.

By this time, Peggy had lost a considerable amount of weight. She had stopped her chemotherapy regimen a month earlier, against doctor's orders. Her head was completely bald, and her eye brows were hairless. She even stopped taking her medication. There was a bottle with 3 pills left on the end table.

Bex kneels down at his mother's side. "Ma! Come on! Let me take you upstairs where it's warm!" he said. "No damnit! How many times I gotta tell y'all I rather stay down here looking at the Christmas tree then be up in that room!" she coughed. Bex grabs some tissue and wipes the blood off of her hand. He tosses it in the waste basket, which was filled with bloody tissues.

Peggy continues to cough. "That's it! As soon as we shovel the jeep out again, I'm taking you to the hospital!" Bex said. "No! I ain't letting them cut me open again! I wanna spend the rest of my days here, with y'all! Now let me be!" she said. "Let her be, fool!" Annie shouted. Bex shoves Annie's head and goes back in the kitchen. "You still a fool!" Annie shouted. Bex puts his gloves back on, and heads back outside. Hakim puts his gloves on too. He walks into the living room. "You 2 want anything?" hakim asked. "Gone get me a beer!" Annie said. "What about you auntie?" hakim asked. "No sweetie." Peggy replied. Hakim heads to the refrigorator and retrieves a beer for Annie. He pops the top for her. "Thank you! Thank you! Thank you!" Annie chuckled. Hakim heads back outside. They continue shoveling.

Later that evening, Bex, Annie and hakim stand outside the house, just looking at the Christmas lights flicker on and off. "That's so pretty! Ain't it fool?" Annie says to Bex. Hakim starts laughing. Bex kneels down and packs a snowball. He throws it in Annie's face. "Oh, you gonna get it now!" Annie chuckles. She packs some snow from off the jeep and chases Bex until she hits him in the back of the head. "Oh, shit! She got you!" hakim chuckled. Bex then makes a snowball and gets hakim in the face. "It's on now!" hakim shouted. Peggy looks through the blinds with tears of joy, seeing them play in the snow. Her coughing continues.

Christmas day had arrived. Annie comes running down the stairs. "Time to open the presents! Ooooh!" she screamed with joy. Hakim comes from out of the bathroom. "Time to open the presents!" hakim said as he grabs a gift with Peggy's name on it. "Here auntie!" hakim said. Peggy unwraps the present. She smiles. "This is beautiful!" said Peggy. The gift was an 8'x 10' picture of Annie, Bex and hakim. "We did it when we took a ride out to the mall last week." Hakim said. "Thank you sweetie!" she said as hakim gives her a hug. "I got jeans, and I got a sweater!" Annie boasted. "Come give mama a hug." Peggy said Annie lands on Peggy, giving her a big hug as hakim opens his present. "Wow! A jewelry box! Just what I needed." Hakim said. "Be careful baby girl before you crack my ribs!" Peggy chuckled. Bex enters the house. "2 houses, and hundred bucks!" Bex shouted. "Come in and get warm baby boy!" Peggy said. "Toby and jenny said they gonna be over later." Bex said. "Oh lord! I ain't got the strength to hear them 2 fuss today!" Peggy said. Bex goes over to the tree and grabs his present. He puts it to his ear, shaking it. "Just open the damn thing!" Peggy chuckled. He opens his gift. It's a wallet. He opens the wallet, and inside is 25 dollars. "What's the money for?" Bex asked. "Didn't you say you would do the landscaping if I paid you? Now I'm paying you!" Peggy said. "Come on ma!" Bex sighed. "You just hold on to that!" Peggy said. Bex goes over and hugs his mother. "I need a drink!" Bex said. "Get me a beer too, fool!" Annie said. "I need something strong myself!" hakim said.

A couple of hours later, Toby and jenny come over to the house. Toby came in staggering with a Santa hat on his head. "Ho! Ho! Ho! Mother fuckers!" Toby shouted. Bex comes running from the kitchen with a folding chair. He sits Toby down in the chair. "Now stay yo drunk ass in that chair!" jenny said. Just as jenny was about to close the door, in steps a big burly white guy. Peggy screamed with joy. "Good lord! Where's my wig Annie?" Peggy shouted. Annie goes to the closet and gets Peggy's wig off the hook. Peggy flops the wig on her head. "Come over here and give me a hug stranger!" Peggy screamed. This big burly man comes through the door, with the look of an alpha male. He goes over and plants a big kiss on Peggy's lips. "Who's that bro?" hakim whispered to Bex. "Man, that's Clint. He's a truck driver that used to mess with ma years ago." Bex whispered.

Clint Rupert was a private jet pilot 15 years before he got into the trucking business. He stood 6ft 5in tall, weighing around 300 pounds, sporting a gray handle bar mustache. He met Peggy a couple of years after spade's death.

"Merry Christmas folks! This can't be little Biron!" Clint said. "Hey Clint. What's up man?" Bex said as he shakes Clint's hand. Hakim steps forward. "What's up? I'm his brother hakim." he said. "What? You went and had another kid on me?" Clint chuckled. "It's a long story!" Peggy said. Peggy started coughing up blood. Annie gave her some tissues. "Y'all don't pay me no mind!" Peggy said. "You wanna beer Clint?" Bex asked. "Ain't nothing like a cold beer on Christmas!" Clint chuckled. Bex goes to fetch him a beer.

"I like that tree!" jenny said. "It's the same damn one I had up last year!" Peggy chuckled. Hakim covered his mouth to keep from laughing. "Who wants a refill?" Bex shouted. "I do!" Toby said. "You ain't getting shit!" jenny said. "Oh come on! It's Christmas!" Bex said. "Oh come on! It's Christmas!" Annie shouted. "We ain't gonna let him leave here and get hurt jenny." Peggy said. "Gone get a drink then!" jenny said reluctantly. Bex runs in the kitchen and makes Toby a drink. Toby tries to stand up, but stumbles. "I'll get my own god damn drink!" Toby shouted. "You stay put buddy. He's coming with your drink." Clint said as he holds Toby up. "Go in the kitchen and turn the radio up loud so we can listen to some Christmas R&B!" Peggy says to Annie. "Yeah! Party everybody!" Annie shouts. Hakim is sitting at the bottom of the steps with a drink in his hand. When the music comes on, Toby gets up and starts dancing. Peggy starts laughing, then starts coughing. "I passed him and jenny on the road, and they said they were on their way here! So I followed." Clint said to Peggy. "Why yo ass ain't call when you got in town?" Peggy asked. "You changed your number!" Clint said as jenny ran into the kitchen. "Where your wife at?" Peggy asked Clint. "We split!" Clint said. "Bullshit!" Peggy said.

In the kitchen, Bex is about to bring Toby his drink. "Here! Go take the money and go get my stuff!" jenny whispered. "Come on! You should've gave me the money yesterday!" Bex whispered. "Stop being like that! Just run down the road real quick! He's home now!" jenny whispered. Jenny didn't realize Annie was standing behind her listening. "No! I'm tired! I shoveled 2 houses today! Plus buddy knows you just as much as he knows me!" Bex whispered. "You know Toby will kill my ass if he found out I was at buddy's house!" jenny whispered. "I'll get it." Annie said. Neither Bex nor jenny heard her. "Come on! Let's go on the back porch! I'll suck you off!" jenny whispered. Bex smiled. "You know I told you we can't do it at my mother's house!" Bex whispered.

Annie goes to the closet and puts on her winter boots and coat. At this time, Clint was whispering naughty words into Peggy's ear, making her giggle. Hakim dozed off for a few minutes while sitting at the bottom of the stairs. Annie is on the porch. She closes the door and starts walking down the road. She finds it hard walking in the snow. She falls to her knees. "Fuck!" Annie shouted.

Back in the house, hakim wakes up, almost dropping his drink. He goes to the refrigorator and grabs a beer to chase down his hard drink. Bex and jenny break up their conversation when hakim enters the kitchen. Hakim noticed that jenny was upset. Jenny heads back to the living room. "What's wrong with her?" hakim asked. "Nothing! She just being a bitch!" Bex said. Bex heads back to the living room as well. Clint and Peggy were hugged up, reminiscing about old times. Toby and Bex were sitting next to each other, talking bullshit. Toby was just mumbling incoherently. Jenny went to go sit at the bottom of the stairs where hakim was. Hakim comes out of the kitchen and kneels down next to Bex to get in on the conversation. Bex was cracking up when he heard Toby call jenny a stinking bitch. Jenny stood up and goes over and smacks Toby in the back of his head. Toby jumps up. "Bitch! You done lost yo mind?" Toby shouted. Bex was so drunk, he fell out of his seat laughing. Hakim was laughing too, but kept jenny and Toby separated. Toby steps on Clint's foot. "Toby! You sick son-of-a-bitch! Go in the kitchen and cool off!" Clint chuckled. Bex gets up off the floor. Peggy grabs Clint's empty beer bottle. "Biron! Biron! Gone in the kitchen and get Clint another beer!" Peggy said. Bex goes into the kitchen and gets the beer. Hakim is working on his 3rd glass of vodka. He becomes fascinated by the Christmas tree lights. Toby looks up at hakim. "What the fuck is wrong with you?" Toby asked hakim. Hakim snaps out of his daze. He storms out to the front porch. Once the cold air hit his face, he becomes more relaxed.

Inside the house, jenny sits next to Toby rubbing the back of his neck. Suddenly, jenny's favorite son comes on. She start snapping her fingers, singing along with the song. "Excuse my darling, but I gotta take a wiz!" Clint says to Peggy. "I think Annie is in there!" Peggy said. "I'll knock on the door!" Clint said. Clint walks into the kitchen and knocks on the door to the bathroom. Clint slowly opens the door and see it's clear. He goes in to do his business. Toby and jenny start arguing again. "I'm gonna kick both y'all drunk asses out if y'all don't stop fighting! It's Christmas! Have fun god damnit!" Peggy chuckled. A minute later, Clint comes out of the bathroom. He goes into the refrigorator and grabs a beer. He goes into the living room, holding his beer in the air. "I just raided your frig!" Clint shouted. Bex waves him off. Go ahead, you family man!" Bex said. "No, I'm drunk!" Clint chuckled. Everybody starts laughing. "Where the hell is Annie?" Peggy asked. "She's probably upstairs sleep!" Bex said. "Gotta use the bathroom again!" hakim said as he comes from outside. "Jenny, Toby, get y'all presents from under the tree!" Peggy shouted. Jenny goes over to the tree and grabs her and Toby's present. Jenny gives Toby his present. Jenny opens her present. "It's a sweater! Thank you!" jenny said as she goes over and gives Peggy a hug. Toby on the other hand, is so drunk, he can't even tare the wrapping open. "Biron! Open that for him!" Peggy said. Bex takes the present from Toby. He opens it. "It's a neck-tie and matching handkerchief!" Bex shouts. "Thank you! Thank you!" Toby shouted. "You're welcome sir!" Peggy said. Toby and Bex shake hands. "Annie got a sweater too, but hers is green. "Peggy said. "What's that smelling good?" jenny asked. "Take the roast out of the oven hakim!" Peggy shouted. "Ok!" said hakim as he grabs the oven mitts off the kitchen counter. He takes the roast out. Clint helps Peggy out of her seat. Peggy looks in agonizing pain as she walks to the kitchen. Clint walks with her. "Let me see what we got here." Peggy said. "Its a little chard on the top, but it ain't burnt." Hakim said. "The veggies on the side look nice!" Peggy said. "It's looks damn good!" Clint said. "Biron! Tell Annie to come down and eat!" Peggy shouted. Bex stands at the bottom of the stairs. "Annie! We're about to eat!" Bex shouted. "Stop being lazy, and go and wake her up!" Peggy shouted. Bex runs up stairs. He gets to the top of the stairs. "Annie! We're about to eat!" Bex shouted. Bex taps on the bedroom door. "Annie?" Bex said. He looks inside and sees that the room is empty. Bex runs back down stairs. He checks the closet and sees that her coat is missing. "Anybody seen Annie leave?" Bex asked. "Last I saw her was in the kitchen!" jenny said. "She ain't there!" Bex said. "Ma! She must've took her coat and walked out the house!" Bex said. "Check the back porch! She probably fell asleep back there!" Peggy said. "She couldn't have! The door is locked!" hakim said. Bex runs outside. He looks down the road in all directions. "Annie! Annie!" Bex shouted into the cold darkness. Bex runs back into the house. "I'll take the jeep and go find her!" Bex said. "Y'all been drinking! Ain't nobody going out in that snow!" Peggy said. "I'm ok. They can drive with me." Clint said. "Get your coat!" hakim says to Bex. Bex runs to the closet and grabs his coat and scarf. Hakim gets his coat too. "We'll be back." Clint said. Clint walks Peggy back to her seat. Hakim and Bex are already outside. Clint jumps into the driver's seat of his SUV. Bex almost falls when his foot sinks into the pile of snow. "Watch it!" hakim said. Bex jumps into the passenger seat. Hakim jumps in the back behind him. Clint's tires spin before they take off. "She probably went to the liquor store! Let's try there first!" Bex said. Peggy watches from the window as they take off. Jenny sits next to Peggy and starts rubbing her back. "They're gonna find her." Jenny said.

About a block away from the house, the guys look in every direction as Clint drives no faster than 20 miles per hour. "It should be easy to find her. Ain't nobody on the streets." Bex said. "Wait! Stop!" hakim shouts. Clint stops. Hakim looks down the dark street. Never mind." Hakim said Clint continues to drive. "Damn its cold!" hakim said. Clint turns on the heat. They are a couple of blocks away from the mini mart when they all spot flashing lights to their right. Clint stops the vehicle. "Ain't that the drug dealer's block?" hakim asked. Bex starts breathing heavy. "Take it easy. I'll drive by slow." Clint said. Clint turns down the block buddy lives on. The closer they get, the more people they see I the middle of the street. Clint had to stop because the street was blocked off by police caution tape. There were 4 squad cars on the scene Bex jumps out of the SUV he almost slips on the ice. Hakim gets out as well. Bex runs through the caution tape. He approaches an officer. The whole block was bright from the flashing lights. "Excuse me officer! Could you tell me what happened?" Bex asked. "A lady was shot! I don't think she made it!" the officer said. Bex starts crying and breathing uncontrollably. He runs pass the officer. "Stop god damnit!" the officer yelled. Bex couldn't hear the officer. He couldn't hear nothing but his own heart beating rapidly. He sees a group of officers standing in a group. He sees 2 girls standing on their porch. "What happened?" Bex asked. "This lady walked up in buddy's house, and he shot her!" the girl cried. Bex ran over to buddy's porch before being grabbed by the cops. He saw a pool of frozen blood in the snow. Bex falls to his knees. The cops grab him, and drag him from the scene. "Are you stupid, running on a crime scene like that?" an officer shouted. A detective walks over to Bex. "Did you know the deceased son?" the detective asked. "Was she wearing a blue coat? Bex cried. "I'm sorry. She was." The detective answered as hakim arrives on the scene. "Who are you son?" the elderly white detective asked. "This is my brother! What happened?" hakim asked. "Annie dead! Annie dead!" Bex screamed while on his knees. "Are you 2 any relation to the victim?" the detective asked. "She was staying with us!" hakim cried. "You've been drinking sir?" the detective asked hakim. Bex stands up. "What the fuck that gotta do with anything?" Bex screamed. The detective's partner, who was a young black woman approaches. "Watch your mouth son! We just want to know if you 2 are able to come down and identify the body!" the detective shouted. The young female detective takes out a pen and pad and jot down information from hakim. Clint comes trotting down the street. "Everything ok?" he asked. "Somebody shot Annie! We gotta go down and I. d. the body!" hakim cried. "Jesus Christ!" Clint shouted. "Are you with them sir?" the female detective asked. "Yeah!" Clint said. "I'm detective brown. I'm going to take them down to I.D. the body. You think you could follow me?" she asked Clint. "I'm parked down the street!" Clint said. "Could you come with me please sir?" detective brown asked hakim. "Come on man!" hakim said to Bex as he picks him off the ground.

After convincing Bex to come down to the morgue, they finally arrive. Bex was silent the whole ride. Once they get to the entrance of the hospital, hakim had to convince Bex to come inside.

Inside the morgue, hakim braced himself for what he was about to see. The body was slid out from the chamber by the orderly. The body bag was unzipped. Hakim tried to stay strong, but fell to the floor when laying eyes on Annie's pale body. She had a hole about 4 inches in diameter in her chest. "We have the owner of the shot gun in custody." Detective brown said.

About a half hour later, Clint's SUV and the detective's car were parked outside of Peggy's house. Bex went inside, while hakim sat on the porch in the freezing weather. The tears on his cheek had frozen. He could hear the screams from inside the house.

A few days later, the police report said that Annie had entered the home of alleged drug dealer, bobby Jones, a.k.a buddy asking for drugs. He thought she came to rob him. He had a shot gun in the closet. He said he went for it and shot Annie in self-defense. The blast from the shot gun knocked Annie back to the ground, where she bled to death. Buddy was let out on 50 thousand dollars bail less than 24 hours later. By the time detectives could get a warrant to search his home for narcotics, his boys moved thousands of dollars of illegal drugs to an undisclosed location.

It was December 31st around 11am, when things went from bad to worse. Peggy's health got so bad, she had to be admitted to the hospital. Bex and hakim new that she wasn't coming home this time. She was hooked up to respirator and tracheotomy tube coming out of her throat. Bex was still in shock over Annie as he stayed by his mother's bedside, while hakim took care of matters at the house. Hakim had only been around these people less than a year, but considered them the most important people in his life. He sat on the sofa gripping Peggy's bathrobe in his arms. Even though she was his aunt, she was definitely the mother he had wished. He gets up from the sofa and walks to the refrigorator. He opens it, and sees that there is only one beer left. Hakim walks outside and stares at the house where Annie and her grandmother lived. There was a for sale sign in front of the house. Suddenly, a blue sports car pulls to the curb. It was buddy sitting in the passenger seat, while one guy from his crew was in the driver's seat. Hakim turns in their direction. He became petrified. "Yo man! I want you to look in the back seat of my ride before you even think about saying or doing anything!" buddy shouted over the loud motor. Hakim realized he was looking down the barrel of a 357 revolver sticking out the window. He couldn't see who was holding the weapon, but he saw that the hand holding the weapon had to be someone with a dark complexion. "Listen here! That retarded bitch came in my house, uninvited! I don't feel bad about blasting her ass either! I wanna tell you, if you and that faggot ass Bex wanna blaze guns about it, bring it! As a matter of fact, I don't wanna see yo bitch asses around here no more!" buddy said as he exhaled small clouds of marijuana smoke. It was freezing outside, but hakim could feel the warmth of urine trickling down his leg. "Let's get the fuck out of here!" buddy ordered his driver. At the same time, parked about a 100 yards away, was the same black van Toby had seen a while ago. The sports car burns rubber down the road. Hakim snaps out of his trance and starts trembling. He looked down and saw sneaker drenched in piss. He quickly runs into the house and sits on the sofa. He starts sobbing like a baby. Suddenly, the phone rings. It rings 4 times before hakim answers it. "Hello?" hakim said. "It's me! You need to get down here to the hospital, Quick!" Bex cried. "Ok." Hakim said in a soft tone. He knew it was bad. He looks down at his pants. He went into the closet. He goes into his duffle bag a pulls out a clean pair of pants, underwear and socks. Hakim runs upstairs. He strips naked and jumps into the shower. As he's in the shower, his fear turns to anger. He starts punching the shower walls harder and harder the more he thinks about buddy and what he said.

About 10 minutes later, hakim comes down the stairs wearing a fresh set of clothes. He took his urine soaked clothes and put them in a garbage bag he took underneath the kitchen cabinet. He then takes his sneakers out to the back porch to let them air out. He found a pair of Bex's shoes which fit perfectly. He grabs the car keys, locks up the house and heads to the jeep.

Hakim arrives at the hospital, he's mumbling to himself on what excuse he could give Bex for taking so long. He goes to the receptionist's desk. There was an elderly white woman at the desk. "Peggy Xavier, room 210." Hakim said. She checks the computer. She shook her head. "You need to hurry up there young man!" she said as she hands him the access pass. Hakim takes the pass and runs for the elevator. He gets out of the elevator on the second floor. He starts trotting down the hall. He stops. He realizes the inevitable. He realized he was too late. Hakim saw his brother sitting on the floor outside his mother's room with his head down. Bex was not alone. He was being comforted by jenny, who was kneeled down beside him rubbing his back. Jenny sees hakim coming towards them. She embraces him with a hug. "Toby and Clint are in the room with her!" jenny says to hakim as she continues rubbing Bex's back. Hakim enters the room. He sees Toby and Clint standing over Peggy's lifeless body. Hakim goes over and hugs Toby. He leaves the room without viewing the body. A group of nurses enter the room to unhook Peggy's body from the monitors and respirators. Hakim stands outside the room across from Bex crying. The orderly comes in the room and covers the body. The staff strolls the body out of the room after getting Bex's permission earlier. Jenny breaks down. Toby consoles her. Hakim goes over and sits next to his brother. "We're gonna be down in the lobby when y'all ready to go!" Toby said. Bex gives a nod to Toby. Clint pats Bex on the shoulder. "I have faith in you young man that you'll get through all of this!" Clint says to Bex. Jenny gives Bex a kiss on top of his head. Toby, jenny and Clint head to the elevator. There was dead silence between to 2 brothers. Suddenly, hakim turns to Bex. "So what are we doing, now?" hakim asked. Bex takes a deep breath. "It looks like I'm gonna have to cremate ma and Annie! I can't afford to do anything else!" Bex said. Hakim looked up at the ceiling, then looks to his brother. "I think you should put the house up for sale, man!" hakim said. Bex frowned at hakim. "Are you crazy? That's my home! When I get enough money, then I'll give them a proper burial!" Bex said. "You don't understand! Some shit might go down if you don't!" hakim said. Hakim sees a woman coming towards them. He taps Bex on the shoulder. They both stand. "Mr. Xavier?" the woman asked Bex. "Yeah, that's me!" he answered as they shook hands. "I'm Olivia Campbell. I'm administrative assistant for this level. We're sorry for your loss, but we need you to fill out some release forms for us." She said. "I'll be down stairs with everybody else." Hakim said.

An hour later, hakim and Bex are back at the Xavier house sitting in the kitchen. Hakim gets up and goes to the refrigorator and gives Bex the last beer. "I don't feel like drinking." Bex said. Hakim unscrews the cap. "Here! Take it…fool!" hakim chuckled. Bex looks at hakim, and starts laughing. He takes the beer and guzzles a third of it down. "Tell me what you was saying about some shit going down." Bex said as he wipe the tears from his eyes. "Buddy rolled up on me. He said he didn't want to see us around here no more." Hakim said. Bex became angry. He stood from his seat. "Man, fuck him! Let's go get this nigga!" Bex shouted. "Calm down! This nigga got an army! We'll be dead for sure!" hakim said. Bex slowly sits back in his seat. "So, we're gonna run?" Bex asked. "Listen. We can lose the battle for now, but if you trust me, and follow my lead, we damn sure gonna win the war!" hakim said. "Man, this nigga killed Annie! You better have a master plan or something!" Bex said. "I do! But, it ain't gonna happen overnight!" hakim said.

It was moments before the New Year. Bex had invited Toby and jenny over to the house to bring in the New Year. Toby had brought over a couple bottles of champagne. Jenny turned on the boom box. She starts snapping her fingers and bopping her head to the music. They gather in the living room to watch the ball drop on TV. Toby grabs some plastic cups from the kitchen. He fills everyone's cup to the rim. Here we go y'all!" jenny shouts. "10,9,8,7,6,5,4,3,2,1! Happy new year!" they all shout at once. Jenny hugs the guys, giving them a kiss on the cheek. Toby hugs hakim and Bex. Bex gives his brother a big bear hug. Bex lifts his cup in the air. "Happy new year ma! Happy new year Annie!" Bex shouts at the top of his lungs. Toby, hakim and jenny lift their cups as well. "Happy new year!" they all shout again. Suddenly, gun shots are heard outside. Hakim ducks quickly ducks down behind the sofa. "It's a hit!" he shouts. Everybody looks at hakim as if he lost his mind. Bex starts laughing. "Sorry bro! Forgot to tell you, we do this every year around here!" Bex chuckled. "What the fuck?" hakim shouted. "We been doing this since I was a boy!" Toby chuckled. More gunfire goes off. "Don't worry though. They shoot in the air." Jenny said. "God damn! Y'all some real hillbillies down here! I can't believe I'm still in Jersey!" hakim shouted.

It was the January 5th of the new millennium. Toby made a promise to Bex that he would take care of the funeral arrangements for Annie and his mother. They both were laid to rest at Clear View Cemetery, located in Vineland. The gang and a few neighbors were silent as a one of the kids of a neighbor sang a heartfelt spiritual song. Jenny broke down, and had to be held by Toby. Bex looked over in the distance and thought he saw Annie standing in a white dress, waving at him. Tears just poured from his eyes. As the singing continued, Bex couldn't hold it together to the point where he had to back off, back to the jeep. Bex gets in the jeep, waiting for hakim to show up.

After the pastor finished his sermon, Annie's casket was lowered into the ground first. White roses were tossed on top of the casket. After a few adjustments, Peggy's casket was lowered on top. More flowers were tossed in.

Minutes later, hakim walks up to the jeep. He was dressed in a white button up shirt and black dress pants. "Ready to roll out?" he asked Bex. "Yeah. You coming to Toby's for the repast?" Bex asked. "Nah! Just drop me off at the house. I can't get used to this shit." hakim said.

The next day around 3pm, the realtor came by the Xavier house. "Mr. Xavier? I'm hector Torres of Atlantic Realtors." He said to Bex. They shake hands. Torres looked around and saw that the living room was empty, with nothing but boxes staked on top of each other. "I see you are all set to move on!" Torres chuckled. Bex scratches his head. "Yeah man, it's time to move on." Bex said. "All right then! Let's take the tour!" Torres said with enthusiasm. Being that the house was so small, the tour lasted no more than an hour.

"Ok Mr. Xavier, the house needs lots of work. The best I can do is one hundred thousand. The appraiser might say different. But, I've been around enough to know that it seems like the right price. If a buyer want to take it as it is, that's what we're looking at." Torres explained. Bex looks around the house. "Alright! Do what you gotta do to make it happen!" Bex said. "Alright! Let's do some paper work and get started!" Torres said.

After Torres leaves the house, hakim comes in the door. "We're ready to roll brother!" Bex sighed. "I know it's hard man, but this is a new beginning for us!" hakim said as he massages his brother's back. "We gonna rule the world. Say it with me!" hakim shouts. "We're gonna rule the world!" both brothers shout. They give each other a hug. "All we gotta do now, is say our goodbyes, and we're out of here!" hakim said.

After hakim and Bex left Toby and jenny's house, they headed to the turnpike north. As they entered turnpike, Bex reminisces about his mother and Annie. His eyes start to tear up until the tears start falling. Hakim looks over and noticed his brother weeping. "Let it out brother. That's the only way to deal with it." Hakim said as he turns on the radio. Coincidently, Peggy's favorite R&B song is playing on the radio. Hakim starts bopping his head to the music. Bex wipes the tears away and looks over at hakim. Bex then starts bopping his head to the music as well. Hakim hits the gas pedal even harder, doing 65 up the turnpike.

It's about 8pm when hakim and Bex arrive in Newark. "Before we stop and get a room, I wanna show you where I grew up at. It's all boarded up, but it's something we gotta see." Hakim explained. Bex nods his as they drive by a bodega. "I used to make my man Curtis stop and bring me out candy from that bodega!" hakim chuckled. They see a couple of young black men on the corner slinging rocks. "Back in the day, niggas like that used to jump when they saw me and Curtis coming down the block!" hakim boasted. They were about a block away from the old building. Hakim notices as they got closer to their destination, that there was a heard of people heading off in the same direction. Hakim hits the brakes. "What's all this?" Bex asked. "What the fuck?" hakim said to himself. He couldn't believe his eyes. His jaw dropped. The building he'd thought was boarded up and abandoned, was totally the opposite. It was reconstructed into a night club. Hakim was in a daze just staring at the giant neon sign on the building. It read BIG SHOTS in bright orange, cursive letters that stretches about 50 feet across the 10th floor. "I can't believe this shit!" hakim shouted as he saw the giant search lights out front sway back-n-forth. "Yo, that's where you used to live?" Bex asked. "Fuck this!" hakim shouts. Infuriated, hakim jumps out of the jeep and heads toward the club. "Hold up!" Bex shouted as he exits the jeep as well.

The line of patrons stretched around the corner. There was a young black man standing in line with his girlfriend, who recognized it was hakim walking towards the main entrance. "I ain't see that dude since we was kids!" the guy says to his girlfriend. There were 3 bouncers standing at the entrance. "Hey, you gotta get in line like everybody else!" one bouncer says to hakim. Bex is standing right behind hakim. "You know who the fuck I am?" hakim shouted. The bouncer pushes hakim back a little. Hakim smacks his hand out of the way. The second bouncer was about to grab hakim, until the 3rd bouncer recognized who he was. The line of people stood in silence. The bouncer whispered in the bouncer's ear who was about knock hakim on his ass. "Wait here for a second!" the aggressive bouncer says to hakim. "You better be who he says you are!" one of bouncers said as the other goes into the club to confirm who hakim was.

Minutes later, the bouncer that was about to attack hakim comes out. "Let him in!" he shouts. "This here is my brother! He's with me!" hakim said. "Alright! He can come too!" the bouncer said reluctantly. Bex has a big smile on his face as he follows his brother through the doors.

Inside the club was packed. Hakim and Bex follow the bouncer down a small flight of stair. Bex noticed that the club was very adult themed. There were projections of triple x movies showing on the walls. There were multicolored studio lights automatically moving in certain patterns. Giant speakers were mounted to the walls and ceiling, blasting dance music at almost ear piercing level. The bouncer, hakim and Bex had to walk sideways to get through the crowd. Hakim looked down at his attire and noticed that his clothes were out dated compared to what everyone else was wearing. There were a lot of patrons gawking at him as he walked by. Bex on the other hand, was impressed at the fast paced crowd mingling and dancing. They walk past the neon lit bar, all the way towards the VIP section. The bouncer unlatched the velvet ropes.

The VIP section was actually a giant glass cubicle, able to occupy at least 20 people. The bouncer made a sharp left pass the VIP section towards a door leading to a back room. The bouncer knocks on the door in a distinct pattern. The door is then opened by another bouncer on the other side. The 3 men enter to see a small room resembling an illegal gambling spot.

CHAPTER 13. KRAYTON

Inside were 5 guys sitting at a poker table. 4 of the guys were black, the 5th guy Hispanic. One of the black guys stands from his seat. "Yo hakim! What's up?" Krayton shouts. He comes from around the table and gives hakim a big hug. "My nigga! I can't believe this shit!" Krayton chuckled. Hakim smiled, returning the gesture. Hakim takes a step back, looking at Krayton. "Man, it's good to see yo ass again!" hakim said. "You must've did some serious benching in the pin! You big as hell!" Krayton said. "Yo man, this here is my brother Bex! This here is my cousin Krayton!" "Yo! It's K boogie now!" Krayton said with a serious look on his face. "Ok! You got that!" hakim said. "Brother? Since when?" Krayton asked. "It's a long fucking story cuz!" hakim said. "Yo! What's up man?" Krayton says to Bex as he gives him a hug. "Yo, let's go somewhere so we can catch up, man!" hakim said. "Oh sure cuz!" said Krayton. He turns towards the guys at the card table. "Y'all gonna have to count me out this hand!" Krayton said. "Fuck that! We gonna finish this hand kid!" said the old guys at the table. "Listen! I got 3 grand on the table, so y'all can split that shit between yourselves! I don't give a fuck!" Krayton said. "You only gotta tell me once!" the old guy chuckled. They all start arguing on how to divvy the money up. "Let's go cuz!" said Krayton. Hakim and Bex follow Krayton to another door that lead to his office.

In the office, Krayton had an oak desk, with a leather chair that resembled a throne. On the other side of the desk were 2 chairs that looked less impressive. On the wall behind the desk, Bex noticed a small replica of the lassenberry coat-of-arms. Hakim looked around the office noticing pictures of naked black women on the walls in various poses. The music muffled once Krayton closed the door. "Have a seat fellas!" Krayton said. Bex and hakim sat down. Krayton goes over and sits in his chair, kicking his feet up on the desk.

Krayton was dressed like a million bucks. He was wearing a silk shirt, silk dress pants, a silk neck-tie and gator shoes. He wore a diamond watch, and pinky ring. "Damn cuz! You let them niggas have your gambling money, and you dripping in diamonds! Life must be good as hell!" hakim said. "Yeah, only big timers rock diamonds these days!" Krayton chuckled. Hakim looked down at his own ring, which was gold. "How long you been out cuz?" Krayton asked. "About six or seven months now." Hakim said. "You get a chance to see your pop?"

Krayton asked. "You're the first one in the family I ran across." Hakim said. "Damn! A lot of shit changed since you've been gone cuz!" Krayton said. "Where's Eddie, my clothes and furniture?" hakim asked as he leans forward putting his arms on the desk. "All that stuff was put into storage. Your pop is staying in Cherry hill." Krayton said. "I saw on the news a while back that Jabbo had passed. Who's helping Eddie out now?" hakim asked. "Sorry to tell you but your pop ain't running the show no more after his stroke." Krayton said. "A stroke?" hakim said. "Yeah. It was serious. He's stuck in a wheelchair now. All fucked up." Krayton said. "So, who's running things now, butch?" hakim asked. "Hell no! Sir Marcus got it now!" Krayton said. "Who the fuck is Sir Marcus?" hakim asked. Krayton sighs. "It's cousin mark. Hakim looks over at Bex. He starts laughing hysterically. He gets out of his seat and starts pacing around the room, still laughing. He stops pacing. "Get the fuck out of here!" hakim chuckled. "Yeah! Sir Marcus runs everything!" Krayton said. "So, you helping him now?" hakim asked. "Nah! He don't want none of the family involved in the game! Not yet anyway." Krayton said as hakim's facial expression turns to anger. "So you just decided to run up in my house and turn it into a fucking night club?" hakim said in a calm voice. "No cuz! It ain't even like that! We got the go ahead from jabbo before he died!" Krayton said. "Who the fuck is we?" hakim asked. "Me and Corey run the place together!" Krayton said. "I can't believe this shit!" hakim chuckled. "We got this place rolling in cash! You see the crowd outside! Check this! We only open on Friday, Saturday and Sundays!" Krayton boasted. "Well since you're doing this good, you can put me in on the action." Hakim said with a deviant smile. "I can't do nothing for you cuz, until I talk it over with Corey!" Krayton said with a smile. Bex and Krayton could see that hakim is really pissed now. Hakim walks around the desk over to where Krayton is and grabs him by the collar. He lifts him out of his chair. Bex jumps from his seat. Krayton tries to break free from his grip, but is too weak against hakim's brute strength. He pushes Krayton up against the wall. "Go ahead a scream for them niggas outside, so they can see me beat yo ass!" hakim shouts. "Come on cuz! It ain't gotta be like this!" Krayton cried. "Me and Bex need a place to stay! We appreciate it if would accommodate us! Cuz!" hakim said. "Alright! Alright!" Krayton stuttered. He reaches into his front pocket and pulls out a set of keys. He takes one odd shaped key off the ring. "Here! It's the key to my penthouse in Manhattan!" Krayton. Said. Hakim snatches the key from him. "Now, where is this penthouse, and what's the number?" hakim asked. "The Empire building, floor P3!" Krayton said. "I think we gonna need some spending money too, cuz!" hakim said. "Ok! Ok!" Krayton cried. Krayton reaches into his other pockets. "It's about 8 grand! That's all I got on me!" Krayton said as he gives it to hakim. "This is how it's gonna go down! We're gonna chill for a few days at yo crib! Within that time, we need you to arrange a meeting for us with mark!" hakim said as he straightens Krayton's neck-tie. Krayton is shaking like a leaf as he nods. Hakim balls up his fists, giving Krayton fake jabs to the gut. Krayton flinches. Hakim smiles. "Just fucking with you cuz!" hakim chuckled. Bex heads for the door and opens it for hakim to pass through. Hakim turns around towards Krayton. "Remember! That meeting better happen, and happen soon!" hakim said before he leaves the room. Bex follows behind. Krayton slumps back into his chair. He's holding his chest.

Outside the club, hakim and Bex walk back towards the jeep. "Damn! That's was easier than I thought!" hakim chuckled. "I thought he was gonna get his boys on us for sure!" Bex said. "Them Lassenberry boys always been punk ass bitches! He'd rather give me the key and money than fuck him up in front of his people!" hakim said. Bex starts laughing. They jump inside the jeep. "Come on brother! Let's check out this penthouse!" hakim said as he drives off.

About an hour later, hakim and Bex arrive in Manhattan. The New York night life was in full swing. They drive their crappy looking jeep down 59th street. "Man, I ain't been to the city since ma took Christmas shopping when I was 10!" Bex said. "For real?" hakim said as they pull up to the Empire building.

The Empire building was considered one of the most luxurious buildings on the upper west side of Manhattan. Socialites call it the building for the young elite. Mostly 20 and 30 something year olds occupied the penthouses. Young "A" list actors, European and Arab royalty are amongst those living there. Krayton depended on the envelopes from his cousin Sir Marcus to maintain residency there.

After giving a tip to the uniformed valet driver, Bex and hakim head to the lobby. There stood an elderly white man dressed in his uniform. He happened to be the door man to the building. "Can I help you gentlemen?" the doorman asked. "Yeah! We're guests of Krayton Lassenberry!" hakim said. "Is he expecting you sir?" the doorman asked. "Nah! He gave us the key to crash here for a few days!" hakim said as he holds the key into the air. "Very well then. Once you enter the elevator, hand over your key to the operator." The doorman said. "Ok, cool!" hakim said. Bex and hakim head to the elevator. "Enjoy the rest of your evening gentleman." The doorman said. Once in the elevator, hakim hands over the key to the elevator operator, who was a young Hispanic man. The operator has an identical key which must enter the slot simultaneously as the key given. Once both key are in their slots, he asks hakim what's his designated floor. Hakim tells him P3. The operator presses the appropriate button. The elevator starts to move.

The elevator reaches floor P3. "Damn this elevator is fast!" Bex said as the operator returns the key to hakim. "Enjoy your evening gentleman." The operator said. "Yeah, you too!" hakim said.

Once the 2 brothers enter the penthouse they are amazed on how elaborate the penthouse was. They walked on a carpet which was covered by wall-to-wall Mohtashem Kashan carpet, one of the most expensive carpets in the world. Bex noticed a grand piano over in the corner. "Look at this! Like that nigga know how to really play the piano!" Bex said sarcastically. Hakim enters one of the 3 bedrooms and noticed a giant bear skin rug on the floor near the fireplace. The thing that really caught Bex's eye was the wood-fired pizza oven. "Yo hakim! You gotta come see this!" Bex shouts

The next day at the lassenberry castle, it was around noon when Sir Marcus was sitting at his desk looking over the books on Galaxy appliance sales. There was a knock on the door. Sir Marcus starts sighing. "Come in!" he shouts. Tony enters the room, dressed in dark-blue suit, carrying his briefcase. "What's up?" Sir Marcus asked tony. Tony takes a seat on the sofa, then crossed his legs. "Your cousin Krayton, I mean K boogie wants to have a meeting with you." Tony said. Sir Marcus chuckled. "Oh really? About what?" Sir Marcus asked. "He didn't say, but he wasn't happy." Tony said. Sir Marcus leans back in his chair, rubbing his eyes. "Alright then. Tell him to be here around 3." Sir Marcus ordered. Tony gets up and starts to leave the office. "Wait a minutes!" Sir Marcus said. Tony leaves the door ajar. "I want you here for the meeting." Sir Marcus ordered. Tony nods. As he's leaving the office, Kimberly enters. She is wearing a long floral dress with shawl draped over her shoulders. Tony bows to her. Kimberly slaps tony on the arm. "You need to stop!" Kimberly chuckled. Tony smiles, then walks away. Kimberly closes the door, then walks over to Sir Marcus. Kimberly leans over and give him a kiss on the lips. Sir Marcus gently puts his hands on Kimberly's belly. "I still can't believe I'm going to be a dad!" Sir Marcus said. Kimberly puts her hands on her hips. "Just makes sure you're there in the delivery room!" Kimberly said with a smile. "I promise." Sir Marcus looks down at her belly and starts rubbing it. She has the look of concern on her face. "I was thinking. Before I start to show, I think we should move the wedding up to an earlier date." She said to Sir Marcus. He grabs her hand and starts massaging her fingers. "Whatever you want to do." Sir Marcus responded. "Well then it's settled! The wedding will be on April 1st. I think the weather should be nice enough for an outdoor wedding!" Kimberly said. "I think we should have the reception outdoors too, to be on the safe side." Sir Marcus said. "Why'd you would you say to be on the safe side?" Kimberly asked. "Remember the last family that held a wedding reception indoors!" Sir Marcus said. Kimberly thought about it for a moment. She smacks Sir Marcus upside the head. "You are mean! That's not funny!" she said. "Hey! The Gatano disaster should be a lesson to us all." Sir Marcus chuckled. Kimberly rolls her eyes. "I'm flying Carmen out here for the weekend to help with the arrangements." Kimberly sighed. "No baby! Just give me a list of everything you need and want, and I'll get tony and his people to get on it! Your job baby, is just to give me an heir and a spare!" Sir Marcus insisted. "An heir and a spare?" Kimberly shouted as she punches Sir Marcus in the chest. "Ouch!" Sir Marcus chuckled.

Later that day, it was 5 minutes pass 3pm. Krayton was sitting in the guest hall of the west wing, waiting to see his cousin. He was dressed in the same clothes he had on the day before. Krayton looked down at his watch. He gets aggravated. There was a NA agent sitting in a golf cart across from him. Suddenly, the NA agent sitting in the golf cart gets a message on the walkie-talkie. "Sir Marcus will see you now. Sir." The agent said. "It's about fucking time!" Krayton says to himself. Krayton jumps into the golf cart. Less than 5 minutes later, the golf cart arrives at the west wing, just outside of Sir Marcus's office. There, another agent stands by the office entrance. Krayton gets out of the cart. He walks toward the doors, in which the agent opens for him.

Inside the office sat Tony Kerouac on the sofa, with his legs crossed. He had a pad and pen on his lap. Sir Marcus was sitting at his desk. Krayton walks over to the desk. Sir Marcus stands and goes over to give his cousin a hug. "How's everything cousin?" Sir Marcus asked. "Everything could be better! Much better!" Krayton said. Krayton turns toward tony. He waves to tony, with a not so genuine smile. "Have a seat cousin." Sir Marcus said to Krayton. Krayton pulls out his chair and takes a seat. "Did my men feed you while you were waiting?" Sir Marcus asked. "Yeah, man." Krayton said. "So, what's up?" Sir Marcus asked. "Hakim is back in the picture!" Krayton shouted. "What'd you mean, back in the picture?" Sir Marcus asked as he folded his hands on the desk. "Man, stop it! You know what I mean!" Krayton shouted. "Krayton! Krayton! Don't sit here and try to read my mind!" Sir Marcus said as he points his finger at Krayton. Krayton starts breathing heavy, shaking his head. "How many times I gotta tell y'all? It's K Boogie, Man!" Krayton shouted. "Whatever! Just tell me about hakim, please!" Sir Marcus shouts. Krayton clears his throat. Hakim came down to my club the last night! He came down with some dude he called his brother, named Bex or something! He wants to have a meeting with you!" Krayton said. "Did he say what he wanted to meet about?" Sir Marcus. "Nah, but I think he's pissed about us turning his home into a night club! That dude is crazy!" Krayton said. "Do you think it's a money issue?" Sir Marcus asked. "When ain't it about money, cuz?" Krayton said. "Where is he now?" Sir Marcus asked. "He and that nigga Bex staying at my place in Manhattan!" Krayton said. "Sounds like you don't want them there." Sir Marcus said. "Hell no! He said he ain't leaving until he talked to you!" Krayton said. "Well, I don't want to talk to him. Not now anyway. Tony!" Sir Marcus yells. Tony stands and grabs a leather bag that was next to him on the sofa. He walks over and gives it to Krayton. "What's this?" Krayton asked. "You said it yourself cousin! When ain't it about money! There's a hundred grand, cash in that bag. Make sure he gets it. Tell him to find himself a nice apartment and go look for a job." Sir Marcus ordered. "Ok." Krayton sighs. "How's Corey as a business partner?" Sir Marcus asked Krayton. "Man, he hires the best DJ's in the Tri-state! He hires top of the line entertainment! He keeps the place packed!" Krayton said. "Good! If there's nothing else, let's call it a day." Sir Marcus says to Krayton. Sir Marcus gives his cousin a hug before he leaves. Before Krayton leaves the office, tony puts his on Krayton's shoulder, turning him around. "You're going to make sure hakim gets the money, right?" tony said with a threatening look. Krayton gulped down the saliva in his mouth. Krayton then storms out of the office. Tony starts laughing. A few seconds later, Krayton runs back into the office. "How the fuck you get out of here?" Krayton shouted. Sir Marcus starts laughing. "Just get in the golf cart and tell the agent you want to go to the main gate." Tony chuckled. Krayton nods and leaves the office once again.

Later that evening, hakim was at Krayton's penthouse with a sexy young lady. He was sitting in a leather recliner wearing nothing but a white bathrobe. The young lady was sitting in front of hakim, on a foot stool wearing a silvery 2 piece bikini and clear stiletto shoes massaging his feet. "Don't forget my pinky toe baby." Hakim said. Suddenly. The door opens. In come Krayton. "What the fuck is this shit?" Krayton shouted. "Hey, what's up cuz? Oh, I asked china here, was she good at massaging feet! She said yes, so here we are!" hakim said. "It's like that now, bitch?" Krayton said. "Man, chill! She was just rubbing my feet! It ain't like she was sucking my dick!" hakim said. "Bitch! Get your clothes on and get the fuck out of my house!" Krayton shouted. "For your sake, I hope you're talking to her!" hakim said. "I meant her!" Krayton said. "You heard the man. I guess you gotta go baby." Hakim chuckled. China puts on her one piece Mini dress. She walks pass Krayton. He grabs her by the arm. "I don't wanna see your ass at my club anymore!" Krayton whispered. China snatched her arm away from Krayton. She exits the penthouse. Krayton slams the door behind her. "So, what did the mighty sir Marcus say?" hakim asked. Krayton tosses the leather bag directly on his lap. "What the fuck is this shit?" hakim asked. "It's yours! Yeah, he said he didn't need to see you!" Krayton said as he goes over to the bar to make himself a drink. Hakim stands up.

He opens the leather bag. "How much is this?" hakim asked. "He said its a hundred grand in there." Krayton said after sipping on his drink. Hakim becomes infuriated. "I wipe my ass with a hundred grand!" hakim shouted. "That's what he gave me! He also said get an apartment and get a job." Krayton said with a smug look. Hakim throws the bag across the room. "Fuck this! I want you to go back and tell his ass again, I wanna see him!" hakim shouted. "Yo! He said that was it! Face it! He runs everything now!" Krayton said as he pours himself another drink. Hakim heads toward the bedroom, knocking over vase. The vase doesn't break. "Be careful! That shit cost me 5 grand man!" Krayton shouted.

About an hour later, hakim comes out of the bedroom fully dressed. Krayton had passed out on the recliner after his third drink. He wakes up feeling groggy. "Give me your car keys!" hakim said. "Where you going?" Krayton asked. "Don't worry about where the fuck I'm going! Just give me the keys!" hakim shouts. Terrified, Krayton quickly tosses hakim his keys to his 1999 Boeman LX. "When Bex gets in, tell him I'll be back in a couple of days!" hakim said before leaving.

After getting Krayton's car, hakim heads south, to New Jersey. He starts punching on the steering wheel. "Now what the fuck I'm gonna do?" hakim whispers to himself.

Within no time, hakim arrived outside BIG SHOTS. One of the bouncers spots him. He trots over to the car and opens the door for hakim, who is shocked that he did it, but goes along with it. "Go park it around the corner." Hakim orders the bouncer. Hakim walks pass the other bouncers at the entrance, this time without any altercation. When he enters the club, he runs into Corey. Corey gives him a hug. "Ever since you been back, You're what everybody's talking about now! It's like you're a legend in these streets!" Corey shouted over the noise. "Tell one of your waitresses to bring me a bottle of your best stuff! I'll be in the back room!" hakim said. "No problem!" Corey shouted as hakim made his way through the crowd. Hakim noticed a guy sitting alone at one of the tables. "Holy shit! Gunz?" hakim said as he gets a closer look. He goes over and taps the familiar face on the shoulder. 2 Gunz looks up. "Oh! My nigga!" Gunz shouts. Gunz jumps from his chair. He and hakim give each other a big hug. "I thought they was lying when they said you was home! When the fuck you get out?" Gunz chuckled. "I got out about 6 months ago!" hakim shouted. "Damn! You looking good! All grown up and shit!" Gunz said. "Man, you don't know how it feels to see a real nigga from back in the day!" hakim said. "Times changed for a nigga like me!" Gunz said. "I see you got some gray up top!" hakim said jokingly. "Man, since yo pop fell off, it's hard for a nigga like me to make some real cash!" Gunz said. "I'm home now! We gonna change all that shit! Follow me nigga!" hakim said. 2 Gunz follows hakim to the back room. There was a bouncer guarding the back room. "Yo! Corey said I can come back here!" hakim said. The bouncer immediately takes out his key and opens the door for hakim.

They both enter the room. Hakim closes the door. "Damn! It's good to see you kid!" Gunz shouts. He and hakim hug again. "Go on and heat a seat!" hakim said as he takes a seat. There a knock at the door. "Hold on!" hakim said as he gets up to open the door. "Here's your bottle you asked for." The young attractive waitress said. "Thanks! Brink another glass for my man here, baby." Hakim ordered. The waitress nods, then leave the room. "Yeah, I come back home, and all this shit is happening!" hakim said. "I don't even know who's running the streets now! All I see is these fucking robots in black suits cruising the streets!" Gunz said. "What happened to elevator crew, roof top crew and everybody else?" hakim asked. "Jabbo told us before he died, for us to stay away!" Gunz said. "For real?" hakim said. "Even Mackie and Chewie was told to break camp! Remember pinky? Well, he tried going into business for himself!" Gunz said. "What happened to him, man?" hakim asked. "They found the nigga head on his mother's porch a while back!" Gunz said when he hears a knock on the door. "Hold on!" hakim said to Gunz. Hakim goes over to answer the door, and takes the other glass from the waitress to give to Gunz. "Thanks baby. I'll holler at you later." Hakim said to the waitress. She leaves. "From what I hear, most of the old crew either got bumped off or went into hiding! Between me and you, we was thinking about sticking up the place!" Gunz confessed. "Who you meant by we?" hakim asked. "Me, Mackie and Chewie! Shit! We come in here masked up, and its wrap!" Gunz boasted. "They're still around?" hakim asked. "Yeah, but they laying low from them clowns in the black suits!" Gunz said. "Guess what? The prodigal son has returned!" hakim chuckled. "What you talking about?" Gunz asked. "I mean I'm here to bring us back to where we belong!" hakim said. "You sure about that?" Gunz asked as hakim cracked open the bottle of Cognac. He pours Gunz and himself a glass. "I wanna make a toast!" hakim shouted. Gunz raises his glass. "To the beginning of a new crew!" hakim said as they tap drinks. So what's the next move? And besides, what you gonna do, that we couldn't do?" Gunz asked after sipped his drink. "You just round up Mackie and Chewie for a meeting. I'll go have a talk with Sir Marcus." Hakim said. "Who the fuck is Sir Marcus?" Gunz asked. "They really kept you out of the loop! Didn't they? Damn!" hakim said. "Man, if you can put cash in my pockets, I'm all ears!" Gunz said.

A couple of weeks later, hakim had set up a meeting for his new crew to gather. It was at a motel in Las Cruces, New Mexico. It was about 105 in the shade that afternoon. Hakim was peeking through the blinds of the air conditioned room. Suddenly, he sees a 98 Boeman mini-van pull up in the parking lot. "They're here!" hakim shouted. Bex comes out of the bathroom. "Listen! Just let me do all the talking! These niggas ain't too bright, but if you get on their wrong side, you're dead!" hakim explained. Moments later, there's a knock on the door. "Open the door!" hakim ordered Bex. Bex opens the door, and in comes 2 Gunz, Chewie and Mackie. "What up my people!" hakim said as he and Gunz hug. "Long time, no see kid!" Chewie said as he and hakim hug. Mackie doesn't say a word. He just gives hakim a big hug as his eyes tear up. "I know! I know! I misses you too!" hakim said. Bex noticed that 2 Gunz had his dreadlocks tied up in a bun. He also noticed that they all 3 had on flip flops. They didn't look dangerous to him. They looked more like middle-aged black men on vacation.

The room was small. There were only 2 chairs in the room, and Mackie and Chewie sat in them. Bex leaned up against the wall with his arms folded.

"Alright guys! I'm glad you all came. The reason why I chose this spot, was because Gunz said those clowns in black were all over the place back home. The plan is simple. We fuck up production out on the streets, so this Sir Marcus won't have a choice but to bring us in on the operation." Hakim said. "What you mean by fuck up production?" Chewie asked. "I mean, we start robbing niggas of their product! But we do it on a sneak tip! After Sir Marcus realizes his people are helpless on the streets, that's when we come in and offer to solve his problems!

Simply put, we create a boogie man so we become the hero!" hakim explained. Chewie looks at Mackie. "Check this out! What if you go to him and he says he don't need yo help? Then what?" Gunz asked. "If bodies start disappearing without a trace, they gonna want some real hardcore dudes on the scene to handle shit!" Bex said. Chewie looks at hakim. "Who the fuck is this nigga?" Chewie asked. "He's my brother! It's a long story! Don't pay him no mind! This is my caper!" hakim said. Bex gets frustrated and walks out the room. Chewie scoffs after Bex leaves. "All I need is for you and Mackie to get y'all hands on some aluminum baseball bats and a van! Make sure you spray paint the windows black!" hakim said. "Why bats, and not guns?" 2 Gunz asked. "Ninjas don't use guns." Hakim said. "Why aluminum bats?" Chewie asked. "Come on! You know well as I do, aluminum bats don't break!" hakim said. "So what's my part in all this?" Gunz asked. "Where gonna need the names and whereabouts of all the street bosses in Newark, especially Bergen street, since it's one of the most profitable spots." Hakim said. "How you know it's the most profitable?" Gunz asked. "You hang out around the club enough, you hear things." Hakim said. "So, if we do all this, what you and yo brother gonna do?" Chewie asked. "We got the hard part! We gotta face the man himself and explain why he needs us! If shit go bad, we still gotta face the man! So, it's our necks on the line! Not yours!" hakim explained. "So if shit goes sour, it don't come back to us? Is that what you telling us?" Chewie shouted. "Yeah! You get to walk away, while me and my brother suffer the consequences!" hakim said. "Sounds fair to me!" Chewie said as he and hakim shake on it. The others agree and shake hakim's hand as well.

A few days later at the corner of Bergen and 18th avenue, it was around 10pm when a young black man named tigger was sitting in his 98 Boeman Sedan. He ran the whole dope spot on Bergen Street from one end to the other. Cocaine, crack, weed, pills and heroin was all under his control. His crew consisted of 30 young runners who brought in about 200 grand a week for the lassenberry people.

Tigger made 10 grand a week, while his runners were paid a grand a week. This caused jealousy and envy not just in tigger's crew, but in every crew throughout Jersey. Tigger brought in his younger brother pooh to watch his back. When tigger wasn't patrolling his turf or getting his refill from tony, he would take his girlfriend on shopping sprees, and to the movies, according to Gunz's surveillance. Once a week he would go to a salon and get his hair braided in corn rolls because he was serious about being well groomed.

This was the night tigger was waiting for his refill on a 10 pound supply of weed, which went fast. At a hundred bucks a once, tigger loved when the white boy would show up and buy it in large quantities.

Tigger was waiting in his car, when he sees a black van pull up beside him. "Damn! That was quick!" he said to himself. He gets out of his car, thinking it was NA agents dropping off the refill. Suddenly, he is snatched inside the van by 2 sets of hands. The sliding door closes. The van slowly drives off into the night. The engine in tigger's car was still running, and his door was left ajar as well.

The next morning, tony was reading the newspaper while being driven to the west wing of the castle on a golf cart. The cart arrived at the door of Sir Marcus's office. Tony gets out of the cart. He brushes off his tailor made suit before he enters the office. Tony knocks on the door, then enters after getting the ok. He sees Sir Marcus sitting at his desk on the computer. Tony slams the newspaper on the desk in front of his boss. "What's up?" Sir Marcus asked as he picked up the paper. "Boeman is up 3%!" tony said. "Brandon put in a lot of hours pushing these cars. Get him on the phone. Tell him to stop by later on tonight so we can celebrate." Sir Marcus said as he put down the paper. "Gotcha!" tony said. "As a matter of fact!" Sir Marcus said while picking up his phone. He dials a number. The call he was making went straight to the answering machine. "Hey terry! It's your brother! We're having a little get together to celebrate a business win! I'll have a car pick you up tonight and bring you to the castle if you're not busy! Bye!" Sir Marcus said. Tony thought for a second. "You playing match maker now?" tony asked. "Who me?" Sir Marcus chuckled.

Sir Marcus had installed on his desk 2 land line phones, besides a mobile phone he carries on his person at all times. One phone is red, the other is black. The red is used to receive calls from high ranking officials from the National Agreement. The black phone is used to send and receive calls from his generals, Butch, Dubbs and Mookie official business only.

Moments later, there's a knock on the officer door. "Come in!" Sir Marcus shouts. Tony stands from his seat. It was one of the NA agents. "Excuse me gentlemen. May I have a word with you Mr. Kerouac?" said the agent. Tony follows the agent out of the office. Tony leaves the door ajar. "What is it?" tony asked the agent. "The supply of marijuana that was supposed to go to the Bergen street crew, never arrived." The agent explained. Tony steps in closer to the agent. Tony had fury in his eyes. What happened to the refill?" tony asked. "The bag is still in our possession sir!" the agent said. "So why didn't it get into the dealer's hands?" tony shouted. Sir Marcus could hear the shouting, but didn't move from his seat. He kept reading the newspaper. "When the agent arrived to make the transaction, the street boss named tigger wasn't there. His vehicle was there, with the motor still running. We intersected the police report. There were no signs of criminal activity." The agent explained. "Wait here!" tony ordered. Tony goes back into the office. He closes the door. "What's the problem?" Sir Marcus asked. "One of our street bosses is missing!" tony said. "Who?" Sir Marcus. "It's tigger! He runs the Bergen street crew! The agent just told me that tigger had a refill of weed coming to him. But he wasn't there at the drop point!" tony said. "We still have the product, right?" Sir Marcus asked with a raised eyebrow. "Yeah! The product is safe!" tony said. "Ok." Sir Marcus said as he scratches his head. "What do you think we should do?" Sir Marcus. "I say we take a look at the B.O.I for a minute!" tony suggested. "You know the combination?" Sir Marcus asked tony. Tony goes to the wall opposite of Sir Marcus's desk and removes an oil painting of a vase. Tony opens the safe and takes out only item that was in there, jabbo's binder of information. He places the binder in front of Sir Marcus. Sir Marcus flips the pages to get to the territory section. He turns to the Newark section. "Ok! This tigger kid runs Bergen Street. He just recruited his brother not too long ago, nick named pooh. The next in line to take over though is this guy named Reggie." Sir Marcus said. "Does he have a rap sheet?" tony asked. "No! It says here he's clean!" Sir Marcus said. "So what's the next move?" tony asked. "Move this Reggie guy up, and send a couple of agents to find tigger. If he's dead, locked up or whatever! I want to know!" Sir Marcus said as he closes the binder. Tony takes the binder and puts it back into the safe.

A week later, the new street boss of Bergen Street, named Reggie was sitting at a booth in a chicken shack the Arabs ran. He was on his mobile phone checking on one of his crew members. Standing at 6 feet, 4 inches tall and weighing 300 pounds, Reggie was a feared young man on the streets. He kept his crew on the streets until the last crack rock or bag of weed was sold. For whatever reason, he allowed his crew to take a break on Sunday.

It was around 8pm. He ordered a 3 piece chicken and fries. "I better have 10 grand in a bag, in my hand by 10 tonight nigga!" Reggie yelled into the phone. Outside, a van slowly pulls in front of the chicken shack. There were no runners standing in front of the chicken shack because Reggie didn't want anyone around him in case the police were going to raid the block. Suddenly. A person dressed in all black, with leather gloves and wearing dark shades, with a hoodies, comes into the shack and throws a brick at Reggie, hitting him in the chest. "What the fuck?" Reggie shouted. The person in black runs outside. The Arab cooks mumbling tom each other in the back. There were no customers in the shack. Reggie gets out of the booth and starts going after the perpetrator. As soon as he steps outside, he sees the person in black run around the corner. Reggie pulls out his pistol and goes after him. As Reggie goes after the person who hit him, another person dressed in black jumps out of the van and whacks Reggie in the back of the head with an aluminum bat. Reggie falls to his knees. He is then whacked again until he falls to the ground, face down. Another person jumps out the van. They drag Reggie into the vehicle. The van takes off down the street. The van stops at the corner. The person that hit Reggie with the brick quickly jumps in the back of the van. The van takes off into the night.

The next morning, Sir Marcus and Kimberly were in their bedroom watching TV. There's a knock on the bedroom door. "Hold on!" Sir Marcus shouted. He puts on his robe. He opens the door and sees tony standing there with a pissed look on his face. "What wrong?" sir Marcus asked. "It happened again! It fucking happened again!" tony shouted. "Calm down!" Sir Marcus said as he closed the door so Kimberly couldn't hear. "What happened again?" Sir Marcus asked. "Another man missing! Reggie!" tony whispered. Sir Marcus sighs. "Damn!" Sir Marcus said. "The last he was seen was at a chicken shack on Bergen! The cooks at the place didn't see anything, or so they say!" tony explained. "Ok! Ok! Who's next on the list to run things?" Sir Marcus asked. "Let me check real quick!" said tony. Tony takes out a note pad from inside his suit jacket. He has a small list of potential bosses to take the place of Reggie. "We got a guy named Laquan and this kid nick named blister!" tony said. "I don't care who you pick right now! We have to have the area covered like now, producing cash!" sir Marcus ordered. "That's the problem now! Word is getting out that tigger and Reggie might be dead! No one else wants to step up to the plate!" tony explained. Sir Marcus closes his eyes, pinching the bridge of his nose. He takes a deep breath. He puts his hand on Tony's shoulder. "Tell Laquan, blister or whoever, that we can offer them protection! Send 2 agents out there to look after them!" Sir Marcus ordered. "That's another problem! The NA only allowed us 8 agents and 6 of them are already guarding the castle! We got the other 2 looking for tigger, remember?" tony said. "Ok! I guess I have to beg that fucking Terrance for more reinforcements! Call back the 2 agents on the tigger case! Send them to protect the next guy!" Sir Marcus ordered. "Ok! Let's give it a shot!" tony responded. Tony jumps into the golf cart. The driver takes off down the corridor. Sir Marcus heads back to the bedroom. He gets back into the bed. "Everything ok?" Kimberly asked. "Nothing for you to worry about baby." Sir Marcus said.

A week later, 3 men were sitting at a table, in the middle of Aves Island. One of the most unusual places in the world to have brunch, which these men were doing.

The Aves Island is small piece of land governed by the country of Venezuela. During storms and rough waters, it has become completely submerged under water. For some reason, these men have picked the perfect moment to meet on this giant rock.

The first man at the table, wearing a white linen suit was Oscar Deltoro Santos. He was the man who supplied the entire eastern seaboard of the United States with pure cocaine. He was the man responsible for Sir Marcus receiving the Order of San Carlos (Knight) medal. The second man at the table, also wearing a linen jacket and pants, was Enrique Rodriguez, the President of the National Assembly of Venezuela. He was 3rd in line as head of the Venezuelan government. The 3rd man sitting at the table was Dragan Serpiente. He was wearing an olive green Gore-Tex body suit.

Dragan was a frail looking old man, whose age was never determined. One time he told Terrance Haggerty about being a young man in the crowd when the Archduke of Austria was assassinated. The Gore-Tex body suit was snug on him, holding his body in place giving the illusion that he was physically fit. He came to the meeting barefoot, having curved long toe nails.

Known to very few, Serpiente was Assistant Supreme Director of the National Agreement. Known to all, he was the actual C.E.O of a major pharmaceutical company in Maryland.

About 100 yards away from where the 3 men were sitting was a Mil Mi-26 helicopter. The men were flown to the island by 3 NA agents. Standing behind Serpiente at attention, were 2 NA agents dressed as waiters wearing white gloves.

"Oh, es un hermoso día para ser caballeros con vida!" Serpiente chuckled. "Usted me quiere decir nuestro aquí para hablar del tiempo?" Enrique Rodriguez asked. "Es Que una agradable para decir al hombre que solo le envía un año de suministro de la medicina el trata-miento del cáncer?" Serpiente asked. "Señor, agradezco lo que has hecho, pero ¿qué es lo que realmente quieres?" Enrique Rodriguez impatiently asked. "Estoy organizando una fiesta al final del año. Todo lo que quiero que hagas es presentarse." Serpiente said.

Serpiente's fingernails were discolored, as were his toenails due to diminishing blood cir-culation. Just like his toenails, his fingernails were as long as talons on a falcon. It didn't deter him from snapping his fingers when he signaled one of the NA agents to hand him a shiny gold envelope. He hands the envelope to Rodriguez. "Ese hijo, es una invitación especial que tengas. Una vez abierto, leerlo, debe quemarlo." Serpiente said. Rodriguez was about to rip open the envelope, until Serpiente slams his old, dried hand on the table. Rodriguez freezes. "No te atrevas an abrir que en mi presencia! Usted espera hasta que Está solo!" Serpiente ordered. Rodriguez quickly shoves the envelope inside the pocket of his suit jacket. "Relájese! Usted podrá disfrutar de to mismo! Prometo!" Santos said as he pinches Rodriguez's cheek. Estoy hambriento! Digamos que tenemos un poco de comida en nuestros estómagos!" Serpiente said in his creepy voice. Serpiente snaps his fingers again. The 2 waiters approach the 3 men pushing dining carts.

The carts had sterling silverware on them, with cloth napkins rolled in napkin rings. The waiters lifted the sterling silver tray covers to reveal the men's food. Santos takes his napkin out of the ring. He places the napkins on his lap. The waiter served him what he had previously ordered. He had a seafood salad sprinkled with white truffle shavings, served with a couple slices of cantaloupe. Rodriguez had pre-ordered an omelet with Patatas bravas. The 2 men tried to compose their look of shock when what they witnessed Serpiente was about to devour. With his bare hands, Serpiente rips apart the body of a live white rat, by first twisting off its head with ease. Once he butterflies the body, he then takes a saucière filled with dark red paste. He pours the paste over the animal carcass. Rodriguez starts to heave, trying his best not to look in that direction. "Sangre bebé!" Serpiente chuckled. Rodriguez and Santos glanced at each other. Santos continued eating.

It was 2pm at the Lassenberry castle, when Sir Marcus received a call on the red phone. "Yeah?" Sir Marcus said. "Pine Barrens, 5pm!" the voice said. Sir Marcus hangs up the phone. "What now?" Sir Marcus says to himself. Sir Marcus gets on his mobile phone. He hears 3 rings, then someone answers. "Tony! I need you here at the castle no later than 3pm!" sir Marcus ordered. He hangs up the phone. He walks outside of his office, he sees one of his agents sitting in the golf cart reading a magazine. The agent quickly puts the magazine away when he sees Sir Marcus. "I want a car ready for me to leave, with 2 agent waiting." Sir Marcus ordered. The agent calls in the order over the walkie-talkie.

The time, 3:34pm. Tony had just arrived at the castle. An agent chauffeurs him down the corridor. Tony jumps out of the cart as soon as it stops. He straightens his neck-tie and grabs his briefcase off the cart. He bangs on the office door. "Come In!" Sir Marcus shouts. Tony enters the office. Sir Marcus was sitting at his desk. "You're late buddy." Sir Marcus said. "You forget. I'm the multitask man around here." Tony chuckled. "How can I forget? You remind me every time! Just get here on time in the future. Please!" Sir Marcus said. "Got it! What are you up to?" tony asked. Suddenly, there's a knock on the door. "What the hell?" Sir Marcus said to himself. Both tony and Sir Marcus looked confused. They weren't expecting anyone. "Come in!" tony said with his hand on his holster. The door opens. In comes Charlie Dalton. "Uh, excuse me Sir Marcus, Sir! The boss wants to see you." Charlie said nervously. Tony sits on the sofa. "Come on Charlie! We're really busy!" tony said. "It's ok Charlie. Bring him in." sir Marcus said in calm voice. Charlie goes back out in the hall. He then brings in Sir Edward.

Sir Edward looked like half the man he used to be. Charlie rolls Sir Edward over towards Sir Marcus. Sir Edward was in his pajamas, with a dark blue blanket draped over his lap and legs. There was a towel draped over his shoulder just in case he started to drool. Sir Marcus gets out of his seat, ad kneels down at eye level to his uncle. Sir Marcus grabs his uncle's clammy hand and starts massaging it. "What can I do for you uncle?" Sir Marcus asked. Sir Edward uses all his strength to leave forward. "Did…My…Brothers… try to tell you…how… to run things?" Sir Edward struggled to say. Sir Marcus wipes the drool from his chin. "How did you know they were going to do that?" Sir Marcus asked. "Because…You…Ain't…Me." Sir Edward chuckled. Sir Marcus stands to his feet. Feeling humiliated, he orders Charlie to take Sir Edward back to his chambers. Sir Marcus and tony could still hear the eerie laughter of Sir Edward out in the hall. "Don't mind him. No one said it would be easy." tony says to Sir Marcus. "Let's go take a ride out to the Pine Barrens." Sir Marcus ordered.

At 5:05pm, Sir Marcus's limo arrives at its destination. There's 2 NA agents at the main gate. The agent in the passenger seat gets out of the limo. He walks up the sentry.

There are exactly 3000 NA agents in existence. They are all of diverse ethnicity, being only males. Decades ago there was a program funded by the National Agreement to have a select group of scientists gather back in the 1920's to take orphans in their infancy. Through dozens of neurological tests, this group of scientists discovered that the herd of infants could be psychologically manipulated into adulthood, through a little genetic altering.

The agent that approached the sentry, removed his dark shades. The sentry removes his shades as well. It took about 3 seconds for the agents to identify each other by staring each other directly in to each other's eyes. The 2 agents then put there shades back on. The sentry then gives the order to open the gate. After the limo driver enters the premises, the gates closes. The limo makes it way down a long gravel road to an alternate entrance, which happened to be huge electronic garage doors.

After passing the garage doors, Sir Marcus gets out of the limo. He buttons 1 button on his suit jacket. He walks through the ware house looking calm and collective. He walks through another set of doors, where he sees a piping system along the walls and ceiling. The pipes weren't just rusted, but was dripping was in random spots.

When Sir Edward came to this place for the first time. He was escorted by an agent who held a key card to access the next room. This time, the National Agreement chief of export production, New Jersey division, Peter E. bellum issued Sir Marcus a key card, which gave him access to the room that held the product. When Sir Marcus entered the room, he sees a wooden chair and desk in the middle of the room. On the desk was a drinking glass with a pitcher of water next to it. "Have a seat Sir Marcus! Please!" a voice said over the p.a. system. Sir Marcus looks around the warehouse. He slowly walks over to the desk. He takes a seat after undoing the button on his jacket. He then gently pushes the glass away from him.

About 8 minutes later, the door on the opposite side of the room opens. Out comes Terrance Haggerty. "Sir Marcus! It's nice to see you again!" Terrance chuckled. Sir Marcus stands. Terrance walks over to him and extends his hand to greet him. The 2 men shake hands.

Terrance is wearing a cardigan sweater over a white button up shirt, with dress pants and wing tipped shoes. Sir Marcus noticed Terrance's ring on his hand. It was a gold ring, with a ruby embedded in it. Terrance looked at his ring. "This was given to me on my 25th birthday by my boss, our boss." Terrance said. "What do you mean or boss?" Sir Marcus asked. "Ok. Since you seemed confused, let me lay it out for you. The agents are there to protect and your immediate family. They are not there to rub out a few thugs." Terrance said. "Listen! I have people on the street disappearing in to thin air! From what I see, those agent s live at my estate!" Sir Marcus said. "The estate? You mean the castle in which the NA built for you and your family for free?" Terrance asked. "I didn't ask for a castle! My uncle did!" Sir Marcus said. "But you have no problem residing there!" Terrance shouted. "So what am I supposed to do without an army to take care of the problem I have?" Sir Marcus asked. Terrance slowly paces back-n-forth. "The job of an NA is not to been seen on the streets for civilians to gawk at!" Terrance said. He stops pacing. "I admit! Once in a blue moon there's a glitch. We had to put down 5 civilians in the past for be overly curious. But, there mandate is surveillance and protecting you." Terrance said. "I need an army! Please!" Sir Marcus shouted. Terrance snaps his fingers. "I've got it! Just get that Butch guy to hunt down the culprits! We don't deal in petty vendettas." Terrance said. "I told jabbo to get rid of those street thugs who worked for my uncle because I thought your agents were professionals!" Sir Marcus shouted. "They are! Believe me, there are. You see, your uncle and your grandfather earned their power! What about you? As they say in the hip hop community, you don't have street Cred my friend!" Terrance chuckled. Sir Marcus had the look of disappointment on his face. "Oh, come now. Just get Butch to do the job for you. Besides, you're his bread and butter." Terrance chuckled. Infuriated. Sir Marcus picks up the drinking glass and throws it against the wall, shattering it. Terrance flinched a little. "Well, I guess this meeting is adjourned." Terrance chuckled. Terrance extends his hand. Sir Marcus doesn't shake his hand this time. "Hey. We're stuck with each other. We might as well make our bond a pleasant one." Terrance said. "You're sick! You know that?" Sir Marcus said. Terrance doesn't say a word. He still has his hand out. Reluctantly, Sir Marcus shakes his hand. "Good! Now you can go, Sir Marcus. Sir Marcus turns away towards the exit to leave. "Hold on a minute! Terrance shouts. Sir Marcus turns around. "What now?" he asked Terrance. Terrance pulls something out of his shirt pocket. "I almost forgot to give you this." Terrance said. Marcus walked back towards Terrance. "What the hell is this?" he asked Terrance. "This my friend, is an invitation to the gathering." Terrance said. It was the gold envelope. "Take it." Terrance chuckled. Sir Marcus snatches it from his hand. "After you read it. Burn it. God help you if someone sees it, or you lose it." Terrance chuckled. Sir Marcus then walks toward the exit. Terrance just stands there, giggling like a child as Sir Marcus leaves.

The next day around noon, Sir Marcus is sitting at his desk reading the financial section of the newspaper. There's a knock on the door. "Come in!" he shouts. In come tony, carrying his briefcase. "What's up?" tony said. Sir Marcus just shook his head as tony places the briefcase on his desk. He opens it to reveal that it was filled with cash. "This is from the Boeman and blush sales this month." Tony said.

Tony did it all. He not only collected Sir Marcus's cut from the businesses, he also made sure lassenberry family members received their envelopes. He changed the rules of the operation by taking the cash from Butch, Dubbs and Mookie before they received their refill.

"2 hundred thousand dollars! Nice chunk of pocket change!" tony laughed. Sir Marcus walks over to the safe. After opening it, he places the cash inside in neat stacks. "I need you to contact Butch for me." Sir Marcus said. "Everything ok?" tony asked. "I want you to go to him in person and tell him I need to see him before the week is out." Sir Marcus said. "You got it." Tony said as Sir Marcus closes the safe. Tony looks down at the newspaper on the desk. He noticed next to it was the gold envelope. He picks it up. "What's this?" he asked Sir Marcus. "That's happens to be an invitation for me from our shadow friends." Sir Marcus said. "Why did you takes this?" tony shouted. "Didn't jabbo warn you about these people? Didn't he tell you how sick they are?" tony said. "Come on! It's just a gathering! What could go wrong at a gathering? Besides, I thinks its best we stay on these people's good side, for the time being!" Sir Marcus said.

That evening, butch was hanging out in his, what he called his man cave. A 4 bedroom colonial house out in Warren County, New Jersey. He stays there once a month to get away from the family. Whenever his neighbors go jogging by or walking their dogs, they would peek through the windows when he wasn't home. The house was empty. Butch only had a sofa, a floor model TV and a frig full of beer. While dozing in and out of his drunken slumber, he noticed headlights piercing through his blinds. He reaches under the sofa cushion and pulls out a Glock 22 and staggers to the window. He peeks through the blinds. He sees that a limo had pulled up into his driveway. He checks the magazine in his gun. It's fully loaded. An NA agent opens the rear door of the limo. He sees tony getting out of the limo. Tony walks up to the door and knocks. With his gun still in hand, butch goes to answer it. Butch cracks the door open. "How the hell you find me out here?" butch asked. "These guys in black suits are like robots! They can damn near find anyone!" tony chuckled. Butch opens the even wider. He looks both ways down the street. "Come on in." he says to tony. Tony noticed that butch was wearing only a t-shirt and boxers. Tony closes the door. "Sir Marcus wants you to stop by the castle before the week is out." Tony said. "Sir Marcus?" butch chuckled. "Something funny?" tony asked. "It's just these titles they've given themselves. That's all." Butch chuckled. Tony didn't find any humor in what he said. "You wanna beer kid?" butch asked. "Why not? I'm not driving." tony said as he looked around. Butch heads to the kitchen, still with the Glock in his hand. He comes back with a cold beer. He opens it in front of tony. Tony takes a big swig. "Ah! That's nice and cold!" tony said as he wipes the beer from his chin. Butch goes over and sits on the sofa. He turns up the volume on the TV. The game is on. "You see that? That nigga can't score for shit!" butch shouted. "This is nice hide out! You gonna keep it?" tony asked. "I'm think I'm gonna give it to my son Kevin after he gets out of college. By the way! Why the fuck you ain't just call me?" butch asked. "The boss said to see you in person." Tony said. "It must be serious." Butch said as his eyes are glued to the TV. Tony looks at his watch. "I gotta go!" tony said as he puts his beer on top of the TV. Butch gets up. "Tell him I'll be there tomorrow then." Butch said as he tony shook hands. Tony leaves.

It was Friday, around in the morning. Sir Marcus and Kimberly were being served breakfast in the east wing by Charlie. There was an NA agent standing guard at the entrance of the dining area. The agents were ordered to take no chances protecting Sir Marcus. Charlie and the kitchen staff were always made to sample the food before it got to Sir Marcus's plate. "Bring my uncle in so he can eat with us." Sir Marcus says to Charlie. Kimberly frantically her head at Sir Marcus. He noticed his fiancée's reaction. "Never mind Charlie. You can go now." Sir Marcus ordered. Charlie leaves the dining area. "Sorry baby! But, I lost my appetite the last time your uncle ate with us!" Kimberly said. "I have to admit. It was pretty grotesque." Sir Marcus chuckled. Suddenly, another NA agents enters the dining area. "Excuse me sir! Mr. Watson is here to see you!" said the agent. "Good! Have him wait outside of my office!" sir Marcus ordered. "Yes sir!" the agent said before leaving. Sir Marcus doesn't rush his breakfast. He and Kimberly continue eating.

About a half hour later, butch was sitting outside the office, when he sees a golf cart coming down the corridor towards him. It was Sir Marcus in the back seat, being driven by an agent. Butch looks at his watch. Sir Marcus gets out of the cart. "Glad to see you!" Sir Marcus said as he and butch shook hands. "Come on in." he says to butch. "No disrespect. But I gotta busy schedule." Butch explained. Sir Marcus ignores him. "Have a seat." He says to butch. "What's this about?" butch asked as he sits across from Sir Marcus. "First, can I offer you a drink or something?" Sir Marcus asked. "I'm good. Just tell me what you need so I can go about my business." Butch said. "Well, since you put it that way, let's get right to it." Sir Marcus chuckled. Butch looks around the office. "I have a problem on Bergen Street. A couple of my street bosses vanished for some reason. I think they've been kidnapped more than likely." Sir Marcus explained. "What's that gotta do with me? You don't think I had something to do with it, do you?" butch asked. "Oh no! I just want you to have some guys from your crew to find out what's happening and take care of it, if you know what I mean." Sir Marcus said. "Trust me kid. I would love to help you, but I don't have the man power." Butch explained. Sir Marcus irritated. "So if my uncle would've asked you to do it, would you say no to him?" Sir Marcus asked. "Listen kid! All my people are dealers! Not killers! Besides, your uncle would've dealt with this without bringing it to my attention!" butch explained. Sir Marcus grabs an ink pen from off his desk and starts scribbling designs on a piece of paper. "What would you think your people would do if your supply ran out? Huh?" Sir Marcus said with a sinister grin. Butch leans forward in his chair. Butch snatches the pen out of his hand and tosses it across the room. "You threatening me kid?" he asked.

In case of an emergency, Sir Marcus had a silent alarm installed on side of his desk. Unknown to butch, he presses the alarm. Within minutes, 3 agents come running in with guns drawn. Butch starts laughing. "So this is what it comes down to kid?" butch said. "I respect you butch, but I run things now! Don't force my hand!" Sir Marcus shouted. "Ok kid! You got it!" butch chuckled. Sir Marcus gives the agents the signal to lower their weapons. After they lower their weapons, butch beats on the desk a few times like a drum. "I'll tell you what kid! Since I've been in the game for a long time, I'll give you a piece of advice!" butch said. "You can leave now." Sir Marcus tells the agents. The agents exit the office. "Get the word out on the streets to the people responsible for this mess, you'll give them a piece of the action. They still gotta go through you anyway! You're the supplier!" butch suggested. Sir Marcus doesn't say a word. He just nods. "Good! Now if there's nothing else, let me get the fuck up outta here!" butch said as he stands from his seat. He looks at Sir Marcus with a smile. "Come on! Bring it in kid!" Butch said as he holds out his arms. Sir Marcus gets up and walks around the desk. They give each other a hug. "We're like family, still!" butch said after giving Sir Marcus a kiss on the cheek. "Tell your uncle I'll come back soon to pay him a visit!" butch said. "Ok." Sir Marcus said as butch leaves.

It was the day Kimberly and Sir Marcus had been waiting for. It was April 1st, 2000 when all 4 wings of the castle were completed in time for the big event.

Sir Marcus woke up to a bright sunny morning. The forecast called for 80 degrees by the afternoon. Sir Marcus stretched as he yawned after getting out of bed. He got had got out of bed in his pajama bottoms. There was a knock on the door. "Come in!" he shouted as he looked out the window at the garden below. In comes Charlie. "The guests should be arriving in a few hours." Charlie said. "Are the chefs and ushers on point?" he asked. Charlie. "Yeah. The best man, bridesmaids, groomsmen and the cardinal are all in the north wing getting ready too." Charlie said. "What about my bride to be?" Sir Marcus asked with a big smile on his face. "She's in the south wing with the hair and make-up people." Charlie said.

The wedding ceremony and reception was going to be held in the court yard. Sir Marcus requested that an additional 20 NA agents be posted on and off the castle estate. They were given strict orders to remain inconspicuous during the festivities.

Sir Marcus had all the participants in the wedding put up at the castle for rehearsal and other preparations. The north wing, with its 15 bedrooms, multiple bathrooms and own kitchen, accommodated everyone involved.

Around noon, guests started pouring into the castle grounds. Friends, family and associates noticed the décor of the courtyard was African themed. Colors and patterns were of West African influence. Kimberly personally took charge of the menu as well. She gave strict orders that she wanted a chef that specialized in West African cuisine. A chef was flown in a week before the wedding. He stayed in the same wing as the rest of the participants. The menu consisted of chicken Yassa, Maafe, Jollof rice, Kenkey, Ndolé, Moin-Moin, Ebà, Acarajé, Tapalapa bread and platters of different appetizers such as Chin-Chin.

Kimberly was in the south wing getting dressed, with an entourage of 10 people. Kimberly wore a Jellabiya white wedding gown fit for royalty, except with trimming of African Kanga patterns.

To follow in his uncle's footsteps, Sir Marcus wore his uniform with the red shoulder sash and green waist sash. His jack boots were polished so, that you could see your reflection. He had all 3 medals pinned on him. Just like Sir Marcus, Charlie, tony and Sir Edward were dressed in their uniforms as well. Sir Edward had only one medal, the Order of the Elephant displayed on him.

The man performing the ceremony was Cardinal Richard Mertel. Cardinal Mertel was Ecclesiastical leader of south Jersey, who was secretly a member of the National Agreement.

The moment had finally arrived. The 150 guests stood to their feet, as the 30 piece orchestra played when Kimberly exited the castle to enter the courtyard. Special guest was Nigerian singer Tiwa Savage who sang a heartfelt ballad as Kimberly made her way to her groom. There were tears of joy throughout the crowd. Kimberly was given away by her on her mother's side of the family.

Terry, Carmen, Samara, Jenna and Kimberly's niece Brea were the brides maids, who wore silk African gowns made of the same print as was on Kimberly's gown. Corey, Big L., Jake jr., Malcolm and Butch's son Kevin were the groomsmen, who wore black tuxedos. Their bow-ties were of Kanga pattern.

After Sir Marcus and Kimberly exchanged vows, some of the guests were feeling uncomfortable after Cardinal said the final words. "Ut benedicerent domino nostro, qui dominator super nos docebit vos lumen! Now you may kiss your bride!" the Cardinal said. "I didn't know mark and Kimberly were catholic!" one guest whispered to her friend. "I don't know what that was!" the other guest whispered. Only half the guests applauded after Sir Marcus planted a big kiss on his bride's lips.

During the reception, Sir Marcus and his bride head to the west wing to change clothes. Once they get inside, Sir Marcus sweeps Kimberly off of her feet, cradling her while spinning around. "I'm a husband now! Soon I'm gonna be a father! I can't believe it!" he shouted. Kimberly starts giggling as her husband spins her. Someone knocks on the door while the couple is enjoying their alone time. Sir Marcus puts Kimberly down. "Come in!" he shouts. In comes tony. "We have to talk! We have to talk, now!" tony said. "What wrong?" Kimberly asked. "Please baby! Change clothes and go out and entertain our guest! I'll handle this!" Sir Marcus said. "Whatever you do, just be careful!" Kimberly said before she kisses her husband. She walks pass tony and leaves the room. "Now, tell me what happened!" Sir Marcus shouted. "Our top man on Bergen street disappeared last night!" tony shouted. "Damn! This shit is getting ridiculous!" Sir Marcus shouted as picks up a chair and tosses it across the room. "I got something else to say!" tony said. "What is it now?" Sir Marcus shouts "April fool!" tony chuckled. "You son of a bitch!" Sir Marcus screamed. Tony starts laughing so hard, he falls to the floor. "Oh, you should see your face, man!" tony shouted. "You bastard!" Sir Marcus chuckled. He kicks Tony's feet while tony continues to laugh. "Go gargle some mouth wash or something! Your breath smells like you've lived in a liquor store!" Sir Marcus said then leaves.

April was the start of the second quarter for Sir Marcus and tony to make the pick-up to refill all the territories. Sir Marcus had to postpone his honeymoon because of the refill. Since Sir Marcus had no general to distribute the refill in Essex county, he had for a time, had to extend Tony's duties. Sir Marcus was pondering on Butch's advice.

It was around 9pm, the day after the wedding. Tony and Sir Marcus were accompanied by 4 NA agents to Port Elizabeth. "We've gotta find someone else to come out here! It's too dangerous for you to be out here on the streets!" Tony said. "I know! I know! We've been over this! Jabbo taught you to test the product, but the NA and the Colombians only sell to me! I've been thinking, we need a guy to run Essex County!

Back when jabbo was the tester, he never used any equipment. Instead, he would randomly dip 2 fingers in a bag of heroin and cocaine and taste it. "This good shit! Pay, and let's go!" were jabbo's words if the product was good, which is was 99% of the time. When it was Tony's turn to test the product, he actually used a test kit for both the cocaine and heroin. Jabbo taught tony that there were 4 grades of heroin. Number 4 being the purist. "It's a 4! Let's do business!" were Tony's words when the product was good.

It was August of 2000, when Kimberly was in her third trimester. Castle Lassenberry was turned into a fortress. The NA allowed the 20 agents during the wedding, to remain at the castle after a failed assassination attempt of Sir Marcus's life.

It was a week later from the incident when hakim was in the back room of the night club BIG SHOTS. It was a Friday night and the place was packed. The music was booming. The ratio of women in the club was 8 to 1, which was very lucrative for the club. Sir Marcus's brother Corey, who was co-owner, was in charge of operating the club that night. Hakim and his crew were playing a game of Texas hold'em in the back room. By this time, hakim had carte blanche of the club. Hakim and his crew had a bar tab in the thousands. He Bex also hosted orgies in the back room from time to time. Not much was said or done about hakim's shenanigans. They had Krayton shaking in his boots, and far as Corey was concerned, hakim brought in a huge crowd that they've have never seen.

It was around 11pm when a Boeman minivan pulled up across the street from the club. 4 men dressed in suits jump out and make their way through the crowd. The 4 had no problem getting into the club. It happened to be Butch and his boys Tommy Bey, Arnold Washington, a.k.a No-No and Butch's cousin Dubbs, who was wearing a trench coat. "Hey butch! Long time, no see!" one of the bouncers said as he shook his hand. "Is hakim up in here?" Butch asked the bouncer. The bouncer didn't say a word. His head just nods. Butch pushed the bouncer out of the way, and made his way inside the club. Butch and his crew make their way through the crowd, while the bouncers run over to tell Corey something was about to go down. "Go over and tell them they can't go in the back!" Corey tells the bouncer. "You gonna have to fire my ass! I ain't getting mixed up in that shit!" the bouncer said. "Well, get your out of here and don't come back!" Corey shouted in his ear.

Butch and his boys head to the back room. The door is locked. Dubbs pulls out a double barrel shot gun from underneath his trench coat. He blasts the door knob, leaving a big gaping hole. Women started screaming. People started running towards the exits, but it didn't matter to butch and is crew. Dubbs kicked the indoor. "Don't nobody fucking move!" Dubbs shouted as Tommy Bey and No-No follow behind, pulling out pistols. Butch is the last to walk in.

Corey found it hard to make his way to the back room. The crowd running in his direction was overwhelming.

In the back room, butch saw the card table filled with stacks of cash. He starts smiling. Butch slowly makes his way over to the table. "Yo! With all due respect butch, you just can't run up in here!" 2 Gunz shouted when he stood from his chair. Butch looks at Gunz. Next thing happened was 2 Gunz was laid out on the floor unconscious. "I still got it!" butch said as he looks at his fist. "Whose next?" butch shouts. Hakim's crew was silent. Hakim steps up to the plate. "If you wanted in on the game, all you had to do is ask." Hakim said in a calm voice. "Sit yo ass down!" butch says to hakim. "You got it." Hakim said with his hands in the air. He slowly sits back in his seat. Guns were pointed at Bex, Mackie and Chewie. Butch sits down across from hakim, and puts his pistol back in its holster. In one big sweep, butch clears the card table of cards, chips, drinks, ashtrays and cash. It all ends up on the floor. "I'm not staying long! I just came to tell you that I want you to stop the dumb shit and tell Sir Marcus to give you a job! You got too much potential son! I don't wanna be a part of killing yo ass either! You belong with us! You were born to be with us!" butch said with a deviant smile. The room is silent. Butch stands from his seat. "Let's go!" he tells his crew. With guns still drawn, tommy and No-No back out of the room first. Butch leaves next, but not without stepping on Gunz's chest before walking out. Dubbs is the last to leave the room. He backs out slowly still pointing the shot gun at everyone. The crew follows butch towards the exit. It was easy to leave the club. Most of the patrons had scattered outside. The 2 remaining bouncer just stand in awe as Butch's crew leaves.

Inside the club, hakim is still sitting at the card table. "Ooh! That was fucking intense!" hakim chuckled. Bex lightly smacks 2 Gunz into consciousness. "Man, we should go after them niggas!" Chewie said. "No! I got a better idea! Bex! Where's Krayton?" hakim asked.

"He should be home. Why?" Bex asked. "We're gonna pay him a visit. Suddenly, Corey comes in the room. "What the fuck you do to my place?" Corey shouted. "It's cool cuz. Just keep doing what you've been doing. Keep the place packed. I'll take care of all the damages. Corey looks around the room and sees all the money and other objects on the floor. "Gunz! Stay here and clean up this shit! I want the rest of y'all to come with me!" hakim said. Bex Chewie and Mackie follow hakim out of the club. "How the hell butch found out it was us?" Bex whispered to hakim. "Don't matter. Real recognizes real." Hakim explained. "You gonna get us killed bro!" Bex whispered.

A couple of days later at the Lassenberry castle, tony and Sir Marcus were sitting in the office. "Kimberly is about due soon. So, I want you to get the word out to as many of my relatives as you can and tell them that I said they should be here in the south wing a few days before her due date." Sir Marcus ordered. "Come on, boss! Babies don't come when expected!" Tony explained. Sir Marcus slams his hand on his desk. "I control everything! Now, go tell them is said to be at the south wing September 9th! Make sure all the beds have clean sheets and the cafeteria is stocked!" Sir Marcus ordered. Tony stands up and nods. "To change the subject real quick. I got word from the streets that Butch and hakim got into some kind of altercation the other night." Tony mentioned. Before Sir Marcus could respond, there was a knock on the door. "Come in!" Sir Marcus yelled. An NA agent enters the office. "What is it?" Sir Marcus asked. "Excuse me sir, but your cousin K boogie, is standing outside the gate demanding to have a word with you. He looks in bad shape." The agent said. "Who the hell is K boogie?" tony asked. Sir Marcus sighs. "Bring him in." Sir Marcus ordered. The agent leaves the office.

Moments later, there's a knock on the office door. "Come in!" Sir Marcus shouts. In comes the agent followed by Krayton. Sir Marcus and tony are shocked to see Krayton bruised and battered. Sir Marcus stands up and walks over to Krayton. "You guys can leave!" Sir Marcus says to tony and the agent. Both of them nod and leave the office. "Have a seat! Can I get you anything?" Sir Marcus asked as Krayton sat across from him. Krayton puts his head down in shame. Sir Marcus goes over to the bar to make his cousin a drink.

Krayton came in the office with his right eye swollen shut and his lip busted. He has dried blood on his shirt. His hand was bandaged up, with dried blood seeping through.

"Tell me what happened!" Sir Marcus said as he gave him the drink. "That hakim is crazy! He said he insist that you so he can to talk business! He said if you don't see him, he'll keep coming at me!" Krayton cried. "Where's Corey?" Sir Marcus asked. "He's good! Hakim said he won't touch him because of you!" Krayton cried. "Because of me, huh?" Sir Marcus said. "He just came and took over my home, and the club!" Krayton said after he gulps down his drink. Krayton walks over to the bar and grabs the whole bottle of Cognac and pours himself another drink. "I knew you 2 weren't cut out for the night life! Just tell Corey you 2 need to sell the place to hakim and be done with it!" Sir Marcus said. Krayton looks at his cousin in disbelief. "Why we gotta run? Just go in and have that nigga killed!" Krayton shouted. "Just calm down!" Sir Marcus ordered. Sir Marcus pressed the button on the intercom. "Tony get in here!" he said as Krayton pours himself another drink. Moments later, tony enters the office. "What's up?" tony asked. "I want you to get in touch with hakim and tell him I'll want a sit down. First, I want you to take my Krayton and get him cleaned up and prepare a room for him in the south wing." Sir Marcus ordered. "Cuz! Its K boogie! Call me K boogie, and why can I stay at my own place?" Krayton cried. "Didn't you just say he took over your place?" Sir Marcus said. "Besides, you'll be safe here." Tony said. "I'm telling you cuz, you gotta kill this nigga!" Krayton cried. "Get him out of here!" Sir Marcus ordered tony. Tony gently grabs Krayton by the arm and escorts him out of the office. "Wait in the hall for a second." tony tells Krayton. Tony closed the office door to have a talk with Sir Marcus. "I hate to say it boss, he's right. I can end this with one bullet to his head." tony said. "No! I'm not doing things like my uncle did in the past! We're going to be straight business men as long as I'm in charge! Understand?" Sir Marcus said. "With all due respect! Your grandfather and uncle didn't get this far by just doing business! I know! I was there!" tony argued. Sir Marcus leans back in his chair, with arms folded. "I understand that you know a lot more than I do, but I'm just curious to see why he would go this far in risking his own life just to see me. Go to him and tell him I'll see him this Monday at mid-night." Sir Marcus ordered. Tony leans over his desk. "You know as well as I do that was him that tried to take you out on the road that day!" tony whispered. "I'm still here. Now go!" Sir Marcus ordered. Tony leaves the office. Sir Marcus takes a deep breath. He goes over and pours himself a drink.

That Monday came. It was around 9pm. Hakim was just waking up from a nap. Bex was asleep in the other room of the penthouse. Hakim enters Bex's room and throws a pillow at him. Bex jumps up in a panic. "Wake yo ass up brother! Tonight, we take over the world!" hakim said with pride. Bex just rolls his eyes and slams his head back on the bed. Hakim goes to the bathroom and strips down naked. He jumps in the shower. Hot water shoots from the fancy shower head as he starts singing to himself.

About an hour later, hakim comes out of the bedroom dressed in an expensive 3 piece suit. Bex on the other hand, was waiting in the living room dressed in a polo shirt, jeans and sneakers. "What the fuck? What happened to that suit you bought?" hakim shouted. "I don't' know about you, but if something jumps off, I wanna be comfortable enough to fight back!" Bex said. "Listen brother! If you're gonna be a big shot, you gotta look the part, even if you're on your way to the grave! Now go change!" hakim ordered. Bex says nothing. He just drags himself back into the bedroom.

About 15 minutes later, Bex comes out of the bedroom dressed in a silk suit as well. Bex adjust the band on his wrist watch. "Now, that's what the fuck I'm talking about!" hakim said as he straightens Bex's neck-tie. "When we get straightened out, then we can go back to South Jersey and take care of unfinished business!" hakim said. "You sound like a villain from a comic book!" Bex chuckled. "Fuck you, man!" hakim chuckled. "What about Chewie and the crew?" Bex asked. "Don't worry. They're already down there, in position." Hakim said.

It was 11:30pm when hakim and Bex arrive in Cherry Hill. Chewie, Mackie and 2 Gunz were parked within eye sight from the castle. Hakim figured that he and Bex might be followed. When they drove up to the main gate, a black Boeman SUV pulled up right behind them. "Damn, you was right!" Bex said. "If we don't come out within an hour, I gave the word for the boys to light this place up!" hakim said.

2 NA agents at the gate approach hakim's car. They already have their guns out of their holsters. "I'm hakim! I'm here to see your boss!" hakim said. "Who's this with you?" one

of the agents asked. "Oh, this is my brother, slash bodyguard!" hakim said as 2 more agents arrive on the scene. "Step out of the vehicle please! Both of you!" the agent on hakim's side ordered. Hakim just smiled as he and Bex exit the car. 2 of the agents push them up against the car and frisk them from head to toe. "He's clean!" one agent said about Bex. "This one too!" the other agent said about hakim. "Let's go gentlemen!" the lead agent ordered. "What about our car?" Bex asked. "It stays here!" the agent said. "Open the gate!" one agent said over a walkie-talkie. The gate slowly slides open. The SUV stayed parked behind hakim's car. Bex and hakim follow 2 of the agents to the golf cart after entering the castle grounds. They all get in the golf cart. The cart drives over the bridge. Bex noticed the moat underneath them. The agent in the back seat of the golf cart hits a remote control that opens 2 huge double doors. Bex looks in awe as they ride down the huge corridor. "God damn, this place is huge!" Bex shouted as he noticed the décor on the walls of the corridor. A few minutes later, hakim and Bex unknowingly drive through the east wing of the castle. Hakim noticed Charlie walking down a side hall with towels in his hands. "Oh shit!" hakim said. "What?" Bex asked. "That was Charlie!" hakim whispered. "Who?" Bex asked. "Never mind!" hakim said. Bex and hakim were astound to see a 20 ft. x 10 ft. mural of the Lassenberry coat-of-arms of the wall before making a left turn down the another corridor.

Finally, they arrive at the west wing of the castle. The agent stops in front of the office entrance. "This is where we get out!" the agent said to hakim and Bex. The other agent stays in the golf cart. The lead agent knocks on the office door. "Come in!" Sir Marcus said from inside. Hakim straightens his neck-tie. The agent, hakim and Bex enter the office. "Come on in guys!" Sir Marcus said in friendly tone. Hakim sees tony sitting on the sofa. "Hey cousin! It's been year's man!" hakim said as he and Sir Marcus hug each other. "You look like you've been working out man!" Sir Marcus said. "This here is my brother Bex!" hakim said. Bex and Sir Marcus shake hands. "Who knew you had a brother?" sir Marcus said. "It's a long story!" hakim said. "I'm just messing with you! I already knew!" Sir Marcus said. "Oh, so you've been doing your homework!" hakim said. "You 2 already know tony!" Sir Marcus said as tony gets up from his seat. Tony shakes Bex and hakim's hands. "Have a seat fellas! Please!" Sir Marcus said as tony goes back to the sofa. "Can I get you guys a late night snack, or something to drink?" Sir Marcus asked. "I'm good cuz." Hakim said. "You gotta beer?" Bex asks. Sir Marcus gives tony a look. Tony goes over to the frig in the corner of the office and grabs a beer. He unscrews the top open and hands it to Bex. "Damn! How'd you know this was the kind I drink?" Bex asked. "Like your brother said, I've done my homework!" Sir Marcus said with a big smile on his face. "Nice and cold too!" Bex said as he takes a gulp. Sir Marcus looks at his watch. "You guys are right on time!" he said. "When it comes to business, I don't bullshit!" hakim said. "I know! I can tell when you tried to assassinate me on the road a while back!" Sir Marcus chuckled. Hakim's jaw dropped as Bex spewed beer from his mouth, on to his suit. "Tony. Get him a towel from the bathroom." Sir Marcus ordered. Tony goes into the bathroom located in the office. He comes out with a head towel. He hands it to Bex to wipe himself off. Bex hands the towel back to tony. Tony puts the towel in the hamper in the bathroom. He then goes over and sits back on the sofa. Before hakim can utter a word, Sir Marcus interrupts. "Don't worry! It's a new day, and I'm still breathing, and so are you!" Sir

Marcus said, still with a smile on his face. "So what's the fuss about you wanting to see me?" Sir Marcus asks. Hakim takes a deep breath. "I came to say that I was born into this world, and that I'm home to take back what is rightly mine!" hakim explained. Tony and Sir Marcus start laughing. "And, what's that?" Sir Marcus asked. "You know as well as I do, that this, all of this was to go to me!" hakim said as a tear trickles down his cheek. Sir Marcus leans forward in his chair. "Well, that's not going to happen! I thought you came here to claim Bergen Street, since you disrupted my business by taking out my guys! Deny it! Go ahead and deny it!" Sir Marcus shouted while pounding his fist on the desk. Hakim starts trembling. "Can I get a drink?" hakim asked. "Tony! Get him a drink!" Sir Marcus ordered. "Make it a double! Please!" hakim said in a faint voice. Tony makes hakim and drink and grabs a coaster. He places the coaster on the desk. Tony hands hakim his drink. Hakim gulps the whole drink down in one shot. Hakim clears his throat. "I earned my way here! I dropped a body before I could get my driver's license! I spent 15 years locked down! That's my résumé!" hakim shouted. "That may be true, but there's no way you'll run things around here! Only the blood of a Lassenberry can take this seat!" Sir Marcus yelled. Hakim places the empty glass on the coaster. "I'm bigger than Bergen Street! You know that!" hakim said as he stands from his seat. "Sit down, man!" tony said as he reaches for his gun. Hakim slowly sits back down. Sir Marcus leans back in his chair, and interlocks his fingers on top of his head. "First thing. You're going to move out of Krayton's penthouse. Second. I don't want you near that club anymore." Sir Marcus said as he presses the silent alarm on his desk. The 2 agents come running into the office. "I'll decide your fate later. Escort these guys back to their car." Sir Marcus ordered the agents. Hakim and Bex stand from their seats. "That's it?" hakim shouted. "You're lucky to be alive! And if you want to stay that way, don't cause any more trouble on my streets! Now get out of here before I change my mind!" Sir Marcus ordered. Hakim buttons up his suit jacket. The agents follow the 2 brothers out of the office.

Tony goes over and sits across from Sir Marcus. "What do you think?" Sir Marcus asks. "The dude got a lot of heart for one. If we give him Essex County, we don't have to worry about anybody screwing with him. That'll keep us out of sight, especially you." Tony explained. "I have a feeling you're right! But, I'm going to let him sweat it out for a while." Sir Marcus said. "I'll have an agent keep an eye on them until you give him the go ahead." Tony said. "Make it happen then." Sir Marcus ordered. Tony leaves the office. Sir Marcus grabs his mobile phone. He presses a button. He hears the phone ring 5 times until someone picks up. "Corey?" he asked. "Yeah?" the groggy voice answered. "This is your brother." Sir Marcus said. "Everything alright?" Corey asked. "Yeah! I want you to listen to me, and listen closely. I want you to sell your part of the club to Krayton." He said. "What? What the hell you talking about?" Corey shouted. "Listen! Something might go down! I don't want you getting caught in the middle of things!" Sir Marcus said. "But I worked hard to get that place off the ground!" Corey shouted. "Just trust me! Ok?" he pleaded with Corey. Sir Marcus clicks off the phone.

It was around 4 in the afternoon on a Friday, when most of the employees at BIG SHOTS arrived to work. There was a total of 20 people that worked for Corey and Krayton from Friday to Sunday. The club generated at least a hundred grand in those 3 days.

The employee roster consisted of 7 bouncers, 3 waitresses, 6 cooks, 3 bartenders and 1 floor manager. Corey would be in charge of the bartenders and bouncers, while the floor manager would oversee the waitresses and cooks.

2 of the waitresses were talking to each other when Corey arrived. "Good afternoon people! Corey said. Everyone returned the greeting. He clicks on the neon sign outside. They noticed that Corey wasn't a suit like usual, but had on sweat suit and sneakers. "Gather around everybody!" Corey shouted. "I got a feeling this ain't gonna be good." One of the cooks whispered to the other. "I guess you fill in the rest of the gang when they arrive!" Corey said. "Is there a problem boss?" one of the bouncers asked. "Something like that. I'm gonna make this quick, so you all can get ready for tonight. First of all, I'd like to say it's been cool to work with you guys. It's been a rough start, but we've pulled it off! You need to give yourselves a round of applause!" Corey leads the group in the applause. "So, you quitting on us?" one bouncer asked. "Yeah, I leaving." Corey said as he fights back his tears. At the moment, Krayton enters the club. He looked tired and disheveled. "Hey everybody!" he shouted to the employees. The workers greetings were faint. Krayton walks over to Corey. "I guess you told them already." Krayton said. "Part of it." Corey said. "So, when he gets here, you can introduce him to the workers he didn't meet yet. I'm going in the back to change. It's been a long night." Krayton said as he puts his cousin on the shoulder and walks toward the back room. "One more thing people! Hakim we'll be taking my place from now on!" Corey said. "Damn! This shit is crazy." One bouncer says to himself. "Listen Corey, man! I can't stay if he's gonna be here!" the bouncer said. "Me neither." Said one of the waitresses. "Hey! If that's your choice, that's your choice! I know what I have to do!" Corey said. Corey goes over and gives everyone a hug before he leaves. One of the waitresses, a sexy Hispanic girl, slips Corey her phone number on a piece of paper. Corey just smiled and put the number in his pocket.

A couple of days earlier, Krayton went to Sir Marcus, practically begging him to have hakim stay around the night club. Besides the Butch incident, patrons kept in line for the most part when hakim and his crew entered the club. Krayton craved the life of a gangster, or being around them.

A couple of hours passed, and no sign of hakim in the club. The employees had already prepared for the crowd that night. Corey had long left the scene, leaving Krayton the lone man in charge. Suddenly, hakim comes strolling in wearing a jogging suit and sneakers. He walks toward the back room. He closes the door and lays out on the sofa. A few minutes later, Krayton storms in. "What doing tonight? Krayton asked. "I don't know about tonight, but I'm letting them bouncers go by next week!" hakim said. "What are you crazy? You just can't come up in here and fire people!" Krayton shouted. "Those useless ass niggas let Butch and his boys just walk up in here and point fucking guns in my grill! They're lucky all they getting is fired!" hakim said. "Now I gotta hire new bouncers?" Krayton asked. "Hell no! I got my own crew for that! Now get the fuck out and get to work, so I get some sleep!" hakim said.

The day had finally arrived for Sir Marcus and Kimberly. It was 2 in the morning, September 13th, 2000 when both the Lassenberry and Jenkins family gathered at castle Lassenberry days before to be there for the birth of the couple's first child.

Sir Marcus ordered the construction of a state of the art nursery in the south wing back in June. A pediatrician with a private practice in Cherry Hill was hired to take up residence at the castle for the past 3 weeks. Her salary of half a million dollars for her stay was over the top from Tony's point of view, but Sir Marcus reminded him once again, that he was the boss, and didn't have to spare any expense for his wife and the arrival of his first child.

It was 4:39am, when the family was rushed to stand outside the nursery. Maggie noticed a dozen agents standing outside the nursery in rows of 2, while being surrounded by a half dozen more agents. "Nobody did all this when my kids were being born!" Big L. whispered. "Quiet!" Maggie uttered as she elbowed Big L. in the ribs.

It was about 6 in the morning, when family members on both sides were becoming restless. Agents set out folding chairs for the family members to sit outside the nursery. Suddenly, Sir Marcus comes out of the nursery wearing light blue scrubs. He takes off his surgeon's mask to unveil a big smile. "It's a boy!" he shouts. All the family members that were still awake stand and applaud. The agents just stand at attention guarding the entrance to the nursery. Kimberly's mother was stopped at the door from by the agents from seeing her daughter. "Just give us a moment ma, then you can go in." Sir Marcus says to Kimberly's mother.

Mark Lassenberry the 3rd was born at the exact time of 6:06 am, weighing in at 8 pounds, 5 ounces. He looked like a Jenkins but had the complexion of his father, with a head full of hair. Tony makes his way through the crowd of relatives and stands face to face with Sir Marcus. "Long live the house of Lassenberry!" he shouts. Family members looked confused as Sir Marcus hugs tony. They didn't know what to make of Tony's outburst. Tony turns toward the Lassenberry and Jenkins family chanting the words over and over until both families follow suit. "Long live the house of Lassenberry!" most of the family members shout. Tyson Richards was silent. He showed no sign of enthusiasm. Tony was still satisfied with the overall response. "Ladies and gentlemen! There will be food and drinks in the north wing of the castle to celebrate this grand occasion! There are golf carts outside these doors to transport you all to banquet!" tony explained.

Later at the north wing, Tyson Richards and his brother Malcolm were eating at the banquet when they were approached by an NA agent. "Excuse me Mr. Richards, Mr. Richards. Sir Marcus would like to see you both in his office at this time." The agent said. Tyson sighs. "I know what this is about!" Tyson said to his brother. Their mother Maggie walks over to them. "Where are you 2 going?" she asked. "Everything's ok ma! We'll be right back!" Tyson said. Tyson and his brother follow the agent out into the corridor, to a golf cart. The agent drives them to the west wing.

Moments later, they arrive at the west wing and exit the golf cart. The agent knocks on the door of Sir Marcus's office. "Come in!" Sir Marcus shouts from inside. The agent opens the door for the 2 brothers. Sir Marcus was sitting at his desk, while tony was standing by his side. Sitting on the sofa, was a nurse who happened to be part of the pediatrician's team. "Have a seat guys." Sir Marcus said. Tyson and Malcolm sit across from their cousin. "What's this about?" Tyson asked. "First of all, I would like to thank you guys for showing up for this precious moment in my life. It means a lot to me and Kimberly. So, thank you." Sir Marcus says. "That's what we're here for!" Malcolm said. "So, what's this meeting about?" Tyson asked. "It's about an extension to the family." Sir Marcus said. "Yeah! We have a new cousin, and you have a son!" Tyson said with sarcasm. "What I really meant, was an extension to, your family!" Sir Marcus said. Sir Marcus hits the button on the intercom. "You can bring them in tony." Sir Marcus ordered.

Moments later, tony walks in with hakim and Bex. "What's up family?" hakim shouts. Tyson stands from his seat. "What the hell is he doing here?" Tyson asked. "Now is that any way to talk to your uncle?" hakim chuckled. "What the hell this fool talking about?" Tyson asked Sir Marcus. "Who you calling a fool, nigga?" Bex shouts as he's about to rush Tyson. Sir Marcus gets in between Bex and Tyson. "Now, everybody just take a deep breath, so we can talk like gentlemen!" Sir Marcus said. "I have nothing say to him! I don't even know why you got this guy in your house anyway!" Tyson said. "Hakim told me earlier that he's a Richards! I've brought in the nurse to see if he's telling the truth! The bottom line is, I need a blood sample from you!" Sir Marcus stated. "You trying to tell me that I might be related to this guy?" Tyson said. "Ah, yeah!" Sir Marcus said. Tyson closes his eyes for a moment, shaking his head. "How is this shit possible?" Tyson asked. "It's simple! Yo granddaddy was fucking around a little too much!" hakim said as he pokes his finger into Tyson's chest. Tyson smacks hakim's finger away. "Say one more thing about my grandfather!" Tyson shouted. Malcolm stands from his seat, ready to defend his brother. "Sit down! Everybody!" Tony said as he takes his gun from its holster. Tyson, Malcolm, hakim and Bex get the message and take a seat. "This is bullshit!" Tyson shouts. Hakim shakes his head showing a smirk on his face. "Now, I brought in Nurse Inez, who take a blood sample from Tyson and hakim." Sir Marcus said. "Don't I have to take a blood sample too?" Bex asked hakim. "Man! If I pass the test, you're automatically related to them! God damn!" hakim shouted. "How long can you have the test results back nurse?" Sir Marcus asked. "You'll have the results back within a week." The nurse said as she takes out 2 syringes from her medical kit.

After the nurse extracted blood from Tyson and hakim, Sir Marcus pays her in cash. Sir Marcus takes out a wad of money from his front pocket and pays nurse Inez 2 grand in large bills. "Muchas gracias Señor!" nurse Inez said. "Es usted muy bienvenido! Por lo tanto, si nos disculpan, voy a tener uno de mis hombres le acompañará hasta su coche." Sir Marcus said. "Come in to escort Ms. Inez to her car." Sir Marcus after pressing the button on intercom. Immediately, an agent enters the office. Ms. Inez follows the agent out of the office. "Since when you learned to speak Spanish?" Malcolm asked. "In this business, I've learned you have to be multicultural cuz!" Sir Marcus said.

The day had come when the tests results were ready, but had to be postponed due to the passing of one of most respected men in the underworld. Frankie Depalma's health had finally given out. He passed at his home surrounded by his wife and children. This left Gino Massoni as the head of the Gatano organization. Just like the other big shots in the past, Frankie's funeral was flocked with crimes bosses and drugs lords from across the country and some parts of Europe.

Sir Marcus and tony were chauffeured out to Brooklyn to pay their respects. It was 2 in the afternoon when the limo arrived at Saint Michaels Cathedral. Sir Marcus was decked out in his black uniform and jack boots. He also wore his green sash around his waist, red sash across his chest, as well as is medals. Tony wore the same identical uniform, minus the medals. Sir Marcus and tony could hear the whispers chuckles as entered the cathedral. He and tony are approached by gatano capo Sal Cotucci. "Can I help you fellas?" Sal asked. "Yeah. We're here on behalf of Eddie Lassenberry, to pay our respects." Tony said. "Wait here." Sal said. Sal walks over to the casket where a group of men and the boss Gino is standing. He whispers in Gino's ear. Gino looks over Sal's shoulder and sees tony standing next to Sir Marcus. Gino smiles, then whispers in Sal's ear. Sal then signals 2 soldiers from his crew to follow him. Sal walks back over to where Sir Marcus and tony were standing. "Ok boys! Spread'em!" Sal said. "Spread'em? We're in church!" tony shouts. "I don't give a shit pal! You ain't going near Mr. Massoni without being searched!" Sal said. "Let's just get it over with!" sir Marcus sighed. Tony was reluctant, but he raised his arms. The 2 soldiers thoroughly frisk tony and Sir Marcus in front of the crowd of people. "He's clean." Said one soldier. "He's clean too." Said the soldier who Sir Marcus. "Follow me boys." Sal chuckled. Sir Marcus and tony follow Sal, as the 2 soldiers follow them. When they approach Gino, gino's whole entourage walks away leaving him standing alone with tony and Sir Marcus. "You 2 look like third world dictators!" Gino chuckled. "Gino Massoni, this is Sir Marcus!" tony said. "So, that's what they call you, huh?" Gino said as he and Sir Marcus shook hands. "How's Eddie doing these days?" Gino asked. "He's still breathing." Sir Marcus said. "That's good to hear." Gino said. "No disrespect to Mr. Depalma and his family, but I also came here to smooth things out between us." Sir Marcus said. "Why wouldn't things be smoothed out already?" Gino asked. "2 of your people were muscling in on Lassenberry Packaging. I had to get a couple of cops on my payroll to keep them away." Sir Marcus said. "Wait a minute kid! There's no need for the heat! The cops can flip on you at any time! Didn't Eddie teach you that?" Gino said. "I just want my uncle Danny to walk down the street without looking over his shoulder!" Sir Marcus said. "Well, since I'm the reigning king of the volcano, I'll look into it! Probably just some wannabes trying to earn their way into the ranks." Gino chuckled. Gino and Sir Marcus shake on it. "Thank you, Mr. Massoni. Now, if you don't mind, I'd like to view the body." Sir Marcus said.

Later that evening at the Lassenberry castle, Sir Marcus and tony were sitting in the office. Tony had a stiff drink in his hand, while Sir Marcus was cradling his son. He gave the nanny the night off, even though she lived in the south wing. Kimberly was out and about with her friend Carmen.

Tony takes a sip of his drink. "I'm surprised gino didn't tell us to fuck off about you're your uncle Danny." Tony said. "Why?" Sir Marcus asked. "It's just that, if I were a mob boss, I'd take every opportunity to grab as much cash as I could, if I'm not in the drug game! That's just me!" tony said then takes another sip. Sir Marcus looks at as he burps his son. "Maybe, all he wanted to be was boss!" Sir Marcus said as tony rests his head on the arm of the sofa. He takes another sip of his drink. "Well, I hope he is truly the boss, so he can keep his chubby fingers out of our shit." tony said.

Elsewhere in an unknown location, Terrance Haggerty, assistant director of the National Agreement, New Jersey Division is sitting in small dark room. The only light in the room was coming from a state of the art computer monitor, radar equipment and LIDAR equipment. Terrance was sitting in a chair naked, covered in blood. He was just staring at a satellite image of the lassenberry castle, while listening to Sir Marcus and Tony's conversation. Lying next to his feet, was a lifeless body covered with a bloody sheet.

"You decided to give hakim Essex County?" tony asked Sir Marcus. Before Sir Marcus can answer, the black phone rings. Sir Marcus thinks for a moment before speaking on the phone. "New Jersey speaking!" sir Marcus said. "New Jersey? Ok, New Jersey! This is southern California! Word is, you got some gang bangers heading your way! These jokers drove out of east L.A. at noon pacific time." The caller said. "How many?" Sir Marcus asked. "About a dozen or so." The caller said. "Thanks for the heads up." Sir Marcus said. "No hay problema. Solo ver su espalda." The caller said before he hangs up. "Damn." Sir Marcus said. "What's going on? Who was that?" tony asked. "I finally figured out a way to put hakim to use! Tell him a need to see him tomorrow night around 6." Sir Marcus ordered tony.

After the phone call the Latino drug lord, Sir Marcus had started a trend that every drug lord would identify himself by his territory. Out of all the drug organizations throughout the country controlled by the National Agreement, Sir Marcus and the Lassenberry organization stood out as one of the most profitable.

The following day, hakim and Bex were on their way to the castle. "This is it! We get to run shit now!" hakim chuckled. "You sure that's what we getting called for?" Bex asked. Why would he waste his time calling us? You need to stop thinking like that brother! What you need to do, is think about snuffing out that nigga who killed Annie!" hakim shouted. Bex didn't utter a word. He just kept driving.

After the drive from Newark, hakim and Bex arrive at the castle. They are escorted to Sir Marcus's office. Hakim bursts in the office with lighthearted attitude, rubbing his hands together. "Alright people! You looking at the next king of Essex County!" hakim chuckled. Tony starts smiling. "Not so fast. Take a seat." Sir Marcus ordered hakim. "What's the deal? The blood work came back positive, right?" hakim asked. "I said take a seat!" Sir Marcus said stern voice. Hakim's attitude went from jovial the anger. He violently pulls out his chair and sits. Bex also takes a seat. "Don't fuck with me! Is Essex county mine, or not?" hakim shouts. Sir Marcus ignores hakim's outburst. "Good news guys! You both are related to the Richards's side of the family! Now, here's the situation. I need you to do something for me to see where your loyalty stands." Sir Marcus said. "Loyalty! Nigga I grew up in this shit! I spent 15 years in locked the fuck up and didn't rat out anybody!" hakim shouted. "You didn't rat out anyone in Sir Edward's regime, but this is my regime! Follow me?" Sir Marcus said as hakim leans back in his chair. "So, what's this act of loyalty I have to accomplish?" hakim asked. "There's some gang bangers from L.A. looking for new territory over here. It's simple. I want you and your crew to stop them." Sir Marcus said. "What if we say no?" hakim asked. "Then you and your crew don't run anything." Sir Marcus said as he opens the drawer to his desk. He pulls out a manila folder. He slid it across the desk in hakim's direction. "The information my people gathered is all in that folder! Now, get to work! Sir Marcus ordered. "I think I saw this shit on TV!" Bex said. "This is fucked up, and you know it!" hakim shouts. Sir Marcus looks at his diamond incrusted watch. "Time is running out fellas! I suggest you get started like, yesterday!" Sir Marcus as he stood from his seat. Hakim grabs the folder. He and Bex leave the office, escorted by an agent. "You think they can pull it off?" Sir Marcus asked tony. "If they can't, just tell the NA your life is in danger." Tony said as he shrugged his shoulders.

Later that evening hakim and his crew were at Newark's Washington hotel. 2 Gunz,

Mackie and Chewie were sitting with hakim around a small table. "Why yo brother ain't here?" Mackie asked hakim. "My brother ain't no killer. We don't need him for this." Hakim said as he opens up the folder Sir Marcus had given him earlier. He pulls out a black and white surveillance photo of the guy in charge of the L.A. crew coming to Jersey. "This nigga here, they call Joseph Jones, a.k.a Killa." Hakim said. "We know this dude!" Chewie said. "We did some work for Eddie lassenberry back in the day, and had to lay low out in Cali for a while! We hung out with some gang bangers out in Watts! This nigga was low level at the time!" Mackie said. "Now, he's trying to start his own shit out here." Hakim said. "So, where the fuck he's staying at while he's out here?" Gunz asked. "I need you to check out all the hotels, drug dens and crack houses in Essex County!" hakim said. Gunz's jaw dropped. "All of them?" Gunz asked. "How you know he'll come to Essex County?" Chewie asked. "This is where the big money is! Speaking of money, I need you to go out to Garden State Parkway. See if you can bribe the video camera operators to show you any California plates." Hakim says to Chewie. "Fuck that shit! Let's just wait until the nigga make a move!" Chewie said. "I second that shit!" Gunz said. "I'm with them Hak!" said Mackie. Hakim looked around the table. "Ok! Ok! We'll wait!" hakim shouts. Gunz smiles as he pats hakim on the back.

It was December 31st, the entire Lassenberry family, minus Danny sr. and his family arrived at the castle to bring in 2001. Kimberly decided to have the party in the north wing.

The north wing was the ballroom area. Sir Marcus had ordered a 15 foot evergreen tree to decorate for Christmas. He had waiters bring up a couple of cases of the his best wine from the north wing cellar

A few weeks earlier, Kimberly and Sir Marcus were in bed one morning. Sir Marcus was talking baby talk to his 4 month old son. "You shouldn't talk to him like that!" Kimberly said. "He's a baby! How else am I going to talk to him?" Sir Marcus said. "Like a human being!" Kimberly said as she plucks Sir Marcus on the back of his neck. Sir Marcus changes the subject. "What's with you telling Charlie you want to celebrate Kwanzaa this year?" he asked. "It's time we've become more culturally aware, for our children's sake!" Kimberly said. "Children?" sir Marcus shouts. "Yeah, children!" she said my family celebrated Christmas for the longest. I don't know about this Kwanzaa thing." Sir Marcus said. "Forget it then!" Kimberly pouts. He looks into his wife's eyes and gives in. "Ok! We can do both then! God!" he said. "Thank you." Kimberly said as heads to the bathroom.

Besides the Christmas tree, there were 7 candles placed in a Kinara on the mantle. The ballroom columns were decorated in Kente cloth colored streamers. There were 7 banners posted on the walls, displaying the 7 principles of Kwanzaa. The rest of the ballroom was finished in traditional Christmas fashion.

Everyone was gathered in the ballroom, 10 minutes before the ball dropped. Charlie had mounted a new 27" flat screen TV on the wall, so everyone could see it from New York.

The same DJ that performed at Sir Marcus's wedding, was hired to play at the New Year's party. This time Kimberly didn't make any music selections. The family danced to R&B and club music. The kids were dancing and jumping around to a popular song, as their elders were laughing and making comments. Maggie was standing on the side with a drink in her hand, watching her grandson victor dance. Your son looks just like his grandfather!" Maggie said to Tyson. Tyson smiled. "You always say that!" Tyson said. "Well it's true!" Maggie said. "Speaking of family! Since we know hakim is family now, who does he look like?" Tyson asked his mother. Maggie went from having a joyful look, to showing a scowl. "I don't give a damn what any blood tests say! That monster is not a Richards! He's a mistake that my brother kept around as a pet!" Maggie said before she storms off into the crowd. "Wow!" Tyson said as his mother walks off.

It was a minute left on the clock before the New Year was to arrive. Sir Marcus and Kimberly ordered Charlie to make sure all the adults champagne flutes were filled. "Come on everybody! Gather around! We have 30 seconds left until the ball drops!" Kimberly shouts. Kimberly and Lula were gathering the kids together to get them in front of the TV. Suddenly, Sir Marcus's mobile phone vibrates in his back pocket. He pulls it out and check the number. The countdown had started. "15, 14, 13, 12!" everyone shouted "New Jersey! Sir Marcus said on the phone. "Yo, it's me hakim! We got him!" hakim said. "8, 7, 6!" everyone shouted. "Speak up! I can't hear you!" Sir Marcus shouts. "3, 2, 1! Happy New Year!!!!" everyone shouted at the top of their lungs. "We got the dude from Cali!" hakim said. The ballroom made a loud echoing noise when everyone started shouting. Sir Marcus cups his hand over his ear. "You telling me this now?" Sir Marcus asked. Kimberly turns to her husband and hugs him, giving him a big kiss in the lips. Kimberly looked upset that her husband didn't react the way she did. She goes over and hugs Joe-Joe. "Say that again!" Sir Marcus shouts. "We're at the Washington Hotel! Room 219! Hurry up!" hakim shouts. At this time, tony is hugging Maggie. He sees Sir Marcus on the phone, looking upset. Sir Marcus sees tony in the crowd and signals him to come over. Sir Marcus then flips his phone closed. Tony makes his way through the crowd over to Sir Marcus. "Just got word from hakim about our friend from California!" Sir Marcus whispered in his ear. "Where at?" tony asked. "Get a car ready with 2 agents! Meet me out front!" Sir Marcus whispered. "Listen! It might be a set up! I'll take the agents with me and take care of it!" tony whispered. "They're in room 219, at the Washington hotel!" Sir Marcus whispered in his ear. Tony puts his hand on Sir Marcus's shoulder. He nods his head and takes off through the crowd and out the exit. Mark sr. walks over towards his son. "Everything ok son?" mark sr. asked. "Now it is! Happy New Year pop!" Sir Marcus said as he gives his father a hug.

About 2 hours later, tony and the 2 agents arrive outside the Washington hotel. "Stay here!' tony orders the agents. Tony walks pass the front desk of the hotel. The clerk was busy on the phone.

Tony gets to the 2nd floor. He gets out of the elevator and makes a left according to the room numbers on the wall. He approaches door 219. He pulls out a small caliber hand gun, and knocks on the door. "Who that?" said the voice on the other side of the door. "It's me." Tony said. 2 Gunz looks through the peep hole. "It's tony! Gunz whispered. Gunz opens the door. Hakim was sitting down watching TV. "Happy New year nigga! Sure took you long enough!" hakim shouts. "It's a foot of snow out there!" tony said. "That's a nice coat! I gotta give it to you! You be dressing yo ass off!" hakims says to tony.

Tony's coat was a black wood trench coat, with a fur collar and belt made from Chinchilla. The hat we wore was a Chinchilla fedora. Tony had all his clothing custom and tailor made to his precise description since he started working for jabbo.

"What's the damage?" tony asked. "They made their move in Irvington! They took out 2 of your runners on Springfield ave, man, but we made all them niggas disappear!" hakim said. "Where is he?" tony asked. "His dumb ass in the bathroom! In the tub!" hakim chuckled. Tony puts his gun back in his holster. He pulls out a pair of thin leather gloves. He puts the gloves on. "You 2, stay put!" tony says to hakim and Gunz. Tony heads to the bathroom. He opens the door to see the man they've been after for a while. Joseph, a.k.a Killa, was sitting in the bathtub, naked. His hands were bound behind his back. His mouth was covered by duct tape. His feet was bound together by duct tape. Tony closes the door, and then takes off his coat in a calm manner. He hangs it up on the door hook, as well as his fedora. He sits on the edge of the bathtub. Tony strips the tape from his mouth. "Please! Please! Let me go! I promise I'll be on the first plane back to Cali!" Jones cried as tony looks around the bathroom. He looks down at Jones. "What was you thinking? You thought you could come all the way from California and run us out of town?" tony chuckled. "No man, it wasn't like that! We just wanted to prove to y'all we could hustle for you! They ran us out of Cali!" Jones cried. "So, you know us!" tony said. "Man, everybody in Watts and Compton know about you and jabbo!" Jones cried. "So that means you know you're not leaving this bathroom alive, right?" tony said. Jones starts sobbing like a big baby. "How old are you?" tony asks. "31!" Jones cried. "I'll give it to you. You got balls." Tony said. "Please let me go!" Jones cried. "Believe me. I want to let you go, but you're too old. Too set in your ways." Tony said. "No! No! I'll change! I swear to god I'll change!" Jones cried.

Jones was a tall skinny dark skinned guy, sporting a short afro. Ever since he was 15, he tatted his forearm with tiny stick figures of how many bodies he put to rest. It could've been 18 stick figures on his arm if hakim and his crew didn't get to him.

Tony frowns as he sees the urine and piles of shit in the tub. While Jones wasn't looking, tony took out a switch blade from his pocket. The blade pops out. "What I want you to do now, is look up at the light fixture and take a deep breath." Tony said calmly. "Oh God! "Oh God! Jones whispered to himself. Jones looks up toward the light. Tony quickly jabs Jones through his temporal bone. The jab was so quick, there wasn't a drop of blood on the blade. Jones starts flipping in the tub like a fish on dry land. About a minute passed when his body stopped moving. Jones died with his eyes wide open. Tony stands up and puts away his blade. He puts on his fedora, then his trench coat. He leaves the bathroom. Hakim stands when tony exits the bathroom. "We good now? I can get Essex, right?" hakim asked. "Get rid of the body and clean up the shit in the bathtub. You'll be notified later." Tony says in a calm manner before leaving the hotel room. 2 Gunz closes the door when he leaves. "That punk mother fucker!" hakim shouts. Tony could hear hakim screaming outside in the hall. He just smiles while walking down the corridor.

It was the 1st of January at 8 in the morning. It was the day of the big gathering that was inscribed on the gold invitation Sir Marcus received a while back from Terrance Haggerty.

Strolling around the ballroom of the north wing in his pajamas, Sir Marcus cradles his son in his arms, and then looks up at the portraits of his grandfather and uncle. There were workers of Latino ethnicity hired to clean up after the New Year's party. There were 2 agents standing at the exit making sure no harm came to Sir Marcus and his son. "One day your picture will be on that wall." Sir Marcus whispers to his son. The baby just looked at his father. Limping into the ballroom was an elderly Hispanic woman. "Buenos días señor Marcus!" she said. "Buenos días Lucy!" Sir Marcus said. Nuestro pequeño prínipe preciosa necesita ser alimentado, y un baño!" Lucy said. "What's that?" Sir Marcus asked. "Bath! Baby need food and bath señor!" Lucy explained. Sir Marcus carefully hands over his son to Lucy. Lucy takes the baby and leaves the ballroom, followed by an agent. It was ordered since his birth, that mark the 3rd be guarded at all times. Sir Marcus looks down at his slippers. "Damnit!" he shouts. Someone had spilled fruit punch the night before. It stuck to the bottom of his slipper. "Come on guy! Somebody clean this mess up, please!

—— CHAPTER 14. THE GATHERING ——

Outside the walls of the castle, wearing a pink cloth jogging suit, Kimberly is on her last lap of her morning jog. She started jogging as soon as she took up residence at the castle. Her regiment consisted of a 10 minute stretch, 40 sits up, and 8 laps around the castle perimeter, which was the equivalent of 2 miles. During her pregnancy, she hired a trainer for prenatal exercises. She comes at the end of her run. At the finish point, was standing a NA agent. He had in his possession a towel and a bottle of water. The agent hands her the towel. Kimberly walks off the burn in her legs. She then walks back and takes the bottle of water. She wipes the sweat from her eyes. Kimberly then jumps in the back of the golf cart. The agent jumps in the driver's seat. He pushes a button on the remote in his hand that opens 2 sliding doors and drives into the castle.

Minutes later, the golf cart arrives at the west wing. "Thank you." Kimberly said. "You're welcome ma'am." The agent said. Kimberly jumps out of the cart and heads to the shower.

10 minutes later, Kimberly comes out the bathroom wearing her monogram bathrobe. She stands in front of the vanity mirror and takes the pins out of her hair to let her dreadlocks flow down her back. She then hears a noise in Sir Marcus's walk in closet. She walks in the closet about 10 feet and sees her husband going through his wardrobe. "Lose something?" she asked. "Yeah! Where the hell is my waist sash?" Sir Marcus shouts. "Do you need to wear it?" Kimberly asked. "Yes! It's part of my uniform!" Sir Marcus explained. He looks on the floor next to his shoes and sees the sash on the floor.

"I'm going to have Lucy iron this a little." Sir Marcus said. "Did she feed the baby?" Kimberly asked. "Yeah, about that! I thought we've talked about you breast feeding!" Sir Marcus said. Kimberly walks up to her husband and puts her arms around him. "I had a change of heart after my nipples started hurting." She chuckled. "I brought you the pump! Use that!" Sir Marcus said. Kimberly rolls her eyes. "Ok then!" she sighs.

Krayton at this time, was at BIG SHOTS with a couple of his employees cleaning up from the New Year's party the night before. They party was a wild locked door event. There were condoms, panties and thongs all over the dance floor.

Minutes later, hakim and his crew come in the club. 2 Gunz, Chewie, Bex and Mackie make their way to the back room, while hakim stands in the door way with his arms folded. He was wearing a long leather trench coat. "Good morning! What's up?" Krayton says to hakim. Hakim doesn't respond. Krayton continues looking over receipts. "What's up hakim?" the employee asks. Frustrated, hakim goes over to the employee and grabs him by the back of the neck. "How many times I gotta tell you to address me as Mr. bates, nigga?" hakim shouted. "Yo hakim, stop it!" Krayton said. Even though the employee was much bigger than hakim, he didn't dare struggle against him. Hakim shoves the employee out the door and closes it. "You ok?" Krayton asked as he trembled in fear. Hakim didn't answer. He just slowly strolls around the bar. He checks the register. It was empty. "Had fun last night?" hakim asked Krayton. Krayton starts acting silly, hoping to calm hakim down. "Yeah! You know how we do!" Krayton chuckled. Hakim steps to Krayton, standing about 5 inches away from him. "Well, I didn't! You're fucking cousin, ain't a man of his word!" hakim shouts in Krayton's face. Krayton stops his silly chuckling. "What happened now?" Krayton asked. "Nothing! Not a god damn thing!" hakim shouted. Hakim walks pass Krayton. On his way to the back room, hakim picks up one of the chairs from a dining table, throwing it against the wall. One of the legs on the chair brakes. "Man! That's solid oak! You know how much that one chair cost?" Krayton shouted. Hakim turns towards Krayton. He stares Krayton down with an evil look. Krayton looks the other way. Hakim enters the back room, and closes the door. Krayton's instinct tells him to go to entrance door. He opens it. There, his employee is standing with a lost puppy dog look on his face. "Man, get back in here!" Krayton shouted.

In the back room, hakim and his crew sit around the poker table in silence. "What's today?" Hakim asked while chewing on a straw. "It's new year's day." Gunz said. Hakim rolls his eyes. "I meant what day of the week!" Hakim said. "It's Monday." Bex said. "Well then, by next Monday, if that nigga Sir Marcus or whatever the fuck he wants to be called don't give me Essex County, I'm taking it!" Hakim said. Except for Bex, the other guys oppose hakim's rant. "Listen man! I know I'm a hard core heavy hitter, but going up against those suit and tie robots, you gotta be insane!" Gunz said. "Well, I'm insane nigga! That nigga ain't never put down a body in his bitch ass life! Now he's in charge of a multimillion dollar dope game! Give me a fucking break!" Hakim said. Bex had his head down, tapping a couple of poker chips together. Hakim smacks Bex on his chest with the back of his hand, real hard. Bex snaps out of his daze. "Listen man! Don't you have some payback for that nigga in South Jersey? You forgot about Annie already?" hakim said. "I don't mean to burst yo bubble brother, but say you take out Marcus, or whatever his name is, do you know his connection, because without that we ain't got a pot to piss in!" Bex said. "Listen to him man, because he's right." Chewie said. There's a knock on the door. "We busy!" hakim yelled. The knocking continues. "Yo! I said we busy!" hakim shouted. The door slowly opens. In comes Krayton, "What the fuck you want?" hakim asked. Krayton looks around at the guys in the room. "I overheard what y'all was saying. I want in." Krayton said in a soft voice. Mackie cups his over his mouth to keep from laughing out loud. Krayton gets agitated. "I'm serious! My cousin turned his back on me one too many times, and I'm tired of the shit!" Krayton said. Mackie couldn't help himself as he claps his hands together laughing. Hakim has a change of heart. "If I need you, I'll call you man." Hakim said. Krayton nods his head, and backs his way out the door. Mackie gets up and slams the door shut. "Now what if he goes back and tell his cousin? Then we're really fucked!" Mackie said. "We really ain't got nothing to worry about man. Trust me." Hakim said.

Miles away, at terry Lassenberry's estate Alpine. Terry is lying naked in her king size bed, but not alone. She smiles and giggles as Brandon kisses on her hands and sucks on her fingers. They had left the New Year's party at the castle soon after the ball dropped.

"What do you think about us being together?" terry asked. "What are talking about?" Brandon asked. "I just, I don't know!" terry said. "You don't want to be with me, after last night?" Brandon asked. "No silly! Of course I want to be with you! It just feels like this whole situation was arranged!" terry said. "I know it does! We're the grandchildren of 2 great men! It seems only right that we get together! It'll be disrespectful for the both of us to break that bond and go off with outsiders!" Brandon said. Terry sits up. "So you're here over a 60 year bond?" terry asked as her eyes start to tear up. Brandon gently caresses her face. "I'm here because I love you." He said. "I love you too!" terry said. They both hug each other. Terry's mobile phone rings. Terry and Brandon are still kissing and hugging. The phone continues to ring. "Let me get that babe!" terry said. She grabs the phone off the night stand. She checks the caller ID as the phone continues to ring. "It's my dad." She said. She presses the button to answer. She puts her finger over Brandon's lips to silence him. "Hi daddy! Why are you up so early?" terry asked. "Your mother and I just wanted to see how you were holding up. You left the party kind of early. We didn't get a chance to give you your new year's hug." Mark sr. said. "I'm fine! Just a little tired from last night!" terry said. "Well, hope to see at the castle this Friday." Mark sr. said. "Why?" terry asked. "Your brother invited us to dinner. I thought he called you!" mark sr. said. "He didn't call me!" terry said. "Well, it's Friday at 6." Mark sr. said "ok daddy! Friday at 6." Terry sighed. "I'll talk to you later young lady. Love you!" mark sr. said. "Love you too daddy!" terry said. "Oh, by the way! Tell my future son-in-law hello." Mark sr. chuckled. "Daddy!" terry shouted. Mark sr. continues laughing before he hangs up. Terry tosses the phone at the edge of the bed. She puts the pillow over her head from embarrassment. "What's wrong?" Brandon asked. Terry takes the pillow away from her face. She starts giggling. She hugs Brandon, and gives him a kiss on the lips. "Everything is just fine!" she chuckled. She kisses Brandon again. "Good! Now go fix me breakfast!" Brandon said jokingly. Terry rolls her eyes at Brandon. "Please! I have a maid!" terry said as she snaps her fingers in the air.

Thousands of miles away in Palermo Sicily, a young Italian man approaches 2 old men sitting outside a café. It was around 4pm. One man is eating Scaccia, while the other is sipping on red wine. The young man passes the man sipping the wine a note. The old man takes the note and unfolds it. He starts laughing. "Cosa è di così divertente?" the man eating Scaccia asked. The other man almost chokes on the wine. "E'ufficale! Massoni è il capo del North Jersey!" the wine sipper said. "Siamo pronti a inviare I ragazzi sopra?" the other old man asked. The wine sipper folds the note back in half. He strikes a match, and then burns the note. "Dirò Don Domenico lasceremo lui mettersi a propio agio." The wine sipper said. The other old man just shrugs his shoulders, and continues to eat. The 2 old men just happened to be capo Luigi Carafa and capo Bramante Cucci. Both are cousins of the late crime boss Gatano and members of the inner circle. The assassin's guild.

It was around 5:30 pm back in Jersey. Sir Marcus is standing in front of the mirror in his bedroom. He's checking himself for any imperfections on his uniform. He straightens all 3 of his medals that were pinned on the left side of his chest. Lucy just finished wrapping the waist sash around him. Kimberly is sitting on the bed, with her son in her arms. "You look like a general baby!" Kimberly said. "Thanks babe." Sir Marcus said as he plucks a piece of lint off of his uniform. "When will you be back?" Kimberly asked. "Tomorrow morning. No later." Sir Marcus said. There's a knock on the door. "Come in!" Sir Marcus shouts. An agent enters the bedroom. "Your limo is waiting sir." The agent said. "Good. Wait for me out in the hall." Sir Marcus ordered. "Yes sir." The agent said. The agent leaves the bedroom. Kimberly stands. "I know it's just for a day, but you be careful and have a safe ride." Kimberly said as her eyes tear up. "What's wrong babe?" he asked Kimberly. Kimberly just shook her head. "Don't pay me any mind!" Kimberly said. She kisses Sir Marcus on the lips. "I love you." She said. Sir Marcus takes his son in his arms. He kisses son on both cheeks. "I love you both." He said. He hands the baby back to Kimberly. He gives her a quick kiss on the lips. "Gotta go!" Sir Marcus said. He walks out the door. Out in the corridor, Sir Marcus jumps into the golf cart. The agent drives off. A few minutes later, the reach the main entrance. Sir Marcus gets out of the golf cart. Before he can leave, he's intercepted by Charlie and Sir Edward in another golf cart. Sir Edward is well strapped in the golf cart, so he doesn't fall out of the cart. "What do you 2 want?" Sir Marcus asked Charlie. "Sir Edward needs to talk to you!" Charlie said. "All due respect uncle, but I have to head out to the airport!" Sir Marcus. "He said it's important that he talked to you, alone!" Charlie said. Sir Marcus just shook his head. "Alright!" Sir Marcus sighed. "Sir! You have to get to the airport!" the agent said in a demanding voice. Sir Marcus steps to the agent. "Listen! You work for me! Remember that!" Sir Marcus shouts. "Yes sir." The agent said. Sir Marcus sits in the driver's seat of the golf cart, next to his uncle. "Tell me uncle. Say what you have to say." Sir Marcus said. As drool falls from the left side of his mouth, tears trickle down his cheek. "What's wrong uncle?" Sir Marcus asked. "Don't…go…please!" Sir Edward cried. "What'd you mean, don't go?" Sir Marcus asked. "It's a…ugly…place!" Sir Edward cried. "This is a big opportunity for us to get the 8 remaining counties! I have to go!" Sir Marcus said. "Don't…go!" Sir Edward said. Sir Marcus can hear the pain in his uncle's voice. He gets out of the golf cart. "Take him back to his chambers and get him cleaned up! I have to go!" Sir Marcus ordered Charlie. Sir Marcus walks out the main entrance, followed by the agent. The limo pulls up. The agent opens the car door for Sir Marcus. The agent gets in the back with Sir Marcus. "To Teterboro!" the agent said. The other agent drives off.

A couple of hours later, the limo arrives at Teterboro airport. There is a private jet waiting on the tarmac, all revved up to take off. An agent walks up to the limo, and opens the door for Sir Marcus and the other agent. They both make their way on board the jet. Sir Marcus and the agent are greeted by the pilot and the sexy blonde flight attendant tiffany. "Welcome aboard Sir Marcus! I'm Captain Tim Gabreski! I'll be your pilot for the duration!" the captain said. Gabreski and Sir Marcus shook hands. "No disrespect. But what happened to Captain Bennett?" Sir Marcus asked. "Oh, he retired just a month ago! Don't worry sir! I come from a long line of pilots!" Gabreski said. "Sound good to me!" Sir Marcus said. "Tiffany here, will show you your seats. Enjoy your flight sir." The captain said. Captain Gabreski walks back towards the cockpit. "Would you gentlemen follow me?" said tiffany. As they follow tiffany to their seats, Sir Marcus can't help notice how sexy tiffany looks in her uniform. She directs them to their seats. "If there's anything you need sir, I'll just be a whisper a way. I do mean anything." Tiffany said with a big smile on her face. She winks at Sir Marcus, and walks away. The agent sits across from Sir Marcus and pulls out a magazine from the seat rack. "Can you read with those shades on?" Sir Marcus asked him. "Yes sir." The agent said. Sir Marcus just shrugs his shoulders. "Ok!" Sir Marcus said. "Will everyone please fasten their seatbelts please? We will be in Maine in approximately 2 hours." Gabreski said over the PA system. Sir Marcus, the agent and tiffany strap themselves in as the turbines get louder. The jet shoots down the runway, and takes off.

As soon as the jet reaches the appropriate height, the captain turns off the seat belt signal. Tiffany approached the 2 men. "Can I get you gentlemen a drink, fruit, of a sandwich?" tiffany asked.

Back at the Lassenberry castle, tony arrives outside the castle gates. He approaches 2 agents guarding the gate. Usually tony walks through the gates with no problem. This time, there was a problem. "Sir Marcus is not on the premises Mr. Kerouac." One of the agents said. "So, what does that have to do with you not letting me pass?" tony asked. "By orders of Sir Edward, no one is to enter the castle walls until Sir Marcus returns." The agent explained. "Are you fucking kidding me, man? Sir Marcus is head of this organization! I'm his second in command!" tony shouted. "Sorry sir. As long as there is a Lassenberry male in the castle selected by the order, his rules stand." The agent said. "Ok! I'll give Sir Marcus a call! Tony grabs his mobile phone from his passenger's seat. He makes a call to Sir Marcus, but doesn't get a signal. "Shit!" tony shouts.

Unknown to most, the National Agreement has inside connections to most major mobile phone companies. All the drug czars, politicians and corporate executives on their way to the gathering in Maine, had their mobile devices remotely disabled.

A couple of hours later, 5 miles above the forests of the great state of Maine, captain Gabreski gets on the PA system. "Would everyone please fasten their seatbelts and prepare for landing." The captain said. The seatbelt signal comes on. Tiffany quickly puts on her uniform blouse, while the same time Sir Marcus pulls up his pants. Before they get to their seats. Sir Marcus gets tiffany's attention. He points to his chin. "You still have a little running down your cheek." Sir Marcus said. Tiffany starts giggling. She takes a hand full of tissue and wipes off the remains Sir Marcus had left. They both hurry out of the restroom, and back to their seats. The agent lowers his shades to stare at Sir Marcus. "Is there a problem agent?" Sif Marcus asked. The agent says nothing. He pushes his shades over his eyes with his index finger.

The jet finally hits the runway. Because the forest is so dense, the runway is not as long compared to FAA regulation runways. Even though its captain Gabreski's first time landing on this runway, he proves himself by landing the jet safely. The jet comes to a complete halt. "Hope you've enjoyed the flight." The captain said over PA system. The seatbelt signal turns off. "Watch your step when leaving the air craft please." The captain said.

At the bottom of the air craft's steps, another agent awaits Sir Marcus. "God! There's a lot of you guys!" Sir Marcus says to the agent. "Would you please follow me sir." The agent said. 20 yards from the jet, a black Boeman limo waiting. The agent that drove the limo, opens the door so Sir Marcus could get in the back along with the other agent. Once the driver gets behind the wheel, the limo takes off on a trail through the woods.

It was close to 10pm. It's was a cold windy night. There was about a foot of snow on the ground, but the road was shoveled down to the pavement. Sir Marcus sees nothing but huge spruce trees on both sides of the road. Sir Marcus was told that the drive would take about 40 minutes. Unlike Sir Edward, Sir Marcus slept the whole ride there. Cocaine was the culprit that kept Sir Edward wide awake and alert.

Finally, the limo reached its destination. The agent riding along with Sir Marcus tapped him on the arm to awaken him. Just like Sir Edward, Sir Marcus was in awe of the scenery. Out of the clearing, there was a beautiful palace.

The palace made the Lassenberry castle look like a log cabin. "This is living!" Sir Marcus said to himself. The limo drives around the enormous water fountain, which was turned off due to the extreme cold. The limo pulls into a designated parking area. Sir Marcus noticed that most of the limousines were made by Boeman Auto. "Business is booming!" Sir Marcus said to himself. An agent pulls up in a custom made golf cart identical to the golf carts at the Lassenberry castle. "I thought my uncle came up with this idea!" Sir Marcus chuckled. The agent ignores his comment. "Climb aboard sir." The agent said. Sir Marcus gets in the golf cart. He leaves the agent that accompanied him from Jersey. Sir Marcus is driven a 100 yards to the main entrance. There were 2 agents standing at the huge double doors. One of the agents press a button on a remote in his hand. One of the doors automatically swings open. Sir Marcus rubs his hands together to calm his anxiety. He walks into the palace. Sir Marcus is escorted towards a podium with a microphone propped on top. At the podium stood a man in a tuxedo, who happened to announce each guest when arriving. He covers the microphone as he asks Sir Marcus how he would like to be announced. Sir Marcus whispers into his ear. "Please welcome Sir Marcus of New Jersey!" the Announcer said. Due to the sophistication of the PA system, Sir Marcus's name was echoed throughout the palace. As Sir Marcus makes his way through the crowd, waiters approached him with sterling silver platters of hors d'oeuvres and champagne flutes and much harder drinks. Sir Marcus was approached by an elderly white guy. "Sir Marcus?" the man said. "That's me. And you are?" Sir Marcus asked. "Peter. Peter Boeman." He said as he shook Sir Marcus's hand. "I remember you from my uncle's ceremony! Finally, I get the chance to meet the man himself, up close and personal!" sir Marcus chuckled. "Pleased to meet you as well young man! At least we don't have to ask each other how's business!" Mr. Boeman chuckled. Mr. Boeman puts his arm around Sir Marcus. "Come, let me introduce you to some of the guys!" Mr. Boeman said. He takes Sir Marcus over to one of the groups that were mingling in a huddle. "Gentlemen! For those who don't know, this is Sir Marcus!" Mr. Boeman said. "How's it going young man? Paul benedict." he said to Sir Marcus. He and Sir Marcus shake hands. "You probably remember this guy! Edgar J. Phine of Galaxy Appliances!" Mr. Boeman said. "It's been a long time young man! How's the family?" Mr. Phine asked. "Everyone's good!" Sir Marcus said as he and Mr. Phine shook hands. Boeman interrupts their conversation. "Obviously you know Senator Brown!" Mr.

Boeman Said. Sir Marcus and the Senator shake hands. "This joker here is Mercer County executive, Anthony Rago!" Mr. Boeman said. "I should've have my assistant tony clue me in more before I came here!" Sir Marcus chuckled. "It's quite alright! You're amongst friends!" Rago said. "This is Tom Mcgovern and bill Tuttlebaum, founders of Upgrade Office Supply." Mr. Boeman said. Sir Marcus shook hands with all the guys in the huddle. Also in the huddle were the Willard brothers, Jeff and Horace, Who were the founders of Lock, Stock and Barrel Defense Contracting. Charles Scott, C.E.O of New World Construction, the man responsible for constructing castle Lassenberry was the last to shake Sir Marcus's hand.

There were over 300 powerful and wealthy men invited as guests to the palace. There was one familiar face that crashed the huddle. Terrance Haggerty walked over asking the guys were they enjoying themselves so far. He was dressed in a sparkling, lavender tuxedo, green bow-tie and a green silk cape. What was really odd was the sparkling green stilettos on his feet. "Hey, What with the get up Haggerty?" Rago asked. Terrance looked upset at first, but started giggling and danced his way over to another group of guests.

As Sir Marcus was trying his best to fit in with the huddle, he sees across the room a chubby Hispanic looking gentleman signaling for him to come over. Sir Marcus reluctantly excuses himself from the first group and goes over to where the Hispanic guy was. "Evening gentlemen!" Sir Marcus said to the second group. "Boys! I want you to meet the man who pioneered the code names for us!" the Hispanic guy said.

The man that called Sir Marcus over to the other group was the same man that warned him about the gang bangers heading to jersey. He was Jose Mendez a.k.a Chi-Chi. Jose was the drug king pin of Southern California. His net worth was reported to be a little over a billion dollars, making him the wealthiest drug czar west of the Rocky Mountains. Just like the Lassenberry organization, Jose was under the thumb of the National Agreement as well. The only difference was that Jose's supplier was the Mexican cartel, while the Lassenberry supplier were the Colombians.

"I want to introduce to you all, New Jersey!" Jose shouted. He and Sir Marcus greet each other as if they were friends for years. From the sound of Jose's voice, Sir Marcus just realized he was Southern Cali. "Thanks for the heads up, man!" Sir Marcus said as he give Jose dap. "No problem! Your enemies are my enemies!" Jose said.

Jose introduces Sir Marcus to the other kingpins in the game. "I'm sure you know New York City here!" Jose said.

The NYC kingpin was Maury O'Neil, who already met Sir Edward at the last gathering. "This is New Orleans over here!" Jose said. Sir Marcus and the New Orleans kingpin shake hands. "How your uncle doing kid? Haven't heard from him since the last gathering!" New Orleans asked. "I can say this. He's still breathing." Sir Marcus said. "Breathing is a good thing!" New Orleans chuckled. Jose went down the line of introductions. "Chicago, Florida, Western Pennsylvania, Denver, Clark County Nevada, St. Louis, Long Island, Georgia, Baton Rouge, Washington State, Dallas, Southern Texas, Oahu, Anchorage Alaska, Juneau Alaska, Upstate New York, Rhode Island, Phoenix and the Fort Hall Indian Reservation. There were so many more drug lords in the room, Sir Marcus just waved to the others in the back ground.

There was one man that didn't need any introduction from Jose. His name was Jacob Dietrich a.k.a the Amish man of Philadelphia. Mr. Dietrich was cast out of the Amish community back in 1960 after being caught with a couple of kilos of cocaine. Soon after, he became the drug under the protection of the Philadelphia mob. Just like Jose, Dietrich's crew weren't blood related.

He kept an Amish appearance by wearing traditional Amish clothing and sporting a long, thick white beard. Not only was he a drug lord, he was known to be a cold blooded killer. A street war was about to erupt between Dietrich and benny Lassenberry back in 1975 when it was apparent that benny was stretching his territory further south. A sit down was conducted and benny came out on top. Dietrich was left was left with the remaining most southern part of jersey. This includes Bex's home town of Bridgeton. This was a problem for Sir Marcus, who wanted the last 8 counties in New Jersey ran by his people. The other problem was that the Lassenberry crew's cocaine connection was from Colombia. While the Dietrich connection was from Mexico. It was the NA that had the final say if a conflict broke out.

"See, you should be over here huddled with us man! Those politicians, corporate types and celebrities think they're better than us!" Jose said to Sir Marcus.

There was a small group of "A" list celebrities huddled over at one side of the room drinking, smoking and having a good time. Sir Marcus knew a couple of them personally. There was movie studio head, G.W. Winters. Standing next to him was action star Jett Connors.

Sir Marcus was in another zone while Jose was talking. All he could focus on was the Amish man. "Say, southern Cali. Introduce me to Philadelphia." Sir Marcus said. "Sure man! No problem!" Jose said. Jose and Sir Marcus walk through the crowd. Jose taps the Amish man on the shoulder while he was chatting with the Milwaukee kingpin. "Philly, I would like you to meet New Jersey!" Jose chuckled. Both the Amish man and Sir Marcus stare each other down for a few seconds. They reluctantly shook hands. "So, New jersey, you've gotten younger over the years." Dietrich said. "I gonna leave you 2 guys alone, while I help myself to the buffet table!" Jose said. Jose walks away. The 2 adversaries stand alone. "If you didn't know it by now, I'm the grandson of benny Lassenberry. I know you've been in the game way before I was born, but I'm here to tell that all of South Jersey belongs to me." Sir Marcus said. Dietrich smiles. He rubs his hand across Sir Marcus's medals. "Nice uniform!" Dietrich said. Sir Marcus smacks his hand away. "Listen old man! You're doing business in my state, and I want you out!" Sir Marcus said. Dietrich starts cracking up. He laughs so hard, he starts coughing. "I can tell you don't follow through on threats, boy!" Dietrich said as he continued coughing. Sir Marcus said nothing. He just stood there for a few seconds, then steps aside. Dietrich walks pass him, still coughing. Suddenly Dietrich clutches his chest and falls to the floor. Sir Marcus is in shock. Everyone turns in their direction. 2 agents runs to the scene. One of the agents feels his neck for a pulse. "No pulse." The agent said. Everyone crowds around. Terrance Haggerty breaks through the crowd. Haggerty kneels down feeling for a pulse. He looks over at the agent. The agent shook his head. "Get him to my office, quick!" Terrance tells the agents. The 2 agents pick up the old man from the floor. 2 more agents come from out of nowhere and help carry the body. "He's fine guys! He just had a little too much to drink! We're taking him to one of the bedrooms until he wakes up!" Terrance chuckled. "You're sure he's ok, man? He looks dead to me!" Jose said. "I'm a doctor! I know when someone is dead or not, and he isn't!" Terrance said.

3 NA big shots approach Terrance. They were Chief of Research, Dr. Alfred Zachmont, Milton Burnhan, NA Finance Director and Earl Shivers. Assistant Finance director. "I like how you think on your feet." Dr. Zachmont whispers to Terrance. "Thank you sir!" Terrance whispered.

As the crowd scattered, an agent walks up to Terrance. "Everything is ready sir." The agent whispered. "If any stragglers are outside, escort them in, and secure the doors." Terrance whispered. "Yes sir. The agent said. The agent walks through the crowd. He snaps his fingers and a team of agents follow him to the exits. Sir Marcus walks over to Jose. "Where the hell are they going?" Sir Marcus asked. "¡Oh hombre! El partido está a punto de saltar!" Jose shouted. "What the hell are you talking about?" sir Marcus asked. "Bro! We're about to be treated like kings!" Jose said.

Terrance goes over to the podium and grabs the microphone. He then walks in the center of the enormous ballroom. "Testing! Testing! Gentlemen! Can I have your attention please?" Terrance shouted. The room went silent. "Was the food good?" Terrance shouts. "Yeah! Everyone shouts. "Are you fuckers pissy drunk yet?" Terrance shouted. "Yeah!" the crowd roared. "Well then, are you ready for some action?" Terrance shouted. "Hell Yeah!" the crowd roared some more. As Terrance was revving up the crowd, agents escorted the stragglers inside the palace. A group of agents with thick chains and sturdy padlocks start securing all the exits. Sir Marcus looks nervous. "What's going on?" Sir Marcus asked. "Man, relax!" Jose said. 2 agents stand by the double doors that weren't chained shut. "Are you ready for some nasty hot sex?" Terrance shouted. "Yeah!" the crowd roared. "I can't hear you!" Terrance shouted. "Yeah!" the crowd shouted even louder. "On behalf of our master, I bring you the sexiest bitches the world has ever seen!" Terrance shouted. Everyone starts screaming and whistling. "Bring'em out boys!" Terrance shouted. Suddenly, the double doors open. Out comes a lineup of sexy young women. 30 to be exact in bikinis.

The men didn't waste any time. Some of them grab the ladies and start groping them and ripping off their bikinis. There was nothing romantic going on here. One guest takes one of the ladies and pushes her to the floor. He unzips his pants, and then takes out his penis. She grabs his penis and starts sucking on it like a wild animal. Another guest bends one of the ladies over a chair and thrusts his penis in her after ripping off her bikini bottom. The guest continue scream and whistle. Jeff Willard grabs a sexy Asian girl by the hair and starts smacking her in the face, until blood seeps from her nose. She falls to the floor. A couple of the other guests run over and start stomping her in her stomach. Her scream for help went on deaf ears. One of the guests squat over her and pulls down his pants. He defecates on her face. Some of the guys start to heave, while others just laugh. Sir Marcus starts to cringe when seeing this.

The majority of the guests preferred women, while others enjoyed alternative pleasures. "For you guys that are in something a little different, I bring you the sexiest studs this side of the western hemisphere! Terrance shouted. Jose at this time, is sitting on the couch getting blow jobs from 2 white girls. Sir Marcus is so distraught from the spectacle, he hides over in the corner, near the bottom of the staircase. The doors to a back room open. This time a lineup of young male models wearing G strings come out. "If you love fresh young dick and balls as much as I do, then go at it boys!" Terrance shouted. Some of the guests were hesitant. "Come gentlemen! Don't be shy! Your secret is safe with us!" Terrance chuckled. Horace Willard grabs one of the young studs by the hand and starts kissing him. After a few lines of cocaine and pills, Willard starts acting more erratic. He grabs the young man's face and rips his nose off with his teeth. The young man starts screaming as 2 more guest piling on him tearing at his face. The guests back away from the young man as he screams for help. He swings and hits Willard in the face. An agent walks over, takes out his pistol. He shoots the young man in the head. All the victims, and some of the guests, even Sir Marcus flinch at the sound of the gun. The young man's body fall face first to the floor. A few guest start to laugh as the body lay on the floor twitching. Everyone continues with their own sadistic perversion. Sir Marcus couldn't believe his eyes when he sees this horrific act. 2 agents come to the floor and drag the body by the feet to a side room, leaving a long trail of blood on the checkered floor. "I guess he won't be Cumming tonight! Get it! Cumming tonight!" Terrance chuckled. One of the young ladies becomes terrified and tries to make a run for the exit. She gets to the door, but can't find a way to get the chains lose. "Hey guys! We've got a fish trying to get away!" Terrance shouts. Suddenly, 2 agents run over to the girl a start beating her to the floor. She is knocked out cold. 2 guests walk over and rip off her bikini and take turns fucking her as she lay unconscious. Mr. Boeman went over in a corner with 2 young studs and told one to fuck the other in the ass as he stood there with his pants down by his ankles masturbating. "This shit is really sick!" Sir Marcus says to himself.

Terrance heads over to a panel on the wall. He opens the panel, and then pressed a couple of buttons. Loud heavy metal music fills the room at very high decibels. Terrance starts jumping up and down, dancing in mercurial fashion. One muscular black stud walks by him. Terrance then jumps on his back, biting his ear until it's ripped from his face. The black stud screams at the top of his lungs. At this time, one of the servants come by holding a serving tray with a display of sharp daggers. 6 of the guests each grab a dagger and commence stabbing the young black man until he falls to the floor. One of the guests, who happened to be an "A" list actor, starts howling like a wolf after completing the horrific act. Terrance then spits out pieces of the ear on to the floor.

One girl runs pass Sir Marcus as she tries to escape up the spiral stairs. One of the guests catches her by the ankle, dragging her back down the stairs. Sir Marcus is so terrified, that he moves out of the way. He turns his head the other way when the guest slits her throat with one of the daggers. Movie star Jett Connors runs up to Sir Marcus naked, drenched in blood. He stands a few inches away from Sir Marcus. "This is fucking living, man!" Connors screams in Sir Marcus's face. Connors then turns around and goes after one of the male victims. Terrance, with a mouth full of blood, noticed that Sir Marcus looked disgusted with what was going on. He ponders with a sinister grin on his face. Terrance goes over to Sir Marcus after taking a glass of Vodka from a serving platter. "Take the edge off, and have a drink." Terrance chuckled. Sir Marcus shook his head. "What, not thirsty? I've got something else that'll knock your socks off!" Terrance chuckled. Terrance runs over to the panel on the wall and turns down the volume to the music. He grabs the microphone from the podium. "Listen up! Listen up!"

Terrance shouted. Only a few guests stand around to listen, while the others continue with their sadistic, bloody acts. Terrance whispers into the ear one of the agents standing next to him. The agent then walk over to a back room and unlocks it. "We've a few young ladies that refused to participate in the festivities! These bitches actually tried to escape earlier! Bring'em out!" Terrance shouts. Those guests who are interested in what's about to happen next, start applauding and whistling. The agent then bring out 3 young ladies chained together by their hands. All 3 ladies are blind folded with duct tape over their eyes. The agent pushes the ladies into the middle of the room. Terrance goes over and removes the duct tape from their eyes. The last young lady to be unveiled shocked Sir Marcus so, that hell fell to his knees. The girls are standing in the middle of the room crying and shaking in terror. Terrance runs over to Sir Marcus and kneels down to him. Terrance covers the microphone so no one could hear his words to Sir Marcus. "Now, you're going to prove to me that you've got what it takes to live in my world!" Terrance whispered. Terrance stands, while Sir Marcus remains on his knees.

What shocked Sir Marcus was that he knew 2 of the girls. One of the girls he knew all of his life. The other girl he didn't recognize, was a tall blonde with a curvy figure. "Hey guys! You can rip the blonde bitch into pieces now!" Terrance shouted over the microphone. 5 of the guests snatch the blonde girl off of her feet. They take her on the couch and start to sodomize her until the couch is soaked with blood. Terrance takes a dagger and tosses it on the floor in front of Sir Marcus. "Now, I want you to take the dagger and rip the guts out of the curly haired one!" Terrance chuckled. Sir Marcus shakes his head. "I'm not doing it, you fucking sick bastard!" Sir Marcus said. Terrance smiles. He walks over to Sir Marcus and puts his lips to his ear. Well, if you don't do it, I'll tell our creative guests to have their way with your cousin! By the way. Your uncle Eddie told me a while back that she was the best piece of ass he'd ever had." Terrance whispered. An agent standing behind Sir Marcus pulls out his pistol and aims it at the back of his head. "If you try to stab me, the agent will blow your head off, and your cousin would still become food for these animals." Terrance whispered. Sir Marcus slowly picks up the dagger and stand to his feet. "Good boy." Terrance chuckled. Sir Marcus gazes at the curly haired girl. He starts breathing heavily. "Go! Go kill that whore bitch!" Terrance shouted. Sir Marcus starts perspiring. He walks over to the frightened girl, with Terrance and the agent close behind. "Gentlemen! Watch as my friend here guts this whore open like the pig she is!" Terrance shouted. Terrance stands behind Sir Marcus. "Kill her! Kill her! Kill her!" he whispered in Sir Marcus's ear. The guests surrounding the scene start chanting along with Terrance. "Kill her! Kill her! Kill her!" they all yell. Tears start to run down Sir Marcus's cheek. "Like I said. You have to have street cred." Terrance whispered. Sir Marcus holds the dagger tight in his hand. He starts trembling. "I'm sorry!" Sir Marcus said to the girl. He screams as he plunges the dagger into the girl's viscera. "Ariel!" Samara screamed. Ariel falls to the floor. The guests applaud and cheer for Sir Marcus. Sir Marcus drops the dagger from his hand, as he stands over Ariel's body. Blood starts oozing from her stomach. A couple of agents grab her by the ankles and drag her out of the room, again, leaving a trail of blood behind.

Samara stands there trembling as pee runs down her leg. "Now, gentlemen! Do you want to see my friend here, cum?" terrace shouted. A few guests applaud and cheer. "I can't hear you!"

Terrance chuckled. "Hell yeah!" the few guests scream even louder. Terrance stands face-to-face with Sir Marcus. "Now, I want you to drop your pants to down to your ankles" Terrance ordered Sir Marcus. "Fuck you!" Sir Marcus said. "You have 3 seconds or she dies a slow, painful death." Terrance whispered. Sir Marcus looks over at samara, as she cries. He slowly unzips his uniform pants. The pants fall to the floor around his ankles. "Good!" Terrance said. One of the agents grab Samara. He stands her in front of her cousin, face-to-face. The agent forces her to her knees. Terrance then grabs Samara by the hair. "Now, I want you to ram your cock into this whore's mouth!" Terrance chuckled. At this point, Sir Marcus's penis is flaccid. He tries to force his penis into his cousin's mouth, but Samara refuses to open up. Terrance squeezes her jaw until she opens her mouth. "Suck it! Suck it! Suck it! Suck it!" The crowd starts chanting. Terrance puts his face closer to Samara's face to get a better view. Sir Marcus starts to moan a little. He looks down at his cousin's beautiful face. He fights the urge not to become erect. Sir Marcus closes his eyes to blind his lust. "Ah, ah, ah! That's cheating! Keep your eyes on her pretty face my friend, or she dies!" Terrance chuckled. Samara looks up at her cousin. "It looks like your cousin needs some assistance. Now grab it!" Terrance whispers in Samara's ear. Samara grabs Sir Marcus's penis, causing it to become more firm. Evidently, Samara was good at what she was doing. Sir Marcus arrived at a full erection. His moans become more intense. "Suck it! Suck it! Suck it! Suck it!" the crowd continues to yell. Samara jerks her cousin's penis faster and faster causing Sir Marcus to explode into her mouth. Terrance laughs hysterically as semen drips down his hand. Terrance then stands to his feet. "Agent! Your weapon!" Terrance shouts. The agent hands Terrance his weapon. Terrance aims the gun at the back of Samara's head. Sir Marcus takes a step back, almost tripping over his pants. He has shame on his face as the crowd applauds. Terrance then pulls the trigger. "Nooo!" Sir Marcus screams. He witnesses his cousin's head being blown away. Her body quickly falls to the floor, but Sir Marcus sees in slow motion. The sound of the gun fire is deafening. Sir Marcus can see the crowd applauding, but can hear nothing. Blood starts seeping out of samara's lifeless body. Sir Marcus falls to his knees. "Samara!" he shouts. Jose walks over to Sir Marcus. "Man, you knew this bitch?" Jose asked. Sir Marcus just stares at Jose, crying. Jose shakes his head, then walks away. The crowd standing around had dispersed.

Besides a semi-automatic pistol and a communications device in their ear, each agent was equipped with a syringe filled a potent anesthetic to knock out their victims once injected. It was kept hidden inside their jacket pockets.

Terrance looks at the agent who handed him the gun. "Agent! Are friend here needs to rest!" Terrance said. The agent pulls out his syringe. He quickly injects it into Sir Marcus's neck. Within seconds, Sir Marcus falls to the floor. The last thing he sees is a young lady being gang banged by 3 of the guests.

Looking up at the top of the staircase, Terrance sees his boss slowly walking down the stairs guarded by 8 agents all around him. "Gentlemen! Gentlemen! Can I have your attention?" Terrance shouted. Most of the guests stop whatever brutal activity they are doing. "I would like to introduce the man who put this all together! My boss, the great Dragan Serpiente!" Terrance shouts on the microphone. Old man Charles Scott, CEO of New World Construction, stands out from the crowd naked drenched in blood, is the first to applaud. Serpiente waves at the crowd as they applaud. He lowers his arms, and the crowd becomes silent. Serpiente reaches the bottom of the staircase. Terrance hands him the microphone.

Serpiente is not wearing his Gore-Tex body suit. Instead, his is wearing a gold skimpy Minnie dress, and a purple wig on his head. Everyone noticed that he came out barefoot, having toe nails resembling talons. Serpiente taps the microphone a couple of times. "Is this thing turned on? Are you turned on?" Serpiente said as he shakes his frail hips. Most of the crowd goes wild with laughter and whistles. "I would like to thank you all for coming out to-night! The Master appreciates your energy by taking this country by storm with raw power and guts!" Serpiente shouted the crowd cheers.

Jose is standing amongst the crowd. He looks up at the top of the staircase. He sees a shadowy figure standing there. The mysterious being puts a hand on the railing. Jose noticed from afar that his hand was pale green and scaly. The fingernails of this being were long and dark.

"Ego illi qui pascitur! Non ad eum pertinent!" Serpiente shouted while staring into Jose's eyes. There were very few applause. It was evident that the guests weren't familiar with Latin dialect. This made Jose feel uncomfortable. "Pero, no temas a mi amigo! Es posible que nos pertenece, pero el mundo es tuyo!" Serpiente said as he points his clammy, disfigured hand at Jose. Jose's eyes tear up. He quickly walks over to Serpiente and kneels down before him. One agent reaches for his pistol, thinking Serpiente is in danger. Serpiente signals him to stand down. Jose gently grabs his hand and kisses the back of it. Serpiente strokes Jose's bald head like a trained pet.

The remaining victims make a dash for the main exit to escape, but the doors are well chained together. The agents on the other side could hear their screams. The screams become fainter minute by minute.

"For those of you who are new to the collective, I give you the gift of all gifts!" Serpiente shouts. His words give Terrance the signal to trot to a secret door.

A short scrawny elderly man in the crowd, stands rubbing his hands together waiting for whatever was to come through the door. "I've been waiting for this moment all evening!" the elderly man said as he salivates. He was wearing nothing but blood stained underwear. His name was Solomon Levine, a.k.a the old man.

Levine has been the overseer of all illegal drug distribution in Florida since Benny Lassenberry first arrived to New Jersey. It is rumored that Levine is the illegitimate son of Serpiente, but no one has confirmed it.

"Gentlemen! On behalf of the master! I give you fresh blood!" Serpiente shouted. Terrance opens the door. Out of the room, a little blonde haired boy, crying at the top of his lungs. The boy couldn't been no more than 5 years old. The boy was totally naked. Terrance grabs him by the arm, and yanks him violently out of the way, causing him to fall to the floor. Levine grabs the boy, and stands him to his feet. Levine starts massaging his back. He kisses the little boy. "This shit here, always made me sick to my stomach!" Lawrence Hall of Chicago whispers to the man next to him. Being forced out of the room, are more little children crying and screaming. Most of the children, about 25 of them, are of African American and Hispanic Descent. Their ages were from 3 to 10 years old. There were a handful of white and Asian kids, who were given to the top guys like Terrance and Levine. The first Caucasian child to come out was personally for Levine.

The NA hierarchy kept the kidnapping of white children down to the bare minimum. Fear of a government investigation would cause the NA structure to crumble if white children were missing in hordes. As for African American children, neglect was common in poverty stricken communities. The Hispanic children were mostly seized at the Mexican border.

Serpiente was told by his master a long time ago that the blood of an innocent child was the fountain of youth. The men who preferred children, were given daggers by the servants. The digestion of blood didn't stop the aging process, but caused the aging to slow down. Serpiente and Levine were living proof of that.

Levine looks at the little boy. He turns him around, examining his body. Suddenly, Levine takes the little boy's arm with one hand and holds his head still with the other. Levine then takes a big chunk out of the boy's throat. The child dies instantly. Blood spews out of the boy's main artery like a fountain. Levine catches the flow with his mouth.

It was around 10 in the morning, Sir Marcus had awaken from his slumber. He jumps up to find himself in a king size bed. The bedroom he was in was lavish. He noticed there weren't any windows to the outside world in this bedroom. Still wearing his uniform, he noticed his pants unzipped and his green sash stained with blood. Still groggy, he staggers out of bed. He holds on to the bed posts to get his balance. He then staggers to the door and opens it. He looks out into the hall and sees nothing but life size statues, suits of amore and fancy paintings lining the halls at both ends. He reaches into his pocket and pulls out his mobile phone. He realizes it's not working. He then makes his way down the hall. He looks down from the top of the spiral staircase and sees an old white man in beige coveralls mopping up the blood stained floor. Sir Marcus then creeps down the stairs. When he reaches the last step, he sees a pile of bodies stacked near the exit, individually wrapped in sheets. Horrified, Sir Marcus collapses to the floor, on his butt. "It wasn't a dream." He whispers to himself. "Sir! Are you ok, sir?" the old man with the mop asked. "Where are those bodies headed?" Sir Marcus asked. "Sorry sir, but that's not for me to answer." The old man said. He continues to mop up the pool of blood. Sir Marcus stands and walks over to the pile of bodies. He noticed that some of the bodies were small. He unwraps the sheet from the face of one of the small bodies. Tears fall from his cheeks when he sees that it was a little black girl. Sir Marcus turns toward the old maintenance guy and tackles him to the floor. Sir Marcus straddles him and balls up his fist, ready to punch him. He looks into his eyes and sees that there is no sign of emotion. It was like he was a machine or in a trance. You're just like the agents!" Sir Marcus said. He gets off the old man. The old man picks up the mop and continues his work as if nothing happened. Sir Marcus walks outside and sees the bodies being thrown in the back of a garbage truck. The truck had no signs on it or a license plate. The agent that accompanied Sir Marcus to Maine appears from out of nowhere. He startles Sir Marcus. "Are you ready to head back to the air field Sir?" the agent asked. Sir Marcus catches his breath. "We're not leaving until I find my cousin's body!" Sir Marcus shouted. "Sorry sir, but we can't interfere with procedures after a gathering." The agent said. "I said I'm not leaving!" Sir Marcus shouts. The agent says nothing. Suddenly, Sir Marcus's vision becomes blurry. He falls to the ground. There was another agent that came from behind and injected him. "Help me get him to the limo." The agent said.

It was January 3rd, around 10:20 in the morning. Sir Marcus wakes up and finds himself in the back of the limo. He looks out the window and sees that he's parked right on the tarmac at Teterboro airport. There is no agent nor private jet in sight. Sir Marcus looks over the front seat and finds that the keys are still in the ignition. Still groggy, Sir Marcus just lays back down until he regains his strength. Suddenly, decides to check his pocket for his phone. He finds out the phone works now. He presses a button to speed dial. Tony's mobile phone rings. Tony is sitting on the toilet reading the paper. He grabs the phone from off the bathroom sink. Tony recognizes the number. "Where the hell you been, man? You have to always stay in contact with me! It's my job to protect you!" tony shouted. "Just shut up, and listen for a minute! Where are you?" Sir Marcus asked. "I'm in West Orange!" tony said. "Ok! Meet me at the castle! I'll be there in a couple of hours!" Sir Marcus said. "I would, but the agents won't let me pass the gates!" tony said. "What?" Sir Marcus asked. "Yeah! Sir Edward gave them strict orders not to let anyone into the castle until you returned!" tony said. "Well, Damnit I'm back! Just stay outside the gates until I get there!" Sir Marcus ordered. "Where are you? I'll come get you!" tony said. "I'm too far away! Just do what I told you! I'm out!" Sir Marcus clicks off the phone.

A few hours later, tony is fast asleep in his car, about a 100 yards away from the castle grounds. He is awakened by a tapping on his window. It's Sir Marcus. Tony rolls down the window. "I thought I told you to meet me outside the gate!" Sir Marcus said. "I thought it would be wise for them not to see me! Something just don't feel right!" tony said. "You don't know the half! Just follow me back to the castle! I'll make it right again!" Sir Marcus said. Sir Marcus walks back to the limo. Tony follows behind in his car. When the limo approaches the gate, Sir Marcus orders the agents to let tony pass. A golf cart awaits them.

Inside the office, tony waits for Sir Marcus to come back from paying Sir Edward a visit. Inside Sir Edward's chambers, Charlie and Sif Edward are eating lunch. Sir Marcus enters Sir Edward's kitchen. He stands there for a moment watching Charlie feed his uncle. He clears his throat to get their attention. Charlie jumps up from his chair, knocking a bowl of fruit on the floor. Sir Marcus shakes his head. "Sir Marcus! Glad to see you back!" Charlie said "So, you 2 were holding down the fort? Where's my wife and son?" Sir Marcus asked. "You…look… like…shit." Sir Edward said. "Answer my question!" Sir Marcus shouted. "She told us that she was taking the baby to her family's island, since she couldn't get in contact with you." Charlie said. Sir Marcus takes out his mobile phone. He presses his wife's number. The phone rings 4 times. Kimberly picks up. "Hey babe! I made it home safe!" Sir Marcus said. "Where the hell have you been? I've been trying to call you since yesterday!" Kimberly shouted. "Sorry babe! I couldn't get a signal from where I was! Why did you leave?" Sir Marcus asked. "I had to! Your uncle was creeping me out rolling up and down the halls in that motorized wheel-chair you bought him!" Kimberly giggled. Sir wasn't laughing. In fact, he didn't say a word. "Hello, sweetie? Are you there?" Kimberly asked. "Yeah babe. I'm here. Listen. Could it be possible for you to stay at the island until Friday?" sir Marcus asked. "Why? What are you up to? Why can't we come home now?" Kimberly asked. "I have some real important business to take care of! You and the baby will just be a distraction!" Sir Marcus said. "Seriously?" Kimberly shouts. "Yes. Seriously." Sir Marcus said in a timid voice. Kimberly clicks off her phone. "Baby? Babe?" Sir Marcus shouted. Sir Marcus puts his phone back in his pocket. He storms out of the kitchen. "Is everything alright? Did I do something wrong?" Charlie asked.

Minutes later, Sir Marcus arrives back at his office. Tony was sitting, reading a magazine. Sir Marcus comes in the office fuming. "Everything ok?" tony asked. "He told me not to go! He told me!" Sir Marcus said to himself. "Who told you not to go, where?" tony asked. Sir Marcus ignores Tony's question. Sir Marcus stops pacing the room. "This is what I want you to do! Go to hakim. Bring him here at mid-night, tonight! Understand?" Sir Marcus said. Tony nods his head. "Are you going to be ok while I'm gone?" tony asked. "Sure! I'll be fine. What you need to do, is take an agent or 2 with you just in case something goes bad." Sir Marcus said. "Got it." Tony said. "I'm about to go jump in the shower. Tony puts on his coat and heads out the door. Sir Marcus sits at his desk. He pulls off his jack boots and unbuttons his uniform jacket. Sir Marcus opens the drawer and pulls out an automatic pistol wrapped in a linen cloth, and checks to see if it's loaded. He then wipes off his finger prints with the cloth and places it back in the drawer. He heads to the office bathroom.

The bathroom was decked out like it belonged in a penthouse. It had marble floors, a separate walk in shower and bathtub, a towel closet and a bidet. What Sir Edward wanted most of all in the bathroom while under construction, was a giant mosaic picture of the Lassenberry coat-of-arms. Engraved into the wall.

Sir Marcus comes out of his uniform, leaving it on the floor. He walks into the shower and turns on the water. After letting the spray down on him, he sits on the shower floor and starts crying. About 8 minutes later, Sir Marcus comes out of the bathroom in a bathrobe and slippers. He picks up his uniform and sash off the floor. He then takes off the medals, placing them on the desk. He pushes the intercom button on the desk. "Agent! Find Lucy and tell her to come to my office!" Sir Marcus said. "Right away sir." The agent said. Sir Marcus goes over to the couch and grabs a magazine from the magazine rack. He takes the magazine back to his chair.

About 15 minutes later, there's a knock on the door. Sir Marcus puts the magazine down. "Come in!" he shouts. In comes Lucy. "You called for me señor?" Lucy asked. "Yes, I'd like you to get me a fresh uniform, underwear, black dress sox, scrubbing brush and black shoe polish for my boots." He ordered. "Would like me to take the uniform on the desk and get it cleaned?" Lucy asked. "Nah, you can leave it there." Sir Marcus said. "Yes señor." Lucy said before she leaves the office.

It was around 5:50 pm when tony finally caught up with hakim. He and Bex had moved into a new apartment in Bloomfield, New Jersey. Tony had just came from BIG SHOTS where he tried to get information on the brothers' whereabouts. One of the female employees told him that they were in Bloomfield, but didn't know exactly where. Tony had received the info from a Gatano associate who hung out at the local pub on Broad Street.

The apartment was a few blocks down from the pub. Tony's limo pulls up in front of the apartment complex. "What a dump!" tony said to himself. One of the agents gets out of the limo and opens the door for tony. Tony gets out and looks both ways down the street. "Yo! Up here, man!" said a voice coming from the apartment complex. Tony looks up at the second floor to see Bex looking out the window. "Open the door! I'm coming up!" tony shouts. Bex comes down stairs, wearing a t-shirt and sweat pants. "Stay here." Tony tells the agent. Tony comes face-to-face with Bex. The 2 shake hands. "How the hell you find us here?" Bex asked. "This is what I do!" tony said. "Hakim stepped out for a minute. He should be back in a few." Bex said. "Can I wait here for him?" tony asked. "Yeah, I guess so!" Bex said. Tony follows Bex upstairs.

Inside the apartment, tony noticed the place decked out with new furniture. There was a huge floor model TV against the wall. Bex was in the middle of playing a video game. "You guys should get yourselves one of those new flat screen TV's. You can hang them on the wall like a picture." Tony said. "Man, this my brother's spot! I'm thinking about buying a house!" Bex said. Tony makes himself at home by sitting on the leather sofa. "You wanna play? I got an extra controller." Bex said. "No thanks. I haven't played in a while. You'll just end up beating me." Tony said. "You wanna a beer?" Bex asked. Tony looks at his watch. "Yeah, I'll take one." Tony said. Bex puts the controller down on the table and heads for the kitchen. He goes into the refrigerator and gets 2 beers. He grabs the bottle opener from the kitchen drawer and opens the bottles. He brings tony his beer. Tony takes a swig. Bex guzzles down half his beer and goes back playing the game. "Which team are you?" tony asked. "I'm the blue one." Bex said.

After 10 minutes of playing, Bex is losing to the computer. Tony takes another swig of his beer. He gulps down the rest. "I can go for another one!" tony said as he hands Bex the empty bottle. Bex pauses the game, takes the empty bottle from tony and makes another run. "Man, you getting your ass kicked!" tony said. Bex comes out of the kitchen with2 more beers. "Man, I'll bust yo ass!" Bex said. Bex hands tony his beer. "Where's that controller?" tony asked. Bex gets up and grabs the other controller from off the top of the TV. He plugs it in, and hands it to tony. Tony takes off his coat, and drapes it over the back of the sofa. Tony takes a swig of his beer. "Let's do this!" tony said. Bex stars the game over for 2 players. "I have to pick my favorite team first." Bex said. "It won't matter home boy! You're about to get your ass ran into the ground!" tony said.

For the next 15 minutes, Bex and tony play the game, with Bex leading the score. "Man, where's the bathroom?" tony asked. "Don't make excuses now!" Bex said. "Seriously! I have to take a leak!" tony said. "Down the hall, to your left." Bex chuckled. Tony heads to the bathroom. Bex takes a swig of his beer. Seconds later, Hakim enters the apartment. "Who the fuck limo is that outside?" Hakim asked. Bex points in the direction of the bathroom while drinking his beer. "Who's in there?" Hakim asked. "It's tony." Bex said. "What the fuck he want?" Hakim asked. "He said he's to see you." Bex said. "How the hell he fined us?" Hakim asked. Tony enters the living room. "Like I told your brother, this is what I do for a living." Tony said while drying his hands with a paper towel. "I hope you came back with some paper towels, because you're out." Tony said. "I know." Hakim said as he lifted grocery bag. "The boss wants me to bring you to the castle at mid-night." Tony said. Hakim puts the grocery bag on the kitchen table. "If he ain't talking about making me the boss of Essex County, we ain't got shit to talk about!" hakim said. "To be honest, I don't know what he wants with you! I'm just here to bring you to the castle at mid-night!" tony said. Hakim just stands there staring at tony. "What you got to lose by showing up?" tony asked. Hakim looks at the clock on the wall. "We got another 5 hours to go then!" Hakim said. "What you gonna do in the mean time?" Bex asked tony. "I'm gonna to finish playing this video game!" tony said. Hakim shook his head. "You eat yet?" Hakim asked tony. "Not really! What's for dinner anyway?" tony asked. "Fried chicken, wild rice and veggies." Hakim said. "Sounds good!" Tony said. "What about the robots outside?" Hakim asked. "Like you said, robots." Tony said. Bex laughs at his comment.

About an hour later, hakim calls Bex and tony to come into the kitchen. They both put their controllers down. As soon as tony enters the kitchen, he takes a whiff of hakim's cooking. "Smells good!" tony said. "I ain't no joke in the streets, and I ain't no joke in the kitchen." Hakim said. Tony and Bex take a seats at the table. Hakim had already set the table prior to them being seated. Hakim comes to the table holding a skillet full of steaming hot wild rice. Does the same with the chicken and veggies. He then takes out a bottle of hot sauce from the refrigerator. "You hood rats love hot sauce!" tony chuckled. "You damn right!" Hakim said. "You must be the first black man that didn't like hot sauce!" Bex said. Hakim takes his seat at the table. "Dig in niggas!" Hakim said.

An hour had passed, and the guys were all on their second helping. Hakim looks at tony. "So, how it feels taking Jabbo's spot." Hakim asked. "It's a lot of work! Between me and you, I really run things. The boss is just a figure head. The rules for these people we're dealing with, is there always have to be a male Lassenberry at the helm." Tony said. "Who made that rule?" Bex asked with a mouth full of food. "The same people that have those robots downstairs protecting us!" tony said. Hakim puts his fork down and wipes his mouth with his napkin. "You mean to tell us that only a male Lassenberry can run Jersey?" Hakim asked. Tony nods his head. Hakim scoffs. "Between you and me, Eddie Lassenberry is the only one in that family with balls! The rest of them are soft!" Hakim said. "Take it easy!" tony chuckled. "No, I'm just saying man! I knew mark and them since we were kids! None of them don't know shit about the streets!" hakim shouted. Tony changes the subject. "Damn, this food is good!" tony said. "Oh! It's like that know?" hakim asked. Tony just smiled before taking a bite of his chicken.

15 minutes later, tony and hakim go back into the living room. Bex stays in the kitchen to wash the dishes. Hakim turns on the TV. "I think the game is on." Hakim said. With a stomach full of beer and a good meal, tony nods out on the sofa. Hakim looks at him and shakes his head. "And he calls us hood!" hakim said to himself.

It was around 10:30pm, when hakim comes out of his bedroom. He sees tony asleep, still. Hakim kicks Tony's foot. Tony jumps up. "What the hell?" tony shouted. "It's about that time man. If we leave now, we can get there by 12." Hakim said. Tony clears his throat. "Ok, let's go!" Tony said. Tony stands and stretches. "Damn! That was a good sleep!" tony said. He puts on his coat. He heads to the door. "I'll meet you down at the limo." Tony said. Hakim heads to the closet and grabs his shearling coat. He snatches his house keys off the coffee table, and leaves the apartment.

When hakim gets outside, he sees an agent standing outside on the sidewalk. "I'll have to frisk you sir before you enter the limo." The agent said. "For real, man?" hakim scoffs as he raises his arms. The agent frisks hakim from neck to ankles. "Did you get a chance to eat or shit since you been out here?" hakim chuckled. "You may enter the limo now sir." The agent said. The limo drives off and jumps on the turnpike south. Tony and the agents were unaware that they were being followed by a black 98 Boeman Sedan.

When tony was fast asleep, hakim made a call from his land line to 2 Gunz. Gunz had arrived an hour before tony had awaken and parked at the end of the hakim's block.

It was about 5 minutes to mid-night, when the limo pulls up to the castle Lassenberry gates. The driver identifies himself, and the gates open. The limo enters the castle grounds. An agent opens the limo door for tony and hakim. They hop on a golf cart driven by another agent, who takes them into the interior of the castle. "I ain't never gonna get used to looking at this shit!" Hakim said.

Minutes later, they reach the west wing of the castle. The golf cart pulls up to the office door. Everyone exits the golf cart. The agent knocks on the door. "Enter!" Sir Marcus shouts. The agent opens the door for tony and hakim. They both enter the office. Hakim sees Sir Marcus sitting at his desk. Sir Marcus stands. He's dressed in a fresh uniform, with all 3 medals pinned on the left side of his chest. "Good to see." Sir Marcus said as he shook hakim's hand. "I hope you brought my ass out here for some good news!" Hakim said. "Have a seat." Sir Marcus said. Hakim takes off his coat and sits down in the chair on the opposite side of the desk. Sir Marcus sits in his chair, while tony takes off his coat and hangs it on the coat rack. Tony takes a seat on the sofa. "How was the ride here?" Sir Marcus asked. "Can't complain." Hakim said. "Can I get you anything?" Sir Marcus asked. "Nah, man. I'm cool." Hakim said. "Where's your brother?" Sir Marcus asked. "He didn't feel like coming." Hakim said. "No? You sure he didn't follow you in the Boeman sedan that was pulled over by the Merchantville Police?" Sir Marcus asked. Hakim's jaw dropped. "These good ol' boys out here in south Jersey love tax free cash!" Sir Marcus chuckled. Hakim raises his hands. "Ok! You got me!" Hakim Chuckled. "Just to let you know, I have cops from a hundred police departments on the payroll. It costs me 5 mill a year to keep them happy and to keep me informed." Sir Marcus said with a smile. "Alright! Alright! I'm impressed!" Hakim said. "I assure you the car is on its way back to Bloomfield in one piece." Sir Marcus said. "Let's get to it! "Why you bring me down here?" hakim asked. Sir Marcus opens the drawer to his desk. He takes out the pistol wrapped in linen, placing it on the desk. "Hold up, man! It ain't gotta go down like that!" hakim shouted with his hands in the air. "Take it easy. It's not for you." Sir Marcus said. Hakim slowly puts his hands down. "Then who's it for?" Hakim asked. Sir Marcus stands from his seat. "Tomorrow, I want you round up all the street bosses in Essex County and tell them you're the man to see from now on to get their refill." Sir Marcus said. Hakim went from shaking like a leaf, to having a smile from ear-to-ear. "You mean I'm the king of Essex County now?" Hakim asked. "No! You're the man running Essex County, for me!" Sir Marcus said. Sir Marcus pressed the intercom button on the desk. "Step into my office agent." Sir Marcus said. Within moments, an agent enters the office. He stands by his boss. "What this agent is going to do, is take you to the east wing of the castle. When you get there, I want you to take this gun and kill the 2 men there. The trick is, you have to make it look like a murder suicide. Then, and only then, will you run all of Essex County." Sir Marcus said. Hakim leans forward in his chair. "That's it? Just snuff 2 bodies, and the job is mine?"

Hakim asked. Sir Marcus nods his head. "Man, I'll kill a thousand niggas for the job!" Hakim said. Hakim stands from his chair. He looks at the gun, then grabs it. He follows the agent out the door. Tony approached the desk "What 2 men? The only guys in the east wing…Oh shit!" tony said. "It had to be done." Sir Marcus says in a calm voice. Tony falls into the chair, putting his head on the desk.

Minutes later, the cart arrives at the east wing. The agent gets out of the cart. Hakim follows the agent to the main entrance. The agent opens the door for hakim. "Walk straight ahead sir." The agent said. Hakim checks the weapon. He sees there are only 2 bullets. Hakim slowly walks down the corridor, checking each room. The agent was following a few feet behind with his weapon at his side. Hakim approached one of the living room. He sees someone sitting in a wheelchair, facing a huge flat screen TV. Hakim slowly walks up behind the wheelchair bound person. He puts the gun to the back of the head of the person. "Hey man! Where's your friend?" hakim asked. The man doesn't move or say a word. "I made some popcorn boss!" a voice shouts out from behind. All of a sudden, Charlie comes into the living room with a big bowl of popcorn. Hakim turns the gun on Charlie. "Oh shit!" Charlie shouts as the bowl of popcorn falls to the floor. "Charlie?" hakim shouts. "Hakim?" Charlie shouted. The agent puts his gun away while standing between hakim and Charlie. Hakim gets a better look at the man sitting in the wheelchair. Hakim shakes his head. Hakim points the gun at Charlie. "Get yo ass over here. Now!" hakim said. "What the hell I do, man?" Charlie cried. "I said get over here!" hakim shouted. Charlie walks over and stands by his boss. Hakim keeps his gun on Charlie. He then kneels down in front of the man he used to call pop. "So, this is how it ends." Hakim said. The agent pulls out his weapon. He points it at Charlie. Sir Edward, sitting in his wheelchair, didn't show any sign of emotion. He just gazed into hakim's eyes. "Why didn't you come visit me in that hell hole?" hakim asked as a tear trickled down his cheek. Charlie was shaking. "Whatever you gonna do man, please don't!" Charlie says to hakim. "Shut the fuck up nigga!" hakim shouted. "Answer me old man! Why the hell you ain't come see me?" hakim shouted. Sir Edward just smiled at hakim. "You think this a joke nigga?" hakim shouted as he pointed the gun to Sir Edward's head. "No…matter…you do… to…me, you will…never… be… a… Lassenberry!" Sir Edward chuckled. Hakim stands, still having the gun at Sir Edward's head. He squeezes the trigger. Charlie flinches. "Oh god, no!" Charlie screamed. The sound of the gun fire echoed throughout the east wing. Sir Edward's head slumps over as if he'd just nodded off. Blood began to drizzle out of his forehead. The back of his head had a huge gaping hole. Hakim walks over to the agent and grabs his pistol. The agent didn't resist. Charlie runs over and drops to his knees in front of Sir Edward's lifeless body. He hugged his boss as he sobbed. Blood began dripping on Charlie's shoulder. Hakim walks over to Charlie and lays down the gun he shot Sir Edward with on the floor next to him. Hakim points the agent's gun at Charlie. "Listen Charlie! I always liked you, but you're standing between me and destiny!" Hakim said. Charlie still had his arms around Sir Edward crying. "You got 2 choices man! Either, take the gun and do yourself, or I'll shoot in the stomach so you die a slow painful death!" Hakim said. Still on his knees, Charlie turns toward hakim sobbing like a baby. "Please! Please hakim! I promise I'll be good! Please don't kill me!"

Charlie shouted. Just put the gun to yo head man, and pull the trigger! It'll end quickly! I promise!" hakim said. Charlie was trembling. He slowly grabs the gun. "Come on Charlie! The quicker you do it, the less painful it'll be!" Hakim said.

Back at the office, Sir Marcus walks over to tony. Tony still crying with his head down on the desk, feels a hand on his shoulder. Tony looked towards Sir Marcus. "We still need him! I still go to him sometimes!" tony cried. "No. we don't need him." Sir Marcus said. Tony sits up straight in his chair. He wipes the tears from his eyes. Sir Marcus takes his hand off of his shoulder. "I run things. Remember that." Sir Marcus said. "I need to go for a walk." Tony said. Sir Marcus nods his head. Tony stands from his seat. He faces Sir Marcus, standing at attention. "Long live the house of Lassenberry." He said in a calm voice. Tony leaves the office.

Outside in the corridor of the west wing, tony walks past an agent sitting in a golf cart. "Can I give you a ride somewhere sir?" the agent asked. Tony didn't say a word. He shook his head and continued down the corridor, heading east. Suddenly, he hears the faint sound of a gun going off. Tony stops and drops his head, and continues his trek.

It was around 6:15am, mark senior is awaken from his sleep. The phone was ringing on his night stand. His wife Tanya was fast asleep. On her night stand was a bottle of sleeping pills and an empty drinking glass. "Hello?" mark sr. said. "Pop. It's really important you and your brothers come to the castle today." Sir Marcus said. "What, what's wrong son?" mark sr. asked as he rubbed his eyes. "I can't talk over the phone pop. Just tell Uncle Jake and Uncle Danny I'll have a limo pick them up later." Sir Marcus. Mark sr. starts to panic. He sits up at the edge of the bed. "Is Kimberly and the baby alright?" he asked his son. "Their fine! Just get dressed, and be ready when the limo comes!" Sir Marcus said. "Ok! Ok!" mark sr. said. Sir Marcus clicks his phone off.

It was around 10am, when mark sr.'s limo arrives at the castle. The agent at the gate gives the signal, and the gate slides slowly open. Mark sr. saw that there were 2 other limos parked on the castle grounds. He is then escorted to a golf cart by another agent. "Where the hell is my son?" mark sr. asked the agent. I'm taking you to him now sir." The agent said.

The golf cart enters the castle. The agent drives down the corridor, heading towards the west wing. Mark sr. holds on tight from fear of falling out of the cart. Within minutes, the golf cart stops in front of Sir Marcus's office. The agent tries to assist mark sr. out of the cart, but mark sr. pushes his hand out of the way. The agent knocks on the office door. "Come in!" Sir Marcus shouts. The agent opens the door to let mark sr. pass through.

Inside the office Danny sr. and jakes sr. are sitting on the couch, while Sir Marcus is sitting at his desk. Tony was leaning up against the wall with his arms folded. "What the hell took you so long?" Danny sr. asked. "Had to make a detour because of construction." Mark sr. said. Sir Marcus stands and goes over to hug his father. "It's good to see you son! Now, tell me what the hell this is all about!" mark sr. said. Sir Marcus takes a deep breath. "This is hard to say! That's why I need you all to follow me, and see for yourselves!" Sir Marcus said. Sir Marcus, his father, uncles and tony leave the office and pile in the golf cart. Minutes later, the driver of the golf cart stops at the main entrance of the east wing. Everyone gets out of the golf cart and follows Sir Marcus through the main entrance. They all walk down the corridor of the east wing, passing several rooms before arriving at the living room. "Brace yourselves." Sir Marcus advised the group. Mark sr. stops in his tracks when he sees a body laid out on the floor, covered with a bloody sheet. He then sees his brother slumped over in his wheelchair, with a huge hole in the back of his head. Jake sr. starts to gag from the horrific smell of death. Danny sr. doesn't show any emotion. He just shook his head. Mark sr. falls to his knees screaming. "My brother! Oh, my poor brother!" he cried. Tony and Sir Marcus struggle to lift the old man from off the floor. Mark sr. had gained a credible amount of weight over the years. Jake sr. walks over to the dead body that was covered. He lifts the sheet and sees Charlie Dalton with a gunshot wound to the temple. Danny sr. stood in the background with his hands in his pockets. "What the fuck happened?" Jake sr. shouts. Sir Marcus walks over to his uncle. "I hate to say it uncle, but it looks like a murder suicide." Sir Marcus said. Jake sr. looks at his nephew with disbelief. "A what?" jakes sr. asked. "I found out not too long ago from one of my men that these 2 were having a lover's quarrel. I'm just saying, maybe that led to this! Sir Marcus said. "A lover's quarrel?" Jake sr. asked. Sir Marcus nods as he gazes at Charlie's body. "Why didn't you call the police first?" Danny sr. asked. Sir Marcus turns to his uncle. "Then what? Have them do an investigation around here?" Sir Marcus asked. "That would've made sense nephew!" Danny sr. said. Sir Marcus ignores his uncle's comment. Sir Marcus noticed that his father was having a hard time standing. "Get my father a chair! Quick!" Sir Marcus shouts at the agent. The agent runs to other end of the room and grabs a reinforced chair with a leather cushion. He brings it over so that mark sr. can sit and catch his breath. "I'll go get him a glass of water." Tony said. The agent helps mark sr. in his chair. Jake sr. looks at his brother's body. "Pop never exposed us to shit like this!" he said to himself. Danny sr. has a smirk on his face. "You're the head of the family fortune now! So, what's your next move?" Danny sr. asked Sir Marcus. Suddenly, tony comes back with the glass of water, and gives it to mark sr. "I know some people that can make this disappear." Sir Marcus said.

Beside the sheet covering Charlie's body, the crime scene was untampered with. The gun was still in Charlie's hand. "Listen nephew! I'm gonna have to step up on this one! It's my brother!" Jake sr. said. "Alright. You all hear that? Uncle Jake is gonna take care of it!" Sir Marcus shouts.

The next day around 2pm, police received reports of a peculiar odor coming from an apartment in Newark. It was an elderly black couple who made the 911 call. When the police arrived on the scene, they had to cover their noses from smell of death. One of the officers kicked the door in when there was no response to their announcement. With guns drawn, they slowly make their way through the apartment. The female officer sees a body lying on the floor as she enters the bedroom. She point her weapon at the figure sitting in the wheelchair. Her partner enters the bedroom. "These guys are stiffs." She says to her partner. The other officer takes a closer look. "Holy shit! You realize who we got here?" the male officer said. The female officer shook her head. "This is Eddie Lassenberry!" he said. The female officer shrugged her shoulders, looking puzzled. "The son of Benny Lassenberry? The guy who used to run all the drugs in Essex County?" the male officer tried to explain. "Oh! Benny Lassenberry! I thought he was put away forever." She said. "He was! After they threw away the key on that guy, I thought I wouldn't hear the lassenberry name again! Now this shit happened!" the male officer said. "I'm no expert, but this looks like a murder suicide to me!" the female officer said.

The bodies of Sir Edward and Charlie Dalton were strategically placed in the bedroom the same way they were found by Jake sr. in the castle. The media was all over the crime scene. It made national news that the son of a former drug lord was involved in a murder suicide. The attorney General of New Jersey had made a public announcement from Trenton that there was a gaping hole in the power structure of the Lassenberry organization. Since the imprisonment of Benny Lassenberry years ago. Now that the body of Eddie Lassenberry was discovered, the attorney general had assured the public that the Lassenberry drug ring was no more.

A week later, Sir Marcus was standing on the outskirts of a land field in Staten Island. He was wearing jeans, a tattered wool coat and worn down hiking boots. He rubs his hands together to keep warm from the frigid air. He stood there watching a flock of seagulls hovering over a huge pile of trash over in the distance. He also sees off in the distance a yellow taxi cab heading in his direction. He looked at his watch. It was 12:05 in the afternoon. The cab driver at high speed, comes to a screeching halt 5 feet in front of Sir Marcus. Sir Marcus doesn't flinch at all. He just stands there with his hands in his pockets. Exiting the driver's side was Terrance Haggerty. He's all smiles. "Didn't mean to scare you!" Terrance chuckled. "You didn't." Sir Marcus said. "I'm talking about what took place at the gathering." Terrance chuckled. Terrance walks over to Sir Marcus. He too was dressed down for the meeting, wearing a flight jacket jeans and sneakers. "Smart location you've picked. I wouldn't never thought of coming to a dump site for a meeting!" Terrance chuckled. Sir Marcus raises his hand in the air. "Put your hands down!" Terrance chuckled. "Aren't you going to frisk me for a wire?" sir Marcus asked. Terrance starts laughing. "Only mobsters and crooked cops do that!" Terrance chuckled. "Not afraid of the law. Huh?" Sir Marcus asked. "Sir Marcus! We are the law!" Terrance continued to chuckle. Sir Marcus shook his head. "Now, let's talk business. "I want the last remaining counties in south jersey." Sir Marcus said. "I don't see why not. The Amish man is out of the picture." Terrance chuckled. "I already know the Mexican Cartel is going to have a problem with it." Sir Marcus said. "True. I don't think the Mexicans would have a problem with letting go of such a small client, when they have all of the West Coast in their grips. But, if they try to disrupt the flow of things, we have people in U.S. border patrol that can make life pretty uncomfortable for them." Terrance chuckled. "That's all I wanted to hear!" Sir Marcus said. He walks away from Terrance. "Need a lift?" Terrance shouted. Sir Marcus shook his head and continued to walk away. "Fucking monster." Sir Marcus said to himself. Terrance's facial expression changes as he gets into the cab. He has nothing but hate in his eyes as he watched Sir Marcus walk away.

An hour later at BIG SHOTS, hakim was sitting in the back room at the poker table running bills through a banknote counter. Across from him was 8 rows of cash stacked 4 inches high. 2 Gunz was standing at the entrance with an Ak-47. Bex had his feet kicked up watching TV. "God damn! It's only been a week, and I got over a million in cash staring me in the face!" Hakim said. "But, what's gonna be left over after you pay off the cops and your people?" Bex asked. "Nigga! This pile right here, is just from Irvington! Imagine when the others come in for their refill! I ain't even count what came in from the Newark crew yet!" Hakim said. "Damn! That's just from Irvington?" Bex asked. Suddenly, the phone on the wall rings. "Pass me the phone!" Hakim said to Bex. Bex sighs as he gets up and grabs the receiver off the wall.

He hands it to hakim. "Hello?" hakim said. Hakim listens to the person on the other end. Hakim had a serious look on his face before he took the phone, but not he has a smile from ear to ear. "Now that's what I'm talking about!" Hakim shouted. He tosses Bex the receiver. "Hang it up!" hakim said. Bex hangs up the phone. "Who was that?" Bex asked. "It don't matter man, because I'm now looking at the soon to be king of Deep South Jersey!" hakim shouted. Bex looks around with an innocence on his face. He then points to himself. "Yeah, you nigga!" hakim shouted. Hakim jumps out of his seat. "You got it man! You got it!" hakim chuckled. Bex stood there in a daze. "How long it's gonna sink in that you're the one? Come here and give your brother a hug!" hakim said. "I got it? I really got it!" Bex shouted. 2 Gunz rolls his eyes. The 2 brothers jump up and down hugging each other, laughing hysterically. 2 Gunz stands at the door with the façade of being happy for the brothers.

CHAPTER 15. 5 GENERALS

It was the 2nd of March when Philadelphia mob boss only known as Mr. Nice, decided to have a sit down with hakim and his crew about Bex. He was a short obese old man with a hair full of gray hair. He spoke with a thick Italian accent. He kept a low profile as an owner of a rundown boxing gym in south Philly. His wife passed away from heart disease back in 1975, leaving him a widower of 4 children. No one, not even the men in his crew knew that he belonged to the inner circle that secretly ran the mafia families throughout the country. It was also a secret that he was a distant cousin of late mob bosses, Luigi Gatano and Alfonse Cucci. Out of all of his illegal activities, shaking down every small business in Philly and getting paid drug money from the Amish man were the 2 most lucrative vices that made him wealthy.

It was at mid-night when the meeting was scheduled to be held at the gym. Hakim, Mackie and 2Gunz pull up in front of the gym, driving a 2000 Boeman Jeep. They are given the signal by a Philly mob soldier to drive around the back entrance of the gym. The car slowly drives around back. "Stay focused boys!" Hakim said sitting in the back seat. There was a security light shining down at the back entrance. Hakim sees another Philly mob soldier standing at the entrance wielding a shot gun. He puts his hand up to signal the SUV to stop. Mackie stops the vehicle, leaving the engine running. The soldier then bangs on the door. 2 more soldiers come out the back door armed with pistols. With guns drawn on the vehicle, one of the soldiers tells Mackie to shut off the engine and exit the car. Hakim slowly steps out of the vehicle first, with hands in the air. "Take it easy y'all!" hakim said. 2 Gunz is the next to exit the vehicle. "Turn around and put your hands on the roof of the car!" the soldier said. Hakim and Gunz puts their hands on top of the SUV. "Get out of fucking car!" the soldier said to Mackie. Mackie slowly gets out of the vehicle with his hands in the air. The soldier grabs Mackie by the collar, with his gun pointed at his forehead. "Easy. Easy!" Mackie said. "Shut the fuck up!" the soldier shouts. He shoved Mackie over to where hakim is. Hakim, Mackie and 2 Gunz are all lined with their hands on the roof of the SUV.

The street that the gym was located, was on a dark industrial side street, far away from the main road. There was only one way out of the back entrance. Hakim and his crew didn't realize it, but it was soon blocked by 2 cars that just pulled up. The soldier with the shotgun covered hakim and his crew, while the other 2 soldiers frisk them from head-to-toe. "They're clean?" the solider with the shot gun asked. The 2 soldiers nod their heads. "Now strip down to your underwear boys!" the soldier with the shot gun said. "Man, its cold as shit out here!" 2 Gunz shouts. "It's 50 degrees to be exact! Now strip, and toss your clothes in the car!" the soldier said. 2 Gunz and Mackie look over at hakim. "Do it!" hakim ordered. Hakim and his crew take their time getting undressed. Hakim tossed his coat in the back seat, but neatly folds his pants and shirt and lays them on the seat. "What are you, some kind of neat freak?" one soldier asked. "That's a 2 hundred dollar shirt, my man!" hakim said.

Hakim was wearing a pair of boxers and a wife beater T-shirt. Mackie is also wearing boxers, but no T-shirt. 2 Gunz on the other hand, wasn't wearing any underwear at all. One of the soldiers whistle at Gunz. "Come on man! No underwear?" hakim said with disgust. "Alright boys! Let's get inside before your dicks shrivel up!" the soldier with the shotgun. Hakim leads the way to the back entrance, followed by Mackie. The soldier with the shotgun opens the door for them. "Keep your hands locked behind your heads and walk straight in and make a left!" the soldier said. One of the soldiers follow the group inside, while the other 2 stay outside and guard the SUV.

Hakim leads the group down a dimly lit hallway, and makes a left. He is told by the soldier with the shotgun to open the double doors. This entrance lead to the main gym area. It was the first time hakim and his crew had been in this place. They noticed old punching bags dangling from hooks, medicine balls on the floor and a filthy looking boxing ring with patches of dried blood on the canvas. They all walk through the gym to another set of doors that lead to a small office. The soldier with the shotgun knocks on the door. "Si accomdi!" the voice on the other side of the door shouts. Everyone enters the office.

The office was actually a huge locker room with lockers lined up against the walls with supply shelves. Hakim sees the man in charge sitting at a card table, with 2 other men sitting on both sides of him. The man sitting on Mr. Nice's left was much younger than Mr. Nice and the other gentleman. Mr. Nice looks at 2 Gunz and shook head with disgust. "Andiamo Ritchie! Hai dovuto portare quella in nudo?" Mr. Nice said. "Pop! It's not my fault he ain't wearing underwear!" Ritchie said. "Grab a towel off the shelf kid!" Mr. Nice said. 2 Gunz grabs a towel and covers his private area. There are a row of folding chairs next to the shelves of towels. "Go ahead and grab a seat!" Mr. Nice said to hakim and his crew. Mackie grabs 2 chairs and unfolds them for hakim and himself. 2 Gunz grabs a chair for himself. Hakim takes the seat in the middle. "Si Può uscire ora Ritchie." Mr. Nice said. "Come on pop! Why can't I stay in on this one?" Ritchie shouted. "Ritchie! Non farmi ripetere me stesso!" Mr. asked said. Ritchie has a tantrum like a child and storms out of the office. "Damn kids! Mr. Nice said. "So, you're Mr. Nice." Hakim said. "And you are hakim?" Mr. Nice asked. Hakim nods his head. "You're the man that's going to be responsible for making back the money I lost on the streets." Mr. Nice said. "It seems that way." Hakim said. "It's a good thing for you that the Amish man died from a bad heart." Mr. Nice said. Hakim folds his arms. "Why is that?" hakim asked. "Because kid, if there was any sign of foul play and then you come to me with this proposal, god help you! Understand?" Mr. Nice said. Hakim scratches his chin. "Point taken." Hakim said. "I want you to meet the man to my right. His name is Augustine. He does business for me out in Camden. He's been with me for years." Mr. Nice said as he pats Augustine on the back. "He will be my liaison between me and you." Mr. Nice said. "The what?" hakim asked. Mr. Nice sighs. "You'll give me my money through him every month!" Mr. Nice said. "Oh, we're talking money now?" hakim asked. "What'd you want to talk about?" Mr. Nice asked. "First I need the names and faces of all the top dealers in your jersey territory." Hakim said. "You plan to kill these people?" Mr. Nice asked. "No. they'll have a choice. Either they work for us or they move out of state." Hakim said. "How soon can you get this operation up and running kid?" Mr. Nice asked. "As soon as you can give me the information need." Hakim said. Hakim and Mr. Nice shook hands to seal the deal. "By the way kid. Who's running the show now that Eddie Lassenberry bit the bullet?" Mr. Nice asked hakim. Hakim looked at Mackie and smiled. He turns back to Mr. Nice. "I would like to know your real name, but I know that's not gonna happen." Hakim chuckled. There was a dead silence in the room. Augustine was shocked that hakim would say such a thing. Mr. Nice bursts out laughing. "I like your style kid! You got a huge set of balls on you!" Mr. Nice chuckled. Mr. Nice then clears his throat. "Now, let's talk money." Mr. Nice said. "Before you say anything, my sources say that the Amish man was kicking up to you a half a mill a month!" hakim said.

During the time that hakim was arranging the sit down with Mr. Nice, hakim went to Sir Marcus to get information on how the Philly crew operated. Sir Marcus then went to Terrance Haggerty and found out how Mr. Nice ran his crime family through NA surveillance. The NA were knew how many made guys were in the Philly crew, and knew how much cash the Amish man was kicking up to them for the past few years.

Mr. Nice smiled at hakim. "It seems you done your homework kid!" Mr. Nice said. "You're not dealing with a dummy! Or should I say, non ha a che fare con un manichino." Hakim said. Mr. Nice and his men jaws just dropped in disbelief. Mr. Nice started applauding hakim. "You're good kid! Just a little rusty saying certain things, but you're good!" Mr. Nice said. "Will a mill a month keep you out of my way and keep you happy?" hakim asked. Mr. Nice just stared at hakim. "Give us a month, and your man here will have a suit case filled with cash!" hakim said. Mr. Nice shook his head. "2 weeks! You got 2 weeks from tomorrow when my guy gives you the info you need!" Mr. Nice said. Hakim sighs. He stands from his seat. "You got a deal. I'll have my guy named Bex make the drop." Hakim said. Mr. Nice stands. His men follow suit. He and hakim shake hands again. "You boys can go now." Mr. Nice said. 2 Gunz tries to hand back the towel. "No kid. You keep that shit." Mr. Nice said. The next day on the 4th, hakim, Bex, Chewie and Mackie were in the back room of BIG SHOTS waiting for Augustine to show up with the names of the dealers they'd have to confront. Suddenly, there's a knock on the door. "Come in!" Hakim shouted. In comes 2 Gunz. "That Augustine dude came by to give you this." Gunz said. Gunz hands hakim a white envelope. Hakim opens it, and inside was a folded piece of paper. Hakim unfolds the paper and reads what's on it. Hakim starts laughing. "What's up?" Bex asked. "This brother, is the name of all the niggas we gonna have to put down! Guess whose name is near the top?" hakim asked Bex. "Who?" Bex asked. Hakim didn't say the name out loud. He just leans over to Bex and showed him the list. "Oh shit!" Bex said. "We're gonna make that nigga top priority!" hakim said. Bex nods his head. "Nah! I think we should save him for last." Hakim said. Hakim folds the paper and stuffs it in his pants pocket. "Forgot to tell y'all, Krayton ain't come in yet, and the delivery guy just dropped off 20 cases of that Steigalhoff beer! Where you want me to put it?" Gunz asked. "Stick'em up yo ass!" hakim said. Mackie and Chewie burst out laughing. Bex just shook his head. "I'm just fucking with you Gunz! Put'em in the basement." Hakim said. Gunz leaves the room with a depressed look on his face. "I still can't believe that nigga 50 years old, and don't wear underwear!" Hakim chuckled. "That's some nasty ass beer!" Bex said.

3 weeks later, on a sunny breezy afternoon in Bridgeton, buddy and his body guard were driving back to buddy's place in a burgundy Boeman sedan. They've just came back from playing a game of basketball at the neighborhood gym. Buddy's body guard, nick named Coal mike, had really dark skin. He was a burley brutish looking guy, standing almost 7 feet tall. He was joked upon behind his back because of his squeaky, high pitched voice. Even when was a corrections officer where Bex and hakim served time, his co-workers used to crack on him behind his back, until he heard one of them making a joke one day. Coal Mike was fired for assault and battery.

"Man, I wanted to smoke that fool for fouling me!" buddy said. Buddy was still in his gym clothes, getting the passenger seat all sweaty, while Coal mike was decked out in a navy blue suit. "Yeah man! You had that kid shaking in his boots!" coal mike chuckled. "Good thing he paid up after his ass loss!" buddy said as he and coal mike give each other dap. "Speaking of money, my supply is getting low, and I still can't get in touch with the Amish man! Shit!" buddy said. "You think somebody took his old ass out?" coal mike asked. "Man, I don't know! All I know, I better get a new shipment from somewhere before all these fiends go somewhere else!" buddy said. Coal mike nods his head.

Coal mike pulls up in front of buddy's place. "Hey man! Who's that dude standing on your porch?" coal mike asked. Buddy squints his eyes to focus. "Oh shit! That's that fool Bex, Who used to live down the road!" buddy said.

Bex was standing on buddy's porch, blocking the entrance. He was dressed in a beige 2 piece suit, with a white button up shirt. Bex had a big smile on his face. "Yo nigga! Didn't I tell you and yo boy not to come around here no more?" buddy shouted. "Remember, when you told me if I ever wanted to get in the game, to come see you first?" Bex shouted. Before buddy could respond, he heard a loud pop. Buddy jumped, turning towards coal mike. He saw blood all over the dash board and on himself as well. "What the fuck?" buddy screamed. Coal mike's head was slumped over the steering wheel. Buddy looked out his window and saw the end of a double barrel shot gun. Holding the shot gun was Mackie. "Get the fuck out of the car! Now!" Mackie shouted. "Ok man! You got!" buddy shouted. Suddenly, Chewie comes from around the driver's side. He yanks the car door open. "You heard the man! Get out the car!" Chewie shouted. Buddy was trembling. "Don't I know you man?" buddy shouted. Chewie shoots buddy in the knee cap with his pistol. Buddy screams from the agonizing pain. Chewie grabs buddy by his sweaty t-shirt and yanks him out of the car. Buddy falls to the ground. 2 Gunz gets out of a car parked 2 houses down. He and Mackie pull coal mike's humongous body over to the passenger's side. "Take the car with the body, far away from here and torch it!" Mackie says to Gunz. Gunz jumps in the driver's seat and drives off. At the legal speed limit. There were a few people standing on their porches, witnessing the whole thing. "What the fuck y'all looking at" Mackie shouted. People started to scatter back in to their houses. Mackie and Chewie pick buddy from off the ground. They drag him inside of his house. They throw buddy to the floor. Mackie kicks buddy in his rib cage, causing him to turn on his back. "Please! Don't kill me!" buddy cried. "Shut the fuck up!" Mackie shouted. Bex enters the house and closes the door.

Mackie and Chewie wore black coveralls, latex gloves and black bandanas over their nose and mouth. "Put him in the chair!" Bex said. Mackie and Chewie each grab an arm and slams buddy's body back into the recliner. Mackie points the shot gun at buddy's face. "Come on Bex, man! I'll give you whatever you want!" Buddy cried. Bex stands there, reminiscing about Annie. Bex starts to panic and runs for the front entrance. "Where the fuck you going?" Mackie shouted. Bex stands on the front steps bent over heaving. "Keep an eye on this nigga!" Mackie says to Chewie. Mackie goes after Bex. "What the hell you doing man? You're gonna be a boss! You better fucking start acting like it!" Mackie whispered. Bex starts breathing heavily. "Fuck this!" Mackie said. Mackie heads back into the house. He walks up to buddy. "Listen! You got 2 choices! Either work for us and continue making money, or die right here, right now!" Mackie shouted. Suddenly, Bex rushes back into the house. He pulls out a small pistol from his waist band. He points the gun at buddy's head at point blank range. "I'm sorry! I'm sorry!" Buddy sobbed. Bex's gun goes off. "Go bring the car in front of the house!" Mackie tells Chewie. Bex just stands there in a daze. He still has the gun pistol pointed buddy's head. "It's ok man!" Mackie said as he slowly takes the pistol from Bex. Mackie hears the screeching of tires outside. "Let's go man!" he says to Bex. Mackie had to grab Bex by the arm. Bex was still in shock looking at buddy's lifeless body. "Come on. We got more work to do." Mackie tells Bex in a calm voice. Bex eventually follows Mackie outside. Mackie and Bex race to the get-a-way car Chewie had drove up on the curb. As Bex was getting in the vehicle, he spotted a black van parked down the street. "Damn! They're everywhere!" Bex said to himself. "Come on man! Get the fuck in before the cops come!" Mackie shouted. Bex gets in the back seat. Bex had a smirk on his face. "We ain't gotta worry about the cops." Bex said in a calm voice.

A few minutes later, an elderly black couple walks up to buddy's gate. They can see buddy's body from outside, sitting in a chair with a hole in his forehead. The elderly woman quickly turns away from the horrific site. Other people in the neighborhood start to gather around. The old man turns to the crowd. "Whatever happened, that boy had it coming!" the old man shouted. He grabs his wife by the hand, leaving the scene. "If they ain't seen nothing, I ain't seen nothing!" a drunken old white guy wearing tattered clothes said. "A couple of teenagers from the neighborhood looked puzzled while listening to the derelict. "I never seen him around here before!" one teenager said to the other. As the crowd scatters while hearing sirens, the derelict calmly walks down the street in the direction of the black van.

Later that evening at hakim's apartment in Bloomfield, Bex is sitting on the couch with a beer in his hand, just staring at the TV. Hakim is standing in the doorway of the kitchen with a beer in his as well. At his feet is a leather suitcase. "We used to sit around drinking bottles of beer all night." Bex said as if he were in a trance. Hakim scoffs at Bex. "Man, you gotta snap out of that shit! I miss aunt Peggy and Annie as much as you do! Now, you got your revenge, it's time to move on!" hakim said. Hakim picks the suitcase from off the floor. "You ain't finished brother! You gotta take this to that Augustine guy tonight." Hakim said. Bex turns to hakim. "You talk about my mother and Annie like you knew them forever. You don't know shit!" Bex said. Bex stands up and takes the suitcase away from hakim. "I already called Mr. nice. I told him there's a big bonus inside from us for taking so long to deliver." Hakim said. Ok. Alright." Bex said. "Now, hurry up! Gunz outside waiting to drive you there!" Hakim said. Bex takes a swig of his beer before leaving the apartment.

20 minutes into their drive, Bex and 2 guns are on their way to meet with Augustine. "Hey man! You think yo brother still mad at me for wearing no underwear?" Gunz asked. Bex looked at Gunz. "What?" Bex asked. "I was just wondering if he was still pissed. From what I see, he picked up a lot of Eddie's ways. I don't want to be the one to piss him off!" Gunz said. Bex looks down at the suitcase. He picks up the suitcase and puts his ear against it. Bex hears nothing. He shows a sigh of relief.

Back at hakim's apartment, hakim's phone starts ringing. He picks it up off the coffee table. He looks at the caller ID. "Yeah?" hakim said. "We received word about what happened earlier. You, and your brother need to be at the castle this Sunday, noon sharp." The voice said. "Got it." Hakim said. Hakim clicks off the receiver and tosses it on the couch. "Now what?" hakim says to himself.

"Damn man! Buddy, Clancy, Lil country, Boon Dock Bobby, Ron Bailey, Mad mike, White boy Stew, even that retired cop! We done took out all the big timers left in South Jersey just in 3 weeks!" Gunz said. Bex didn't pay any attention on what Gunz was saying. He unlocks the latches on the suitcase. He slowly opens it. Bex sees the contents. He starts laughing. On top of the pile of cash was an 8"x 10" black and white photo of a bundle of dynamite sticks with a timer. The timer was counted down to zero. There was writing on the photo with a red marker. "You must learn to trust me." The writing said. Bex tosses the photo out the window.

Another 20 minutes had passed, and 2 Gunz and Bex arrive at the rendezvous point in Camden. Bex enters the bar, which happens to be a mob social club and heads straight to the back. He passed a table where a few wise guys were playing cards. He quickly glances at them without making eye contact. They had no problem staring him down though. This made Bex walk even faster towards the back. He enters the back room. In the room Augustine is sitting by himself at a booth reading a thick paperback book. When he sees Bex enter the room, he takes off his reading glasses. He creases the last page he read and closes the book. Bex places the suitcase on the table in front of him. He sees that Augustine looked pissed. "Why can't you black guys conduct business on time?" Augustine asked. "Chill! I got the money right here!" Bex said. "Yeah! After the fucking original due date!" Augustine shouted. Bex sighs. "My brother put a bonus in there for your pain and suffering! Happy now?" Bex said. "That bonus is for the boss's pain and suffering! What about my pain and suffering?" Augustine shouted. Bex shook his head. He digs in all of his pants pockets and pulls out wads of money. "I got 5 grand here! Take it!" Bex shouted. A couple of Augustine's soldiers hear the shouting and come running in the back with guns drawn. "Tutto bene qui cap?" one soldier asked. Augustine nods his head. The 2 men put their guns back in their holsters and leave the room. "Every time you're late, expect to get taxed kid." Augustine said. Bex storms out of the room. He returns to the car. "Let's go!" he orders Gunz.

Sunday came around, when Bex and Hakim were on their way to castle Lassenberry. They both were dressed down in jeans, sneakers and leather jackets. Bex was driving, while hakim was checking the magazine in his pistol. "I don't even know why you brought that with you! You can't get it pass the gate!" Bex said. "I can tell right now you ain't no gangster brother. They don't let us in, we'll just turn our black asses around. Don't forget man, they need us now." Hakim said.

Within minutes, Bex pulls up to the gates. An agent walks up to the car. "Can I help you sir?" the agent asked. "Yeah. I'm hakim and this is Bex. We have an appointment to see Sir Marcus. Tell'em I'm packing, and I ain't coming in without it." The agent takes off his shades. He stares hakim directly into his eyes. "I'm serious man! Go tell'em!" hakim said. The agent puts his shades back on. Wait here gentlemen." The agent said. The agent walks over to where another agent is standing. They both go back-n-forth on what to do about the situation. One agent gets on his com link. After 5 minutes, hakim and Bex become restless. "Yo! We ain't got all day man!" hakim shouted. 3 more agents arrive on the scene. All the agents in up in a huddle talking amongst themselves. "Tell Sir Marcus to get y'all some new suits! When the last time y'all had them cleaned?" hakim chuckled. The agents ignore hakim's taunts. A few minutes later tony comes out on a golf cart driven by an agent. He's decked out in a gray silk suit and tie. He jumps out of golf cart. Hakim could see that he had rage in his eyes. Tony orders the agent to open the gate. Tony walks up to hakim's vehicle. "What's the fucking problem?" tony shouted. "I'm packing, and I ain't coming in unarmed!" Hakim said. Tony looks over at the agents, then turns to hakim and Bex. He then calms himself. "Listen. Since Sir Edward's demise, these people think we don't have what it takes to hold things together. Shit! Sometimes I don't think we have what it takes. But, we are the ones running things now. I know you grew up in this game, just like I did. Plus, we all know you're a bad ass. But, we have to keep up appearances. So please, hand over the gun, and let the agents frisk you so we can do business." Tony whispered. Hakim chuckles. "You must have a lot of bitches riding yo dick man! You're one smooth talking nigga!" hakim chuckled. Tony smiled and shrugged his shoulders. Hakim hands the pistol over to tony. "Now, was that hard?" tony said.

Inside the walls of the castle, the golf cart pulls up to Sir Marcus's office. Hakim noticed that there were 2 agents guarding the door. Bex, hakim and tony get off the golf cart. One of the agents opens the door. "After you, gentlemen." Tony said. Bex enters first. Hakim is shocked once he enters the office. He takes a step back, backing into tony. "Easy! Watch my shoes!" tony said. Hakim sees that Sir Marcus isn't the only one in the office. Sitting opposite of Sir Marcus's desk was Butch and Dubbs. Next to them, bound to his wheelchair was Mookie Vasquez. "What's this all about?" hakim asked. Sir Marcus stands up. Welcome gentlemen!" Sir Marcus said. Bex looked nervous. "Calm down kid. This ain't an ambush." Butch says to Bex. Tony shuts the office door, leaving the agents outside. Sir Marcus opens the drawer to his desk and pulls out a small black box. "Gentlemen! I want to say that Hakim Bates and Biron Eric Xavier have rapidly proven themselves worthy to join our inner circle." Sir Marcus said. "Thanks man! We appreciate it!" Bex said. Hakim just rolls his eyes. "Butch. Would you and Dubbs stand please?" Sir Marcus said. Sir Marcus open the black box. He hands Bex a ring. "This ring was designed and passed down from my grandfather. It represents the elite in our organization. Wear it with pride. You might have to adjust the size." Sir Marcus said. "Thanks again man!" Bex said as he and Sir Marcus shook hands. Sir Marcus takes the other ring out of the box. He hands it to Hakim. "This belonged to Sir Edward. Now it belongs to you." Sir Marcus said. Hakim looked stunned. He couldn't take his eyes off the ring. "Hey man. It's not haunted." Sir Marcus said. Everyone except for Bex start laughing. Hakim snaps out of his trance. "Very funny! Ha! Ha!" hakim said. Hakim puts the ring on. "It's a little loose." Hakim said. "You can have it made to fit later. But, you must wear it at all times from then on." Sir Marcus. "I'll take care of it first thing tomorrow." Hakim sighed. Hakim and Sir Marcus shake hands. "Good! Now that we're all here, let me run down the territories so no one gets confused on what's what. "Shouldn't we all know this by now?" Dubbs asked. Sir Marcus gave Dubbs an evil look. Dubbs just puts his head down. Butch consoles his cousin by rubbing his back for a few seconds.

"Now. Butch runs Sussex, Passaic, Bergen, Warren and Morris Counties! Hakim runs all of Essex County! Mookie runs both Hudson and Union Counties! Dubbs runs Hunterdon, Somerset, Middlesex, Mercer, and Monmouth Counties. Last top complete the circle is Bex, who runs Burlington, Ocean, Camden, Salem, Atlantic, Gloucester, Cumberland and Cape May Counties!" Sir Marcus said.

Tony had set up as silver platter with 7 glasses of Cognac on it. He approached each man in the office, allowing each of them to grab a glass. Sir Marcus grabs his glass first. Tony is last to grab his glass. He puts the platter on the desk. "I would like to make a toast!" tony shouts. Everyone raises their glass. "To the 5 generals! May they reign to make lots of money for a long time!" tony shouts. "To the 5 Generals!" everyone shouted. They simultaneously gulp down their drinks. Bex goes over and grabs the bottle of Cognac. He fills everyone's glass once again. "I wanna make a toast this time!" Bex shouted. Hakim rolls his eyes, shaking his head. "Could y'all raise y'all glasses guys?" Bex asked. Butch and hakim reluctantly raise their glasses after everyone else does. "I would like to thank the man that made this all possible! To Sir Marcus!" Bex shouted. "To Sir Marcus!" They all shout. Everyone gulps down their drink. Sir Marcus puts his empty glass on the platter. "I just want to thank you guys for coming out for this little ceremony. When you leave here, I just want you all to be careful out there. I mean that." Sir Marcus said. Hakim approached Sir Marcus. "Yo. Thanks for the ring man. Now I gotta get up here." Hakim said as he and Sir Marcus shook hands. Hakim was about to leave the office, but his path was blocked by tony. "What's your problem?" hakim asked. "Bex! Get over here!" tony said. Bex walks over toward tony and hakim. "Since you guys are in the inner circle now, I'm going to say this one time and one time only. When you enter or exit a room with Sir Marcus present, you will say these words loud and clear. Long live the house of Lassenberry! Long live Sir Marcus! Understand?" tony said. Hakim had the look of disbelief on his face. He closed his eyes for a second, while pinching the bridge of his nose. "Ok man, whatever." Hakim said. "Well, I'm about to get out of here myself." Butch said. "I'll leave with you guys!" Mookie said. "Long live the house of Lassenberry! Long live Sir Marcus!" the 5 generals shout simultaneously. Butch had a smirk on his face when seeing hakim's lack of enthusiasm. Each general shook Sir Marcus's hand as they left the office.

"Wow that was something!" Sir Marcus said as he unbuttoned the top button of his uniform. "You think we're gonna have a problem with him?" tony asked. "Who hakim? Nah! He's been dying for that position for a long time." Sir Marcus said. "No. he's been dying for your position for a long time." Tony said.

That evening, Sir Marcus was lying in bed with his wife watching TV. He dozes off, falling into a deep sleep. Kimberly gets out of bed and heads into the next room to check on the baby. Shortly after, Sir Marcus starts tossing and turning in bed. In his dream state, he sees people walking the streets in a zombie state of mind. His dream then switches to seeing Terrance walking towards him naked, carrying his deceased cousin Samara. She is covered in blood. Suddenly, her eyes open. She looks at Sir Marcus. "Help me!" she said in a haunting voice. His dream then switches back to the streets of Newark. The people on the streets were naked and covered in blood. Thousands of naked people drop to their knees, before Sir Marcus begging for help, while he sits on a throne made of human body parts. His dream then changes quickly to seeing his cousin Krayton descend from the clouds with black demon wings attached to his back, flapping in the wind. In his dream, Krayton is also wearing a black robe. He hovers above Sir Marcus. He tells Sir Marcus if he helped the people, he dies. Suddenly, Sir Marcus awoke from his nightmare in a cold sweat. He looks around and sees that the TV is still on showing an infomercial. He looks at the clock on the wall. It's 1:36. Sir Marcus sits at the edge of the bed in his pajama bottoms. He looks around the huge bedroom, breathing heavily. He then hears Kimberly on the baby monitor singing a lullaby to their son. He starts chuckling.

It was April 30th 2001, when Sir Marcus, Kimberly and the baby were near the end of their vacation. Sir Marcus had told Kimberly that they would spend the remaining weeks of April on their honeymoon touring Europe and North Africa. This was Sir Marcus's way of making up for all the lost time he and Kimberly missed together due to the life of being a drug lord.

It was the remote island of Cabrera where Kimberly wanted the family to stay for their getaway. Cabrera happened to be a territory of Spain. Sir Marcus more or less rented out the entire island for his wife and son. Lucy had accompanied the couple, along with 6 agents. 3 of the agents were ordered by tony to dress as tourists and to keep a safe distance from Sir Marcus and Kimberly if they decide to go site seeing. Baby mark was being cared for by Lucy, and guarded by an agent when the couple wanted to have time alone.

Sir Marcus and Kimberly traveled Mali, Tunisia and Egypt during their tour of North Africa. Sir Marcus was almost brought to tears when he laid his hands on one of the Pyramids of Giza for the first time. During their tour of Europe, the couple visited Milam, Madrid, Paris, London and even Moscow. A professional photographer from Spain was also hired to come along with them to take dozens of pictures of them standing in front of ancient ruins, posing with the locals and indigenous people. From riding the London eye, to riding camels. In the African Desert, Sir Marcus and Kimberly enjoyed every moment of their vacation.

Back in the United States, tony was holding down the fort for the organization. This time there was no one who had the authority to keep him out of the castle in Sir Marcus's absence. Tony had access to all the sensitive materials pertaining to the Lassenberry family businesses, including what Jabbo called the B.O.I, all the money laundering deals set up by the NA, the Lassenberry family oversees accounts, the list of all the public and law officials on the Lassenberry payroll, which were all locked away in a reinforced iron safe with an electronic combination. The safe was located in the dungeon 2 levels below the castle. Sir Marcus had also left in Tony's possession, the name of his successor in case of his demise. There was also the safe in Sir Marcus's office tony had access to in case of an emergency. The safe held a little over 10 million dollars in cash. The cash was used to bail out high ranking members of the organization like hakim and Butch if convicted by the courts.

Tony was in the office watching TV when the red phone started ringing. He just stared at the phone for a moment before picking it up. "Shit!" tony said to himself. He knew it could only be bad news if the red phone was ringing.

Back on the island of Cabrera, Sir Marcus was sitting at the edge of the harbor by himself taking in the view of the Mediterranean Sea. The sun was setting as he closed his eyes when a strong breeze came in his direction. It was a peaceful moment for Sir Marcus. While his eyes were closed, all he could hear was the sounds of the sea, he started taking deep breaths. He was about to go into a meditated state until he was approached by one of his agents, who was wearing Bermuda shorts and a t-shirt. "Sir! Your have an important call from Mr. Kerouac." The agent said. Sir Marcus still kept his eyes closed. "Tell him I'm busy." Sir Marcus said. "But it sounds urgent sir." The agent said. Sir Marcus opened his eyes and turns towards the agent. "Agent! Tell him I'm busy!" Sir Marcus shouted. The agent just nods his head and walks off back to the lodge. Sir Marcus just stares at the sea.

The next day, Sir Marcus's private jet lands at Teterboro. All the passengers on board were still asleep expect for Sir Marcus, who had a worried look on his face. There were 2 limousines waiting on the tarmac. As soon as Sir Marcus departs the aircraft, he is approached by an agent. "Mr. Kerouac is waiting in the limo for you sir!" The agent shouted because the turbines were still revved up. "What?" Sir Marcus shouted. The agent points to one of the limos. "Kerouac!" the agent shouted. "Ok!" Sir Marcus shouted. "I'll take your family back to the castle with me in the other limo!" the agent shouted. Sir Marcus gave the agent the thumbs up. The jet's turbines come to a halt. Kimberly comes out the jet with the baby in her arms. Lucy comes out, followed by the agents carrying the luggage. "I'm going back in the limo with tony." Sir Marcus said. "Is everything ok?" Kimberly asked. "We have some business to catch up on. I'll see you back at the castle later." Sir Marcus said. He gives Kimberly a kiss. He kisses his son on the head. Sir Marcus walks to the limo where tony is, followed by 2 agents. As soon as Sir Marcus gets in the limo, he can already tell that tony was pissed at him by the look on his face. "You can all go in the limo with my family." Sir Marcus ordered the 2 agents. "But sir. Who's going to protect you?" one agent asked. "Just do what I said agent." Sir Marcus said. "Yes sir." The agent said. The burly agent closes the limo door and heads back to the other limo. Tony's driver takes off. "What the hell is your problem?" tony shouted. "Calm down! I'm still the boss last time I checked!" Sir Marcus said. "Calm down? I got a call from some NA guy named Peter something or other yesterday!" Tony said. "Bellum." Sir Marcus said. "Whatever! He told me that a group of rebels in Afghanistan had assassinated our connection and took over the poppy fields!" tony said. Sir Marcus sighed. "I guess we have to get in touch with General Magus then." Sir Marcus said. "More bad news! I was told his plane was shot down over Afghan air space by an RPG right after Qadir's murder!" tony said. "What else did he say?" Sir Marcus sighed. "That's it! He just hung up! I tried to get to contact Terrance, but he won't speak to me!" Tony said. "I'll call him when I get to the castle." Sir Marcus sighed. "Why does it feel like I'm more upset about this then you are?" tony asked.

Back at the castle, Sir Marcus and tony head to the office. The first thing Sir Marcus does is get on the red phone. He can hear the phone ring on the other end. "Come on! Pick up! Sir Marcus said to himself. Terrance picks up. "Ah, Sir Marcus! Good to hear from you!" Terrance chuckled. "Why the hell are you so happy? I'm sure you've received the bad news!" Sir Marcus said. "This just opened up a new door for us my friend! We have enough product to supply you for the rest of the year! All you have to do, is sit back and enjoy the fireworks!" Terrance chuckled. "What fireworks?" Sir Marcus asked. Terrance hangs up. "Hello! Hello!" Sir Marcus shouted. "What happened?" tony asked. "This guy is really sick!" Sir Marcus said. "What did he say?" tony asked. "He said he can supply us for the rest of the year. Then he said enjoy the fireworks. Whatever that means!" Sir Marcus said. "Well, if he's not panicking, neither should we." Tony said. "I feel something real bad is about to happen!" Sir Marcus said. Tony slaps Sir Marcus on the back. "Whatever happens, you're still the boss!" tony said. Sir Marcus rolls his eyes. Tony then snaps his fingers. "Oh, I almost forgot! Butch and Dubbs need a refill on weed!" Tony said. Sir Marcus nods his head. "Let me check on Kimberly and the baby, and change out of these clothes." Sir Marcus said. "How was your vacation?" tony asked. "It was great! The photographer must've taken a million pictures!" Sir Marcus said with a smile on his face. "Cant' wait to see them!" tony said. Sir Marcus leaves the office.

For the next few months, it was business as usual. Sir Marcus was in his office going over some paper work, when tony walked in with a briefcase. He opens it. Inside were stacks of cash. "200 grand! This is your take this month from all the dive bars!" tony said. "Ok. Put it in the safe." Sir Marcus said. "Want me to give Brandon a call about the Steigalhoff sales?" tony asked. "Ah, no. It can wait until tomorrow." Sir Marcus said. He pulls out a set of keys from his desk. "Where you headed?" tony asked. Sir Marcus zips up his sweat jacket. "Going for a drive." Sir Marcus said. "By yourself?" tony asked. "Why not? Besides! Nobody knows who I am!" Sir Marcus said. "You need an agent with you. Seriously." Tony said. "I'm taking one the old cars from the garage. I won't have to worry about getting car jacked." Sir Marcus chuckled. "You need a body guard!" tony insisted. "Just put the money in the safe and take the rest of the day off. That's an order!" Sir Marcus said. He leaves the office.

Outside, Sir Marcus is driver to the garage by an agent in a golf cart. "Are your sure you want to go out alone sir?" the agent asked. "I quite sure of it agent." Sir Marcus said. The agent opens the garage with a remote control. The garage is constructed to hold up to 20 vehicles. It had its own repair shop, 2 gas pumps and air and vacuum machines. Sir Marcus starts the ignition to a 92 Boeman hatchback. The agent gets on his com link, ordering the gates to open. Sir Marcus then drives off the premises. He gets on the main road, which leads to the turnpike. He heads north.

After driving through the streets of Newark and Irvington, Sir Marcus finds himself pulling over to the curb. He starts sobbing after witnessing all of the harm he contributed to in the streets. He's seen people walking the streets looking like zombies from the effects of their drug addictions. He wipes the tears from his eyes and continues his drive. After a while, he ends up in Bloomfield. He stops at the red light. He sees a white guy standing on the corner, leaning against a telephone pole nodding out. The man has a lit cigarette dangling from his mouth. Sir Marcus just shook his head. The light had turned green. He takes off down the street. While driving on Broad Street, he noticed the people sitting outside of a restaurant. It was 3 in the afternoon when he decides to park the car to get a bite to eat. He goes in to place and orders a sandwich and fries. He takes his tray of food outside to a table to eat.

Sir Marcus took a bite from his sandwich, when he heard someone calling him. "Yo Marcus!" the voice shouts. Sir Marcus looked up and saw that it was hakim standing over him. Hakim was wearing a 2 piece suit, gator shoes and a diamond incrusted watch. "Holy shit! What you doing out here?" Hakim asked. Sir Marcus noticed that hakim was wearing his ring. "I was just riding around and decided to stop here and get something to eat." Sir Marcus said. "You know I live a couple of blocks down the street! You should stop by sometime! I order from here a lot! Mind if I sit with you?" he asked Sir Marcus. "Yeah, I kind of do mind. I just want some free time to myself, without all the attention." Sir Marcus said. Hakim just looks at Sir Marcus with a sinister smile. "I guess you're right! You don't wanna bring attention on yourself, especially being out here alone!" hakim said as takes one of Sir Marcus's fries from his plate and eats it. Sir Marcus looks around to see if anyone noticed. "I guess I'll get up with you later!" hakim chuckled. He walks away. Sir Marcus watches as hakim jumps into his vehicle. Sir Marcus gets infuriated and tosses is food in the trash. He quickly heads for his vehicle and drives off.

It was around 6 in the evening when Sir Marcus returned to the castle. He walks down the corridor Of the East wing, while being followed be an agent driving a golf cart. "Are you sure you don't want to be driven to your destination sir?" the agent asked. "For the last time, no!" Sir Marcus said as he continues to walk. Within minutes, Sir Marcus arrives at the East wing entrance. Since the demise of Sir Edward and Charlie, there was no need to have an agent posted at the entrance. Sir Marcus opens one of the double doors. "Stay here!" Sir Marcus sad to the agent. Sir Marcus walks in the middle of the empty room that used to be Sir Edward's bedroom. He starts crying and falls to his knees. "I have to make things right! I have to make things right!" Sir Marcus cried.

It was August 30th, when Sir Marcus and tony were in the office counting out a large sum of cash and placing small stacks in envelopes. "Are you sure you want to do this boss?" tony asked. "Yeah, I'm sure!" Sir Marcus shouted. Tony placed the last envelope in a large duffle bag. Sir Marcus hands tony a piece of paper. On the paper, Sir Marcus had written down the names of all the churches and charities that he wanted the money to go to. The cash was originally meant to be disbursed to the Lassenberry family members. It was a total of 1.4 million dollars in the duffle bag. Tony grabs the bag and leaves the office.

A couple of days later, Krayton was at his pent house in New York waiting for his for his envelope to arrive as usual. It was 3 in the afternoon, and no sign of tony, or anyone from his disbursing team. Krayton became impatient and made a call to his cousin. The phone rings 3 times before someone answers. "Lassenberry residence. Kerouac speaking." Tony said. "Yo tony! Its K boogie! Where's my envelope, man?" Krayton asked. "Who?" asked Tony. "It's Krayton! Where's my envelope?" Krayton shouted. "No envelopes will be given out for the next 2 months, by orders of Sir Marcus." Tony said. "What the fuck? What you mean, no envelopes?" Krayton shouted. Tony hangs up the phone. "Hello!" Krayton shouted. Krayton then makes another call. The phone rings a couple of times. "Lassenberry residence." The voice said. 'Put my father on the phone!" Krayton said. "Hold on please." The voice said.

The person answering the phone was Jake seniors live in housekeeper. She was an elderly woman from Haiti named Edwidge. She the third housekeeper hired by Jake Sr. within the past 5 years. Edwidge took the cordless phone to her boss, who was outside on the terrace reading a book. "It's your son Krayton on the on the phone sir." Edwidge said. She hands Jake sr. the phone. "I already know what you're going to say! Your brothers call earlier." Jake Sr. said. "So what's going on pop?" Krayton asked. "I have no idea what's going through your cousin's head right now. I've been getting calls from a lot of the family. Even your aunt Lula called all the way from a movie set from Vancouver!" Jake Sr. said. "So, what we gonna do about it?" Krayton shouted. "There's nothing we can do! Your cousin is in charge of the family finances! He's probably going through something! Just give him time! I'll talk to you later." Jake sr. said. Jake sr. hands the phone back to Edwidge. "I'm not taking any more calls for the day." Jake sr. said to Edwidge. "Yes, Mr. Lassenberry." Edwidge said. She leaves, leaving Jake Sr. so he can continue his reading.

Sir Marcus's financial boycott didn't just end with family members. Shortly after, he refused to buy products from Boeman Auto, Blush Cosmetics, Steigalhoff Brewery and Galaxy Appliances. Within a week, the heads of these corporations started making complaints to the head of NA research and development, Dr. Alfred Zachmont in turn, brought it to Terrance Haggerty's attention.

It was September 10th when Sir Marcus's red phone started ringing. Sir Marcus was sitting at his desk at the time. He had his hand on the receiver, but didn't pick up just yet. Tony was standing nearby. "Going to answer it?" tony asked. "I guess, there's no way around it." Sir Marcus sighed. He picks up the phone. "Yeah?" Sir Marcus answered. "I've have 2 things to say to you! Cut the bullshit, and start buying! Don't make any flight plans tomorrow!" Terrance said. Terrance hangs up the phone. Sir Marcus hangs up. "What did he say?" tony asked. Sir Marcus had a worried look on his face as he taps his finger tips on the desk. "Make a call to Brandon. Tell him, to resume business as usual." Sir Marcus said. Tony just nods his head.

The next morning, Sir Marcus is awaken from the sound of his wife crying. She is sitting at the edge of the bed cradling her son as she watched TV. "What's wrong babe?" Sir Marcus asked. "2 planes just crashed into the twin towers!" Kimberly cried. Sir Marcus slid to the edge of the bed, next to his wife and son. "Monsters! All of them! Sir Marcus said as he gazed at the TV. "What are you talking about?" Kimberly asked. "Nothing." Sir Marcus said. Sir Marcus puts on his robe. "Where are you going?" Kimberly asked. "To the office. I'll be back in a few." Sir Marcus said as he strokes his son's back. He puts on his slippers and looks at the clock on the wall. It was 9:58am. Suddenly, Kimberly screamed after watching the South Tower collapse, causing the baby to cry. Sir Marcus didn't comfort his wife. He stood watching the TV for a few seconds, then leaves the bedroom.

Moments later at the office, Sir Marcus grabs the remote and clicks on the TV. Every channel Sir Marcus turned to, showed the horrific act of terrorism. He makes call on the red phone. Seconds later, Terrance picks up the phone on his end. "What the fuck did you people do?" Sir Marcus shouted. Terrance just started giggling like a mad man. "We needed a reason to get back the poppy fields! Now, we have one!" Terrance chuckled.

Months earlier, Dragan Serpiente gathered a few high ranking officials of the National Agreement from around the country to decide on how to regain control of the poppy fields in Afghanistan without unveiling their agenda. Former Essex County Executive Blake Hamm had ran for New Jersey Senator a couple of years earlier, winning by a landslide. His win was mostly due to NA connections, Hamm quickly became a rising star with his colleagues in the senate. His recent rhetoric of Islamic extremists planning to attack the United States just came to fruition. Senator Hamm and his colleagues also convinced an unpopular president to fund a private army to find the perpetrators.

The plan was for the private army, who were actually specially trained NA agents to guard the poppy fields. The puppet Afghani government would hire local tribes to harvest the fields. U.S. forces unknowingly were there just for propaganda to give the American people a sense of security.

Being a part of the conspiracy, Terrance couldn't help but boast to Sir Marcus on how 4 planes were electronically rigged to be taken over by remote. One of the planes missed its target due to a malfunction in the remote. The government wrote it off as an act of heroism by the passengers. Sir Marcus and Terrance were at the land field they've visited a while back when Terrance exposed the plot. Sir Marcus puked his brains out right in front of Terrance after he spoke. Terrance just burst out laughing.

All the events that followed, didn't distract Sir Marcus from using his power to slow down sales of narcotics throughout New Jersey. He would secretly hire outsiders to sabotage and rob incoming shipments of heroin. Not even tony new of his deeds.

It was the beginning of October, when around mid-night Butch was on his way back from Port Elizabeth with a refill. He had 2 suitcases filled with pure heroin. He was being driven in a Boeman SUV by his driver Sam Post. Sitting in the back seat wielding a shotgun was body guard Arnold Washington, a.k.a No-No. "When we get to the lab, make sure that new girl strips down naked! No bra and panties!" Butch said to No-No. Suddenly, a dump truck comes from out of nowhere and crashes into the SUV. The shotgun goes off. Sam's head is splattered into small fragments. The SUV runs off the side of the road. It crashes into a huge tree. Smoke comes from under the hood. "Oh shit!" Butch shouted. He sees flames coming from the hood he quickly releases his seatbelt. "Get the suitcases!" he said to Arnold. Arnold was in a daze. His head was slammed hard on the back of the head rest. Butch gets out of the Vehicle. He opens the back door and grabs the 2 suitcases. The SUV is now engulfed in flames. "Arnold! No-no!" Butch shouted. Butch has the 2 suitcases in his possession, but refused to put them down to save Arnold. Butch runs far away from the vehicle as possible. The SUV then explodes. The force of the blast knocks butch to the ground. Butch sees the dump truck heading in his direction. He gets up and grabs the suitcases. He makes a run for it. The dump truck catches up with him. While the truck is still moving, a man in a black ski mask jumps out and tackles butch to the ground. The dump truck stops. The driver gets out. He too is wearing a black ski mask. He also has 2 baseball bats in his possession. Butch and his attacker get up from the ground. The suitcases are out of Butch's hands. He and the attacker get ready to go at it hand-to-hand. "Come on! You just fucked with the wrong nigga!" Butch shouted. The driver of the dump truck runs up and tosses one of the bats to his partner. "Get the suitcases!" the driver shouted. The other attacker swings his bat at Butch. Butch ducks and hits him in the jaw, knocking his attacker out cold. The driver comes from behind and hits Butch in the back with his bat. "Ah, you mother fucker!" Butch screamed in agonizing pain. The driver then takes another whack at Butch's kneecap. Butch falls to the ground. The driver goes over to his partner and smacks into consciousness. The attacker awakens. "Come on! Let's get the suitcases and go!" the driver shouted. The 2 attackers grab the suitcases and make a run for the dump truck. Butch sees them running off, but can't get off the ground to go after them. He massages his injured knee. The dump truck takes off down the road. Butch pounds his fist on the ground. He hears sirens wailing. He sees the flashing lights in the distance. "Fuck!" Butch says to himself.

About a couple of hours later at BIG SHOTS, hakim receives a call on his mobile phone. "Hello." Hakim said. "You know you a dead nigga, right?" Butch said in a calm voice. "What the hell? Who is this?" hakim asked. "You know damn well who the fuck this is! I'm the nigga you just robbed!" Butch said. "Wait! Wait a minute! You got robbed too?" hakim asked. "What the fuck you saying?" Butch asked. "A couple of punk asses just stuck me for my product on the way to the club!" hakim said. "You better not be lying to me boy!" Butch said. "I swear man! Why would I pull something like that twice?" hakim said. Butch was silent for a moment. "If you ain't do it, then who did?" Butch asked.

Elsewhere, Bex just walked into the home that used to belong to his former enemy, Buddy. Bex purchased the house 2 weeks ago. The house was empty. There was no furniture, but a card table and 2 folding chairs. Hakim had talked Bex into purchasing the place as a safe house. The only difference between Buddy and Bex, was that Bex put money orders in the mailboxes of everyone one the block to keep things quiet.

Bex, toby, Clint, and toby's stepson Calvin were at the house that night when someone dressed in black and wearing a black ski mask broke into Clint's truck and stole Bex's 2 suitcases of heroin. Calvin was the first to run outside when he heard glass breaking. Bex is right behind Calvin. The back passenger window was broken out. Calvin and toby look inside the truck. "I told you to bring them in the house with us!" toby said. "Fuck!" Bex shouted as he kicked the side of the truck. Bex takes out his mobile phone. He presses speed dial. "Yeah!" hakim answered. "Man, someone just robbed me of my shit!" Bex said. "Join the club." Hakim said. "They got you too?" Bex asked. "They got Butch, Dubbs, and I bet Mookie got hit too." Hakim said. "What we gonna do now?" Bex asked. "Me and Butch gonna arrange a meeting with Marcus, and see if we can get a refill on the refill." Hakim said. "I don't know, man! If 10 suitcases of pure heroin go missing, I know I wouldn't trust us!" Bex said. "Just wait for the call to come to the meeting." "What I'm gonna do about Mr. Nice?" Bex asked. "Come out yo pocket and pay the nigga!" Hakim said before hanging up the phone.

The next evening, a shipment of heroin was being transported to the NA facility out in the Pine Barons. The 3 camouflage army trucks were driving down the desolate road, only a few miles from their destination. Suddenly, 2 men in black coveralls and wearing black ski masks stand out of the bushes off the side of the road. The 2 mysterious men had in their possession an RPG. The 2 men loaded the grenade launcher and aimed it at the first truck in the convoy. The man loading the rocket gave his partner the signal to fire. The first truck was destroyed completely. The 2 men reloaded the RPG. The second vehicle swerved around the first vehicle. The man with the RPG didn't have time to focus on his target. Coincidently, the attacker hit his target's rear wheel, causing it to flip on its side. The third truck swerved around what was left of the first truck. It picked up speed escaping the attack. The RPG attackers realized no one had survived the in the 2 trucks. They ran off into the weeds in different directions.

At the NA facility, Peter Bellum was sitting in his office looking at his wrist watch, waiting for the shipment to come. Suddenly, there's a loud banging on his door. He reaches for his side arm. While having the gun aimed at the door with one hand, he reached for the door knob with the other. Peter quickly opens the door. Standing in the door way was his assistant, nick named the Troll because of his odd appearance. He was trying to catch his breath. "Sir! 2 of the trucks were ambushed!" Troll said. Peter puts his pistol back in its holster. "Where?" Peter asked. "A few miles down the road!" Troll said. Peter grabs his suit jacket from off the back of his chair. "Sound the alarm and lock the facility down!" peter shouted. Troll runs off. Within minutes, the whole facility was shut down and secured. 12 agents, all carrying sub-machine guns, escort peter to the gate. 2 cars pull up to the gate. "4 of you stay at the gate! No one gets pass the gate unless I come back with them! Everyone else, follow me!" peter said to the agents. Peter and the rest of the agents pile up in both cars, and head out to where the ambush occurred.

A few days later, all 5 of Sir Marcus's generals meet with him at the garage in Ocean View. The generals were ordered to come alone. Mookie showed up with Dubbs. Dubbs assisted Mookie with his wheelchair. There were no body guards, and no tony. All 6 men stood in a small room in the back of the garage. It was around 2 in the morning. "Why the hell we're meeting here?" Bex asked. "When your brother notified me, I figured we needed total secrecy, even away from the agents." Sir Marcus explained. "Let's get down to it! What are gonna do about our missing dope?" Butch asked. Sir Marcus noticed that Butch was using a walking cane. "I brought you guys here to tell you that we need to lay low for a while, and not move any product until I give the word." Sir Marcus said. Everyone looked at each other in awe. "You lost yo fucking mind?" hakim shouted in rage. "Calm down and show some respect!" Butch said to hakim. "Show some respect? You gotta busted leg, and this nigga talking about laying low! Fuck that!" hakim shouted. "Come on man! We're on the same team." Dubbs said. "I know all of you are not hurting for cash! Everyone here is a millionaire! I know you all have pills and weed left to push on the streets! Live off of that, until I decide what I'm going to do next!" Sir Marcus said. "Con el debido respeto, señor Marcus, corro una tripulación de animals locos! Lo único que mantiene a raya es el flujo de caja proveniente de la cocaína y la heroína!" Mookie said. "What the hell he just say?" Bex asked. "Mookie. Just trust me." Sir Marcus said. "All I know is, whatever my cousin is down with I am too!" Dubbs said. Hakim rolls his eyes. "Alright guys. This meeting is adjourned. "Long live the house of Lassenberry! Long live Sir Marcus!" everyone but hakim shouted. "Hakim! Say it!" hakim looked around the room at everyone. They were waiting for his response. "Long live the house of Lassenberry. Long live

Sir Marcus." Hakim said with a little enthusiasm. Everyone leaves the garage except for Butch and Sir Marcus. Butch gently puts his hand on the back of Sir Marcus's neck. "What's wrong kid?" Butch asked. Sir Marcus started trembling. "I…saw…him!" Sir Marcus whispered. Butch looked puzzled. "Who?" Butch asked. "The devil! I saw…the devil, and he's real!" Sir Marcus. Sir Marcus starts sobbing. He puts his arms around Butch for comfort. "I'm not made for this! I can't live this life! I keep seeing all that crazy shit in my dreams over and over again!" Sir Marcus cried. Butch starts rubbing Sir Marcus's back. "Take it easy kid. Take it easy. Everything's gonna be alright. Stop crying. You're a Lassenberry for Christ's sake!" Butch said. Sir Marcus pulls away from Butch. "He was right Uncle Eddie was right! He told me not to go! He told me!" Sir Marcus cried. "What are you talking about kid?" Butch asked. "I… killed my uncle! I killed Sir Edward!" Sir Marcus cried. Butch shook his head. "I'm sorry about your leg!" Sir Marcus cried. Butch was silent. His eyes started to tear up. "I'm sorry!" Sir Marcus cried. "I don't wanna hear anymore!" Butch said. Sir Marcus falls to his knees. "Please…forgive me!" Sir Marcus cried. "Get yo ass up!" Butch said with rage in his voice. Sir Marcus stands. "It's gonna be ok kid!" Butch said as he wipes the tears from Sir Marcus's eyes. "Get yo self together, and let's get out of here!" Butch said.

It was around 8 in the morning, when Butch was sitting at his man cave residence in Warren County. All the lights were turned off in the house. The only source of light came in through the blinds from the street lights. Butch was sitting on the sofa butt naked. He just sat there staring at the TV, even though it was turned off. He had a glass of liquor in his hand. On the end table next to him was empty bottle. On his lap was a shotgun. Tears were streaming down his cheek as he took a gulp from his glass. He sat there reminiscing about the old days when he and Eddie Lassenberry were running the streets of Newark. He starts to laugh, thinking about the good times for a moment, and then starts crying again.

A few days later, it was around 6 in the morning when tony was getting dressed at his home in West Orange. He stands in front of the mirror in his bedroom fixing his silk neck-tie. He turns towards the bed looking at the young white woman that was asleep. He puts on his suit jacket and heads down stairs. He grabs his house keys off the key hook on the wall. He heads outside to the garage. He gets in his vehicle and starts the engine and hits the remote to raise the garage door. He backs out of the garage, down the driveway. He sees a Boeman sedan in his rear view mirror blocking the driveway. He stops the car and reaches in the glove compartment and pulls out a pistol. He quickly checks the clip. He jumps out of the car and points the pistol at the Sedan. The car door slowly opens. Out comes Butch with his hands in the air. "Take it easy man! It's just me!" Butch shouted. Tony still had his pistol pointed at Butch. "I don't give a shit! Nobody comes to my house uninvited!" tony shouted. Tony takes a quick survey of his surroundings. "Who's with you?" tony asked. "I came alone! There's some important shit we gotta talk about!" Butch said. Butch slowly lowers his arms. "Listen man! You really wanna do this out here?" Butch asked. "How'd you find me?" tony asked. Butch started smiling. "You have your sources finding out shit, and I have mine!" Butch said. "How do I know this ain't a set up?" tony asked. "You don't!" Butch shouted. Tony cocks back the hammer on his pistol. "Either we go inside, or you shoot me, and have a whole bunch of niggas coming after yo ass!" Butch shouted. Tony looks around his surroundings. He then lowers his weapon. "Let's go inside then!" tony said. Butch limps up the driveway. Tony leads him to the front door. They both enter the house. Tony slams the door shut. He points the gun at Butch. "Now strip!" tony said. "Man, have you lost yo high yellow mind?" Butch shouted. "I know about the game as much as you do old man! You could be wired! Now strip!" tony said. Butch shook his head in disbelief. "Ok!" Butch said. He slowly gets undressed. "T-shirt and underwear too!" tony said. "Man, you're paranoid!" Butch said. "That's how I lasted so long in this life! Now strip!" tony said. Suddenly, the young woman that was in Tony's bed, comes down stairs in a robe and slippers. "Sweetheart! What's going on?" she asked. "Nothing baby! My friend and I were just about to talk business! Go back upstairs and get dressed!" tony said. He reaches in his pants pocket and pulls out a wad of cash tied in a rubber band. He tosses it to the young lady. "That's about 3 grand! Take it and go shopping or something!" tony said. "What's going on?" she asked. "Damnit woman! Just go back upstairs and get dressed!" tony shouted as he kept his eye on Butch. The young blonde runs back upstairs. "Finish stripping!" tony said to Butch. Butch takes off his t-shirt and underwear. Tony looks down at Butch's private parts. "She got you excited, huh?" tony said. "Fuck you man!" butch said. "Let's take a walk down to the basement!" tony said. Tony waives his gun, signaling Butch to walk. They both head down into the basement. Tony clicks on the light switch on the wall. Have a seat!" tony said. There was a wooden chair near the wall. Butch noticed something peculiar on the chair. "Hey man! Is that dry blood?" Butch asked. Tony chuckled. "This used to be Jabbo's house. This is where he would bring people to…let's say…interrogate." Tony said. "I ain't sitting in that shit!" Butch said. "Well stand then!" tony said. Butch takes a deep breath. "We got a problem! Your boss! Our boss, ain't built for this life!" Butch said. "No shit! Tell me something I don't know!" tony said. "In so many words, he confessed at the last meeting he was responsible for me and the other generals getting jacked for our product." Butch said. Tony shook his head in disbelief. "Bullshit!" tony said. "It's no bullshit! I did my homework, and found out he hired some punks from New York to do the job! Think about it kid! Why would I come here and lie, and try to fuck up everything we've built?" Butch explained. Tony scratched his head, trying to absorb this information. "He said he saw some fucked up shit at some party he went to a while back!" Butch said. "The gathering" tony said to himself. Tony puts his gun away. Tony falls on his butt. He starts laughing hysterically. "This ain't no time to lose it kid!" Butch said. Tony stops laughing and clears his throat. "I tell ya man, it was all so easy when jabbo was here." Tony said. "You sound weak kid! Ain't no more room for weak niggas in this shit! I'm going back up stairs and get dressed!" Butch said. Butch leaves the basement. Tony is still on the floor, looking bewildered. "I'm tired. I'm really tired." Tony said to himself.

When tony finally decides to stop wallowing, he heads up stairs. He goes into the kitchen where Butch is sitting at the kitchen table. "We need a new boss." Butch said. Tony sighs. "I agree. What's fucked up about it, these robots formed a pact with the Lassenberry family. Only a male Lassenberry can take that spot." Tony said. "So what you're telling me is that we're fucked." Butch said. Tony nods his head. "I need a drink!" Butch said. Tony doesn't say a word. He goes into the living room. Moments later, tony comes back in the kitchen with 2 shot glasses and a bottle of rum. "Oh, I see you brought the good shit!" Butch said. Tony sits down across from Butch and pours Butch and himself a shot. He sets the bottle on the table.

"A toast!" tony said. They both raise their glasses. "Long live the house of Lassenberry!" he shouts. "Long live the house of Lassenberry!" Butch shouted. They both gulp their drinks. Tony pours another shot for Butch and himself. They gulp down their drinks. Tony looks at his wrist watch. "Now, let's start this little think tank before I get a call from the castle." Tony said.

CHAPTER 16. 1224T

A couple of days later, tony is sitting in his car. He was parked on an industrial street in Elizabeth, New Jersey. It was around mid-night. Tony had been parked out there for about an hour. The street was quiet and desolate. The street light above him illuminated the area. There were tractor trailers parked across the street from there were a pile of old tires next to him on the sidewalk. He looked at his wrist watch. He sighs. "What the hell is taking him so long?" he said to himself. Seconds after tony said that, the street light went out. Tony starts to panic. He looks at his rear view mirror to see if someone was creeping up on him. Coming from around the corner were 2 black vans. One of the vans parks a few inches behind Tony's car, while the other van backs up a few inches in front. The headlights from the van behind him lit the area. Tony had his pistol on his lap. Suddenly, 2 agents from each van get out and aim their weapons at Tony's car. "Lay any weapon you have, on the roof of the vehicle Mr. Kerouac!" one of the agents shouted. Tony slowly places his pistol on the roof of the car. "Now, step out of the vehicle slowly, with your hands in the air!" the agent said. Tony opens the car door, and then steps out of his vehicle. "Step away from the car!" the agent said. Tony walks away from his car, with his hands still in the air. One of the agents trots over to Tony's car and retrieve the gun from the roof. Another agent goes over and frisks tony from head-to-toe. "He's clean." The agent said. "It's all clear." Another agent said in his walkie-talkie. Moments later, a black limo comes from around the corner. It drives pass tony and the agents and make a quick U-turn. "Get in the back seat Mr. Kerouac." one of the agents said. One of the agents' opens the limo door for tony. Tony climbs in the back and sees Terrance Haggerty sitting across from him. The 4 agents surround the limo with their backs to it.

Mr. Kerouac! What makes you overstep the boundaries of protocol?" Terrance chuckled. "First of all! Why the hell you find everything so funny?" tony asked. "It's simple. I'm disturbed!" Terrance chuckled. Tony just shook his head. "What's on your mind Mr. Kerouac?" Terrance asked. "Our organization needs a new leader. I thought it would be the right thing to inform you." Tony said. "Here's the deal Mr. Kerouac. Unless you convince Sir Marcus himself to find a successor, or convince another male with the last name Lassenberry to take his place, I guess you're stuck with him." Terrance chuckled. "That's insane!" tony said. Terrance straightens his neck-tie. "Unlike you animals, we live by a blood oath." Terrance said. "He's telling his top guys to lay low and not sell anything!" tony shouted. Terrance leans in toward tony. "Like I said. You better find a Lassenberry to replace him. If he dies and there's no male lassenberry to replace him, you and all the top guys in your organization will stand in front of a firing squad. Literally. Now get the fuck out of my limo." Terrance said in a calm voice. Tony slowly exits the limo. The agent hands tony back his gun. All 4 agents trot to their vehicles. The limo takes off. The vans take off, leaving tony standing in the middle of the street, in the dark. Suddenly, the street lights come back on. Tony gets nervous and runs to his car. He turns on the ignition and floors the gas pedal.

Later that day, tony arrives at the castle. An agent chauffeurs him down the corridor of the west wing in a golf cart. Moments later, they arrive at the office. Tony gets out of the cart and knocks on the office door. There is no answer. He turns the door knob. The door is locked. Tony turns to the agent sitting in the golf cart. "Is Sir Marcus in his office?" tony asked. "No sir. He's in his bedroom." The agent said. Tony looks frustrated. "Why the hell didn't you tell me in the first place?" tony asked. "You didn't ask sir." The agent said. Tony runs up the stairs. He walks down the corridor. He knocks on the bedroom door. "Enter!" Sir Marcus shouted. Tony enters the bedroom. He sees Sir Marcus lying in bed wearing a t-shirt, covered with a comforter from the waist down. "Is everything alright boss?" tony asked. "You're my eyes and ears! You tell me!" Sir Marcus said. He had the TV remote in his hand. Tony just stood there while Sir Marcus was flipping channels. He stops when he comes to the news. The local news shows a gang of young Hispanic boys from Union City being arrested on a drug bust. "You see that? We're the cause of that. We're the cause of all of that bullshit in the streets!" Sir Marcus shouted. "Boss. We didn't arrest those kids. The cops did. We didn't force those kids to sell the product. They chose the life. Just like me, and just like you." Tony said. "Kimberly and I had a fight. She took the baby and went to stay with her sister." Sir Marcus said. Tony looked around the bedroom. He looked at Sir Marcus. "What's really wrong boss?" tony asked. Sir Marcus cleared his throat. "Since that gathering with those people, I haven't been feeling well." Sir Marcus said. "Did you eat something? You want me to call the doctor to come here?" tony asked. "Haven't you heard a word I've said?" Sir Marcus shouted. Tony drops his head and starts massaging his temples. "Where have been? You were supposed to be here hours ago!" Sir Marcus said. Tony had a smirk on his face. "I was…entertaining a couple of fine ladies!" tony said. "That sounds like you." Sir Marcus chuckled. Tony then rubs his hands together. "What you want me to do boss?" tony asked. "I want you to take the keys off the night stand here. Then, I want you to tell the chef to make me a plate of fish and chips and have one of the agent bring up." Sir Marcus said as he was yawning. "What do I need the keys for?" tony asked. "I want you to go to the office. Go into the safe and take out a million dollars, and go bail those kids out." Sir Marcus ordered. "What? They're part of Mookie's regime! That's his problem!" tony said. "I'm making it my problem now! Now, go do what I told you to do, and don't forget about my food!" Sir Marcus said. Tony was silent as he walked over and grabbed the keys from the night stand. He noticed that Sir Marcus's ring was on the night stand as well. He remained silent and headed towards the door. "Wait a minute!" Sir Marcus said. Tony turns around. "There's too much light in here. Close the drapes." Sir Marcus ordered. Tony goes over to the window and closes the drapes. Tony heads to the door once more. "Hey!" Sir Marcus shouted. Tony turns around. "You think I should've kept Charlie around?" Sir Marcus asked. "You can't be serious!" tony said before walks out and shuts the door.

While driving in his way to Union City, tony pulls out his mobile phone. He pressed the speed dial button. The phone rings 4 times. "Hello?" the voice answered. "Yeah Butch! It's tony! I want a meeting with all the 5 generals at the Kenilworth spot in 3 hours!" tony said "I'm out shopping with my daughter!" Butch said. "Remember what we talked about? Well, we need to settle it, like now!" tony said. "What happened now?" Butch asked. "Just cut the shopping spree short and gather the others at the Kenilworth spot!" tony said. Tony clicks off the phone. He tosses the phone on the passenger seat.

About a half hour later, tony arrived at the Union City police precinct. He picks up his mobile phone. He dials a number. "Union City Police Department." The voice said. "Yes. Can I speak to Chief Ortiz please?" tony asked. "May I ask whose calling? The voice asked. "Tell him that Mr. Kay would like to speak with him please." Tony said. "Hold please." The voice said. A few minutes later, Chief Ortiz comes to the phone. "Chief Ortiz speaking." He said. "Hey chief! It's the cash cow! I need you to come around the corner, across the street from the liquor store!" tony said tony clicks off his phone. "Hold my calls. I'll be back in a few minutes." The chief said to the dispatcher.

Chief Ortiz was a tall, thin Hispanic man in late 50's. He wore a buzz cut and always had a pair of shades propped up on his head. He walked out of the precinct in a nonchalant manner down the street. Around the corner he sees tony sitting in his car. He gets in. tony drives off. "How's it going chief" tony asked. "Never mind that! What is it?" the chief asked. Tony reaches in the back seat and drops a duffle bag on the chief's lap. "I need you to release those boys you arrested today." Tony said. "What boys?" the chief asked. The Spanish kids on the news!" tony said. The chief unzips the duffle bag. "Oh, those Spanish kids! These punks must be really important to you!" the chief said. "Nah! This is coming from up top." Tony said. "I'll see what I can do." The chief said. "I also want their wrap sheets tossed out." Tony said. "Some of those kids have priors!" the chief said. "It doesn't matter. Toss'em!" tony demanded. The chief pulls out a wad of cash from the duffle bag. "For this, they can be born again!" the chief said. "So, how's life treating you?" tony asked. "The wife wants me to build a pools for the grandkids." The chief said. "Above or in ground?" tony asked. The chief looks down at the duffle bag. "¡Dos mío! With this, I can build a fucking lake!" the chuckled. Tony starts laughing. Tony drives around the corner and stops in front of the precinct parking lot. The chief gets out, with duffle bag in hand. "Take it easy chief." Tony said, "Don't forget my monthly street tax tomorrow." The chief said tony nods head and drives off. "Greedy bitch!" tony said to himself.

It was around 4pm when tony and the 5 generals met up at the Kenilworth spot, which happened to be a warehouse owned by the Lassenberry family. Mookie was the last to show up. He was assisted by one of the guys in his crew. Once inside the warehouse, Mookie told his assistant to stay in the car. All in attendance gathered in a circle. "Man! It smells like a dead mouse in here!" Dubbs said. "Come on tony! I'm tired of traveling around the globe to these meetings!" hakim said. "Calm down and listen!" tony said. "What's the meeting for man?"

Hakim asked. "The boss is failing under pressure. He's not going to last in this game." Tony said. "Well then, we'll just kick him to the curb and do the damn thing ours selves!" Dubbs said. "It's not that simple!" tony said. "Why not?" Dubbs said. "Benny took some type of oath with the connection! They won't accept no one to take over but a male Lassenberry! This shit is bigger than all of us! The coke, heroin, weed and pills can only come through a Lassenberry!" tony said. "None of them Lassenberry cats don't know nothing about the game!" butch said. "Yeah! All they do is go shopping and spend money we bled for!" Dubbs said. "The worst part is, if we try to take him out ourselves, we'll be put down!" tony said. "Are you fucking serious?" butch shouted. "I was told personally, a firing squad! "This guy wasn't fucking around either!" tony said. "Fuck that! I guess we go to war then!" Dubbs shouted. "Don't be stupid! We're running a drug ring, not an army! Like I said! This shit is bigger than all of us!" tony said. The room was silent. Hakim breaks the silence. "I got a Lassenberry for us." Hakim said. "Who? "Tony asked. I can't say right now! Just tell the boss man that you got everything under control!" hakim said. "Who you got in mind?" Bex asked. "Just trust me! I'll tell you when the time is right!" hakim said. Tony pulls out his wallet from his back pocket. He reaches into his wallet and pulls out a business card. "If you find a Lassenberry, he'll need this." Tony said. Tony gives the card to hakim. Hakim reads the card. He has a scowl on his face. "Stephan's House of Style?" hakim said. "Yeah! Tell him I sent you! Have Stephan suit up our new mystery boss ASAP! While you're at it, you and your brother need to get fitted for a uniform too!" tony said. "Why we gotta wear some uniform?" Bex asked. "To keep up appearances! To make this new boss feel like he has real power! That's why!" tony said. "All y'all had to go through this shit?" Bex asked. Butch shrugged his shoulders. "Yeah." Was Butch's response. "You sure you can pull this off Hak?" Dubbs asked. "Don't worry! I got this!" hakim said. "I guess this meeting is adjourned!" tony said. "Ok! Let's not stand around, and do the damn thing!" hakim shouted. "Long live the house of Lassenberry!" tony shouted. "Long live the house of Lassenberry" everyone shouted. This time, hakim shouted with enthusiasm. They all leave the warehouse. Tony made sure the warehouse was locked and secured.

It was Sunday around 3 in the morning. Krayton and his employees had locked the doors after the last of the patrons left. It was a full house that evening. Krayton, the head bouncer and the bartenders stayed behind as the other employees left the club with their pay in hand. Krayton came out of his own pocket to pay the staff. Exhausted, he slumped back into one of the chairs, while the bartenders counted the registers. BIG SHOTS had raked in 100 grand that evening.

It was 2 days after the meeting at Kenilworth. There was a banging on the main entrance door. "We're closed! Come back next week!" the bouncer yelled through the door. The banging continued. It became louder and faster. The bartenders became nervous. The banging continued. "Go see who that is, and tell them to go away!" Krayton said to the bouncer. The bouncer cracks his knuckles and walks toward the door. He unlocks the door and cracks it open. One of the guys on the other side of the door pushes his way inside. The bouncer saw who it was and stepped back. 2 men make their way in. "Oh shit! The Loa brothers!" Krayton said to himself.

The Loa brothers, Tony and Jimmy were associates of the Gatano crime family. They were struggling earners for the family. Tony, who was short and scrawny looking, was the older of the 2. He was around 25 years old at the time. His brother jimmy was a tall burly Neanderthal, about 6 foot 5, weighting about 300 hundred pounds. They were straight up criminals, but hard of hearing. Gino had warned his people not to touch Lassenberry businesses.

"Hey Krayton, my man! How's business?" tony asked. Krayton stands up. "First of all, my name is K boogie! Man, what you guys want?" Krayton asked. Tony and jimmy start laughing. "Ok, K boogie! We just came to see if you needed any help with security! We noticed you had a packed house tonight! Probably made a shit load of money too!" tony said. "I ain't hiring anybody, especially not tonight!" Krayton said. Tony grabs a candle bowl from off one of the tables. "It'll be a shame if this place got torched because someone didn't wanna pay their street tax." Tony said in a calm voice. The bouncer started breathing heavy as jimmy stepped to him. Jimmy was a few inches taller than the bouncer, but the bouncer was just as burly. Tony looked back. "Take it easy jimmy! We just came to talk business with our friend K bugger!" tony said. "Its K boogie!" Krayton said. "Whatever!" Tony said. "Listen! You know who I'm with, and I know who you're with! So, just leave. Please!" Krayton said. "Ok. 10 grand and we're out of here, forever." Tony said. The bartenders hide the cash behind their backs. "I ain't got it like that!" Krayton said. "You're a Lassenberry! You got it like that, and then some!" tony said. Tony throw the candle bowl at the bar, causing the bartenders to duck. The bowl smashes a few bottle of liquor. "Yo man! What the fuck is wrong with you?" Krayton shouted as his hands were trembling. Tony picks up another bowl. "I told you I would never come back! Just give us the cash, and we'll be our way!" tony shouted. "I don't think so bitch!" a voice from out of nowhere shouted. Everyone looked toward the main entrance. There was a shadowy figure standing in the door way. The figure came into the light. It was hakim standing there. He slowly walks over to jimmy, looking him up and down from head to toe. Jimmy steps back. Hakim just walked pass him with a smirk on his face, as if jimmy wasn't a threat. "You girls can leave!" hakim said. The 3 bartenders quickly drop the money on the bar counter. They grab their jackets and purses, hightailing it out of the bar. "See you ladies Friday!" hakim said as the girls run pass him. "Hey Hak, my man! What's up?" tony said. "What the fuck you doing here tony? Last I heard, you and jimmy here ain't get your buttons yet! So that means your freelancing! That means, my crew can fuck y'all up and don't have to worry about retaliation from Gino!" hakim said. Tony looked nervous. Hakim steps to tony, standing about a few inches away from Tony's face. "Next time you come here, you better be buying a drink or doing the 2 step with some bitch!" hakim said in a low calm voice. Tony smiled. "I can tell when I'm not wanted! Jimmy! Let's get the fuck out of this shit whole!" tony said. "What about the money?" jimmy asked. "Fuck the money! It ain't worth not getting made." Tony said. "Bye!" hakim said. Tony turns to Krayton. "You get to keep your money, K boogie!" Tony said. Tony and jimmy leave the club. The bouncer closes the door. Hakim walks behind the bar and pours himself a drink. "Thanks man. That was good fucking timing." Krayton said to hakim. Hakim gulps down his drink. "You can go home man. I got it from here." Hakim said to the bouncer. The bouncer grabs his jacket and looks both ways down the street before leaving. Hakim pours himself another drink. He gulps it down. "Have a drink with me, nigga!" hakim said. Krayton walks over to the bar and sits on the bar stool. Hakim grabs another glass and pours Krayton a drink. Krayton raised his glass. "To us!" Krayton said." To us! Hakim said. They both gulp down their drinks. Hakim takes out the business card tony had given earlier. He passes it to Krayton. "What's this?" Krayton asked. I made an appointment for us tomorrow to go to Stephan's House of Style over in the city." Hakim said. "Man, since my fucking cousin stopped with family allowance, I ain't got that kind of money to throw away on an expensive suit!" Krayton said. "We ain't going shopping! You, Bex and I are going out there to get our uniforms!" hakim said. "What the hell you talking about, uniforms?" Krayton asked. Hakim smiled. He pours himself and Krayton another drink. "We got the go ahead from up top. Your family needs a new boss, and you're it nigga." Hakim said. "Get the fuck out of here!" Krayton shouted. "Serious, man!" hakim said. "Don't fucking play with me, man!" Krayton said. "Tomorrow, we get our uniforms. In a few days, we head out to the castle." Hakim said. He could see Krayton get all teary eyed. "You can't be crying like a bitch and run a half billion dollar dope game!" hakim chuckled. "I can't believe this shit!" Krayton cried. "Drink up nigga!" hakim said. Hakim and Krayton gulp down their drinks. "Now, go home and rest up." Hakim said. "I gotta close out the register and lock up!" Krayton said. Hakim grabs half the cash from the counter. "This here, is my payment for saving yo ass from them Guido niggas!" hakim said. Krayton sighs. "Oh, come on man! I need that money!" Krayton said. "Nigga! In a few days you're gonna run the whole state of New Jersey's dope game! Take yo ass home!" hakim said. Suddenly, Krayton went from upset to having a smile from ear to ear. He gives all the money to hakim. He grabs his jacket. "Don't forget to lock up! You know what, fuck it! You can have this place! I got the whole state now!" Krayton chuckled as he left the club. Hakim gets on his mobile phone. He dials a number. The phone rings 3 times until someone picks up. "Yo tony! It's me. You can come get yo 10 grand tomorrow. You deserve an award for best actor." Hakim said. "Just pay me brother!" Tony said. "Stop crying! I got you! Peace!" hakim said. Hakim hangs up.

Later on that day, Tony Kerouac arrived at the Lassenberry estate or Mark, the father of Sir Marcus. He had made a call earlier to have a talk with Sir Edward's 3 brothers. All 4 men are sitting in the man cave of Mark sr. having drinks. "Now tell me why my sons' not answering my phone calls? His mother is worried sick!" Mark sr. said. "I think he's going through some type of depression, Mr. Lassenberry." Tony said. "Mark! Your son has to realize, there's a multi-million dollar enterprise he's running. This is not the time to be weak." Danny Sr. said. Mark Sr. starts coughing. Everyone could hear the mucus in his throat. "Be careful what you say little brother! That's my son you're talking about!" Mark Sr. said. Danny Sr. rolls his eyes. "I just came to tell you all, if you give me a few days, I'll get him to come around." Tony said. "What about our envelopes? We're all missing a couple of payments!" Danny senior said. "Take it easy!" Jake sr. said. "I'll see if he'll give me the order to make the payments, but we're having trouble with the cash flow right about now." Tony said. "So, what are you telling us?" Danny sr. asked. "The bottom line is, if my people can't get theirs, you can't get yours." Tony said. "We appreciate you coming to us like this tony, but don't think you're taking control of what my father created." Danny sr. said. Tony chuckled. "Mr. Lassenberry! I know my place. Your nephew is the boss. I take orders from him." Tony said. "What about my kids? I haven't heard from my daughter in a while! Danny jr. is still missing! I need you to go find them!" Danny sr. said. Tony puts his drink down on the coaster. He stands, and buttons his coat. "Like I said Mr. Lassenberry, I take orders from your nephew. Good day gentlemen." Tony said. Tony shows himself out. Her gets in the limo. The agent drives off.

The next day around 3pm, Krayton was standing in front of a body size mirror getting his measurements for his uniform. Bex and hakim had already been fitted. Stephan had a hard time finding the same buttons for Krayton's uniform, but he eventually came through. Moments later, the cobbler arrives with 3 pair of black jack boots, all polished and ready to be sold.

The cobbler's name was Vaun, Stephan's ex-lover. They've remained friends for business's sake. Vaun was a tall, thin Asian guy with a purple Mohawk. Through Stephan, he became famous for his custom footwear. Vaun handed the 3 men their footwear, which was the appropriate size for each man. "Cool!" Bex said.

Saturday had come. It was a cold and windy morning. Sir Marcus was walking the corridors of the castle in his pajamas. He was whispering to himself. There was an agent following not too far behind in a golf cart. In his hand, Sir Marcus had an empty bottle of wine. He threw the bottle of wine at the agent, barely missing his head. The bottle shatters against the wall. "Get the fuck away from me!" Sir Marcus shouted. The agent made a quick U-turn on the golf cart, heading back towards the west wing.

Tony was in the office going through paper work. He had finally talked Sir Marcus into giving him access to the family's oversees accounts and the B.O.I, as jabbo called it. Suddenly, there was a knock on the door. "Come in!" tony shouted. The agent enters. "Sir. Sir Marcus is on another drinking binge again." the agent said. Tony looked at his wrist watch. "Shit! Get someone to help you, and get him a cold shower! Give him a sedative and Have his uniform laid out! Now go!" tony ordered. 'Yes sir." The agent said. The agent leaves the office. Tony is shuffling the papers into a neat pile. Tony makes a phone call on the black phone. The phone rings several times before someone picks up on the other end. "Krayton! It's me tony. You have your uniform made?" tony asked. "Yeah man! I'm good to go!" Krayton said. I need you at the castle tomorrow before mid-night. I'll have a limo pick you up at your penthouse." Tony said. "Can't wait man!" Krayton chuckled. Tony hangs up the phone. Tony then picks up the red phone. After 3 rings, Terrance picks up on the other end. "Hey buddy! How's tricks?" Terrance chuckled. "Do you know who this is?" tony asked. "Tony! I am aware of everything!" Terrance chuckled. "I have your so called heir to the Lassenberry throne!" tony said. "Great! That's just great! I'll be at the castle tomorrow before mid-night to make it official!" Terrance chuckled. Tony's jaw dropped. He was in awe. "How did you know when to come here?" tony asked. Terrance just laughs hysterically and hangs up the phone. Tony hangs up the red phone. He becomes paranoid, looking around the office for listening devices. After a few minutes, he finds nothing. He sits himself in Sir Marcus's chair. He takes out his mobile phone. After pressing in a phone number, he then presses a 3 digit code. After 4 rings, someone picks up. "Industrias Santos." The woman on the other end said. "Tengo que hablar con el jefe! Código 1224t!" tony said. "Por favor, mantenga como puedo verificar el Código." The woman said. "Gracias." Tony said.

After Sir Edward had taken over the Lassenberry organization, Oscar Deltoro Santos, head of the Caballeros de fortuna cartel had issued Sir Edward and jabbo codes to contact him in case changes occur in the their operation. Years later, Sir Marcus and tony received a code as well.

15 minutes had passed. Tony was getting restless staying on the phone. He was about to nod out from boredom. The woman returns on the phone. "Hola!" the woman said. Tony jumps from his seat. "Yes! I'm here!" tony said as he rubbed his eye. "Verificación complete. Espere Por favor." the woman said. Tony looks at his wrist watch. "God damn!" he said. Moments later, Santos picks up the phone. "1224t. cómo puedo ayudarle?" Don Santos asked. "¡sí! Llamando para decir que ha habido UN cambio de mando en Jersey." Tony said. "¿Esto ralentizará negocios? Recorder lo que sucedió la úlitima vez!" don Santos said. "Te lo prometo, señor! Estraremos listos para el próximo envoi, como estabas previsto!" tony said. "Muy bien! Voy a tener a mi gente organizer una reunión con el nuevo jefe! 1224t! No me decepciones de nuevo!" Don Santos said with rage in his voice. "Señor entendido!" tony said. Don Santos hangs up. Tony tosses the phone on the desk. He starts to pace the room. "Fuck!" tony shouts.

The next morning, tony wakes up. He had slept on the couch in the office. His clothes were wrinkled. He looked at his wrist watch. It was 5am. Tonty runs his fingers through his curly hair. He heads to the office bathroom to take a leak. He goes over to the mirror. He leans over the sink, and looks up at the ceiling. "Damn Jabbo! How the hell you do this for so long?" tony said. He turns on the faucet and splashes water on his face. He grabs a towel from the towel rack and pats his face dry. Tony leave the office and heads upstairs to Sir Marcus's bedroom. There were 2 agents posted outside the bedroom. "Morning." Tony said. "Morning sir." Both said simultaneously. Tony enters the bedroom. He sees that Sir Marcus's bed wasn't slept in. looks on the other side to the bed and sees Sir Marcus curled up on the floor in the fetal position shaking. "Sir Marcus! Boss!" tony shouted. Tony went back and closed the door. Tony stands over Sir Marcus. He looks up at tony. "I can't sleep! I keep seeing their faces! Screaming and running for their lives!" Sir Marcus cried. Tony goes over and gently helps Sir Marcus off the floor. "Come on Boss! Get it together!" tony said. "I don't want this life! I don't want this life!" Sir Marcus cried. Tony sits Sir Marcus on the edge of the bed. Tony sits next to him. Sir Marcus eyes were blood shot red. The 2 agents enter the bedroom and close the door. "Please tony! Don't let them put that stuff in me again! I'll do anything!" Sir Marcus cried. "Listen boss. After tonight, all the nightmares and pain will go away. Trust me." Tony said. Sir Marcus puts his arms around tony. Tony puts his arms around Sir Marcus and starts rubbing his back. He looked over and saw Sir Marcus's uniform draped over the chair, and his jack boots on the floor polished to perfection. Tony pulls away from Sir Marcus, while still holding his hand. "Listen! Listen to me! If Kimberly calls, tell her to stay with her relatives! After tonight, I'll set it up so you can be with them. But for now just relax. Relax." Tony said. "Just stay with me! Please, don't leave me!" Sir Marcus said. Tony puts his arms around Sir Marcus and cradles him back-n-forth. Tony signals one of the agents to come closer to him. Tony reaches inside the agent's jacket pocket and pulls out a syringe. Tony injects the syringe in the back of Sir Marcus's neck, pressing down on the plunger. Sir Marcus flinched. His eyes bulge. He stares tony in the eyes as he loses consciousness. Sir Marcus falls back on the bed. Keeping his promise, tony stayed by his side. He laid down next to Sir Marcus and closed his eyes, with the syringe still in his hand. The 2 agents leave the bedroom, closing the door behind them.

There were 30 agents assigned to Sir Marcus at the castle. Their quarters and birthing area were on the third floor of the north wing of the castle. Like a well-oiled machine, the agents had switched shifts guarding the bedroom.

Both Sir Marcus and tony were fast asleep, when a loud knock on the bedroom door awakens tony from his slumber. Tony went to the door. He sees that there were 2 different agents at the door. "Krayton Lassenberry is at the gate sir." The agent said. Tony rubs his eyes and scratches his head. He looks at his watch. It was 11:45pm. "Shit! Let him pass, and have him escorted to the office!" tony said. "Yes Sir." The agent said. The agent speaks into his com link. "Bring Mr. Lassenberry in, and escort him to the west wing office." The agent said. Tony closes the door. He goes over to Sir Marcus, who was still asleep. "Sir Marcus! Boss!" tony shouted. Tony leans over Sir Marcus. "Sir Marcus!" tony shouted. There was no response from his boss. He repeatedly taps Sir Marcus on the cheek. Still, there was no response. The taps turns into slaps. "Don't die on me now!" tony said he runs into the bathroom. He comes out with a glass of cold water. He pinched Sir Marcus's nose. He poured the water down Sir Marcus's mouth. Sir Marcus jumps up coughing, and spitting out water. "Wha- what the hell?" Sir Marcus shouted. "You have to get in uniform, like right now!" tony said. "What happened to my pajamas?" Sir Marcus shouted. "I took them off so you can run into the shower real quick! Now, get dressed!" Sir Marcus looks up at tony, still coughing. He nods his head. Sir Marcus staggers into the bathroom. He turns on the shower. Tony reaches into his pants pocket and pulls a bottle of prescription pills.

5 minutes later, Sir Marcus comes staggering out of the bathroom wrapped in a towel. "Here! Take this!" tony said. "What's that?" Sir Marcus asked. "You're still groggy from the booze. This will straighten that out." Tony said. Reluctantly, Sir Marcus goes into the bathroom, turns on the faucet. Tony follows him to make sure he takes the pill. Sir Marcus swallows the pill. He cups his hands under the faucet. He slurps up a hand full of water.

About 20 minutes later, Sir Marcus was being escorted down stairs by tony and 2 agents. They approach the doors of the office. One of the agents opens the door for Sir Marcus. When he enters the office, he sees his cousin Krayton standing by the desk with 2 more agents. Terrance was sitting on the couch with his legs crossed. Krayton was dressed in the same identical uniform as his cousin, minus the medals. Krayton smiled at Sir Marcus. Sir Marcus stood there with an empty emotionless look on his face. Krayton took this non response as his cousin being upset with him. "With all due respect cousin, I'm just here to keep things moving forward!" Krayton said. Suddenly, there was a knock on the door. "Come in!" tony shouted. An agent enters the office. "The 5 Generals are at the gate sir." The agent said. "Bring them to the office agent." Tony said.

Outside of the castle, 5 limousines were allowed to pass the gate. Butch, Mookie, Dubbs, Bex and hakim were individually chauffeured on the to the castle grounds. They were all individually driven into the castle walls on golf carts, followed by 20 agents at 2 abreast, trotting behind wearing riot gear, wielding sub-machine guns.

Minutes later, the 5 generals enter the office, all dressed in the same uniforms as Krayton and Sir Marcus. They were told by tony to stand side by side like soldiers, with Mookie at one end, bound to his wheelchair. To further their unity, tony was instructed to tell the 5 generals to shave their heads and facial hairs.

Sir Marcus was aware of his surroundings, but didn't have the will to react to what was about to take place. "After tonight, you'll be free from all of this." Tony whispered to Sir Marcus. Tony takes Sir Marcus by the arm and leads him to the desk. Tony had 5 documents laid out on the desk. He gives Sir Marcus a ball point pen. Sir Marcus just stares at tony as a tear falls down his cheek. Tony takes his hand, forcing Sir Marcus to sign off on all 5 documents. Tony then signals Krayton to come over on the other side of the desk and sign his name on each document under Sir Marcus's name. At this time, Terrance stands. He walks over toward Krayton. "Could you stand in the middle of the room please?" Terrance asked. Terrance faces Krayton, standing a few inches apart. Tony shuffles the documents into one pile. "State your given name!" Terrance said. "Krayton Lassenberry." Krayton said. "Do you swear on your life and on the lives of those you love that Lassenberry blood flows through your veins?" Terrance asked. "Yes, I do." Krayton said. "Look to your right." Terrance said. Krayton turns his head, staring at the 5 generals. "Do you recognize these men who are about to be your loyal followers?" Terrance asked Krayton. "Yes, I do." Krayton said. "From this day on, how do you wish them to address you?" Terrance asked. Krayton turns toward the 5 generals. At this time tony removes Sir Marcus's ring from his finger. "From this day, you all will address me as…Edward the 2nd!" Krayton shouts. Tony walks over, standing between Krayton and the 5 generals. He places the ring on Krayton's right ring finger. "Long live the house of Lassenberry! Long live Sir Edward the 2nd!" tony shouted. "Long live the house of Lassenberry! Long live Sir Edward the 2nd!" the 5 generals shouted simultaneously. After that was said, Edward the 2nd guts his eye at hakim. Hakim then reaches into his left jack book, pulling out a small pistol, which could be concealed in the palm of one's hand. He walks up behind tony, and points the pistol at the back of his head. At point blank range, he pulls the trigger. Edward the 2nd was the last face he laid eyes upon before he fell to the floor. "That's the end of that shit." Hakim said. Terrance starting jumping up and down, giggling like a child. "I love this!" Terrance chuckled. Edward the 2nd puts his hand on hakim's shoulder. "Now, we're even, man." He said to hakim. Suddenly, Sir Marcus starts come around and into focus. He sees these men standing around dressed in the same uniforms like himself. Still woozy from his trance, he becomes frightened seeing his right hand man face down on the floor. He then sees hakim and his cousin standing over his body. It didn't take Sir Marcus long to figures out what took place. He quickly runs out of the office. Out in the corridor, he sees a platoon of NA soldiers standing in 2 rows of 10 facing each other. Frightened, Sir Marcus runs in the other direction, down another corridor. "Don't worry about him! Where can he go?" Terrance chuckled. Hakim walks over to the bar and pours 7 glasses of Scotch. He passes them out. He raises his glass. "To my man, Edward the 2nd! May he rule forever!" hakim shouted. Everyone taps glasses then drinks. Terrance snaps his fingers signaling the agents in the office to remove Tony's body. "Would you excuse us gentlemen? I would like to talk to your new boss for a while to discuss some things!" Terrance said. Edward the 2nd takes the documents from off the desk. The generals puts their glasses down on the desk. "Long live Sir Edward the 2nd!" they all shout. Edward the 2nd shook hand with each general as they left the office. Hakim was the last to leave out before he is hugged by Edward the 2nd. "The world is yours now, nigga! Don't fuck it up!" Hakim said. Edward the 2nd just smiled. Hakim leaves, leaving the pistol on the desk. Terrance sits on the couch with his drink in his hand. "Have a seat! It's your desk now!" Terrance chuckled. Edward the 2nd takes a seat at his desk. "I think I can get used to this!" he said. Terrance crosses his legs. He takes a sip of his drink. "You have a lot to catch up on buddy! There's a lot to know running a half a billion dollar business!" Terrance chuckled. Edward the 2nd looked shocked. "You said a half billion?" he asked. "Yes, and it's yours now!" Terrance chuckled. "Shit!" Edward the 2nd said. "But there are some rough edges that need to be smoothed out before you can breathe easy." Terrance chuckled. "What's that?" Edward the 2nd asked. Terrance clears his throat. "As we speak, another order is on its way to take back control of the narcotics business from your family. I've assigned the 20 NA soldiers out in the corridor to be under your command to give you some leverage. Gee! Ain't I a nice guy?" Terrance chuckled. Edward the 2nd didn't say a word. He just sat trembling, barely able to drink his glass of scotch.

About a thousand miles away, as high as 5 miles in the air, a private jet heads towards the United States. The passengers were 10 men of Italian descent. One of the passengers was Don Fernando Domenico. He was sitting next to one of his soldiers. The soldier's mobile phone rings. He answers it. He listens to the person on the other end for a few seconds, and clicks the phone off. "Don Domenico. Gino Massoni è stato catturato." The soldier said. "Ottimo. Appena Siamo sistemati in, riprendiamo ciò che è nostro!" Don Domenico said.

THE END?

About the Author

Daniel Webb believes most conspiracy theories are, for the most part, true. He was born in Newark, New Jersey, and served in Desert Storm. Since 1994, he has worked as a letter carrier for the Bloomfield, New Jersey, post office.

Printed in the United States
By Bookmasters